THE MI
BEANFIE

Half of Joe's gardens and half his fields
shriveled in a drought, even though Indian Creek
practically formed a swimming pool in his living
room. In fact, Milagro itself was half a ghost
town, and all the old west side beanfields were
barren, because over thirty-five years ago, during some complicated legal and political maneuverings known as the 1935 Interstate Water
Compact, much of Milagro's Indian Creek water
had been reallocated to big-time farmers down
in the southeast portion of the state or in Texas,
leaving folks like Joe Mondragón high and much
too dry.

But then one day Joe suddenly decided to
irrigate the little field in front of his dead parents' decaying west side home (which Joe still
owned—in itself a miracle) and grow himself
some beans. It was that simple. And yet irrigating that field was an act as irrevocable as Hitler's
invasion of Poland, Castro's voyage on the
Granma, or the assassination of Archduke Ferdinand, because it was certain to catalyze tensions
which had been building for years, certain to
precipitate a war.

❧

"Tender and comic, mad and sly, real and funny,
touching and hilarious . . . excellent!"
—*Publishers Weekly*

CRITICAL ACCLAIM

FOR **MILAGRO**

THE
Milagro
Beanfield
War

by John Nichols

Illustrations by Rini Templeton

BALLANTINE BOOKS • NEW YORK

Library of Congress Catalog Card Number: 74-4409

ISBN 0-345-29533-1

This edition published by arrangement with
Holt, Rinehart and Winston

Manufactured in the United States of America

First Ballantine Books Edition: February 1976
Eighth Printing: October 1983

If I am not for myself, who will be for me?
Yet if I am for myself only, what am I?

—Hillel

Prologue

"What's that little half-pint
son of a bitch want to
cause so much trouble for?"
—Some people of Milagro

꿎

Many people in the Miracle Valley had theories about why Joe Mondragón did it. At first, the somewhat addlebrained but sympathetic sheriff, Bernabé Montoya, figured it was just one more irrational manifestation of an ornery temperament, of a kid, now almost middle-aged, with a king-sized chip on his shoulder, going slightly amuck. The Frontier Bar owner, Tranquilino Jeantete, said (with a sardonic wink) that Joe did it because he was hungry for an enchilada made from honest-to-God Milagro frijoles, with some Devine Company cojones mixed in. Nick Rael, the storekeeper, figured Joe might have done it because he could not pay the ninety-odd dollars he owed the store; or else maybe he did it just out of sheer renegade inbred spite, hoping to drive up ammo sales at the same time he put Nick out of business. The chief perpetrator of the Indian Creek Dam, Ladd Devine the Third, who held Milagro's fate in his hand like a fragile egg, considered what Joe did a personal assault on his empire, on the Indian Creek Dam, and on that egg. And the immortal old man, Amarante Córdova, who lived on the west side of the highway in the ghost town neighborhood, believed Joe did it because God had ordered him to start the Revolution without any further delay.

Whatever the case, if there were mixed opinions on the matter, there were also mixed ideas about what the consequences might be. "What's that little half-pint son of a bitch want to cause so much trouble for?"

some said. Others quietly intoned: "I'm not saying it's good, I'm not saying it's bad. Let's just wait and see what happens." Still others on both sides of the Indian Creek Dam question armed themselves and prepared for war, while the governor and the state engineer down in the capital chewed their fingernails, wondering how to maintain their own untenable positions.

Of course the final consensus of opinion, arrived at by both those who were for Joe Mondragón and those who were against him, was that in order for him to do what he did and thus precipitate the war that was bound to follow, Joe had to be crazy. People also figured only a miracle could save Joe from his foolhardy suicidal gesture.

Yet Milagro was a town whose citizens had a penchant not only for going crazy, but also for precipitating miracles.

Take, for example, an early nineteenth-century sheepherder named Cleofes Apodaca and the scruffy sheepdog he irreverently called Pendejo, which, translated loosely, means "idiot" or "fool"—or, translated more literally, means "pubic hair."

Today, Cleofes Apodaca might qualify to be called the Patron Saint Crazy of Milagro.

Almost from the start, when Cleofes was but a child, everybody had predicted a bad end for him. In those bygone days a bishop visited the Milagro parish about once every five years, and when the bishop came he confirmed all the small fry in town. It was the bishop's habit, right after confirming a child, to deliver the kid a cuff on the cheek, thus reminding him or her that he or she must always be prepared to suffer for religion. When the bishop laid a soft right to the plump cheek of little Cleofes Apodaca, however, the future sheepherder uncorked a retaliatory haymaker to the holy man's chin, causing the prelate to tumble over backward, striking his bald pate against the baptismal font. And from that day forth people figured Cleofes was in trouble up to his eyeballs.

For a long while, however, Cleofes led a fairly normal, if somewhat lonely, life. His neighbors kept their distance, claiming he had El Ojo, the "evil eye." People especially steered their babies away from Cleofes, afraid that if he admired the kids or tickled them under their fat chins, the children would sicken and grow humps. If the plants in somebody's garden suddenly withered or became infested with mites and aphids, the owner of that garden had a tendency to blame Cleofes Apodaca's evil eye. Pregnant women walked a mile out of their way just to avoid Cleofes and thus ensure that their offspring would not be born missing a nose or a finger or some other priceless appendage.

Folks also came to believe that at night this loner, who had slugged the bishop and named his dog Pendejo, turned himself into a black mongrel that waded along the irrigation ditches committing genocide on frogs. For this reason, during the first half of the nineteenth century, you seldom heard frogs at night in Milagro. In fact, for over a decade, when Cleofes Apodaca was in his prime, frogs were as scarce in that town as camels and gold bullion.

One farmer insisted Cleofes was responsible for the birth in his flock of six two-headed lambs in one springtime. But the most unusual anomaly accredited to this solitary rogue's evil eye was the job done on one of Timoteo Mondragón's goats, which was born with both a vagina and a penis, but no testicles. For years this schizoid beast pranced around the goat pen eagerly mounting any female in sight while at the same time it was being mounted by the billys. This made for a very unstable and confusing situation in the herd. In fact, pretty soon all the females became infertile, the billys impotent, and Timoteo's huge flock dwindled away to nothing—all because Cleofes Apodaca's evil eye had caused the hermaphrodite to be born.

Cleofes was also a stickler for eating the first slice of everything, even though evil spells always resided in the first slice; and he had a nasty habit of letting white geraniums bloom on his windowsill, even though white geraniums were a surefire invitation to death. Adding insult to injury, the arrogant aloof sheepherder never carried a little chunk of oshá in his pants pocket to ward off poisonous snakes.

"Sooner or later Cleofes is gonna get it," his superstitious peers whispered fearfully. And sure enough, they were right.

The downfall began when one day Pendejo disappeared. And Cleofes, who had never married, was heartbroken. He searched high and low for the dog, up in the Midnight Mountains, out on Strawberry Mesa, down in the Rio Grande gorge. But Pendejo had vanished from the face of this earth. Cleofes prayed to the saints for his dog's safe return. He begged the Santo Niño de Atocha to find his dog. And, because traditionally the Santo Niño wore out many shoes walking around the countryside performing miracles and errands of mercy, Cleofes began to sew little shoes for the small carving of this saint which occupied a niche in the church. In fact, it soon got so that every other day the balmy sheepherder showed up at the church with another pair of tiny shoes for the saint. This ritual continued for months, until the shoes formed a huge pile surrounding the santo, and trickles of miniature footwear were spreading out underneath the pews. But the Santo Niño refused to give Cleofes Apodaca back his beloved Pendejo.

In the process of becoming such an industrious cobbler, the sheepherder neglected his animals, his fields, his house—everything had fallen into disrepair. Seeing this, the townspeople rubbed their hands, smirking as they cackled smugly: "Okay, *now* Cleofes is getting it back in spades for clobbering the bishop." At about this same time too, frogs reappeared in the irrigation ditches, and folks once more heard them singing at night, obviously because the old sheepherder had become so busy stitching miniature clodhoppers for the Sainted Child and otherwise trying to bring back Pendejo that he no longer had time for his nocturnal canine patrol of the waterways.

Following his shoemaking phase, Cleofes began to traipse around the county carrying a little statue of Santa Inéz del Campo, who was supposed to find missing animals. But with her he struck out as badly as with the Santo Niño de Atocha. To boot, he wore out his own shoes and blistered his feet until they bled. Then he tramped around barefoot, weeping and sobbing and beating his breast and tearing his hair, while microscopic parasites crawled out of horseshit piles and penetrated up into his bare feet and entered his bloodstream, lodging eventually in his guts, in his stomach, and in his liver. Some enterprising filarial worms, having worked their way up into his eyeballs, started making him blind, and he grew very gaunt and miserable. Confused, the sheepherder invoked Saint Anthony's aid, even though that saint possessed nowhere near Santa Inéz's power when it came to locating lost pets.

Then suddenly, one stormy summer day, Cleofes heard Pendejo barking. Which gave him great joy except for one minor consideration: the barking came from underneath the ground in an alfalfa field where a thousand graceful, noisy birds called killdeer were nesting. No matter, though, the sheepherder grabbed a shovel and set to, vehemently attacking the earth under which his dog apparently was trapped.

For countless mornings and afternoons, through new moons and full moons and old moons, through rainstorms and starry evenings and windy days, Cleofes wielded his spade, digging deeper and deeper toward his beloved friend who never for a moment ceased barking, whining, growling, yipping, and whimpering, as dogs will when eagerly awaiting the arrival of their masters. At first the nesting killdeer screeched and whistled in alarm, flying frantically in all directions and repeatedly dive-bombing the mad sheepherder dressed in rags, who paid them no mind. But after a while the birds got used to the digging, resettled upon their freckled eggs, and hatched out ten thousand little killdeer that scurried around Cleofes Apodaca's pit peeping hysterically. Meanwhile, curious townspeople gathered along the edges of the field, fascinated by the absurd scene, eagerly awaiting Pendejo's arrival. When they realized his appearance was not to be immediately forthcoming, men and women brought buckets which they turned upside down to sit on, or they rode horses to the site and sat astride their mounts bemusedly looking on. Pretty soon an enterprising fellow named Carlos Lavadie (the great-great-granduncle of the present-day bastard Eusebio Lavadie) lugged over two dozen wooden chairs, which he rented out for a duro each. By the time the Pendejo affair was resolved, Carlos had become a very rich man, who subsequently sired a line of the town's most hated patróns.

Never for a moment did Pendejo quit barking and whining; so Cleofes kept digging. He unearthed bones and arrowheads and beautiful clay pots; he tossed out lovely silver goblets and mammoth gold coins, and stones that sparkled, full of stars. In fact, he discovered the treasure of the Seven Cities of Cibola which had drawn Coronado north from Mexico not so many years before. But the sheepherder merely chucked all these iridescent artifacts into a great gleaming pile and flailed away some more with his shovel. In due course he extended long ladders into the hole. Laboriously, step-by-feeble-step, he lugged earth-filled pails up the rungs and dumped them onto the huge mound rising beside his hole. The baby killdeer matured and migrated away. The rainy season came and went and golden aspen leaves skippety-hopped across the field into his hole. Then a frost glazed the ground—winter came; relentlessly, the dog pleaded to be set free; unflaggingly, Cleofes persevered. To survive, he ate worms and snails and other sluggish, deaf, and blind little creatures that inhabited the soft, mysterious soil.

All at once Cleofes struck a hot spring. In an instant the pit filled with steaming mineral water; the crazy sheepherder drowned; the treasure of the Seven Cities of Cibola disappeared; *"Que milagro!"* spectators cried; Pendejo stopped barking; it began to snow; and for days a chorus of joyful, almost-drunken frog chug-a-lugging drowned out the neighborhood magpies, roosters, dogs, and coyotes.

Yet for years afterward, according to the most imaginative storytellers, air bubbles kept rising to the surface of that hot spring, and a lone buzzard was said to have circled nonstop directly above the spot for a decade. Then the water evaporated and the earth rose, so that not even a small depression marked the terrain; and nowadays nobody knows in which field the befuddled sheepherder dug his fabled hole.

But Cleofes Apodaca was not the first Miracle Valley-ite to go drilling into Mother Earth. The legends also tell of a Milagro pastor who went crazy tunneling toward a bell that was ringing underneath his church. This happened, a very long time ago, when bells were almost impossible to come by in the New World, and this particular priest, José González Sinkovich, who hailed from Sevilla (by way of Prague), went mad just from longing for a bell to sanctify his religious edifice.

That is: Padre Sinkovich had wanted a bell so badly for so long that one day he simply began to hear a joyful bronze tolling beneath the dirt floor of his humble mud church.

The padre grabbed a shovel and lit into the floor like a hound going after a rabbit. Immediately he started unearthing bones, as it had been the custom during the early days to bury the dead inside the House of God. Pretty soon Padre Sinkovich, who had unearthed enough skeletons to start a mail-order Halloween business, was staggering around with bloodshot delirious eyes, furiously booting innumerable bones every which way as the magnificent tintinnabulation somewhere down there literally drove him bananas. For a month his flock tried to worship among the foxholes and fibulas and tibias, but finally the pealing of the bell began to hurt everyone's ears and they all became temporary atheists; which suited Padre Sinkovich to a T, since he no longer had time to spare for his congregation. Hoping to speed up matters, he hired a dozen Chamisaville Pueblo Indians to help with the digging. Day and night they chipped and hacked, pickaxed and burrowed deeper, uncovering whitened bones by the ton while the deranged clergyman rambled about, frothing like a lunatic. Then all the Indians got spooked and quit, whereupon the padre locked the church from inside. And on he excavated, around the clock, babbling incoherently as he searched for his melodious bell that never for a moment stopped BONGING! BONGING! BONGING!

Eventually, though, Padre Sinkovich undermined the very foundations of his church, which collapsed on top of him, writing finis to another droll chapter in Milagro's history.

There were many other strange doings and bizarre myths, legends, and fairy tales that, taken loosely together, had wound up giving the town and the Miracle Valley their names. For example, there were even the present-day accounts of how a man named Onofre Martínez lost his arm, and of how a tiny woman called Ruby Archuleta killed a deer with her bare hands.

But of even greater interest, and perhaps also much more germane to the pending story of the war brought about by Joe Mondragón's illegal actions, is the incredible saga of the immortal old codger Amarante Córdova, who had played seven-card stud poker with Death ever since 1880, winning every hand.

Part One

"You can't buy bullets with food stamps."
—Nick Rael

❦

Amarante Córdova had thirteen children. That is, he and his wife, Elizabeth—known as Betita—had had thirteen children, who either still were or had been Nadia, Jorge, Pólito, María Ana, Berta, Roberto, Billy, Nazario, Gabriel, Ricardo, Sally, Patsy, and Cipriano. Betita, who had never been sick a day in her life, died in 1963, on November 22, on the same day as President Kennedy, but not from a bullet in the head. She had been outside chopping wood during a lovely serene snowstorm when suddenly she set down the ax and began to walk along the Milagro–García spur out onto the mesa. In recalling her death later Amarante would always tell his listeners, "You cannot imagine how beautiful it was that afternoon. The snow falling was as serene as the white feathers of a swan. When the ravens sailed through it they made no sound. You looked up and the big black birds were floating through the snowflakes like faint shadows of our forefathers, the first people who settled in the valley. The tall sagebrush was a lavender-green color because there had been a lot of rain in the autumn, and that was the only color on the otherwise black and white mesa, the pale lavender-green of the sage on which snow had settled. You remember, of course, that Betita's hair was as white as the snow, and she was wearing a black dress and a black woolen shawl that Sally, our daughter who was married to the plumber from Doña Luz, knitted for her on a birthday long ago."

Slowly, taking her time, Betita walked across the mesa to the rim of the gorge. "And there she stood on the edge looking down," Amarante said. "For a long time she was poised there like a wish afraid to be uttered. The walls of the gorge created a faded yellow glow to the flakes falling eight hundred feet down to the icy green river below. Ravens were in the air, circling, their wings whispering no louder than the snow falling. It was very peaceful. I was at the house, I never saw her leave. But when she didn't come in with the wood after a while, I saddled up that lame plow horse we used to have called Buster, and went after her, following her tracks in the snow. Just as I left the road to enter the chamisal an owl dropped out of the darkening sky, landing on a cedar post not ten yards away. An owl is a sure sign from the dead, you know, and it was right then I knew she had disappeared into the gorge. When I arrived at the rim an enormous raven was standing where she had last stood, and when he saw me he spread his wings, which were wider than my outstretched arms, and floated up like a good-bye kiss from my wife into the lazy storm. Next day we opened the church, only the second time that year it was used, not to say prayers for Betita, but to burn candles and shed our tears for the President who had died in Dallas. But I lit my candles for Betita, and nobody noticed. Three months later her body was discovered on the bank of the river two miles below Chamisaville."

The Córdova sons and daughters had scattered, as the saying goes, to the four winds. Or actually, only to the three winds, eastward being anathema to the children of Milagro, whose Mississippi was the Midnight Mountains, that chain running north and south barely a mile or two from all their backyards.

Nadia, a waitress most of her life, first in Doña Luz, then Chamisaville, wound up in the Capital City barrio, dying violently (and recently) at the age of sixty-one in a lover's quarrel. Jorge emigrated to Australia where he tended sheep, same as at home. Pólito, who spent his life wandering around, getting married three or four times and taking care of sheep in Wyoming,

Montana, and Utah, had died young of the flu. María Ana wanted to be a dancer, took the train to San Francisco, and after years of strenuous work, heartbreak, and small roles in the city ballet company, she hurt her back and wound up teaching in an Arthur Murray studio. Berta married an Anglo who raised lemons in California, and, curiously, they never had any children. Roberto, Billy, and Nazario became farm workers, mechanics, truck drivers, dishwashers, and short-order cooks in and around Los Angeles; they all raised large families, and although between them they'd had nine sons in Vietnam, only one of Billy's kids, Rosario, had been killed. Gabriel, who miraculously metamorphosed into a run-of-the-mill featherweight boxer in the army, turned pro after his discharge, was known as the Milagro Mauler during his short and undistinguished prime, and died in a plane crash in Venezuela. Ricardo had stayed on as a rancher in Milagro, although he spent half his life in the lettuce, sugar beet, or potato fields of southern Colorado, or else with the big sheep outfits up in Wyoming and Montana. Two of his sons, Elisardo and Juan, had died in Vietnam; another boy was stationed in Germany. Sally married a plumber in Doña Luz and had eleven kids herself, one of whom became a successful pop singer in Mexico City, but never sent any money home, not even after the plumber died when a black widow bit him while he was creeping around somebody's musty crawl space on a job. Patsy, the most beautiful and the sharpest in school, ran West to join a circus, became an Avon lady instead, and died with her husband and all their children except Peter (who was in a Japanese hospital at the time recovering from wounds received in Vietnam) in a head-on car crash in Petaluma. And little Cipriano, the baby of the family, born in 1925, who went farther than everyone else in his education, and, in fact, had just obtained a full scholarship to Harvard when he was drafted, was vivisected by a German machine gun during the first eighteen seconds of the Normandy D-day landings.

All his life Amarante had lived in the shadow of his

own death. When he was two days old he caught pneumonia, they gave him up for dead, somehow he recovered. During his childhood he was always sick, he couldn't work like other boys his age. He had rheumatic fever, chicken pox, pneumonia three or four more times, started coughing blood when he was six, was anemic, drowsy all the time, constantly sniffling, weak and miserable, and—everybody thought—dying. At eight he had his tonsils out; at ten, his appendix burst. At twelve he was bitten by a rattlesnake, went into a coma, survived. Then a horse kicked him, breaking all the ribs on his left side. He contracted tuberculosis. He hacked and stumbled around, hollow-eyed, gaunt and sniffling, and folks crossed themselves, murmuring Hail Marys whenever he staggered into view. At twenty, when he was already an alcoholic, scarlet fever almost laid him in the grave; at twenty-three, malaria looked like it would do the job. Then came several years of amoebic dysentery. After that he was constipated for seventeen months. At thirty, a lung collapsed; at thirty-four, shortly after he became the first sheriff of Milagro, that old devil pneumonia returned for another whack at it, slowed his pulse to almost nothing, but like a classical and very pretty but fainthearted boxer, couldn't deliver the knockout punch. During the old man's forties a number of contending diseases dropped by Amarante's body for a shot at the title. The clap came and went, had a return bout, was counted out. The measles appeared, as did the mumps, but they did not even last a full round. For old time's sake pneumonia made a token appearance, beat its head against the brick wall that evidently lined Amarante's lungs, then waved a white flag and retreated. Blood poisoning blew all his lymph nodes up to the size of golf balls, stuck around for a month, and lost the battle.

Amarante limped, coughed, wheezed; his chest ached; he spat both blood and gruesome blue-black lungers, drank until his asshole hurt, his flat feet wailed; arthritis took sledgehammers to his knees; his stomach felt like it was bleeding; and all but three of his teeth turned brown and toppled out of his mouth like acorns. In Milagro, waiting for Amarante Córdova to drop dead became like waiting for one of those huge sneezes that just refuses to come. And there was a stretch during Amarante's sixties when people kept running away from him, cutting conversations short and like that, because everybody *knew* he was going to keel over in the very next ten seconds, and nobody likes to be present when somebody drops dead.

In his seventies Amarante's operations began. First they removed a lung. By that time the citizens of Milagro had gotten into the irate, sarcastic, and not a little awed frame of mind which had them saying: "Shit, even if they took out that old bastard's other lung he'd keep on breathing."

A lump in his neck shaped like a miniature cow was removed. After that a piece of his small intestine had to go. There followed, of course, the usual gallbladder, spleen, and kidney operations. People in Milagro chuckled "Here comes the human zipper," whenever Amarante turned a corner into sight. His friends regarded him with a measure of respect and hatred, beseeching him to put in a good word for them with the Angel of Death, or whoever it was with whom he held counsel, even as they capsized over backward into the adobe and caliche darkness of their own graves.

But finally, at seventy-six, there loomed on Amarante's horizon a Waterloo. Doc Gómez in the clinic at Doña Luz sent him to a doctor at the Chamisaville Holy Cross Hospital who did a physical, took X rays, shook his head, and sent the old man to St. Claire's in the capital where a stomach specialist, after doing a number of tests and barium X rays and so forth, came to the conclusion that just about everything below Amarante's neck had to go, and the various family members were notified.

The family had kept in touch in spite of being scattered to the three winds, and those that were still living, including Jorge from Australia, returned to Milagro for a war council, and for a vote on whether or not they could muster the money to go ahead with their father's expensive operation. "If he doesn't have this operation," the Capital City doctor told them, "your father will be dead before six months are out."

Now the various members of the family had heard that tune before, but all the same they took a vote: Nadia, María Ana, Berta, Sally, and Billy voted for the operation; Jorge, Roberto, Nazario, and Ricardo voted against it. And so by a 5–4 margin Amarante went under the knife and had most of his innards removed. He recuperated for several weeks, and then, under Sally's and Ricardo's and Betita's care, went home to Milagro.

But it looked as if this time was really *it*. Slow to get back on his feet, Amarante had jaundice and looked ghastly. He complained he couldn't see anymore, and they discovered he had cataracts in both eyes, so Ricardo and Sally and Betita took him back to St. Claire's and had those removed. Thereafter, he had to wear thick-lensed glasses which made him look more like a poisoned corpse than ever before. His slow, creeping way of progressing forward made snails look like Olympic sprinters. The people of Milagro held their collective breath; and if they had been a different citizenry with a different culture from a different part of the country, they probably would have begun to make book on which day *it* would happen. In fact, the word had spread, so that down in Chamisaville at the Ortega Funeral Home, which handled most of the death from Arroyo Verde to the Colorado border, it became common for Bunny Ortega, Bruce Maés, and Bernardo Medina to wonder, sort of off the cuff during their coffee breaks, when Amarante's body would be coming in. And eventually, although she did not go so far as to have Joe Mondragón or one of the other enterprising kids like him dig a grave out in the camposanto, Sally did drop by Ortega's in order to price coffins and alert the personnel as to what they might expect when the time came.

One gorgeous autumn day when all the mountain aspens looked like a picture postcard from heaven, Amarante had a conversation with Sally. "I guess this old temple of the soul has had it," he began with his usual sly grin. "I think you better write everybody a letter and tell them to come home for Christmas. I want to have all my children gathered around me at Christmastime so I can say good-bye. There won't be no more Navidades for me."

Sally burst into tears, she wasn't quite sure whether of relief or of grief. And, patting her father on the back once she had loudly blown her nose, she said, "Alright, Papa. I know everybody who's left will come."

And *that* was a Christmas to remember! The Celebration of 1956. Jorge came from Australia with his wife and their five children. Nadia journeyed up from the capital with her lover. María Ana took off from the Arthur Murray studios in San Francisco, flying in with her husband and four children. Berta and the lemon grower took a train from the San Jose Valley. Roberto, Billy, and Nazario, their wives and fourteen children and some grandchildren, drove in a caravan of disintegrating Oldsmobiles from L.A. And Sally and the remaining two of her brood still in the nest motored up every day from Doña Luz. People stayed at Ricardo's house, at what was left of Amarante's and Betita's adobe, and some commuted from Sally's in Doña Luz.

They had turkeys and pumpkin pie, mince pie and sour cream pie; they had chili and posole, corn and sopaipillas and enchiladas and empanaditas, tequila and mescal, Hamms and Coors and Old Crow, and in the center of it all with the screaming hordes revolving happily about him, chest-deep in satin ribbons and rainbow-colored wrapping paper, so drunk that his lips were flapping like pajamas on a clothesline during the April windy season, sat the old patriarch himself, dying but not quite dead, and loving every minute of it. His children hugged him, whispered sweet nothings in his ear, and waited on his every whim and fancy. They pressed their heads tenderly against his bosom, muttering endearing and melodramatic lovey-doveys, even as they also anxiously listened to see if the old ticker really was on its last legs. They took him by the elbow and held him when he wished to walk somewhere, they gazed at him sorrowfully and shed tears of both joy and sadness, they squeezed his feeble

hands and reminisced about the old days and about
the ones who were dead, about what all the grandchildren were doing, and about who was pregnant and
who had run away, who was making a lot of money
and who was broke and a disgrace, who was stationed
in Korea and who was stationed in Germany . . . and
they joined hands, singing Christmas carols in Spanish,
they played guitars and an accordion, they wept and
cavorted joyously some more, and finally, tearfully,
emotionally, tragically, they all kissed his shrunken
cheeks and bid him a fond and loving adios, told their
mama Betita to be strong, and scattered to the three
winds.

Three years later when Jorge in Australia received
a letter from Sally in Doña Luz, he replied:

> What do you mean he wants us all to
> meet again for Christmas so he can say
> good-bye? What am I made out of, gold
> and silver? I said good-bye two winters
> ago, it cost me a fortune! I can't come
> back right now!

Nevertheless, when Sally a little hysterically wrote
that this time was really *it,* he came, though minus the
wife and kiddies. So also did all the other children
come, a few minus some wives or husbands or children, too. At first the gaiety was a little strained, particularly when Nazario made a passing remark straight
off the bat to Berta that he thought the old man
looked a hell of a lot better than he had three years
ago, and Berta and everyone else within hearing distance couldn't argue with that. But then they realized
they were all home again, and Milagro was white and
very beautiful, its juniper and piñon branches laden
with a fresh snowfall, and the smell of piñon smoke
on the air was almost like a drug making them high.
The men rolled up their sleeves and passed around
the ax, splitting wood, until Nazario sank the ax into
his foot, whereupon they all drove laughing and drinking beer down to the Chamisaville Holy Cross Hospital where the doctor on call proclaimed the shoe a

total loss, but only had to take two stitches between Nazario's toes. Later that same afternoon there was a piñata for the few little kids—some grandchildren, a pocketful of great-grandchildren—who had come, and, blindfolded, they pranced in circles swinging a wooden bat until the papier-mâché donkey burst, and everyone cheered and clapped as the youngsters trampled each other scrambling for the glittering goodies. Then the kids stepped up one after another to give Grandpa sticky candy kisses, and he embraced them all with tears in his eyes. Later the adults kissed Grandpa, giving him gentle abrazos so as not to cave in his eggshell chest. "God bless you" they whispered, and Amarante grinned, flashing his three teeth in woozy good-byes. "This was in place of coming to the funeral," he rasped to them in a quavering voice. "Nobody has to come to the funeral." Betita started to cry.

Out of the old man's earshot and eyesight his sons and daughters embraced each other, crossed themselves, crossed their fingers, and, casting their eyes toward heaven in supplication, murmured, not in a mean or nasty way, but with gentleness and much love for their father:

"Here's hoping . . ."

When, five years later, Jorge received the next letter from Sally, he wrote back furiously:

NO! I just came for Mama's funeral!

On perfumed pink Safeway stationery she pleaded with him to reconsider, she begged him to come. For them all she outlined their father's pathetic condition. He'd had a heart attack after Betita's death. He had high blood pressure. His veins were clotted with cholesterol. His kidneys were hardly functioning. He had fallen and broken his hip. A tumor the size of an avocado had been removed from beside his other lung, and it was such a rare tumor they didn't know if it was malignant or benign. They thought, also, that he had diabetes. Then, most recently, a mild attack of pneumonia had laid him out for a couple of weeks. As an afterthought she mentioned that some lymph nodes had been cut from his neck for biopsies because they thought he had leukemia, but it turned out he'd had an infection behind his ears where the stems of his glasses were rubbing too hard.

Jorge wrote back:

> What is Papa trying to do to us all? I'm no spring chicken, Sally. *I* got a heart condition. *I'm* blind in one eye. *I* got bursitis so bad in one shoulder I can't lift my hand above my waist. And I've *got* diabetes!

He returned, though. He loved his father, he loved Milagro. Since the last time, Nadia had also died. The other surviving children came, but none of the grandchildren or great-grandchildren showed up. Times were a little tough, money hard to come by. And although maybe the old man was dying, he looked better than ever, better even than some of them. His cheeks seemed to have fleshed out a little, they were even a tiny bit rosy. Could it be their imagination, or was he walking less stooped over now? And his mind seemed sharper than before. When Jorge drove up the God damn old man was outside chopping wood!

They shared a quiet, subdued celebration. Most of them had arrived late and would leave early. And after they had all kissed their father good-bye again, and perhaps squeezed him a little harder than usual in their abrazos (hoping, maybe, to dislodge irrevocably something vital inside his body), the sons and daughters went for a walk on the mesa.

"I thought he said he was dying," Jorge complained, leaning heavily on a cane, popping glycerin tablets from time to time.

"I wrote you all what has happened," Sally sighed. "I told you what Papa said."

"How old is he now?" asked Berta.

"He was born in 1880, qué no?" Ricardo said.

"That makes him eighty-four," Billy said glumly. "And already I'm fifty."

"He's going to die," Sally said sadly. "I can feel it in my bones."

And those that didn't look at her with a mixture of hysteria and disgust solemnly crossed themselves. . . .

For the Christmas of 1970 only Jorge came. He bitched, ranted, and raved at Sally in a number of three-, four-, and five-page letters, intimating in no uncertain terms that he couldn't care less if his father *had* lost all the toes on one foot plus something related to his bladder, he wasn't flying across any more oceans for any more Christmases to say good-bye to the immortal son of a bitch.

But he came.

The airplane set down in the capital; he took the Trailways bus up. Ricardo, who was recovering from stomach surgery but slowly dying of bone cancer anyway, met him at Rael's store. Sally came up later. Jorge had one blind askew eye and poor vision in the other, he was bald, limping noticeably, haggard and frail and crotchety. He felt that for sure this trip was going to kill him, and did not understand why he kept making it against his will.

Then, when Jorge saw Amarante, his suspicions were confirmed. His father wasn't growing old: he had reached some kind of nadir ten or twelve years ago and now he was growing backward, aiming toward middle age, maybe youth. To be sure, when Amarante lifted his shirt to display the scars he looked like a banana that had been hacked at by a rampaging machete-wielding maniac, but the light in his twinkling old eyes, magnified by those glasses, seemed like something stolen from the younger generation.

The next day, Christmas Day, in the middle of Christmas dinner, Jorge suffered a heart attack, flipped over in his chair, his mouth full of candied sweet potato, and died.

Bunny Ortega, Bruce Maés, and the new man replacing Bernardo Medina (who had also died), Gilbert Otero, smiled sadly but with much sympathy when Sally and Ricardo accompanied the body to the Ortega Funeral Home in Chamisaville.

"Well, well," Bunny said solicitously. "So the old man finally passed away."

"No-no-no," Sally sobbed. "This is my brother . . . his son! . . ."

"Ai, Chihuahua!"

And here it was, two years later more or less, and Joe Mondragón had precipitated a crisis, and Amarante Córdova had never been so excited in his life.

One day, during his Doña Luz daughter's weekly visit, Amarante told her, "Hija, you got to write me a letter to all the family."

Sally burst into tears. "I can't. I won't. No. You can't make me."

"But we have to tell everyone about what José has done. They must see this thing and take part in it before they die. Tell them the shooting is about to start—"

So Sally dutifully advised her surviving siblings about what Joe Mondragón had done; she informed them that the shooting was about to start.

Maybe they read her letters, maybe they only looked at the postmark, but to a man jack they all replied: "Send us your next letter *after* Papa is dead!"

"That's the trouble with this younger generation," Amarante whined petulantly. "They don't give a damn about anything important anymore."

&

Joe Mondragón was thirty-six years old and for a long time he had held no steady job. He had a wife, Nancy, and three children, and his own house, which he had built with his own hands, a small tight adobe that required mudding every two or three autumns.

Joe was always hard up, always hustling to make a buck. Over the years he had learned how to do almost any job. He knew everything about building houses, he knew how to mix mud and straw just right to make strong adobes that would not crumble. Though unlicensed, he could steal and lay his own plumbing, do all the electric fixtures in a house, and hire five peons at slave wages to install a septic tank that would not overflow until the day after Joe died or left town. Given half the necessary equipment, he could dig a well, and he understood everything there was to understand about pumps. He could tear down a useless tractor and piece it together again so niftily it would plow like balls of fire for at least a week before blowing up and maiming its driver; and he could disk and seed a field well and irrigate it properly. "Hell," Joe liked to brag, "I can grow sweet corn just by using my own spit and a little ant piss!" He could raise (or rustle) sheep and cattle and hogs, too, and slaughter and butcher them all. And if you asked him to, he could geld a pony or castrate a pig with the same kind of delicate authoritative finesse Michelangelo must have used carving his *Pietà*.

Joe had his own workshop crammed full of tools he had begged, borrowed, stolen or bought from various friends, enemies, and employers down through the years. In that shop he sometimes made skinning knives out of cracked buzz saw blades and sold them to hunters in the fall for five or six bucks. At the drop of a five-dollar bill he could also fashion an ornate Persian wine goblet from an old quart pop bottle. Then again, if the need arose and the money to pay for it was resting lightly on his main workbench like an open-winged butterfly taking five, Joe probably could have invented the world's tiniest dart gun, to be used by scientists for crippling, but not killing, mosquitoes. Just to survive there had to be almost nothing Joe couldn't or would not at least try to do.

The Mondragón house was surrounded by junk, by old engines, by parts of motors, by automobile guts, refrigerator wiring, tractor innards. One shed was filled with wringer washing machines, and when Joe had the time he puttered over them until they were "running" again; then he tried—and often managed— to sell them . . . with pumps that went on the fritz (or wringer gears that neatly stripped themselves) ten minutes after Joe's three-month warranty (in writing) expired. This presented no problem, however, because for a very small consideration Joe was more than willing to fix whatever broke in whatever he had sold you.

In a sense, Joe was kept perpetually busy performing minor miracles for what usually amounted to a less-than-peanuts remuneration. Still, when something, when *any*thing was wrong in town, when a pump was frozen or a cow was sick or the outhouse had blown down, the call went out for Joe Mondragón, who would defy rain, hail, blizzards, tornadoes, and earthquakes in order to skid his pickup with the four bald retreads and no spare to a stop in your front yard and have the thing or the animal or whatever it was temporarily patched up and functioning again. Reeking of energy like an oversexed tomcat, Joe was always charging hell-bent for election around town in his old yellow pickup, like as not with a beer clutched tightly in one fist—arrogant little Joe Mondragón, come to fix your trouble and claim your two bits, who didn't take no shit from no body.

But he was tired, Joe had to admit that. He was tired, like most of his neighbors were tired, from trying to earn a living off the land in a country where the government systematically gathered up the souls of little ranchers and used them to light its cigars. Joe was tired of spending twenty-eight hours a day like a chicken-thieving mongrel backed up against the barn wall, neck hairs bristling, teeth bared, knowing that in the end he was probably going to get his head blown off anyway. He was tired of meeting each spring with the prospect of having to become a migrant and head north to the lettuce and potato fields in Colorado where a man groveled under the blazing sun ten hours a day for one fucking dollar an hour. He was tired, too, of each year somehow losing a few cows off the permits he had to graze them on the government's National Forest land, and he was tired of the way permit fees were always being hiked, driving himself and his kind not only batty, but also out of business. And he was damn fed up with having to buy a license to hunt deer on land that had belonged to Grandfather Mondragón and his cronies, but which now resided in the hip pockets of either Smokey the Bear, the state, or the local malevolent despot, Ladd Devine the Third.

Usually, in fact, Joe did not buy a license to hunt deer in the mountains surrounding his hometown. Along with most everybody else in Milagro, he figured the dates of a hunting season were so much bullshit. If he hankered for meat, Joe simply greased up his .30-06, hopped into the pickup, and went looking for it. Once a Forest Service vendido, Carl Abeyta, had caught Joe with a dead deer, a huge electric lamp, no license, and out of season to boot, and it cost Joe a hundred dollars plus a week in the Chamisa County Jail. In jail he half-starved to death and was pistol-whipped almost unconscious by a county jailer, Todd McNunn, for trying to escape by battering a hole in the cheap cinderblock wall with his head.

Joe had been in jail numerous times, usually just for a few hours, for being drunk, for fighting, for borrowing (and consuming) Devine Company sheep, and each time it had cost him fifteen or twenty-five dollars, and usually he had been manhandled, too. The corrections personnel laughed when they clobbered Joe because he was funny, being so small and ferocious, weighing only about a hundred and twenty-five pounds, kicking and hitting, trying to murder them when he was drunk, and when he was sober, too. Sometimes they tried to hold him off a little for sport, but Joe was too dangerous, being the kind of person —like the heralded Cleofes Apodaca of yore—who would have slugged a bishop. So they tended to belt him hard right off the bat and then let him lie. Joe had lost a few teeth in that jail, and his nose had been operated on by police fists, clubs, and pistol butts so as to conform to the prevalent local profile. Outside the jail Joe had broken fingers on both his hands hitting people or horses or doors or other such things. "I ain't afraid of nothing," he bragged, and thought he could prove it, although when he said that his wife Nancy hooted derisively: "Oh no, that's right, you're not afraid of *any*thing."

But Joe was tired of the fighting. Tired of it because in the end he never surfaced holding anything more potent than a pair of treys. In the end he just had his ass kicked from the corral to next Sunday, and nothing ever changed. In the end half his gardens and half his fields shriveled in a drought, even though Indian Creek practically formed a swimming pool in his living room. In fact, Milagro itself was half a ghost town, and all the old west side beanfields were barren, because over thirty-five years ago, during some complicated legal and political maneuverings known as the 1935 Interstate Water Compact, much of Milagro's Indian Creek water had been reallocated to big-time farmers down in the southeast portion of the state or in Texas, leaving folks like Joe Mondragón high and much too dry.

This situation had caused a deep, long-smoldering, and fairly universal resentment, but nobody, least of all Joe Mondragón, had ever been able to figure out how to bring water back to that deserted west side land, most of which, by now, belonged to Ladd Devine the Third and his motley assortment of dyspeptic vultures, who (not surprisingly, now that they owned it) *had* figured out a way to make the west side green again.

But then one day Joe suddenly decided to irrigate the little field in front of his dead parents' decaying west side home (which Joe still owned—in itself a miracle) and grow himself some beans. It was that simple. And yet irrigating that field was an act as irrevocable as Hitler's invasion of Poland, Castro's voyage on the *Granma,* or the assassination of Archduke Ferdinand, because it was certain to catalyze tensions which had been building for years, certain to precipitate a war.

And like any war, this one also had roots that traveled deeply into the past.

For several hundred years, and until quite recently, Milagro had been a sheep town. Nearly all the fathers of Joe Mondragón's generation had been sheepmen. There was no man, however, and there had been no men for more than a hundred years, perhaps, who had truly made a living off sheep, the basic reason for this being that Milagro was a company town, and almost every herder, simply in order to survive as a sheepman, had been connected to the Ladd Devine Sheep Company. And being a sheepman connected to the Devine Company was like trying to raise mutton in a tank full of sharks, barracudas, and piranha fish.

For this, the people of the Miracle Valley had the U.S. Government to thank. Because almost from the moment it was drawn up and signed in 1848, the Treaty of Guadalupe Hidalgo, which not only ended the war between the United States and Mexico, but also supposedly guaranteed to the Spanish-surnamed southwestern peoples their communal grazing lands, was repeatedly broken. Shortly after the war, in fact, the U.S. Congress effectively outlawed their communal property, passing vast acreages into the public domain, tracts which then suddenly wound up in the hands of large American ranching enterprises like the Devine Company. Later, during Teddy Roosevelt's era, much remaining communal territory was designated National Forest in which a rancher could only run his animals providing he had the money and political pull to obtain grazing permits.

Hence, soon after the 1848 war, most local ranchers found themselves up to their elbows in sheep with no place to graze them. In due course the small operators were wiped out either from lack of access to grazing land or from trying to compete with the large companies that now dominated the public domain and Forest Service preserves. The sheepmen who survived did so only by becoming indentured servants to the large companies that controlled the range and the grazing permit system.

In Milagro, this meant that since the last quarter of the nineteenth century most sheep ranchers had been serfs of the Devine Company, which, during the seventies and eighties, in one of those democratic and manifestly destined sleights of Horatio Alger's hand (involving a genteel and self-righteous sort of grand larceny, bribery, nepotism, murder, mayhem, and general all-around and all-American nefarious skulduggery), had managed to own outright, or secure the grazing rights to, all the property on the Jorge Sandoval Land Grant in Chamisa County.

At the end of each year since this takeover, every sheepman, woman, and child in Milagro had discovered themselves heavily in debt to the Devine Company. In fact, after an average of ten years under the sheep company's tutelage, just about every man, including men like Joe Mondragón's father, Esequiel, had owed the rest of whatever resources he might accumulate in his lifetime to whichever Ladd Devine happened to be sitting on the family nest egg at that particular moment.

Of course, the Ladd Devine Company had not only been interested in land and sheep and its company (now Nick Rael's) store. It owned controlling interests in both the First National Bank of Chamisaville and its Doña Luz branch. The Dancing Trout Dude Ranch and Health Spa had been operating on the Devine estate up in Milagro Canyon ever since the early twenties. When the Pilar Café was constructed across from the company store in 1949, it was a Devine operation. And when, more recently, the Enchanted Land Motel was built on the north–south highway to handle the new breed of pudgy tourists who simpered by in their baroque apartment houses on wheels, it was a Devine-financed and Devine-controlled operation.

To be truthful, the Devine Company, which had gotten fat on sheep, was not dealing in wool anymore. The company had much more interest in a project called the Indian Creek Dam, a structure—to be located in Milagro Canyon—that was considered the essential cornerstone of a Devine development endeavor known as the Miracle Valley Recreation Area.

A dam in Milagro Canyon had been the dream of both Ladd Devine Senior and the present caudillo, Ladd Devine the Third, who took over the Devine operation when his grandfather (who was eighty-nine at the time) was caught alone and on horseback up beyond the Little Baldy Bear Lakes in an early autumn snowstorm back in 1958. Ladd Devine the Second, a profligate and playboy who married five times, put a bullet in one ear and out the other on the Italian Riviera at the age of thirty-nine, thus accounting for

Ladd Devine the Third's early ascendancy to the throne.

The Ladd Devine Company had started drawing up plans for the recreation development about the same time people were losing their water rights and beginning a wholesale exodus from the hapless west side. The original Ladd Devine had not objected much to the unfair 1935 water compact shenanigans, which somewhat damaged his sheep operations by driving many of his herders elsewhere, because he was too busy buying up those herders' momentarily worthless land at bargain-basement prices. In this way, during the years immediately following World War II, when the water compact really began to be enforced, almost all the abandoned and apparently worthless land on the west side passed into Devine hands.

And now—*Que milagro!*—the Indian Creek Dam was conveniently going to restore water rights to the west side so Ladd Devine the Third could bless the few surviving small farmers of Milagro with a ritzy subdivision molded around an exotic and very green golf course.

The dam would be built across Indian Creek at the mouth of Milagro Canyon, establishing a mile-and-a-half-long lake whose easternmost shore would extend up to within hailing distance of the Dancing Trout's main lodge. And the dam—or paying for it, that is—would be made possible by creating a conservancy district whose boundaries, for taxation purposes, would incorporate almost all the town's largely destitute citizens.

Wherein lay a rather profound rub.

At least one person understood this rub. Hence, right after Ladd Devine the Third announced plans for the Miracle Valley Recreation Area (which would include the Indian Creek Reservoir, the Miracle Valley Estates and Golf Course, and the Miracle Mountain Ski Valley) by erecting an elaborate wooden sign on the north–south highway just below town, the old bartender at the Frontier, Tranquilino Jeantete, began telling anybody who would listen:

"You watch. The conservancy district and the dam

is a dirty trick. Like the 1935 water compact, it's one
more way to steal our houses and our land. We'll be
paying the taxes for Ladd Devine's lake. And when
we can't pay our conservancy assessments, they'll take
our land and give it to Devine. And that fucking Zopilote will sit up there on his throne in his fucking castle
putting pennies on our eyes as they carry us to the
camposanto, one by one."

But most farmers, completely baffled by the complexity of a conservancy district, did not know what
to do. Should they hire a lawyer and fight the vulture?
Or should they just sit tight and let this terrible thing
happen the way terrible things had been happening
now ever since the 1848 war, trusting that, like Amarante Córdova, they could somehow, miraculously,
survive?

In the end, after much talk and many heated arguments, the people shrugged, laughing uneasily and a
little ashamedly. "That conservancy district and that
dam," they philosophized, "will be as hard to live
with as Pacheco's pig."

Pacheco being an enormous, shifty-eyed, hysterically lonely man who—in the time-honored tradition
of Cleofes Apodaca and Padre Sinkovich—had been
losing his marbles at a vertiginous rate ever since his
wife died six years ago, and who owned one of the
world's most ornery sows, an animal he could never
keep penned. For years it had been a regular thing in
Milagro to see unsteady, mammoth Seferino Pacheco
staggering across fields or splashing through puddles
in the dirt roadways, searching for his recalcitrant
porker, which was usually inhaling a neighbor's garden or devouring somebody's chickens. Pacheco was
forever knocking on front doors and back doors and
outhouse doors, asking after his sow. And people
were forever shouting at, and shooting at, and throwing rocks at Pacheco's gargantuan, voracious animal.
Yet for a long time the pig had led a charmed life,
nonchalantly absorbing high-powered lead lumps in
its thick haunches, or else—it being also a rather swift
pig—escaping on the run unscathed. "Maybe that
marrana carries a chunk of oshá in her cunt that pro-

tects her from poisonous people," Onofre Martínez once giggled. And because the pig, with Pacheco gimping crazily after it, had become such a familiar sight all over town, sayings had grown out of the situation. Such as: "He's more trouble than Pacheco's pig." Or: "She's got an appetite like Pacheco's pig." And again: "It's as indestructible as Pacheco's pig."

And of course: "That conservancy district and that dam will be as hard to live with as Pacheco's pig."

Which is about where things stood when Joe Mondragón suddenly tugged on his irrigation boots, flung a shovel into his pickup, and drove over to his parents' crumbling farmhouse and small dead front field in the west side ghost town. Joe spent about an hour chopping weeds in the long unused Roybal ditch, and then, after digging a small feeder trench from Indian Creek into the ditch, he opened the Roybal ditch headgate at the other end so water could flow onto that fallow land.

After that Joe stood on the ditch bank smoking a cigarette. It was a soft and misty early spring morning; trees had only just begun to leaf out. Fields across the highway were still brown, and snow lay hip deep in the Midnight Mountains. Milagro itself was almost hidden in a lax bluish gauze of piñon smoke coming from all the fireplaces and cook stoves of its old adobe houses.

Last night, Joe recalled, the first moths had begun bapping their powdery wings against his kitchen windows; today water skeeters floated on the surface into his field, frantically skittering their legs.

The Trailways bus, with its lights still on, pulled off the highway to discharge and pick up a passenger. And the water just kept gurgling into that field, sending ants scurrying for their lives, while Joe puffed a cigarette, on one of the quietest lavender mornings of this particular spring.

❧

About fifteen and a half minutes after Joe Mondragón first diverted water from Indian Creek into his parents' old beanfield, most of Milagro knew what he had done. Fifteen and a half minutes being as long as it took immortal, ninety-three-year-old Amarante Córdova to travel from a point on the Milagro–García highway spur next to Joe's outlaw beanfield to the Frontier Bar across the highway, catty-corner to Rael's General Store.

Back in 1914 Amarante had been Milagro's first sheriff. And he still wore the star from that time pinned to the lapel of the three-piece woolen suit he had been wearing, summer and winter, for the last thirty years. The only person still inhabiting the west side ghost town, Amarante lived there on various welfare allotments (and occasional doles from Sally, the letter-writing Doña Luz daughter) in an eight-room adobe farmhouse whose roof had caved into seven of the eight rooms. Until the year before Jorge from Australia keeled over with his mouth full of candied sweet potato, Amarante had gotten around in a 1946 Dodge pickup. But one summer day he steered it off the gorge road on a return trip from a wood run to Conejos Junction, was somehow thrown clear onto a ledge, and from that spectacular vantage point he watched his rattletrap do a swan dive into the Rio Grande eight hundred feet below. Since that day Amarante had been on foot, and also since that day, come rain or come shine, he'd walked the mile from his crumbling adobe to town and back again, babbling to himself all the way and occasionally lubricating his tongue with a shot of rotgut from the half-pint bottle that was a permanent fixture in his right-hand baggy suit pocket.

On this particular day, as soon as Amarante had safely landed his crippled frame on a stool in the huge empty Frontier Bar and fixed a baleful bloodshot eye on the owner, eighty-eight-year-old Tranquilino Jeantete, he said in Spanish (he did not speak English, or read or write in either language):

"José Mondragón is irrigating his old man's beanfield over there on the west side."

Tranquilino turned up his hearing aid, and, after fumbling in his pockets for a pair of glasses, he perched the cracked lenses on his nose, muttering, "Eh?"

"José Mondragón is irrigating his old man's beanfield over there on the west side."

Tranquilino still couldn't hear too well, so he muttered "Eh?" again. Neither man's pronunciation was very good: they had six teeth between them.

Ambrosio Romero, a burly carpenter who worked at the Doña Luz mine, sauntered through the door for his morning constitutional just as Amarante repeated: "José Mondragón is irrigating his old man's beanfield over there on the west side."

Ambrosio said, "Come again? When are you gonna learn how to talk, cousin? Why don't you go down to the capital and buy some wooden teeth? Say that once more."

With a sigh, Amarante lisped, "José Mondragón is irrigating his old man's beanfield over there on the west side."

"Ai, Chihuahua!" Ambrosio made his usual morning gesture to Tranquilino Jeantete, who slid a glass across the shiny bar, selected a bottle, and poured to where Ambrosio indicated stop with his finger.

In silence the miner belted down the liquor, then belched, his eyes starting to water, and as he left he remarked: "What does that little jerk want to do, cause a lot of trouble?"

Ambrosio went directly from the bar to Rael's store where he bought some Hostess Twinkies for a midmorning snack at the mine, and also casually mentioned to Nick Rael, "I hear José Mondragón is irrigating over on the other side of the highway."

Nick's instinctive reaction to this news was, "What's that little son of a bitch looking for, a kick in the head?"

Four men and two women in Rael's store heard this exchange. They were Gomersindo Leyba, an ancient ex-sheepman who would, for a dollar, chauffeur anybody without wheels down to the Doña Luz Piggly-Wiggly to do their shopping; Tobías Arguello, a onetime bean farmer who had sold all his land to Ladd Devine the Third in order to send his two sons to the state university (one had dropped out to become a career army man, the other had been drafted and killed in Vietnam); Teofila Chacón, the mother of thirteen kids, all living, and at present the evening barmaid at the Frontier; Onofre Martínez, a one-armed ex-sheepman who was known as the Staurolite Baron and also as the father of Bruno Martínez, a state cop; and Ruby Archuleta, a lovely middle-aged woman who owned and operated a body shop and plumbing business just off the north–south highway between Milagro and Doña Luz in the Strawberry Mesa area.

These six people scattered like quail hit by buck-shot. And by noon, many citizens engaged in various local enterprises were talking excitedly to each other about how feisty little Joe Mondragón had gone and diverted the water illegally into his parents' no-account beanfield.

And by and large, the townspeople had three immediate reactions to the news.

The first: *"Ai, Chihuahua!"*

The second: "What does that obnoxious little runt want to cause trouble for?"

And the third: "I'm not saying it's good or bad, smart or stupid, I'm not saying if I'm for or against. Let's just wait and see what develops."

At two that afternoon an informal meeting convened in Rael's General Store. Attending this meeting were the Milagro sheriff; an asthmatic real estate agent named Bud Gleason; Eusebio Lavadie, the great-great-great-grandnephew of Carlos the ringside-seat millionaire, and the town's only rich Chicano rancher; the storekeeper, Nick Rael; two commissioners and a mayordomo of the Acequia Madre del Sur—Meliton Mondragón, Filiberto Vigil, and Vincent Torres; and the town's mayor, Sammy Cantú.

The sheriff, forty-three-year-old Bernabé Montoya, had held his job now for nine and a half years. All four of his election victories had come by three votes —27 to 24—over the Republican candidate, Pancho Armijo. Bernabé was an absentminded, rarely nasty, always bumbling, also occasionally very sensitive man

who dealt mostly with drunks, with some animal rustling, with about five fatal car accidents a year, and
with approximately seven knifings and shootings per
annum. He also reluctantly assisted the state police,
once in the spring and again in the fall, during their
raids on the Strawberry Mesa Evening Star hippie
commune, during which raids they confiscated maybe
five hundred marijuana plants that later mysteriously
turned up in the pockets of Chamisaville Junior High
School kids. Bernabé had arrested Joe Mondragón a
dozen times, and had personally driven him down to
the Chamisa County Jail twice. In earlier times Joe
and Bernabé had run together, and the sheriff still
admired his former pal's spunk, even though Joe was
a constant hassle to the lawman's job—a troublemaker, a fuse that was always, unpredictably, burning.

Bernabé had gloomily called this meeting because
he sensed a serious threat in Joe's beanfield. He had
understood, as soon as he heard about the illegal
irrigation, that you could not just waltz over and kick
out Joe's headgate or post a sign ordering him to
cease and desist. Because that fucking beanfield was
an instant and potentially explosive symbol which no
doubt had already captured the imaginations of a few
disgruntled fanatics, and the only surprise about the
whole affair, as Bernabé saw it, was, how come nobody had thought of it sooner?

"So I don't really know what to do," he told the
gathering. "That's how come I called this meeting."

Eusebio Lavadie said, "What he's doing is illegal,
isn't it illegal? Arrest him. Put him in jail. Throw
away the key. Who's the mayordomo on that ditch?"

Vincent Torres, a meek, self-effacing old man,
raised his hand.

"Well, you go talk to him," Lavadie huffed. "Tell
him to cut out the crap or some of us will get together and break his fingers. Or shoot his horses.
I don't see what all the fuss is about."

A commissioner for the Acequia Madre, Filiberto
Vigil, said, "Don't be a pendejo, Mr. Lavadie."

The other commissioner, Meliton Mondragón,

added, "What kind of harm does anybody think this really might do, anyway?"

"It's a bad precedent," Lavadie said. "This could steamroll into something as unmanageable as Pacheco's pig. Any fool can see that."

"Are you calling *me* a pendejo?" Meliton Mondragón asked.

"Not you personally, no. Of course not. But it's obvious the question isn't whether to let this go on or not. The only question is, how do we stop it?"

There was silence. Nobody had a suggestion.

At length, Bernabé Montoya said, "If I go over and tell him to stop he'll tell me to shove a chili or something you know where. If I go over to arrest him he'll try to kick me in the balls. And anyway, I don't know what the water law is, I don't even know what to arrest him for or charge him with or how long I could hold him. I know as soon as we fined him, or he got out of the Chamisa V. jail, he'd go back to irrigating that field again. It seems to me it's more up to the water users, to the ditch commissioners and the ditch bosses here, to stop him."

"Well, have them talk to him, then," Bud Gleason said. "How's that sound to you boys?"

It didn't sound that good to the boys. The two commissioners and the mayordomo shrugged, remaining self-consciously silent.

"For crissakes!" Lavadie suddenly exploded. "What a bunch of gutless wonders we got in this room! If you all are too chicken to do it, I'll go talk to that little bastard myself. There's no room in a town like ours for this kind of outrageous lawlessness—"

Five minutes later Lavadie's four-wheel-drive pickup lurched into Joe Mondragón's yard, scattering chickens and a few flea-bitten hounds.

A cigarette lodged toughly between his lips, Joe emerged from his shop tinkering busily with a crowbar.

"Howdy, cousin," Lavadie said.

Joe nodded, eyes crinkled against the cigarette smoke. Nancy opened the front door and stood there, flanked by two big-eyed kids.

"I came over to talk to you about that field you're irrigating on the other side of the highway," Lavadie said.

"What interest you got in that beanfield?" Joe asked.

"I figure what's bad for this town, whatever stirs up unnecessary trouble, is bad for all of us, qué no?"

Joe shrugged, inhaled, exhaled, and replaced the cigarette Bogey-like between his lips.

"I just came from a meeting we had over in Nick's store," Lavadie said. "We decided that since it's illegal to irrigate those west side fields, we ought to tell you to quit fucking around over there."

Joe delicately flicked the head off a small sunflower with the crowbar.

"Well—?" Lavadie said.

"Well, what?"

"What's your answer to that?"

Joe shrugged again. "Who says it's me irrigating over there?"

"I guess a little birdie told somebody," Lavadie grunted sarcastically.

"Hmm," Joe commented.

"So what's your answer?" Lavadie demanded.

Joe spit the cigarette butt from his lips and, swinging the crowbar like a baseball bat, expertly caught the butt, lining it across the yard at his antagonist, missing him only by inches. "Maybe you better quit fucking around over *here*."

Lavadie flushed, but kept his cool. "Are you or are you not going to stop irrigating that field?" he asked.

Joe smiled blandly. "The real question is, are you or are you not gonna get off my property, Mr. Lavadie?" He advanced a few steps flexing the crowbar.

Lavadie hastily backed up to his truck. "What are you doing . . . are you threatening me?"

"This is my property," Joe explained matter-of-factly.

"Well, goddamn you . . ."

Lavadie slid behind the wheel of his truck and started

it up. "I'll go over there myself and see that not another drop goes into that field," he threatened.

"You do and won't nobody show up for work at your place tomorrow, Mr. Lavadie," Joe said quietly. "Your hay and your corrals might get burned by accident, too."

Lavadie fumed silently for a full ten seconds before jamming the gearshift into reverse and bouncing backward out of the yard.

"And—?" Bernabé Montoya politely inquired several minutes later.

Lavadie, pacing around the sheriff's living room, shook his head nervously. "What do you think, Bernie? Could he really get people to stop working at my place? Would he have the guts to burn my hay?"

"Sure. Maybe. Who knows?"

"I'd be up the creek without a paddle if that happened." Lavadie picked his nose. "This is more complicated than I thought. That little shithead's got no respect, does he?"

"Nope."

Following an awkward pause, Lavadie said, "I think maybe I better back out of this, Bernie. I think maybe the best thing right now is I shouldn't get involved, qué no?"

"Suit yourself, Mr. Lavadie."

"It's just I didn't realize—I had no idea . . ."

After Lavadie had slunk off, Bernabé slouched out to his pickup, tuned the radio to mariachi music coming from KKCV in Chamisaville, and steered onto the highway, turning south. Like everyone else in town, he automatically fired an obscene gesture (known as a "birdie") at Ladd Devine's Miracle Valley Recreation Area sign. Almost immediately after that he shuddered going over a painted cattleguard on the road, muttering to himself, "It sure beats me how a handful of white stripes can fool cows like that." Then, smoking thoughtfully, he listened to the radio and allowed his eyes to drift half-assedly around the landscape as he drove the fifteen or so miles to Doña Luz. In a field some kids were flying kites. Magpies hunkered atop flattened prairie dog carcasses along the shoulder. A few miles farther, the sheriff had to stop for some cows stupidly milling around on the highway. After that he tried to think about Joe's beanfield, but quit because already it made him uncomfortable to confront this thing; he had no idea how to deal with it. It was a situation like this, in fact, that could cost him his job. If he blew it, which was more than likely, that three-vote margin over Pancho Armijo every two years could dissolve into a landslide victory for his opponent.

So he had decided to try and pass the buck.

Two men occupied the tiny cinderblock state police headquarters at Doña Luz: a crew-cut good ol' boy state cop, Bill Koontz, and a young good-looking radio dispatcher, Emilio Cisneros.

Bernabé leaned against the counter behind which the two men sat—Koontz reading a comic book, and Cisneros typing up some forms—and he lit another cigarette.

"What's new up in the boondocks?" Koontz asked lazily. "Who shot whose cow last night?"

Bernabé smiled tiredly. He disliked the state police; he was also slightly awed by them. They were well-equipped men with an organization to back up their actions, and he himself was a loner with one stupid deputy. Any difficult crime he always referred to the state police: in fact, they wound up processing most of his arrests. Accident victims always awaited state cars to take them to the medical facilities in the south. All the same, he disliked going to cops like Bill Koontz for help or advice because that usually meant he wound up siccing them on his own people. And although nothing much ever really came of that, it made him uncomfortable all the same.

Now he said thoughtfully, "I came down here because I got a problem."

Koontz smiled. "So what else is new?"

"This one is kind of funny."

"Shoot," Koontz said.

"Well, there's a guy up in my town, maybe you know him—Joe Mondragón—"

"Sure, I know that S.O.B. What's he up to now?"

"He's irrigating his old man's beanfield on the western side of the highway."

"So—?"

"None of the land over there that used to have irrigation rights has irrigation rights anymore. I don't know the whole complicated story of how it happened, but it's got to do with the 1935 water compact."

"Sounds to me like the ditch boss, the one you people call the major domo, ought to handle this kind of thing," Koontz said. "What could we do about it?"

"Maybe you don't understand." Bernabé scratched behind one ear. "It's not like he's just irrigating this little beanfield. There's a lot of people in Milagro, you know, who aren't too happy with the way things are changing there, or down in Chamisaville, or all around the north. Up in Milagro—you've been along the Milagro–García spur, haven't you? You've seen the houses people used to live in out there, the old farmhouses, and all those fields?"

"That's a ghost town, man. Only that crazy old fart —what's his name—the little waffle with the badge and the suit, lives in those ruins—"

"Amarante Córdova."

"Yeah. He's the only one lives over there."

Bernabé drifted away from the counter over to the door, where he stood, hands behind his back, staring at the highway. The thought crossed his mind that he ought to handle this thing himself, because after all he more or less understood and had sympathy for the situation. On the other hand, if he handled the situation himself, suppose he butchered the job (a likely supposition), what then? At least if he gave it to the state cops he was off the hook.

Facing Koontz and Emilio Cisneros again, he said, "The thing is, irrigating that field is symbolic, the way I see it. People are bitter over how they lost their land and their water rights. And this sort of act, small as it may seem, could touch off something bigger."

Koontz said, "What do you want us to do?"

"I don't know. Frankly, I don't know what to do about it. It's not like you can just go in and arrest him or fuck up the beanfield or something. I mean, this is too *close* to everybody——"

Koontz frowned. "I'm not sure I understand, Bernie."

"Why don't you talk with somebody else," the sheriff suggested. "Talk with Bruno Martínez when he comes in. Better yet, get in touch with Trucho down in the capital. This is his sector, isn't it? Tell him to call me."

"For what? For a little loudmouthed troublemaker who's trickling a couple gallons of water into a crummy beanfield?"

Bernabé mumbled, "Ah, screw it then, I guess I'll handle it myself," and walked out to his truck.

Emilio Cisneros said, "If I was you, Bill, I'd call Trucho."

"Why?"

"Because I think he'd want to know. I don't think you really understand what Joe Mondragón is doing."

"You honest to God think I oughtta call Trucho?" Koontz asked uncertainly.

"Sure. The least he might do is talk with the state engineer. You let Bernie Montoya go back up there and handle something as sensitive as this on his own and he's sure to blow it badly. That sheriff is so stupid his boots were on the wrong feet, did you notice?"

"Okay. So maybe I'll call Trucho, then . . ."

Xavier Trucho, the third highest ranking cop in the state, in charge of the entire northern sector, said, "Repeat the whole thing to me again, Bill. Slowly. I want everything you can remember that honky-tonk Cisco Kid told you."

"It ain't much," Koontz said, suddenly nervous about the beanfield. "There's just this little guy, Joe Mondragón, who's cutting water into some deserted field isn't supposed to have water rights on the west side of the highway, in that ghost town part of Milagro, that's all."

"I think what I'll do," Trucho said, "is talk with the state engineer. Seems to me his office ought to handle it. I'll get back to you——"

And when he got back Trucho said, "Listen, Bill,

this thing could be a little antsy, but for the time being we're gonna steer clear of it. Bookman's—the state engineer's—office will handle it, or at least try to. So why don't you drive up to Milagro and tell that Montoya ape to keep his boots from getting muddy over there on the west side, okay? You might also stop up at the Devine place and let them know we're aware of the problem. And Bill—?"

"Yeah?"

"The key word is tact, alright? The key thing right now is to play this cozy. I mean, lay off Joe Mondragón, and let's keep our uniforms as inconspicuous as possible up there. Be nice to Bernie Montoya. People start getting the bright idea something is cooking, Bookman feels, it'll only aggravate the situation, and we're liable to find ourselves up to our ass in Mexican hornets. Okay?"

"Okay," Bill Koontz said, puzzled by the respect people seemed to be developing for Joe Mondragón and his puny beanfield. He turned, asking Emilio Cisneros:

"What does a little jerk like that want to cause this kind of trouble for?"

"I dunno," the dispatcher said, smiling faintly, curiously. "Let's just wait and see what happens."

❧

The Dancing Trout Dude Ranch was a thirty-eight-room adobe palace set in a cluster of cottonwood, Russian olive, weeping willow, cedar, and aspen trees on the banks of Indian Creek and surrounded by lush green meadows and apple, pear, apricot, and plum orchards that extended for miles back up into the Milagro Canyon.

Ladd Devine the Third was not so opulent.

Standing five foot nine in his cowboy boots, tipping the scales at one-forty-five, he had a bland, regular, and slightly good ol' boy face and a bland, regular, slightly good ol' boy way of speaking. He was the kind of man who worked hard, enjoyed circumventing risks, and avoided the limelight. He drove a pickup truck and kept a sharp authoritative eye on pretty much everything that went on at his spread. He also often spent up to twelve hours a day in his third-floor office constantly telephoning various parts of the town, county, state, and nation. At all times this sawed-off, unflamboyant man knew exactly where his affairs were at.

The Ladd Devine empire had been established by his grandfather, a boisterous whoremongering outdoors man who drank his bourbon straight from the bottle and cursed a lot. But once the corporate conglomerate was established, Ladd Devine the Third had been the perfect man to tone down the operation and keep it barging along smoothly; and also, incidentally, to build it into something really powerful.

This is not to say that Ladd Devine the Third hadn't inherited a couple of his grandfather's quirks. One was the airplane he often piloted himself out of the Chamisaville airport. The other was his wife, Flossie, a six-foot-tall "honeydear" woman from an Odessa, Texas, oil family, who wore Neiman-Marcus skintight, flare-cuffed, gold lamé, western cowgirl pants and stacked her peroxide-blond hair in a three-story bouffant. She had a body to match her garish looks, and with the ton of makeup she swabbed on daily, Flossie Devine looked to be on loan from the Lido, or else some kind of rent-a-tart from Las Vegas, Nevada. But Flossie was actually a placid, gentle soul. Her time she whiled away riding plump thoroughbred horses, playing bridge and solitaire and Scrabble, and drinking too much champagne or beer or whatever else happened to be around and open at the time. Flossie was a quiet lush, though, usually going to sleep right after dinner, and she had never done her husband dirty.

After an avocado salad lunch on the day Joe Mondragón first began to irrigate his beanfield, Ladd Devine's starched and prissified personal secretary, Emerson Lapp, scuttled like a nervous crayfish into the Devines' private den.

"Bad news downtown," he said. "Something funny is happening, Mr. D. It looks like trouble to me."

"Calm down, Em," Devine urged quietly. "You

want a bit of Irish coffee? Flossie and I were just having a cup, weren't we, Flossie?"

"Maybe you better hear about this right away," Lapp wheezed. "You know this guy downtown, his name is Joe Mondragón? He worked up here once, maybe four, five summers ago. He was on that cesspool crew you hired and during the time they worked we kept missing things, remember? A couple of aluminum siding panels, a few tools, some of that rough-cut lumber we were using on the stables extension. After maybe three weeks you narrowed the thefts down to Joe and fired him."

"Oh yes." Devine nodded. "He was a real wise guy."

"Well, he's cutting irrigation water into his father's piece of property over there on the west side."

"What was his father's first name? A lot of Mondragóns lived over there."

"I don't remember. But you don't own it, Mr. D. This Mondragón was one who wouldn't sell, remember? The old man—Joe's father—he went around raising a big stink back then, telling people not to sell. His son is a troublemaker, first class."

"Then what you're saying, Em, is that this Joe Mondragón is illegally irrigating his father's land, or his own land as the case may be, over there on the west side."

"Exactly. And I don't like it. He could stir up something nasty. Those people down there, they're tense enough as it is over this dam proposition—you know, and the conservancy district. If you ask me, and you'll pardon my French I'm sure, Flossie, he could start a fucking war if this isn't handled correctly and disposed of quickly and efficiently."

Devine pursed his lips, thinking for a moment. Then he picked up the telephone at his elbow and called the sheriff.

"Hello, Bernie? Ladd Devine. Say, listen, my friend, my secretary Mr. Lapp just came in with a story about this character, what's his name? this Joe Mondragón fellow he says is diverting irrigation water into one of those fields on the west side."

"He speaks the truth," Bernabé said, covering the mouthpiece as he whispered to his wife, "Carolina, get me a couple aspirins, will you? This is getting worse."

"Well, tell me then, Bernie. Do you think there's any possibility an apparently random action like this could have serious consequences?"

"Maybe. I dunno, Mr. Devine. But that's been on my mind, I can promise you."

"Did you go have a talk with Joe?"

"Well, it's this way, sir. Joe would have told me to jump in a lake before I opened my mouth."

"You could arrest him, couldn't you?"

"I figure until I understand better how the people here feel, Mr. Devine, and whether there's more than just one person involved, it might be foolish to start driving folks down to the Chamisa V. cooler. You know, some fanatics in town are just a little bit tense about your dam, sir—"

"It isn't *my* dam, Bernie. It would be controlled and operated by the people."

"Sure, sure. But of course you're aware of some of the sentiments floating around down here anyway." Masochistically, the sheriff chewed up the aspirin in his mouth, making a horrible face that startled his wife.

"I see." Devine thought for a moment. At length he said, "Bernie, I suppose you're right. At least for now."

"Basically, there's not much to do now, the way I see it, sir. Just lay low and see what develops, is my motto."

"Right. I'll keep in touch, Bernie. Good-bye."

"That guy—" Emerson Lapp cast his eyes to the ceiling. "It walks, it talks, it carries a real gun, so it calls itself a sheriff," he groaned sarcastically. "What did he have to say: 'Let's just lay low for the time being and see what happens,' I'll bet."

"Don't be nasty, Em." And, as Devine dialed another number, he told his secretary, "See if you can't drum up Horsethief Shorty and Jerry G., okay? I think Jerry G.'s down in the pony corral with some kids. Shorty might be over in the bunkhouse, it's his afternoon off. Tell them to come up for a short talk. And Jim Quintana, too—is Jim around? Hello, Harlan—?"

Emerson Lapp started to say, "Jim Quintana's out with that Kildare party from Lubbock—" but cut it short on a brief hand signal from his boss, who was talking to Harlan Betchel, manager of both the Pilar Café and the Harlan Betchel (Buck-A-Fish) Trout Pond behind the café.

Glumly, the secretary nodded so long to Flossie and left the room.

"Look, Harlan, a matter's come up that I think we should discuss. Do you think you could drive up here in, say, about ten minutes, for a short meeting at the ranch? You can leave Betty in charge. It won't take long."

"Sure, Mr. Devine. I could do that except the missus has the car, and she's down in Chamisaville doing the weekly shopping at Safeway."

"You can go over to the Forest Service office and hitch a ride with either Carl, or—what's that new man's name?"

"You must be talking about Floyd Cowlie, sir."

"Right, Floyd Cowlie. Tell me, is their truck outside the office, can you see?"

"Yup. Just sitting out there, Mr. Devine. In fact, only ten minutes ago they pulled in from having it serviced at Jake's Enco in Doña Luz. It had a leak in the oil pan they picked up on the Little Baldy road yest—"

"Then you can ride up with them, Harlan. I'm going to call them right now, so why don't you hustle over there pronto?"

"Sure thing. Right away."

Devine dialed the Forest Service office. Carl Abeyta answered.

"Carl, this is Ladd Devine. Right—thanks. Look, I'd like both you and Floyd to come up to my place right away for a short meeting. It's about that Joe Mondragón beanfield on the west side. Harlan Betchel's going to catch a ride with you boys because Greta is down in Chamisaville with the car. I'll expect to see you soon—"

"Whatever you say, sir. We'll be right over."

After that, while his wife pensively sucked on a sour lemon, Devine called the Enchanted Land Motel manager, Peter Hirsshorn, who promised to come right up, and then he dialed long distance to his lawyer and partner in crime, Peter's brother Jim. Briefly he outlined to the lawyer the situation insofar as he understood it, and asked Hirsshorn what his initial and instinctive gut reaction was.

"I dunno, Ladd. *I'm* not worried, if that's what you're after. Both of us have lived here all our lives, you know. We understand these people. You can probably smoke out the situation as well, if not better, than anyone else around there. My initial, gut-level response would be to keep close tabs on the situation, on Joe Mondragón, but for the time being stay cool, don't push the panic button. I'm assuming what he wants is to have his action legitimized by some kind of nervous or hysterical or authoritarian attention. So don't play his hand, Ladd, and I kind of feel the whole thing will die down."

"Thanks, Jim. Got to sign off now, here come Shorty and Jerry G."

Jerry Grindstaff, a foreman of the Dancing Trout, was a tall, lanky, fifty year old with a weather-beaten Oklahoma face and an air of the old-time rodeo cowboy about him. Horsethief Shorty Wilson, the other foreman, was a short, bowlegged, foxy-looking, white-haired man from Plainfield, New Jersey, who'd come out West forty years ago to be a cowboy, had traveled the rodeo circuit for about three years as a clown, and then been signed on one wild drunken night by Ladd Devine Senior, and he had been with the Devines ever since. Where Jerry G. was no-nonsense, taciturn, practically zombielike, Horsethief Shorty was a boozing, tall-story upstart with a propensity for never making the same mistake twice. Of the three men in the room, only Horsethief Shorty spoke Spanish.

"Don't tell me, Ladd, lemme guess," Shorty said

cheerfully. "That sawed-off ex-pachuco José Mondragón has went and cut water into a beanfield he owns on the west side of town, and you called us together right now because you got an uncomfortable inkling that that man irrigating that field at this particular time spells Trouble with a capital T—am I right?"

"You're right, Shorty," Devine said, although his words did not come out altogether friendly; with Shorty they never did. He had grown up and grown middle-aged with Shorty, but he had never really liked or absolutely trusted the man. Shorty's brass balls didn't disturb him as much as the man's uncanny familiarity with the entire workings of the Devine empire. And while Shorty usually ate with the help (whereas Jerry G. often dined with Devine, Flossie, Emerson Lapp, and other Devine functionaries), it was his habit right after lunch to amble obnoxiously into the boss's den and spend fifteen or twenty minutes with the *Wall Street Journal*. Over the years he had invested in stocks and bonds, and Devine suspected Shorty was currently worth a nice piece of change. Devine also suspected that if he himself had not shown an interest in the Devine enterprises, old Ladd Senior would have bequeathed the operation to Shorty—lock, stock, and barrel.

Most probably because his grandfather and Shorty had been alike as two peas in a pod, Devine was also somewhat awed by Shorty. And he harbored a feeling, which had been riding shotgun with him all his grown-up life, that if Shorty were ever removed, for one reason or another, from the Devine Company, the whole empire would come tumbling down.

Hence, he tolerated Horsethief Shorty and, while wincing at his uncouth cowboy appearance and his loud and sometimes lewd mouth, Devine nevertheless dealt Shorty into all high-level conferences; to a very great extent, he counted on his Spanish and his way with the local people to keep a finger on the pulse of the Miracle Valley.

The Forest Service truck jolted up the white gravel drive, and Flossie excused herself to greet the new arrivals at the door and usher them in. The men exchanged hellos and then Devine briefly reviewed the situation, asking each man what he had heard on the grapevine, what the thought Joe Mondragón's act might portend, and what he, Ladd Devine, ought to do about it.

"It's illegal," Floyd Cowlie said. "Why doesn't Bernie arrest him? I mean, forgetting for the moment that probably the only thing Bernie ever arrested was his own development."

"Well, people are nervous," Devine said, refusing to snigger along with the rest of them. "This dam, this conservancy district has the farmers down there on pins and needles. Arresting Joe Mondragón for a symbolic act like this could start something nasty."

Carl Abeyta laughed. "Who you trying to kid, Mr. D.? The people in this town—they're my people, qué no?—I know these people. They're not gonna go off half-cocked just because José Mondragón gets arrested. Shoot, I can't think of anybody who wouldn't send three cheers your way for cutting that punk down a little. Things aren't as tense as you think, Mr. D. I know. They're my people. qué no?"

"Excuse me, but what are you gonna learn from your so-called fucking people, seeing as how you work for the Floresta?" Horsethief Shorty chuckled, an obnoxious light twinkling in his dark eyes. "Shit, man, half the farmers who go to bed at night in this town dream of hanging you up by the balls for becoming one of Uncle Sam's Mexican honchos. Don't you remember what happened back in Buddy Galbaldon's time during the Smokey the Bear statue riot, I'm surprised that fat green truck of yours doesn't blow up every morning when you step on the accelerator. These people wouldn't confide in you, in that uniform, Carl, if you was César Chávez, Pedro Infante, Cantinflas, and Lee Trevino all rolled into one."

"Uh, Harlan—?" Devine asked, moving uncomfortably on.

"Mr. D., the people in this town like you. In fact, I wouldn't be surprised if you found out someday they really *love* you. I mean, you put this place on the map, didn't you? And now with this Miracle Valley project, why, they're gonna owe to you everything they got—"

"Which won't be nothing new," Shorty interrupted, flashing a bright impudent grin at his boss.

"No, I think whatever you decided to do, they would back you up," Harlan insisted. "I know *I* sure would. And Nick Rael, that's the way *he* feels—"

"Which isn't too surprising," Shorty said, "considering that Ladd here's got so many notes on Nick's business, not to mention the mortgage on his house— shit, fellas." Shorty bit off the end of a cigar, rolling it in his puckered lips for a moment before he scratched a match on his zipper and lit it. "I got nothing against Nick, understand, but he's owed the Devine operation so much for so long that all he's got on his mind now is how best to kiss ruddy bums from here to Christmastime so's to build up credit until Valentine's Day, and I wouldn't trust his opinion any more than I'd trust you, Harlan, to dish me up a piece of cherry pie for breakfast that wasn't made from fruit in a can."

Flossie giggled. She loved Horsethief Shorty. In fact, she had always wanted to make love with Shorty. Once, a long time back, when her husband was away and the help more or less off for the day, they got drunk together, her and Shorty, under some weeping willows, drinking bourbon, seated in mammoth wooden armchairs built by an alcoholic local santo carver named Snuffy Ledoux, who had left town years ago (during the Smokey the Bear statue riot, in fact) to seek his fortune in the capital. When they both had a mellow buzz on, laughing and giggling intimately together, Flossie asked, "Can I take my clothes off, Shorty, and would you diddle me if I did?" And Shorty's eyes popped open wide as he exclaimed, "Shit, Flossie, I ain't *that* drunk!" When she burst into tears, he went over and tenderly cuddled her head for a moment, crooning, "Listen, honey. It ain't what you maybe think, and it sure ain't nothing personal. But all my life I've had the bad habit of sticking my tool into anything that would spread its legs or its cheeks or open its mouth, and right now, much as I hate to admit it, I got a dose." She never learned if that was true or not, but he went on and unpinned her hair, letting the long yellow curls flow and bounce around her shoulders, and then he sat on the thick grass in front of her while they talked about screwing and other things. Some talk was sad, some funny. Shorty recounted terribly raunchy stories about the whorehouse in Juarez and Agua Prieta and Nogales; he also gave her the straight poop on a couple of women he had loved. She didn't have anything approximating his experience, but she told him about groping around in the back seats of enormous convertibles with crew-cut boys in tuxedos who sucked on her big breasts like newborn babies. They became very close that afternoon, like brothers and sisters, and at one point Shorty unzipped his fly, letting her ogle his wong for a minute; after that she unbuttoned her blouse and pried out a breast for him to inspect. He went and kissed the nipple, which touched off her tears again, but nothing else happened. Since then they had been close, and sometimes Flossie talked to Shorty about things that bothered her, or else she just described to him the nebulous thoughts floating like lazy tropical fish through her brain, and she never felt Shorty was mocking her, not even silently in his mind. They had much in common, being both lonely and sad, but comfortable; and they felt at ease with each other; and somehow, God knows how, they had handled it perfectly for a long time, so that no chisme or rumor had ever linked them in a compromising fashion.

"Jerry G.," Devine said. "What do you think?"

Jerry G. furrowed his brow, pursed his lips, and for a long time said nothing. Eventually he dislodged the following:

"I think this small act is part of a larger problem which could become serious."

"That's it?"

Not one to adorn an opinion, Jerry G. nodded.

"What would you do about it?"

Again he frowned, steeped in plodding, methodical,

concentrated thought. At the end of this session, he drawled:

"I hate to say 'Let's just wait and see how the thing develops before making a move,' but I'm afraid that's all I can think to say right now."

Ladd Devine settled back. "Anybody here got any idea why he did it?"

"Why does that little bugger do anything?" Carl Abeyta said.

"Anybody else?" Devine asked.

"He's curious to see what'll happen," Shorty suggested. "I don't think he knows why he did it himself. One thing for sure, nobody put him up to it. But if I was you I wouldn't let nobody, least of all nobody from the valley you don't trust for sure, see those plans for the conservancy district where you and Nelson Bookman got almost all that new water made possible by the dam going into that beanfield acreage you been buying up over on the west side for a golf course ever since the 1935 water compact killed all the little farmers over there."

Devine blew cigarette smoke carefully out through his nose. Then, leaning forward abruptly, he said, "Well, boys, for the time being I guess that's it. Sorry to put you out, but this meeting is already over. I think for now we'll simply have to wait and see how things develop—"

And the last of the men had just departed when the phone rang.

Peter Hirsshorn, manager of the Enchanted Land Motel, blurted, "Hey, Ladd? Look. Listen, I'm really sorry. But we've had an accident down here. The couple in 12B—well, the guy, he's from someplace around Austin, he's a fishing nut. They were gonna go over to Betchel's Buck-A-Fish highway robbery, catch a few moron trout, and this guy, his name is Carson, Phil Carson—he's in space electronics or something—well, he was outside beyond the pool, casting with his new rod, trying it out or practicing or something, with one of those big grasshoppers on it, you know? The ones Fred Quintana ties that Harlan sells in the café, he had one of those on, a number six which I know is crazy—for the Rio Grande, maybe, but not Harlan's mud puddle—but he had it on anyway, dry casting it on the lawn like I said, and he just got it caught in his ear. The hook went all the way through his fucking ear. So instead of coming up to your place I had to drive him down to the clinic here in Doña Luz. That's where I'm calling from, and I'm really sorry . . ."

"Don't worry about it," Devine said. "No sweat. Everything is under control."

ॐ

Five men were seated around a large oval table in a conference room off the governor's office in the state capitol. There was the governor himself, a tall, heavily built man with small nervous eyes that never really looked at anybody and a cowboy twang when he spoke, a successful rancher who had parlayed a number of hunches into some successful oil interests, and close—but largely disguised—ties to several big-time land developers who were moving into the state. He walked slowly and spoke slowly, and almost everything he said publicly was bland, or a cliché, or just plain stupid. Yet, though ridiculed by the press and slandered unmercifully by his enemies, he had come out on top in a very crooked election and he could control a political machine better than any person in the state had ever controlled one, and he was worth over four million dollars.

The other men with the governor in the room were the state engineer, Nelson Bookman; a lawyer from the state engineer's office named Rudy Noyes; a short swarthy aid to the governor—his bodyguard, actually —called Myron Cloon; and an undercover agent for the state police. The agent, Kyril Montana, was a tall, sunny-looking Anglo with straw-colored hair and wide blue eyes, an all-American nose, straight thin lips, and an athletic physique. He had a nice smile, a pretty wife who had been runner-up in a state beauty contest fourteen years ago, and two good-looking kids. Kyril Montana wore a neatly pressed pink shirt, a bolo tie, beige, tapered western pants, and cowboy boots, and he carried a pack of filtertip cigarettes in his shirt pocket over the heart. In overall appearance he came on like a young, good-natured cowboy. He had been a cop for over fifteen years, however, and he was very sensitive to police work and to people's attitudes about the police. He was not a gung-ho cop; he wasn't quick to make an arrest, or to pull a gun, or to nail people just on general principles. He had done several stints on the narcotics beat at the state university, mingling with kids, acting like a student, drawing up detailed lists of drug users and their connections, but he had never set up a massive bust of psychedelic dopers or pot smokers. Even when there had been political pressures to arrange something that would grab headlines and squash longhairs for a while, Kyril Montana had played it cool, had kept maneuvering through the drug subculture hoping to nail the hard-drug pushers and suppliers, and he had usually managed to keep his superiors off his back until he finally had one of the big fish, until he finally had tiptoed through the smack or cocaine hierarchy to a source. Then, as quietly as possible, he had set up the bust, and more often than not it was so clean and so quiet that hardly anyone realized what had happened, the agent receiving no publicity at all. Occasionally he had been called off assignments when his superiors felt he was proceeding too cautiously. But the agent took these periodic lumps without comment, and in this way he had survived. He was a good cop, a cynical but not unhappy man. He liked his children and was true to his wife. With her he rarely talked shop. They played golf together and went out often—to movies, to the theater occasionally, to triple-A baseball games, and to the state university football games. Their sex together wasn't that imaginative, but it was all right, still satisfying. They were a clean-cut couple with clean-cut kids, a suburban house with a water sprinkler on the manicured front lawn and a small pool in back, and the agent himself was a clean-cut professional cop who managed to keep his work surprisingly free of depressing fuckups.

The state engineer, Nelson Bookman, and his personal special assistant, Rudy Noyes, knew more water

law than the rest of the state put together. For the
past seventeen years Bookman had been the state
engineer, meaning he was more responsible than any
other person or group for what water the state had
obtained during that time through interstate pacts
and reclamation projects and so forth. Rudy Noyes,
who was still young at thirty-six, had been with the
office, had, in fact, been Bookman's personal sidekick,
apprentice, and mouthpiece for eleven of those seventeen years. During that time they had weathered the
heaviest political storms to sweep the state. They had
also sweated, plotted, finagled, begged, twisted, and
driven their way to what they felt was their state's
fair share of Colorado River Basin water; they had
made deals with Texas and California, with Arizona
and Colorado and Utah; and they had created lobbies
in Washington to have dams built and rivers chan-
neled; they had set into motion adjudication suits to
determine how much water people did or did not have
in all areas; they had literally decided how the rivers
would run and which people must benefit the most
from those rivers. In so doing they had constantly
played the state's southern agribusinessmen off against
the small northern farmers, and somehow they had
come through. The conservative farmers in the south
hated State Engineer Bookman and his little sidekick,
Rudy Noyes, because they felt the north was getting
too much water—in fact, they felt *any* water allo-
cated to the north was wasted water. If Bookman and
Noyes explained that the northern farmers owned
priority rights because they had been using the water
for centuries, the southern farmers pointed to their
cotton and grain fields, asking, "But who's growing
cash crops, who's providing the stuff for export, who's
keeping the state's economic head above water?" And
you couldn't argue with that. Farming in the north
was subsistence farming, nothing more; and nothing
could be less.

But the farmers in the north hated Bookman and
Noyes also because those two had betrayed their water
interests and rights, they had worked deals whereby
much of the north's centuries-old water rights had

gone to the southern agribusinessmen, and they felt
that Bookman and Noyes, more than any other state
political figures, headed those forces most responsible
for the death of little towns like Milagro, whose residents spoke a different language from the people of
the south.

But Bookman and Noyes did not have it in for the
Northerners. They divided up the state's water—as
nearly as was possible—in direct relationship to a
region's political clout and economic pull. It was that
simple, and it meant that by dealing with the realities
of the given situation, Bookman and Noyes had quietly
overseen the transfer of water and water rights from
the small-timers in the green northern valleys to the
big businessmen and development enterprises in the
flat plains and deserts of the south. Both Bookman
and Noyes believed in the American concepts of
"growth" and "progress"; hence, they could see no
justification for the small farmers' wrath. "Why don't
those fucking old-fashioned irrelevant Tinkertoy coyotes face up to the economic realities?" was the way
Bookman usually put it. "Who do those pathetic illiterate old geezers think they are, sitting on one-acre
beanfields, demanding more water, when there's a
man down south with an eight-thousand-acre farm
that's crying to be irrigated?"

Noyes, a skinny red-headed man, never said much.
And certainly not in public. He wore impeccable
three-piece Brooks Brothers suits, Bostonian loafers,
and staid horn-rimmed glasses, and he knew the law.
He sat beside Bookman at Interstate Streams Commission meetings—when, say, the environmentalists
were trying to defeat a Bureau of Reclamation water
salvage project—and while Bookman, who knew
more than anybody else about water, was tearing apart
his opponent's arguments, Noyes never said a word,
unless Bookman, without even turning sideways or
taking his eyes off a particularly offensive ecology witness, asked, "What's the law on that, Rudy?" And
then Rudy Noyes would state the law, precisely,
clearly, and flawlessly, and usually as he stated the
law he would be riffling through the state's book of

statutes or water laws or whatever until, just at the moment he finished talking, he would land on exactly what Bookman wanted, and he'd read that too, clipped, sharp, without faltering, and with no extraneous comments added.

In this way, Bookman and Noyes had been a formidable team. They always had on hand more information, more facts to support their theories and their projects, than did the other side. They scared people with their efficiency and their knowledge. Bookman used language like a scalpel. He cut carefully and cleanly, never misstepping, building arguments that were irrefutable, even if erroneous or morally repugnant. He could do this not just thanks to his own critical intellect, but because in Noyes he had a wizard of a researcher with a photographic mind and an absolutely articulate way of laying out a thing during the closed, man-to-man skull sessions lasting up to an hour the two had every day between nine and ten in the morning. In a sense, or at least in one important —the most important—area, they had more political power than the governor. The governor was a land man. He understood a lot about how to speculate for land, graze it, subdivide it, make it pay dividends. But still, the land in a desert state was worth nothing without water, and Bookman and Noyes controlled the water. In their back pockets, they had the arteries of the state, the rivers and streams, the creeks, and the ponds and the reservoirs that created its valleys of life. All that was in their hands, their heads, their legal notebooks. However they planned their water, that is how and in what directions the state would grow.

Now these men, the governor, the undercover agent, Kyril Montana, the state engineer, Nelson Bookman, and his special assistant, Rudy Noyes, and the governor's aide and bodyguard, Myron Cloon, were gathered in the conference room of the governor's office for a very specific reason, and that reason was Joe Mondragón.

"Alright," said the governor. "Here's a half-pint son of a bitch cut water he has no rights to into a half-pint field that'll never grow a decent bean, and what the hell are we going to do about it?"

"Let's review the facts first," Bookman said, and he wasn't talking to the governor, but rather to Kyril Montana, who was sitting back comfortably with his hands folded under his chin, politely listening. "The facts are that this man's name is Mondragón—Joe A. Mondragón. He's a general handyman who lives and has always lived in Milagro. He has four pieces of land, only one of which has irrigation rights, the acre directly surrounding his house. His other pieces are five acres of sageland in the eastern section of Milagro known as Coyote Arroyo and another 1.7-acre piece near the north–south highway that never had any rights so far as our office knows. After that there's this piece in question, seven-tenths of an acre. It's fed by a ditch they call Roybal's ditch that comes off the Acequia Madre del Sur that used to have a headgate on Indian Creek. There has been no water in Roybal's ditch for fifteen, twenty years. We have aerial photographs proving this. When the 1935 Interstate Water Compact was set up, all the land on this ditch was adjudicated, and all the people made an offer of no rights. We could do this because so many farmers from Milagro had never filed title to their rights with our office. Now it's normal procedure, in a case such as this, for people to come into the office with proof of water rights if they disagree with our officer. At the time of the compact this land under question was owned by Esequiel Mondragón, Joe's father. He never came in, never signed the adjudication papers, and so we made a default judgment of no water rights. There was never any trouble. At that time I think the old man was sick with malaria and had quit working his fields anyway; later he raised a stink. But, in fact, this particular field in question, during the Second World War, lay fallow for longer than four straight years, and so automatically, according to state law, lost its rights anyway. But in any any case, those fields along Roybal's ditch, all of which were given no rights offers, simply fell from usage completely when people understood what had happened. Many people—in

fact, most small farmers in that part of town—have
sold their land to Ladd Devine, the heir to the old
sheep company and the present-day developer of the
Miracle Valley Recreation Area project, which includes a luxury subdivision on the west side land
that would be built around a Robert Trent Jones golf
course. Hence, when we consider this problem and all
its ramifications, we've got to keep in mind that what
could be seriously compromised, not only by Joe
Mondragón's beanfield, but also by mishandling the
affair, are Ladd's interests, and—quite frankly—the
interests of this office also. We've worked hand in
hand with Ladd Devine for a long time, and I personally feel that his Miracle Valley project can open
up the north to a progressive economic development
on a scale that we would not even have dared to
dream about five years ago. All this is tied in with
the Indian Creek Conservancy District and Dam, of
course, which I won't go into right now except to
state an irony in the situation. Which is that once we
create the conservancy district and build that dam,
Joe Mondragón will receive water to irrigate his field.
Of course, he may understand—I don't know, and *I'm*
certainly not going to tell him—that with development
of that golf course and the subdivision, his land value
and the taxes and conservancy assessments on it are
going to skyrocket so high he'll never be able to raise
the cash for those costs by growing beans. And, since
the chances are a million to one against his ever being
able to raise the capital to develop that small plot,
he'll wind up having to sell out or else he'll simply
lose it to the state, which would, of course, pass it on
to Ladd Devine where I'm afraid it belongs. That's
the nature of the situation, and the people up there
understand it instinctively, although they certainly
don't understand the finer points nor the mechanism
that can bring all this about."

Bookman paused, lighting a cigarette, slightly re-
arranged the single sheet of eight by eleven typing
paper that lay in front of him, and continued.

"Now for whatever reasons, a short time ago Joe
Mondragón decided to irrigate his field. This was

around the fifteenth, I think. He probably spent an hour cleaning Roybal's ditch to the point where it diverted into his seven-tenths of an acre, then opened the headgate on the Acequia Madre del Sur and flooded the field. Apparently no one was around. At least nobody stopped him."

The governor stood up and went to the window where he paused, both hands in his pockets, staring thoughtfully down at the capitol parking lot jammed with cars. But none of the other men moved. Only the state engineer was smoking and the smoke from his cigarette curled quietly in the still air.

"The Roybal ditch has no mayordomo," Bookman continued. "It's been out of use too long. The mayordomo on the Acequia Madre is a man called Vincent Torres, who's a cousin of Mondragón's."

"They're all cousins up there," the governor's aide said. "They been inbreeding up there for centuries. It's a wonder they're not all insane."

There was no response to this comment from the other men, all of whom thought Cloon an insufferable dolt. Bookman went on.

"It's a cinch Mondragón didn't ask Vincent Torres for permission to irrigate. We've had an investigator up there twice already, and he's spoken with Torres both times, and both times Torres has acted shocked, as if he can't believe Mondragón is irrigating. So our man took him to the field and he just scratched his head and said he'd keep an eye out and let us know if he caught anybody . . ."

"Bullshit," mutttered Cloon to himself, to nobody.

Bookman said, "Our man spoke with the two commissioners on the Acequia Madre, Meliton Mondragón, also a cousin, and Filiberto Vigil, no relation. They likewise registered surprise, and stayed surprised when our people took them to the field."

"It's a conspiracy," Cloon muttered, and Kyril Montana allowed just a flicker of annoyance to ripple his brow. The governor continued to stare out at the parking lot, where a man was flitting from car to car testing doors, and then, as Bookman continued, the governor saw the man open a door and lean in quickly, rifling through a glove compartment, and the governor never said a word to interrupt the state engineer, nor moved a muscle nor an eyelash while the car was ransacked.

."We saw Mondragón next," Bookman continued, "and he denied everything. He wouldn't come to the field with us, said he was busy. He was working in his shop, welding together a horse trailer. We gave him copies of the offer of judgment clearly stating he has no water rights on that land and then left because he was growing hostile."

"What do you mean by hostile?" Kyril Montana asked.

"He threatened to kick my man's butt out of there. And he said if any more feds came around his place bothering him when he was at work, he'd 'dust their asses with buckshot' because they were trespassing on his private property."

The governor turned, chuckling briefly, walked back to his chair, and sat down. Kyril Montana smiled quietly.

"We've talked with some other people in Milagro," Bookman said. "With the mayor, Sam Cantú, with the sheriff, Bernabé Montoya, with the general store manager, Nick Rael. They were all upset about the thing, but didn't exactly know what to do about it. They referred us back to the commissioners of the Acequia Madre del Sur and the mayordomo; all were downright sullen and hostile. A rancher we talked with, an Anglo named Ray Gusdorf, who owns a small spread at the mouth of Milagro Canyon just below Ladd Devine's Dancing Trout ranch, told us he minded his business and the other people in town minded theirs and that's the way he liked it. In short, in one way or another everybody seemed to know about this situation, but nobody was willing to take the bull by the horns."

Cloon got up and approached the window. He was a short, wiry-haired, stocky man, strong and agile, with a smooth slick face and bored eyes, and a short flat .38 in a shoulder holster you could see whenever he leaned slightly forward and his sport coat lapel fell away from his chest. Resting one foot on the low windowsill, he gazed grumpily down at the parking lot.

"Alright," said Kyril Montana. "So tell me exactly what the nature of the problem is."

"We've gone back to Milagro twice since then," Bookman said. "After he irrigated that first time, Mondragón plowed the field and then disked it and planted it. With beans. With irrigation trenches beside each row. By now those seeds should be sprouting. The third time we went up the earth in the field was wet and green grass was growing around the edges, and, more sparsely, down along the ditches. Obviously the field was receiving water regularly."

"Hey," Cloon muttered from over at the window. "There's a bastard down there robbing cars."

Kyril Montana said, "So—?"

Bookman leaned back with his hands clasped behind his head: "So we almost served him with papers to show cause that he has water rights on that piece of land."

"What's the procedure for that? What exactly does that mean?" the agent wanted to know.

"He'd have thirty days to prove he has water rights to that piece of land. If he couldn't prove it, the state could order him to stop irrigation. There'd be a hearing before a special water master, of course. But it would be open and shut; our records confirm that. Problems might be witnesses to testify that Mondragón is irrigating his own land. But we have more than enough evidence, I don't foresee any difficulties there. Otherwise, if—after the hearing—he continued to irrigate, we'd have to arrest him, I suppose. And that could get sticky. Which is why we're still holding onto those show-cause papers."

Bookman took his hands from behind his head, shook another cigarette out of the pack on the table before him, and lit it.

"Sticky, you understand, because there'd be a lot of attendant publicity, maybe hostility, which could hurt the conservancy district, the dam, and the whole Miracle Valley setup with Ladd Devine. It's a tricky business to try and implant a tourism-oriented development in the middle of a hornet's nest, in a tense situation that might be violent, that would certainly have racial overtones. It could even develop into a minor revolution of sorts. Those people up there have traditionally had long fuses, but they do have fuses as any of you gentlemen who's studied this state's history a little knows."

"What makes you feel there'd be so much publicity?" Kyril Montana asked.

"Well, for one thing, and maybe we can discount this as no threat, there's a lawyer," Bookman said, leaning back again, taking his time now. "He happens to be Joe Mondragón's lawyer, and he also sometimes writes articles for a small monthly paper published in the capital here, *The Voice of the People*. Maybe you've read it?"

"Sure," the agent said. "I've glanced through a few copies."

"Alright. Now, this lawyer, he's a strange fellow, a displacement from the East Coast. He worked in Colorado for a while, in Alamosa, in the Legal Aid program up there. Then he moved to Milagro. He's thirty-seven years old, married to a twenty-nine-year-old Chicano woman—they have two kids. He has an informal practice up there after a fashion; in a quiet way he defends the poor. He's not a raving liberal, though he has done cases for chickens, tomatoes, and cucumbers. But never—as far as I know—for land, so he's acquired a certain trust up there, I imagine. We've crossed with him twice on water rights issues. He's articulate but not that good. I sense that he's as frightened of rocking the boat as we are. Of course, he may be a better lawyer than the last time we faced him in a small matter over a year and a half ago, I don't know."

"What's his name?" the agent asked, taking a small pad and a cheap ball-point pen from his shirt pocket, and when Bookman said "Charley Bloom," Kyril Montana started to write it down, then suddenly stopped, nodding, and put his pen away.

While this went on the governor sat passively in his chair, hands folded in his lap, little eyes lost beneath his brows, staring at the edge of the table, at the tip of a boot, at nothing. Myron Cloon slumped down in a chair by the window, chewed off a finger-nail, and began playing with it in his teeth.

"I take it you had in mind a specific article he did for the *Voice*," Kyril Montana said, lighting a ciga-rette and blowing the smoke out slowly.

"Right. Naturally, he's talked with his client. He's talked with a lot of other people up there, also, and he wrote a story, not implicating anybody, but in a general way running down Ladd Devine's relationship to the town, the conservancy district and the dam and so forth, the poverty of the Miracle Valley, all that. It's a very technically vague but emotionally clever story. Rudy—?"

Rudy Noyes placed the folder he had been holding in his lap on the table, flipped it open and neatly extricated a Xeroxed copy of the typewritten article, which he turned around in his hands much like some-one turning a knife around so the handle would be first, and handed it across the table to Kyril Montana.

"He treats it like nobody knows who's irrigating the field. He makes it out that the entire town is irri-gating the plot. It's a propaganda article, a socialist tract in a way, I suppose, but it might be effective. He's done some research into the 1935 water compact, also gotten a number of quotes about how bitter the small farmers up there feel over their land and water situation."

Kyril Montana wrote something down in his note-book.

"Nobody, or at least hardly anybody, reads the *Voice*," Bookman said after a pause. "I don't think their readership is much more than fifteen hundred, maybe two thousand, and half of that is from out of state—you probably know that as well as we do."

The agent nodded.

"But you never can tell," Bookman added. "We don't want this to blow up into something symbolic. If we could stop publication of Bloom's article, that would be nice—but I don't see how we can. We can buy it up—we'll do that—no problem. It would be bad, though, if the regular media got hold of it and decided to play it up. Now that's your department more than mine, you know the people, you have the information—"

Kyril Montana nodded again and jotted a few more notes on his pad. Bookman waited until he was through writing before resuming.

"Like I said, we don't want this to blow up into something symbolic. The way things stand right now, that lawyer's article is romantic bullshit, the town is not really behind Joe Mondragón. But they're not against him either. I've talked with Ladd Devine, and of course he knows there's a deep-rooted underlying resentment in that town, and that the Miracle Valley project is going to have to tiptoe into Milagro like a drunk husband with his shoes off. Still, most of those people are scared stiff of authority. They're tough, sure, else they wouldn't have survived up there this long, but they don't want trouble. Yet they are also curious right now. I'll wager some are really drawn to Joe Mondragón. He's a town character. He's feisty, he talks a lot, talks big, fights to back up his words. He's a little bulldog, that's what he is, and I'll tell you frankly, I don't want to misjudge his capacity for drawing those people together and causing trouble. He doesn't know it but he might be a leader. And what my office wants, what I personally hope for, is that we can end this thing before some of these old galoots up there take it into their heads to join him. Maybe it doesn't seem so now, but that's potentially one hell of a volatile area up there, in the north . . ."

Kyril Montana said, "What are his chances of proving he has water rights to that field?"

"Zero. He has no rights."

"Suppose at a hearing your special water master was to find that Joe Mondragón did have water rights to that field—wouldn't that help you out of the situation?"

"The rest of the fields Devine doesn't yet own, including maybe four or five acres he needs for that golf course but hasn't gotten yet, would immediately come under irrigation," Bookman said, "making it that much harder to consolidate the entire area."

"The problem is," said the governor, "that this man has to be discouraged before we ever even get to the hearing stage."

Cloon suggested, "So scare him."

"I don't think he's going to scare that easily," Bookman said.

"Buy him off," Cloon rasped.

Irritated, Bookman stubbed out his cigarette and continued to address Kyril Montana. "Two, maybe three things," he said. "First, we should see if there's any way to squash the Bloom article. I doubt there is so we'll make arrangements to corner as many copies of the magazine as possible. Then we should probably check out the lawyer himself."

Kyril Montana said, "And then——?"

"And then we go after Mondragón. I don't know that much about how it might be handled. That's your department. We go to Milagro, maybe, talk with people, find the weak links. Maybe float a little money, see who nibbles, make a few promises, I don't know. Seed a rumor. Mondragón has a hair-trigger temper. Get him to assault someone, an official or our office perhaps, or a cop—put him away for a time until things cool down. I don't know exactly how, but I don't think it would be too difficult."

Through all this the governor, who was good friends with everybody present, seemed not to be paying attention, and Cloon suddenly appeared to fall asleep. Rudy Noyes sat impassively beside Bookman, and Kyril Montana studied the wire binding holding his small notebook together.

At length the agent said, "Do you think if he lost the hearing he would quit?"

Bookman said, "I know he wouldn't. Sooner or later we'll have to arrest him."

"How do you know he won't quit?"

"I've just got a feeling," Bookman said. "I know the north, and something like this has been building for a long time. The war never ended in 1848, you know. We simply don't want this hearing and we don't want to arrest Joe Mondragón for using water that he lost in 1935 to grow beans today. The worst thing we could do is make him a martyr."

The governor said, "What do you think, Ky?"

Kyril Montana put his notebook away and stubbed out his cigarette. "I'm not sure. Maybe I'll go up there. Study the town, talk a little. I've got a close friend in real estate up there, we'll chat. I think we already have a file on Bloom. I'm not positive he's got a vulnerable profile, but if memory serves me there's a couple of decent-sized holes in his life. So although right now I can't say for sure, perhaps we'll start with the lawyer."

They all got to their feet then and returned to their separate offices.

ॐ

There were no windows in Amarante Córdova's remaining one room: long ago he had adobed them up solid to preserve heat. All the same, he awoke on this morning, as he did every morning, at first daylight and slowly commenced his day, climbing out from under about twenty-five pounds of crazy quilts and old army blankets and hastily drawing on his sloppy old suit over his patched, foul-smelling long underwear. Then he took a shot from a half-pint brandy bottle, and before rolling a cigarette, hefted a couple of piñon logs from a corner stack and stuffed them into his twelve-dollar Sears tin heater. Usually the coals from the night before were still so hot in the heater that after a minute, if he just dropped a lit kitchen match in there—which he now did—the logs burst into flame.

This accomplished, he swung the circular cover back on the stove, unbolted and opened his door, and stood in the doorway a moment assessing the day. The view from this one opening into his room was a view like many another in Milagro. A well housing in the front dirt yard, a rusty 1949 Oldsmobile with bullet holes across the windshield sinking on its rims nearby, big yellow tumbleweed skeletons scattered among a few sunflowers, then the raggedy cottonwoods along the creekbed across the road and the majestic snow-capped Midnight Mountains beyond.

The old man coughed, scratched his balls, snagged a coffeepot with one arthritic paw, and shuffled over to the hand-dug well. Letting the bucket drop slowly to the water thirty feet below, he only a quarter filled it, then slowly, resting after each tug, pulled the bucket up and tipped some water into the coffeepot, which he carried back and set atop the heater.

Next, he proceeded cautiously around his dwelling to the backyard outhouse. And while he camped there with the door open so he could watch the turquoise-silver bluebirds flying about his crumbling farmhouse, he also slowly and shakily, though in the end expertly, rolled a cigarette and lit in, contentedly puffing away as he crapped.

After that, Amarante creaked around to his room again and made a cup of instant coffee, poured some brandy into it, and for almost an hour, while the day began, he sat on a white stump next to his front door, bathed in the early sharp sunlight, letting his eyes go bleary as he sipped the piping hot, spiked coffee and rolled and smoked another cigarette. During this time he talked to himself about his wife, his children—those still living and others dead and gone. He also carried on long, intricate, nonsensical dialogues with his good friend Tranquilino Jeantete, and with God, a number of devils, a few saints, and the Virgin Mary. And another thing during this quiet breakfast time: he had the habit of remembering scenes, moods, geography, little moments—memory blips—that had occurred yesterday or maybe fifty years ago. And so he would picture green fields full of confused and immobile meadowlarks during a late May snowstorm; or he would recall the way lightning had exploded jaggedly all around the Chamisaville drive-in theater when his daughter Sally had taken him to a John Wayne movie fifteen years ago; or maybe he would see his wife, Betita, straining, holding his hands, turning purple and howling with her legs spread wide, crushing his hands (she broke his finger once) during the birth of a child. . . .

And on this morning, as on other recent mornings after he had put on his thick-lensed eyeglasses, Amarante also observed Joe Mondragón several fields away, irrigating his bean plants.

The old man watched Joe's work with interest, with a certain feeling of pride, even with a kind of reverence. Amarante had been born on Milagro's west side, in this same house when it was intact; he had worked the fields that now lay fallow about him, and someday he would die on the west side, in his room, or from a heart attack while splitting wood, or maybe he would freeze to death in a ditch some sparkling winter night on his way back from the Frontier Bar—but whatever, Amarante had stuck with the west side through all the thick shit and all the thin shit, saying good-bye to his neighbors one by one while refusing to budge himself, until he had wound up alone with the swallows and the bluebirds and the crumbling houses whose rooms were full of tumbleweeds. Then here, suddenly, was a stubborn, ornery little bastard who had decided to put some life back into the west side. And as Joe Mondragón's bean plants started to grow, Amarante fixed his eyes on that patch of green, feeling excited and warm and a lot less lonely, too.

It hadn't taken long, though, for Amarante to realize that Joe's beansprouts were really going to stir up something in Milagro.

And so on this morning Amarante had a special plan. Spending less time than usual on the stump beside the front door, he drank only one cup of coffee and forewent his customary wood-chopping session. In its stead he hastily gummed down two Piggly-Wiggly tortillas wrapped around some tiny Vienna sausages, made sure a full book of food stamps was stashed safely in his inside breast pocket, and then from a peg driven into the mud wall over his bed he removed a cracked leather gun belt and holster, which he buckled around his skinny waist.

From a tin box on whose cover fading blue asters had been painted Amarante then removed a well-oiled revolver, an old, very heavy Colt Peacemaker. His father had given him the gun eighty years ago: it was the weapon he'd carried as sheriff of Milagro. Amarante had never discharged it at anybody; in fact, the gun had rarely been used, even for target practice. But it had always been, and yet remained, his most cherished possession.

The old man fitted this monumental weapon into the holster, made certain his sheriff's badge was pinned correctly to his suit lapel, and hit the road.

Shoulders hunched, leaning way forward, Amarante stomped with a rickety bowlegged gait along the potholed dirt path, eyes fixed straight ahead, absolutely determined—once in motion—to let nothing break his feeble rhythms until he had arrived where he planned to go.

He stopped once, however, near Joe's beanfield, swayed uncertainly for a moment before leaving the road, climbed up the Roybal ditch bank, and carefully picked his way over stones and dry weeds to where water left the ditch and entered the field.

He waved at Joe, who was leaning against his shovel, and Joe called, "Howdy, Chief. What's with the pistol this morning?"

Grinning toothlessly and gesturing with his hand, Amarante offered Joe a shot of cheap brandy. So Joe splashed over and fastened onto the bottle, tipping it to his lips while the old man squinted his eyes and watched eagerly, nodding happily as the young man drank.

"*Ai, Chihuahua!*" Joe said. "What is this crap, burro piss?"

Amarante cackled and sucked off a swallow for himself, then patted his gut. "It's good for you," he said. "Keeps you warm."

"So how come the hardware?" Joe asked again.

Winking conspiratorially, Amarante put his bottle away and laid a hand on Joe's shoulder. "I'll be back soon," he said. "I'll take care of you. I'll take care of this field."

"Sure, you do that for me, Chief." Gently, Joe cuffed the old man's face. "You and me together, friend, we'll keep those bastards at bay, qué no?"

Abruptly, Amarante plunged toward the road. But he halted a couple of times, and, looking back, muttered, "I'll be right back . . ."

In town a few minutes later, instead of heading as usual for the bar, he hoofed it directly into Rael's General Store and, pulling the gun from its holster, laid the weapon atop the rubber change mat on the counter in front of Nick Rael.

"Hello, Pop," Nick said, wondering, what in hell is this old looney up to now?

"What kind of bullets does this take?" Amarante asked. "I forget."

After Nick had turned the gun admiringly over in his hands once or twice, he set it back on the rubber mat again.

"Why buy bullets?"

Amarante was a little confused; he could hardly hear anyway. "What kind of cartucho?" he asked again. "I want to buy some shells."

"Sure." Nick swung out from behind the counter, ambling across the store to his ammo shelves. "But what for?"

Following Nick, the old man watched with interest as the storekeeper, after searching among the ammunition for a moment, selected a box of .45 shells, which he slapped into Amarante's hands. Back at the counter the old man asked, "How much?"

"Three dollars and twenty-nine cents, plus fourteen pennies for the governor, equals three-forty-three altogether," Nick said bemusedly. "What are you gonna do, Pop, go hunting for bear?"

"How much?"

"Three-forty-three!" Nick fairly shouted into his ear.

Grinning, Amarante produced the food stamp book and, while Nick looked on incredulously, painstakingly tore out four one-dollar stamps which he laid carefully on the counter.

Nick pushed them back toward the old geezer, shaking his head. "Hey, Grandpa," he explained. "You can't buy bullets with food stamps. You got to pay me money."

Puzzled, Amarante held up the stamps. "What's the matter with these? They're no good?"

"They're for buying *food,*" Nick rasped. "You can't use food stamps for bullets. You need *money.* Real dollars."

Amarante scrutinized the pieces of paper in his hand. At length he said, "This is money."

"For food, yeah," Nick sighed. "They're only good for food, man."

"I don't want food. Only these bullets."

"Then put those food stamps away and gimme three dollars and forty-three cents," the storekeeper said.

The old man laid the food stamps on the counter again. "This is the same as money," he explained.

"Aw, come on, Pop. You know as well as I know that there's some things you can't buy with food stamps. You can't buy dog food or beer or nonedible stuff like shampoo or toothpaste or razor blades."

Smiling, Amarante picked up the shells and dropped the box in his pocket.

"Hey wait a minute——" Nick started to grab the old man's arm, but let go quickly. "Money," he said, moving his lips exaggeratedly as if talking to a lip reader. "Not food stamps, you dumb old coot—money. I need *money* for those shells."

Once again, Amarante nodded toward the food stamps on the counter, hoisted his gun and jammed it carefully into the holster, touched the front brim of his rumpled hat by way of saying good day, and lurched off.

Cursing as he did so, Nick snatched up the food stamps and slapped them into the space under the black plastic cash pan in the till.

Amarante teetered into the Frontier Bar, saluted his comrade, Tranquilino Jeantete, tugged himself onto a stool, placed the pistol and the box of shells on the bar, and, while Tranquilino watched, he slowly and very carefully loaded the gun.

"What do you want to load a gun for?" the bartender asked. "Life isn't hard enough, you're out looking for more trouble?"

His feeble hand resting lightly atop the mammoth

gun lying on the bar, Amarante said, "Sometimes it's necessary to carry a gun."

"I bet you can't even pull the trigger," Tranquilino replied petulantly. "You're not even as heavy as a little bag of dried-up aspen leaves."

"I can shoot this gun."

"And what could you hit—a dead elephant from two feet away?"

"I can shoot this gun."

"Your brains are scrambled," Tranquilino said. "The defunct ones from the camposanto must be dancing around in there. You're going to give all us rotten old bastards a bad name."

"Sometimes a man should carry a gun."

"Who do you think you are?" the bartender accused. "Pancho Villa? The Lone Ranger?"

Offended by his friend's bad taste, Amarante looked stonily straight ahead, his wrinkled old hand still lying firmly atop the gun.

"Put the safety on, at least," Tranquilino finally grumbled in a more gentle, friendlier tone. "I don't want any bullets flying around my bar."

Refusing even to acknowledge that he'd heard, Amarante remained stiff backed, his shriveled sunken lips as tight as he could make them.

After a long silence, Tranquilino creaked onto his feet and fetched two glasses, filling both a third full of cheap bourbon. Placing one glass next to Amarante's gun hand, he said, "Let's both have a drink to your stupid gun."

Amarante cracked no smile, but he did move his hand from the gun to the glass, and the two old-timers drank.

About half an hour later, as his friend left the bar, Tranquilino called, "Hey, Pancho Villa, you forgot your cannon!"

Amarante returned, almost daintily lifted the weapon off the bar and stuck it in the holster, and then suddenly they both started to laugh.

"Shit," Tranquilino cackled after they had each survived minor coughing jags brought on by their

laughter. "Carrying around all that extra weight I bet
you get a heart attack!"

Out in the sunshine Amarante swayed and blinked.
The road was littered with squashed grasshoppers; and,
their wings crackling, a number of live grasshoppers
sailed through the air back and forth across the road
as if the summer sun, having thawed out their nearly
frosted bodies, had set them abruptly to sizzling. A
pickup carrying plumbing for a frame house being
built by a Texas couple in the canyon slowed down
and stopped, and the woman from the Strawberry
Mesa Body Shop and Pipe Queen, Ruby Archuleta,
poked her red bandannaed head out the window.

"Hey Amarante. What are you going to do with
that gun?" she asked.

He grinned, tipping his hat to her. "Hello," he said.
"How are you today, Mrs. Archuleta?"

She pointed. "How come the hardware, cousin?
Who you gonna plug?"

"A Thanksgiving turkey," the old man suddenly
barked. "A big Thanksgiving turkey."

Ruby arched her eyebrows, laughing again, ground
the stickshift into first, and, with the admonition
"Make sure it's pointed in the right direction before
you squeeze the trigger!" she bolted her truck away.

Whereupon Amarante Córdova, shining in a trium-
phal light, pirouetted clumsily in the middle of the
plaza area to acknowledge the attention and admiration of any other onlookers. But at this moment the
heart of town, such as it was, was deserted. Disappointed, the old man toppled painfully into gear,
bumping into Seferino Pacheco, who had tears in his
eyes.

"My pig is gone again," Pacheco moaned.

"Fuck your pig! Fie on your pig! Death to your
voracious pig!" the old man spat, circling huffily
around the stunned, slope-shouldered Pacheco.

"She was in her pen just this morning," Pacheco
called. But Amarante couldn't have cared less—he
was heading home.

The old man reached the highway just as the sheriff
was turning in. Bernabé Montoya's pickup coasted a

little past him, and, without even looking around, Amarante could tell the truck had stopped. Guiltily, he waddled across the highway.

Bernabé negotiated a tight U-turn, paused to let a two-ton flatbed, piled high with hay bales from Colorado, zoom down the highway, then crossed the road and pulled over slightly ahead of Amarante.

The old man halted. For effect, Bernabé took his time slouching out of the cab.

"Uh, how come you're wearing that antique buffalo gun?" the sheriff wanted to know.

Unable to think of answers, Amarante just stood still, his hat off in the presence of the law, grinning and wheezing laboriously, playing the fool.

"Excuse me," Bernabé said, gently lifting the pistol from its holster. When he'd ascertained that it was loaded he rolled his eyes wearily to the sky, moaning unhappily. "What's happening all of a sudden that this town is filling up with troublemakers? What kind of charge does a wrinkled little old prune like you, Mr. Córdova, get out of walking around with a two-thousand-year-old shooting iron on your hip and your pockets full of bullets? What do you want to do, incite this poor town into another Smokey the Bear santo riot or something? Take the bullets out of the gun, Mr. Córdova—" And here the sheriff actually removed the cartridges himself, plip-plopping them into the old man's palm.

"If it's loaded," he explained sorrowfully, shoving the gun carefully back into its holster, "it can go off. Hang it back on the wall where it belongs, Mr. Córdova. Please, huh? Nobody wants violence."

Amarante said, "I can go home now?"

"Yeah, sure. Whatever you want . . ." Bernabé backed up, hesitating momentarily at the door of his truck, disturbed by the old man who was grinning absurdly in his direction. But finally, with a shrug and a worried *"Ai, Chihuahua,"* he climbed behind the wheel and effected another U-turn.

Amarante waited until the sheriff was gone before moving on. Slowly he rattled along the dusty road to where he had to climb the Roybal ditch bank, and once he had accomplished that he teetered along the bank to the field.

Joe was gone. Amarante surveyed the damp earth, the glistening green bean plants, the faint yellow irrigation foam left around the stalks, the mud cracking softly in some freshly watered rows. A few robins, starlings, and blackbirds were still scavenging. The old man trundled off a ways into the shade afforded by dusty, silver-leafed cottonwoods and sat down on a log.

Spastically, dropping a half-dozen bullets, he reloaded the gun, placing it on the log beside him. Next he rolled a cigarette, and, quietly smoking, he listened woozily to faint meadowlark songs drifting melodically on the clear summer air.

From here on in, he thought, if anybody like Eusebio Lavadie or Zopi Devine tried to mess with José Mondragón's beanfield, they would have to reckon with Amarante Córdova first.

But he was sleepy, his head buzzed drowsily. Grasshoppers crackled, a locust buzzed, a woodpecker blammed against a faraway hollow tree. Somewhere, too, a chain saw was droning.

Amarante lowered himself so that his back pressed against the log on which he'd been sitting. The gun he laid carefully in his lap. His eyes flickered and were about to close when he noticed something odd hovering over town. For a moment the thing was so out of place that his mind could not translate what it saw. Then he realized that, even though no rain had fallen at all for the past few days, the arching vision, shining faintly but unmistakably over Milagro, was a rainbow.

Too tired to worry about such a sight, Amarante fell asleep. But no sooner had he begun to snore than that queer rainbow appeared in his dream, shimmering faintly in the hot dry air muffling Milagro, and a few minutes later an angel showed up to complicate the miracle.

No shining angel with a golden halo straight from Tiffany's, a French horn, and wings fabricated out of pristine Chinese swansdown arrived to bless Amarante's fertile imagination; rather, a half-toothless, one-eyed bum sort of coyote dressed in tattered blue jeans and sandals, and sporting a pair of drab moth-eaten wings that looked as if they had come off the remainder shelves of a disreputable cut-rate discount store during a fire-damage sale, appeared.

This grisly sight limped along the Milagro—García spur pausing every now and again to blow its bulbous gray nose onto a greasy unhallowed sleeve, after which it rumbled and choked for a while like an old crone dying of TB.

"Hey, Angel," Amarante called out in his dream. "What's a rainbow doing over our town on a sunny day like today?"

The angel, startled by Amarante's voice, froze stiff with its ears lying back flat; and then, realizing there was no immediate danger, it turned to observe the puzzling natural phenomenon.

"Who knows, cousin," the coyote apparition mumbled at last. "Maybe it's because for once in your lives you people are trying to do something right."

Abruptly, then, the angel disappeared. And Amarante went on to dream he was on a horse, carrying a rifle across the pommel of his saddle, tracking a deer through snow in the high open country around the Little Baldy Bear Lakes.

❧

Bernabé Montoya, his face screwed up with concern, lumbered into Rael's store. "Hey, Nick," he almost whined. "How come the old geezer's wearing that prehistoric revolver?"

Nick shrugged. "It's that beanfield, Bernie. Some-body should go talk with José in no uncertain terms before it's too late."

"The last time he wore that rig was during César Pacheco's trial over in Ojo Prieto, wasn't it?" the sheriff mumbled dejectedly, more to himself than to the storekeeper.

"He's out of his head," Nick said. "He don't know what's going on. Of course, he puts that thing on when he votes, too. And for the Feast of San Isidro."

"But there's no holidays this week, Nick."

"He doesn't know that. Maybe he thinks it's time for next month's Chamisaville fiesta."

"The goddam thing was *loaded*." Bernabé stripped the paper off a Milky Way candy bar. "That gun was stuffed full of live ammunition, can you believe it?"

"I know. He bought shells from me earlier. With food stamps."

"Food stamps?"

Dolefully, Nick shrugged. "It turned out to be easier," he grumbled by way of explanation. "That old bastard's as stubborn as Pacheco's pig."

Bernabé retrieved a Nehi orange from the soda bin. "Shit," he observed. "Something is rotten in Chamisa County."

"Oh, I don't think he'll hurt anybody," Nick said, "He can't even pull the trigger."

"Where there's a will, there's always, sooner or later, some kind of way," Bernabé scowled, loudly scuffing his boot heels as he ambled mournfully out of the store. "I wish to Christ him and José would drop dead."

As Bernabé Montoya propelled himself disconsolately off Rael's porch wishing that Joe Mondragón and Amarante Córdova would drop dead, a mottled-green, 1953 Chevy pickup, with a huge three-legged German shepherd perched arrogantly on the cab's roof, clanked to a stop on the other side of the dirt area that passed for the town plaza. And as this scruffy vehicle coasted noisily to a colorful exhaust-belching halt, it happened to obliterate from Bernabé's view the lone parking meter in town.

This meter had been the brainstorm of the mayor, Sammy Cantú, his two councilmen, Bud Gleason and Ricardo P. Córdova (a second cousin of Amarante Córdova's son, Ricardo A. Córdova, who was still being slowly dispatched by bone cancer), and the sheriff, Bernabé Montoya.

The parking meter's purpose was to earn funds for the sheriff so that law and order might prevail in Milagro. Supposedly, donations to the meter would buy gas for Bernabé's truck and provide dimes for the sheriff's on-the-job official phone calls, which he often made from the pay phone on Rael's front porch.

Since its installation two years before, however, the parking meter had rarely collected dimes. Most motorists simply parked elsewhere. One reason they usually parked elsewhere was because one-armed Onofre Martínez, the Staurolite Baron and father of Bruno Martínez the cop, always parked his mottled-green, 1953 Chevy pickup in front of the meter.

Although he never contributed a dime.

This had led to what might be called a feud between Onofre and the sheriff.

In fact, for two years hand-running, almost daily, and in spite of the three-legged shepherd's fang-baring snarls, Bernabé had been ticketing Onofre's perambulating junk heap. The tickets he wrote out were long and convoluted and very elaborate. They were printed on stiff, expensive paper, and each ticket pad cost the town two dollars and sixty cents. Hence, every time Bernabé wrote out a parking violation on that meter it cost him twenty cents in citation paper, ink, and his own valuable time to do so.

The fine for illegal parking in Milagro was fifty cents. But Onofre Martínez was not about to cough up four bits for the privilege of being ticketed in front of the Pilar Café, especially since his own son Bruno had developed into such a rotten apple by joining the state police. Thus, each time Bernabé affixed a citation to his windshield, Onofre plucked the ticket out from under the wiper with his left—and only—hand, bit down on one edge of the glossy cardboard, and commenced ripping it to shreds.

For two years now, in all seasons, these shreds had lain like a perpetual New Year's Eve confetti all across that hapless dusty area in the middle of the Rael's General Store–Frontier Bar–Pilar Café downtown commercial center of Milagro.

Onofre Martínez had as good a reason as any man for shredding parking tickets.

"Listen," he enjoyed telling Bernabé Montoya every time the sheriff sighed, almost cried, and in a desultory halfhearted manner threatened Onofre with hellfire and damnation for his belligerent lawless attitude, "I'm seventy-nine years old, I got one arm, I had three wives, I got four brothers and a sister still living, six of both sexes already dead, I got six children —three girls and three boys, one a mental retard, and one who went to school and became a Communist, and another who shamed my name by becoming a state chota—but anyway, all my kids are living, and I got sixteen grandchildren and some great-grandchildren, too, and ever since I learned how to drive the same year they invented cars I been parking where I wanted to park and nobody ever tried to make me pay money to do it, especially not my own son (so why you?), and I'll be goddamned if I'll start now. You can't teach an old dog new tricks, so screw you, Bernabé, go put the bite on somebody else."

In answer to this, Bernabé usually tried to reason with Onofre. The sheriff's reasoning went like so:

"Alright, you one-armed, bandy-legged pipsqueak, pubic hair, and maricón. If you keep violating the law like this, if you keep deliberately committing a crime in the eyes of the law and in the eyes of your long-suffering fellow citizens, I'll make sure they lock you in the Chamisa County Jail for a hundred years in a row, and I'll tell Ernie Maestas to personally see to it there are worms and fly larvae and things like that in every piece of food you eat!"

Onofre Martínez's reaction to Bernabé's reaction, first off, was the reaction of just about all the poor people in Milagro to just about any statement from a cop. But then, calming himself, Onofre would offer these philosophical comments about crime and punishment:

"If you try to arrest me, Bernabé, you know what's gonna happen? First of all I'm gonna plead innocent. Then I'm gonna get a lawyer; I'll get Bloom. Then we're gonna have a trial. Maybe in the end I'm guilty, but you know how much it's gonna cost Milagro to take me to trial? More money than that parking meter could shit at you in twenty years."

Which was a true statement: Onofre Martínez knew his rights.

And anyway, how could Bernabé Montoya expect to reason with a man who had named all his three sons Onofre after himself: Onofre Carlos (called Bruno Martínez), the one who became a chota; Onofre Jesús (O. J. Martínez), the retarded one who delivered the Capital City *Reporter* to the people of Milagro; and Onofre Tranquilino (O. T. Martínez), the one who got educated and became a Communist.

"You keep giving him tickets, though," Sammy Cantú growled morosely, "and one of these days we'll think of something. Maybe we can get an OEO loan from the government to prosecute that son of a bitch."

By rough estimates, it had cost the town approximately two and a half to three dollars a week for over two years just to ticket Onofre Martínez. Nobody else, no citizen from Milagro, that is, parked in front of the meter because there was ample parking elsewhere. Even tourists seldom patronized the meter because the rest of the "plaza," not to mention all the dusty side streets in town, were open to their monstrous automotive freakshows.

In fact, since it was first installed at a cost of two hundred and thirty-six dollars to the Milagro exchequer, that parking meter had received only fourteen dimes, eight nickels, and eleven pennies.

Or exactly one dollar ($1) and ninety-one cents ($.91).

To date, the meter had cost the town as follows:

Purchase and installation charges	$236.00
49 traffic violation citation books at $2.60 per book	127.40
Repair bills paid out to Joe Mondragón when teen-age hoodlums (i.e., Joe himself or Benny Maestas, in which case they split the take) jammed the meter with slugs or plowed their trucks into it under cover of darkest night	189.75
For a grand total of	$553.15

In private, Bernabé Montoya, Sammy Cantú, and the two council members, Bud Gleason and Ricardo P. Córdova, christened that parking meter "The Wart on the Asshole of Milagro."

Publicly, however, the parking meter had to stay so long as the mayor, the council, and the police force were locked in a life-and-death struggle with Onofre Martínez. Admittedly, they did not know how to nab, stab, or otherwise stop that one-armed lunatic without throwing away a fortune in legal fees and court costs, but they kept hoping desperately that some kind of *deus ex machina* would intercede for them.

To all the stubborn parties obstinately concerned with this matter, it was The Principle of the Thing.

Still, Onofre Martínez was not a bad, vile, or vindictive hooligan. Rather, he was something of a poet, an inventor of on-the-spot ballads called corridos, and at one time he had been able to read and write in both English and Spanish. In the old days these peculiar talents had made him the official letter writer in the village, since until the latter stages of the first half of the twentieth century literacy had been a rare phenomenon in Milagro. Hence Onofre had written a thousand love letters for a thousand lovers, and he had also read those love letters to the persons who received them. For this service he had been paid both by the sender and by the recipient; and so Onofre had certainly garnered his share of whatever was passing for loot—chickens, hog cracklings, a bag of jerky —in his time.

Nobody, including Onofre himself, knew how he learned to read and write—certainly he had never attended school. But all at once, when still a child, Onofre had awakened able to read. His sudden skill was a miracle of sorts, on a par with the unexplained underground barking of Cleofes Apodaca's lost sheepdog Pendejo or the bell whose ringing caused Padre Sinkovich to undermine the foundations of his very own church.

Onofre Martínez could no longer write, however, because he had lost his literate arm, and he had no more been able to transfer literacy to his left arm than Bernabé Montoya had been able to wheedle a fine out of Onofre for all those parking meter violations.

Maybe not a miraculous, but certainly a rather curious, story lay behind Onofre's dearth of an appendage.

The normal way to lose an arm, leg, or whatever in Milagro was by having it mangled in tractor sickle bars or crushed beneath a horse. The deputy sheriff, Meliton Naranjo, had lost a finger when, as he was fussing with a fan belt in a truck, his kid had climbed behind the wheel and turned the motor over. Cristóbal Mondragón, Joe's third-youngest brother, had half his pinkie bitten off when he lost hold of the nose twitch on a horse he was worming. Tranquilino Jeantete had lost one ear tip to frostbite during the same long-ago winter that the Strawberry Mesa Body Shop and Pipe Queen operator, Ruby Archuleta, killed a deer with her bare hands. Marvin LaBlue donated half his left thumb to a scissors jack at the Body Shop and Pipe Queen, and Claudio García dedicated the first joint of his right hand's middle finger to that same beastly machine. Many arms, pieces of tongues, and parts of legs had been left by various Milagro residents in the rear seats of their head-on collisions with cows and horses on the north–south highway. And back in the late 1700s, so the story goes, an old man who had been courting a witch suddenly lost his penis, but not his life, to a lightning bolt that struck from a quiet winter snowstorm.

And each generation, of course, owned somebody who had lost an eye to a BB gun.

But Onofre Martínez claimed to have lost his arm to butterflies.

At least, that's the way Onofre himself liked to tell the story when he had an audience of children and other gullible creatures who believed in werewolves, flibbertigibbets, and miracles.

"On the day it happened, all morning I'm irrigating my fields, so by lunch time I felt real tired. I went and sat down under a tree and ate a burrito and an extra piece of cheese. Then, just as I'm dozing off, along comes a big orange butterfly and lands on my arm, on the part called the bicep, up here. I didn't move, and she sits there with her wings open, and after a minute I notice she's putting some sticky stuff on my skin, and in this sticky stuff there's a bunch of little white bumps, which after another minute it hits me are her eggs. Eventually she flutters away and I'm left with this little sticky circle on my arm full of teeny white huevos. I was curious so I didn't brush them off. I went home, and for the next few days I'm real careful not to move my arm, you know, so as not to disturb the eggs. Then one morning I woke up and the eggs had hatched into little gusanos and these little gusanos had already eaten a hole in my arm. They looked like maggots. It didn't hurt though, so I let them go ahead. They ate right into my arm and disappeared and not a drop of blood came out of the hole, I guess they sucked it all up along the way. It still didn't hurt, so I'm just waiting for something to happen, being careful not to move my arm too much, of course. After a while I notice they're eating up all the meat under the skin of my lower arm. But still, don't ask me why, it didn't hurt. And these little gusanos are growing and getting real fat, until pretty soon I didn't have any more meat in my arm down there, and then a couple of them gnawed through my bone up by the bicep, up here, and my arm fell on the ground. Which is when they started flying out of my arm like out of a cornucopia, all these beautiful crimson butterflies, flying all around me like hungry bats for a minute until the wind blew them up into a tree. And for just a minute, even though it was August, a little snow fell on the cottonwood trees and on those blood red butterflies. The snow was so cold it killed all the butterflies in a wink, and they fell from the tree onto the ground like autumn leaves. I picked up my arm, which only had the skin intact with the rest hollowed out, thinking maybe it would make a good wind sock at the Chamisa V. airport. But I tumbled into a ditch on the way home and lost it. This happened a long time ago before you were born. Maybe dogs ate what was left of my arm, or perhaps tecolotes used it to line their nests. . . ."

But anyway, on this particular summer day Bernabé Montoya walked out of Rael's just as Onofre's mottled-green, 1953 Chevy pickup with the three-legged dog on top hiccupped to a stop at the town's lone parking meter and, with a dispirited—call it a lonely—*"Ai, Chihuahua!"* the sheriff reached for his citation pad. Bitterly he began to write, thinking as he did so that if ever all the cantankerous streaks in people like Amarante Córdova, Joe Mondragón, and Onofre Martínez were united behind a common cause, there would be much more than all hell to pay.

Onofre's three-legged shepherd leaped to the ground as the Staurolite Baron slammed the door, and, with a triumphant grin riding on his face like a soaring hawk, Onofre pulled out the driver's side windshield wiper, making it that much easier for Bernabé to slide his ticket into place. After that, staggering swiftly forward like a man about to fall flat on his face, Onofre chugged toward the Pilar. On his way up the steps he encountered Bud Gleason, decked out in a madras sport coat and bow tie, coming down and Onofre tipped his cowboy hat good day with his invisible arm. At least, Onofre always insisted he used his nonexistent right hand to tip the hat, and it certainly *looked* that way, because his left and visible arm never swung up from his other side. Skeptics, though, said the hat tip was just a trick Onofre had learned to do by wiggling his scalp.

Yet at least one person in town, Joe Mondragón, claimed that he had once had his lip split in a Saturday night argument at the Frontier by the invisible fist residing at the end of Onofre's invisible arm.

∽

For years many stories and quite a few unconfirmed rumors about the Strawberry Mesa Body Shop and Pipe Queen tycoon, Ruby Archuleta, had circulated between Milagro and Doña Luz. Some folks swore she was a witch; a few misguided harpies insinuated she had poisoned or otherwise murdered the three husbands who had died on her. Various highly impeachable sources suggested that Eliu Archuleta, her eighteen-year-old son, was actually the offspring of an affair between Ruby and the expatriot santo carver who had disappeared right after the Smokey the Bear statue riot, Snuffy Ledoux, a clandestine relationship that supposedly occurred while her second husband, Sufi Menopoulous, a Greek who had owned the Eagle Motel on Route 26 leading east from Chamisaville, lay dying of cancer at St. Claire's Hospital in the capital. Then again, for years a few hardcore gossips had whispered that Eliu was actually the product of a virgin birth.

Getting down to more verifiable facts, though, Ruby Archuleta was an uncertified midwife who had been safely delivering babies since 1940. She also qualified as one of the best fishermen in the area and was a deer hunter supreme. And whenever raspberries ripened in the local canyons a thousand jars of Ruby's raspberry jam appeared almost instantly on the shelves of Rael's store in Milagro, Benny's in Doña Luz, and the Flowering Wheat Health Food Store in Chamisaville, and she raked in the dinero hand over fist.

This dynamo measured five feet two inches tall, was forty-nine years old, and her misty red hair had mostly turned to gray. With her son Eliu, her gigantic lover, Claudio García, and a roly-poly hillbilly mechanic named Marvin LaBlue, she lived in a mud-plastered railroad tie house situated on a hill overlooking the Body Shop and Pipe Queen, an enterprise inherited from her first husband, a charismatic hustler named Ray Mingleback, who had drowned on Halloween night, 1958, when his Rolls Royce dove off the north–south highway into the Rio Grande about twenty miles below Chamisaville.

In the Archuleta house candles always flickered, and santos—some made from cornhusks, a number fashioned by Ruby herself, and still others carved by that disillusioned expatriot Snuffy Ledoux—lined the walls. Curious people from all over the state, running the gamut from well-known artists to shadowy hunted outlaws, continually stopped in transit to share a meal with Ruby and her crew; they puttered and chewed the fat, embraced Ruby affectionately, and pushed on at dawn. An aura of mystery and of knowledge surrounded Ruby Archuleta, and so of course the average Milagro citizen both envied and resented her, both loved her and hated her guts, thought she must be a Communist, refused to have his automotive or plumbing needs catered to by anyone else . . . and nobody knew Ruby very well although everyone had known her all their lives.

Actually, there was nothing that peculiar about the Body Shop and Pipe Queen (as some jokers occasionally called her). Awake each morning at five, Ruby dressed in a work shirt, weathered jeans, and cowboy boots, cooked breakfast for the men, tied her long hair up in a red-checkered bandanna, and marched outside to start overhauling cars or organizing plumbing jobs. She cut pipe and welded metal joints, installed shocks and stripped down engines— you name it. Whatever Claudio García, Marvin La-Blue, or her son could do, Ruby could do better. Hence, though a small-time operation, like everything else Ruby tackled, the Body Shop and Pipe Queen was the best operation of its kind in the country. And not because this tiny woman with dusty green eyes, a sharp nose, high cheekbones, and severe, beautiful lips possessed the sort of witchcraft that could produce giant beanstalks and golden eggs either—she just worked bloody hard. She shouted orders, made split-second decisions, helped to manhandle machinery, operated the wrecker in all kinds of weather, and when she needed parts or supplies she jumped in a truck and whizzed down to the capital and got them —and to hell with the U.S. Mail!

Men had trouble accepting Ruby's strength; they were flabbergasted by both her loveliness and her vitality. Many who did not peg Ruby for a witch called her The Ant because she was so busy all the time, and because it almost seemed that she could lift and manipulate objects ten times her weight and size.

There was one story about Ruby Archuleta everyone in Milagro took for the gospel truth. The incident occurred, so the self-appointed historians drawled, when Ruby was a young woman living alone close to the Rio Lucero at a point on the mesa where the stream ran in the open, unhidden by trees, for about two miles before plunging into a gorge that deepened abruptly as the water cascaded toward the Rio Grande.

It was the middle of a very bitter winter, so the story goes. A terrible winter for the sheep and for all other animals. Cattle far out on the mesa died when hay could not be trucked in. For weeks on end the windows of all the houses were patterned with elaborate jungles of ice. Although piñon fires burned in stoves day and night, dwellings stayed barely warm; outside, trucks would not start. People were snowed in for weeks, some nearly starved. And bear and deer wandered miserably down from the high country, seeking food.

Despite the severe cold, every morning at daybreak, before lighting a fire or cooking breakfast, Ruby emerged from her house stark naked with her soft red hair coiled across her pale shoulders, and headed for the river where she splashed briefly in a small pocket of rushing water. The river below this pool was smoothed over, icy, frozen solid.

On the one particular day of this story, Amarante Córdova, on horseback and searching for a rabbit or a deer, happened to top a rise about a quarter mile from Ruby's digs just in time to observe her trip to the river. Naturally, never before having blundered onto such a wonderful sight, he couldn't believe his eyes. So what could he do but gape as she ducked into that turbulent pool in front of the iced-over river? Then, as Ruby jumped from the water, Amarante noticed a deer tiptoeing through the sagebrush fifteen yards from where the woman had bathed. The instant Ruby spotted the buck she charged after it. Frightened, the deer veered through the sage, aiming in a northerly direction toward the river. Of course, when the animal struck the smooth ice its legs splayed and it skidded, unable to regain its balance, no longer able to flee. Catching up, the young woman flung her arms around its neck, moved her hands higher, and grabbed the antlers. For a moment both the deer and the woman were fused together, as frozen and as straining as the winter air, Ruby's hair already a glaze of transparent crystals, her breasts powdered with white ice; then she snapped the buck's head sharply back, breaking its neck, and the blood suddenly gushing from the animal's mouth covered her icy body as she lifted the deer and carried it back to her house.

The killing of that deer was a story which had become legend. Joe Mondragón's beanfield was another story which might also one day grow to the proportions of myth. And it happened that shortly after Joe cut water illegally into his field, Ruby Archuleta, her son Eliu, Claudio García, and Marvin LaBlue stopped to cast a first appraising and appreciative glance at Joe's field. For an extended pensive moment Ruby stood with her hands on her hips, an ash growing long on the cigarette held tightly between her unpainted lips. Even after the men grew bored and returned to listen to the truck's radio, Ruby stayed by the field, thinking about that damp earth, those fragile beansprouts.

And when finally she rejoined her crew at the truck, Ruby was grinning broadly. She hoisted herself spryly into the back, then suddenly broke into happy laughter.

"I knew José Mondragón couldn't go through his entire life," she sang, "without attempting one great thing!"

~§

Joe Mondragón (who, after the initial euphoria wore off, had begun to wonder if his beanfield might be such a great thing after all), was sitting on a bench fixing a boot to the inside of his pickup's left rear tire, when a mangy, flat-headed, obscene-looking, bow-legged, vomit-yellow male cat with its ears rotted down to bloody nubs from frostbite, and sporting a grotesque pair of enormous furry black balls, stiff-leggedly entered the yard, trailed by (but apparently oblivious to) three angry and very noisy magpies who were pecking at its tail and raising an intolerable ruckus.

Out of habit, Joe picked up a rock and winged it at this apparition of feline death warmed over, missing by a mile. The magpies flapped away, but, unfazed, the cat merely halted and settled down, tail wrapped comfortably around itself, contemplating Joe through unperturbed, sleepyish snake eyes.

"Hey, scram!" Joe hurled the six-inch-long buttend of a two-by-four at the cat. But again the projectile landed way off its mark, and the animal didn't flinch.

Joe trotted inside, returning to the yard a few seconds later toting a package of Chinese firecrackers. Lighting the main fuse, he tossed the entire package at the scruffy intruder, setting off a berserk orchestration of flash-bangs. The cat roused itself as a matter of protocol and arched lazily, politely frizzing the fur just behind its snake-shaped head, and when the dust had settled and the gunpowdery smoke had drifted across the yard, the animal sat down, sleepily closed its eyes, and commenced purring as it gently kneaded the dusty earth.

"Well, I'll be goddamned." Joe had to admire a tomcat with that kind of balls. So, muttering "Fuck you, gato," he went back to his boot.

After a while the animal stood up, stretched, sauntered casually across the yard, and disappeared into the henhouse.

"Okay, friend, enough is enough!" Joe grabbed a hoe with which to chop the obnoxious cat in two, and entered the henhouse expecting to catch the animal stalking one of his prize egglayers.

Instead, the ragged tom was curled up in an egg box, contentedly snoozing.

Joe leaned his hoe against the wall and scrutinized this battered old refugee for a moment, wondering, what the hell kind of omen is this, anyway?

Then, retreating to the house, he popped open a tallboy and slumped at the kitchen table, watching Nancy mop the floor. Their three kids, Billy, Larry, and Luisa, were flopped acrobatically around the living room avidly gooning at the television.

Because he felt mean and unsettled, Joe barked, "How come those kids are watching TV?"

Nancy kept right on mopping. "Ask the kids, not me."

Joe glowered at her. "What's the matter with you today?"

"Nothing's the matter with me that wouldn't be better if you went back outside where you belong."

Joe smirked unpleasantly and drank. Then he snarled, "You kids get out of here, understand?"

They shifted their sweet arrogant little gazes over to their father, then to their mother—who merely shrugged at them while wiping a strand of hair off her forehead.

"What's the matter?" Joe growled. "You didn't hear me? I'll go get a belt."

"Aw, c'mon . . ." Larry, the eldest, whined. "Ma said we could watch TV."

"I'm gonna call up Joe S. Mondragón's Radio and TV Repair in Chamisaville and have that damn thing repossessed," Joe spat. "I didn't raise my kids to sit around the house in the middle of summer lapping up that garbage. And anyway, you're learning too much English. So get out of here. All of you. *Beat it!*"

"What's the matter with *you* today?" Nancy wanted to know.

"Nothing's the matter with me. I came inside to have a beer in peace—turn it *off*, Larry! Yeah, just like that—*all* the way off. Now beat it, huh?" And to his wife: "How come you use so much pneumonia every time you mop the floor?"

"Ammonia, dummy!" Nancy grinned, leaned the mop handle against a counter, fetched herself a tallboy from the fridge, and sat down opposite him at the table, deliberately popping the top in such a way that foam splashed into her husband's face. "Hey," she said calmly, suppressing a giggle but not the sarcasm in her voice, "what's the matter with my rough tough little cream puff this afternoon?"

Without moving to wipe the foam off his forehead

and nose, Joe threatened quietly, "You're gonna wish you hadn't done that."

"Yeah, I bet." Nancy sucked in a third of her can, gulping loudly, and released a noisy satisfied sigh. "I'm scared, José. I'm trembling I'm so scared."

They sat in silence for a minute, Nancy smiling at Joe, Joe staring at his beer can and drawing pictures with his finger in the puddles on the table.

"Stella Armijo called," Nancy said after a while. "She said she talked with Betty Apodaca, and Betty told her she was in the Pilar waiting on tables and overheard Horsethief Shorty Wilson talking to Harlan Betchel, and Shorty told Harlan Bernie Montoya went to the state chota pendejo factory in Doña Luz about your beanfield. That was a long time ago, before those jerks from the capital came up. Lydia Martínez called too, and she said when she was mopping up over at Pedro Hirsshorn's Land of Enchantment whorehouse for tourists she heard Pedro "the Pedo" himself talking with Zopi Devine on the telephone, and she said afterward the Pedo told Nick Rael that the Zopilote was gonna fly down to the capital and talk with the governor about your beanfield."

Sarcastically, Joe said, "Thanks for all the wonderful information."

"Charley Bloom called too. He thinks you two should talk things over some more."

Joe shrugged, trying to appear nonchalantly caustic instead of scared stiff.

"I guess everybody is scared," Nancy said.

"I don't see what over," Joe grumbled.

"If you ask me, you're scared too."

"Who asked you?"

She retorted, "Actually, maybe you're right. Who needs to ask about what's so obvious?"

Joe looked up at her. "What do you want," he proposed quietly, "a punch in the mouth?"

Reaching across the table, Nancy laid her hand gently over his. "You and whose army, José?"

"I'll hit you so hard," Joe said, "they'll stop you in El Paso for speeding."

"So? I'll hit you back. What do you think I am,

afraid of you? I'll stab you in the back if you hurt me. I'll shoot you in self-defense. You don't think I won't—? Feel my muscle."

"*Ai, Chihuahua,*" Joe whined miserably, withdrawing his hand from under hers and resting his chin unhappily in both hands. "I had to marry a scorpion."

"Eusebio Lavadie called too," Nancy informed him.

"That's the fifth time in the past two weeks." As an afterthought Joe muttered unconvincingly: "I'll bust his nose."

"He apologized again."

"Whatta you mean, he apologized again?"

"He just said to tell you he hadn't understood all the facts back in the beginning and to let you know he was sorry."

" 'Sorry,' " Joe moaned sarcastically. "He's 'sorry.' He struts around with his tongue sticking up the Zopilote's whosit and with a machete in each hand cutting off everybody else's whatsits. His father Meliton was the lousy patrón of this hapless burg who invited old man Devine to come on in and suck the blood out of our veins and the marrow out of our bones, and he's 'sorry.' "

"He's scared," Nancy said. "Just like you and me."

"Speak for yourself, numskull."

Finishing her beer, Nancy snagged Joe's, killing it also. Too depressed to protest, he grumbled, "Thanks for all the support."

"I'm behind you, sweet."

"That's what I need." Joe grinned a little in spite of himself. "Your poisonous mouth behind me. That should keep me out of trouble, alright."

"All you *got* right now is my mouth." Nancy's eyes flashed in a fierce, tender way. "You better treat me with respect."

"Since when did you ever treat me with respect?"

"Ever since I knew you, amor," she replied languidly, fetching two more tallboys from the fridge.

Joe flexed his hands. They were scarred, bruised, calloused, greasy; one fingernail was black and blue and coming off—some hands. He could see his name in blinking neon lights: *Featuring* JOE MONDRAGÓN

AND HIS MISS AMERICA HANDS! He cast a surreptitious glance at Nancy's hands and they weren't much better: red, tough, scratched, clobbered, the fingers permanently bent from being wrapped around mops, wrench handles, shovels, and the like—she could work as hard as him, maybe even harder . . . so why didn't she buy some of that pink creamy gunk they were always hyping you with on TV? And Joe had a flash, then, of their wedding day eight years ago, driving all around town in those cars covered with paper pom-poms and colored streamers, honking their horns, with the kids and dogs running after them, and all the people waving from their houses and gardens and from the wet green fields—

"Oh, hell," Joe griped. "I just dunno . . ."

And he wanted to discuss with her the funny way he felt. Like he was so tired and played out and uncertain of where he'd been going ever since he was a kid that he actually occasionally wanted this bean-field thing to blow up into something where he would wind up walking out his front door with a rifle blazing, only to be riddled for once and for all by their fucking bullets in return. The thing was, Joe had never had a firm grasp on anything, he had never really understood his own motivations, he had never had an idea where he was going. He didn't even know if he loved Nancy or his children. However he operated, he had operated instinctively. And mostly it was all too much work. He was exhausted from waking up apprehensive every morning of his life. And he envied his wife one thing: she loved him and she loved their brats, and that was her life—to feed them, keep house, and fight to protect them. She understood—maybe not exactly where she was or where they were going—but she understood the boundaries of her life, and the tasks that needed doing within those boundaries.

They sat there in silence finishing up their second tallboys, moving into thirds. The kids sneaked in, turning the TV back on, and neither parent paid attention. Outside it began to thunder a little, a few raindrops fell, then a wind blew the clouds back over the mountains. Joe had an urge to make love, but that was something he had never tried in broad daylight, not while it was still light out and work could be done.

"We owe on the pickup, the washing machine, the TV, and the refrigerator," Joe announced glumly.

"Don't worry. I mean, you know—what else is new?"

" 'Don't worry.' " He glared at her, this time with real hostility. "I been worried ever since I was born."

Nancy was a little drunk. "Screw your self-pity, José. Go tell it to the sheep."

"Speaking of sheep, how we doing for meat?" Joe asked a few minutes later.

"Not so good. In fact we don't have any."

"Well, I guess I'll go kill one of those kids, then."

"I'll help . . ."

Reeling a little, bumping into each other, they went out to the goat pen.

"You tie up the kid," Joe said. "I forgot a knife."

While he plodded back for the knife, Nancy caught a small brown billy, tying its left hind leg to its left front leg, then she fastened the right hind leg to a metal hook in the low ceiling of the dilapidated tool shack next to the goat pen. When Joe returned with the knife and a clean plastic bucket, he was trailed by the kids, all three of whom loved a good butchering. He gave Nancy the bucket and, without a word, clamped a hand around the dangling kid's muzzle; then with one stroke he laid open its throat and held the animal for a moment, with the blood gushing over his fingers and into the bucket Nancy held, until the body quit twitching. Nodding, then, he let go and went to the doorway. There he licked the hot blood off his fingers and watched as that ugly yellow cat calmly devoured a small water snake over by the irrigation ditch.

Joe felt more uncomfortable than he had in ages. Danger, maybe even evil, floated on the air, thick as the scent of fox. But, not knowing what to do about it, Joe just stood there, quietly licking his fingers clean and not thinking, because in the final analysis he understood no more about life and death and politics and love and the human soul than the next man.

·∾

Nick Rael's wife Dorothy had divorced him some years back; she currently lived in Chamisaville with three of their four children, Buddy, Sonny, and Lizzie Rael, and Nick lived in Milagro in a modest adobe house right next to the store with the fourth kid, Jerry, and his eighty-nine-year-old mother. Jerry was as normal as any other awkward fourteen-year-old adolescent, but Nick's mother, Mercedes, was another story altogether. "All her marbles are loose," the locals were fond of saying, "and you can hear them rattling when she walks around town at night."

Actually, Mercedes Rael wasn't much for walking around town at night, but occasionally she did manage to jump the picket fence surrounding Nick's house and yard and go for some protracted aimless strolls, either up into the mountains, in which case a posse usually had to be formed to hunt her down before she starved to death, or else sometimes she liked to wander down the middle of the north–south highway dressed in whatever she happened to ·be wearing at the time, which could run the gamut from elaborate floor-length lace nightgowns and puffy lounging robes, to nothing. More than once the various lawmakers and town officials had suggested to Nick that he should either lock his mother up in the house every day while he was next door in the store and every night while he was asleep, or, better yet, deposit her in the state funny farm down in the capital and make everybody involved rest that much easier.

But Nick wasn't about to commit his mom to the state bin, or even lock her up in the house all day. "If I lock her up," Nick had explained more than once to more than one exhausted sheriff or state cop after a three-day search for Mercedes, "she gets clusterphobia. And when she gets clusterphobia she starts lighting matches. Once she set herself on fire, and another time she set her mattress on fire when I had her tied to the bedpost. If you take the matches away she starts to eat things, any things. Once she ate half the feathers in a pillow when I left her locked up all day. Another time she drank an entire bottle of tequila I had hidden way back in a corner cupboard. I'm telling you, boys, it's better if she can move around. She likes to be out in the yard—"

Mercedes did indeed enjoy being out in the yard. But she didn't just lie about on the grass or in a hammock or a rocking chair like your average eighty-nine-year old woman. She took an active interest, for example, in Nick's flower garden, often eating the heads off the daffodils and hydrangeas, also off the lilacs and roses when those plants bloomed. If the class foliage had all gone to seed, she crawled around on her hands and knees eating dandelions when they bloomed; or else she spent hours blowing apart the seedlings on those she had—for one reason or another—missed. She was an abnormally spry little old lady, too, and thus was often spotted high up in the few Chinese elm and cottonwood trees Nick had growing around his tidy place; she would spend hours making faces at the hummingbirds and magpies that had nests up there.

But by far and away the quirk which had given wrinkled, half-bald, almost ninety-year-old Mercedes Rael her most far-reaching fame was her habit of throwing stones at people.

The old lady derived such pleasure from this activity that Nick indulged her to the point where he was constantly ordering high-priced white gravel bits to replace the gravel walk leading from his front gate to the front portal. This walk was the old woman's ammunition dump, and she used it so regularly that Nick had to lay down a new path about once every four or five months.

Mercedes never hurt anybody throwing these stones, although occasionally she annoyed the living daylights out of certain local individuals who were her constant targets. Harlan Betchel was one of these targets; Peter Hirsshorn another; Jerry Grindstaff a third. Whenever the Forest Service boys, Carl Abeyta and Floyd Cowlie, moseyed on over to the store for their midmorning Dr. Pepper and gossip break, she would stand behind the gate, or behind the low white picket fence on either side of it, pelting them with the expensive white pebbles. Mercedes was a refined little bat, though, and she never attacked by flinging handfuls of pebbles; that would have been unspeakably crude. Instead, she threw one pebble at a time, almost delicately, although over the years she had developed a rapid-fire accuracy that was something to marvel at, if you did not happen to be the object of her attention.

Others who drew her fire (you could hardly say they were drawing her wrath because she was always perfectly composed during these pebble flurries, smiling blandly and sweetly like a decrepit grandma serving up tea and ladyfingers) included anyone in a policeman's uniform; all the deliverymen who brought goods to the store, to the Frontier Bar, or to the Pilar Café; the Trailways bus and its driver and passengers; and anybody who worked for Ladd Devine. She never threw stones at Tranquilino Jeantete or at Amarante Córdova or at Onofre Martínez or at Panky Mondragón or at Seferino Pacheco. And although she usually threw stones at dogs or other animals that wandered past the Rael home into the plaza area, she never attacked Pacheco's pig, because the first time she had pelted the huge sow it charged her, broke down the gate, knocked her to the ground, and had her arm in its mouth up to the elbow before Nick came bounding out of the store with a crowbar in his hand to save the day.

Mercedes also never chucked pebbles at kids, because kids nowadays had no respect for their elders and were liable to return her fire.

There were always a few people gathered within range on the porch of Rael's store, chewing the fat, comparing government checks that had come out of Mercedes' son's post office in the back of the store, or else just sitting around drinking beer and pop and listening to Nick's radio, which he usually kept tuned loudly to KKCV in Chamisaville. So the old lady was always standing on the store side of the white picket fence picking her shots among those congregated on the porch, and this had been going on for such a long time that nobody really noticed Mercedes anymore, nor paid much attention to the white pebbles that bounced harmlessly among them like hailstones.

Harlan Betchel was probably the only person in town who'd never been able to acclimate himself to the pebbles of Mercedes Rael. Maybe it was because he'd been a huge, gawky, chubby, and highly disliked kid, and the old lady's pebbles reminded him all too much of the persecution that had dogged the heels of his unhappy childhood. Whatever the case, Harlan was the one person in town who genuinely hated Mercedes Rael; he was the one person in town who never volunteered to go out and scour the mountains whenever she got lost in them; he was the one person in town who kept sticking the needle into Bernabé Montoya and into the state cops to have them stick the needle into Nick to have him commit her to the state hospital down in the capital. Harlan had once even gone so far as to write an anonymous letter to the head of the state Health and Social Services Department, a woman named Ursula Bernal, asking her to force Nick to commit this ding-y octogenarian who was making life unbearable for everybody in Milagro, but the HSS head had never even sent an underling up north to check out the situation.

Almost every other time Harlan Betchel decided to cross the plaza area from the Pilar Café to Nick's store, he would veer out of range of the old lady standing expectantly behind the fence and shuffle nervously around by the Frontier Bar and Forest Service headquarters. But even then, as he swerved back up onto the porch, Mercedes usually managed to uncork a half-dozen infinitely annoying gravel bits that plinked around his feet before he attained her son's door.

When he did not see the crazy old bag standing by the gate or behind a section of fence, Harlan naturally strode straight across the plaza area. Sometimes, however, this lack of caution backfired, because Mercedes would be on all fours hiding behind a lilac bush or some tulips, and she would pop up with her pitching

arm going like balls of fire as soon as Harlan entered
the invisible but well-marked sphere of her range, and
without fail her sudden appearance, plus the accuracy
of her pellets, would give the big blubbery man such
a start that on several occasions he actually fell down
from surprise, and he almost always emerged from
these sneak attacks with his heart thundering in a
terribly unhealthy manner.

For years now, Nick Rael had been telling Harlan,
"Throw something back at her, for crissakes, then
she'll stop it." But Harlan had always considered himself too much a gentleman to take up arms against a
little old lady.

There came a day, however, when the café manager cracked. Preoccupied by uneasy thoughts stem-
ming from the Joe's beanfield business, Harlan forgot
—on his way across the plaza area to buy cigarettes
at Rael's (where they were cheaper than in the café
machine)—to swerve around by the Frontier Bar and
the Forest Service headquarters, and one of Mercedes' tiny white pellets' drilling him in the ear took him
so by surprise that he actually stumbled over sideways
with a yelp. As soon as he realized what had happened, Harlan began to scramble about in the dust
looking for a projectile big enough to wing at Mercedes, who merely regarded his curious antics with a
blank, bemused expression. Harlan could locate nothing much larger than a pea, however, until suddenly
he sat up, removed a loafer from his foot, and flung
it wildly at the old lady, who forgot to duck, thus
allowing the shoe to clock her squarely in the forehead. Of course Harlan, even in his rage, had never
expected, or intended, to hit her, and the sickening
BLONK! that resulted from this meeting between his
loafer and her noggin resounded with a terrifying
echo all around the plaza area, causing him to lurch
up with a terrified squeal just as Mercedes gave a
quizzical burp and keeled over, out cold.

"Nick!" Harlan bleated, rushing toward the white
picket fence. *"Nick, Nick, I just killed your mother!
I just killed your mother!"*

Nick hollered, "Just a sec, I gotta ring up this purchase!" and then after he had handed Horsethief Shorty Wilson his change, the storekeeper trotted into the Rael front yard, where Mercedes hadn't moved a muscle or twitched an eyelash for over two minutes, and where Harlan Betchel was holding onto his loafer as gingerly as if it had been Lizzie Borden's blood-stained ax.

Curiosity had led Horsethief Shorty to follow Nick, and now he asked, "What the hell did you do, you bully, you beaned the little old lady with your shoe?"

"You always told me, Nick," Harlan stammered. "You always said—"

"Yeah, sure, Christ," Nick responded, "I know, I know. I didn't think you'd clobber her with a boot, though."

"It's not a boot, it's a loafer . . . I . . ."

"Wasn't there no little stones or anything handy?" Nick asked glumly, feeling for his mother's pulse, and —perhaps all too quickly—finding it, strong as the pulse of an ox.

"She ain't dead," Shorty said.

"H-how can you tell?" Harlan blurted. "H-how do you know?"

Shorty, who had knelt on the other side of the body, thrust his recently purchased snuff tin under her nose and then held the tin up for Harlan to observe, saying, "See? She's breathing. There's a moist film on the tin. That's one way I can tell. The other way is I can see her chest heaving up and down like a bellows. The third way I can tell is there's funny little wrinkles all around her mouth from trying not to smile. You ask me, Nick, this deaf old bat is playing possum."

Nick nodded, shouting, "Come on, Mom! We know you're awake! You can get up now!"

Harlan gaped. "You mean she's okay?"

"Well, she's gonna have a lump on her forehead for a few days," Nick said. "But other than that I guess she'll be alright—"

And Mercedes was okay. But she never again chucked pebbles at Harlan Betchel. Harlan, however, never knew for certain that she wasn't going to throw

something at him, for it seemed that she was always
there whenever he crossed the plaza area, only now
instead of throwing gravel bits at him with one of
those sweet moronic smiles on her ancient features,
she glowered sternly from under lowered eyebrows
while letting the little stones run through her fingers
from hand to hand, threatening him more by her
abstention than she had before with her open attacks.
In fact, the looks she gave him were so severe, Harlan began to fear she was planning how to cook his
goose, say, with a gun, and he knew this was more
than possible because Nick had weapons galore lying
around his place; the old woman wouldn't even have
to use ingenuity to get hold of one.

Harlan's trips to and from the store became a hundred times more nerve-racking than before. He soon
found himself back skirting around by the Frontier
Bar and the Forest Service headquarters, but now he
felt uncomfortable in this approach too, because if, as
her threatening monkeyish expression seemed to suggest, she was planning to murder him with one of
Nick's myriad household pistols, no detour short of
a mile was going to save him.

Harlan wished Mercedes would go back to chucking stones at him. In fact, he often caught himself
silently begging her to revert to her old form of harmless torture.

But maybe Mercedes' feeble mind still knew a thing
or two about psyching out her opponent. In any case,
she stuck to her guns, and come rain or come shine,
whenever Harlan Betchel was crossing the plaza area
she was out there, silently frowning and glowering and
running the white pebbles through her fingers, mercilessly driving the café manager toward an early grave.

And somehow it all connected up to—in fact Mercedes' cruelty and cunning were savagely focused by
—the existence of Joe Mondragón's pathetic little
beanfield.

ॐ

After the meeting in the governor's conference
room, Kyril Montana went to work. First, he requi-

sitioned the Bloom file. There wasn't much on the lawyer. A native of Longmeadow, Massachusetts, a graduate of Harvard Law, Bloom had been married once before, to a rich young Bostonian named Sherri Pope, a Radcliffe graduate with a master's in education. Divorced nine years ago, they had one child, Miranda, who lived with her mother and stepfather in the suburban Boston area. The divorce had apparently been a drawn-out, sticky affair, but the file contained few details.

Bloom had been in the state five years and was presently married to a young Chicano woman, Linda, maiden name of Romero, whose hometown was in the San Luis Valley of Colorado. Their children, both girls, were six and two and a half years, respectively —Pauline and María. The file had been started on Bloom at the time he defended a vocal land-grant heir, one César Pacheco, a part-time plumber from Ojo Prieto, sixteen miles west of Milagro. Pacheco, considered a militant activist by police agencies in the north, had been arrested on a drunk-driving charge, possibly authentic but probably not, and during the course of the arrest he had stabbed a county police officer—Pete Sandoval—once in the chest, inflicting a minor wound.

Bloom had created an imaginative and effective defense, something few lawyers would have dared, considering the political overtones of Pacheco's involvements, not to mention the fact that he had stabbed a cop. Starting with the assumption that Pacheco had attacked Sandoval in self-defense, Bloom put together a string of witnesses, testimony, and circumstantial evidence which had so incriminated Sandoval that the trial almost became a forum for protests against police brutality in the north. In the end, of course, Pacheco was convicted of resisting arrest, assaulting a police officer with a deadly weapon, using obscene and abusive language, being drunk and disorderly, and so forth, and he was presently serving a five-year term in the state penitentiary.

The cursory check on Bloom's character and background that had been run during and after the Pacheco

trial produced several memoranda covering two dis-
cussions the undercover arm of the state police had
had with state bar officials concerning Bloom's quali-
fications and credentials, all of which were in order.
At the time, pending further development of Bloom's
career—which up until the Pacheco trial had been
orderly and quiet—it was decided that nothing should
be done, no pressures brought to bear on Bloom or
on his practice, such as it was, by the Bar Association.
In general, the various people in the capital, in Milagro, in Colorado, and in the East who'd been contacted about Bloom had opined that he was no
crusader and that he would not follow up the Pacheco
case with more of the same fire and brimstone. This
turned out to be an accurate appraisal of the lawyer's
then immediate future, now his receding past. After
the Pacheco case and up until this Joe Mondragón
thing, Bloom had once again comfortably immersed
himself in the endless petty squabbles, divorces, and
mundane litigations of the poor people of Chamisa
County.

After going through the file Kyril Montana picked
up the telephone, and the first calls he placed were
to Boston and Longmeadow, Massachusetts. Once he
had defined what he was looking for to his contacts
in the East, he put on his sport coat and left the
office, walking twelve blocks across town to the *Voice
of the People* office, which was on a quiet tree-lined
street not far from the veteran's cemetery.

Curiously, although there was nobody in the four-
room building, the front door was open, and so the
agent walked inside. In each room he found a desk,
an electric typewriter, a telephone, and a mess.
Mounds of paper were scattered around, ashtrays and
wastebaskets were filled to overflowing, and, where
visible, the flat olive carpeting was freckled with cigarette burns. Back issues of the *Voice* in cardboard
boxes lined the hallway leading to a bathroom in the
rear. Beside the bathroom, in a large closet-type area,
was a lot of darkroom equipment, including a valuable photo enlarger. Across one wide desk that apparently belonged to the business manager were

scattered a half-dozen open envelopes: among them were notices from the phone company, from an office-supply rental firm, from the landlord, from a printer, and from the Library of Congress Copyright Division. Skimming the contents of each envelope, Kyril Montana learned that the *Voice* owed the Sierra Bell Telephone Company $197.53, and that their phones would be turned off if they didn't make arrangements to fork over the cash immediately; the office-supply firm was threatening suit to obtain $503.00 for back rent on three electric typewriters; the landlord wanted last month's rent; the printer was demanding $670.40 for the past two issues; and the Library of Congress Copyright Division wanted $108.00 for failure to pay the $6.00 filing fee for the last eighteen issues of the magazine.

Kyril Montana jotted this information down. Then he went from cardboard box to cardboard box selecting back issues, and within minutes he left the office carting twenty old issues of the magazine under one arm. Stopping for coffee and two burritos with green chili in a café near the central plaza, he leafed swiftly through all twenty magazines, marking the stories that carried a Charley Bloom by-line. Back in his office he skimmed through each Bloom article, underlining paragraphs here and there, and after that he composed a short profile of the lawyer's largely innocuous subject matter which he typed up on his own machine.

This done, the agent read through the Xerox of the typewritten article on Joe Mondragón's beanfield that Rudy Noyes had given him at the meeting in the governor's conference room; he made a few notes on this, had another Xerox of it run off and placed in the Bloom file, then contacted both the local FBI office and the Treasury Department's Alcohol, Tobacco, and Firearms Division to see if anyone had a photograph of the lawyer, but there he struck out: until this moment, apparently, nobody had ever seriously considered Charley Bloom a dangerous person.

Toward the tail end of the following afternoon phone calls came in from both Massachusetts towns, and the scoop on Charley Bloom was everything the agent could have hoped for. During one seven-year period the lawyer's tax returns had been audited, challenged, and taken to court annually. He had paid fines galore, and the whole business was not yet straightened out. He had messed up regularly on his alimony payments, too, and there was still a great deal of confusion in the matter of who in the family could declare the daughter, Miranda, whom both Bloom and his first wife had named as a dependent on their returns for six years.

Their divorce, as the file indicated, had been a doozy. First, Sherri Bloom had contested it. Bloom's lawyers had countered by threatening to take Miranda and have Sherri declared insane, or at least incapable of being a parent. Bloom's wife then accused him of adultery; in return he accused her, first of frigidity, then of sexual promiscuity with at least three other men. In the end Sherri Bloom's side had concocted an atrocious lie, threatening to accuse Bloom in court of attempting to have sexual relations with his eleven-year-old daughter. They never had to make this fabrication a matter of public record, however: their letter to Bloom accusing him of this deed did the trick— he finally dropped out of the fight as if poleaxed. At the time of the divorce the Blooms had been eighty-three thousand dollars in the hole; there followed bankruptcy declarations and a substantial loss of valuable suburban property. It had been a very ugly situation, a bad divorce. Obviously, Charles Morgan Bloom had come out West in order to begin a new life.

Kyril Montana wrote all these things down, then he typed them up for the file. After that he made one phone call to a particular person, and finally, a little after 6:00 P.M., he said good-bye to several men in the office and drove home. On his way he stopped by the *Voice of the People* office, which, though dark, was still unlocked. When he arrived home the agent made a last short business call, then changed into sports clothes and went out to have a cocktail with his wife beside the pool.

That night the *Voice of the People* offices were routinely burglarized, the three rented electric typewriters and the enlarger stolen. These machines were discovered by the police the next day abandoned in a dry arroyo on the western edge of town. Although the typewriters were brought in unharmed, the enlarger was hopelessly smashed. The typewriters were not returned to the *Voice of the People,* but instead were handed over to the rental company that owned them. That same day the rental company filed suit against the *Voice* for $503.

Still, three days later the *Voice* published an issue. The day after that the magazine was mailed out to one thousand, two hundred, and eleven subscribers, half of whom had not renewed their subscriptions but were getting the magazine anyway, and during the next four days about fifteen hundred copies of the paper were distributed to eleven towns located in the top northern quarter of the state.

The issue turned out to be the most successful ever in terms of newsstand sales. In fact, within several days it was almost entirely sold out. But the *Voice* staff didn't know this. Once the magazine was inefficiently hauled from town to town and drugstore to drugstore in a rattletrap pickup driven by a vague long-haired poet named Jamey Carruthers, nobody from the *Voice* kept track of it until Jamey Carruthers came around again a month later to collect and distribute once more. So no one, least of all Charley Bloom, realized that the magazine had been quietly bought up by three men traveling in one car over Jamey Carruthers' route, nor did the *Voice* staff realize that the copies, once bought, were to be quietly burned in the backyard barbecue pit of a Capital City man named James Vincent who occasionally did odd jobs and the like for the undercover wing of the state police.

This James Vincent, a portly and nervous son of a bitch, lugged all the cardboard boxes of bought-up *Voices* into his backyard, which was dominated by a huge concrete barbecue pit flanked by feathery tamarisk trees. Vincent set down the last of four cardboard boxes with a grunt, then went inside for some lighter fluid. On his return, he carefully lifted all the magazines from the boxes and set them in separate piles atop a redwood picnic table beside the pit.

It was a windless, absolutely clear and sunny day. Although in an understandable hurry to incinerate the magazines, Vincent paused for a moment to stare at a tiny yellow-breasted warbler flitting about in the green mist of the left-hand tamarisk tree. Relaxing for a moment, he started to relight his cigar.

But as James Vincent touched a match to the tip of what Mrs. Vincent always called the "permanent pig turd" clenched between his false teeth, a miniature tornado—known locally as a dust devil—twirled down the street, whipping up little cones of last autumn's Chinese elm leaves and making neighborhood dogs slink off on their bellies. The dust devil suddenly veered off the pavement into the Vincent yard, grabbed up the yellow-breasted warbler, the pyrotechnician's cigar, and all one thousand, four hundred, and eighty-one copies of the *Voice* in its voracious little wind funnel and, after that, with a graceful hop it sailed over the right-hand tamarisk tree heading toward one of the capital's main thoroughfares.

"Wait a minute!" James Vincent cried.

And he had only just plunged into the house to make a frantic phone call when a frantic phone call was placed to him.

"Are you out of your mind?" Kyril Montana said icily into the phone. "Did you hire a plane to scatter them all over the city?"

"I can explain," Vincent stammered in terror.

"I wouldn't make book on that," the agent hissed sarcastically.

"It was a dust devil. No shit, I'm not kidding. A fucking goddam dust devil!"

"That's hard to believe, Mr. Vincent. Very hard to believe indeed."

"Could I lie about it?" James Vincent wailed. "Man, how *could* I lie about a crazy thing like this?"

"Well, we've got eight people over in the La Loma–Manzanillo area picking up those magazines. But some of them fell into backyards, onto portals, and roofs—"

"I couldn't help it," James Vincent moaned. "It

happened so suddenly. It was an act of God. I was just gonna start drenching them with lighter fluid. How could I help it, I'm some kind of supernatural weatherman? I never saw it coming. The chances were ten million to one a thing like this could happen."

"Well, I assume we've got it under control," the agent said disgustedly, and hung up.

"Luck," James Vincent groaned to himself, to nobody, not in his wildest dreams realizing how prophetic his statement would turn out to be: "I got the kind of luck even a rattlesnake wouldn't strike at."

Kyril Montana sat at his desk, slowly shaking his head. He was perplexed, also pissed-off. He hated allocating jobs, he wished he never had to depend on other people to perform some of the services necessary in his work.

But by the time he picked up the jangling phone in order to receive a broadside in his right ear from his boss, Xavier Trucho, the agent felt better; so much better, in fact, that when Trucho finally paused to suck in a gasping breath, Kyril Montana, who by nature was a fairly humorless man, found himself laughing.

"But it was an act of God," he joked. "The chances were ten million to one that a thing like this could happen."

❦

Charley Bloom was a tall, affable, sincere, although somewhat wishy-washy and also quite tormented man. He spoke gently, had a soft smile and an outwardly relaxed, controlled, and sort of scruffy demeanor. But he was also a man torn between deeply conflicting ideals, who harbored a profound resentment against many things that had been embedded in him during the early years of a puritan New England upbringing. This resentment surfaced on those rare but awful occasions when he blew his cool, and then for brief, holocaustic moments he could be like a mad dog or a murderer; and for days afterward, afraid of himself and worried about his sanity, he would be contrite and terribly ashamed.

For six years, fresh out of law school and then not

so fresh out of law school, employed by his father-in-law's successful Boston law firm, Bloom had struggled, not only to consolidate a kind of upper-class establishment "security," but also to rationalize life with the beautiful woman who was his first wife and with whom he could neither relate nor communicate. Basically, both Bloom and Sherri Pope were talented, educated, sensitive people who, before their marriage, had been so completely versed as social beings that neither could muster the guts to face up to anything. Sherri's dream was to become an even better-known, more glamorous bigshot in Boston's social arena; and, depending on his mood, her desires either coincided with or were directly in opposition to what Bloom lusted after as opposed to what he felt was "useful" and "good." They both resented the marriage because it exposed—to each other, if not to society at large—their own immaturity, moral weaknesses, and intellectual shortcomings. And, after only a year and a half together, even before Miranda's birth, Bloom's temper tantrums had suddenly exploded out of nowhere to become an almost monthly event. On several occasions he slugged his wife, hating Sherri for the way her presence constantly had him split down the middle. As soon as she recognized the nature of her husband's unhappiness, Sherri knew they were doomed and reacted accordingly by commencing one, and then several, affairs. How they kept up appearances for four more years until the disastrous divorce Bloom, for one, had never been able to ascertain.

When the lawyer deserted the East Coast after that divorce he was a stunned human being, a twenty-nine-year-old man on the block and ready to give up. He wished to sever all his roots into positions of privilege; and he never wanted to be intimately involved with another person again. He drifted here and there—Aspen, Colorado, was the town where he holed up the longest. Eventually some of the divorce's trauma wore off or at least receded enough so that the casual observer would not notice, and Bloom merged himself timidly again with the currents of his time. There was a strange epoch during which he indulged in much kinky sex with a number of transient Aspen girl friends, but after that he drifted back into paralegal work, and finally into a Legal Aid position in the southern rural valleys of Colorado. At first his job was simply a way to mark the days while his wounds healed or his life slowed down to a crawl, whichever; but after a time, during his travels—which took him to towns like Saguache and Monte Vista and Fort Garland—he timidly allowed honest attachments into his life again: first, for the poor people in general whose rights he was defending, and eventually for one of them specifically, a gentle skittish woman named Linda Romero.

Their romance progressed at less than a snail's pace. Bloom was still so touchy about intimacy that for a half year they hardly exchanged monosyllables over cups of instant coffee in the Romero kitchen when he came to talk with Linda's brother, Johnny, who was up once on burglary and then again on armed assault charges. Linda herself was a timid, mistrusting, yet also quite sensual woman who not long before he met her had been engaged to a child-hood sweetheart; it was an affair that had ended bitterly and with a terribly traumatic abortion. Thinking themselves cynical about, and not a little afraid of, life, neither Bloom nor Linda wished to become involved again for a long time.

So, as is natural in these situations, they fell in love. And before either understood exactly what had transpired, a justice of the peace in Antonito, Colorado, was signing their marriage certificate; a few minutes later they exploded into violent lovemaking in the back seat of Bloom's VW bus parked on a deserted side road near La Jara. Their short, erotic honeymoon took place that same night in a white cottage across the street from the tiny Jack Dempsey Museum in Manassa, Colorado. In the morning, astonished with themselves and terrified for their futures, they drove back toward Alamosa; the roads were decorated with fat autumn pheasants and strikingly beautiful yellow-headed blackbirds. For both, their bodies aching from last night's almost brutal sexual assault on

each other, that drive to Alamosa the morning after
was a cherished, nearly sacred moment. Bloom especially thought it the best possible omen for the start of
a new life. He sincerely believed that by marrying
this good woman, the product both of a tough lower-
class upbringing and of a rich communal culture very
unlike his own, he was breaking with an establishment
past, a liberal-conservative tradition that had always
hung him up. Already he felt almost self-righteous
about his new life because it was going to be Down
to Earth, Humble, Unpretentious, *Real*.

Yet Bloom and his wife had existed on tenterhooks
with each other for years now. Within six months their
physical attraction for each other suddenly waned;
they lost a sexual rhythm together, becoming clumsy
in bed, self-conscious, and then abruptly withdrawn.
After that, as products of very different backgrounds
they were continually scared stiff of hurting each
other's feelings; hence they understood and tolerated
their respective foibles almost to the point of obse-
quiousness. Neither ever lost his or her temper; and,
terrified of blowing their lives again, each begging the
other for some kind of emotional security, theirs became a kid-gloved marriage of major proportions.

To Bloom's private horror, he discovered almost
immediately that far from being proud of, or even
content with, her Chicano heritage, Linda almost hysterically wanted out of her poverty-stifled past. In
order to serve his rural clients, most of whom spoke
Spanish, Bloom had painstakingly learned to speak
that language well—but Linda had what almost
amounted to an aversion toward her mother tongue.
She insisted on speaking English with him, so much
so that when Bloom tried to speak Spanish he accused him of wanting to mock her, make her angry,
upset her days. In point of fact, Linda aspired to certain illusions of security offered by those establishment
traditions and values which had created an insupport-
able tension between the lawyer and his first wife.
Thus, instead of a way out for Bloom, Linda threatened to reaffirm the roots he badly wanted to destroy.
And their dilemma was instantly this: he desired what

he thought she had been, whereas she desired what she thought he had been. Immediately both of them felt cheated and they began to resent each other, although they kept their mouths shut, praying for some kind of miracle to come along and straighten things out or at least fashion a workable compromise.

In spite of their different attitudes, hopes, and goals, they gradually—though neither could have explained how—reached a functioning détente. After thinking about it for a while, Bloom rationalized that he did feel some gratitude for not now being obliged to make the radical commitments he had always feared. And in the end, daring even to have children, their relationship evolved into a polite standoff. Bloom continued working for the poor, and, although far from poor himself, he was still able to feel at least as moral about his work as Linda felt about immersing herself totally in raising a middle-class American family. Understanding the inherent weaknesses of their arrangement, they remained aloof from others, cultivating few friends, keeping their own lives relatively simple—on an even keel, so to speak—by avoiding close ties both with themselves and with their neighbors.

In light of these survival tactics, after Bloom broke from the Legal Aid program and moved to Milagro to begin a more relaxed private practice, and, more importantly perhaps, to help Linda set up a home safely removed from her family connections, the lawyer's involvement in the César Pacheco case went completely against the methods by which they had learned to handle their marriage. It was one of those commitments that occurred because of Bloom's deep-seated dissatisfaction, which often made him profoundly uncomfortable with a lifestyle that seemed much too inherently selfish.

The Pacheco case, then, was a reaction against a life that had become too comfortable, too safe. Hence, even though terrified of political commitments, Bloom had gone out on a limb and it had cost them. During the course of that nerve-racking trial, Linda saw his temper for the first time. One evening shortly after

Bloom had returned from court, some stray dogs attacked and killed several of their chickens. When the lawyer realized what was happening he grabbed an ax, lunged outside bellowing dementedly, trapped one attacking dog inside the chicken pen, and literally hacked the squealing mongrel to pieces.

So those were the tensions he had and might always have inside himself, and after the Pacheco trial and the dog incident, Linda had never trusted her husband again.

Pacheco's trial had been four years ago. Today the Joe Mondragón affair threatened once more to upset the tenuous stability of their lives. This time the client was a friend; the favor could not be refused. Despite Linda's cautious approach to people, she and Joe's wife had become more than just neighborly acquaintances. And although Bloom had always tended to shy away from Joe's hot head, he also admired Joe from a distance for the fighter he was, and he had done a number of routine legal favors for the Mondragóns —tax returns, mortgage and loan agreements, plus several trips to the Chamisa County Jail to bail Joe out. In return the Blooms had received bottles of homemade chokecherry wine, a leg of mutton, Halloween pumpkins, even hay bales for their two Shetland ponies, Orangutan and Sunflower.

Of course, Bloom thought on reflection, one of his worst blunders was the article on Joe's beanfield he'd done for the *Voice of the People*. In fact, all the articles he had written for the *Voice* added up— Bloom suddenly felt—to a mistake on his part. At the start he had agreed to write them because the paper's editor, a Capitol City lawyer named Sean Carter, was a friend who often did law library research and other favors for Bloom; and too, Bloom assuaged the liberal side of his conscience by providing those informative, slightly renegade articles free of charge. By and large the Milagro lawyer's articles had been fairly innocuous—generalized summaries of welfare problems, advice on how to pay less income tax, on how to apply for and receive food stamps. Taken within this context, the beanfield article represented a departure from the lawyer's norm—so much so, in fact, that as soon as he saw it in print Bloom wished to Christ he could pull it back, erase it, disclaim ownership, forget about the whole thing. Because at heart he felt he did not have the guts, or maybe even the desire, to put his money where his mouth was. He had grown too accustomed to playing things safe, even if he did not enjoy them that way; and if he rocked the boat now, his home, his family life would be the first thing to collapse. In retrospect, all his writings had done were to make him that much more politically and professionally vulnerable. "En boca cerrada," Nancy Mondragón had one time told him with a wry wink, "no entran moscas." Meaning: "If you keep your mouth shut, flies won't enter."

But then, all during the time Bloom had known Joe he had understood that sooner or later the relationship was going to lead to trouble; and who knows, perhaps that is even why he had protected their friendship. When it happened, then, when Joe danced by after the fact to announce with pride what he had done, Bloom almost gratefully dropped an arm around his neighbor's shoulders, saying, "Don't worry, man, if they come down on you we'll fight them every inch of the way." Though, of course, as soon as Joe left he reconsidered, wondering was he crazy to encourage such a hopeless and inflammatory act? Whereupon, afraid for his own hide, Bloom almost (but not quite, thank God!) called Joe up to tell him to quit playing childish games.

About the situation Linda understood two things: why her frightened husband had refused to cop out when for the health of them both he should have, and also what grave consequences might develop from the affair. And she deeply resented the fact that Bloom could jeopardize their fragile marriage in this way.

Thus immediately, two minutes after Joe dropped by with the news about his west side beanfield, Linda and Charley Bloom were very much on edge with each other, waiting for the sky to fall.

"Do you really want to do this?" Linda asked in a

small, uneven voice. "Do you really want to become involved?"

"Of course. I mean actually of course not, I suppose. I mean . . . I don't know . . ."

Later that same afternoon Bloom walked out back to survey his small, secure kingdom. There was his garden and the Rototiller with which he'd turned it over. There were his irrigation boots and a spade for cutting water out of the Acequia del Monte into his back field, or into his apple and plum trees, or into his garden. There were the two beehives Onofre Martínez had built and which the one-armed man cared for, supplying the Blooms with honey as a kind of rent. And there was the chicken coop Linda and he had built together, and the chickens wandering in the yard.

Bloom sensed all of it was terribly tentative, doomed. A time bomb was ticking at the heart of their outwardly placid, inwardly unstable little family universe, and he was afraid.

Naturally, Linda's lack of support pissed him off.

And he could feel his temperature rising as with her eyes, but never again with her voice, she urged him to back out while the backing was good.

When Bloom read his beautiful girls, Pauline and María, their bedtime stories, he nearly burst into tears. Having blundered into something he really did not *want* to do, simply because it was something that probably *ought* to be done, he was terrified of the dues that would have to be paid.

And when he and Linda went to bed at night they clung together wordlessly, waiting for unseen fatal blows to split open their skulls.

One weekend afternoon, the lawyer was outside on his front lawn desultorily hacking away at some piñon with a dull ax when Joe Mondragón's pickup entered the drive like a crippled jet fighter and made a one-point landing that stopped just short of plowing into the woodpile.

Straightening up, Bloom greeted Joe the way a timid cat might greet a very large fat rat. Joe smiled back, waving hello, and jumped nervously down from the cab, tossing a white package one-handed jumpshot style across the hood of his truck toward Bloom, who dropped the ax but bobbled the package anyway.

"What the hell is this?"

"Goat meat. We just killed a cabrito. It's good. You'll like it."

"So what's happening?" Bloom asked.

Picking up the ax, Joe ran his thumb along the edge. "Jesus Christ!" he exploded. "Why don't you sharpen your fucking ax, Charley? You'll kill yourself trying to break wood with this thing."

Bloom shrugged, grinning foolishly: "What can I say?"

"I got a file." Joe fetched it from the toolbox cached underneath what was left of his front seat, sat down on that seat with the door open, and began to sharpen the ax.

"You came over just to give me a package of dead goat?" Bloom asked suspiciously, fearing the worst.

"I dunno . . . you know," Joe said. "I just wondered if, well, if you read up anymore on water law, shit like that."

"I know one thing," Bloom said.

"Yeah? What's that?"

"The inspection sticker on your truck here expired a year and a half ago."

Joe looked up blandly, readjusting his cowboy hat. "So what?"

"Don't you ever get a ticket for that?"

"Not so far. Who's gonna be stupid enough to try and give me a ticket? Nobody in this town would be driving if we had to keep our stickers up to date. Bernie Montoya, *his* sticker expired two years ago!"

Bloom shrugged hopelessly. He couldn't stand such blithe defiance of petty laws. It was arrogant and stupid and caused a lot of useless trouble. And because Joe was stupid and arrogant he was no doubt also going to make a lot of stupid and useless trouble for Bloom, which the lawyer was going to let him do because he felt guilty, or noble, or was just too chickenshit to refuse a case that was doomed from the start.

Joe turned the ax over, starting to file along the

other edge. He said, "Hey, Charley, why don't you run down for me again what the law is about that water, okay? Just so I can get it straight in my mind."

Bloom settled uncomfortably into an old wooden chair he had been meaning for months to refinish, and for the umpteenth time summarized the 1935 Interstate Water Compact and the state water laws in general, detailing how, legally, the state could go after Joe if he kept irrigating on the west side, by calling a hearing and so forth. He explained what the special water master could and probably would try to do to Joe, and he wrapped up his brief narration by observing, "You understand, of course, that we've got about as much chance of winning this as a one-legged man has of winning an ass-kicking contest."

Joe had listened intently, grinding hard with the file, and when Bloom finished he quit sharpening the ax. They sat silently for a moment while Joe (wanting to scream because it was all still a muddle in his mind) lit a cigarette, and Bloom (wanting to scream because he had seen his explanations flying like scared doves into one of Joe's ears and out the other) stuffed and lit a pipe.

Eventually, Joe said, "I got some free time the next couple days, you got anything else around here needs fixing?"

The lawyer shook his head. After all, the more he accepted, the more he would be obliged to offer, and he was already in well over his head, thanks anyway.

Jumping out of the truck, Joe leaned the ax against the woodpile. "Well," he said hastily, avoiding Bloom's eyes, "you lemme know when you got something around here needs fixing, okay? And I'll let you know when those bastards try to arrest me or send me a summons in the mail or something, okay?"

"Okay," Bloom said, making an effort to smile. "Thanks for the cabrito, Joe."

Behind the wheel of his truck, Joe metamorphosed instantly into a cocky madman, jauntily tipped his hat, and catapulted his jet fighter back onto the public road, leaving the lawyer engulfed in a robin's egg blue exhaust cloud. Bloom brushed the poisonous fog

away from his face, went over to check the ax blade
. . . and promptly cut his thumb.

Sucking on his thumb, Bloom entered the kitchen
and tossed the cabrito package to Linda. When she
asked "What's this?" he rolled his eyes to the ceiling,
mock moaning, "Goat meat. Kid goat meat."

"Well, at least it's not venison."

Linda popped the package into their refrigerator's
freezing compartment which already held quite a few
gifts from Joe Mondragón—namely, three packages
of venison (one of which was two years old), some
brown trout wrapped in tinfoil, a small hunk of smoked
rattlesnake, and an entire (nicely skinned, perfectly
dressed) jackrabbit.

Confronted, as he sucked on his thumb, by this
freezer compartment full of what Linda (and, yes,
himself a little, too) considered inedible goodies,
Bloom didn't know whether to laugh or cry.

~§

How Charley Bloom felt was nothing compared to
the thoughts roiling in Herbie Goldfarb's brain. Herbie
Goldfarb being a twenty-two-year-old conscientious
objector and VISTA volunteer from Brooklyn, New
York, and a recent graduate of CCNY where he'd
majored in English literature. Herbie planned to go
to graduate school, but had reasoned upon graduation that he ought to take a year off and see the
world. And if you did this by joining VISTA, which
qualified as an alternate service to the draft, you were
much less likely to find yourself suddenly in the army
seeing that part of the world which included Vietnam.
So Herbie had spent a few weeks in the East boning
up on VISTA lore, and then he'd been shipped on a
bus with six other peagreen do-gooders to Chamisaville, where he had wanted to be stationed. But it
turned out Chamisaville had arranged for the six volunteers to be scattered into deserving remote areas,
and so that's how come Herbie found himself, quite
early one summer morning, descending from the Trailways bus at Rael's store in Milagro with a guitar in
one hand and a suitcase full of books and sneakers

and T-shirts and Levi's in the other, and the mayor, Sammy Cantú, who was supposed to meet him, didn't.

So began what Herbie later on in his life would refer to as "that nightmare summer." He tried to call up the mayor, only to discover Cantú had no phone. When he entered the store to ask Nick Rael for help, Nick just cocked his head suspiciously, asking "Who are you?" and then "What's VISTA?" and then, incredulously, "You came here to *teach* us things?"

Herbie spent a couple of hours out on the porch after that, blushing every time a local resident, who was usually practically vibrating with what Herbie interpreted as hostility, approached the store. And when some older men tipped their cowboy hats, mumbling, "Buenos días, cómo le ha ido, amigo?" it suddenly dawned on Herbie that maybe these people he had come to help spoke Spanish. And sure enough— they did. And he didn't.

Not one word.

Somewhat dumbfounded by this revelation, Herbie stared at the thousand confetti bits of torn-up parking meter tickets littering the plaza area, and tried to ignore the sweet little old lady in a nearby yard who was methodically stoning him with minuscule gravel bits.

About ten o'clock on that first morning a pudgy, cheerful, prosperous-looking man wearing a suit and a bolo tie emerged from a late model Plymouth that had just parked in front of Herbie, and, on his way into the store, tipped his cowboy hat and smiled, saying in English, "Hi there, how you doing?" By then Herbie was desperate, and so, leaping at the chance to converse with a relatively friendly English-speaking person, he blurted, "Excuse me, sir, but maybe you can help me, I'm looking for Mr. Cantú."

The man said, "Sammy Cantú, Bill Cantú, Meliton Cantú, Felipe Cantú, Amarante Cantú, Eloy Cantú, or Chemo Cantú?"

"Isn't your mayor named Cantú?" Herbie asked meekly.

"Sure." The man really grinned. "*I'm* the mayor.

My name is Sammy Cantú. What can I do for you, young man?"

"Uh, Mr. Cantú, my name is Herbert Goldfarb, I'm the VISTA volunteer."

The mayor regarded him blankly.

Herbie mumbled, "Didn't anybody tell you about me?"

Sammy Cantú squinted semisuspiciously, asking, "What's a VISTA volunteer?"

"Mr. Cantú," Herbie blurted, "I'm supposed to come and live here for a year. Mrs. Appleby down in Chamisaville, she said that all the arrangements were made, if I would only just check in with you when I got here."

"What do you mean, arrangements?" the mayor asked.

"Well, you know. A place to stay. People to talk with in the beginning about setting up some programs . . ."

"In Milagro?" Sammy Cantú looked really puzzled. "You mean nobody told you I was coming—?"

The mayor shrugged. "Nobody told *me*. But that doesn't mean nobody told nobody. Maybe somebody told somebody, but they didn't tell *me*."

"Well, what do you think I should do—" Herbie almost burst out crying.

"You say you're supposed to live here for a while?" Herbie nodded.

"Well, I know a place you could live if you're not too particular. My wife's brother, he's a cousin of Pancho Armijo, and when Tranquilino Armijo died he willed Pancho the big house, and Annie's husband, the brother Felix, he was willed this little one-room kind of smokehouse next door. It doesn't have no fireplace, but there's one of those Monkey Ward tin stoves in there, you could keep warm, and there's a ditch runs in back of the house usually has water in it you could drink so long as nobody farther up the line is using it in a field, and the rent probably wouldn't be very steep."

"Sure. That sounds great!" Herbie almost shouted, and proceeded to gush over with thanks.

He might have saved his applause for a more appropriate moment, though. The place was minuscule, it had one small, very high-up window, no electricity, and it was always cold. Skunks lived under the floorboards. The chimney of the tin stove wouldn't draw properly and it took him an hour to start a fire. Herbie owned no truly warm clothes because, having associated "Southwest" with "desert," he had figured the temperature would always be hovering around eighty-five degrees. Instead, he was living in a mud hut at seventy-four hundred feet, surrounded by twelve- and thirteen-thousand-foot snowcapped mountains, and the temperature, in June, even in July, dove to the high thirties and low forties with regularity at night. When it rained, which was almost every day for a while, his dirt roof with sunflowers growing in it leaked. Then winds that blew day and night, sucking the moisture out of the earth and knocking over old dried-up cottonwoods (one of which splintered his outhouse), kept driving sand into his sensitive eyes. And, with sties in both eyes and a cottonwood tree in his lap, his asshole aching from diarrhea that probably came from drinking irrigation ditch water, Herbie soon found himself all too often seated in his open-air outhouse (which he only dared use at night), wondering if it would take as long as two months before he cracked.

When he cleaned the house on his first day in it, Herbie discovered three black widow spiders. Next week their relatives were spinning new webs in the corners and between the legs of the tin stove. Because the hut lacked electricity he read by candlelight, literally hundreds of six-penny candles were soon set obscenely into pop bottles on the floor beside his sleeping bag. His only furniture was the suitcase, on end beside the window during the day, the chair on which he constantly perched reading Malamud, Katherine Anne Porter, Hemingway, F. Scott Fitzgerald, James Joyce, Isaac Bashevis Singer, Virginia Woolf, Henry Miller, and Joyce Carol Oates.

Asleep, Herbie dreamed the black widows were getting him. When he patronized the outhouse late at night he was terrified rattlesnakes would end this experiment in social consciousness; or else one of his brooding savage neighbors, thinking him a deer, would send his college-trained, intellectual brains foaming into the air with a slug from a .30-30.

One day his southern neighbor, Joe Mondragón, loafed over. Herbie was outside in the yard, sitting on a rock, playing his guitar. Joe said, "Hey, man, that's a pretty nice-sounding guitar, lemme have a whack at it." Herbie handed the instrument over and, with one foot on the rock, Joe stroked a few chords—he couldn't play worth shit. But then he started singing and Herbie had never heard a voice like that—lusty and high, almost piercing, but especially melodic too, singing in Spanish songs that to Herbie seemed rare and exotic, although he could have found them on any $1.79 Al Hurricane or Tiny Morrie record in the Chamisaville Whacker's store.

Joe said, "This is a nice guitar, you mind if I borrow it, just for a day? I want to sing my kids to sleep tonight."

"Sure," Herbie said, desperate for friends. "Go ahead. Keep it as long as you like. I don't play it that much anyway."

"Well, when you want it, holler," Joe said.

That was the last Herbie saw of his guitar. It disappeared into the Mondragón house and never came out again. Maybe Joe had forgotten about it, or maybe the kids had busted it. "If that's the case," Herbie mumbled to himself, "of course the Mondragóns can't pay . . ." And so to save everybody embarrassment Herbie never went over to ask for his guitar back.

In fact, the more he thought about it the more Herbie became convinced the kids had busted his guitar. They were terrors, those little Mondragón brats. The oldest one, who looked about six, got his kicks from hiding behind a big rabbitbrush bush at the Mondragón boundary fence and winging BBs at Herbie or at Herbie's window with a homemade innertube slingshot. Herbie never landed on the kid for this because he was afraid of the parents, even though several times in the beginning, after the guitar-lending incident, Nancy had come over with things for him to eat—a bowl of chili, another of posole, a bag of hot sopaipillas. He had thanked her profusely, wondering if they were payment for his splintered guitar. "Come on over and eat with us or watch television whenever you want," Nancy said brightly, but Herbie never took her up on that. Mostly because he was too shy, and because also he had been brought up in a society where such invitations were often largely a matter of social course and not to be taken that seriously. After a while Nancy stopped bringing food, and Herbie never went over. Of course, it did not occur to him others might be just as shy as himself.

And as for the guitar? Several times Nancy chided her husband, saying, "José, you got to give that poor boy back his guitar." But Joe pooh-poohed her concern. "He said keep it as long as I like. When he wants it back he's gonna holler—"

On another day early in Herbie's stay, a huge pig wandered into the Goldfarb yard. Herbie picked up a rock, but instead of running away the pig charged, and the volunteer had to run for his life, leaping high into the cottonwood that lay across his splintered outhouse.

Presently a hulking, crazy-eyed man toting a stiff lariat appeared on the scene. Without introducing himself he grumbled, "Oye, primo, ayúdame con esta pendeja marranita cabrona."

"I'm sorry," Herbie said, "but I don't speak Spanish."

Seferino Pacheco stopped, looking vaguely askance and threateningly at the Easterner perched in the fallen cottonwood.

"How come you don't speak no Spanish?"

"I never learned. I didn't realize so many people spoke so much Spanish so much of the time around here."

Pacheco grunted. "Well, help me catch this pig, will you?"

The pig wandered through the open door into Herbie's house. Exclaiming triumphantly, Pacheco leaped forward, slamming shut the door. Then he turned around and sat down on the small concrete stoop, rolling a cigarette while the pig went crazy inside, banging against the wall, crunching into the stove, squealing and grunting and bellowing—almost like a mule, Herbie thought. And then it was suddenly quiet in the little house.

"When it calms down I'll put this rope around it," Pacheco explained.

"I think your pig is eating my books," Herbie offered nervously. The window was so small and so high he couldn't look in to verify his fears.

"What kind of books?"

"Oh, you know, different people, mostly fiction . . ."

"You got anything by Hemingway?" Pacheco asked.

Herbie was a little taken aback. "Sure . . . I mean, yes, I got a couple . . ."

"You ever read *Old Man and the Sea?*"

Herbie nodded. "Sure . . ."

"That was a good book," Pacheco said. "My wife, she read it to me. I never learned to read. She read *To Have and Have Not* to me too, but I thought it was a bullshitty book. She read me a lot of stuff and a lot of it I liked. I'm the most learned illiterate man in this town. I know about people like James Joyce and Scott Fitzgerald and John Steinbeck. Me, I enjoyed especially books like that *Of Mice and Men* and *The Red Pony*. And *The Grapes of Wrath*. That's the kind of Anglo stuff people like me can relate to a little, I guess you'd say. But there are a lot greater writers than Steinbeck. You ever hear of Juan Ramón Jiménez, or read his book *Platero y Yo?* For that they gave him a Nobel Prize. Or how about Pablo Neruda? Or the Guatemalan, Asturias? Or the Argentinian, Jorge Luis Borges? My wife, she read all those people to me. Federico García Lorca. And how about the epic poem that boxer wrote, *Yo Soy Joaquín?* And you know what we did once? We left this town for a month and drove across the country, just to see the Orozcos in the Dartmouth College Library—"

Pacheco halted, cocking his head, belaboring Herbie with a crusty, almost evil eye. Then he said:

"Sometimes, after she died, when I used to get down

to the capital, I'd listen to the records and tapes in
the blind people's library. I knew a guy who worked
there and he didn't mind. But I don't get away from
this place anymore—I lost my mobility. I'm a little too
crazy to function on the outside, I think. How do
you like your neighbors?"

"I don't even know my neighbors."

"You got Pancho Armijo over there, and José
Mondragón behind us. Armijo, every two years he
loses the sheriff race to Bernie Montoya by three
votes. Which is okay because Bernie's not too smart
but he's not mean either—he's a good person to have
for sheriff. His way of keeping the lid on is by steering
clear of people's affairs. José Mondragón, he's another
kind of fish. He's got such a hot head you'd think he
was plucked off a chili plant instead of born natural
like the rest of us. He's one of those little guys likes
to beat the shit out of big guys. When he was high
school age he used to kick my Melvin down one side
of the playground and up the other side every recess
time. Melvin got killed in Korea. The only thing people around here are professionals at is producing
cannon fodder for that pendejo Tío Sam. Later on
José and me we built frame houses together when
the mine first came into Doña Luz, so we got to be
friendly. And now I can't hold any grudges. Except
if somebody asked me to name the six people in
town who, if that big pig in there ever got into their
fields, would most likely not only kill it but have the
animal butchered and packed away in their freezers
before I even knew about it, I'd have to say he would
be one of them."

Uncomfortable with this lopsided, wild-eyed man,
Herbie said, "Excuse me, sir, but I really am afraid
your pig is eating my books."

The look Pacheco cast his way practically nailed
Herbie to the cottonwood trees behind him. It was
part angry, part hurt, but mostly unhappy and very
lonely. Then Herbie realized that Seferino Pacheco
had made himself comfortable on that stoop with an
eye toward talking, and all at once the volunteer re-
gretted pushing the panic button, but he couldn't pull

back his words. And he *was* worried about his books.

Pacheco stood up, carefully opened the door, and darted inside. In due course, after a brief but noisy scuffle, he emerged with the pig trussed in a curious way, the rope around its neck and one leg so that it hobbled meekly along beside its master, grunting complacently.

Herbie said another thing he immediately wished he hadn't: "Isn't that pig big enough to slaughter?"

Pacheco returned a self-effacing, almost apologetic, somewhat embarrassed smile. "If I killed this miserable hog, then I wouldn't have an excuse, qué no?"

Later on in Herbie's western summer, as things—instead of developing—remained more or less the same or got worse, he wished Pacheco's pig would come around once more so they might chew the fat again. But it never did. Hence, he spent most of his time reading in his dismal room, wishing he could play his guitar, walking the three hundred yards to town for groceries—and somehow he just couldn't begin. He couldn't approach people, talk with them. He never saw the affable mayor again. Everybody seemed so far away, unreachable. He was a Connecticut Yankee in Milagro's court, and a blind man could see that whatever he might know enough about to teach somebody would be totally irrelevant to these people. He felt ashamed, and when he went out for walks he hunched his shoulders, wanting to be as invisible as an insect with diaphanous wings. People who actually would have been very friendly had he dared talk with them seemed sullen in his eyes: he imagined them kneeling before ornate little altars in their bedrooms at night, praying for him to take a powder—and he wanted to go home.

Once a week he hitchhiked to Chamisaville for lunch with the other volunteers, and for a shower at the KOA Kampgrounds a mile north of town. "Hey," one kid said, "I found this dynamite old guy who's teaching me Spanish." Another, a woman, gloated. "This really suave old lady is teaching me how to make tortillas." But basically they all felt sheepish and so out of their element it was crazy. "This is a great experience for all of us," Herbie said, "but what are we doing for the people?"

When he returned to Milagro from these Chamisaville trips and hurried, hunched over, to his miserable home, Herbie plunged back into literature with a vengeance, wrote long sorrowful letters home to a girl friend and to his parents, plinked imaginary lackluster rhythms on his forgotten, stolen, or busted guitar, and cursed the remote people and their remote village and especially himself for being unable to cope. Most of all, though, he cursed the skunks under his floorboards whose perpetual low-key stink was driving him insane—his eyes continually watered, his nostrils had become raw and almost bloody.

So sat Herbie Goldfarb, alone in his one-room house in the eye of a gathering storm, reading Hemingway, Joyce, McCullers, and Flannery O'Connor, the only inhaling and exhaling lump in Milagro oblivious to the fact that something was beginning to get ready to hit the proverbial fan.

Part Two

"United we flounder, divided we flounder."
—Benny Maestas

❧

Inevitably, Kyril Montana paid a visit to Milagro. He came in, one the north–south highway driving an unmarked state car, a beige, four-door Ford Galaxie which had a police radio and a .38 police special in the glove compartment. The agent rarely carried a gun on his person, and he had never had occasion to fire a gun at another human being. He was, however, an expert and deadly shot, a good hunter, also a conservationist. He was very careful about shooting the right kind of deer in the right season, and never violated the point system on ducks and upland game. He usually applied for a special elk and bighorn sheep permit, and such were the rules of the game within the various state agencies, that he was always granted a permit, and he always got his sheep or his elk. Too, the agent was an excellent bow hunter; and he sometimes went with an old college friend—the Milagro real estate agent Bud Gleason—varmint calling. But he was not into overkill, and there was nothing bloodthirsty about his hunting habits. A careful and cautious man who picked his shots, never drank while carrying a firearm, and always stayed in shape, Kyril Montana thoroughly enjoyed the outdoors with or without a gun. He was a member of the Isaac Walton League, the Sierra Club, and Ducks Unlimited. He loved to backpack with his family on weekends, and he had an intricate professional knowledge of many mountain ranges in the state.

133

Kyril Montana was also a person who usually traveled with a plan. In hunting he always sized up the territory ahead, he always took into consideration all the factors involved before moving in on his game. He liked to set things up, and had an abhorrence of blundering along without having considered the alternatives well in advance. He was a person who laid an extensive—sometimes his superiors felt too extensive—foundation, before attacking the heart of a matter. His caution in the past may have cost him an arrest or two, but he had rarely, if ever, made a serious mistake.

So when the agent steered his unmarked car off the north–south highway into the western section of Milagro, he had a plan, and his plan was first of all simply to "case the joint," as it were. On the seat beside him, on top of a clipboard holding papers, photographs, lists, and names of Milagro citizens, he had a large map with the houses of perhaps a dozen people —among them Joe Mondragón's and Charley Bloom's —inked in.

He drove west on the Milagro–García spur, a dirt road partially shaded by some cottonwoods and Russian olives growing alongside Indian Creek. The agent was so familiar with the map and with the landmarks he should be looking for that he never had to stop the car to orient himself. He knew exactly how far it was from the north–south highway to the Acequia Madre del Sur headgate; and once he spotted the headgate, it was no problem, despite the clustering trees and some patches of tall flowering rabbitbrush, to trace the route of the acequia to where the Roybal ditch branched off, creating a thin lush path directly to the small field, green and almost garish now between bordering patches of dusty earth, where Joe Mondragón's bean plants were arrogantly growing.

Kyril Montana experienced little emotion when he saw the field for the first time. He did not entertain the crosscurrents of conflicting emotions that were often aroused in others upon sighting "the enemy." In fact, it would never have occurred to him to consider Joe an enemy. Instead, he was a problem to be dealt with, and an interesting problem at that, and people like Joe were why Kyril Montana found his work enjoyable. So he never changed the pace of his car as he drifted quietly past the green, shimmering beanfield.

Beyond Joe's field, and as the road curved north along the course of Milagro Creek, no land had been irrigated for years. Magpies drifted from cottonwoods across the deserted road, and bluebirds and swallows flitted in and out of abandoned adobe farmhouses. Rusting car hulks cast the only shadows across deserted yellow yards; in many places barbed wire had snapped between fence posts and now curled frozenly toward the sky. The timbers of small corrals were broken, well housings aslant, outhouses blown over and destroyed. When the road swung away from the stream course heading back toward the north–south highway, the ruins tailed away to the west. Still, you could make out the old irrigation ditches which had once fed the larger and still-fenced bean- and alfalfa fields, dry and dead now but for tumbleweed and numerous yellow bun-shaped snakeweed bushes and sparse tufts of gramma grass. The land here was flat, flowing into a sagebrush terrain as you approached the highway again, leading to piñon foothills and the high mountains in the east, to the gorge and a formation of delicate gray and beige mesas in the west.

Back on the highway, Kyril Montana drove a mile and a half south to the eastern turnoff into town where the surviving population of Milagro was settled. He cruised past the Pilar Café, the Frontier Bar, the Forest Service headquarters—and that was it. Some kids gathered along Rael's porch sucking on Dr. Peppers glanced at the car as it stirred up a small storm of parking ticket confetti; Mercedes Rael chucked a few pebbles that pinged off his hood; and a three-legged German shepherd, leaping off the roof of a rattletrap pickup, charged after the agent's vehicle for a few yards, barking furiously.

Then a huge pig was standing in the middle of the road. The agent braked, but the pig stood pat, challenging the automobile. Not wishing to call attention to himself, the agent gave the horn a brief beep, then drove right up to the pig, which snorted desultorily, refusing to move on. So Kyril Montana lurched his car forward and hit the animal; it toppled over with a surprised squeal, scrambled quickly to its feet, and lumbered bluntly off the road.

As the houses petered out, the agent nosed his car onto a dirt road that twisted up the side of Capulin Hill past a small deserted elementary school, continuing on up to the white Milagro water storage tank, which had numbers—'68, '70, '71—painted all over it by graduating Doña Luz Junior High School classes: students who went on to high school were bussed farther south to Chamisaville.

Parking in the tank's shadow, Kyril Montana sat behind the wheel of his car looking over the town. A compact, simple unit, Milagro was cut in two by the north–south highway, a curious division of green here and desert there—Entre verde y seco, the agent thought: Between what's lush and what's dry. And there was Joe Mondragón's beanfield, completely out of place to the west, an absurd green bauble in the otherwise desolate landscape slated to become a posh golf course. But on this side of the highway green fields led directly up to the road's eastern shoulder— an unnatural setup; obviously the result of a strange, possibly a bad, law.

The agent scrutinized the town, getting it down right in his mind, giving himself time for everything to register, the houses of people he didn't know and the houses of those in whom he was interested, the network of irrigation ditches and small dusty roads, the minuscule orchards and small herds of sheep and horses. He watched where a jeep, a pickup, an old Chrysler, a young man on a horse went; he followed, for a moment, the movements of a woman hanging wash on a line; and then he shifted his attention to two teen-age boys mixing mud and straw in a shallow pit for adobes.

Kyril Montana stayed beside the water storage tank only until comfortable with his *feel* of the place, then he started his car and swung around and down the hill to take care of business.

Except for Bud Gleason, all six men present were afraid of Kyril Montana, or at least unnaturally nervous in his presence. They were gathered in the real estate agent's living room, and among them were the sheriff, his deputy Meliton Naranjo, the mayor, Nick Rael, and Eusebio Lavadie. Kyril Montana sat on a comfortable couch with his clipboard on a low coffee table in front of him, and the other men were spread around in various chairs, each man nursing a beer, compliments of Bud Gleason, who had arranged the meeting.

"This is a simple matter," the agent said quietly. "Or at least it should be a simple matter. And I'd like to go through it quickly because I don't want to take any more of your time than is necessary. You all know Joe Mondragón. At least I'm assuming you all know him—" he looked up and swiftly around.

"We all know him," Lavadie said somberly, and the other men nodded yes, muttering agreement, some smiling, some looking grim.

"Alright." The agent pressed open the spring on his clipboard, extracting six issues of the *Voice of the People,* which he gave to the man on his left, Sammy Cantú, with a nod to pass them around. "First of all, or rather after this meeting, all of you should read the article in this magazine, an article written by a Milagro resident, the lawyer Charley Bloom."

"Sure," Lavadie said. "Charley Bloom. He lives here."

"You know him? Do all of you know him?"

"I do," Lavadie said. And Bud Gleason nodded. "I sold him his house." The others shrugged or shook their heads.

"Okay." The agent paused dramatically for a second as the magazine went around, then he plunged into a brisk summary of the problem. "Joe Mondragón, as you may or may not know—though I'm assuming you all *do* know, and if you don't you will by the time you finish that article—Joe Mondragón has diverted some water from the creek on the west side of the highway, and for a while now he's been irrigating a small beanfield over there, which is strictly illegal, as Sheriff

Montoya here knows, and as Mr. Naranjo knows too, and as the rest of you are probably aware also. There is in this case, however, a problem, a delicate sort of situation which exists—an extenuating circumstance. We know that some people here in Milagro support Joe Mondragón despite the possible grave consequences, and simply to arrest and jail Mr. Mondragón for his flagrant illegal actions would probably cause more trouble than it would cure. I'm sure all of you are aware of that—I mean, you know this town much better than I do—you're aware of what's going on. Yet what's going on, at least insofar as we see it down in the capital, is not something that most of you in this town fully understand. In fact, I think whatever support Mr. Mondragón has is coming from citizens who honestly do not question his motives—"

Kyril Montana paused to let that sink in.

"—who do not question his motives, who believe that all Mr. Mondragón wants to do is lodge a protest against, say, the 1935 water compact by growing a field of beans."

Most of the men were waiting now, quietly, not so much with the attention of men waiting to learn something new, but rather with the guarded attention of men who understand exactly what is being driven at and where everyone stands, but are wondering how it's going to be worded and what their commitment to what must follow is going to have to be.

"Alright. As far as it goes maybe that's part of it. You men grew up with Mr. Mondragón; I did not. But I think you should know certain facts that we are aware of down in the capital, and I think that you should think very carefully about those facts and what they could do to your lovely town here. In the first place, after you've read that article, you'll understand a little more about Charley Bloom. Read the entire magazine and you'll understand even more. You'll understand, I think, that Mr. Mondragón isn't acting entirely on his own. In fact, we have reason to believe that this beanfield is not even Mr. Mondragón's idea, but a plot hatched up by the lawyer Charley Bloom."

A few men nodded. Bud Gleason sneezed. The others sat quietly, waiting.

"Charley Bloom and his wife Linda have lived in this town how long?" Kyril Montana asked.

Bernabé Montoya shrugged, glancing up at Lavadie; Sammy Cantú frowned, guessing, "Four years? Five years? I don't remember . . ." Bud Gleason blew his nose and then recalled, "Summer of 1966. That's when I sold them the house."

"Six years," the agent said slowly, enunciating deliberately. "Six years only, but after six years he's writing articles like this. After six years a relative newcomer, an outsider, is in cahoots with Joe Mondragón; maybe—who knows?—against Joe Mondragón's wishes, or maybe Joe Mondragón is an unwitting victim, I don't know; but anyway, I think it'll become painfully obvious to all of you, as it has become painfully obvious to us, that Charley Bloom has a plan for stirring up trouble in this town, and unless you people take measures to see that he and Joe Mondragón are discouraged from persisting in this matter, there are going to be serious consequences for Milagro."

The agent stopped, casting about, trying to measure his progress. Then he said: "Alright, I'm assuming everyone here remembers the Pacheco trial four years ago."

"Pacheco," Nick Rael muttered petulantly. "We got more Pachecos around here than we got fleas. Who Pacheco? Meliton? Leroy? Eloy? Teodoro? Jaime? Hippólito—?"

The men in the room laughed nervously; Kyril Montana smiled as he removed newspaper clippings and some Xeroxed sheets of those same clippings from his clipboard.

"César Pacheco, the militant," he noted, passing out the original articles and the Xeroxes. There was a short silence as the men glanced over the stories, and then Sammy Cantú vigorously nodded his head.

"Sure. We all remember this. César, he's not from here. But he has cousins here. Adelita Trujillo, she's his cousin. And Mary Ann Roybal, too. And Seferino

Pacheco and his brother Ben, they're all his cousins. They went over to that trial. Me, personally, I didn't go. I had really bad hemorrhoids back then, so I didn't drive around too much, I—"

"Bloom has been relatively quiet since then," Kyril Montana interrupted. "Until now, that is. He's planning to defend Mondragón if a hearing is held on this matter—"

"Well, there's no way he can win," Eusebio Lavadie said matter-of-factly. "He's crazy to even try."

"Legally, of course, he—they—the two of them don't stand a chance," the agent said. "But they're not worried about that. They just want to get it into court—"

"As a kind of propaganda trick, qué no?" Lavadie ventured.

"Absolutely. They figure if they can get it to the hearing stage—which gives them at least a few months more for organization, you understand—if they can do that they can recruit a lot of people to their side."

"And if that happens," Sammy Cantú said quietly, "I suppose we got trouble."

"You're damn right. You'll have a lot of trouble."

"So? . . ." Bud Gleason asked.

"I want you to know several things about this lawyer that perhaps you all are not aware of." Kyril Montana removed two photographs and some Xeroxes of a one-page document from his clipboard. Passing out the first photograph, he informed the group, "Mr. Bloom was married before, when he lived back East, to the woman in that photograph, whose name—whose maiden name, anyway—was Sherri Pope. As you can see she was, I'm sure she still is, a very lovely woman."

He handed out the other, smaller photograph.

"They had one daughter, and this is a picture of her. Her name is Miranda."

The agent's photograph of Miranda Bloom had been taken when she was a nine-year-old kid complete with freckles and braces and her hair in beribboned pigtails.

"When they got divorced," Kyril Montana said

carefully, "and understand, please, I'm not telling you gentlemen these things to titillate you or because I like chisme, because I don't, I dislike it very much. But I want you to understand the people we're dealing with—or at least that *I* . . . that we down in the capital are dealing with at this time. When they got divorced there were some nasty proceedings, namely a very savage battle for custody of this lovely child, which in the end Mr. Bloom lost quite suddenly when it was revealed that he had attempted on several occasions to sexually molest his own daughter—that's her photograph—Miranda Bloom."

"*Ai, Chihuahua,*" Eusebio Lavadie, who was looking at the photograph, muttered.

The agent handed around a Xeroxed copy of the letter sent by Sherri Pope Bloom's lawyer to her husband, accusing Bloom of the act so described and threatening to make the accusation public if he did not give up his daughter.

Then Kyril Montana leaned back. "So that's the kind of person we're dealing with," he said. "There may be others too, so perhaps I should say that's the kind of people who are using your neighbor, Mr. Mondragón, as a pawn in their lethal game—"

After the other men had left, Kyril Montana stayed around for a few minutes to shoot the breeze with Bud Gleason and his wife, Bertha. Before they could launch a conversation, however, the Gleasons' wiseacre eleven-year-old daughter, Katie, clumped down from her room and started banging away on the living room piano, until her mother screamed, "Alright, already, enough is enough, we got guests, go outside and kill frogs!"

The noise stopped. Bright-eyed Katie appeared in the doorway. "You do not have guest-*s*," she said haughtily, really working over the final *s*. "You have a gues-*t*."

"What, I didn't tell you to go outside?" her mother growled, setting two cups of coffee and half a fruitcake on the kitchen table where the men were seated.

"How come I couldn't be at the meeting?" Katie asked nastily.

"Because little pitchers have big ears," Bertha sighed. "Now beat it."

Katie flounced through the living room and out the front door, which slammed shut with a thunderous bang behind her. Then, before either Bud, Bertha, or Kyril Montana could open their mouths, the child screamed back in a high voice:

"What are pennies made out of?"

And in a lower, bellowing voice, she answered herself:

"Dirty copper!"

"A sweet child," Bertha said to Bud. "How come God blessed us with such a sweet child?" Then she said, "Listen, Kyril honey, I don't mean to pry, but what's the point of trying to put the fear of God into this town—we don't have enough trouble already?"

Bud answered for his friend: "The point is, Bertha, to stop things before they really get started."

"By putting the evil eye on Charley Bloom? You'll pardon me, I know my place, I wasn't really listening to what you said, and I'd keep my mouth shut anyway, you know that, but by tomorrow morning the ditches are maybe gonna be lined with corpses because of this meeting."

Bud, who was more than a little nervous (Just wait'll I get *you,* Katie, he was snarling to himself), looked at the agent, raising his eyebrows and lowering his eyelids in order to project a helpless and foolish *Oh-Jesus-look-what-I-have-to-put-up-with-all-the-time* grim, as he shrugged.

To Bertha, Bud said, "You don't know about these things, and I don't either; it's not our line of work."

"I'll say it isn't." A big Italian-looking Polish woman, Bertha stood by the stove eyeing both men over her cup of coffee.

"Listen," she added, "don't get me wrong. Especially *you* don't get me wrong, Kyril honey, because I don't want you or any of your flat-footed compatriots hiding out in my closets with tape recorders and hand grenades, thanks anyway. But I mean, like, I'm

married to one of the biggest horse thieves in the valley, I know which side my bread is buttered on, I'm
with you 100 percent. It's just World War III shouldn't
start in my backyard, know what I mean?"

Kyril Montana smiled. "Don't worry, it won't."

"That's easy for you to say, you don't live here."

Bud was irritated. "Oh cut the crap, Bertha. Forget
it. Nothing's gonna happen. Jesus. You could turn an
ant into a dinosaur."

She rolled her eyes at the ceiling.

The agent started to say something, but was interrupted by Katie, who was running circles on the small
lawn outside the kitchen window, shrieking "Oink!
Oink!Oink! Oink!Oink!Oink!" at the top of her voice.

"Oh my God, that *kid*!" Bertha exclaimed, stifling a
big grin as she did another eyeroll.

"Well, don't just stand there—" Bud fumed at her.
"Honestly, Ky, I'm so sorry . . ."

"The kid is a kid," Bertha said. "Kids are like that,
why worry? Someday she'll grow up, someday our
friendly local Gestapo will make her apologize—"

"We all should live so long," Bud groaned. "Ky,
I'm really sorry . . ."

The unflappable Kyril Montana smiled. "Don't
worry, man. What the hell. Now listen, I gotta go.
So just keep your phone open, okay? And lemme
know if you hear anything—"

The two college friends shook hands. Bertha said
good-bye, but for some reason she and the agent had
never touched, not even to shake hands. "Say 'Hi'
to Marilyn," Bertha said. "And don't run over any
little Chicano farmers on the way out—"

Bud glared at her the way a priest might glare at
a parishioner who had farted loudly during the Mass.

And the last thing Kyril Montana heard as he
pulled away from the house was that annoying kid
screaming, "What are pennies made out of?" And
answering herself: *"Dirty copper!"*

But his spirits were unruffled as he drove south,
turned west onto Strawberry Mesa, and spent maybe
twenty minutes in the Evening Star hippie commune
hogan of a newly arrived freak called Lord Elephant.

After that, the agent drove on to Doña Luz. There he pulled into Louie's roadside café, ordered some rolled tacos, an enchilada, and a cup of coffee, bought cigarettes from a vending machine, and then punched out fifty cents' worth of country and western tunes on the jukebox.

While smoking a filter cigarette and waiting for his order to arrive, in his mind he played over the faces of those men in Bud Gleason's house reacting to his information, and to his personal conclusions about that information, on the lawyer. The agent was quite certain of Eusebio Lavadie. Among the others he felt good about Bud Gleason, in spite of Bertha and the kid—after all, he and Bud were friends. He felt all right about the deputy sheriff and Nick Rael, too. The sheriff, Bernabé Montoya, disturbed him, but he did not know exactly why. And the mayor was a total loss, a scared jackrabbit, but one who at least would not talk. By and large, then, everything had worked out okay. He had made the plant, and soon all of Milagro would know about Charley Bloom. Then perhaps events would take their proper course with no more need of interference from him.

Several hours later, when Kyril Montana walked through the front door of his comfortable home in an all-white suburban section of the capital called Piñon Knoll, his wife Marilyn greeted him with a courteous hug. Their two kids, eleven-year-old Burt and thirteen-year-old Kelly, were gone; the former at Boy Scouts, the latter at their country club, working out in the Olympic-sized swimming pool. So the agent changed into his bathing suit and went out back for a swim. Having removed a frog from the pool with a long-handled net, he walked to the end of the diving board and stopped. Beyond his own redwood fence and a number of hard-plastered adobe or fake adobe houses, the sun was creating a vast and lovely panorama in the sky, a feast of gold and russet, daffodil and rouge. In the north, wispy and cottony streaks extended down from fiery clouds, a gorgeous pink rain falling.

Kyril Montana observed this for a moment, feeling good about things in general, about his own slim body, then he took a fine deep breath and dove beautifully into the cool water.

Soon Marilyn came out wearing a turquoise bikini, carrying a gin and tonic in each hand. Setting the drinks down on a white tin table, she joined her husband in the water. They swam together and kissed again and the agent made a leisurely pass at his wife, calmly giving a couple of pumps to her nice-sized breasts. She laughed and swam away on her back for a few feet, then circled around, breaststroking quietly to him. They kissed once more and flicked a little water at each other and rubbed noses, chuckling together, standing in about five feet of softly lapping water, enjoying the peaceful evening.

᠗

In Milagro, only the Dancing Trout, the Forest Service headquarters, and the Enchanted Land Motel had private telephones: all other town residents were on an archaic system of party lines installed so as to resemble a Tower of Babel built with electronic spaghetti. Often as many as seven families were on the same line, and somehow the phone company had never gotten around to providing a private signal system; hence, most phones in town were constantly ajangle with one set of coded rings or another. At any given moment at least a dozen phones in Milagro were off their hooks and out of their cradles, while perhaps another quarter to a third of the town's residents were listening clandestinely to the conversations of everyone else.

This made for a rumor mill and information network of substantial sophistication.

Naturally there were many people (like Bernabé Montoya) who could never remember their own signal codes and were thus constantly picking up the phone whenever it rang, a situation that had over the years ignited a great many long-standing and hotly contested feuds.

Other people—unused to telephones all their lives until immediately after World War II when the present system was installed—still, some twenty-odd years later, automatically answered anything that gave off an urgent blast.

And still others, unable to tolerate the continual ringing going on in their houses, often left their phones off the hook for hours, occasionally days, which was an open invitation to get murdered.

The present mayor, Sammy Cantú, had achieved his high office by promising to force the Sierra Bell Telephone Company to update the party line setup in Milagro. He defeated the previous incumbent, Eloy Martínez, who himself, by promising to straighten out the phone situation, had defeated the then-incumbent Orlando Mondragón, who had likewise, several years before that, ridden to victory on a platform of NO MORE PARTY LINES!

Much as the people complained, however, the tangled party line setup had become part and parcel of Milagro's communication and rumor systems, and as such, people had come to depend on it. For example, Bernabé Montoya often tuned into his own party line after some local atrocity (such as the stealing of a cow or the raiding of a corn patch) in order to find out who did what, and how, and to whom.

Hence, practically the moment Kyril Montana's unmarked Galaxie cruised unobtrusively into Milagro, it appeared on the town's telephonic radar screen, and its progress was tracked with interest by many of the town's inhabitants. Nick Rael inadvertently let the cat out of the bag when, somewhat flustered, he called Sammy Cantú to say he'd just seen a car with a chotalooking person in it go by, and was the meeting going to take place earlier than had been prearranged or what? Sammy Cantú assured him the meeting would take place at the preordained time, maybe the agent had simply arrived early in order to look the town over and get his bearings straight. This particular conversation was overheard by Stella Armijo and Sparky Pacheco, and also by Eusebio Lavadie's half-deaf wife, Fabiola, who mistakenly thought the phone had rung a short, two longs, a short and a long, instead of a long, one short, two longs, and a short, as it actually had. When she hung up, she mentioned cas-

ually to her husband that apparently some sort of
police agent had arrived in Milagro for a meeting and
she wondered vaguely why, and with whom. Lavadie
immediately flew into a rage and called up Bernabé
Montoya. "Bernie," he shouted into the phone, "that
stupid storekeeper and the mayor have been blabbing
to each other over the phone about that agent's visit
and the meeting at Bud's!" This enraged statement
was overheard by Ray Gusdorf's wife, Jeanine, Onofre
Martínez's retarded son, O. J., several Romeros, an
Esquibel, and the mayor's oft-married sister, Isabel
Cantú Martínez Mondragón Córdova. Within seconds,
then, at least half the village was peeping curiously
out from behind various curtains, half-opened doors,
and trees, observing the police agent as he bumped
into Pacheco's pig and later climbed up Capulin Hill,
and still later as he drove back down to Bud Gleason's house for the meeting.

No covert military tribunal, Secret Service snoopers,
or police group could have devised half as compre-
hensive or effective a Distant Early Warning System.

☙

They were gathered in Joe Mondragón's yard: ten
men and the two women, Ruby Archuleta and Joe's
wife, Nancy. Nobody had called a meeting. Joe was
working that morning on a tractor belonging to Ray
Gusdorf who, though an Anglo, spoke fluent Spanish
and had been failing at farming and failing at trying
to run sheep (yet somehow surviving) just about as
long as anyone else in the valley. At about 10:00 A.M.
Ray and his neighbors Tobías Arguello and Gomersindo Leyba, who had a stake in the tractor because
Ray was going to cut and bale their alfalfa fields, had
come over to see how Joe was progressing. Then
Ruby Archuleta and her gang of Claudio García, her
son Eliu, and Marvin LaBlue had stopped by to deliver some cut-rate tin roofing Joe was using to build
a sunshade for tourists on the shore of Harlan Betchel's
(Buck-A-Fish) Trout Pond; they had also come to
discuss the plumbing needs for an A-frame taco joint
Joe had contracted to help build with funds being

skimmed off the top of the Custer Rural Electric Co-op down in Chamisaville. The other four present were Jimmy Ortega, a baby-faced kid who was always hanging around Joe's shop, helping out and learning a lot; his insolent, jiving friend, Benny Maestas, a Vietnam veteran on parole for throwing a beer bottle through the window of Bruno Martínez's state police car four months back; an elderly sad-sack bag of bones, Juan F. Mondragón, Joe's great-uncle, who just liked to hang around watching the work and spitting tobacco at the cats or chickens that wandered through the yard; and Johnny Pacheco, a handsome long-haired Milagro kid in his mid-twenties who played in a Chamisaville rock band called the Hotshots. Johnny had arrived two hours earlier with an amplifier almost as tall as himself that needed fixing.

The topic under discussion this morning, as Joe tinkered with the tractor's innards, was Kyril Montana's top secret visit to Milagro and his top secret meeting in Bud Gleason's living room.

"I guess they're kind of worried down there," Ray Gusdorf said. "I guess somebody down there don't know whether to crap or get off the pot."

Joe grinned. "They better be careful. Next time they send that chota up here he might fall in a well."

The old men chuckled, the young men cackled, thinking that was a funny statement for Joe to make.

Ruby Archuleta asked, "What's Bud Gleason's stake in all of this? He ought to know better, it seems to me."

"Oh, hell, that Bud Gleason," Tobías Arguello said. "He'd sell the boots off his mother's corpse. If there wasn't but one piece of land left in the country, and that was his own, with his house on it and everything, he wouldn't think twice to put it on the block."

"Somebody ought to leave a dead horse on his doorstep," Joe said, grunting as he turned a wrench.

"He'd tie a pink ribbon around it and try and sell it to the vultures," Benny Maestas laughed.

"All the same, he's got no right to let that cop in his living room," Claudio García observed.

Gomersindo Leyba said, "Knowing Bud, he probably rented his living room out at six dollars an hour to that state cop."

"What was the name of the chota again?" Ruby asked.

"Somebody said Montana."

"Like the state of Montana? With a name like that, he's Chicano?"

"Nope. I heard Anglo. And his first name's Ken."

"Carl. I heard Carl."

"Ken or Carl, where's he from, the capital?"

"That's what I heard."

"But who sent him up here?"

"The chotas. Or the governor. Who knows? Why do they always send those bastards up here?"

"I never saw him around before, though."

"You seen one chota you seen them all."

Ruby Archuleta, seated on an old engine block and smoking a cigarette, said, "They send him up like that, saying those things he said at that meeting, they must mean business. That guy didn't just come up here to look at the scenery."

"How come Lavadie was there? Is he a cop too? I didn't know he was a cop."

"He ain't a cop, for crissakes. He was there for Zopi Devine."

"What's the Zopilote got to do with all this?"

"Well, most of it's his land over there, where he's planning to build that golf course when they put in the conservancy and the dam, qué no?"

"I ain't irrigating his land," Joe said. "That field ain't his field, it's my field."

"It's the state engineer's office sent the chota, that's who. They're worried about their lousy dam."

"Well, how's my beanfield gonna hurt their dam?" Joe sneered.

Ruby said, "Probably they consider this some sort of organized resistance, or symbolic act."

"Who organized it?" Joe asked petulantly. "I didn't organize it. I didn't talk to nobody. If I'd talked to anybody they would of told me not to stick my neck out. Nobody organized nothing."

"All the same, they're pretty worried," Benny Maestas grinned. "Those chotas are walking around with their pants full of little itty-bitty goat-sized chota turds. They think this is a revolution."

Everybody had a hearty laugh over that one.

"Maybe the Zopilote feels it's a challenge or something," Tobías Arguello said. "Maybe this Montana fellow knows something we don't."

With a stick Ray Gusdorf drew a line in the dirt. "Actually they probably just want to get us all stirred up and confused and at each other's throats so that nothing bad or organized *could* happen around here."

"What you all ought to do," Johnny Pacheco said, "is get up some morning around 4:00 A.M. and irrigate the whole west side."

"*Ai, Chihuahua!* Are you crazy, man?" Joe's great-uncle gagged as if he had just swallowed a cat. "They'd set up a machine gun in front of Rael's store and kill the whole bunch of you when you came back across the highway. What do you want to go and fool around with those bastards for? They'll slit your throats without even saying hello if you start acting crazy like that."

Tobías Arguello rolled a cigarette. "Yeah, maybe you shouldn't irrigate that field, José. Maybe innocent people will get involved. Or even hurt."

"That's my field," Joe snarled. "I didn't ask for help. Did anybody hear me call for help? I just felt like doing what I did, that's all. Who heard me ask for help?"

"Nobody," Ray Gusdorf said. "At least I didn't."

"I don't need any help," Joe said. "I never needed anybody's help. Tell *that* to them chotas."

"Maybe you're going to need help, though," Ruby mused.

"What for? I mean, tell me the truth, who really could care less about a crummy beanfield and a couple gallons of water?"

"That Carl Montana for one."

Joe dismissed the cop with an arrogant wave of his hand, "Screw him."

"Now wait a minute," Marvin LaBlue drawled. "Now this thing isn't just that simple, is it? I mean,

I don't know, but I sure don't think it's just this simple."

"It isn't," Ruby said. "And we're all involved. José, I don't care what you say, that beanfield belongs to all of us."

"When I harvest those beans *I'm* gonna eat those beans myself. Because those are *my* beans. I paid for the seed. I bought the gas for the tractor to turn over the earth."

Silence ensued for a minute, while Joe angrily ripped a few things loose from the tractor's engine and unloosened a couple of bolts.

"United we stand," Eliu Archuleta said, "divided we fall."

"Oh screw that Yankee Doodle bullshit," Benny Maestas growled. "United we flounder, divided we flounder."

"But what's true is the truth," said Gomersindo Leyba.

Juan F. Mondragón grumbled: "Me, I don't want trouble. Every time one of *us* gets mad at one of *them* we go out and kill another one of *us*. Now you tell me, where's the sense in that?"

"There is no sense in that."

"Damn right there's no sense in that."

"That's how come we should kill the chota, qué no?"

"Kill, kill, kill," Nancy muttered sullenly. "Five days ago I told José, I said 'José, I want to cook a turkey, go cut me off the head of one of the turkeys.' So did he take the ax—who, José? Oh no, he's from the Ford car company and he's got a better idea. He takes the pistol. He's gonna *shoot* me a turkey. All the turkeys, they're gathered over by the sheep pen, only there's just one arthritic old ewe over there, and five or six lambs we're bottle-feeding; they're lying in the straw, and the turkeys are out front. So José, he shoots the turkey. Only maybe he didn't aim so good or something, because the turkey does a back flip, and flops all around for a minute, and then starts running around in the field, gobbling and going crazy, and all the other turkeys fly up into that big tree over there and don't come down for three days, and one of the lambs is bleating like a stuck pig because the bullet passes right through wherever it hit the turkey and goes into the lamb, and one of the other lambs is so scared it runs into the wall and breaks its neck. So José had to shoot the other lamb he'd wounded, and then *I* had to take the shotgun and run down that damn crazy turkey—and then what happened? I broke a filling on a piece of buckshot when we ate it! So don't talk to me about kill, kill, kill. I'm sick of it!"

Joe said, "Who asked you to talk?"

Nancy's eyes flashed. "I'll talk when I want to talk."

"Nobody's going to kill a chota," Ruby said.

"Maybe I will if he messes with my field," Joe snarled.

"I'm not going to back you up with any shotgun," Nancy threatened.

"*Ai, Chihuahua!*" Joe threw up his hands.

"It would be crazy to kill a chota," Claudio García reasoned. "Anybody who wants to kill a chota should see a doctor, because when you start thinking like that it's time to turn in the old brain for a new one."

"Well, what was that bastard doing up here laying down that rap against José here?" Benny Maestas wanted to know. "I'll go get that pendejo. What's his address in the capital?"

Ruby said, "The thing is, they probably think we're united. They probably think we're all together in this."

"You really think they're that dumb?" Nancy asked bitterly.

"Well, we *are* in this all together, qué no?" Tobías Arguello mumbled passionately. "*I'm* behind José. I'll help you irrigate that field, José."

Joe shrugged. "A baby could irrigate that field. Amarante Córdova could irrigate that field with both hands tied behind his back. It's set up so good you don't have to do a thing, you just cut in the water and twenty minutes later it's done."

"In the old days—" Juan F. Mondragón began.

"Old days, old days—bah. This ain't the old days

anymore," Joe snapped. "The old days been here and gone."

"In the old days people were more together," the old man insisted.

"In the old days a hundred throats were cut every Saturday night, and money was as rare as a rattlesnake higher than eight thousand feet, and everybody dropped dead from TB before they were forty." Joe grimaced his teeth at his great-uncle. "Look at your mouth, Tío, it's empty. And you come from the old days. But look at my mouth, it's full of gold and silver and almost all the choppers I was born with. I'm gonna be chewing a steak when they say my rosary!"

"All this doesn't have much to do with the bean-field," Ruby complained.

"Just leave me in peace about my beanfield," Joe sulked. "People start helping me, sure as hell it'll get screwed up."

"The fact remains," insisted Ray Gusdorf, "that that Carl Montana fellow had a meeting at Bud Glea-son's with Bernabé and Lavadie, Meliton Naranjo, and—who else was there?"

"I heard the Zopilote himself."

"No, he wasn't there."

"What about Horsethief Shorty?"

"I didn't hear he was there either."

"And Jerry Grindstaff—?"

Those that had heard something shrugged.

"Sammy Cantú was there," said Gomersindo Leyba.

"Sammy Cantú couldn't punch his way out of a paper bag."

"But he was there, qué no?"

"Yeah, I heard he was there."

"Mostly who he talked about, as I understand it," said Ray Gusdorf, "was Charley Bloom. And of course you, Joe. He said irrigating that beanfield was your idea and his."

"Bullshit." Joe fumbled for the right-sized wrench in his toolbox. "That's a lie. I never talked to any-body about it, I just went and did it. If I'd talked about it with somebody, we'd still be talking about it and arguing and fighting about was it good or bad or smart or stupid or whatever. If nobody around here had talked about what we were all gonna do the past two hundred years we wouldn't all be hanging by our fingernails like we are today."

"So what are we going to do?" Marvin LaBlue drawled laconically. "We aren't just going to sit around on our fat duffs and do nothing, are we?"

"What can we do? Who made a move?"

"They made a move. They sent the chota."

"The state engineer's office sent a couple of their jerks to me and I told them to go to hell," Joe said. "It was as simple as that. If this chota came around to see me, I'd tell him to go share a piece of hell with the state engineer's idiots."

"If you hadn't told them to go to hell we wouldn't be in all this hot water," the great-uncle bitterly complained.

"Hot water?" Joe popped his eyes. "Where's the hot water, Tío? What has happened?"

"You'll see," the old man pouted, retreating. "Pretty soon . . . I hate to think about it. You'll see."

"It's my affair," Joe said. "Why is everybody worried about my affair? I can handle it."

"No, it's our affair," Ruby said firmly. "It's your beanfield, but it represents all our beanfields. That dam is gonna hurt all of us, and we're all gonna pay those conservancy district taxes, and there isn't anybody here who hasn't been screwed by Ladd Devine."

"What does all that got to do with my beanfield?" Joe snapped. "I didn't say I had a beef with the Zopilote."

Benny Maestas laughed. "Wow, you people are too much. This is just too heavy. *Chi-hua-hua!*"

Gomersindo Leyba offered an opinion: "But José, you see, the trouble you started will affect us all. They think we're united. That's how come they sent the chota. To scare us so we won't be united anymore. If they knew you were almost alone, José, they would break you in half like a matchstick and Ernie Maestas would throw you in the Chamisaville jail and eat the key."

"I ain't scared," Joe bragged.

"I am," Ruby said.

Everybody looked at her, and there was a moment of silence.

"Me too," Nancy admitted. "I'm scared. I don't care what José says. Suppose they kidnap the kids—"

"Oh Jesus, nobody's gonna kidnap the kids!"

"Well, I don't know . . ." Nancy murmured uncertainly.

Johnny Pacheco was disturbed by the sudden seriousness of the moment. "Ah, it'll all blow over. Soon as you quit irrigating that useless field everybody will forget about it."

"That field stays irrigated." For emphasis, Joe spat.

"I don't know. Maybe you should quit doing it," Tobías Arguello said. "Maybe it isn't worth it."

"He speaks the truth," said the great-uncle. "Everybody knows it isn't worth it. For a lousy sack or two of beans?"

Ruby stood up. "I think it's worth it."

No one else said anything.

"And I think, whether we know it or not, that we're united," the Body Shop and Pipe Queen operator said gently. "I mean, how in God's name can a bunch of sorry types like us live together in the same damn valley for three hundred years without being united? So there's got to be a meeting."

"What do you mean a meeting?"

"Of everybody. We'll open the church . . ."

"Trouble," groaned Juan F. Mondragón, "here comes trouble, big as an elephant, to flatten us all."

❧

Precisely these same sentiments were churning up the troubled mind of the sheriff as he guided his pickup onto the north–south highway, gave the finger to Ladd Devine's pompous Miracle Valley sign, flinched uncomfortably as his vehicle's tires whirred noiselessly over the painted cattleguard, and then gunned it down to Chamisaville.

It was noon, a lazy summer day. The Chamisaville *News* staff had gone to lunch; five drunks, three of them burned and twisted Indians, the other two bloated, sour Chicanos, were resting in a shady portal between La Paloma Liquors and the deserted *News* office. Farther on some teen-agers halfheartedly chopped at weeds along an irrigation ditch behind the junior high school football field bleachers. Beyond them, in a town park, Anglo mothers and fathers spilled from VW buses and bugs to pick up their kids who had been in a Monday–Wednesday playgroup. A sprinkler was going on Jim Hirsshorn's lawn; Bernabé accorded the office a lackluster birdie as he glided slowly by, pinned down now in the tourist traffic, all but immersed in adobe dust.

By the time he reached the Kachina Motel the sheriff felt shitty, like he should have phoned Vera and canceled their appointment. But he had been chasing after tail on this strange clockwork schedule for so many years it had become a habit that couldn't be broken, even if he did not enjoy it that much anymore. So he parked and slumped out of the truck with a wistful sigh, locked up, and ambled slowly into the Kachina Bar's purple gloom, bought a pint of Old Grandad from the bartender, Teddy Gallegos, checked his watch to make sure he wasn't early, and went out back to 12G, on the other side of the swimming pool.

"It's open," Vera said, and he walked in. She smelled like daffodils and reminded Bernabé a little of the chubby, sexy Mexican actresses who played bit parts in taco westerns. Her face once had dark, very Indian features, but it was puffed out of shape now, sensual still, but well over there on the sad side of her early forties. Her pitch-black hair was nice, hairdresser tousled especially for him, and she had small pearls in her earlobes, like a little girl. She wore a dark yellow jersey, a short brown miniskirt, stockings, and high heels. Her body's dumpling plumpness made warm and cuddly what could have looked nasty and cheap, and she was okay, a lonely and pretty gentle woman underneath. She understood Spanish but couldn't speak it anymore, talking instead in a slurry English, so he spoke in English—"Hey, how you doing?"—as he went to where she was sitting on the

bed and leaned over and kissed her, sliding his hand
in a perfunctory way up the inside of a thigh, while
she briefly touched his crotch and smiled the way she
always smiled, strained like a person either worried
about dust in the air or about to cry.

Seating himself at the dressing table, Bernabé peeled
the sanitary cellophane wrappers off two glasses and
poured them each a drink. She took her glass without
comment, stirring the straight bourbon with her finger, and sipped reflectively while the sheriff also
sipped. Eventually she asked, "So how's Carolina?"

"Oh, you know, what the hell. She's okay." Everything with Bernabé's wife was always pretty much
the same from one day to the next.

"I saw her in the Safeway, when was it I was there
with Bert. On Tuesday? I think it was Tuesday."

"I guess that's when she came down, I don't remember."

Vera said, "Huh . . ."

They sat in silence after that, sipping slowly, in no
real hurry to go anywhere, do anything. Except Bernabé would have loved to talk. This was nothing unusual with him, he had always wanted to talk with
the women he bedded. But all his life he'd found
that the women in his affairs were exactly like Carolina; some kind of mystery about them or an aura
about them, or some kind of barrier erected by the
macho culture in his blood made it impossible for
him to converse. Often they prattled like guinea hens
to him, baring their souls (as he so fervently wished
to bare his) while he listened; that's all it ever
seemed he could do, just listen. Even if the words
roiling in his guts caused miserable cramps and gas
pains, even if tormented confessions battled against
the backs of his teeth like bats trying to escape a cave
at dusk, he couldn't speak. Wanting to talk, all he
could do was hearken to their patter . . . and lay
them . . . and hearken some more. And every time he
located a new lady he did so with a hunger that was
not half as sexual as it was social—desperately he
wanted to communicate, get things off his chest, share
secrets, confess, bare all, ask for advice, probe and

interrogate, let loose torrents of rage, or maybe even release whatever it was he might have to say about love. But he was terrified; he had visions of his own awkwardness, of how clumsy he would sound, of how startled and ashamed the women would be. And so he kept his trap shut.

Often the sheriff looked at himself in the mirror. Not to primp, comb his hair, shave, or to practice sneering. He simply stared at himself. Bernabé Montoya, forty-three years old and the two-bit bumbling sheriff of Milagro, who had a million questions to ask people about things but had never asked them, who was growing old all bottled up, who would never have considered confronting men with his dilemma, and who had been unable to forge a repository for the gathering pronouncements of his stormy soul in the arms of a hundred clandestine paramours.

With dumpy, warm, sometimes shrill, often soft Carolina snoring dispassionately beside him, he'd had dreams. To be sure many of these dreams, especially of late, depicted one-armed Onofre Martínez tearing up Bernabé's fucking parking tickets in front of Milagro's lone parking meter. But other dreams dealt with Bernabé Montoya, the human piñata. Wrapped in gaudy holiday paper he twirled giddily at the end of a silver thread, while all the women he had ever humped on the so-called sly, jaybird naked and glistening like the butterplump, self-basting turkeys you could buy in the Safeway, pranced underneath him, blindfolded and wielding wooden bats with which they struck the piñata Bernabé. Back and forth he swung as they giggled and whacked, their droopy breasts and wide sagging buttocks joggling and flopping like beached fish, but none could ever bash him hard enough to split his guts, allowing his candies and pieces of silver, in the shape of eager words, question marks, and pathetically confused babblings, to cascade all around them, making small bruises on their spreading brown flesh like the marks from summer hailstones—

Right now Bernabé was especially curious about, and afraid of, Kyril Montana. But he was also curious

about the things that made all human beings tick. He
had an irresistible need to dissect people and study
their mechanisms; he had almost an artist's desire to
cut open their hearts (the way he cut open fish stomachs to check their feed) in order to discover what
kind of secrets might come bulging out. Whenever he
came into contact with dead bodies, with shocked and
staring car-accident victims, say, or with a hippie OD
frozen beside the highway in winter snow, he stared
long at them, trying to discover knowledge about life
and death, trying to catch sight of a soul, perhaps,
that was late in flapping off to heaven, trying to pene-
trate the camouflage that had protected their real
personalities during life. Death awed the sheriff because he'd always had an inarticulate but very pas-
sionate reverence for the life of people. And, no
matter how healthy a perfectly normal man, how
bright and shapely a woman, he sensed they were
twisted, one-eyed, half-crazed, crippled beings, awash
in subterfuge, aflutter with ominous ideas and devious
thoughts—like himself—with furtive hungers and reck-
less desires and arcane yearnings that were almost
supernatural, a murderer's row of outwardly pleasant
and monotonous dumdums. It was an incredible mystery to Bernabé why people did not go off their
rockers every five minutes.

But all this he sensed; he didn't *know* anything,
not really. Not about people, not even about himself
or Carolina. He had always wanted to learn, though,
always wanted to ask a million intimate questions he
had never formulated, let alone popped; perhaps because he understood people would always be afraid
to answer, or else they would stab him with butcher
knives for daring to imply that they were what they
really were. Then too, Bernabé did not know what
he wanted to learn; he had no idea where or how to
start . . . it was all so haphazard and vague. In his
lifetime the sheriff had never really forged any starting points; his sluggish brain was like a transistor
radio whose batteries kept running low on juice during the most crucial broadcasts; his life had been

belabored by melancholy endings that occurred before page one.

Vera said, "Saturday, I think it was, I went over to Laura Martínez's, you know, the sister of William, the assistant manager at Safeway?"

"Yeah." Glumly he nodded.

"We picked crab apples. I'm gonna make jelly. I went over with Mary Ann Trujillo, the one who's a secretary for that lawyer, Timmy Morris, you know, Tomás' daughter, the one that went to college."

"Which Tomás? I know six Tomás Trujillos."

"The one who used to sell coal. You know, out by the Ranchitos Bar."

"Oh, that Tomás. The tuerto, the one with the eye that points at the birds."

"No, that's his brother Pete has the funny eye."

"I thought Pete moved to El Paso. Who told me he moved to El Paso?"

"No, that was Pete Trujillo from Cañon. Pete Trujillo, Tomás' brother, always lived in Llano. He's the one who had the peacock, and then his little daughter, Isabella, got run over by the school bus, so he gave the peacock to that Anglo with the funny last name, Flipper or something, and the Anglo shot himself in the hand when he was out hunting, but he never even knew about the bad luck of peacocks, and nobody told him—"

She talked. He poured them both another drink and listened, not listening. He was thinking about Kyril Montana, who made him extremely nervous, and about Joe Mondragón's beanfield, and about the state cops, and about Amarante Córdova and Carolina, and Eusebio Lavadie and Ladd Devine and Horsethief Shorty, trying to put together the pieces of what worried him so profoundly. And then about halfway through his second drink he got up and went over to her and, standing between her legs, pulled up her sweater and began fondling her breasts, and a moment later they undressed and the sheriff climbed on top of her like some slow and weary, big but fragile animal about to mate in the sand of a lonely beach after a long, exhausting swim through dangerous ocean waters.

He couldn't get a hard-on, though. He lay between her legs as limp as the dangle on a castrated horse, with strange scared screams on his lips but only nervous grunts coming out for her to hear, while she cooed softly and smoothed her hands over his back and kept from complaining even though his heaviness hurt her some.

Finally, with a wry, sardonic little shudder, Bernabé said, "Welcome, ball fans, to the World Series of Sex," and he pushed down a little, dropping his thick lips over one breast. She held his head but did not press it into her. After a while he fell asleep, and she lay there holding his head, deriving a small but important comfort, even faintly smiling as she stared at the ceiling.

ﻬ

Milagro awoke early. Although the sun rose late because the town lay at the base of high mountains, most citizens were up long before the first bright rays fell across the narrow eastern fields of pasture hay and alfalfa. In the predawn summer gray, vehicles, most of them old pickups with their lights on, pulled out of the hard-packed shiny dirt yards and began threading through the town's narrow back roads. Some trucks carried hay bales which farmers dumped into dusty corrals or into minuscule overgrazed plots for horses and sheep. Other trucks headed back along the many primitive dirt roads that led to National Forest land where permit cattle grazed. A few people headed up toward jobs at the Dancing Trout Dude Ranch in Milagro Canyon. But most trucks—their occupants ritualistically saluting Ladd Devine's Miracle Valley sign with obscene gestures—headed south on the main highway to jobs in the Doña Luz mine, or to tourist-oriented shitwork in the motels, hotels, and restaurants of Chamisaville.

One truck, this particular morning, crossed the highway onto the Milagro–García spur and stopped near Joe Mondragón's beanfield. Joe himself hopped out, grabbed a shovel from the back and proceeded, in a few minutes, to divert water from Indian Creek into the Roybal ditch that led to his illegal field. Walking a little ahead of the flow he chopped at a few grassy tufts in the ditch, cut a water snake in half, then stood on the bank watching the clear cold liquid surge into the furrows between his bean plants.

And standing there during the blue pastel moments before dawn, Joe harbored feelings he hadn't had since he was a kid. He felt truly tough and arrogant, indestructible and happy. His beanfield, purely and simply, was beautiful. And for a few seconds he experienced an almost embarrassing and awkward sensation of well-being and importance. Like he was the King of the Castle. Number One—

El Numero Uno.

And if illegal use of Indian Creek water brought down the wrath of the gods in the state capital, so be it. Fuck Carl or Ken or whatever the hell his first name was Montana! Joe—all five feet six inches of him—could kick the living shit out of all comers, and especially out of any two-bit, lambe, pistol-packing chota! He would rip the tin stars off their marshmallow chests and chew them up in his mouth and spit them back, in the shape of bullets, at those blue-suited faggots!

Stature. Maybe that's what Joe felt for the first time in a long time. And maybe that's what this beanfield could impart to a down-in-the-dumps, dog-eared town like Milagro. Of course, nobody talked or even thought about it in that way. In fact, despite the building tensions, hardly anybody had even admitted to Joe they knew the beanfield existed. Most people still did not want to get involved. They wanted to lie back and see what might happen before they committed themselves either to the right or to the left. They wanted to see if Joe could get away with it. They were waiting for a sign from God that it was all right. In fact, thought Joe, they were a bunch of scared-stiff goatherds and sheep-fucking drunks who sure as hell weren't going to throw their hand in with anybody until they understood what kind of shit was going to come down on them. *Then* they would form their allegiances. Yessir, *then* they would all drive down to Anglada's Floral City in Chamisaville and load up with gaudy plastic bouquets to heap on Joe's rocky mound in the Milagro camposanto! *Then* they would putter around dressed in black and shedding saccharine tears and talking about how "Triste" was "La Vida," and about how Dios would pay up debts to Joe Mondragón in heaven for the terrible suffering he had done on earth.

Laughing, Joe seated himself on a dead cottonwood trunk near his beanfield, lit a cigarette, and watched the rattletraps heading down the highway toward menial fifty-cent-an-hour, maybe a dollar-an-hour, at most a dollar-sixty, a dollar-eighty-an-hour jobs in Doña Luz and Chamisaville. A bunch of lousy chambermaids, cooks, and babysitters, Joe thought. And abruptly the strangest feeling he had ever known came over him; as suddenly as a summer hailstorm in the mountains, it caught him by surprise, and it damn near made him fall over backward. Just like that, something tender he had never felt before took over his bones and seeped into his guts like a golden molasses, making him want to cry.

Which was a hell of a spooky thing to happen to Joe, because about the only time he ever cried was when he chopped onions to sprinkle on Nancy's enchiladas, or when he ate a real hot jalapeño.

No getting around it, though: suddenly he held a profound tenderness for his people, that's what it was. His people. His gente. His bunch of inbred, toothless, tubercular, flea-bitten, illiterate vecinos, sobrinos, primos, cuates, cabrones, rancheros, and general all-around fregado'd jodidos.

Suddenly he loved the people he lived with, he cared about their lives. And this feeling, this *tenderness* oozing throughout his body, made him almost weak.

Then, while magpies jabbered like a bunch of excited monkeys in the branches overhead, and with two sparrowhawks quiet on the telephone lines across by the highway, Joe fell into a peculiar reverie. His childhood, something he had all but forgotten, drifted out of a dim, misty place, clouding his mind and his heart, working on that softness he felt within, prodding him gently, releasing frail human sensitivities Joe had always scorned.

He was with his father, Esequiel Mondragón, a small stoop-shouldered and very quiet person who had lonely pale-green eyes and silky gray hair. On horse-back, they were driving their sheep home from summer pasture fifty miles west, far on the other side of the Rio Grande gorge. Three dogs circled around the sheep, barking, keeping the animals in order. His father didn't say much as they rode through the dust behind the slow-moving herd; he simply chewed tobacco and sat hunched over in his saddle, all of his attention, in a vague sleep-eyed way, on the sheep. Joe was riding bareback. On either side of them, in the Curandero Valley, aspen trees were a lovely buttery yellow, shivering in the Indian Summer breezes. Several times they spotted small bunches of mule deer moving along the upper meadow slopes near the tree line. For eight days they were together with the sheep, heading home. Slowly, they descended along a rocky trail into the gorge, the sheep moving single file, and, once in the gorge, they came across a rattlesnake, which his father killed so Joe could skin it. Later he tanned the skin and made a belt; he had worn it for years.

Today, that road in the Curandero Valley had been paved; there was a fancy new bridge over the gorge, and you were not allowed to drive your sheep along the road anymore. The state had also bulldozed some lakes in the valley and stocked them with rainbow and cutthroat trout, and there were half a dozen manicured campgrounds along the route.

Joe remembered summer nights with his father and the sheep in the high mountains, on the steeply sloping alpine ridges where the marmots with their bushy tails ran for cover in the rocks and small gray pikas stared at him while he sat unmoving in the grass. There was the summer his father shot a bear. And the coyotes howling, which had scared him as a kid until he got used to it and until he began to travel with a

.22, killing the coyotes. But the bobcats had always scared him with their now-guttural, now-piercing and effeminate, bloodcurdling screams. And his father's scare gun firing at intervals throughout the lightning-ribbed night to scare away all predators . . . but you were not allowed to use those scare guns anymore.

He was four, maybe five years old, and he had never seen a rattlesnake. His dad stopped their old truck and pointed to a snake in the Conejos Junction road. It was dusk, the snake gleaming dustily in the yellow headlight beams. While Joe peered through the cracked windshield his father got out with a stick and poked at the snake to make it coil, then he tried to make the snake strike, but it wouldn't strike the cold stick. Finally, though, he goaded it into striking by tapping its nose, and only then did the snake give a warning buzz. His father explained to Joe what poison was and warned him to always stay away from this kind of snake. Then, as a strange dispassionate afterthought, he hit the snake with the stick, breaking the serpent in two or three places, and crushed its head under his boot heel. They drove over it and continued on. Later Esequiel gave his son a piece of oshá, warning him to carry it in his pocket at all times as protection against rattlers.

His father hunted as all men hunted. Joe remembered being on horseback with the old man, heading up through snowy hills, looking for elk and deer. And he remembered his father stripped to the waist and covered with blood, gutting an elk that was strung up on a homemade block-and-tackle rig in the backyard, and then later his father was almost hidden inside the huge animal, washing it out with the hose.

He remembered sitting in the back of the pickup on wild-strawberry summer evenings heading down to the fiesta in Chamisaville. Nighthawks dashed around in the darkening sky as the truck rattled southward. Joe was spit-polished and clean, wearing a chartreuse cowboy shirt and new boots, and as they chugged along he took potshots at roadside prairie dogs with his .22 and never hit a one, so far as he could determine—the truck bounced too much.

Esequiel Mondragón had been a strange man. A silent man who never got drunk at the fiesta, who herded sheep, who sometimes was gone all summer, following the sheep for outfits in Montana and Wyoming or doing seasonal farm labor up in Colorado, and then all winter he hung around doing odd jobs like Joe himself now did odd jobs, and somehow getting by.

In the autumn they went fishing together. The old man never taught his son how to fish. In the beginning, only he carried a rod and Joe tagged along, observing and learning. His father fished with flies that he tied himself at home. The streams were small and so narrow you could jump right across them, and his father crept up along the banks all hunched over, sometimes snapping out his line instead of casting, or else, wearing irrigation boots, he walked up the center of the stream in the shallow places. When the fish hit he jerked them out quickly so they wouldn't get tangled up in roots and dead branches. The fish were only seven or eight inches long, and when Joe was young they were all beautiful native cutthroats. But then when he had reached his teens about all they ever caught were German browns, because the big logging companies that cleared roads in the forest and clear-cut areas had dropped slash into the tiny streams, ruining the cutthroat's habitat.

Later, Joe learned how to fish those streams, and how to tie his own flies. Then he and the old man worked the streams together, in the late autumn mostly, when early snows speckled with yellow aspen leaves lay on the ground, and the water was icily cold, and little gray dipper birds flew up ahead, splashing through the water and disappearing in the deep places, walking along the bottom, and then popping up onto rocks again.

His father never carried a creel. He stashed the fish in his front shirt pockets, and then in his coat pockets, and in his pants pockets, if necessary. They came home with fish bulging out of their clothes.

After his father died Joe didn't fish much, and the times he did go, he went with friends and lots of beer

and plenty of worms. Or he shot them with a .22.
The streams were crawling with tourists by then, except for very high up where the bank underbrush was
so thick you could hardly get to the water. But mostly
Joe had quit fishing: there were too many other more
important things to tend to, apropos earning a living.

Joe had gone every spring with his father to clean
the irrigation ditches. The grass in the fields was still
yellow, the trees naked, but the ground no longer
frozen. Killdeer ran around in all the fields, screeching, whistling, trying to lead you away from their
eggs. They chopped the edges of the ditches and dug
mud out of the bottom to build up the sides. They unearthed frogs that were still in hibernation and so
groggy they could hardly move. His father struck a
kitchen match with his thumb and dropped it in the
dry grass alongside the ditch and the grass flared
quickly, smoke drifting across the fields, past the cattle
and horses and placid sheep. They worked all day on
a ditch, drinking beer, until they were bone tired and
the ditch was clean, with its banks built up strong
again.

Nowadays, Joe always paid a kid five bucks to work
on the ditch that irrigated his backyard, and everybody else did the same, and the kids did a shitty
job.

Joe pictured his father and mother on snowy mornings out in the yard, splitting wood. By the end of
autumn they had stacks of piñon higher than the
house, and that was the only heat they used. Now, he
still heated part of his house with piñon, but they had
a butane heater too.

And Joe recalled how his father would walk along
the potholed driveway with him in the mornings to
catch the school bus for the Doña Luz elementary
after the Milagro elementary shut down for good. Joe
would break the ice in all the puddles while his old
man, smoking a cigarette, patiently waited. After a
rain the driveway was crawling with worms, and Joe
crushed every one of them under his heels. His father
looked on and never commented on that, but now suddenly, Joe had the uneasy sensation that his father

had disapproved of such wanton murder. Certainly Joe
had never seen his father kill anything, except for
meat, or unless it was poisonous—his father would
swerve a truck almost unconsciously to squash a rattlesnake or a tarantula on the road.

Pigs. Esequiel Mondragón shooting them in the
head. And then tying them up to bleed. And scalding
the pigs in huge tubs of boiling water. These days Joe
got a lot of his meat precut and packaged from the
feedlot up in La Jara, Colorado.

During his father's last few years Joe had gone with
him often up to Colorado, up to the auctions in Monte
Vista and Alamosa and other towns in the San Luis
Valley. Farmers were just starting to go out of business
up there, and his father always attended those auctions. You could get everything from fence posts to
lambing pens to refrigerators dirt cheap. Very vividly
Joe could see his father and a hundred other intent
men walking from pile of goods to pile of goods,
hardly talking, their brows deeply furrowed, listening
carefully to the auctioneers' wild, incomprehensible
jabber, his father occasionally bidding on something
by just barely tilting his head to let one auctioneer
or the other know he was in.

Joe still traveled north to those auctions, and he
usually drove back with his pickup full of junk. But
it wasn't for his home, his animals, and such. Mostly
it was stuff he sold to a couple of friends who had
tourist-type antique and secondhand stores down in
Chamisaville.

His father had not been a religious man; only once
a year did he attend church, the one time each year
that a service was held in the Milagro church. Otherwise, people went south on Sundays to Our Lady of
Guadalupe in Doña Luz. But this one time each May,
on the day of San Isidro, who was patron saint of all
farmers, they opened the small adobe church in town.
The service was at night and there were little bonfires
all along both sides of the road on the way to the
church.

His father had had a couple of beehives in the
back field too. And his father had loved to shoot

baskets with him at the elementary school's outdoor court in the cool misty summer evenings after supper. And the family had often gone together into the hills to pick raspberries, and they would come home with big jars stuffed full of the red fruit. And his mother always heated green chilies on trays in the oven, and then they all sat at the table, peeling off the browned skins. . . .

Bernabé Montoya coasted his pickup to a stop in back of Joe's truck and got out. Joe waved, and then watched suspiciously as the sheriff walked along the Roybal ditch bank up to the borders of his beanfield.

"Morning." Bernabé said, leaning nonchalantly against a cedar fence post.

"What are you up to, cousin?" Joe said guardedly.

"Oh, nothing much, nothing much. Just out and around, you know. Just out and around, checking on things."

"Hmm," Joe said, and they both watched water flow into the field for a while.

"Uh, there was a fellow up here the other day from the capital," Bernabé said. "He talked with a group of, you know, people from around here."

"That undercover son of a bitch with the photographs driving the unmarked Galaxie?" Joe said.

"Oh. You heard."

Joe smiled. "Somebody mentioned it, but I had forgotten about it until now."

"Hey, José," Bernabé said gently. "Lots of people are worried about this little beanfield."

"You don't say."

"I suppose you're gonna keep on irrigating?"

"Yes, sir."

The sheriff, hardly an hour into his day, was already tired and dispirited. He lit a cigarette, offering one to Joe, who said "No thanks, I got my own." And, removing a pack from his front shirt pocket, Joe lit a weed.

At that moment a foot-long brown trout washed into the field and began floundering in the shallow water. Joe got up and grabbed it, bashing its head against a rock. Then, sitting back down, he took out his pocket knife and proceeded, quickly and deftly, to gut the fish.

"There's a whole bunch of important powerful people down south who are pretty nervous about this field, José," Bernabé reiterated.

Silently, stoically, Joe thumbed up the guts, grabbing intestines and tearing them out, chucking the glop into the water.

"I'm kind of nervous about it too," Bernabé said.

Joe swished the fish in the water a few times to clean it out, and sat back down again.

They smoked. Joe got up once more, and, with his hoe, diverted the water into a new row.

"This is just asking for trouble," the sheriff said.

"This was my father's field, Bernabé, you know that." Joe pointed to a ruin. "We used to live in that house."

"That was before," the sheriff said.

"It was before you became sheriff, too," Joe said.

"I earn a living," Bernabé said sadly.

They smoked some more. The sheriff flicked his butt into the water.

"So why did you come over here at 6:00 A.M.?" Joe finally asked, grinning. "To help me irrigate?"

"I came over to ask you to stop this before it gets out of hand," the sheriff said.

"That's what I thought. Fuck you."

"I came over to warn you that some people in this town are gonna try and stop you from irrigating this field."

"Other people are on my side," Joe replied quietly.

"This town is uptight enough, José. Already we're too much set against each other. Why make it worse?"

"This is my land. Who made the laws that said I can't irrigate my land? I didn't put my Juan Hancock on any papers like that."

"The man who was up here wasn't kidding around, José. He's a dangerous man."

"If you go to any more meetings with that man tell him, for me, will you, to stick a finger up his ass and then suck it like a popsickle stick afterward."

With a resigned sigh, Bernabé lit another cigarette.

"Not too long ago we used to run together," he said.

Joe shrugged. "Things change."

"As a friend maybe you would do this thing for me."

"What thing?"

"Quit irrigating this little no-account field."

"Why talk about what isn't gonna happen?"

"I won't protect you, then," Bernabé said testily. "You're gonna mess up my job, you know that? So I hope they beat you so hard your kidneys bleed."

"I can take care of my kidneys."

"I can't arrest you because that will only cause more trouble," Bernabé said. "And anyway, I'm afraid of you. I mean, I can't arrest you for illegally irrigating this field, and you know that and I know that. We're not stupid. But if something happens to you or to this field, I don't have to arrest anybody else, either. I'm sorry, but I think that's the way things stand right now . . ."

"You're trespassing on my property," Joe said.

Sadly, Bernabé backed up. "What do you want to go and cause this trouble for?" he asked unhappily. "We had a peaceful town here . . ."

Joe said nothing.

Bernabé snapped away his cigarette, and, after directing a halfhearted obscene gesture at Joe, turned and headed for his pickup.

Fifteen minutes later, when the field was almost entirely watered, a state fish and game truck driven by Carl Abeyta, with Floyd Cowlie in the passenger seat, parked directly behind Joe's pickup. The two men sauntered over; Carl Abeyta wore a gun.

"Heard you been fishing," Carl said to Joe in English. "You got a license?"

"Check your own records and you'll learn the answer," Joe replied in Spanish, picking up his hoe.

"Speak English," Carl said. "Floyd here don't speak Spanish."

"A la chingada con tu y tu amigo gabacho," Joe said.

"You *don't* have a license," Carl said in Spanish.

"So what?"

"We're gonna have to fine you then."

"What for?"

"For that fish you got in your possession."

"Fish?" Joe exclaimed incredulously. "Who's got a fish?"

"Tell him to speak English," Floyd Cowlie said, swinging under the nearby fence. "Where's that fish, Joe?"

Joe shrugged and addressed Floyd in Spanish: "I don't know what you're talking about, you fucking goat."

"Hey, I know that word," Floyd growled angrily.

"We heard you had a fish," Carl said quickly.

"Maybe what you need is a new hearing aid," Joe said.

"We got it from a good source."

"Hey, you," Joe said to Floyd Cowlie in English. "You're trespassing on my property." With the hoe, he advanced toward the man. "You got until I count three to haul your ass onto the other side of that fence with your pal. Did anybody give you a warrant to search my property?"

Floyd backed under the fence; Carl dropped his hand onto his gun. "Listen," Floyd said, "we know you got a fish." He snagged his shirt on the barbed wire, cursed softly, unsnagged himself, and straightened shakily beside his partner.

"You bastard," Carl Abeyta hissed in Spanish. "We'll get you."

"You and whose army?" Joe chuckled.

Without another word the two walked back to their vehicle.

"What are you Florestistas looking for—" Joe shouted gleefully after them, "another Smokey the Bear santo riot?"

Then Joe cut the water back into the river and sat for a moment longer while the sun rose higher and water seeped into the ground around his bean plants. At the far corner of the field some blackbirds and three magpies were wading in the water and muck, hunting for choice tidbits. High overhead, aflame in the early-morning sunshine, a vulture quietly circled.

Joe felt saucy, in control, cool. On top of the world. Everybody else and his brother was either an idiot or a chicken compared to Joe Mondragón.

And for a moment he had wonderful delusions of grandeur.

But later, as he drove past the Miracle Valley sign, defiantly shaking an obscene finger at the announcement of Ladd Devine's dream, Milagro's nightmare, Joe suddenly felt scared stiff again. And a vision popped into his head: of the Zopilote and Jerry G. and Horsethief Shorty and that Carl Montana and the state engineer, Nelson Bookman, all sitting around a campfire up by the Little Baldy Bear Lakes, roasting miniature Joe Mondragóns skewered like hot dogs on aspen twigs over their campfire.

⊌§

Billy Ray Gusdorf, known simply as Ray these days, was a lean, quiet man who, in a lean and quiet way, believed in God. He never prayed, so to speak, or went with his family to church, but he had a kind of awe for what was alive, a respect for everything from horses to chickadees that amounted to the sort of general all-around respect for the world and its creatures that others might take for a belief in God.

Ray hadn't always been thus. In fact, back during his youth, he had been a pretty cantankerous son of a bitch. He was born in the cattle country near Mexico, and raised by a family that had run beef and then gone into cotton when the big Bureau of Reclamation dams completely transformed the plains country. Eventually old man Gusdorf had gotten royally skinned when the bottom fell out of cotton, and he wound up relegated to a sharecropper's role forever after. Billy Ray's childhood, then, consisted of sorrowful years in tarpaper shacks, much ill health, and general all-around human disaster. Under these deteriorating conditions the child—early on—had developed into one ornery hellion.

Thirteen, fourteen years old, and he drank, he smoked, he swore, he ruined little girls and ran with ruined women, and by the time he was seventeen, his daddy fresh buried and his mom on the outs with TB, it looked for sure like Billy Ray was either going to rewrite the legend of Billy the Kid, or else die trying.

Then a few things happened which, when added up, turned the wild youngster into an entirely different person. First off, his entire family, along with nine other members of the Glen Mark Baptist Church, were wiped out by a single lightning bolt which hit the cottonwood they had sought shelter under during a storm that was washing out their church picnic. Billy Ray did not go to his justly deserved reward along with the rest of them because he was off in an abandoned shack with a lady parishioner shouting "Glory Hallelujah!" at the exact moment his family and neighbors got fried.

After that, for the first time in his life, Billy Ray started wondering about the Lord, whom he'd previously always considered a kind of stern Santa Claus. He was so shook up that he hit the road, and for some reason that road aimed due north five hundred miles, leading up out of flat plains and the desert country into high mountains, and—maybe a year after the death of his family—to a job at the Dancing Trout Dude Ranch, guiding tourists on horseback through the summertime Midnight Mountains. Ladd Devine Senior hired him on for the same reason he'd hired on Horsethief Shorty Wilson, namely, he liked and trusted hellraisers, blasphemers, whoremongers, and loud-mouthed alcoholics, knowing exactly how to keep the edge off by paying them fair and feeding them well to boot.

All went okay at the ranch for a few months. Billy Ray continued his off-hours boozing, brawling, and other sundry endeavors. Then one morning he woke up with the first autumn snow alighting gently on the ground outside. Billy Ray threw on a shirt, some jeans, and his boots, walking outside into something he had never experienced before; and he just stood there, letting that first snowfall gather in his hair and on his shoulders. And after it stopped he still remained there, because he had never before even vaguely approximated such a wonderful and wonder-struck affinity for a horse, a mother, or a whore, let alone for an act of weather.

Subsequently, while going through lazy autumn chores, battening down the dude ranch's hatches for winter, Billy Ray, abstracted, moved almost in a reverie, pausing often to gaze mystifiedly into the mountains, where he could see the gray velvet smirches of early snow falling.

Came one morning, then, shortly before Christmas, when Billy Ray slipped on a dude ranch backpack, hung some snowshoes on the side of it, and walked into the mountains. He hit snow early, donned the snowshoes, and pushed on, meandering upward. The first night, still in thick timber, he instinctively made a little snow cave, wrapped himself in a blanket, and slept warmly in his icy cubbyhole. Next day around noon he reached the high open valleys around the Little Baldy Lakes, which were invisible under ten to fifteen feet of snow.

The silence within the alpine bowl was unbelievable. Icy white, sunny, and mute, the expanse everywhere was almost entirely unmarked except for faint feather patterns where a little bird had pushed off; or for tiny mouse tracks trickling across the still, shimmering snow.

Billy Ray ate a few raisins, a tortilla, nothing else. Expressionless, directionless, more than awed, he moved about in the high country valleys, occasionally sucking on little snowballs, stopping often to listen to the inaudible hum, the fantastic and unhearable *crinkle* of that pristine frozen landscape. And again, he stopped often simply to absorb by osmosis the immense grandeur, loneliness, majesty, and both frail and cruel beauty of his surroundings.

For several days he plodded that way, aimlessly searching for nothing, in no hurry, a minuscule curious specter inching around in that peaceful winter country, absorbing something, taking it in—indelibly— for all time. Sometimes long fan-shaped snow sprays were spun off the mountaintops by high winds. Other times the mountains and valleys and forest were as still and as quiet as hawks in the air, a mile high, drifting. Occasionally, when caught in the exact eye of this bleached and motionless crystal expanse, Billy Ray's limbs went weak from sheer joy. And at one point during an impeccably white noon he closed his eyes and nearly fell asleep standing up in the middle of a sloping, unblemished snowfield; he almost died.

Practically no living things crossed his path during those days in that universe of gorgeous frozen light. A small bird here, a skittish mouse—nothing more. At night, huddled in his snow holes with the starry darkness absolutely dumb overhead, he slept like a puppy behind a warm stove, like a cat on a sunny windowsill, like a baby fresh from its mother's breast.

And it was during those nights that the Billy the Kid legend died.

Three days passed: after them, Ray Gusdorf quietly emerged from the Midnight Mountains a different human being—mature, introspective, curiously subdued. He quit work at the Dancing Trout, fell in love with and married Jeanine Juniors, started his own small spread as close to those mountains as he could, had one kid, and then a whole bunch of children in rapid succession, learned Spanish and became a respectable citizen, a silent man, but understood and well liked. Ray had arrived, as few people have the good luck to arrive, at home.

Since then, all through the subsequent years, Ray had carried those three days in his heart; they were constantly being pumped anew with his blood throughout his veins and arteries; and although he had never since returned to the winter country, it was as if he had somehow remained up there forever.

"For three hundred years, maybe longer," Ray said to Joe Mondragón one evening while they were both sitting on Rael's porch, the one killing a Pepsi, the other working on a beer, "the people around here have starved to death, but somehow they always survived. Now comes a ski area, probably motorcycles, winter snowmobiles, a subdivision, and so forth, jobs for everybody say Bud Gleason and Ladd Devine, money in the bank . . . and in five years we'll all be gone."

He paused thoughtfully, watching diners move about the café across the plaza area. Then he turned his head sideways, focusing on the mountains that loomed over the town, the same mountains that were nestled in his heart.

"I figure I can live with hunger," he said gently, "a hell of a lot better than I could ever live with fat."

❧

The phone rang; Charley Bloom answered. It was his lawyer friend and also the *Voice of the People* editor, Sean Carter, calling from the capital with some bad news.

"Christ, are we ever up shit creek without the old proverbial paddle," Sean began.

Bloom prickled with a sudden chill: "How so?"

"Well, to begin with I think we have to suspend publication."

Bloom's heart leaped back up from where it had fallen; he didn't dare speak, he just waited.

"The machines got stolen, you know all about that."

"Sure." And to make himself sound convincing, he added: "Those bastards."

"I can't get 'em back unless I come up with that bread, but who am I, Jesus Christ tearing apart loaves and fishes and dollar bills—?"

"I'll type up some stuff," Bloom offered unenthusiastically, cursing his hypocrisy. "There's other people with typewriters."

"Of course, man. Thanks. But that isn't the half of it."

"Give me the rest then."

"You sitting down—?"

"Oh come on, Sean, cut the melodrama."

"Mirbaum, the printer, he sends me a bill for six hundred and eighty fat ones today, with a little note attached, to the effect that either we cough up the bread or else he doesn't print the next issue."

"What about John and Mary?" They were the typesetters.

"I talked to them. They're okay for another issue, except we owe them two hundred and ninety bucks, and they're about to go under, too, so I feel kind of guilty about that."

"How much do we have in the bank?"

"What are you, Charley, a comedian? The last time I dared look it was a hundred and fifty, something like that. Tish went back East to see her folks or an old boyfriend or somebody, so that means we can't get the July and August renewals out until she comes back. But that ain't all——"

"Don't tell me," Bloom sighed, outwardly morose, inwardly almost ecstatic, sensing that at the end of this telephone call he was going to be off at least one hook. "Lemme guess. Adams suddenly decided he wants his back rent or out we go." Adams was the landlord.

"Congratulations. I guess you work for the *Voice* a little you become almost psychic about these matters."

"Well what's with that bastard?" Bloom said, trying to sound irate. "I thought him letting us use his building was an arrangement of love. He's floundering in gold, he doesn't need our rent!" It was the right tone of voice, Bloom knew; he had come across.

"Who knows?" Sean mumbled. "Maybe somebody talked to him, maybe he got scared, I don't know. That burglary freaked him a little. He's afraid next time it'll be a fire. I mean, that robbery was no accident. Oh, and by the way. Guess what?"

"Don't tell me, I think I've had enough."

"The phone company called up this morning. I got until 4:30 P.M. to hit Sierra Bell—bless her electronic titties!—with a check for three hundred and eighty bucks, otherwise tomorrow morning we start communicating with smoke signals and tom-toms."

Bloom tried to sound bitter: "What else? Is there anything else? What happened with all those foundations?"

"We sent out thirty-eight letters. Nobody had any bread they wanted to lay on our stellar organization."

"I thought Manny Gale was going to get in touch

with that guy in Boston—what's his face?—you know, the one with all the *z*'s and *x*'s in his name."

"You don't mean Cartright?"

"Yeah. And fuck you."

"I dunno. I'm not sure. You can never trust a radiclib. I haven't even seen Manny, either, for the past three weeks. His car broke down; they busted him for carrying a couple of joints in the glove compartment, then he broke up with Tania, and shit, I guess things just fell apart in general."

"There was another person, a woman, Mrs.—you know. The artsy-craftsy philanthropist who lives practically next door to you on Camino de los Arbolitos."

"I saw her. You think I'd miss a trick? It was beautiful. I sat in a six-hundred-dollar chair in a hundred-thousand-dollar house whose walls were lined with Fritz Sholders and Georgia O'Keefes, sipping raspberry wine, listening to the old bitch sing the poverty blues."

"But didn't she offer to throw a party, or organize a benefit or something?"

"In the first letter she wrote—yes. But when we talked she wasn't that hot to trot. I dunno, suddenly she had reservations about the *Voice*. She talked about how we're becoming a little too radical, irresponsible, shit like that. We were losing our objectivity. But then she had a great idea for a soiree."

"I bet."

"She said, why didn't we set up a cocktail bash in her home, invite all the heavies, make a pitch. And then, because you gotta have entertainment at these shindigs, you know what she suggested—?"

"I'm afraid to ask."

"A tap dancer."

"A what?"

"A fucking tap dancer."

"*No!*"

"Yeah. Can you picture it? We get all the heavies stoned, and then hit 'em with a tap dancer. Wow! And the other great idea she had was why didn't the editorial board of the *Voice* write a best-selling political sex novel."

"Oh Christ, man. What did she suggest we call it, *Naked Came the Candidate?*"

"There's more," Sean said almost gleefully.

"Go ahead. I'm alright." You *bet* he was all right.

"A letter arrived this morning by registered mail, from the firm of Slosser and Bendix, representing guess who?"

"That AMPEX subdivision on the San Gervasio reservation."

"Bingo."

"They're going to sue for that article Jane Moran did last month?"

"Double bingo."

"But how can they do that? What did she say that they could sue for? Where's the libel?"

"Honesty is no defense," Sean said pleasantly. "You know that."

"I'll be damned," Bloom said quietly, trying to modify the sensations arising in his body that were almost akin to joy.

Sean said, "Again, I think somebody talked to them. I called Herb Slosser—I mean, Herb and me, we were in Harvard Law together, weren't we? I called him, I said, 'Herb, what goes?' He was really uptight, evasive. He mumbled something about he couldn't afford not to advise them to do it. His partner, Bendix, you know, he's got a big piece of the AMPEX action."

"So what are we going to do?" Bloom asked.

"I'm not sure. Mostly, there's nothing we can do. The *Voice* is dead. Who do you know who's crawling with money he wants to give away? I've hit up everybody I know, and the good people are honestly all tapped out. We'll have to suspend, the way I figure it, until we can raise the bread, and in the process, no doubt, we'll lose the second-class mailing permit. I'll put out a letter, of course, to all the subscribers, with the sustainer plea—you know. But we've already hit on our sustainers twice this year."

"Oh shit," Bloom muttered sadly, wanting to shout "Hallelujah!" After all, he was out of it, then—*with honor*.

"I'm sorry. Listen, Charley, I wanted you to know

because you've been close to the paper, but I get off now. If you're working on another piece for the twenty-fifth deadline, don't kill yourself. Because unless a miracle happens, we're not coming out next month."

"I wasn't working on an article," Bloom said, his voice literally dripping with false disappointment, phony gloom.

"Well, if you do write something, send me a carbon. I'd really dig reading it no matter what . . ."

They said good-bye, then, and Bloom cradled the phone with a smile lighting up his features like a photographer's floodlamp. He was free . . . out of it . . . released!

Someone knocked on the door and Bloom went to answer. Standing on the welcome mat was a small, ruggedly pretty Chicano woman of about fifty whom he had seen around. Then, even before she extended her hand, saying hello and giving her name, he remembered that she was the Body Shop and Pipe Queen owner, Ruby Archuleta.

"Sure, come in, sit down, please. I'll get you some coffee—"

"I don't got the time right now to come in," Ruby said. "I just wanted to ask a favor."

"Of course. What is it?"

"There's gonna be a meeting in the church about the conservancy district and about that dam. We'd like your help, you know? José Mondragón, he says being a lawyer you know pretty much all there is to know about it. He showed me that article you wrote in the magazine, and I liked it very much. José says, too, that you got maps and you got books and things that could help explain it to the people. We want you to come to the meeting and help us to understand better this thing that is happening in the valley—can you do that?"

What could he say? With every voice in his body, heart, and soul screaming *No!* he said, "Yes."

She smiled and shook his hand again, telling him that when the word had been spread and the people had talked among themselves a little more, the meeting would take place, and she would let him know exactly when that would be. Then she walked quickly back to her truck.

The lawyer, stunned, sat down. And for a long while he remained very still with his head in his hands, feeling doomed. He had been released, and then abruptly rejailed. He had lived the short happy life for no longer than a heartbeat.

"I should have told her to go to hell," he moaned aloud in the quiet kitchen. "Why can't I tell people to go to hell? I'm not a decent human being, so why do I keep pretending to act like one?"

But then all at once his misery parted just long enough to allow another emotion its brief moment of glory. Because—to tell the truth—he also felt flattered.

"People like me," Bloom whispered aloud with a wry melancholy smile, "are called Yo-Yos."

❧

In the early days there had been no Santa Claus or Easter Bunny to decorate the sacrilege, piety, or greedy whimsy of Milagro's various religious seasons. In their stead, the Abuelo, a shady and gnarled old man— more closely related in spirit to the bogeyman than to old Saint Nick—scrambled around in the winter or spring shadows, trying to lay his icy fingers on irreligious little kids who strayed from the straight and narrow. When he latched onto a victim, the hairy old Abuelo, who dressed in rags and occasionally smoked a cigar, made the kid kneel on the ground, whipped him heartily with a cat-o'-nine-tails, and then ordered the child to say his prayers. If the youngster didn't know his prayers the Abuelo was liable to kick him around in the snow until his body became a white ball, or else he would burn off the tip of the kid's frosty nose with his cigar.

For dozens of decades the Abuelo had hung around at one festive time of year or another, beating up kids or shining flashlight beams into burros' eyes until they went crazy, and in general causing a great deal of malicious mischief.

But as the modern age intruded upon Milagro,

bringing with it the Cinemascope and Technicolor versions of Santa Claus and the Easter Bunny and cutesy Day-Glo Halloween skeleton suits, the ferocious Abuelo began to fade from the sanitized scene like the image in an old tintype.

Still, every town, and particularly a town with a heritage of crazies like Milagro, needs some sort of bogeyman, banshee, witch, frog-eating Cleofes Apodaca shaped like a dog, or Abuelo with which to terrorize children during the holiday seasons, and also with which to explain many of the unexplainable things that happen year-round in the neighborhood.

Of course, Pacheco's pig in certain ways had become just such a scapegoat, taking up some of the slack created by the Abuelo's demise. But long before Pacheco's indestructible sow rose to prominence in the townsfolk's fertile imaginations, another phantom was born to roam through the Miracle Valley wreaking all manner of curious havoc.

This phantom was Onofre Martínez's missing arm.

As legend would have it, Onofre Martínez's missing arm floated around town doing nasty deeds because it had been eaten by butterflies or by dogs or by snakes or by coyotes . . . but whatever the case, it had never received a proper Christian burial. And, bitter over this, the arm had sworn to plague the town for eternity in revenge.

In this capacity, of course, the arm served a traditional and useful purpose. Mothers told their very young children all about El Brazo Onofre, and, once the child's imagination had thoroughly grasped the image of that powerful, invisible, and very evil appendage drifting through the Milagro air searching hungrily for nasty things to do, mothers tried to extract obeisance from their small fry by threatening: "You watch out, Alfredo; if you're not a good boy El Brazo Onofre will choke you in your bed tonight—" Or: "Eat your stew, Eloy, or tonight El Brazo Onofre will open your window and steal your piggy bank—" Or again: "Adelita, you better be a good girl over the holidays or else El Brazo Onofre will strangle Santa Claus and you won't get no presents."

Occasionally, El Brazo Onofre could be a good phantom. Thus, all during the boxing career of Amarante Córdova's son Gabriel, it was said that the Milagro Mauler's most special punches, the ones that gained for him all his victories, were usually the invisible haymakers landed by Gabriel's patron saint —El Brazo Onofre. And teen-age kids from Milagro who boxed down in the Chamisaville High School always winkingly attributed their victories to the fact that they had had El Brazo Onofre in their corner.

If you went into it at all, El Brazo Onofre actually possessed quite a diverse character. Once, as a small child, when caught by Nick Rael walking out of the general store (then the Devine Company Store) with his pockets stuffed full of stolen candy bars, Joe Mondragón had automatically, instinctively squealed: "I didn't do it! I didn't know I even had those candy bars! I was framed by El Brazo Onofre!"

And when Joe, or Amarante Córdova, or any other men in town sneaked into the National Forest to set a fire so all the men in town would have hard work at good pay for a while, they always stood around afterward with their hands in their pockets gazing innocently up at the sky, lips pursed, carelessly whistling "Dixie" as they declared the fire must have been set by that unconscionable rapscallion, El Brazo Onofre.

This ubiquitous appendage also had quite a sex life. Milagro boys claimed there were no true virgin girls in Milagro because El Brazo Onofre liked to prowl around at night invading the bedrooms of little Ana Marías who were just beginning to bud or flow, as the sayings go, and apparently the hand at the end of El Brazo Onofre was always stimulating these diminutive females into very erotic nightmares.

Then again, there were some people to be found, mostly among the town's adolescent boys, who often leeringly suggested that El Brazo Onofre was a maricón that went hither and yon jerking off the young males in Milagro, thus accounting for about 95 percent of the village's wet dreams.

All this, then, by way of background to the envelope which turned up on Ladd Devine the Third's desk one morning, and to the note inside that envelope, scrawled in a semi-illegible hand, that said:

> El Brazo Onofre is looking for you, Mr. Zopilote Devine, and when it finds you, you son of a bitch, it's gonna choke you to death.

Devine walked out of his office and down the hall to Emerson Lapp's office and over to Emerson Lapp's desk. Settling the note dramatically in front of his startled secretary, he asked:

"What the hell is this?"

Lapp read the note, scanned it again, then wrinkled his upper lip, squinched his nose until the bridge was thoroughly grooved, and weighted down his entire prissy face with a formidable, puzzled frown.

"Christ, Mr. D., you sure got me. What's this El Brazo Onofre?"

"El Brazo means 'The Arm,'" Devine said. "I don't know what Zopilote means."

Emerson Lapp turned the piece of paper over, turned it back, reread it again, and shook his head. "It's stupid, Mr. D. It's silly. It's not serious. It's somebody's idea of a joke."

Devine reread the note, observing: "I don't think it's very funny."

Next, he showed the message to Jerry G., who also shook his head, looking very serious, and had nothing to say. Who or what the hell was El Brazo Onofre?

"Onofre's Arm," Horsethief Shorty murmured, perplexed, biting his lips to keep from laughing, lacking an answer for once. "Maybe they mean Onofre Martínez's missing arm, that's the first thing pops into my mind. But what kind of significance they've given it sure beats me. Must be something private to them, and it must be pretty private if I never heard of it."

"What does this word 'Zopilote' mean?"

"Vulture. Buzzard."

"Oh."

The fifth person to read Ladd Devine's note was the sheriff, Bernabé Montoya. He was sitting on Rael's porch drinking a Dr. Pepper while keeping an eye on things, when the front tire of a Dancing Trout pickup almost clipped the tips off his feet, and Devine draped an arm out the window, allowing the threatening note to glide off his fingertips into Bernabé's lap.

"What kind of rotten joke is this, Bernie?" he asked angrily.

Bernabé read the note, and as he did so, unseen by Devine, an *Ai, Chihuahua!* about the size of a dinosaur quietly fumbled up the sheriff's queasy esophagus and mutely dissipated itself into the heavy summer air. For a second Bernabé thought he had better explain the myth of El Brazo Onofre; but on second thought, he wondered, Why begin, for crissakes?

Slowly, the sheriff shook his head, pretending to be very puzzled. "What's this, Mr. Devine? It sure is weird. Who's this Brazo Onofre?"

"You mean you never heard of Brazo Onofre?" Devine asked suspiciously.

"Never in my life," Bernabé swore, still ponderously shaking his head, trying to win an Oscar for his interpretation of a bewildered frown.

"Well, if this is somebody's idea of a joke, I don't think it's so God damn funny," Devine said.

"Is this a note you received, sir?" Bernabé asked politely, handing it back to Devine.

"In the mail. This morning." Lips pressed firmly together, Devine scanned the note again. "I wonder whose handwriting this is," he said tightly.

Bernabé shrugged, trying to repress the intuition he had about what was coming next.

Devine said, "Wouldn't you classify this as some kind of peculiar death threat?"

"I wouldn't say that, sir. To me, it seems just like somebody's idea of a prank."

"The writer called me a son of a bitch," Devine said softly. "And the writer also threatened to choke me to death."

Commiseratingly, Bernabé nodded, mentally booting himself in the ass for sitting on Rael's porch out in the open at 11:00 A.M. in full view of all traffic heading to or from the Dancing Trout Dude Ranch.

After a pause, Devine asked, "What would you do about a note like this, Bernie?"

"I'd sit on it," the sheriff said. "I mean, you know, not literally. I just wouldn't do nothing."

"What would the state police do?" Devine asked frostily.

Bernabé released another gargantuan though inaudible *Ai, Chihuahua!*, and, fearing for his career, his voice almost a moan, he said, "They sure wouldn't come into town and go around asking people to write on pieces of paper and then compare those pieces of paper with your note, sir. If you wanted somebody to want to kill you, that would be a good way to get them to be that way."

Devine said, "Alright, Bernie. Thanks for your valuable time." He turned abruptly around in the plaza area and drove home.

The note which arrived next morning said:

Maybe some night El Brazo Onofre will creep through your window, Mr. Zopilote Devine, and tickle you under your armpits, and take all the money from your wallet, and then drive a big fat knife through your fucking heart.

Ladd Devine stapled the two notes and the two envelopes they had come in together, slipped them into a manila folder, and filed them under *E* for "El" in his personal correspondence file.

Notes arrived almost daily after that. Devine cursed silently to himself and filed them away. Maybe the fan letters were only a prank, but they upset him; each one jarred his day a little when it came, and he found it difficult to recover afterward. He did not tell Flossie about the notes, however, nor did he again mention them to Emerson Lapp, although the secretary knew of their existence since he always handled and sorted the mail before passing it on to his boss.

Late one afternoon at the height of the El Brazo Onofre deluge, Devine turned to his wife. "Let's go for a fly," he said gently. "Would you like that?"

"Oh Ladd," Flossie murmured happily. "Can we really?"

"Sure. Get your coat."

"May I take this drink along?"

"As you wish, my dear."

She fetched her coat, a fluffy white imitation-fur carcoat, and, bracelets jangling, her champagne glass in one hand, a bottle of bubbly in the other, followed him out to the main garage where he chose a Ford station wagon for the trip down to the airport. Their drive to Chamisaville was quiet, the radio turned on softly to music, neither speaking to the other. They parked at the small airport, and while Devine talked over weather conditions with the manager, Chet Premminger, Flossie sat in the car listening to the radio and sipping quietly from her glass, staring through the spotless windshield at the wide and glorious sagebrush expanse leading up to the green and white mountains.

Then she walked to the plane with her husband. There was little wind; in a moment they were airborne. Flossie saw it all through a peculiarly lazy alcoholic dream. She was not unhappy to be who she was, she thought, living with whom she lived. Yet ever since she had been a little girl she hadn't known what to do with herself. When her mother said go out and play, she merely drifted around the yard, or lay on the lawn, daydreaming about nothing in particular, wondering what to do. Everything had always been very rosy, very taffeta and vague, and only half-troubled. On horses she walked, simply forgetting to spur them into a trot, a canter, a gallop, having no desire to be thrilled. Somebody always put the saddle on and took it off, and somebody else had always curried the animals for her. And she had been drinking steadily, now, for a very long time.

Devine flew the plane without talking. Once over the mountains they saw a herd of about fifteen deer in a high open meadow. Later they caught sight of tiny circular lakes, the sun glaring bright silver off their still surfaces.

Flossie gazed, holding her glass carefully so that

none of the champagne spilled. Her husband kept them very steady.

"This is nice," she said. "Thank you, dear. This was a nice idea."

"Yes," Devine said, smiling as he patted her knee. "I thought you might like it."

"Let's go see the ranch."

Moments later they flew over the Dancing Trout, and over Milagro, and they circled over it all again.

"Honey," Flossie said suddenly, her carefully penciled eyebrows descending, coming together in a little frown. "Is what we do wrong?"

"I don't understand."

"Oh, you know. The ranch. The company. The Miracle Valley project. We own *every*thing, love."

"Nonsense. We don't own everything. And what we do own, why, we worked pretty darn hard for it."

"I guess I don't understand things," Flossie said, sipping from her glass. "And of course you're right, we worked really hard for it . . ."

"So don't worry," Devine said. "Let's drop the subject. Do you want to see the Little Baldy Lakes?"

She smiled. "That would be fun."

They flew over the nine lakes, silver baubles in green alpine bowls. In spots the rocky sides of surrounding peaks still displayed some snow.

"Sometimes I'm afraid it's all wrong," Flossie suddenly dared to whisper as they came off the mountains and over juniper and then sagebrush terrain again.

"Nonsense," Devine said a little testily.

"It does make me sad, though, the way you men talk together about those things," Flossie said. "Joe Mondragón is so *poor,* isn't he? Doesn't—well, doesn't, *don't,* I mean . . . don't things ever make you sad?"

"Everybody becomes upset from time to time. You know that."

She smiled and reached over, affectionately touching his shoulder. "They're going to have a meeting—"

"I know all about it and I don't want to talk about it."

"I wonder if they'll talk about us . . ."

"I said we won't talk about that."

"I'm sorry." She settled back, murmuring, "I don't know why, sometimes I get so silly. I'm so comfortable all the time. I'm always warm and I'm always comfortable. I thank you so much for all of that. Isn't it beautiful over there? Look, you can see our shadow. Let's fly down in the gorge."

Devine steered the plane westward, dropping carefully down between the gorge walls. Sunlight was fast leaving, but they still had plenty of light to fly by. Swallows zipped away from the plane. Startled, several fishermen looked up, mouths agape; suddenly, giddily, they waved. There were sections where the river flowed slowly and serenely; in other areas it was a white foam crashing through a course of enormous boulders. They flew under the bridge spanning the gorge west of Doña Luz, the road that crossed it heading toward Ojo Prieto and points beyond.

When they pulled out of the gorge, Flossie poured a touch more into her glass. "That's one of my favorite places to fly," she murmured.

Her husband turned the plane around and they flew back through the high plateau sunset, orange and powdery blue, brilliant and soft and different everywhere, the mountains crimson for a few seconds, then dark purple, suddenly black, nighthawks flying below them over the sage; and once they saw, or at least Flossie thought she saw, a coyote running. The plane skimmed in low, teetered just slightly, and bounced along the runway.

Flossie wandered back to the car and, while Devine spoke with Chet Premminger about servicing the plane, she leaned on the hood, staring at what was left of the sunset, a few crimson and orange ribbons in the west, with mesas and gentle mountains silhouetted black like on corny picture postcards.

It was dark by the time they headed away from the airport. The heating system purred loudly. Flossie clicked on the radio to soft dance music, then opened the glove compartment to find an emery board for filing down her nails. Instead, her hand landed on a gun. Startled, she removed it, a .38 police special; and loaded, too.

"What the heck is this?"

"I put it there," Devine said. "Leave it alone."

"But what for? You never carried a gun in the car . . ."

"Well, you never can tell," her husband said in that special threatening tone of voice he used to indicate a discussion was over.

And so they drove home to Milagro. In silence. In the dark.

&

Meanwhile, as some people tiptoed around slipping loaded pistols into their glove compartments, and as other people anxiously awaited the meeting called by Ruby Archuleta, the VISTA volunteer Herbie Goldfarb was quietly heading toward a nervous breakdown.

And he was going crazy, not because of Joe Mondragón's beanfield, but first of all because of snakes, and secondly because of his next door neighbors' rabbits and chickens.

The snakes Herbie began to notice shortly after he had established himself in his pathetic redolent smokehouse. More specifically, he really noticed them when, upon sliding into his sleeping bag one night, his feet jammed up against a squirming pile of chilly coils. Squealing hysterically, he grappled clear of the sleeping bag, crashed blindly into the wall and bounced onto the floor, almost fainted, and started to cry. Eventually, though, Herbie had the presence of mind to drag his sleeping bag outside and shake it hard; he shuddered as four skinny little water snakes blinked puzzledly up into his flashlight beam.

Next morning, Herbie awoke to find two small snakes snoozing in the middle of his floor. Grabbing them by their tails, he dropped them almost instantly, blurting falsetto eeks because they had wriggled back up to nip him with their toothless little mouths. And then, trembling uncontrollably, the volunteer spent the next eight hours mixing mud in a wheelbarrow (borrowed from Joe Mondragón) and caulking up all the inside holes around the foundation of his "home."

"I never saw so many snakes in my life," he chattered nervously to Joe, who merely shrugged and loaned him a shovel, saying, "If they bother you, just chop the little motherfuckers into pieces with this."

"Oh, I wouldn't want to kill them," the pacifist said unhappily. "I mean, they're not poisonous or anything . . ."

Scornfully, Joe said, "Suit yourself."

Three days later, with an anguished groan, Herbie chopped his first snake in two: it had been curled up on his sleeping bag, happily snoozing in the glow of his bodily warmth, when he awoke. After hacking it apart, though, he almost vomited as he watched the two halves wriggle frantically in the dust. Desperately, Herbie banged away at the serpent with his shovel until all the pieces were stilled. "Don't tread on me," he remembered sickly. And: "United we stand . . ."

Suddenly the snakes were everywhere. Short, skinny, and harmless, they were still snakes. They became a bona fide nightmare. They were the first creatures Herbie saw when he opened his door each morning, sunning themselves on his stoop or lethargically arranged in the dust beside his house with green webbed feet poking out of their mouths and their eyes popping out of misshapen heads as they tried to swallow frogs. Usually they slithered under his house or off toward the irrigation ditch whenever his shadow fell across their bodies. Occasionally, though, they coiled up like rattlesnakes and hissed, scaring the volunteer half to death. And these he chopped up with a fatalistic but raging vengeance.

The days grew warm, the snakes multiplied like guppies. They surged over the irrigation ditch banks like Mongol hordes of yore. Herbie walked on tiptoe, eyes trained on the ground, terrified. Abhorring the violence in his blood, he nevertheless allowed his shovel to become like a killing instrument from the

French Revolution. And, dreaming that snakes were crawling in his eyes and out his nose and through his body like a hose, he woke up whimpering, hollow-eyed, his body and his spirit swiftly flagging.

Then, at the height of the snake plague around Herbie's stinking bungalow, a miracle occurred. A moth-eaten, dog-eared, sleepy-eyed, bow-legged, nausea-yellow cat beleaguered by angry noisy magpies appeared one morning and systematically started to butcher the snakes. The cat showed up early and sat in the dust beside the house, ignoring the magpies that kept pecking its tail as it waited for the snakes to emerge and start sunning themselves. When a reptile was drawn forth by the sun's warm rays, the cat quietly walked over, placed a paw slightly behind the snake's head, bit through its tiny skull with a nonchalant crunch, and passively chewed up the rest of its short squirming body as if chomping up a licorice stick.

Within a week this grubby yellow animal had committed genocide on the snakes, blitzing Herbie's digs. Whereupon, with an unperturbed flick of its flea-bitten tail, the cat—still hounded by a brace of black-and-white birds—disappeared.

Which is precisely when the chicken slaughter began.

Herbie's next door neighbors Pancho and Stella Armijo owned about thirty young chickens. Earlier in the springtime they had purchased unsexed mail-order chicks because the birds came cheaper unsexed. Naturally, about half the batch had grown up to be roosters, which would one day be killed and put into the freezer. But there was no point in killing them until they started crowing and nailing the pullets and fighting each other.

True to his run of luck this particular summer, Herbie just happened to settle in Milagro at about the same time the Armijos' fifteen roosters came of age. And so, abruptly, starting every morning about three, there began a racket—to which the Armijos were apparently inured—that sounded to Herbie (hollow-eyed, gaunt, and aching from night-long bouts with dog-bark and skunk-odor and snake-nightmare in-somnia) as if a herd of raging, feathered monsters the size of buffaloes, uttering bloodcurdling war whoops, were about to stampede through his grim hovel, reducing everything to pulp and ashes. To combat the ruckus, Herbie first stuck fingers in his ears, then he tried some tiny cotton wads. But the cock-a-doodle-dos pierced both his thick adobe walls and the cotton wadding, and in short order the shrill cries had made his exhausted brain feel all foamy, like a vanilla milkshake.

As the sun rose each morning, the fifteen roosters quit heralding dawn and started their mortal combat. They scrawked, bleated, screamed, flapped, and flut-tered, slashing at, and bashing into, each other's eye-balls and jugular veins. While the roosters shrieked, the hens scrambled helter-skelter, commenting shrilly on the action: they clucked hysterically; they cackled obscenely; sometimes their alarmed voices were like machine guns.

Finally, as—unable to stand the fowl cacophony any longer—Herbie crawled dazedly clear of his raunchy sleeping bag and opened his creaking door to launch a feeble protest into crisp early-morning breezes, the fucking began.

And that was a hullabaloo to end all hullabaloos!

As the volunteer swayed in his doorway, dust and feathers from the dawn combat clogged the air and, like as not, a piece of bloody plumage would drift into Herbie's nostril, condemning him to chest-wrenching sneezes for the next six hours. Be that as it may, red-eyed and dully cringing in his doorway, Herbie could only stare helplessly at the sexual holo-caust taking place in his neighbors' pen. For the roosters, after months of peaceful childhood and ado-lescence, had suddenly become inhabited both by dev-ils and by an insatiable appetite for feathered pussy, and this combination caused them to go positively gaga with lust. Some of the hens tried to escape, flapping and scrawking like puritanical virgins run-ning amuck; others crouched and spread their wings, popeyed and gurgling as the roosters jumped them, grabbing the backs of their heads with cruel beaks, tearing shoulder feathers out with their claws, humping away like medieval stir crazy beings in an amoral time of plague. Chickens collided and shrieked; they catapulted sideways, rolling and tumbling and flopping in agony and in ecstasy; feathers exploded into the air as if shot from cannons, and droplets of blood—as if spewed by underground geysers—littered the air with crimson.

Stunned by the erotic Armageddon, Herbie teetered abjectly, miserably, totally befuddled. Before the first week was out, all the hens had bloody heads and bare, pimply backs. And it was then that the abattoir scene commenced.

With a hammer and two threepenny nails in hand, Stella Armijo emerged from her low adobe farmhouse one morning while Herbie reclined on his front stoop trying to read a book. Crossing her yard to a large rust-colored stump, she quickly drove the two nails side-by-side into the block, then sat down on a nearby sawhorse to sharpen her ax with a file. When Herbie first heard that melody of the file against axblade steel, he should have retreated to the gloomy insides of his stinking little house. Instead, a strange compulsion held him where he was and, already queasy, doomed to witness the crude brutal demise of his early-morning tormentors, he waited for the sword to fall.

Stella had shut the chickens inside their coop the night before. Now she entered the shack carrying an empty burlap feed sack. An outraged commotion followed. Blowing breast feathers off the bangs covering her forehead, Stella emerged moments later lugging a bulging sack, which she carted over to the rust-colored stump. There, forsaking all preliminary rituals, the woman withdrew a rooster, stepped onto the mouth of the sack so the other birds couldn't escape, fitted the rooster's head between the two nails and, holding the bird by its legs, she pulled the body out until the neck was taut; then raised the ax and with one crunchy blow—*shtok!*—she beheaded the chicken and chucked the body unceremoniously into a nearby pile of wood chips where the wings flapped crazily as blood—driven, no doubt, by the heart's last fervid memories of yesterday's torrid balling—spurted from the neck.

It was like that, one after another—*shtok! shtok! shtok!*—the blade repeatedly tunking neatly through feathers, flesh, and bone so quickly that even before Herbie could go into shock over the first execution, the last had been performed. A pair of bloody wings staccatoed out a final energetic protest and fell still, and only a pair of warty yellow legs still quivered . . . and kept quivering . . . and continued quivering endlessly, like appendages somehow related to tuning forks.

After perfunctorily wiping her hands on her apron, Stella trotted inside, returning shortly with a large cauldron of boiling water. She dipped each beheaded rooster in the water, then plucked it so savagely Herbie winced at each tear, at the sound of damp feathers popping from thick puckered skin. Then she drove a long knife into each carcass's ass, twisted the blade once, reached inside, and, with a single sharp jerk, yanked out the guts and tossed them to the Armijos' ugly, pug-faced, cocker-bodied dog, Esperanza, who greedily gobbled them up while Herbie's own guts did loop-the-loops.

The chicken yard was noticeably subdued the rest of that day. Hens, slouching around mooney-eyed and sad, pecked desultorily at little bugs; the surviving roosters lay in small craters of dust and curdled lust with their heads tucked back between their shoulder blades, the hothouse riots in their blood considerably cooled by chill presentiments of mortality, their doomed fertility dripping from once brightwild eyes like tears. Somehow, incredibly, they all suddenly looked almost senile, feeble beyond belief. And Herbie, who only yesterday had dreamed of wringing all their necks, dreamed today of kidnapping them so no more would die such cruel, degrading deaths.

Next morning, following the 3:00 A.M. cock-a-doodle delirium and the 5:00 A.M. civil war, there came a 7:00 A.M. death orgy. This time Herbie stayed put in his pestilential sleeping bag. All the same, he shuddered, his body actually twitching spasmodically with each resonant *shtok!* as he learned that imagining a scene is often worse than being an actual spectator to it.

When finally the volunteer roused himself and staggered outside, there was nothing but blood on the ground and feathers scattered everywhere like apple blossoms. A dusty gloom hung over the chicken pen where the five remaining roosters uneasily preened their gorgeous feathers as they waited for the Angel of Death to chop, pluck, and disembowel their youthful, awakening bodies.

Right about then, Herbie realized that the large raised pen beyond the Armijos' chicken compound was a rabbit hutch. And as his eyes focused on all the gentle gray shapes slowly hopping around in that compartmentalized wire pen, his heart did another flip-flop. After all, if the roosters were dying like flies, could the bunnies be far behind?

His premonitions soon proved to be grounded in fact. Came a morning when—half in a doze, exhausted from lack of sleep—Herbie heard a curious thock-crunch sound, then a faint plop, followed by a nauseating scuffling noise. He sat up, immediately the thing happened again; thock-crunch . . . plop . . . scuffle-scuffle-scuffle.

Fearing the worst, Herbie tiptoed to his door and opened it a crack. There stood Stella Armijo, a two-foot piece of lead pipe gripped tightly in her brawny fist, over by the bunny bin, methodically annihilating the cute little critters.

One by one, and quite gently, she removed them from the hutch, set them on a thick wooden table, stroked them a few times to ease their dread, and then—*thock-crunch!*—busted their stupid little brains apart with a single curt blow of the pipe and dropped their quivering bodies onto the ground—*plop*—where their legs continued to kick and skid for a moment in the dust: *scuffle-scuffle-scuffle.*

When she had a pile of seven, Stella gutted and skinned and cleaned the rabbits as unconcernedly as she had denuded and disemboweled the roosters. After that, drenched to the elbows in bunny gore, she sat down and smoked a cigarette with a placid, beautiful look on her broad face, a look so queer and detached it made Herbie's testicles whimper as they shrank up higher into his shriveled scrotum.

But after a certain number of rabbits had been pogrommed, an almost supernatural peace descended over the neighboring barnyard.

It was a peace that only lasted about eight minutes. Because as soon as all the rooster feathers and bunny fur had been blown from the chopping block dust into the tangled branches of the cottonwood vivisecting Herbie's outhouse, the Armijos' dog, Esperanza, went into heat. This meant that every one-legged, mangy, half-blind, oversexed, lice-infested, ferocious or whimpering, crippled or groveling or man-eating canine entity within fifteen miles, whose olfactory senses and/or penis were functioning, appeared and laid siege to the Armijo house in hopes of getting a shot at Esperanza.

To complicate matters, on the same day Esperanza went into heat, Pancho Armijo came home with a brown milk goat. This wasn't his idea—Pancho hated goats. But Stella wanted the milk for yogurt. So Pancho locked the goat in the shed next door to the henhouse, which was also surrounded by the chicken pen's wire fence. The goat walked around the shed once, then jumped through the glass panes in the upper half of the door. And, after circling the chicken wire pen once, it took two dainty steps backward and, with an effortless leap, sailed over the four-foot-high barrier. The goat then trotted into Herbie's yard and ate a copy of *Portnoy's Complaint,* which the volunteer had carelessly left on his front stoop during a foray into town for baloney, beer, and cheese.

Stella Armijo boarded up the shed door, caught and reimprisoned the goat, strung two barbed wire strands above the chicken wire, and released the goat again.

Meanwhile, about thirty of the world's most pathetic mongrels were slinking around the immediate neighborhood with hard-ons. Herbie had just bought a bicycle, which Joe Mondragón had resurrected from the town dump, and the dogs pissed over it so much it got rusty in a day and all the paint peeled off and the black rubber tires bleached out white. The dogs also peed on Herbie's shack, but the permanent skunk smell on the premises was so strong the volunteer hardly noticed.

Pancho Armijo had tied Esperanza to a rope in the front yard, and whenever he or Stella caught mutts creeping on their filthy bellies toward her, they stampeded out of the house shooting birdshot from a .410 shotgun. So for a while there was sporadic gunfire, followed by earsplitting yelps, and this went on both day and night. Herbie writhed and tossed in his sleep; he began to duck—asleep or awake—at the slightest noise. In fact, he hardly dared exit, even for food, lest a wayward shotgun pellet nip his delicate aesthetic life in the bud.

Despite this birdshot barrage, the male dogs kept sneaking around with their slanty bloodshot eyes dripping vile lusting mucus, and with their swollen testicles pulsating anxiously. They were jealous of each other also; hence, the general pandemonium was continually being garnished by one snarling dogfight or another, all taking place just outside the perimeter of shotgun range.

At least four dogs made it to the Promised Land daily. At which point truly demented melees occurred. The first time he heard the sort of uproar these dogs made scoring, Herbie raced outside to discover that three sex-starved hounds were trying to hump Esperanza at once. She howled, maybe from pleasure, more likely from pain, as the males fought among themselves, going for each other's jugular veins while their hind ends pumped wildly, searching for a hole. One hand clasped to his head, Herbie had leaned weakly against his wall, overcome by such abandoned savagery, when Stella Armijo sailed through her portal with the shotgun, both barrels of which she emptied at the two fleeing curs. The third, which was the only one to have struck paydirt, had also somehow gotten stuck and could not withdraw. Wailing terrifiedly, he thrashed about in the dust, taking poor Esperanza with him, kicking his legs insanely, trying to dismount and run, while Esperanza, in pain now and squealing hysterically, snapped frenziedly at him with her sharp teeth.

Stella took her time reloading the gun, then ambled over to the mess and kicked the male so hard his penis tore loose from Esperanza, catapulting him end over end three times; and, before he could regain his feet, she blew his brains out.

Then, while Stella dragged the dead animal into the back field, heartless Esperanza just sat there in the dust, unconcernedly licking her cunt.

Later that same day, about the time Herbie had finally recovered enough from the morning's trauma to eat a can of beans, the new milk goat ate a hole in the chicken wire pen allowing eight prize egglayers to walk out into freedom where they were promptly drawn and quartered (in another shrieking, yelping, feather-flying extravaganza) by the same rabidly panting dogs gunning after Esperanza's tail.

Herbie's teeth chattered, and he wondered: Am I beginning to suffer from shellshock? Will they send me for R and R in Japan?

Next day, a skinny German shepherd that had been lured into the vicinity by Esperanza's scent caught a paw in the bear trap Pancho Armijo maintained under the rabbit hutch to catch any stray dogs that developed a taste for his cottontails. Esperanza was locked in the house, both Armijos were gone, and so the trapped dog wailed in pain all day, each of its woeful howls like an arrow piercing Herbie's sensitive breast. Several times he traipsed over to aid the dog, but even though he had good intentions and tried to convey this by talking soothingly and offering the animal hash to eat, the dog only bared its fangs, and Herbie couldn't get close.

Toward 3:00 P.M., unable to stand the racket any longer, the volunteer stumbled over to the Mondragón's house, where he blurted out the situation to Nancy, who fetched a pistol from a kitchen drawer and followed Herbie to the hutch.

When the dog saw her it quit yowling, its eyes grew heavy-lidded, almost sad. Although its neck hairs continued bristling, it looked almost friendly, almost gentle, damn near serene. Nancy cocked her gun, taking careful aim at the quiet shepherd, and when the gun went off the dog's legs splayed out in four directions dropping it onto its stomach dead as a doornail.

"That's what somebody should do to the Zopilote," was Nancy's only comment as she nodded tersely to Herbie and jogged home to hang up her laundry.

Two days after that, just as Herbie was beginning to think a cease-fire had been declared, Stella Armijo, Joe Mondragón, and Onofre Martínez castrated the Armijo's three little pigs. The deballing occurred quite early one morning, shortly after Herbie had at last achieved a sort of painful, but at least semicomatose, state. The sound that jarred the volunteer from his reveries was a terrified bleating squeal such as movie vampire victims are wont to make as the fangs of cackling necrophiliacs puncture their breasts or jugular veins. Jolted upright, Herbie—from force of habit —released a petrified squeak himself, then staggered to the door and opened it a crack. He was in time to watch as Joe, straddling a hog-tied animal, made a second slit in the pig's scrotum, reached inside, and tugged out one testicle, cut a cord, and chucked the testicle to another hobbled pig nearby, who promptly ate it.

Herbie retreated; he huddled in a fetal position atop his sleeping bag. If I survive this, he thought, it will be a miracle; and he wondered if things would have been more peaceful in Vietnam.

❧

The Milagro church stood on the west side, at the end of the original town square, fronting a wide open space lined on both sides by lovely old houses with wide portals, the town's long-ago heart, deserted now, dusty, dilapidated, and forlorn.

But on this day an old man named Pancracio "Panky" Mondragón, no relation to Joe (although he was the grandfather of one of Nancy's first cousins,

Larry Mondragón), turned a large iron key in the
massive rusted lock and pushed the door open, allowing a bright flood of eastern sunlight to dance in and
start raising havoc with the dusty air. Once he had
opened the door, Panky stood there, gazing fondly
at the simple church. A Warm Morning Ben Frank-
lin stove occupied the centermost floor space; a few
rows of rickety wooden benches were aligned on
either side of the stove. The altar was covered by a
simple linen cloth; above it hung a plain wooden
cross. Two arched, narrow, plain glass windows were
set into the side walls. Between the windows some
ancient wooden santos, and a couple of newer ones
that had been carved and painted by the expatriate
Snuffy Ledoux, were hanging.

Bluebirds fluttered high in the beams where they
had nests, and Panky spent a few minutes scraping
up their droppings with a trowel. As he was finishing
this job, the people began to arrive. First, old Amarante Córdova, wearing his mammoth pistol, limped
between ghost houses and down the plaza to the steps
of the small mud-plastered church.

"Hi, cuz," Panky muttered, and, as the two shook
hands, Amarante said, "This is a great day for the
church. This is a great day for the people."

"The people are just cutting their throats," Panky
pontificated sourly. "They are as crazy as Pacheco's
pig."

Amarante feigned astonishment.

"Well, so I came to cut my throat along with the
rest of us idiots," Panky cackled sardonically, slapping Amarante's shoulder, the force of his blow almost knocking them both over.

Next, Ruby Archuleta and the rest of the Body
Shop and Pipe Queen bunch arrived, followed closely
by Joe and Nancy Mondragón, Joe's brothers Cristóbal and Billy, and Joe's shop rats, Jimmy Ortega and
Benny Maestas. Between them the two teen-agers
supported the great-uncle, Juan F. Mondragón, who
muttered dire warnings of doom every inch of the way
from the pickup to the pew. Ray Gusdorf showed up
with his neighbors Tobías Arguello and Gomersindo

Leyba. Tranquilino Jeantete came, as did his night-time barmaid at the Frontier, Teofila Chacón, who had seven of her thirteen children in tow. After her, the Staurolite Baron with the infamous missing arm, Onofre Martínez, appeared, gestured obscenely at his son Bruno Martínez, the state cop (who was parked nearby keeping an eye on things), and entered the church. Others who came early were Amarante Córdova's dying son, Ricardo; the man who cooked for Harlan Betchel in the Pilar Café and tied fishing flies on the side, Fred Quintana; the Pilar waitress, Betty Apodaca, and her husband, Pete; and a lot of old men with names like Sparky Pacheco, Eloy Mascarenas, Floyd Gabaldón, Felix Ruiz, Amadeo Valdéz, and Paul Romero.

By the time Charley Bloom arrived, perhaps fifty pickups and other vehicles in various terminal stages of decay were parked in front of the church between the empty crumbling houses; and at the eastern end of this improvised parking lot, Bruno Martínez and Granny Smith lounged sloppily against their state police car, indolently smoking cigarettes.

Bloom had to park close to the cops. With his arms full of rolled-up hydrographical survey maps, he got out and started for the church. Granny Smith moved toward Bloom and, nodding at the maps, asked, "What's all that crap for? What's this meeting about, anyway?"

"It's just some stuff," Bloom mumbled, hurrying —almost sprinting—toward the church.

"Hey, wait a minute—" Bruno called, but Bloom refused to acknowledge that he had heard. By the time the lawyer reached the steps, however, he was trembling almost uncontrollably, although nothing else had happened.

Still, Bloom figured as he entered the church that he was now truly a marked man. And he wanted to throw his maps at all the shriveled old bastards waiting patiently with their crumpled sweat-stained hats in their laps for him to arrive; he wanted to do that and then run away.

Amarante Córdova was already talking to the approximately seventy-five people present, most of them either middle-aged or quite old men, interspersed by a few women, and maybe a dozen kids.

"We didn't ask for this problem," Amarante croaked in his garbled Spanish. "It came and landed on us like an eagle lands on a prairie dog. But we aren't gonna be like no prairie dogs, we're not gonna dig a hole and hide our heads from the Zopilote and his Zopilotitos, Jerry Grindstaff and Harlan Betchel and Jimmy Hirsshorn and other people like that. We're gonna *fight*!"

He paused, coughed, and nobody stirred. It was hard to tell if they had heard—probably most of them, being so old, were pretty deaf, and even if they weren't deaf, it was six of one, half-dozen of the other as to what Amarante, with his three teeth and un-grammatical, butchered, ninety-three-year-old Spanish, was saying in the first place. But everyone had the air, at least, of listening respectfully.

"I'm not gonna faint in the middle of the road and wave a white handkerchief!" Amarante suddenly hollered, but then he started to cough so dramatically he couldn't continue his flamboyant oration. In fact, the fit gathered so much steam so swiftly that he had to stagger over to the altar and grab hold of it to keep from falling. At which point everybody in the church leaned forward expectantly, no doubt thinking in unison: Ahah! *Now* is when the crafty old devil is finally going to perform for us the miracle of drop-ping dead!

But although Amarante could not recover, neither was he about to die. And finally Ruby Archuleta and Onofre Martínez ushered him to a seat in the first pew, where he sat hunched over with tears in his eyes, intermittently rumbling for the duration of the meet-ing.

Ruby Archuleta then took the floor. "Listen, friends," she began. "You all know what's been hap-pening in the valley. You remember when this church was the heart of a town that no longer truly exists. You remember the days when we were not rich, but when poverty was different, not a thing to be ashamed of, and we got along okay. You remember when we had a certain freedom, and you know we don't have it anymore, and you remember when our children grew up and stayed home and raised their children in Milagro. Well, look at us now. We're a congregation of old men and old women and where have all our children gone?"

She paused, pacing back and forth in front of them.

"Listen, my friends, my cousins," Ruby continued quietly. "My little grandmothers and my little grandfathers. I love you. But when I wake up in the morning sometimes I want to cry. I think of recent history, and then I think of this Indian Creek Dam and the Indian Creek Conservancy District, and I know that if they come about it will be the end for most of us. And I cannot bear to let this happen without a fight. We are old, and many of us are tired, we have been on welfare too long, and food stamps have sapped our pride and dulled our fighting spirit. I know the conservancy district and the dam are difficult to understand, but our response to complexity can no longer be, 'Well, that's just the way things are, what can we do about it?' I have spent too much of my life watching bad things happen to us, to my people. I know our problems. And at this point I think we have become a little like land that has been overgrazed, or like land that hasn't been planted correctly or fertilized for many years, and so it has lost its richness, becoming thin and weak and played out; there are no more vitamins in the soil, and all the crops growing out of it are poorer each year—"

Ruby stopped, losing the thread, confused in her own metaphor, aware of saying incorrectly what needed to be said. She was scared, too, because she had never really spoken to a group before, and because she was worried that a woman should not be saying these things, and that maybe because she was a woman with a mysterious history who lived outside the town proper they would refuse to listen.

Suddenly she changed her tack.

"Look, I'm not saying it right, I know that I'm not our leader. I want to do what's good and I want to fight in whatever way the people want to fight, that's all. I'm speaking now because we haven't chosen a leader. But maybe there's somebody who can speak better than me, who would like to talk now about these things?"

They stared at her impassively, in absolute silence, for a good thirty seconds.

"Alright," she said gently. "I had an idea before I came to the meeting. I was hoping maybe we could form ourselves into a group, and I thought we might call our group something like the Milagro Land and Water Protection Association, I don't know. We'll think about that, and maybe we can have an election at the end of the meeting or sometime soon. Maybe, too, we can elect the officers of our association, if we choose to make ourselves that, and we can discuss future meetings. But right now I asked somebody to talk to us, because he has written articles about this dam and he understands the conservancy district better than me, and perhaps he can help us all understand the technicalities, so we'll know what we're up against. As you know, he lives with us here in Milagro, and I consider that he is on our side—"

Charley Bloom went to the front; Ruby smiled and shook his hand and sat down—he faced the people. Their familiar faces were neither hard nor soft. Searching for glints of humor, for smiles, for compassion, he could not find any. Their faces seemed so old, so dark, calling forth overworked clichés about the earth and the sky and the wind. Old, wrinkled, simple, profound. Bloom was afraid of these neighbors, feeling simultaneously superior and less of a man. God help him not to sound either patronizing or defensive! He knew they were weary and frightened, too, but on no one face did this seem evident, and he was afraid that he broadcast it from his body as if someone had painted him a Day-Glo chickenshit yellow that shone in the dark. Although he knew many of them must lead confused and desperate lives (wasn't his own wife Linda an example?), he still could not help but feel they were confident men and women who believed in themselves, holding in their lives to truths that were self-evident and irrefutable. He sensed, too, that they were unafraid of danger and of dying, and this they held over him more than anything. A part of him knew he was wrong, knew that he did no credit to these friends and neighbors (as he had done no credit to his wife) by romanticizing them just as they probably romanticized him, but he couldn't help it. He envied them because they were different from him, and because, despite their poverty, their language and their culture seemed to offer a viable and dignified alternative. Looking at them, he translated their faces into a strength he had once hoped somehow to marry into.

But then, too, there was this thing in Bloom: at heart, and especially today after that tête-à-tête with Bruno Martínez, the lawyer did not want to commit himself to these hostile, impervious old people; he had no desire to carve some kind of niche for himself on the state police shit list because of their dead houses and their pathetic abandoned beanfields.

But he was willing to do it anyway, and he really did not understand why. He was simply caught, trapped, wishy-washy, doomed.

Apologizing for his bad grammar, Bloom began to speak in Spanish, knowing even as he did so that his Spanish was much more formal and correct and classical than their own; knowing also that he could read books and newspapers in Spanish, and write letters in that language, whereas most of them could not; they were illiterate in Spanish as well as in English; very few had progressed as far as the fifth or sixth grade.

Ruby Archuleta and her son Eliu, Ricardo Córdova, and Tranquilino Jeantete held up the maps while he spoke. Tracing the conservancy district boundaries, the lawyer showed where the dam would be constructed, and then ran down who owned each piece of land within the district. He repeated himself, talking slowly, trying to make a very confusing thing simple and clear. He tried to make them understand technically what they all knew instinctively, that they were going to be taxed heavily for water which would be used mostly by a very few people, and those people would by and large be connected with the Devine empire.

Leaving the maps, then, Bloom talked about the history of the north, about land grants and how they had been lost, strayed, or stolen, divvied up. He named thieves and quoted statistics, working hard to relate what he knew of the far past and the near past to the present. He spoke of sociological trends in Chamisa County, in the entire United States. He ran down for them a history of other conservancy districts in the state which had effectively destroyed subsistence farmers by forcing them into cash economies where they could not compete. He did everything possible to probe and expose the hypocritical rhetoric surrounding the Indian Creek Dam—the state engineer's pronouncement, for example, that it was "the only way to save a dying culture." He tried to demonstrate how the conservancy district and the dam was just one more component of the economic and sociological machinery which for a long time had been driving local small farmers off their land and out of Chamisa County. He quoted figures about per capita income and median incomes; he outlined what the real costs of the dam could balloon into, and broke those costs down to an amount per acre, per year, per person, regardless of that person's wealth. He explained how the proposed Ladd Devine Miracle Valley project would drive their land values sky high, and what that would do to their taxes. He told them that when middle-class or wealthy people from other states bought expensive vacation homes up in the canyon or around the golf course on the subdivided west side, they would want a school for their children, sewage systems, a cleaner water supply, and for that *all* the people of Milagro would have to pay. And once the ski valley was completed there would be pressure to raise taxes for a better road up to it. And Bloom did his best to question the myth that this development would bring wealth to every inhabitant, and jobs and security for all. For forty years, in Chamisa County, there had been a tourist boom: and yet most of the profits went into a few pockets at the top. Skilled construction workers and technicians were always brought in from outside. For the poor and the rural people little had changed, except that in taking service jobs for low wages they no longer had the time to work their land, and so had often wound up selling it, only to discover themselves poorer than before, with not even the security of their own land and a home on it to take the sting out of a poverty as bitter as Chamisa tea.

"In 1950 this county was 85 percent Spanish-surnamed people," Bloom said quietly. "Now it's only 60 percent Spanish-surnamed and declining fast. In 1950 the per capita income was eight hundred and seventy dollars a year; now it's one thousand two hundred and eight dollars, but that increase isn't because people are making more money, it's largely because of inflation. Actually, everyone, all the rural people, are a little poorer than before in spite of the tourist boom these past fifteen or twenty years . . ."

In the end he petered out. Their faces, perhaps paying close attention, perhaps not, never seemed to change. He couldn't tell if he was making a point, helping to explain the specific workings of what they already understood all too well in general, or if he was talking to seventy-five or a hundred walls. Judging from their expressions it occasionally seemed as if they heartily mistrusted him and hardly believed a word he was saying. Then he picked up on hostility: they were thinking, he thought, What right does this smart aleck have to come in and tell us what is happening, and what is going to happen, to our lives?

He stopped.

"Hay preguntas? Yo puedo tratar a explicarles qualquiera cosa que tal vez no entienden."

There were no questions. Incredibly, after an hour of talking, there were no questions. People shifted, coughed, did not take their eyes off him, but still seemed not to respond. He hadn't even made a dent. Embarrassed, hating them, and hating himself for getting into this thing, for butting into their affairs, for daring to think he had any answers (let alone the courage of his convictions) after only a few years in their town, Bloom sat down, thoroughly ashamed.

After thanking him, Ruby Archuleta asked, "Who wants to speak?"

Tobías Arguello creaked erect. "We are a peaceful people," he said, his voice trembling. "We don't play the Anglos in their own game because they are possessed by the devil. I have a gun, but I use it only to hunt for food. I detest violence. I don't want no more Smokey the Bear santo riots. I'm also a good American. I fought for my coutry in the First World War. I love being an American, and I am proud. I think maybe if we are violent, we are un-American. I am a man of peace. So we should be peaceful. If we don't watch out, Snuffy Ledoux will come back and start another riot. Thank you."

Sparky Pacheco stood up and, hat in hand, nervously croaked, "These goddamn Anglo bastards like the Zopilote will steal our land and everything else, our babies, and our tractors, and even—please excuse me—our testicles if we don't say 'Stop!' I for one hope Snuffy Ledoux comes back to start another Smokey the Bear santo riot!"

A smattering of voices croaked feebly: *"Que viva Snuffy!"*

Another old man said, "The gabachos, and especially their lawyers, are always deceiving us. They are full of lies."

And, a little stronger this time: *"Que viva Snuffy!"*

Panky Mondragón growled ferociously: "We deceive ourselves. We're full of our own hypocrisy and lies. For years we have stolen our land from each other and from the Indians. Men are men and women are women, to hell with the colors and languages. Charity begins at home."

A woman, Lilian Chávez, said shyly: "I am ashamed of Nick Rael and Eusebio Lavadie, and all the others who work with the Zopilote. They have betrayed my race. All the same, though. God forbid we should have another Smokey the Bear santo riot in this town."

"Que viva Snuffy!"

"Wait a minute!" Onofre Martínez stammered excitedly, emotionally placing his only hand on Ray Gusdorf's shoulder. "This is my neighbor, and he is a gringo, not even a little bit coyote. But he's been in the valley as long as I remember, and I consider him to be of my people. And that white man over there who told us these things about the dam and the conservancy and showed us the maps, I consider him to be of my people, too, even though he is a lawyer, and even though he speaks a funny Anglo Spanish you can hardly understand. But I believe he at least tries to speak the truth, and a lawyer who does that should get a big gold medal to hang around his neck. I don't consider Nick Rael to be of my people, because he works against my interests, I think. He's too busy counting money to care about the people. So I don't believe this is a brown against white question. This is only one kind of people against another kind of people with different ideas. There are brown and white people on both sides. Remember, too, there are brown chotas as well as white chotas and brown políticos as well as white políticos. People are people. My own son will roast in hell, I hope, for becoming a chota. The brown and white people on our side are better people because they are on the correct side, that's all. And if I am ashamed of Nick Rael it's only in the same way I am ashamed of Jimmy Hirsshorn and the Zopilote. If there was no Zopilote or Jimmy Hirsshorn, in their places would be a Mr. González and a Jimmy Pacheco, I think. And if I love my brother Tobías, it's only in the same manner I love my brother Ray, here, who is a good neighbor and a good human being, even if he isn't even part coyote. Let that be understood by everybody, please. And another thing: if Snuffy Ledoux comes back to start another Smokey the Bear statue riot, I'm gonna be the first to shake his hand. Que viva Snuffy!"

"Que viva Snuffy!"

And when he sat down, Onofre stared fixedly ahead, lips trembling—for he had spoken.

"Who else wants to speak?" Ruby asked.

"I wanna speak," Joe's brother Cristóbal said. "I nominate my brother José to be president of the Milagro Land and Water Protection Association."

Joe leaped up. "Oh no you don't, not me! I ain't no president!"

"You're the one with the beanfield!" Cristóbal shouted. "You started all this! If the state chotas stick a bullet in my ear, it's because of your pinche beanfield!"

"Bullshit! I didn't start nothing! *I* didn't call for this meeting! *I* didn't ask for nobody's help with my beanfield! What am I, crazy to ask for help from mental retards like you?"

"It's because he won't ask nobody to help him that he endangers us all!" Fred Quintana said.

Joe spluttered: "Oh Jesus Christ. If that's the way it's gonna be, as soon as this meeting is over I'm going to start up my tractor and drive it to the west side and plow up that beanfield and get all you people off my back!"

"You do, José," his wife Nancy threatened, "and I'll shoot you! I'll put ant poison in your enchiladas!"

"Wait a minute!" Ruby cried. "Wait just a minute, *please*—"

"We should tie José up and throw him in a closet before he wrecks everything!" Seferino Pacheco bawled.

"That's *my* beanfield!" Joe howled. "That's my private *property!* Nobody here's got a right to tell me what to do with my property!"

"Well, we'll kill you if you plow under those beans!" Sparky Pacheco fairly screamed.

There ensued a sudden silence as these words echoed in the church. By now, half the congregation was standing.

"Well . . ." Joe pouted, "I still ain't gonna be no president."

"There wasn't even a motion on the floor to make ourselves an association," Ruby soothed. "This is no time to vote for a president when there's nothing to be president of."

"Why are we shouting at each other?" Tobías Arguello asked softly. "We should be peaceful."

Panky Mondragón explained, "We're not shouting at each other anymore, so siddown."

Tobías held his ground. "I got a right to speak. This is an open meeting—"

"But we're not shouting anymore," Panky snarled. "So you can siddown. And besides, you're blocking my view."

"When I'm ready to sit down, I'll sit down—"

"You siddown!" Panky shouted, waving a fist. *"We're not shouting anymore, dammit!"*

Lilian Chávez asked, "How can we steal eggs from the Zopilote's nest when you idiots are fighting about who's shouting or not?"

And Onofre Martínez stood up again. "Outside, my evil son, the state chota, is having a good laugh because we're all growing donkey ears in here. Now you take me personally, I get sick to my stomach whenever that chota son of mine has a chuckle at my expense. So I'm sorry to say that if everybody doesn't shut up pretty soon and sit down, I'm gonna barf."

For some reason, Onofre's attitude, tone of voice, words, or all three taken together did the trick. Muttering unhappily, everyone sat down, folded their hands in their laps, and returned their quiet, sullen (though pious) attention to the front.

"Alright," Ruby Archuleta said calmly. "Does anyone wish to talk quietly and in turn, first about this Milagro Land and Water Protection Association, and second about electing leaders?"

Tranquilino Jeantete arose, taking forever to adjust his hearing aid and clear his throat. "These are probably good ideas but we should think about them and talk among ourselves for a while before deciding."

The rest of the gathering nodded, murmured, stirred about, ready for fresh air.

"Alright," Ruby said quietly, frowning warily. "Then I guess this meeting is over."

"Que viva Snuffy!" Sparky Pacheco cried, as everyone else got up to go.

◦౭

In the evening, after the church meeting, Joe Mondragón finished eating supper and, with his six-year-old son Larry in tow and a basketball under one arm, he walked up the road to the elementary school basketball court at the foot of Capulin Hill.

Usually on summer evenings before dark there would be enough men and boys around for a game. But today only Benny Maestas and Jimmy Ortega, and Joe's twenty-eight-year-old cousin, Floyd Mondragón, were at the court laconically shooting baskets. After mumbling subdued hellos, Joe stood at the edge of the dirt court with Larry's hand tucked tightly into his own, reluctant to step out and begin. The sunset, rosy, orange, nacreous in spots, flecked with pastel blues and streaks of lavender and blood, reflected gorgeously in those few school windows not yet broken. From this vantage point slightly above town you cauld see uninterruptedly across the mercury-colored mesaland, pocked occasionally with juniper bushes, bisected by that thin dark crack of a gorge, and stretching westward for smooth, dusty-soft miles to the dim ice cream-mound mountains and buttes beyond which the sun was slowly floating into its kaleidoscopic oblivion. In the foreground, black silhouettes, the two boys and Joe's cousin, moved in a lazy kind of athletic ballet. In a drowsy, almost slow-motion way they dribbled once or twice, stuttered their bodies in that lovely, almost awkward, jerky syncopation peculiar to basketball players, and pumped, moving heads and shoulders in careless automatic fakes, then rose casually off their toes and shot, the ball leaving their delicately fluttering fingertips and hanging for a long time in the air like a black moon—

Joe lit a cigarette and stepped onto the dirt court; Larry sat down and began building a road in the dirt. Sometimes a lot of kidding went on during these evening sessions; usually people felt noisy, obscene, or full of horseplay. But tonight they nodded, barely speaking to each other as they moved loosely around on the court, seldom breaking into anything more energetic than a brief trot, keeping the two balls floating lazily toward the basket, which had no net, only a bent rim. Joe entered automatically into the low-key rhythm, grunting occasionally, making the briefest of small talk, and taking care not to exert himself. It was a relief not to be in a competitive situation, not to be driving wildly, fighting, swearing torrents, sticky with dust. So he made baskets, and walked around getting out the kinks from an afternoon spent behind an acetylene torch, passed to the others and received passes from them, loped in for almost gentle lay-ups, or raised one knee lifting off his other toe for drowsy hook shots, and he felt okay, flipping his cigarette away only when it threatened to burn his lips and lighting another almost immediately.

It was a warm evening—the two boys had taken off their shirts, and after a while Joe stripped also. The sun departed altogether, leaving the mesaland black, but the mountains still glowed. A persistent flicker called; some nighthawks, flashing bright white spots on their narrow, knifelike wings, dipsy-doodled overhead. The moon was already up, round, white, and beautiful like a thin transparent wafer. Mosquitoes had been out in force for a while, but after the sun died they were chased into hiding by the suddenly crisp darkness. Then the night grew chilly and the players put their shirts back on.

The moon shone brightly and stars were scattered like luminous snowflakes in the pale cloudless sky. They were all used to shooting baskets in this kind of white night. There was no sound now in the early-night hush, except for their feet scraping laxly through the dust, their clothes rustling as they grunted softly and sent the ball toward the basket. Shadows to each other, they flowed gently through the velvet air, momentarily at peace, working together, in tune.

But then Joe noticed something. The others were deferring to him, allowing him the clean shot, giving him back the ball more often than they gave it back to each other. When Joe shot they held the other ball so as not to interrupt his effort. Small gestures, to be sure, but suddenly Joe recognized them for what they were, gestures of respect, and they bothered him a little. What was happening to his life? Was he turning into somebody special? This wasn't the first time he had noticed. Would they force him to become a leader? A president?—*Ai, Chihuahua!* He didn't want their respect; they could take their responsibility and shove it. After all, if he had made such a mess out of his own life so far, what was the point of implicating others?

Plus he was afraid. The whole thing had gotten out of hand. He would like to have punched his brother for making that fucking suggestion in the church, and Ruby Archuleta wanted to pass around a petition, and down in the capital the políticos and the chotas and who knew who else were trying to figure out how to brand his ass—

Not—of course—that Joe didn't sort of enjoy the attention. After all, wasn't it about time somebody aroused this apathetic community's penchant for fire and brimstone? But Joe still could not foresee what might happen, he had no idea how to handle a big crisis if one developed, and he wished somebody else would be the leader in this thing. Like Ruby Archuleta; or even Charley Bloom, what the hell—fight Anglos with Anglos. Anybody except himself, that is, because frankly, he was too scared and too stupid to handle it.

Fuck it, Joe thought. And he quit playing because their subtle deferential treatment made him nervous. Larry was sitting happily on a mound, staring at the sky, singing "Twinkle, Twinkle, Little Star." Joe seated himself on a metal crossbar to which a seesaw had once been attached, popped open a beer his cousin Floyd had brought, and smoked a cigarette while the others continued to pad quietly around, dreamily and contentedly shooting baskets in the vibrant, sweet-smelling dark.

What happened next none of the basketball players could later agree on. But a number of men ("There was only three," Floyd said; "There must of been at least a dozen!" Joe insisted) suddenly burst from the darkness and beat the living daylights out of Joe and his cousin and the two teen-agers. Straight off, Joe caught a chain across his face and dropped like a sack of potatoes—for a second he blacked out. Both Benny Maestas and Jimmy Ortega were whacked with crude clubs, and Benny's nose was broken; Jimmy sustained a huge bruise on his arm trying to ward off the blows. Joe's cousin Floyd was banged once in the ass, then he took off like an antelope down the hill, and the men didn't bother to chase him. And that was all: in half a minute the rumble had ended, their attackers disappeared.

Little Larry was sitting in his sandpile crying, Joe was doubled over on the ground gasping, Jimmy Ortega was wailing about his arm, and Benny Maestas, his face covered with blood, his eyes staring at a damp switchblade knife in his hand that he thought maybe he had stuck into one of those bastards, was propped against a basket pole, snarling epithets.

"They were Chicanos," Joe said bitterly fifteen minutes later, slumped in a kitchen chair while Nancy sponged off his face and rubbed salve into his ribs. "I heard those mothers say something in Spanish."

"Screw you, they had Anglo accents," Benny Maestas spat bitterly. "They smelled like hippies to me."

Floyd Mondragón was still trembling. "What did they want to do that for?" he whined miserably, ashamed at having fled.

"They wanted José," Jimmy Ortega groaned from the living room couch. "The Zopilote must of sent those sons of bitches to get José."

Benny Maestas was still staring at his knife with the dried blood on the tip. And then—only then—did he notice the small hole and circle of caked blood around it in his Levi's. "Oh shit!" he exclaimed, whipping loose his belt and dropping his pants and staring at the deep puncture in his thigh: "I fucking stabbed *myself*!"

◆

One-armed Onofre Martínez lived with his three-legged German shepherd in a three-room adobe house only three hundred yards from the center of town.

The house was set on a half-acre landscaped like Shangri-la. No place in town had more gimcracks, doodads, and gewgaws crammed into less space in a more orderly fashion than Onofre's spread. He called it Chateau Martínez: at least, that's what the fancy wooden sign (sculptured years ago by the presently absent santo carver Snuffy Ledoux) over the front gate said. The gingerbread universe beyond the gate boasted a little Astroturf lawn, a dozen fruit trees, several aspens, some cottonwoods, a few Chinese elms, a horse corral, a half-dozen beehives and a shack for processing honey, a toolshed and a small lush garden growing corn, squash, beets, chilies, pumpkins, and strawberries, a picturesque well housing near the front door, a patch of raspberries so the bees could make raspberry honey, a chicken pen containing eight pullets, three turkeys, and a guinea hen . . . and there were also flower beds everywhere, not to mention birdhouses and hummingbird feeders and the dozen or so bats that were always snoozing behind the green wooden shutters flanking all the windows. To boot, Onofre's TV antenna was so tall, so elaborate, so pronged, and so replete with squiggling copper and aluminum tubing and boosters, that it looked like a DEW-line radar interceptor in Greenland. Onofre's half-acre also had room for seven of the widest and highest piles of piñon firewood in the county. All this was surrounded by a white picket fence built so sturdily that the Chateau Martínez was the only place in town which had *never* been desecrated by Pacheco's pig.

Inside the house Onofre had a large library of both Spanish and English detective novels, an upright piano, and the best reception on his mammoth color TV set of anyone in the county.

Day and night, Onofre's house usually buzzed with grandchildren and great-grandchildren: he gave the orders and they carried them out. For example, two great-grandchildren, Chemo and Chepa Martínez, aged seven and nine, always rode with Onofre in his truck when he collected honey from the twenty hives he had scattered around the Milagro area. Some older grandchildren helped him—for a small cut—to process the honey, which was later sold either in Rael's store or directly from the Chateau Martínez.

Onofre was also Chamisa County's chief dealer in staurolites, a big tourist business in Rael's store and in several trading posts and gift shops in Doña Luz and Chamisaville. Onofre's prominence in this trade had long ago earned him the title of the Staurolite Baron. Staurolites, also called Fairy Crosses, being a certain type of crystal (shaped like a perfect little cross and ranging in size from small pinkie to fat thumb) peculiar to the hills around Milagro and having a rather extensive folklore. Onofre couldn't have cared less about the folklore, however. At least twice a week, during dry spring, summer, and autumn days, Onofre loaded his truck with grandchildren and great-grandchildren and barreled up one canyon or another to hillsides positively reeking of pulverized rocks among which a diligent kid, given four or five hours and a dime per salable staurolite, could usually find at least a dozen of the lovely little curiosities. In turn, Onofre sold the crystals to Nick Rael and other commercial entrepreneurs for fifty cents, and the entrepreneurs unloaded them to tourists for a buck apiece, maybe even more.

Staurolites, then, were a lucrative deal to everyone concerned.

As was the piñon wood which Onofre collected, again aided by his great-grandchildren, who usually received a flat dollar per pickup load for their efforts. Onofre either dumped the wood in one of his mammoth piles (which were even advertised in the Chamisaville *News*), or else sold directly—often at twenty-five dollars a pickup load—to the Dancing Trout or to the middle-class artsy-craftsy and retired families down in Chamisaville. His own people could not buy from Onofre at those prices: they were used to paying five dollars, at the most a sawbuck, for a pickup load of piñon.

Onofre also knocked down a tidy dollar here and fifty cents there by helping Joe and Nancy Mondragón run their hamburger, Italian ice, and corn dog stand down at the Chamisaville Moto-Cross races one Sunday a month during the summer and autumn. In point of fact, Onofre was this operation's main bookkeeper, even though his left arm was illiterate: he spent hours telling Nancy what to write in the books, and how to write it, and how to cheat and disguise and rearrange for tax purposes, and so forth. Onofre's other duties included being the chief procurer of the stand's beef, which he bought mainly from the hippies at the Evening Star commune on Strawberry Mesa. Though bad ranchers, and even worse farmers, the hippies were rich—their commune was floated by a member's father, the chairman of a huge international corporation—and thus they indulged themselves by raising pathetically inadequate gardens and by growing cows. Although the Evening Star commune had only been around a few years, its college-educated freaks had nevertheless beaten the system out of cattle permits on some very rich terrain adjoining acreage controlled by Eusebio Lavadie. Hence, although they were badly overgrazing this land and losing most of their calves to colic or coyotes, their herd presently sported some real fat beef on the hoof, and Onofre, knowing exactly how to play on their white middle-class guilt, always managed to drive the price down until the hippies were practically selling Joe Mondragón his Moto-Cross hamburgers for nothing. Many townspeople treated the hippies in a similar fashion, looking upon them as a sort of manna from heaven, hiring them—for example—to make adobes, because the freaks learned fast and were willing—again out of middle-class guilt, and also because they were independently wealthy anyway—to labor eight or ten hours a day at what amounted to slave wages.

There was a saying that the Evening Star hippies were the only farmers in the Miracle Valley rich enough to turn over their gardens and cut their fields by hand.

Well, Onofre Martínez was a shrewd man; also an ornery S.O.B., as evinced by his attitude toward Milagro's lone- parking meter. And, like all the other old men in town, Onofre was also a little bit gaga.

The Astroturf lawn in front of his house Onofre had won in a cereal boxtop jingle contest, but he had paid hard cash for all the plants in his elaborate and colorful flower gardens, and they were all plastic. "If I could afford it, I'd put in plastic fruit trees, too," Onofre told anybody willing to listen. "I mean, when was the last time my trees bore fruit? I, for one, can't remember."

A fair enough (and typical enough) reaction to the orchard situation in Milagro. For although every family in Milagro had fruit trees, virtually all of these fruit trees bore fruit as often as the women of Milagro bore quintuplets. The Death of the Fruit Tree Blossoms, a ritual that took place every spring, had been known to drive some people more than a little ding-y. At best, the ritual set farmers to gnashing their teeth so hard and so often that almost all the people of Milagro who still had them owned teeth which were very irregular, chipped, and loosened by the gnashing that ran rampant during apple blossom time.

The ritual Death of the Fruit Tree Blossoms began toward the end of every March when, after a long hard winter, warm air coursed lovingly into the Miracle Valley, leading all the fruit trees to believe spring was just around the corner. And, believing this, their sap began running, their buds grew fat, their branches suddenly burst forth into flowers. The air became redolent from apple and pear and plum blossoms, and the locals started wandering around in shirt sleeves, made lazy and soporific and horny by the perfumed air. Farmers greased up their tractors; Nick Rael ordered garden seeds, summer hoses, irrigation boots; and cows groaned and fell down and bore their calves.

Whereupon, inevitably, as certain as death and taxes and the enlargement of Ladd Devine's empire, there ensued a final week of frost and frequently snow that turned into blizzards, and people who had not brought their cows in to calf had those calves frozen to death, and all the fruit tree blossoms were killed, and the subsequent summer came and went without so much as a boo! from a single pear, apple, or plum.

Herein lay another complaint the people had with

the educated and tricky thugs who were trying to form a conservancy district in order to build the Zopilote's private swimming lake behind the Indian Creek Dam. "With more water you can grow fruit like crazy from your fruit trees," the thugs' mellifluous voices crooned.

Which made any upright, true blue Milagro citizen, knowing the odds in favor of the early Death of the Fruit Tree Blossoms, just about vomit.

Still, for centuries, because of one masochistic spiritual or genetic flaw or another, Miracle Valley residents like Onofre Martínez had persisted in growing fruit trees, and even in hoping each year that this year a false spring would not set up the trees to be butchered by the little winter that always occurred after the false spring.

In a way, the Milagro fruit trees were related to the town's horses. And here too Onofre Martínez was a case in point. He owned a horse, which he kept in a little corral at the rear of his half-acre Shangri-la. This horse knocked off a bag of Staminoats every few weeks and two flakes of an eight-flake hay bale (costing a buck in a wet year, two bucks in a dry one) every day. On top of this the horse chewed up vitamin blocks as fast as Onofre could pitch them in, and of course the animal was always licking away at a salt block. Other than these activities, however, the horse did nothing, and, except for its shit, which Onofre's great-grandchildren Chemo and Chepa shoveled onto his vegetable garden, it was basically a worthless animal. Onofre had not ridden his horse in ten years, and the grandchildren and great-grandchildren only rode it a few times each summer. It was an old horse now, fat and half-blind, and it had spent most of its life in that little corral, just eating and moving its bowels. To be sure, Onofre talked to it each day, patted its nose, wormed it when it had to be wormed, trimmed its hooves when they needed trimming, dug mud out of the hooves when mud needed to be dug out, and curried the horse as well. But other than that the animal just paced around in the corral back there, sort of like an appendix, and just as useless, too.

For every inhabitant of Milagro, there existed a

horse like the one belonging to Onofre Martínez. Charley Bloom had once put it this way in a *Voice of the People* article:

> You walk along the narrow roads of Milagro in the spring and early summer sunshine. The small fields are green with alfalfa, timothy, and clover. At one house, a man with a wooden pallet called a "hawk" is scraping adobe mud off this hawk with a trowel and smoothing it against a wall. It is calm in Milagro; there is a feeling of uninterrupted history everywhere. In each of the half-acre and quarter-acre pastures one or two horses are grazing. For in Milagro, a man who is too old to ride, or his children who would rather speed in cars, still keep a horse or several horses. They switch them from small field to small field, and, no matter what, they will scrape together the dollars to buy hay bales for the winter months to feed their horses. There is something vestigial about the horses of Milagro. Occasionally, you see a man on a horse walking toward the Midnight Mountains, or two children riding bareback. But mostly the horses are just there, useless, parasitic, grazing in the overgrazed fields, because there have always been horses in Milagro. They can make you sad, these horses that nobody rides much anymore; or they can stand proudly and beautifully as a kind of symbol of a people who refuse to die.

But start throwing this kind of penny ante sociology around in front of Onofre Martínez, try to explain to him the significance of his old, fat, half-blind mare out back in that tidy corral, and he would listen politely for a while, until finally, catching you in a pedantic or scholarly pause, he would observe, "You're just farting words." Then he would start a conversation about something else. A man who kept a horse, to Onofre's way of thinking, was as natural as a man who unbuttoned his fly and pried out his pecker before, instead of after, taking a leak.

Onofre called his horse Balena, a word that means "whale."

Another thing about this one-armed man: Onofre Martínez was as close to Seferino Pacheco as anybody in town. Occasionally, Pacheco came over to the Chateau Martínez, not under the pretext of looking for his sow (because how could his sow transcend that airtight picket fence neatly surrounding Onofre's property?), but simply to stare at Onofre's color TV, or maybe to stare at his piano.

That piano had once belonged to Pacheco's wife, who could play it like a nightingale can sing. When she was still alive, that woman used to play for Pacheco every afternoon at five, and he would lie on a couch with his eyes closed, positively enraptured, his soul drifting around the room like a pink, helium-filled balloon. Sometimes she soothed him with classical music, sometimes she played popular songs, singing along in her husky melodic voice. In summer, the music would float out on the evening air, reaching the neighboring houses. Back in those days, Joe and Nancy Mondragón and Pancho and Stella Armijo and Sparky Pacheco and others who lived close to the Pacheco adobe used to stop whatever they were doing and listen to Pacheco's wife at the piano. And most of these people still counted those peaceful evening concerts among their most cherished memories.

But then Pacheco's wife died, and Pacheco sold the piano for a song to Onofre Martínez, who had planned to hustle it at a huge profit to a moneybags down in Chamisaville. But for some reason he kept putting off the sale. Maybe he remembered those musical evenings which had been so beautiful they had even lulled all the hummingbirds at his feeders—the tiny birds had lined up on branches and actually seemed to drift off into tiny buzzing dreams while Pacheco's wife caressed the ivories. And besides, Onofre fancied himself a bit of a whiz at the keyboard, too. In fact, it was Pacheco's wife who taught him for free back when she gave lessons to any kid in the valley eager to learn. Mostly, Onofre liked boogie-woogie, and so she taught him that. But then his right arm mysteriously disappeared, leaving him with nothing but a boogie-woogie walking bass. Nevertheless, Onofre still enjoyed playing his walking bass, and although he never gave concerts at 5:00 P.M., his neighbors often heard that jive bass coming from the Chateau Martínez around dusk. Nobody stopped work to listen, though, because Onofre had always been a lousy piano player, even with two hands, and he still tunked out basically atonal numbers.

Of course, Joe Mondragón would swear on a stack of Bibles, if you asked him to, that he had awakened at least twenty times in the middle of the night these past five years and heard both the walking bass *and* the treble runs *at the same time* carrying across on the clear black air to his startled ears.

So that was another story to file with all the previous fables about Onofre's missing arm.

But anyway, Seferino Pacheco occasionally visited Onofre's house, not to hear him play the piano—God forbid!—but simply to stare at Onofre's miraculous boob tube, and also occasionally to listen to his friend read.

It was in this, the literary area, that their acquaintanceship really suffered, however. Namely, because Pacheco could not stand the way Onofre, reading aloud in Spanish, pronounced his *c*'s and *z*'s. He pronounced them with the Castilian *th* sound, that is, with a lisp, an affectation peculiar to many of the Miracle Valley's old-timers, whereas it could not be found farther south in Mexico. The reason for this being that Onofre's and Seferino Pacheco's ancestors had come from Spain four centuries before, traveled to this godforsaken place in the high Rockies, and then been cut off from civilization for three hundred years, thus maintaining many of the purities in their Spanish language and in their Spanish customs.

But Pacheco hated that fucking lisp. He could hold his tongue, listening to Onofre read, only for about ten minutes. Then he would explode; and the two men would engage in knockdown drag out verbal fisticuffs, which usually terminated when Pacheco called Onofre a *"screaming elitist fairy!"* waking up all the bats behind their custom-made bat shutters as he stormed out of the place. Pacheco usually did not stop there, either. Turning at the gate, he always added: "An Astroturf lawn! And plastic flowers! *That proves I'm right!*"

After a Pacheco visit, the hummingbirds were usually absent from the Chateau Martínez for several days, or until the atmosphere calmed down enough so that they could zip here and there without striking air pockets caused by Pacheco's epithets.

"Someday he'll kill me for lisping," Onofre said to Joe Mondragón one afternoon while they were selling hamburgers and cotton candy at the Chamisaville Moto-Cross race, which was, as usual, taking place on a nonvisible track fifteen feet from Joe's trailer; the cyclists lost, as always, in a dust storm.

"If he does, why don't you will me your piano?" Joe said. "I want my kids to learn more culture than they can get on Herbie Goldfarb's guitar."

"I'm not gonna die, I don't think," Onofre said, "until I've played taps, on that piano, for Zopilote Devine."

ॐ

Two nights after the basketball court rumble, while Joe and Nancy Mondragón were making love, a bullet crashed through their living room window and thudded into the other side of the bedroom wall, causing the plastic crucifix above the bed to fall on Joe's head.

Jumping out of bed, Joe grabbed a rifle from the corner and charged through the front door. A car, trying to get away, was spinning its tires, stuck in the mud. Joe aimed his rifle and fired—but nothing happened because he had failed to load up. Forgetting that the car's occupants were armed, and brandishing his own gun by the barrel, Joe galloped toward the vehicle, planning to beat them all to a bloody pulp with the stock of his weapon. As he raced across the yard, however, their tires caught and, jolting clear of the gooey rut, the car plunged down the road.

"You bastards!" Joe yelled, flinging his gun after them: it landed with a splash in a puddle.

Bernabé Montoya sat up in bed and tapped Carolina's shoulder. "Hey," he muttered groggily, "did you hear a rifle shot?"

His wife rolled onto her back and spent a befuddled ten seconds stretching open her sleep-caked eyes. "What?" she mumbled. "What did you say?"

"I thought I heard a rifle shot."

Carolina sat up. "I didn't hear anything. I was sound asleep."

Bernabé laid one hand gently against his head. "I got a lousy headache," he moaned. "This town is giving me whatta you call them?—migraines. Joe's beanfield is gonna give me an ulcer."

"I'll fix something," Carolina said, climbing dutifully out of bed and slipping her feet into some fluffy pink slippers.

"Just gimme a couple aspirin," Bernabé said. "No fancy remedies, huh?"

"Don't worry, I'll fix you something better than aspirins," she insisted quietly, shuffling determinedly out of the room. "Remember: an ounce of prevention . . ."

"*Ai, Chihuahua . . .*" Bernabé whimpered, settling back. *Oh Jesus Christ Almighty,* he wailed silently, terrified of the old-fashioned remedy she was sure to turn up with, and he was certain to drink, in about ten minutes.

Occasionally—in fact, better make that often—her old-fashioned ways touched him. For example, he usually carried a little piece of oshá in his pants pocket. Not because he put it there himself, understand, but because she always slipped it in when he wasn't looking. In the old days, people had carried around these little chunks of wild parsnip root to protect themselves from poisonous snakes, and so what if rattlesnakes had always been as rare as money in Milagro? Bernabé was forever throwing away the oshá that turned up almost daily in his pockets, and Carolina was forever replenishing the supply, and neither of them ever mentioned the matter to the other.

But what really drove Bernabé out of his skull was Carolina's way of talking. Actually, Carolina didn't talk too much at all, but when she did open her mouth it seemed sentences never emerged, only aphorisms, called "dichos."

Hence, when Bernabé remarked, "You know, Carolina, I really wonder about Horsethief Shorty Wilson sometimes," she would respond with: "Hay lobos con piel de oveja." Which meant: "There are wolves who parade about in sheep's clothing."

Or if he said, "I wonder, sometimes, if I'm really handling José's beanfield correctly," she assured him, without even looking up from her colcha embroidery: "El que hace lo que puede no está obligado a más." Meaning: "He who does what he can isn't obligated to do any more."

Again, if Bernabé happened to mention, over a plate of carne adobada, that Joe Mondragón was a pig-headed son of a bitch who wouldn't listen to reason, Carolina was certain to chirp: "El que no agarra consejo no llega a viejo." That is: "He who can't take advice, won't live to a ripe old age."

Then if Bernabé continued to attack Joe's recalcitrance, she would probably add, "You can lead an ass to water but you can't make him drink."

The few times Bernabé had tried to break down the political and social situation in town, talking about how little land and money the farmers really had, Carolina had rather consistently observed, "Quien poco tiene poco teme," which means, "He who has little has little to fear."

And on those days when the sheriff was sick and tired of the whole thing and just came home early and put his feet up and proceeded to get drunk on a six-pack, she moaned at regular intervals: "Tiempo perdido los santos lo lloran," but at least he had the guts to pay no attention. Let the damned saints cry over all the time he was wasting.

That was another thing, of course. Their house, a kind of southwestern religious Smithsonian Institution, was crammed full of bultos and retablos, carved saints and painted saints, bleeding saints and saints wearing little cloth capes on which roses and moons and stars were embroidered, and saints carrying silk shoulder pouches, and saints with angels driving their plows through the earth behind them, and saints with gourds full of sacred water and baskets overbrimming with sacred bread—they had santos in their household like most of Milagro's dogs had fleas!

Yet among all these pious wooden dolls there was one Bernabé liked. It had been carved by that alcoholic expatriate responsible for the Smokey the Bear santo riot, Snuffy Ledoux. It was a plain wooden santo with no name, and, contrary to the other carved or plastic saints, it was grotesque. The eyes bulged like mad frog's eyes; the huge ugly nose was bent all out of shape; the lips were fat and twisted into a half-gurgle, half-scream; the big awkward hands gripped the figure's chest arthritically, in terror. Bernabé had bought it off the distinguished sculptor for a bottle of cheap tokay twelve years ago. But he liked it a lot; maybe he even loved that santo. Because it looked to the sheriff like a man who was full of a million questions he would never dare ask, a million opinions he would never dare offer; that ugly wooden carving looked to Bernabé Montoya like another human being with a kindred soul.

The one real fight Bernabé and Carolina had had in their life together occurred because of the saints. It had been an abnormally dry year (every other year in Milagro was an abnormally dry year, alternating with all those abnormally wet years), and so one day, during the Death of the Fruit Tree Blossoms time, Carolina carried their San Isidro out into the back field asking him to encourage it to rain on their cucumbers. Well, sure enough, it rained all right, then the rain turned to snow, and the snow turned into a blizzard, so Carolina ran outside with their Santo Niño de Atocha, begging him to queer the blizzard before the cucumbers and the fruit trees were destroyed, and so the blizzard stopped and it began to rain again and the rain froze and tree branches fell down onto everything, and some cows Bernabé had up in the canyon froze to death. Whereupon suddenly, gnashing his teeth so hard little pieces of porcelain literally spewed from his mouth, the sheriff jumped up and grabbed an armload of her saints and threw them into the holocaust. Carolina shrieked, plunged into the storm, retrieved her precious little statues, and cried for three days.

But God forbid they should ever yell at each other. Bernabé dreamed of that, though. He dreamed of leaping suddenly out of an armchair and throwing his clenched fists over his head as he bellowed, "Carolina, shuttup!" Or: "Carolina, you piss me off!" Or again: "Carolina, go to hell and take the saints and the dichos with you!"

Except that underneath he loved her very much, loved her plump gentle flesh, her quiet way of sewing, cooking . . . of being true. He was grateful, too, for the way she had of never really reproaching him for anything. Despite Vera Gonzáles down in Chamisaville and a hundred others before her, Bernabé felt loyal to Carolina. Their children were grown up and gone, they were both entering middle age, and yet their sex wasn't all that bad either. In fact, Bernabé periodically lusted after her way of making love with him whenever and however he wanted, in a slow, sensual, gratifying way, or else allowing him his "perversions" when he wanted them, doing things to or with him in a quiet, mystical, almost unbearably religious and sexy manner, if that's what he needed. Bernabé did not even mind it too badly when, after a really good tumble during which neither of them had thought about contraception, Carolina rolled heavily out of bed, and, as she tiptoed in her lethargic yet sexy way toward the bathroom to douche herself, said to him: "A stitch in time saves nine, you know . . ."

Bernabé knew.

Right now, Carolina returned to the bedroom and handed over a glass. What was in it—?

"Just some whiskey and a little ground-up oshá,"

she explained tenderly, adding of course: "An ounce of prevention is worth a pound of cure."

Bernabé closed his eyes, steeled himself, and drank. But no matter how hard he tried, he couldn't pretend her phony potion had cured him. In fact, his headache was straightaway multiplied by three. But how could he tell her the stuff she gave him didn't work?

And, caught in his eternal dilemma, Bernabé started thinking about how people always tried to kid each other. This led to thoughts—as he lay there tensed, waiting for another gunshot—about the ways people tried to fool animals. And painted cattleguards came to mind.

For some strange reason, Bernabé had never been able to accept the fact that painted cattleguards actually worked. A real cattleguard, consisting of ten or fifteen steel rails or two-by-fours set six to eight inches apart and laid across a dug-out section of road, kept cows, afraid of plunging a hoof between the rails and maybe breaking a leg, from crossing. A painted cattleguard, however, was just that: nothing more subtle or elaborate than a group of evenly spaced white stripes painted across a macadam road. They were also about five hundred dollars cheaper to build than real cattleguards.

One such ersatz cattleguard adorned the north-south highway a few hundred yards below Ladd Devine's Miracle Valley development sign. And every time Bernabé drove over those twelve white stripes, he flinched and, shaking his head, muttered to himself: "It beats me how a handful of white stripes can fool cows like that."

Bernabé likened the painted cattleguard to the sort of stickers—"Protected by Acme Burglar Alarm System"—store owners who could not afford burglar alarm systems put on prominent display in their business windows.

Or to those signs—"Beware of the Dog"—that suburban folks too cheap to invest in a ferocious mutt, but nevertheless terrified of burglars, displayed on their lawns.

Or then again, Bernabé figured a painted cattleguard might be said to share a common soul with a shapely woman who wore falsies.

And Bernabé wondered: Did the painted cattleguard concept have some relationship to artificial insemination, also?

Or how about its relationship to the plastic flowers in Onofre Martínez's garden that so confused his myriad hummingbirds? Too, how about its relationship to Onofre's invisible arm?

Of course, ultimately, painted cattleguards were like Bernabé Montoya himself, pretending to be a sheriff, when actually the title Bumbling Misfit might have suited him better than did his badge.

I oughtta take a week's vacation, Bernabé thought, and use it to teach Lavadie's cows how to cross that cattleguard.

The sheriff couldn't stand to see cows fooled by that phony cattleguard. In fact, it just about broke his heart to see any thing or any person tricked into believing in something that wasn't real.

Once Bernabé had mentioned his uneasiness about the painted cattleguard to Nick Rael.

"Listen," Nick said. "A bandido walks into a bank, he's got a gun in his right hand, he asks for the teller's money or her life. Maybe the gun in his hand is carved out of soap, maybe it's just one of those clever replicas you send away for, maybe it's nothing but a lousy cap pistol. On the other hand, who knows for sure it ain't a real gun? And who wants to be the chump to find out, is it the real McCoy or isn't it the real McCoy?"

"I see what you mean," Bernabé said.

"Well, that's the way it is with Lavadie's cows and that painted cattleguard," Nick said.

Still, the whole thing unsettled Bernabé. He sensed an inherent unfairness residing in that painted cattleguard. How come, if you couldn't fool a horse or a man or a goat with such a simplistic phony design, you could nevertheless twist the tail, udder if it had one, and both horns off a cow with it?

Bernabé rolled the concept of painted cattleguards around in his brain the way a lapidary rolls a rough stone around in a rock tumbler to make it smooth. Bernabé never could take the rough edges off that concept, though, the way a lapidary's tumbler could take the rough edges off his rock, making almost any mineral chunk shine like a jewel.

So Bernabé never truly understood the deep-down discomfort caused in himself by that painted cattle-guard.

Nobody else understood his discomfort, either.

One day Bernabé decided that the painted cattle-guard just south of the Zopilote's Miracle Valley sign had a lot in common with Joe Mondragón's beanfield.

Or should that be vice versa?

Bernabé, for one, didn't know.

But he tormented himself like this over useless questions all the time.

People said because of this nonsensical bent, the sheriff was driving himself bananas. Why worry, they reasoned, about something so irrelevant? If a thing worked, it worked. And painted cattleguards had always worked just like a little piece of oshá in the pocket had always kept away poisonous snakes. Start questioning why a thing that worked worked, people warned, and you were asking that thing to stop work-ing. The time to start worrying about how things worked was when they broke down or fell apart, and not before.

Seferino Pacheco understood, though. Several years back he had told Bernabé: "Six hundred years ago maybe you could have grown up to be somebody like Michelangelo."

"Who was Michelangelo?" the sheriff asked.

Disgusted by such philistine ignorance, Pacheco re-considered. "On second thought, maybe you wouldn't of grown up to be somebody like Michelangelo. Maybe even six hundred years ago you just would of grown up to be somebody in the tradition of our own Cleofes Apodaca or Padre Sinkovich. Maybe you just would of grown up to be somebody like yourself, all the time tripping over the hem of your own toga."

Bernabé had asked Nick Rael: "Who was Michel-angelo?"

"He was an ancient philosopher," Nick teased, "who believed that men's souls were round like apples, the color of pearls, and had little white wings."

Well, on the night a bullet went through Joe Mondragón's window, Bernabé studied Joe's beanfield, and he studied the painted cattleguard, and he wondered about the relationship between them, but he never really got anywhere with either.

His headache only grew worse.

The sheriff would have liked a mind that could deal with abstract thoughts and ideas. Instead, he possessed a mind capable of tinkering with things just enough to make them impossibly confusing and himself so dissatisfied with his own intellectual inadequacies that he would never be happy.

As a teen-ager, Bernabé had taken apart a 1939 Plymouth, but he had never been able to get it back together again.

"A fool and his reason are soon parted," Carolina once said reproachfully.

"*Ai, Chihuahua,*" the sheriff had grumbled.

Finally, on the night a bullet knocked the crucifix off the bedroom wall onto Joe Mondragón's head, Bernabé drifted back into an uneasy sleep. He dreamed about the piñata Bernabé, and about all the naked women he had ever loved hitting him with sticks. They flailed away, giggling and prancing, their breasts bouncing like happy puppies, while Bernabé twisted and twirled, reversing direction with every blow, eyes closed, hugging his knees, spinning this way and that way, getting all black and blue, and unable to burst no matter how hard he tried.

❧

Ladd Devine sat on the edge of a mahogany table; Jerry Grindstaff stood over by a window; Emerson Lapp was seated at an antique rolltop desk with a pen in his hand and a pad of legal-sized yellow paper in front of him; two state cops, William Koontz and Onofre Martínez's shameful offspring, Bruno Martínez, were perched uncomfortably side by side on a delicate brocaded couch; located across from them on a stiff divan were the two Forest Service personnel, Carl Abeyta and Floyd Cowlie; and Horsethief Shorty was lounging in a wing-back chair with one leg dangling over an arm, smoking a cigar. Emerson Lapp had a headache because of Shorty's cigar. He always got headaches from Shorty's cigars. In fact, Shorty himself often gave Lapp a monumental headache. It had something to do with Shorty's overall smell, sloppy bearing, and arrogance, and the way Ladd Devine tolerated all this. Lapp himself would not have tolerated Shorty for a minute. Neither of the two cops nor the Forest Service people nor Jerry G. would have tolerated Shorty either. And as for Shorty?—he just sat there languidly chewing on his cigar, basking—as he always had—in their hostility.

Devine said, "Jesus H. Christ."

There was silence in the room, everybody except Shorty—who was grinning almost imbecilically—wearing their longest faces.

Devine continued: "I'd like to know who was the dumb jerk took a shot at Joe Mondragón's house, I really would."

Again there was a profound, maybe guilty, silence in the room.

Eventually Shorty said, "You don't suppose, do you, that it might have something to do with that Secret Service baboon your friends in the capital sent up here, do you?"

"I don't know and I don't give a shit," Devine said. "But when people start throwing hot lead around this town like that—well, Christ. What do they think I'm sinking my money into this Miracle Valley project for, for kicks? Is that what they think? Do they think I'm sticking my neck out just so the bottom can fall out because a lot of trigger-happy hoodlums have turned the valley into a shooting gallery?"

"We're gonna try and find out who did it, sir," Bruno Martínez said, practically choking on that "sir," because he happened to dislike Ladd Devine as much as the next man and besides, he thought he knew who had fired that bullet.

"Well boys I sure hope so," Devine said. "Because

that's all we need right now is a lot, or even just a little, slaphappy stuff like that. As it is, if this gets out to some of my backers——" With a handkerchief he wiped his forehead. "And I mean it, too. I want you fellows——" he nodded at the two cops "——to put the word out, understand? Shorty, you too. You know how things stack up around here."

"What *did* happen at that meeting with the undercover flatfoot?" Shorty asked. "How come I wasn't invited?"

"We weren't there either," Bill Koontz said.

"I don't know who sent him," Bruno Martínez added. "You ask me, downstate should keep their noses out of this."

"Looks to me like a case of the right hand not knowing what the left hand is doing," Shorty drawled.

Emerson Lapp said, "This whole affair has become rather unbelievably sticky."

All heads turned toward Lapp, all eyes except Shorty's assessing him with the dull disdain of macho eyes confronting a little Lord Fauntleroy.

Irritated by the distraction, Devine broke in, "Explain to me, Shorty, will you? just what you know about the meeting they had."

Shorty shrugged. "They called a meeting; I wasn't invited to that one either. The lawyer Bloom, he got up and explained the dam, the conservancy district, and your role in this town."

Devine blurted, "Who the hell does Bloom think he is?"

"He thinks he's so scared he almost fainted in front of all those people," Shorty said with a wide grin.

"You know, Shorty, this really isn't that amusing," Devine observed.

"Amusing?" Shorty arched his eyebrows. "Excuse me, Ladd——" Both Jerry G. and Emerson Lapp flinched, as they always flinched when Shorty used their boss's first name. "Excuse me, Ladd, but this whole situation is pretty fucking funny, if you ask me. Downstate doesn't know what upstate is doing; everybody in the valley is totally confused and disorganized; we're trying to get it together and they're trying to get it together, and nobody knows what to do, including the state's most influential song-and-dance team of Bookman and Noyes. In fact, nothing has happened but everybody's hysterical, and all because an un-educated half-wit Mexican decided to grow a half-acre field of beans."

"Shorty," Devine remarked patiently, "what do you suggest we might have done about that meeting?"

"We could of set up a .50-caliber machine gun and shot the old geezers as they tottered out," Shorty grinned, touching a match—arrogantly lit on his fly zipper—to the end of his cigar.

In the ensuing quiet, Emerson Lapp expelled a long exasperated sigh.

At length, Jerry G. said, "If we let them get away with stuff like this meeting, they'll just get worse."

"What do you mean?"

"I mean they'll just get more confident."

"And if we attempt to sabotage their next meet-ing—?"

"They might burn down the Dancing Trout," Shorty said glibly.

"So what do we do?" Devine asked.

"Ignore them," Shorty proposed. "What's that phrase I heard an educated man once use about this country—the 'Tyranny of Tolerance'?"

"Oh God, Shorty," Emerson Lapp muttered under his breath. "You're so erudite."

"There must be a way to control this thing." De-vine looked to the cops, then to Floyd Cowlie and Carl Abeyta.

"Maybe there's some way we could forbid them to open the church again, because it's unsafe or a health menace or something," Bruno Martínez suggested un-convincingly.

"They'd come up here and hold their meetings on the Dancing Trout baseball diamond," Shorty asserted gleefully.

"Shorty," Devine said, "I think I'd like a little more out of you than sarcasm."

"Ladd, you know I've always given you 110 per-cent."

Emerson Lapp rolled his eyes to the ceiling and banged his pencil down against the legal pad. Jerry G. shifted uncomfortably, moving his eyes nervously from Devine to the cops to Shorty.

"I think maybe the lawyer is one of their really weak links," Devine said.

"Maybe you're right. He's a chickenshit, so far as I know, from the word go."

"Just how far do you know, Shorty?"

"Not very. I see him around. We never officially met."

Ladd Devine stood up and paced toward the rolltop desk, turned, and walked back to the table. "I could talk with him," he said. "I'm not sure what I'd say, though."

"You could offer to buy him off, or threaten to cut him up into little pieces and feed him to the loan sharks."

"Very funny," Devine murmured, glumly eyeballing Shorty.

"As I see it, there's an inherent problem in all this." Shorty suddenly swung himself up so that he was seated on the arm of the chair. "You want to pull the rug out once and for all from under the people in this valley, Ladd, and you don't really give a shit how you do it, with guns or with money, with state cops or with hired hoodlums—speaking of which, what's the name of that police strong-arm junkie out at the Evening Star, anyway—Lord Rhino? You might ask him about who fired the shot at Joe's place. But anyway: if you can just wipe 'em out with pieces of paper covered with legalese, so much the better. The problem is: how to do it without pulling the rug out from under yourself, right? That's all. That's what's under discussion here. Very simple."

Wearily, Devine looked at Shorty. Then he looked at Jerry G., whose gaze fell to the floor. Then he looked at Emerson Lapp, whose eyes also dropped to the floor. After that he looked at the two cops, who became very interested in the hands in their laps. The Forest Service men also abruptly commenced scrutinizing their thighs. So he looked back at Shorty, who was looking fearlessly back at him, and Devine realized that if he was going to make it safely through this mess he would have to put a lot of his eggs in Shorty's basket.

With that, Shorty said, "Say, Ladd, why don't you have Floyd and Carl here set a forest fire?"

"Hey, just a minute!" Carl Abeyta stiffened self-righteously and stifled an urge to lunge across the room at Shorty. "What the fuck are you talking about?"

"Setting a fire," Shorty said calmly. "Christ, that's one of the few ways those men down there have earned a living around here. I know of a dozen guys from town, the past twenty years, who've gone up and set the trees on fire. For crissakes, man, it's—what is the pay now? Two-fifty an hour around the clock? Three dollars? And the Forest Service—God bless Smokey the Bear!—packs in potatoes and all the fresh-killed beef you can eat. You want to get this town's mind off that beanfield, light the forest and hire all the heavies to put it out. And keep lighting little fires here and there—"

"Oh, hey, Shorty," Carl Abeyta whined. "Don't you have any idea of how much money we get for trees when we sell them to timber companies?"

Shorty said, "Okay, then. Ladd, why don't you build maybe four more cottages down there beyond the tennis courts?"

"Why should I? We don't need them."

"You could hire maybe fifteen people from town to work on them, building the frames, laying foundations, making adobes—"

"I'm not sure I follow."

"If you're paying them they aren't gonna slit your throat, are they?" Shorty was suddenly angry at his boss, at the dude ranch, at himself. "I'll go down there myself and offer Joe Mondragón two months of work he can't possibly refuse. Buy your toilets, all your plumbing materials from Ruby Archuleta's Pipe Queen and there's another few leaders of this thing on your side. It's time to throw the peasants a bone, Ladd."

"It doesn't make sense to construct houses I don't need. That would just be money down the drain."

"Why not call it insurance?" Shorty said, nodding to the cops, and then to Emerson Lapp, as he walked out.

The room stayed silent while Devine lit a small cigar.

"What's eating Shorty?" Carl Abeyta finally asked.

"What's eating all of us," Bruno Martínez noted sourly. "I can't even visit home for a meal these days; my old man throws me out of the house."

"With just one arm?"

Bruno nodded and shrugged. "He sics that fucking three-legged mastiff on me even before I get out of the police car."

"Ah, what the hell," Devine sighed. "Let's break it up for now, my friends . . ."

After they had gone, Devine and Emerson Lapp remained alone in the room.

"It's a bitch," Lapp said reflectively, tapping his front teeth with the eraser tip of his pencil.

"Yeah." Devine loosened his belt, unlaced his shoes, and set his stocking feet up on a glass coffee table. "You're right, it sure is a bitch."

The boss let his guard down now, as he did but rarely, and then usually only when alone, or occasionally—as now—with his longtime secretary.

"Yessir," Devine repeated, "it sure is a bitch." And he added, "Em, do you think it can be done?"

"Oh for God's sake, Mr. D., of course it can be done."

Devine smoked his cigar quietly for a while. Then he chuckled: "Hey, let's you and me ride on up into the hills and set that forest on fire, Em."

"Why don't we go ahead and burn down the Dancing Trout while we're at it, Mr. D."

Devine guffawed, sputtered a little, giggled once or twice. "Better yet, Em, let's just burn down the town and pave it over for a parking lot."

The secretary shrugged, smiling painfully; they lapsed into silence for a minute.

"Now you take my grandaddy," Devine began again

abruptly. "There was a remarkable man. He never flew in an airplane. You know why? He said to me, he said: 'Always go on the ground, Laddy'—that's when I was a kid he said that. He said, 'Always go on the ground, Laddy, otherwise you'll lose contact with everything important.' And I think people down there, around here, I think they actually liked the crusty old son of a bitch."

"Things were different then, Mr. D. People were different."

"Oh, my grandaddy sucked blood," Devine said. "You can bet he sucked blood. He hurt people in a big way. He had a cruel and brutal style."

Again the secretary shrugged. "I guess it's the nature of the beast."

"Yes, I suppose so . . ." A great fatigue suddenly swept over Devine. "Oh shit," he mumbled. "I loved that old bastard, Em, I really did. He had class, you know? I don't have any class. Or not much, anyway. Sometimes I wonder if I have any class at all—I don't think so. I don't think people like me much, but I don't even think they hate me, Em, do they? I think I'm just neutral. I'm a neutral S.O.B. An anonymous tycoon. And you know how that feels—?"

Lapp, surprised by his employer's sudden dive into a maudlin mood, did not reply.

Devine grinned: "It just feels neutral," he chuckled. "Not good, really. Not bad, either . . ."

But, incredibly, there was a tear in one eye. And Emerson Lapp—horrified—quickly left the room.

"My old grandaddy," Devine called after him. "My old grandaddy, he would have set the forest on fire! Did you know, Em, that *he once slit the throat of a Mexican whore who tried to rob him and then he let her have it while she bled to death on the floor!*"

⌇

Kyril Montana and Bud Gleason met in the Conquistador Lounge of the La Fonda Hotel in the capital for lunch.

"Listen, Ky," Bud began nervously as soon as they

had ordered drinks, "things are beginning to get awfully uptight back home."

"In exactly what way?" the agent asked, leaning forward slightly.

"Well, for starters it looks as if a kind of informal Chicano organization is starting up, I don't know for sure. There's rumors galore, but it's hard to pinpoint anything. They had a meeting, though—you probably already know about that. On your side they're organizing, too. Somebody fired a shot at Joe Mondragón's house a few nights ago. Also, Joe and some friends were beaten up at the old elementary school basketball court about a week ago."

"I knew about the meeting," Kyril Montana said, noting that Bud had said "on *your* side," instead of "on *our* side," and he told himself he had better keep a sharp eye on his old college pal. Bud owed him a loyalty beyond old school ties, however, because several times in the past the agent had fed him information about certain land and real estate deals around the capital that had allowed Bud to buy into, and capitalize on, some fairly lucrative developments. Kyril Montana had also helped Bud out of one ticklish situation involving federally controlled interstate land sales in which Bud had become embroiled during his earlier days when he was based in the capital.

"Who fired that shot, Bud? Who beat up Joe and his friends?"

Bud shrugged, eyes bobbing unhappily. The waitress arrived with a martini and a bloody mary. The undercover agent took a quick sip of his drink and handed it back to the waitress. "I'm sorry," he said politely, "but you tell the bartender to mix this thing the way I asked for it, easy on the salt and Worcestershire, and with a single, not a double shot of vodka, okay?"

The waitress, a pretty girl who flustered easily, apologized, "Oh, I'm so sorry, sir," and "Of course, sir," and hurried away.

Kyril Montana said, "So do you know, or don't you know, who attacked Joe?"

"Well, not for sure," Bud mumbled, toying nervously with a fork. "You know . . . not me, of course.

What?—I got a heart could take that? Shit no. But maybe Eusebio Lavadie did it, or one of Devine's foremen, the quiet weird one named Jerry Grindstaff. Maybe Harlan Betchel was involved, maybe not. Nick Rael, too, he could of been in on it, him and an off-duty cop, say Bill Koontz or Granny Smith—I dunno. There's a lot of talk, you understand, but nobody really knows. A name I've heard a couple of times is this Lord Crocodile or Lord Lion or something who lives out at the Evening Star commune, but then you'd know more about that than me. They had a meeting, though, Joe's people, Ruby Archuleta, and they're bound to retaliate, and you wanna know the truth, I'm a little scared. Things have never been tense in quite this way before."

"If they retaliate and get caught, and Joe Mondragón is with them, which is likely, then it will be over."

"I'm not sure people are reacting the way you think they ought to react," Bud cautioned.

"Those people are conservative, they're also scared and confused, so much so that I doubt they could ever really join forces together. The few renegades, like Joe, they're going to flush themselves into the open, and we'll hog-tie them, we'll have them put away in no time. I think 90 percent of the people in Milagro are begging us to nail them and end that irrigating and restore things to an even keel."

"What good is an even keel," Bud complained, "if I'm in a grave?"

The waitress returned with a new bloody mary, and the police agent took a sip, nodding to her that it was all right as he said: "Aren't you getting a little het up over nothing, Bud?"

Bud knocked off the martini and called the waitress over to order another. "Yeah, maybe I am, I dunno." He handed her the glass, then abruptly sneezed and pulled out a handkerchief, fumbling with it around his nose. "But I'm just not sure you know those people up there, Ky. I *live* in that town, remember. Okay, so I live behind a six-foot-high wall in an adobe mansion surrounded by spruce trees, and I got more land than twenty of those poor bastards put together, but

I been dealing with them for years, I been selling and buying their land, and right now I'm tied heavily into Ladd Devine's Miracle Valley project, which I stand to come out of sitting very pretty, unless the whole ball of wax gets blown to smithereens by a bunch of trigger-happy Chicanos or cops or whatever. I mean, tourists are finicky people, Ky. They got a tendency to keep away from wherever there's a war going on."

"When we have Joe Mondragón it will be over," the agent said. "And in the meantime, if people are as confused and uncomfortable about things as yourself, well, they aren't going to organize in any viable way, believe me."

"All I can say is you better nail Joe pretty fast, then," Bud said bitterly, tying into his second martini the instant it alighted on the table, "before he's got half that fucking town stuck to him and his beanfield like flies to flypaper."

"How's Katie?" the agent asked.

"Oh Christ!" Bud's chubby face lit up with a rueful grin. "Listen, I'm sorry about that when you came up, I really am . . ."

Kyril Montana smiled gently as he fitted a filter-tip cigarette between his lips and, snapping on a lighter that invariably worked on the first try, lit it. "That was no problem. Really. Now, tell me about this woman, the one who runs that Body Shop place— Ruby Archuleta. You say she's talking about a petition? . . ."

At home that evening, though, Kyril Montana felt a little out of sorts. He understood what to expect from Bud Gleason and what not to expect; and he had gotten not only what Bud had to give, but also what he owed. The fact that a shot had been fired at Joe Mondragón's house did not particularly upset him either; if those primitive bastards started shooting at each other for real, it might create a publicity problem, true, but at the same time it could not fail to bring things to a head that much sooner.

The agent's family was gathered around the pool on this dusty peaceful evening. All his life Kyril Mon-

tana had cultivated the habit of leaving his job at the
office: once home, he relaxed; he became a family
man. Tonight, however, Bud Gleason—his shifty eyes,
his shot nerves, the way he belted down martinis
against a heart specialist's orders—nagged at the back
of his brain. No matter, though. He was home. So he
changed into a swimsuit and sat for a moment in a
metal chair beside the pool, watching his healthy kids
perform. While his thirteen-year-old daughter Kelly,
an exceptional young athlete, swam measured laps, his
eleven-year-old son Burt kept flipping gracefully off
the diving board. The agent had taught each child how
to swim, and how to swim well; now he was teaching
his son to dive. In college, the agent had been a first-
string diver on the swimming team; he had almost
qualified for the Olympics.

Watching Burt perform a relatively simple forward
one-and-a-half, the agent criticized: "Son, that was a
sloppy tuck; you didn't go into it tight enough."

"Aw, sir, I'm kinda tired—" Burt grinned infec-
tiously.

"If you're tired, take a rest. When you're tired,
that's when accidents happen. Also it's a bad habit to
do a thing sloppily."

His wife asked if he wanted a drink, the agent
replied, "No thanks, I had one at lunch with Bud
Gleason, and I think in a minute I'd like to do a little
diving myself."

Marilyn smiled, ."Suit yourself," and settled in a
nearby chair with her drink. Burt dried himself off and
went inside, returning in a moment dragging a TV on
a butler's cart onto the patio. He turned to a program
he enjoyed, and lay on an air mattress on his stomach,
watching the show. Kelly was still doing laps at a
steady pace, and watching her, both Marilyn Montana
and her husband shared the hope that their daughter
might one day soon be Olympic material: her swimming coach felt she was that good.

The agent roused himself and strolled over to the
diving board. He went out to the end, then strode
back three steps, measuring his approach distance.
Turning, he stood very still, concentrating on the up-

coming dive, and then he walked out to the end,
lifted his right foot in a pump and pumped his arms
once as he came down and lifted off the board, letting
the spring in it catapult him almost straight up, and
when he was at the apex of his rise he snapped into
a tuck position and was around one-and-a-half times
in an instant with his eyes alertly wide open directly
above the end of the board; he came out of it swiftly,
but not so fast that there would be an abrupt un-
gainly snap or jerk in his dive, and glided down,
missing the end of the board by inches, entering the
water with hardly a splash.

All her life Marilyn had been awed by that preci-
sion and beauty in her husband, in his body. She had
rarely, if ever, seen him make a mistake off the diving
board. He never clowned around. "Occasionally, you
might get off too directly over the board," he had once
told her. "But if your eyes are open, you can always
push off and avoid an injury. I never had an injury."

Kyril Montana broke the surface smiling, and he
directed that smile at his wife. Kelly had halted at
the shallow end in order to watch her father's dive.

"You were beautiful, Daddy," she called out. "You
were like a bird and a fish all rolled into one." Her
voice positively sparkled.

"Yeah, sir," Burt echoed from his mattress. "That
really looked good."

They had a lovely quiet time at the pool. When his
program ended, Burt turned off the TV and rolled it
back inside, disappearing into his room. Some robins
landed on the small lawn beyond the shallow end,
hunting for evening worms. The bell of an ice cream
truck tinkled over the wall, fluttering in the cooling
evening air almost like a butterfly. Kelly returned to
her laps, gliding tirelessly through the water. The
agent did a few more dives, a backward twisting one-
and-a-half, a half-gainer, and a beautiful soaring swan
dive, all of them executed in what appeared to be an
effortless manner. Each dive gave Marilyn a surge of
joy, a warm feeling of pride in her man who never
made a mistake.

There was peace and tranquillity here; a sense of

goodness and security; an almost exciting atmosphere of togetherness and love.

᪐

Up north on that same evening, things were not so calm. The sky was overcast, threatening rain, when Joe Mondragón's rattletrap pickup skidded to a halt on the Strawberry Mesa Body Shop and Pipe Queen grounds and Joe hopped out and strode swiftly up the slope to where Claudio García and Marvin LaBlue and Ruby Archuleta were seated on various stumps outside the house, quietly smoking. Marvin LaBlue had a big battery-powered shortwave radio beside him, tuned softly to WBAP, a country and western station in Fort Worth–Dallas. Joe nodded hellos to Marvin and Claudio, and addressed Ruby.

"I just had a talk with Horsethief Shorty, who says they're gonna build four more cottages up there at the Dancing Trout, and the Zopilote wants to hire me and maybe fifteen other people. Shorty said I might even head the crew, and what plumbing they use and like that, they're gonna buy from here."

"Why did you come to me?" Ruby asked quietly.

Joe hesitated. "Well . . . I guess mostly because Nancy thought I'd better."

Ruby laughed. "So what do you think?"

"I think that son of a bitch is going to pay three, four dollars an hour to maybe fifteen, twenty people, including me, for a couple months, maybe longer," Joe said unhappily.

"And that would be a lot of money."

Joe nodded, feeling more uncomfortable than he had in ages. And though he had not articulated to himself what was coming, he'd felt it in his bones ever since Horsethief Shorty had squatted down near Joe's shop, using a stick to scribble the facts and figures in the dirt while Joe listened, practically drooling.

Defensively, Joe protested, "If I don't do it, he'll just get somebody else."

"If you don't do it, and I don't supply the plumbing, and if it isn't you or us that does the hiring, he's not gonna build those cottages," Ruby said adamantly, knowing she spoke tripe, because Devine could just go hire himself a crew from Doña Luz or Chamisaville if he wanted.

"How do you know?" Joe said angrily, not angry at her as much as he was angry at himself for being so confused about the whole fucking thing.

"I can feel it," Ruby said. "I can see it plain enough."

"We could take the work and just not let it make a difference."

"I think if fifteen people in this town were earning three dollars an hour for eight or ten or twelve hours a day, it would make a difference," Ruby said. "José, for a long time you and me and the people of this village, we have—or rather we should have—been at war with that man."

Joe faced away from her, knowing she spoke the truth, and hating her guts for being right. He had a very strong desire to say, Well, tough titty, Missus Archuleta, I'm heading up there first thing in the morning to sign myself on anyway. You see, me and my wife and kids, we're tired of eating stewed tennis shoes instead of meat.

Ruby said gently, "José, they shot a bullet through your window. It could have killed somebody."

For a moment they all just listened to the lonely strains of a hillbilly guitar a thousand miles to the east, and the sound of that guitar mixing in with the songs of the local crickets made it a terribly peaceful, terribly quiet time.

"You want some coffee?" Ruby asked. "Or a beer?"

"No, thanks." Joe squatted, automatically picking up a twig and beginning to scratch in the dirt.

"It's just a bribe, José."

"Well, how many years have we been complaining among ourselves that that bastard won't hire locals for his construction and shit, and now he's doing it," Joe blurted, "and why should we refuse?"

"Because of the situation. Because in this context it's a bribe. He's hiring us to work only because he doesn't want us to fight him. He's hiring us to work to protect his interests, not ours. He's hiring us to work so he can get his conservancy district and his dam and his Miracle Valley Golf Course that will put all of us out of work for good."

Joe wrote Fuck You in the dirt, crossed it out, and said, "Three dollars an hour."

"I suppose if we don't take his offer," Ruby said thoughtfully, "he'll try to hire others. And of course our most desperate people will grab at the chance, why shouldn't they? Who isn't so poor he doesn't need that loot? If nothing else, just the *question* of should we work on those houses or shouldn't we will set us further against each other; it will create resentments in those who finally work and in those who refuse. . . . So it's a very clever offer," she concluded, her voice suddenly tired, reduced to a despondent whisper. "That foxy son of a bitch."

They were quiet again, smoking: the radio announcer dedicated a song to Chuck, a Consolidated Freightways driver zooming along the highway somewhere east of Ponca City.

"So," Ruby said.

"So . . . I dunno," Joe said. *"Chihuahua."*

"We should decide, José. You and me. We should decide right now."

Joe looked up, startled at the tone of voice she had used saying "we."

"Oh hell . . ." he said.

They waited.

"Fuck it," Joe mumbled uncomfortably. "Turn off that music, will you Marvin? Christ, goddam hillbillys. Get Juárez or Mazatlán or someplace decent."

Marvin, who loved country and western music, took no offense. He fiddled with the dial a moment, landing on some mariachi music that was as equally redneck and sappy in its own way as were the cowboy songs. Joe grumped, "That's better. *Je*sus."

Claudio García shifted, rolling a smoke. A cat moved through the darkness carrying a live mouse it would kill in a minute. Down below a wind fluff stirred up some greasy newspaper pages; you could smell fresh oil on the air.

Joe said, "What happens if I refuse to work for that bastard?"

"Two things. Wait and see if Shorty approaches anybody else. Maybe he won't, it's hard to tell. We keep our mouths shut about it, though, just in case—for whatever reasons—they only wanted to plant that seed in you. If they'll take anybody because they're really serious about those cottages, then we'll have to try and explain to people why they shouldn't go, why they should boycott the Dancing Trout."

Joe bit his lip and wrote a few more obscenities in the dirt. "I don't know," he murmured fitfully. "I just don't know." He felt miserable. He actually had a pain in his gut from the tension. He couldn't believe that somehow he would not be working on those cottages earning three dollars an hour. Christ, maybe if he got back in Devine's good graces he could actually tie into some kind of steady livelihood for once—

"None of us really knows," Ruby said. "Things just have to become different, that's all. And those cottages wouldn't make the right kind of difference. The whole plan is as destructive as Pacheco's pig."

Softly, Joe said *"Chihuahua"* again.

Claudio García picked his nose.

The honky-tonk mariachi music was getting on Joe's nerves. "Why don't you just turn off the radio," he ordered.

Marvin complied.

They listened to the crickets.

And then something happened. A tiny sparkling light no bigger than a child's pinkie fingernail floated through the troubled air between them like a miniature star. Joe gasped; so did Claudio García and Ruby. It was a sign, an omen, an incredible, mystical thing. They gaped at it the way they might have gaped at a sudden apparition of the Virgin of Guadalupe spreading roses around the Body Shop and Pipe Queen buildings.

"What . . . the . . . hell . . . was . . . that?" Joe whispered, awed, a little afraid.

Marvin LaBlue, the only Easterner among them, drawled, "Don't panic, folks, that was just a little bug. Back home we call 'em fireflies. That little critter must be a thousand miles off course."

A thoughtful silence followed this information. Then Joe finally spoke again. "Alright," he said, abruptly standing and throwing his stick away. "I guess you're right . . . maybe."

With that he said good night and strode swiftly down the hill. But once inside his truck he felt so unfairly cheated that he damn near broke a finger clobbering the dashboard.

After Joe roared away, Marvin LaBlue turned the radio on to WBAP again. Ruby stood up and Claudio García followed her inside to their bedroom. There she turned to him and Claudio cuddled her in his mammoth arms. They undressed in the soft blue darkness that smelled of cinnamon, oregano, and sagebrush, and, atop the covers, they made love, Claudio's enormous dark bulk curling mutely around that small tough little woman—he crushed her gently in an embrace she always thought might stop her heart. And then she sucked this inarticulate giant into herself and wept at the love, and at the pain as, in a way, he tenderly almost killed her.

❧

A slow-pitch softball league operating in Chamisa County included two teams from Milagro: the Saints, who were made up largely of players from the town, including Charley Bloom, Eliu Archuleta, Johnny Pacheco, Jimmy Ortega, Benny Maestas, Claudio García, and Joe Mondragón, and the Angels, who were largely a Devine conglomerate, and for whom Horsethief Shorty, Nick Rael, Bernabé Montoya, and Harlan Betchel and his anemic seventeen-year-old son, Albie, played. The balls and strikes were usually called by Ruby Archuleta.

These two teams, which were currently fighting each other for the cellar (the Mormon church from Chamisaville occupied first), happened to meet a couple of days after Joe Mondragón rejected Ladd Devine's offer to build cottages.

About fifteen minutes before game time Joe's pickup

jolted into Herbie Goldfarb's yard and screeched to a halt: impatiently, Joe honked his horn. Herbie staggered out the door like a man about to be snatched by the Gestapo.

Joe leaned from the window. "Hey, Goldy. You play softball?"

"I used to . . . I mean . . . you know . . . dicking around . . . fraternity stuff."

"Let's go then. Come on." Already Joe had it in reverse, backing around.

"But—"

"Let's fucking *go*," Joe snapped, leaning across the seat to open the passenger door. "We haven't got all day."

Like a zombie on the way to his own beheading, Herbie climbed in.

"Punch the button," Joe said, popping the clutch, "else the door'll open."

Herbie already knew that, though, as, reaching wildly for the handle of the outswinging door, his head tunked painfully against the jamb.

Joe had a theory about driving: namely, if you didn't goose it hell-bent for election no matter how shitty the road, you would never get anywhere on time. And if the car or truck fell apart because of this rough treatment, no sweat, Joe was an expert mechanic, he could fix anything in a jiffy because in the toolbox under his seat he had everything from an infinite variety of wrenches to tubes of liquid aluminum.

Hence he drove with his hands clamped to the wheel, his head permanently ducked so it wouldn't go through the roof of the cab, and his ass perpetually in the air; and nobody could deny that he sure as hell got where he was going in a hurry. Though how Joe could see out the spider-web cracks decorating the windshield was a mystery to Herbie Goldfarb, and why they didn't suffer three or four blowouts on the way to the ball field the VISTA volunteer never knew.

They skidded to a stop at the loveliest ball park in Chamisa County, the only ball park with a grass infield and outfield—in fact, the only ball field with grass,

period. It was located, of course, about a hundred
yards below the tennis courts on the Dancing Trout
grounds.

This particular ball game began, as the games between these two teams were apt to begin, with the
Saints batting around one and a half times, and with
Herbie Goldfarb garnering the distinction of making
two of the Saints' first two outs. With not even half
an inning over, then, the Saints were ahead, seven to
nothing, and Horsethief Shorty—the old pro—trotted
in from third base to replace Albie Betchel on the
mound. Shorty retired the side, though not before he
had clobbered Joe Mondragón between the shoulder
blades with a throw (off Joe's bunt) that Shorty at
least pretended he'd meant for the Angel first base-
men, Joe's chickenshit cousin, Floyd Mondragón. At
the moment of impact, Joe stopped on a dime, turned,
began to charge Shorty, pulled up short, ripped off an
obscene finger as he screamed a string of obscenities
in Spanish, and then he almost slugged his cousin
Floyd when the first baseman picked up the ball and
tagged Joe out.

At this point both benches emptied and converged,
and the twenty or so fans watching joined the fray.
While numerous loud threats were exchanged, and
some halfhearted pushing and shoving went on, Ruby
Archuleta lazed over to a grassy slope, sat down, and
bemusedly smoked a cigarette.

In due course order was restored and the game
resumed, moving briskly into the bottom half of the
first inning. Joe, the Saints' first pitcher, promptly
winged an overhand bean ball at Harlan Betchel, who
staggered clear of the batter's box, pointing his bat
accusingly at Joe.

"Hey!" he called angrily. "This is slow pitch. This
isn't fast ball." And, appealing to the ump: "Hey,
Ruby, he's not allowed to throw that fast."

"Que no la tires tan rápido, José," Ruby hollered
nonchalantly, tilting her head back to blow out some
cigarette smoke.

Joe lobbed the next one in so slow that Harlan
swung about four seconds too soon, and, all off-

balance, he lost hold of the bat, which zoomed forward on a dead line for the pitcher's head. Joe reacted quickly enough—but in flattening himself onto the mound he put a tooth halfway through his tongue.

Even before Joe was up, Harlan had begun to retreat, yelling, "That wasn't on purpose, damn you, Joe! *That wasn't on purpose!* I'M SORRY!"

Joe charged about halfway to home, obscenities and blood flying out of his mouth like shotgun pellets, but he pulled up when Bernabé Montoya stepped in front of Harlan, shouting, "Play the goddamn game, José, or get the hell out! Or get the hell arrested for assault and battery, I don't care!"

So furious that the veins on his forehead bulged and he felt dizzy, Joe nevertheless limped back to the mound, gestured a couple of times to God, and threw a relatively decent pitch which Harlan hit over Eliu Archuleta's head for a home run.

The sheriff popped up to the second baseman, but then Floyd Mondragón and Nick Rael hit back-to-back doubles, a kid named Rúben Tafoya walked, Albie Betchel was hit (unintentionally) by a pitched ball, and Horsethief Shorty singled.

Joe set the ball down in the hollow in front of the rubber and walked out to second, thumbing at the mound as he growled to Herbie Goldfarb, "You pitch."

"Me—?"

"Go ahead. Before it's over everybody will pitch."

Herbie, much to his astonishment, dealt up a double-play grounder to the first batter. At least, it should have been a double play. The shortstop, a junior high school kid named Bobby Maés, scooped up the ball and tossed underhand to Joe Mondragón, who, instead of firing it on to first, lowered a shoulder and drove himself savagely into Horsethief Shorty, who was trying to throw a block on him to queer the double play.

The ball spurted out of what followed, almost a cartoon blob of dust with furiously pounding and kicking hands and feet revolving out of it, and the Angels' bench emptied as the Saints' team sprinted in. All except for Herbie Goldfarb, that is, who stood on the mound, mouth agape, more or less terrified, and wondering what God had wrought. Charley Bloom and Marvin LaBlue grabbed Joe; Bernabé Montoya and Nick Rael tugged off Shorty.

"You're grown *men*!" Bloom shouted, almost hysterical himself. "And this is a *game*!"

"Fuck this game, that son of a bitch tried to kill me," Joe squealed, his voice skipping up a few registers like it always did when he was enraged.

Shorty just smiled, cool as a cucumber in spite of a split lip. And, allowing his goading smile to grow into a truly nasty chuckle, he said in Spanish, "Just play the game, José. Hitting the second baseman to break up the double play, that's just part of the game, man."

"For crissakes, this isn't the majors," Bloom complained. "Is this the majors? We're not even in shape, some of us are old men—is the point to kill each other?"

"Fuck it. Screw these bastards. Let's call it off," Harlan Betchel said disgustedly. "In fact, if Joe stays in, count me out of it. He's got too many hornets up his ass tonight and Bloom is right. You people want to kill each other, count me out."

"Yeah," Floyd Mondragón agreed, "there's no point to this. This isn't a ball game, this is a war."

"Ah, come on," Nick Rael said, "let's get on with the game."

"Not if he plays," Joe hissed, pointing at Shorty.

"Not if he plays," Harlan Betchel grumbled, aiming a bat at Joe.

"Are you threatening me with that bat?" Joe snarled.

"Oh shit," Bernabé Montoya snapped, gently pushing Joe back.

"I don't care who plays, I'm not playing," said Johnny Pacheco. "This is no fun. A game should be fun."

They mingled around, bickering petulantly for a moment; tempers died; the game commenced again. Herbie Goldfarb served up a home run, a deep fly out, a triple, and then Harlan Betchel laid a nice bunt down along the first base line. The first baseman charged the ball, and Herbie, perhaps acting on some latent instinct that was a holdover from a previous incarnation, stumbled over to cover the bag at first, in itself a good idea. But he placed himself directly behind the center of the bag, and at about the same time that he received the ball from the first baseman, he also caught all two hundred and ten pounds of Harlan Betchel, frantically legging out his bunt like a rusty runaway locomotive.

The onrushing Betchel express didn't just knock Herbie down: it knocked him to earth so hard that he bounced, and, after trampling over him like the proverbial herd of thundering buffalo, Harlan toppled to the ground himself. Both Charley Bloom and Joe Mondragón probably would have reached Harlan in a photo finish, if Joe hadn't stumbled halfway there and gone flying.

As Bloom and Harlan, and then Joe, collided, both Bernabé Montoya and Nick Rael were running toward the rumble, yelling hoarsely, "The game is over, you bastards! *The game is over!*"

Joe was practically sobbing when they dragged him off. "The pendejo wants to kill us!" he bellowed. "That asshole wants to murder us all!"

"Oh, come off it," Harlan whined defensively. "Look where that kid was standing. I'm allowed to try for a hit. He's not supposed to stand there."

"Anyway, it's over," the sheriff said. "This is no game. Everybody's too uptight."

"Don't look at me," Horsethief Shorty drawled smugly. "I'm not uptight."

"A baseball bat up your—" Joe shrieked in Spanish. "You'll get yours."

"Oh hell, José, go home," Bernabé said. "Go home and grow up. You alright, kid?"

Herbie was sitting there, pinching his nose. "I think so . . . my nose is kind of sore."

"Listen, I'm sorry," Harlan apologized. "But that was a dumb place to stand. I couldn't stop myself. Drop in at the café sometime, I'll give you a free egg sandwich, or a hamburger, or a milkshake, whatever you like."

"Oh jee*zus*!" Joe spat blood. "You know where the Pilar's hamburgers come from, Goldy? From Louie Baca's glue-factory horses down in Chamisaville. And sometimes from the monkeys that croak in the Capital City zoo!"

"It's over," Nick Rael said glumly. "Is it all over?"

Claudio García loomed over everybody. He could only speak in Spanish. "Hey José," he chuckled. "Maybe if you hadn't ducked back there that bat would of knocked some sense into your head."

"Very funny," Joe growled, patting his bloody lower lip, wincing with each pat.

Having returned to her spot on the grassy knoll, Ruby Archuleta said cheerfully, "This game is called on account of attempted murder."

"It ain't that funny," Bernabé Montoya groused.

Herbie Goldfarb picked himself up and, letting out a deep breath, he announced: "I'm going to *walk* home—"

He got lost, though. Somehow, landmarks changed with dusk as he meandered down the bumpy dirt road toward town. Or maybe he had been so shook up he just couldn't pay close enough attention. A number of times he halted to gawk at the transparent and magnified moon balanced atop a nearby mountain like a ball on a seal's nose. Then it was the night-hawks that astonished him, those beautiful falcon-winged owl-colored birds, dashing after insects, beeping in a raspy, loud monotone. Down lower, where an Indian Creek feeder streamlet crossed under the road and the valley floor's marshy fields began, at least a dozen bats in the air actually frightened him. Their high sonic calls were audible; and sometimes they flew so close to his head that he could hear their leathery wingbeats.

Abruptly it was dark, and Herbie had no idea how to thread the intricate maze to home. To make matters worse, dogs started barking as he walked by. Some actually pranced savagely onto the road, raising an unbelievably raucous stink. One pack of jabbering

mutts charged across a field, threatening first to deafen
him, then to trample him to death, then to tear him
slobberingly, teeth-clickingly from limb to limb. But
they skidded to a stop at their owner's barbed wire
boundary, and sat there, howling and gnashing their
teeth until he turned a corner.

Next, two friendly simpering hounds crawled out of
a ditch, and, limping badly from broken legs and
crippled hips, from BB or real gunshot wounds, they
cringed along—tails between their legs—at his heels,
whining unctuously, half-creeping, half-slinking, looking up at him beggingly from the sides of their
whitened eyeballs, flinching whenever he just slightly
stumbled or gave them an angry glance; starved for
affection (not to mention for a bowl of Gaines Meal,
for a rabbit, or for a can of Friskies). When Herbie
finally snarled at these groveling outcasts, who reminded him too much of himself, ordering them to go
home, they flattened onto their bellies and dragged
themselves in the dirt, pleading for just a speck of
human kindness, and—surprised by his reaction—the
volunteer discovered that he wanted to kick them in
their sly-eyed, obsequious guts; he wanted to bust
some more of their ribs.

Later, Onofre Martínez's powerful three-legged
German shepherd charged off its porch like an enraged water buffalo, jumped over the picket fence,
and hung on the volunteer's heels. Practically on tip-
toes, Herbie begged the dog to go away, to leave him
alone. But the massive dog refused to heed his whimpering request until he crossed some invisible boundary
beyond which the savage cur would not travel.
As suddenly as it had attached itself, it quit dogging
his heels and sat down, staring after him with eyes
drowsily half-closed, contented and serene, maybe
even purring.

Other dogs stayed on their porches, happy to mark
his appearance and departure with passive earsplitting
symphonies. Their barks set off a chain reaction, so
that as Herbie limped fearfully by any given adobe,
usually about fifteen or twenty insane animals were

announcing his existence to the rest of the world at large.

Thinking that cutting across a field would lead closer to home, Herbie found himself suddenly surrounded by cows—which he took to be bulls—and by two of the biggest, shaggiest horses he had ever laid eyes upon. The cows gazed at him with a sort of threatening idiotic placidity; the horses peered down their long snouts like curious, intelligent gods.

Desperately, Herbie started to back up. The cows remained in place, but the two horses were interested; they lumbered toward him in a huge friendly manner. Ducking backward through a fence, Herbie caught a sleeve on a barb, tearing the shirt in his panic to reach safety. The horses stopped at the wire and rumbled a little, but apparently decided not to barge through the flimsy barbed strands and trample him to death.

Eventually, sighting on the small cluster of garish mercury vapor lamps in town, Herbie made it to Rael's store, and from there he knew the way home.

But the skunks were flirting or fighting or whatever underneath the floorboards, making sleep impossible; his eyes burned and his brain felt as if it had been wrapped in hot green chilies. Dogs barked and were silent and barked some more. At one awful point, every kind of canine voice imaginable cut loose, rejoicing, wailing in pain, some barks offering challenges, others announcing, with fear or ecstasy, the hectic gang-banging of females in heat. Toward midnight, coyotes on the western mesa sang their falsetto tunes and were answered. And so, how the hell could an Easterner, used to nothing more hysterical than police sirens and fire engines and cars honking and women screaming "Rape!" and muggers thudding their fists into gurgling victims, get any sleep?

Around 2:00 A.M. a small brown bear wandered into town, and the security dog Harlan Betchel kept locked in the Pilar Café, a Doberman named Brutus, went wild. The bear stared at Brutus for a while, then clumped up the road leading to Herbie Goldfarb's redolent adobe shack. It so happened that at the time

the bear strolled through, Herbie was camped in his
open-air outhouse. But the bear padded silently across
the dirt yard without giving him so much as a tumble,
and kept right on going until it hit the juniper-piñon
cover of the foothills.

When Herbie finally slept that night, Hieronymus
Bosch never had such chilling nightmares.

∽

Joe Mondragón owned four cows, three horses, and
ten sheep. His personal earthen property, on which
he might have grazed these animals, consisted of one
irrigated acre around his house, five sageland acres in
the Coyote Arroyo section of Milagro, one and seven-
tenths acres of sageland and sparse gramma grass near
the north–south highway, and the seven-tenths of an
acre on the west side where his beans were growing.

The sum total of vegetation on this land was enough
to keep one cow in food for approximately sixteen
days out of every year.

Hence, in order to keep his other livestock functioning, Joe had to supplement their diets with hay bales
bought locally or from outside or with hard-to-come-
by grazing permits which allowed him to fatten them
up on government grass, or by playing a frustrating,
frantic, and never-ending game of musical pastures:
that is, by switching his livestock from one small field
to another small field to another small field in town,
renting these fields from neighbors or borrowing them
from friends. This was the most common way for
animals to survive in Milagro, though also one of
the most tenuous, since almost everyone else also
owned animals of one sort or another that they were
simultaneously and continually switching around, too.
Thus, just about every small pasture was overgrazed
and had been overgrazed ever since the government
and the Ladd Devine Company appropriated most of
the rest of the county some one hundred years ago.

Joe had a permit to graze two head of cattle in the
National Forest from June through October. Only
twenty-five years ago, Joe's father, Esequiel, had
had a permit to graze one hundred sheep and sixty

cows in the National Forest. Joe had inherited this permit from his father (promptly losing 10 percent of the animals allowed on each permit through an official attrition policy akin to inheritance taxes), and down through the last fifteen years he had seen the number of animals allowed on it steadily reduced through some kind of governmental bureaucratic black magic, until he had grazing rights for only two cows left from that rich heritage bequeathed to him by his father.

Joe's case was not unique: all Milagro was in more or less the same boat. Everybody could remember those days when, even though they had lost much communal land, they had still been allowed permits to run cattle and sheep and goats galore in the National Forest. And everybody was a little stunned by how these permits had been miraculously whittled away, until today almost nobody, except for Eusebio Lavadie and Ladd Devine, had the right to run much more than a token animal up there in the tourist and timbering country, which was so green and lush the odor coming off it into Milagro on the evening breezes could make a skinny horse just about scream.

One way the permits had been reduced was simply by annually upping their costs by about two cents per head. An even quicker and more popular way to shave permits was by impounding cattle that strayed out of their designated government areas (or off private land onto the unfenced National Forest), and fining people exorbitantly to get them back. Along with the fine (which was usually twenty dollars—the lifetime savings of most town residents), the head count on a rancher's permit was often cut as punishment; and in this way the small farmers' permits had been reduced to almost nothing over the past years in order to make room in the forest for the far more lucrative tourists and big-game hunters and timbering interests.

Joe's animals survived because Joe hustled twenty-eight hours a day to keep them alive. But also they survived because they were tough. No animal in Joe's herds, or in Milagro for that matter, except for the sheep, were ever allowed into any structure that resembled a shed or a barn. Hence, on a typical winter morning when the sun rose, any number of fuzzy white beasts could be seen moving stiffly around in the white fields, their fur frozen solid, snow piled high on their backs, their eyelashes looking like Christmas tree branches. Often it rained on a January evening and then froze an hour later, so that the horses and cows became ice sculptures that could not move until they were thawed out some fifteen hours later by the next day's sunshine. Other times, on chill winter mornings, cattle and horses might be seen standing very still in the boggy vegaland, having been frozen into place overnight, and—again—they were waiting for the sun to melt the icy ground so they could recommence pawing through the snow for food.

Like everyone else in town, Joe was also constantly engaged in the aforementioned game of musical pastures, begging friends and neighbors and even enemies for the right to rent or use their fields for one or more of his animals for one or more days, weeks, or what have you. Thus, at any given time he might have two cows on a permit up in the forest, one cow in Panky Mondragón's quarter-acre backyard, the other cow in with Bernabé Montoya's cows up on Bernabé's canyon land, one horse eating hay at home and another horse in a half-acre pasture belonging to Nick Rael, the third horse on a tether beside the highway eating the Right of Way grass for nothing, and his ten sheep spread into groups of three, three, and four each, grazing in overgrazed pastures belonging to Pete Apodaca, Ray Gusdorf, and Seferino Pacheco, respectively. Meanwhile, of course, Pete Apodaca had both his horses in a pasture rented from Eusebio Lavadie, and Ray Gusdorf had his seven cattle split up into groups that were on a Forest Service permit, in a Nick Rael field, in Joe Mondragón's backyard, and running loose (by "accident") along the same lush highway Right of Way on which Joe's tethered horse was grazing.

Since Eusebio Lavadie had more pastureland than everyone else, people were always trying to work deals whereby their animals could graze on his grass for a nominal fee. Lavadie himself owned many animals, but he had permits to graze them on either Bureau of Land Management or National Forest land, so his own bottomland could be rented out to others, which he was only too glad to do. Naturally, he charged exorbitantly for the right to graze on his land, and was thus able to pay for his BLM and National Forest permits and turn a tidy profit to boot. Which was the unhappy way the ball had been bouncing in Milagro for quite some time, and which was just another reason Eusebio Lavadie was not a particularly well-liked person in the Miracle Valley.

Given the situation, much illegal grazing went on in the Milagro area. Joe Mondragón often cut a horse or two loose onto the BLM land controlled by Eusebio Lavadie, and Ray Gusdorf often cut his own fences so that his cows could wander by mistake into the Dancing Trout's verdant pastures. In fact, fences were constantly being snipped accidentally so that skinny cows, horses, or sheep might wander off their owner's mini-dustbowls into their neighbors' less parched fields. Quite often the irate neighbors responded by shooting the offensive intruders, but such shootings amounted to pyrrhic vengeance, because the law read a person had to fence animals "out," not "in" and thus if a rancher shot an animal that had wandered onto his property, the blame for it being on that property was always the rancher's, never his neighbor's, and the rancher always wound up shelling out in spades in court for destroying his neighbor's livelihood.

This law held true for private property owners only, however. For if a private cow happened to wander out of its barren pasture onto National Forest land, the cow's owner, and not the Forest Service, was to blame.

One day a cow belonging to Joe Mondragón walked through a rusty fence surrounding Seferino Pacheco's back field and wandered up the Milagro Canyon road past the Dancing Trout, turned left into a lush meadow owned by the United States of America, and was immediately impounded by Floyd Cowlie and Carl Abeyta, who lassoed the gaunt animal and led it back into the stock pen behind Forest Service headquarters in town, and then dutifully sent Joe a gleeful letter announcing that if he didn't pick up his cow and pay the twenty-dollar fine within five days, the cow would no longer be his. The letter also mentioned that since this was the third time a Mondragón cow had been discovered poaching on government greenery, the amount of cattle allowed on Joe's permit, number 37765, was being reduced from two to one.

The letter was posted in the Milagro Post Office at the back of Rael's store, and the postmaster, Nick Rael, threw it into the mail bag which would be picked up by Teddy Martínez and taken to Chamisaville for sorting and canceling, a process that might take two days, and then Teddy Martínez would bring the bag of Milagro mail back up to Rael's store, where it would sit for a day or so until Nick, or his kid, Jerry, got around to putting it out in the boxes.

Before all this could happen, however, Joe showed up at Pacheco's to drop a salt block into the field, and when he discovered his cow had flown the coop he started screaming at Seferino, who just glowered lopsidedly at him during the five-minute tirade. When Joe finally stopped for air, the big morose drunkard said, "José, I let you put that sick cow in my field for nothing, so I didn't have no obligation to mend no fences."

"Sure, you let me put it in for nothing," Joe snarled. "There wasn't no grass in that field you could charge me for anyway!"

"Well, why did you put it there in the first place, then?" Pacheco wanted to know.

Joe threw a fistful of dirt on the ground, unleashed a string of curses by way of an adios, and stomped off to search for his skinny animal.

It was on his way back into town after a fruitless search that he caught sight of the cow munching on a bale of mildewed government hay in the pen behind Forest Service headquarters. And when Joe saw his cow in that corral his heart almost stopped, because he knew straight off that, not only was the steer's freedom going to cost him twenty dollars he didn't have, but also a permit head as well.

So Joe went home and got drunk. After about his third beer he fetched his .30–06 from the bedroom and loaded it up; then he went back into the kitchen and laid the rifle across the table and popped open another tallboy, getting himself revved up to do what just about anybody else in town in his position would have done, given tradition and the nature of these particular circumstances.

"What are you getting ready to do, José?" Nancy asked warily, knowing only too well what her husband was getting ready to do.

"I'm gonna go over to Pacheco's place and shoot his fucking pig and his fucking chickens and maybe even his fucking self for letting my fucking cow get out of that fucking field," Joe said.

Nancy sighed wearily and sat down at the table, absentmindedly sticking her pinkie in the gun barrel's snout.

"Oh, you are so stupid, José," she said. "The Floresta is kicking you in the butt, so what do you do, you go and kick Pacheco in the butt. Then maybe Pacheco will go and kick Onofre Martínez in the butt, and to get back at him Onofre will charge Ray Gusdorf three times what he should charge him for a load of wood, and in retaliation Ray Gusdorf will tell Pete Apodaca to take his cows out of Ray's field, and Pete Apodaca will give his wife Betty a black eye or a broken arm in payment for *that,* and meanwhile Floyd Cowlie and Carl Abeyta will be rolling around on the Floresta office floor laughing about what a lot of dumbbells we all are."

Joe stared at her, hostility gleaming out of his eyes.

"Well, where am I gonna get that twenty bucks?" he asked acidly. "Maybe God will leave it under my pillow tonight?"

"I don't know," Nancy pouted. "But I'm sick of the way it's always a hundred of us who wind up paying that measly twenty bucks, and you still lose another cow off the permit."

Joe polished off his beer, hoisted up the rifle, and

said "I'll see you around" as he kicked open the kitchen door and staggered out, murder humming through his blood.

About halfway to Seferino Pacheco's house, Joe hit the brakes hard and skidded to a stop. Then he popped the clutch, lunged forward, and stalled.

And he just sat there in the truck in the middle of the dirt road, thinking.

Onofre Martínez's mottled-green, 1953 Chevy pick-up with the three-legged German shepherd on the cab roof and Onofre behind the wheel, and with his great-grandchildren Chemo and Chepa in back, came down the road toward Joe and lurched to a stop: Onofre waved and then beeped for Joe to pull over a little, and Joe gave him the finger.

Onofre turned off his truck, got out, and walked over to the driver's side of Joe's vehicle.

"What's up, cousin?" he asked warily. "What's the matter with you?"

"I had a cow in Seferino Pacheco's field and he let it get out, and now it's eating mildewed hay in that fucking corral in the back of the fucking Floresta office."

Onofre whistled softly, almost gently, the way all people in Milagro had a tendency to whistle whenever they learned about a disaster of such gigantic proportions.

Then he asked, "But how come you're sitting in the middle of the road like this?"

"I dunno," Joe said, puzzled over his own indecision. "I was going over to Pacheco's place to pay him back for letting my cow get loose."

Onofre said, "What's the point of that? All of us are always paying each other back when the Floresta arrests one of our animals. So then instead of just one person suffering, two people or three people or four people or twenty people all suffer, and the Floresta just sits in their wood-paneled office having a good laugh about what a bunch of lamebrained idiots the lot of us are."

"Yeah, I know," Joe said. "Nancy was just telling me."

Onofre's eyes narrowed, growing a little sleepy-looking as he suggested casually: "You'd think that someday somebody in this town would have the intelligence to lay the blame where the blame deserves to be laid, qué no?"

"I suppose so," Joe said, his own eyes narrowing a little in that sleepy, thoughtful manner—

One-half hour later a small cluster of pickups belonging respectively to Joe Mondragón, Onofre Martínez, Ray Gusdorf, the Body Shop and Pipe Queen, and Sparky Pacheco appeared at the corral behind the Forest Service headquarters, and after Marvin LaBlue and Sparky Pacheco had opened the corral gate, Joe lassoed his cow.

Both Floyd Cowlie and Carl Abeyta came hurrying out the back door of the office shouting, "Hey, what the hell do you men think you're doing?"

"I just came for my cow," Joe said. "No problem." And he grinned.

"That's right," Onofre Martínez confirmed, "he just came to pick up his cow."

"Well, you'll have to come into the office and sign a form," Carl said. "Have you got the twenty bucks?"

"I think this time I'll just take my cow without signing the forms or paying the twenty bucks," Joe observed calmly, casually tying the other end of his rope to the pickup bumper.

"Hey, hold on a minute," Floyd Cowlie protested. "Just what the hell do you think you're doing?"

And, dropping a hand onto his gun, Carl Abeyta called loudly, "Come on, Joe, you know that ain't regulations." Then more softly, to his partner: "Floyd, you hustle into the office and give Bernabé a call—"

As Floyd Cowlie headed back into the office, Joe said, "Carl, this is my cow and I don't got the twenty bucks to pay for it, and you can take your regulations and shove them."

"Goddammit, you men are breaking the law, do you know that? This is a felony. You can be thrown in jail. I'll hand you your pimpled asses on a silver platter—"

"You do that, Carl," Onofre Martínez drawled,

"and I got a feeling you'd be transformed overnight into the equivalent of a jackrabbit on a target range."

Joe grinned at Carl, swung into his truck, and moved off slowly, leading the cow out of the corral. Claudio García dropped off the fence and shut the gate. Whereupon Carl Abeyta drew his gun.

As soon as Carl drew his gun, he realized it was 130 percent the wrong thing to have done. But once it was out, how could he stick it back in the holster? And anyway, once it was out, and once he had shouted, "Okay, you bastards, you're under arrest for stealing government property!" how could he have sheathed the weapon without inviting them to point their rifles at him (there were eight weapons visible, either tucked in the crooks of their arms or arranged menacingly in pickup window racks) and perhaps even discharge a bullet or two in his direction?

There followed a particularly quiet standoff. None of the men moved, but they all harbored looks of disdain which suggested that nobody considered Carl was pointing anything much more menacing than a popgun. They also knew what Carl knew, namely, that if he so much as fired one shot at them, the death of Bonnie and Clyde would read like a Walt Disney fairy tale compared to the annihilation of Carl Abeyta and Company.

The group was assembled in this manner when Bernabé Montoya drove up. As soon as the sheriff assessed the situation, he sighed heavily, wishing to hell that he'd never had a phone installed in his living room. Then he opened the cab door, slouched out onto the ground near the corral, and said, "Carl, why don't you holster that gun before somebody gets hurt?"

Carl stammered, "If I do, Bernie, they'll kill me."

"Oh cut the crap," Bernabé said. "Not while I'm around nobody's shooting anybody, qué no, boys?"

The boys let their eyes shift vagrantly over to Bernabé, and they gave him a cluster of cool, sleepy-eyed glances that almost made him shiver. Then they allowed their eyes to float back over to Carl, who was so drained he looked like an Anglo.

"Well, how about if somebody told me what the problem is here?" Bernabé proposed.

"Joe there, he's stealing government property," Carl said.

"You stole *my* property," Joe snarled.

"I take it that cow is what all this fuss is about?" Bernabé said.

"We impounded that cow yesterday," Floyd Cowlie explained. "And Joe over there, he refused to pay the fine, and now he's stealing it out of our corral, and this corral is U.S. Government property that those men broke into, and until such time as Joe pays for that cow the animal is government property."

"Carl," Bernabé suggested, "first off, why don't you sheathe that fucking pistol, because as far as I can see it's just creating antagonism."

"Not on your life, Bernie. I do and they'll shoot me down in cold blood."

"Aw, for crissakes," Bernabé muttered disgustedly. "Hey, you boys, if Carl puts away that gun are you gonna shoot him in cold blood?"

And to a man, smiling faintly, chillingly, loving the act, the boys all just slightly nodded their heads yes.

Bernabé figured he better try a different tack. Addressing Carl, he said, "Uh, I guess you found that cow up in the forest, that's why you arrested it, qué no?"

Carl swallowed dryly and just barely tilted his head yes, keeping his eyes all the while on the "boys."

"And you found it up there yesterday, is that right too?"

Floyd Cowlie answered: "Yup, that's right."

"Now José," Bernabé said carefully, "when was it that cow got out of Pacheco's field, do you remember?"

"It was yesterday," Joe said, keeping his eyes on Carl Abeyta instead of shifting them over to the sheriff.

"Well, perhaps you found that cow before it even ate a handful of government property," Bernabé said to Carl, "and so maybe you didn't have no right to arrest it since it hadn't yet technically broke any of the rules."

Carl let his eyes flick over to Bernabé, who had dropped his eyes to where his boot tips—pointing outward from being on the wrong feet—were scuffing self-consciously in the dust.

The district supervisor asked, "What are you driving at, Bernie?"

"What I'm driving at is I don't think there's any way to prove that cow had actually trespassed the legal amount of time on government land, so in all fairness you oughtta just let José take it home, and if you sent him one of them letters you oughtta kill the copy in your files, and forget about the fine and the permit reduction, and then everybody will be happy, qué no, boys?"

This time the boys grinned, muttering, "That's right, Bernie," or "Que sí, sheriff," things like that.

Carl protested, "Bernie, you're a damn fool, you don't know your ass from government law in this case."

The sheriff remarked, "It's your ass that has got a bullseye painted on it right now, Carl."

Whereupon Floyd Cowlie hissed in Carl's ear, "Do like he says, you idiot, what are you trying to do, get us both killed?"

Put that way, Carl suffered a reluctant change of heart. "Well . . . uh, okay, Bernie. I guess maybe you're right. I hadn't exactly considered things in that light."

"I didn't figure you had," Bernabé said, daring to look up now as he added, "So how about stashing that firearm, okay?"

"Sure," Carl said amenably, slowly and gingerly slipping the pistol back into the holster. "Course, I wouldn't of shot nobody," he laughed. "Shit, you boys know that." He couldn't quite bring himself to uncurl his fingers from the grip, however.

The boys didn't say anything, so Bernabé prompted, "Hell, you boys knew that, right?"

"Rrrrriiiiggggght . . ." the boys mumbled slowly, reluctantly letting it out.

"Okay. So why don't we break it up now, huh? José, you take that skinny heifer back home, or back to Pacheco's place, and see if you can't keep better track of it next time."

With that, carefully unwinding, the men got into their pickups, started their engines, and slowly pulled away from the corral. By way of an adios, Joe tooted his horn and waved gaily at the sheriff and the two Forest Service personnel, then led his cow up the road at a brisk trot.

Bernabé grumbled, "I oughtta arrest you, Carl, for pulling that gun. What's the matter with you anyway?"

"But did you see what they did? They just came by and took that cow. In a hundred years nobody ever did anything like that. I could take every one of those bastards to court—"

"Sure you could. And I could sit tight at home out on the front porch in a rocker with my boot heels up on the railing while they had another Smokey the Bear santo riot, or did you forget about that? And then when it was all over I could mosey on down to the camposanto with a wine jug tucked under my arm and help them dig your and Floyd there's graves."

Carl squatted and picked up a handful of dirt, letting it trickle through his fingers, thoughtful as he replied, "Nothing like this ever happened before." As he spoke, a bird, a little pine siskin, flitted through the corral fence, zipping low to the ground, and for some reason did not register Carl's bulk in its way. Carl never saw it coming, either, and when the hapless bird banged head-on into his ear he gave a startled yelp, tumbling over sideways as if struck by a bullet. The siskin landed upside down several feet away, and lay on its back in the dust, flopping and kicking spastically while issuing pained chirrupy gurgles.

"For chrissakes!" Floyd Cowlie exclaimed.

But none of them could move, not Bernabé nor Floyd, nor Carl lying on his side with his head in the dust, staring at the gasping bird.

Suddenly the siskin righted and ruffled its feathers, shaking out the dust as it blinked a few times, and then with a hotshot rocketing little explosion it took

off again, only to collide immediately with a corral
post and bounce back into the dust knocked out cold.

Astonished as he was, Bernabé went over and
picked up the bird and frowned at it, unable to sum-
mon the proper words for the occasion.

After a moment the intrepid siskin opened its eyes
and shivered, coming back to life. When Bernabé figured it was in possession of all its faculties, including
that of flight, he threw it up in the air, expecting that
it would take off.

Instead, the bird never once flapped a wing, plowing back to earth like a shot, causing a minuscule
explosion of dust when it smacked into the dirt, breaking its neck.

"Nothing like *that* ever happened before either,"
Bernabé finally managed to croak.

৵

As everyone knows, Smokey the Bear is a symbol
of the United States Forest Service. And for almost
a hundred years the United States Forest Service had
been the greatest landholder in Chamisa County, although most of the land it held had once not so very
long ago belonged to the people of Milagro. And,
since the Forest Service's management of its recently
acquired property tended to benefit Ladd Devine the
Third, big timber and mining companies, and out-of-
state hunters and tourists before it benefited the poor
people of Milagro, the poor people of Milagro tended
to look upon Smokey the Bear as a kind of ursine
Daddy Warbucks, Adolf Hitler, colonialist Uncle Sam,
and Ladd Devine all rolled into one.

Many years ago, the alcoholic expatriate santo
carver Snuffy Ledoux, who was so poor at that particular moment in time that he was practically baking
and eating his own Monkey Ward boots, had contracted with the then District Forest Supervisor Buddy
Gabaldón (Carl Abeyta's predecessor) to mass produce a line of little foot-high wooden Smokey the
Bears, which Buddy planned to sell to tourists who
stopped by Forest Service headquarters for maps and
fire permits, snakebite kits and bug repellent, and so

forth. Snuffy had contracted to make the Smokeys for a buck and a half apiece, and Buddy sold them for three dollars.

As it turned out, these hand-carved and hand-painted little Floresta talismans moved like hotcakes. But not exactly in the way the district supervisor had had in mind.

No tourist ever wound up with a little wooden Smokey. Because as soon as they went on sale in the headquarters, people from town began stealing them off the counter. So Buddy put them inside the glass display case, whereupon the locals actually began to pay money for them hand over fist. Buddy couldn't believe how popular Snuffy Ledoux's wooden Smokeys were. They were so popular, in fact, that one day a one-armed bandit with a black kerchief over his face, accompanied by a huge and ferocious three-legged German shepherd, marched into Forest Service headquarters, flung an empty feed sack on the counter, pointed the business end of a .45 automatic at Buddy Gabaldón's Adam's apple, and suggested Buddy stuff all the Smokeys he had in stock into that bag, which Buddy—who had a great lust for his own life—was more than happy to do.

The question, of course, was: Why were these statuettes so popular with the local folk? And the answer was: People were treating those pudgy, diminutive Floresta santos the way one might treat a voodoo doll. In short, they kicked the little Smokeys around their houses; they poured kerosene on the little Smokeys and lit them; they hammered nails into the little Smokeys; and in a great many other imaginative and bestial ways they desecrated Snuffy Ledoux's carvings in hopes of either destroying the United States Forest Service or at least driving that Forest Service away from Chamisa County, and, in particular, away from Milagro.

When Snuffy Ledoux realized how popular his carvings had become, he decided to break his contract with Buddy Gabaldón, who was more than happy to accommodate the artisan because he—Buddy—hadn't logged a decent night's repose since the armed robbery of his Smokey stock. Still and all, the contract Buddy signed with Snuffy had been forged in the sluggish and self-righteous bowels of the United States Government's implacable bureaucracy in Washington, D.C., and in order to terminate this contract, Buddy had to explain things to headquarters back East, and naturally headquarters back East replied, "Nonsense! If they're selling like hotcakes, the contract should maybe be renegotiated, but never terminated!"

There was no way, however, that Snuffy Ledoux wanted to renegotiate that contract. In business for himself (though guided by the managerial genius of Onofre Martínez), he could sell the Smokeys directly to the people for three greenbacks a shot, thus earning a buck and a half more than he had been earning per santo in his deal with Buddy.

The original contract, however, called for Snuffy to supply a certain number of Smokeys, and at the time he decided to go into business for himself Snuffy had only supplied Buddy with half the statuettes called for in their legal agreement. Which was again okay with Buddy, who lived in Milagro and thus represented a kind of everpresent moving target. Hence, whatever Snuffy and the other townsfolk wanted to do with those little Smokeys, God bless 'em and Merry Christmas and far be it from Buddy to interfere.

The new arrangement wasn't okay with Uncle Sam, however. Namely, because Uncle Sam, thanks to Buddy Gabaldón, had shelled out a couple of hundred dollars to Snuffy Ledoux as an advance against all those Smokey the Bears Snuffy planned to produce, and here was Snuffy welshing on his word. Uncle Sam also suspected that Buddy Gabaldón was lying about the whole thing. "They use them for *voodoo* dolls?" the Regional Director Tommy Bascomb screamed, via the telephone, into Buddy's right ear. "You got to be kidding!"

"Why don't you come up here and see for yourself," Buddy whimpered.

"You're darn tootin I'm gonna come up there and see for myself," Tommy Bascomb threatened. "And

I'm gonna start proceedings against that Ledoux character if he refuses to come across!"

Ai, Chi-hua-hua! Buddy Gabaldón hung up the phone and he felt like barfing.

He also felt as if suddenly his life wasn't worth a plug nickel.

A few days later Tommy Bascomb guided his big, shiny green, U.S. Government Regional Director's Forest Service truck to a stop in front of the Milagro district headquarters and clomped inside. Two minutes later he walked out again accompanied by Buddy Gabaldón, and they pulled away from the headquarters heading for Snuffy Ledoux's humble adobe abode on the west side of town.

"How about stopping at my place first," Buddy suggested.

"What for?" Tommy asked.

"I want to pick up my rifle, my pistol, and a few hand grenades. You never can tell."

Tommy Bascomb scoffed, parked in front of Snuffy Ledoux's decrepit hovel, and the two men strode inside, Bascomb brandishing a rolled-up copy of the government's contract with Snuffy like a knight's lance, Buddy all hunched over and just about walking sideways in order to present as small a target as possible.

Snuffy greeted them with the openhearted good humor and warmth he usually reserved for rattlesnakes, gila monsters, and the bubonic plague. He was sitting in the middle of a dark room surrounded by maybe a hundred and twenty foot-high statuettes of Smokey the Bear. Onofre Martínez and Amarante Córdova were off in another corner painting the Smokeys. Tommy Bascomb unrolled the contract and thrust it under Snuffy's nose, and Snuffy sniffed it and then squinched down his eyebrows, pretending to study the various clauses the regional director so self-righteously proffered. Buddy Gabaldón knew Snuffy couldn't sign his own name, let alone read, or write, or even speak English, but Buddy was so busy trying to remain inconspicuous in the background that he didn't bother to inform Tommy Bascomb of this fact.

"According to this contract," Tommy Bascomb said,

"you owe the United States Government one hundred and ten more Smokey the Bears, for which you have already been paid."

Snuffy shrugged and, in Spanish, suggested the regional director place one of his fingers somewhere and then afterward suck on it like on a popsicle stick.

"What did he say?" Tommy Bascomb asked Buddy.

"He says he begs to differ with you but he feels he has already fulfilled his contract obligations," Buddy whimpered.

"Bullshit. If he's gonna give me the runaround, the government will simply attach what is the government's due. Help me cart these little statues out of here."

Thus, when Tommy Bascomb drove his big green government truck away from Snuffy Ledoux's house, the back of it was filled up with a hundred-and-ten Smokeys. He and Buddy transferred the Smokeys from the truck to the back room of the district headquarters, and when Buddy locked up after they had finished this job, he kissed his fingertips and touched them tenderly to the wooden door of his office, saying good-bye to the building which had housed his hopes, his dreams, and his paycheck for almost a decade.

Next morning, sure enough, many things had happened. To begin with, the throats of the three Forest Service horses in the corral behind headquarters had been slit, and a little Smokey statuette had been shoved halfway up the ass of each dead horse. Likewise, the tires on Tommy Bascomb's big green government truck had been slashed, the slogan CHINGA SMOKEY! had been painted all over his vehicle, and another santo had been whittled down so it could be jammed up the truck's tailpipe. The remaining Smokeys had perished in the fire that had quietly, without any alarm being given, burned the district headquarters to the ground.

Tommy Bascomb stared at the carnage, then he started to cry.

"I guess there must of been a short circuit or something in the wiring," Buddy Gabaldón mumbled lamely.

And that was the Smokey the Bear statue (or santo) riot.

And that was also the morning Snuffy Ledoux skipped town, never to return.

Buddy Gabaldón was subsequently relieved of his Milagro post and transferred to the regional director's office in the capital where he became a mere bureaucratic cipher, plowing through mountains of paper work at half his former salary. Sometimes he mourned the good outdoor life at top pay that had been his in Milagro, but after a while the security of his capital job came to outweigh what he had lost, and he forged a separate peace with the disaster that had cost him his former post.

Now it happened—arriving finally in the present (the present being approximately three days after the softball game that was called on account of attempted murder)—that an equipment request from an outlying station, namely, the Milagro station, came across the desk of Buddy Gabaldón's co-worker, Pete Casquabel, in the Capital City regional headquarters office they shared.

"Hey, get a load of this OETB-15 double-zero form!" Casquabel exclaimed.

"What's in it?" Buddy Gabaldón asked, running a hand through his sparse graying hair.

"It's a request from a guy named Carl Abeyta in the Chamisa County Milagro district headquarters for a bunch of bulletproof vests. Now what the hell do I do with a thing like this?"

"Lemme see that form." Buddy frowned, bit his bottom lip, scratched his head, and eventually—solemnly—floated the paper back to Casquabel.

"Just process it with a green flag," he said quietly. "If I know Milagro, I think we better grant them their last request."

Part Three

"We will be like the Vietnamese."
—Ruby Archuleta

❦

By noon on the day after Joe Mondragón "stole" his cow back from the Forest Service, Nick Rael was able to confirm a definite run on ammunition. It began when Tranquilino Jeantete, even before opening the Frontier Bar, entered the store and purchased a box of .30-30 ammo, also a carton of .22 shorts. Next Joe Mondragón himself came in asking for two boxes of .30-30s and one box each of .45s, .270 rifle shells, .22 longs, and 16-gauge number 4 shotgun shells on credit.

Nick dialed *M* in his credit box and informed Joe that as soon as he paid up the ninety-six dollars he owed for groceries, he could have the ammo on credit.

Joe said, "What do you mean ninety-six bucks? Lemme see that bill!"

Nick showed him the bill. "That's your signature," he said very politely.

Joe glared at him. "I got to have that ammo, Nick. You know as well as I do some son of a bitch put a slug through my living room window the other night, and I have to defend myself."

"When you deliver me the money for your bill, I'll be glad to put you on credit again."

Joe snarled, "Maybe the next bullet will knock out that plate glass window you got up front, Nick."

"Is that a threat—?"

"Nobody's issuing any threats. You just better sign

me up for them shells or who's telling what kind of trouble might happen, that's all."

Nick picked up the phone behind the counter and dialed a number. "Hello, Bernie? Nick here, over at the store. Listen, maybe I got a problem. José Mondragón, he's over here, wants to buy some bullets, but he hasn't paid up his bill so I can't extend him any more credit. He's a little pissed-off by this fact and has made a couple of what I'd call threatening statements. Maybe you'd—"

"Fuck you," Joe said. "Forget it."

"Did you tell the sheriff somebody shot a hole in your house," Nick called after Joe.

"Tell him yourself," Joe snapped, kicking open the screen door. "He probably fired the shot himself."

While Joe was on the porch, angrily thumbing two dimes into the soft drink machine, Bud Gleason's Chevy Blazer pulled up in front of the store. Bud swung down from behind the wheel, and Horsethief Shorty ambled around from the passenger side.

" 'Lo," Bud said, keeping his eyes straight ahead as he entered the store. "Hola, José, que 'stasaciendo?" Shorty grinned cheerily, catching the screen door as it started to close, and he followed the real estate agent inside, some pebbles chucked by Mercedes Rael plinking at his heels.

Bud Gleason purchased a box each of .270 rifle bullets and .357 magnum pistol shells. Shorty selected a box of .32s on credit, also some .22 longs.

"You know," Shorty said as he signed the Dancing Trout's charge account sheet, "you better hang that Mexican target out there on your porch someplace else, Nick, or you're liable to wind up with a front wall full of holes and a leaky pop machine."

The men had a good laugh. Nick, for one, quit laughing about seven minutes after Bud and Shorty had left—that is, his mirth died in conjunction with the flamboyant return of Joe Mondragón, who barged into the store accompanied by five big stern-looking people, two of whom carried rifles.

"Hi, cousin," Joe said. "I come to purchase a little ammo."

"Me too, cousin," each of the other men crowed. The biggest of them, six-foot-six-inch Claudio García, approached the counter, opened the breech on his scope-fitted .30-06, and showed it to Nick.

"See?" he said. "It's empty. It ain't got no more bullets."

Whereupon this entire group, excluding Nick, laughed heartily. Then they stocked up on ammo, and Joe gleefully affixed his signature to the charge sheet while Nick fumed. This accomplished, and wishing to affirm that he was a scrupulously honest person who always paid his debts, Joe fished in his pocket for a nickel, which he dropped insolently on the counter, explaining, "I had a soda the last time around and forgot and took the bottle home—here's your fucking deposit, Nick."

The six men had purchased a few other odds and ends, candy bars, Slim Jims and jerky and piñon nuts, and now they hung around for a moment, unwrapping stuff and with exaggerated politeness practically tiptoeing across the store to discard the little wads of crumpled paper in the waste can, while they kept up a running superinnocent patter on the weather, the hay, the sheep and cattle, the tourists and whatnot, and Nick stood behind the counter with eyes as dark as thunderheads and his mouth frozen in a hating— but polite—little smile.

Eventually, the men scuffled arrogantly onto the porch, sitting around a little longer out there, drinking pop and, in loud voices that were sure to drift back inside to Nick, shooting the breeze about how nice and quiet and peaceful and friendly it was here in Milagro.

In due course, they moseyed off into the nearby narrow roads and alleyways. After them, it was mostly singles who came in: a few more Dancing Trout employees; Fred Quintana, the fly-tying short-order cook from the Pilar Café; the Enchanted Land Motel's manager, Peter "The Pedo" Hirsshorn; and a number of old men, among them Sparky Pacheco, Onofre Martínez, Juan F. Mondragón, Panky Mondragón, Ray Gusdorf, and Martín Arguello. Most of these old duffers purchased a single box of ammunition for a .30-30 rifle, joking as they did so about either the fish, grasshoppers, prairie dogs, coyotes, butterflies, or rattlesnakes they were planning to kill.

Around eleven-thirty, Charley Bloom threaded his way through the members of the Senile Brigade still trading gun stories on the porch and entered the store. Nick watched him with interest. Obviously terribly nervous, the lawyer walked around almost aimlessly, up and down Nick's aisles, looking over the food a little too carefully, pinching this and handling that, putting everything back until finally he selected from the cooler a six-pack of beer which he clunked down self-consciously on the glass counter beside the cash register. Only then did he pretend to notice the used guns on prominent display along the top shelf of the counter behind which Nick stood. Carelessly, almost gaily, the big bluff lawyer said, "You know, Nick, for quite some time now I've been meaning to buy a gun. Nothing fancy, of course, just a little something to keep around, to carry in the glove compartment, you know, just in case—"

"Sure," Nick said. "I know."

"What kind of gun would you suggest for that sort of thing? Like, what kind is that one over there, in the corner?"

"That's a .32," Nick said. "That's the kind they call a Saturday night special."

"Oh." Bloom blushed. Suddenly he couldn't believe that he had not only grown up in America, but also had grown half-old in it without ever having fired a gun. "What about that one?" he asked.

"That's a .45 revolver," Nick said.

"Jesus. That's a big mother gun."

"You want to see it?"

"Sure. Why not?"

Nick handed it to Bloom, who turned it over kind of helplessly in his hands.

"How do you load it?" he asked finally.

Nick flipped back the shell guard and showed him.

"Doesn't the cylinder come out? I thought the cylinder was supposed to come out."

"Nope, you just push down the ejector rod here—see? Like that. For spent shells. If they're not spent, they're heavy enough to just fall out."

"Nothing happens when I pull the trigger," Bloom said.

"It's a single-action revolver. You got to pull the hammer back."

"How come the cylinder won't go around?" Bloom laughed nervously. "In the movies they always spin the cylinders around."

"Pull the hammer back two clicks."

Bloom pulled it back two clicks and tried to thumb the cylinder around.

"I guess I was wrong. Try three clicks," Nick said.

Bloom tried three clicks, but it still didn't work.

"Here, lemme see."

Nick took the gun and fiddled with the hammer, pulling it back to various stops, but he couldn't get the cylinder to turn.

"Shit," he muttered with a disappointed smile. "I guess I'll have to strip the fucker down and see what's the matter."

"What do the bullets for a gun like that look like?" Bloom asked.

Nick pried open the flap on a carton of .45s and stood a cartridge up on end on the counter.

"Christ, that's a big shell, isn't it?"

"Yeah. Maybe for you the best gun I got is this one here." Nick removed a .22 with a four-inch barrel. "It's light, you can carry it around easy, your wife, she could handle it too. It's a double action."

"What does that mean?"

"You can shoot it either by pulling the trigger or by pulling back the hammer. You could squeeze the trigger six times in a row and get off six shots."

"Oh."

Bloom held the gun, managed to rotate the cylinder and even spring it out, click it back in; then he pushed the ejector rod in and out of all the chambers.

"I don't know," he said indecisively. "I know this sounds funny, but I just never owned a gun before."

"You came to the wrong place not to own a gun," Nick said. "You wanna see something?"

Nick unbuttoned the two lowest buttons on his shirt and pulled the tails out of his pants, exposing a wide scar tissue patch that covered a large part of his stomach and continued under his belt down across his abdomen.

"Jesus," Bloom whispered.

"My cousin did that to me when I was seventeen," Nick said matter-of-factly. "He shot me with a .38. He was drunk."

Bloom felt sick. "That . . . that must have been something."

Nick shrugged and buttoned up, tucking in his shirt-tails.

Then the storekeeper said, "So?"

Bloom set the .22 down carefully on the glass beside the .45. "I dunno," he mumbled. "I just never owned a gun. There's something weird about buying a gun. You know? I mean, why am I even looking at weapons in the first place? I guess I'm a little paranoid. Things are getting a bit jumpy in this town. But who's to say a gun like this, carrying it around in the car—maybe I'd just be more uptight. I mean, once you get one, that changes your status, doesn't it? And suppose somebody has a beef with you. If he knows you own a gun he'll come after you with a gun. But if you don't own a gun . . ."

"Then it's much easier to kill you," Nick said. "If he knows you have a gun maybe he'll be too chicken to ever come around at all."

Bloom stared at the guns for quite a while. When he broke the silence, it was only to mutter unhappily, "Six of one, half-dozen of the other. That's the way everything turns out, isn't it, Nick?"

The storekeeper leaned back, folding his arms, and stared sideways out the front window, faintly whistling a tune.

Bloom handled the .22 again, asking, "What's the best way to shoot one of these?"

Nick smiled. "Keep it pointed away from your own head."

The lawyer chuckled as if appreciating the joke. "No, I mean, how do you hold it? Would you rest the barrel across your other fist like this?"

"If you wanted to burn the shit out of your hand, I guess that's how you'd do it."

Bloom thought: This wise bastard is making fun of me. He said, "So how's the best way to hold it?"

The storekeeper shrugged. "Hold your arm out straight, I guess. Maybe hold your wrist with your other hand. I dunno. Usually, if you're shooting people, they're pretty close so you don't have to aim much. Just point it in their general direction and shoot."

"I hadn't really planned on shooting people," Bloom said tightly.

"What else you gonna shoot with that kind of hand-gun?"

Nervously, Bloom flickered a glance at Nick, then at the gun in his own hand. "Ooh . . . I guess not," he said suddenly. "I guess I don't really want a gun." He let go of the weapon like a hot potato. "I'm sorry—"

"You don't have to apologize," Nick said.

Bloom walked out—ashamed at having exposed himself, his weaknesses, his fear—just as Bernabé Montoya walked in.

"Lemme have a box of .38s," the sheriff grumbled dejectedly, taking an Eskimo Pie from the ice cream freezer.

"You're lucky I got any left."

"How come?"

"Today I been selling ammo at about two hundred times the normal rate I usually sell it."

"Wonderful," the sheriff groaned, stabbing his teeth through a hunk of the ice cream bar. "That's really good news. That makes my day. Who fired that bullet at José's house the other night?"

"He go to you about it?"

"Would he go to a rattlesnake about it—?"

"I don't know who did that. I was at home. In bed. I didn't even hear the report."

"Sure. Everybody was at home in bed. I guess that bullet must have been fired by El Brazo Onofre."

"I wouldn't know," Nick said. "I just know I sold enough ammunition already today to start our own little Vietnam here. You were at the meeting at Bud's with that Wyoming guy."

"Montana. And screw him." The sheriff licked the wooden ice cream stick clean, flipped it in the general direction of the wastebasket, and selected another Eskimo Pie.

"The God damn state police and the God damn state engineer should keep their God damn noses out of our God damn affairs," he grumbled heatedly. "We should of sat this thing out with little or no fanfare. But oh no, they had to push a panic button. Now you just wait and see what happens. Put the bullets on my card, Nick, and don't sell any ammo to José or any of those other bandits."

"He already came back," Nick said. "With five others, including Claudio García, and two of them had rifles."

"Did they threaten you?"

"Well, not exactly . . . but you know how it is."

"How much did you sell them?"

"Couple of .30-30s, an ought six, .38s, .270s, like that."

"Ai, Chihuahua."

Outside, the sheriff sat on the porch for about five minutes, chewing up a pack of Juicy Fruit, tossing out each stick of gum as soon as the flavor left. An ill wind, blowing no good, was rising. What he ought to do was take his lovely tin star over to that bastard Pancho Armijo and let him have the fucking job.

While Bernabé was sitting there, sorrowful-eyed and whining Seferino Pacheco limped into focus.

"Hey!" the crazy drunk shouted, wavering unsteadily in front of the sheriff. "You seen my pig?"

"Screw your pig!" Bernabé snapped, bolting up and striding past the huge woozy man, who teetered around a bit more, watching the sheriff depart, then staggered over to the porch and sat down with a thud, holding his big miserable head in his big, but curiously delicate, hands.

The VISTA volunteer, Herbie Goldfarb, all sneakers and CCNY sweatshirt, came nervously down the road; Pacheco surveyed his approach with a narrowed, suspicious eye. Herbie carried a knapsack on his back, and after he had shuffled obsequiously past Pacheco with his arm upraised to avoid the flurry of pebbles from Mercedes Rael, he ferreted nervously among Nick's wares, loading up on corned beef hash, bean dip, potato chips, powdered milk, and the like, all of which he would lug home in the mildewed knapsack.

At the counter, Nick—who usually refrained from speaking to Herbie because he wanted the skunk smell out of his store as fast as possible—had an idea. So he asked, "How's it going up at your place?" And Herbie, startled, grinning too wide, said, "Oh, okay, I guess. You know. I'm having a little trouble getting started, but I imagine that pretty soon I'll get into the swing of things. I'm learning Spanish, but I haven't really practiced on anybody yet. I'm still very self-conscious about it."

Nick proceeded quickly to the point: "Aren't you getting tired of those skunks up at your place?"

"You're not kidding I'm tired. I can't sleep anymore. My eyes water all night long. I feel sick twenty-four hours a day."

"I think what you need is a gun," Nick said.

"A gun? What would I do with a gun?"

"Put those skunks out of their misery, for one."

"Do you really think so?" Herbie's heart hammered at the thought of actually owning, let alone pulling the trigger of, a gun.

"Sure. Christ, you wouldn't catch me sleeping three minutes on top of a bunch of stinking skunks. It'll give you the GIs, after a while your skin will peel, your eyes will puff almost shut, and you'll have to move out."

"What kind of gun would a person use to kill a skunk?" Herbie asked meekly.

"How much money can you spend?"

"I don't have much. Only about seventy-five dollars right now."

"Well, how about this .38?" Nick chuckled. "It belonged to a nice little old lady who never drove it over forty."

"Beg your pardon?"

"A joke," Nick explained. "Seriously, I'll give it to you for forty bucks, box of ammo included. You can't go wrong. And anyway, living out there where you do, next door to Mad Dog Joe Mondragón on one side, and Thrill Killer Pancho Armijo on the other side, I'd think you would want something for self-protection. Also, you never know when a bear might come around, or something like that, trying to get into your bacon and beans. Me, I wouldn't be caught dead in a wide open frontier town like this without some kind of self-protection, you want my honest opinion."

"But how would I kill the skunks?"

"There's a hole, ain't there? Under the edge of the house somewheres?"

"Sure, there's two big holes that I've noticed."

"Well, that's how they got under there in the first place. What you want to do, see, is sit down a little ways away, round about suppertime, and just blow them apart when they poke their heads out. Or hell, stick your hand down the hole and blast off a cylinder or two. Even if you don't hit anything, skunks are pretty smart, they're bound to get the idea."

"I never owned a gun before," Herbie said.

"Every man should own a firearm," Nick admonished. "Christ, I got my first gun when I was eight years old. A .22 rifle. By the time I was nine I could thread a bullet up a prairie dog's ass and out his nose from thirty· yards away while he was on a dead run. I killed my first deer when I was twelve."

"You really think this type of gun would be the kind to use on a skunk?" Herbie said.

"Sure. You could use it on just about *any* kind of skunk," Nick sniggered.

"I guess maybe I'll buy it then," Herbie said abruptly, his heart racing like a stuck throttle.

"You 'guess maybe,' or you actually want to buy it?"

"Yes, alright, I mean, I'll buy it," Herbie—flustered —mumbled. "Would you show me how to load it, and how it works and everything?"

Fifteen minutes later Herbie Goldfarb, pacifist, conscientious objector, VISTA volunteer, walked out of there like a young man who had just lost his virginity, the gun and a box of bullets tucked down snug in his pack among the corned beef hash and Spam cans, peanut butter, Bunny bread, and beer. It felt to him as if he had just undergone some powerful rites of passage and now belonged to the western mountains instead of to the East Coast, fair-haired college culture. He was so eager to be home that he almost broke into a trot, pack and all. But then, envisioning the spectacle that would be, he slowed down, and, uncomfortably aware of the Chicano faces following his progress with utter disdain, if not out-and-out hatred, he walked slope-shouldered and humbly the rest of the way home.

There, having opened and drained a beer, he straightaway loaded the gun, and, moving swiftly before second thoughts could sabotage his determination to rub out the skunk colony that was making his life so miserable, he kneeled at the larger of the two entrances to their lair, shoved down his arm, leveled the gun as best he could, and pulled the trigger.

The first explosion hit him with the wallop of a bomb, the sheer volume of sound scaring him so much that he shrieked, yet somehow he managed to pull the trigger again, driving a slug up through his own wooden floor, and with the third shot the gun kicked right out of his hand and he tumbled over backward, expecting the house, or at least the nearest wall, to collapse violently on his head.

In the Pilar Café, Bernabé Montoya knocked over his coffee cup, spilling the hot fluid onto his egg salad sandwich as he cried *"Oh shit it's beginning!"* and dove off his stool. Grabbing a .38 from a shoebox on the shelf under the cash register, Harlan Betchel leaped after the sheriff out the door. Bernabé swung up behind the wheel of his pickup, and Harlan just made it into the passenger seat as the sheriff gunned the truck, spinning his wheels and veering in a sharp U-turn that almost sliced off Seferino Pacheco's knees. They careened into the narrow lane that led to Joe Mondragón's house three hundred yards up the road.

"Get that gun off the rack!" Bernabé panted. "There's a clip in the glove compartment!"

As he complied with the order, Harlan gasped, "It's out at Joe's place, isn't it?"

"Where else, goddammit!"

Tires squealing, they thundered into Joe's yard, and as they did so Joe bolted out his front door, hunched over and running fast, carrying a rifle like a marine gutting it up a Pork Chop Hill, dashing behind a huge cottonwood. Even before Joe reached the tree, however, Harlan was diving out of the truck, his .38 blazing in Joe's direction. Bernabé tumbled out of his door, tripping and crashing belly first into the dirt, then he scrambled up into a squat and backpedaled frantically until his shoulder whacked against a tire, and he spun, duck-waddling hysterically toward the rear as he heard Joe return Harlan's fire, Harlan bellowing and scrambling rearward too as a slug splintered into the other side of the truck, and, plunging around the tail of the pickup from opposite sides, the two men collided head on, each of their weapons —Harlan's .38 and the sheriff's rifle—discharging, though somehow missing, both of them. "You idiot!" Bernabé raged, slugging Harlan clumsily in the chest. *"It's Armijo!"* Joe screamed from the tree. *"He shot at me! What are you shooting at me for?"* "Where is he?" Bernabé hollered. *"I dunno!"* Joe shouted back. *"He's over there somewhere though, he fired three times!"* "Are you hurt?" *"No, but no thanks to you, God damn you, Betchel, are you crazy? You point that gun at me again I'll blow off your balls—!"*

"He . . . he had the gun . . . he was running . . ." Harlan blubbered, ashen-faced, about to faint.

Joe leaped out from behind the tree and scrambled pell-mell across the open space, diving practically into their laps in the shelter of the truck.

"I'm sorry . . ." Harlan stammered. "I didn't think . . ."

"What would Armijo be doing this for?" Bernabé gasped, all out of breath, his heart thundering so hard he thought his chest would explode.

"I dunno. He shot three times," Joe blurted. "I never even saw the bastard. I was watching TV."

"Where did the bullets hit?" the sheriff asked.

"Your guess is as good as mine." Joe crawled up front and peered around the edge of a tire. "I can't see a fucking thing over there. Maybe he's lying on the roof, the bastard, behind the fire wall—"

Actually, Pancho Armijo and his wife Stella were lying on the floor beside their telephone table, Pancho with a rifle in his hands, and Stella manning the telephone.

"Hello, Carolina?" she gasped. "Where's Bernie? José Mondragón is shooting at us! He's gone crazy! He's shooting at us for no reason at all!"

"What? What? *What?*"

"Where's Bernie!" Stella shouted. "They're going to kill us over here!"

"Try the Pilar!"

Stella tried the Pilar. Betty Apodaca answered. "Where's Bernie?" Stella sobbed.

"He just ran out!" Betty babbled excitedly. "There's a shooting over at Joe's and the Armijos!"

"*I'm* Stella Armijo!" Stella wailed. "And I don't see Bernie anyplace around here!"

"But where are you?"

"On the floor beside the telephone table!"

"Well, tell Pancho to look out the window—"

"But they'll shoot him in the head!" Stella cried. "They'll shoot him in the head!" And she hung up.

"Oh shit," Pancho Armijo moaned. "Oh shit, oh shit, oh shit." The weapon in his hand was empty. He hadn't a single bullet in the house. That madman José Mondragón was going to gun them down in cold blood because they didn't have a single bullet in the house.

Their phone rang and Stella answered. It was her talkative good friend Mary Ann C. de Baca down in

Doña Luz, who, before Stella could get a word in edgewise, was wondering if she could contribute a cake or some chocolate chip cookies or something to the Hospital Ladies' Auxiliary bake sale down in Chamisaville this upcoming Saturday.

"I can't," Stella sobbed into the telephone. "We're being shot at, they're trying to kill us, good-bye!"

At the store, Nick dialed the Dancing Trout. Emerson Lapp answered. "They're shooting it out at Joe Mondragón's," Nick shouted breathlessly into the phone.

"Who's shooting what out? And who's this?" the secretary wanted to know.

"This is Nick at the store. Bernie and Harlan just went over in Bernie's pickup! I heard six, seven shots at least! You better get Mr. D.!"

Emerson Lapp ran outside. A pickup, with Horsethief Shorty at the wheel and Jerry Grindstaff and a cowboy named Hugh Slocum beside him, both holding rifles tensely between their knees, barrels pointed at the ceiling, and with two younger hands—Tommy Gallegos and Richard Tafoya—in the back clutching guns, roared by, gravel flying.

"Where you headed?" Emerson Lapp called.

"There's a gunfight down at José Mondragón's!" Tommy Gallegos yelled excitedly.

At the first sound of shots, Charley Bloom set down a cup of Campbell's tomato and rice soup and almost sobbed to Linda at the table across from him, "God help us now, it's beginning."

"What's beginning, Daddy?" Pauline piped. "Tell me what's beginning?"

Bloom got up and went to the open doorway.

"Where did they come from?" Linda asked.

"Where did what come from, Mommy? Where did *what* come from?"

"Joe's place," Bloom answered. He could see, across several fields and through a few young Chinese elms to Joe's house, the jumble of outbuildings and rusted machinery and the ten-foot-high piles of piñon.

"What do you think is happening?" Linda asked, terrified.

"What's happening, Daddy?" the child echoed. "What's happening, what's *hap*pening?"

"I don't know . . ."

"What are you going to do?" Linda wailed.

"I don't know." And Bloom waited, unable to act. Suddenly there was a loud popping bang, and then a heavier but also sharper explosion that ricocheted across the valley. That was followed a few seconds later by another hollow pop and sharp gunshot almost in unison. And then silence.

Bloom waited, still unable to move, hardly thinking. He was too scared and too chicken to act, and he abhorred the deep-down feeling of relief in himself, for this must mean, surely, thank God, it signaled the end of the affair.

The Dancing Trout pickup rattled past Nick Rael and then passed three older men legging it on the double up the road toward Joe Mondragón's house. It skidded to a halt behind Bernabé Montoya's pickup, and the five men who hopped to the ground were surprised to find Joe Mondragón hale and hearty and in the companionship of the sheriff and Harlan Betchel, all with their guns pointed past Herbie Goldfarb's shack toward Pancho Armijo's cozy little farmhouse.

"Pancho!" Bernabé yelled. "Cut the shit and walk out of there, hands on your head, toss the weapon out in front of you!"

"Bernie!" Pancho shouted back. "Is that you?"

"Who the fuck do you *think* it is?"

"This is a hell of a way to win the next election, then!" Pancho shouted. "Trying to kill your opponent!"

"You just come out with your hands on your head, Pancho, and don't forget to toss out the gun ahead of you. There's twenty-five of us out here, and if we have to rush the house and somebody gets hurt it won't go well for you!"

"Where's José?" Pancho yelled.

"He's right here, he's alright, you didn't hit him!"

"*I* didn't hit him?—of course not! I never *shot* at him! He shot at *me*! I didn't shoot at anybody!"

The sheriff fired a hairy eyeball Joe's way. Joe said, "Don't look at me. That man's lying."

"You come out of there, and then we'll see what's what!" Bernabé called.

"I got Stella with me!"

"Tell her to come out too!"

With ten guns trained on his front door, Pancho Armijo tossed his unloaded rifle out into the dirt yard, then both he and his wife, their hands clasped atop their heads, emerged, babbling Hail Marys, into the bright sunshine.

The sheriff, Joe Mondragón, Harlan Betchel, Horse-thief Shorty, Jerry Grindstaff, Hugh Slocum, Richard Tafoya, Tommy Gallegos, three old men from the Frontier, and Nick Rael advanced slowly toward the Armijos, and as they did, passing the corner of Herbie Goldfarb's bungalow, they came upon the sight at which both Stella and Pancho Armijo were staring aghast.

For there was Herbie, seated in the dirt at the side of his house, banging his head to try and drive the high-pitched, scary ringing from his ears.

He looked up at them all, puzzled, and during the last few seconds before it dawned on him what he had caused to happen, he lifted up his right hand, gingerly trying to wiggle the thumb, explaining to Bernabé Montoya, to them all:

"I was trying to shoot the skunks under my house. But I think I sprained my thumb."

❧

About two hours after the gunfight at Herbie Goldfarb's, as Charley Bloom saw Ruby Archuleta's plumbing truck pull up outside his house, he wished to hell that he'd driven down to Chamisaville that afternoon to Xerox some deeds and other papers at the Legal Aid office there. Because if Ruby wanted something from him, it could only spell trouble, and after today he wanted no part in the kind of trouble her desires were certain to cause. Yet how to escape?—he let her knock before opening the door.

"Can I talk with you a moment, Mr. Bloom?"

"Sure, sure, come on in . . ." Bloom was all smiles, expansive, a good guy, a wonderful lawyer: Champion of the Poor.

Ruby scraped her feet carefully, flicked a cigarette butt away, and entered the kitchen, sat down at the table.

"You want coffee? Or a beer?"

"A beer is okay, thanks." Ruby lit another cigarette, inhaling deeply. Bloom popped the top for her and sat down on the other side of the table.

Ruby said, "I need some help to write a petition. We're gonna pass around a petition, you know? Against the dam and the conservancy district. Also I want to know if we can hire you . . ."

"Who's 'we'?"

"The Milagro Land and Water Protection Association."

"Are you incorporated? In what ways do you exist?"

Ruby smiled toughly and leaned back, tapping her head. "Up here we exist, Mr. Bloom."

"That's not enough."

"It's a start."

"How do you plan to grow?"

"I've talked with the commissioners and the mayordomos on all the ditch systems. They listen, they're talking with each other now. Nobody knows for sure. Some are very bitter, others are angry, everybody is afraid. To fight this thing takes money and we have no money and people are afraid of anything that calls for money. But they understand what's happening here. By talking at the meeting you helped. Still, they don't trust me, they don't trust you. If Snuffy Ledoux came back tomorrow they probably wouldn't trust him. They don't even trust themselves. Many think it's hopeless to oppose the Zopilote. But there is José's example that won't go away. People are watching him; they're watching you too, waiting to see how you will act when the chips are down. Maybe nobody will sign my petition, I don't know, we'll see. But it's a first step, you know? After the first step comes the second step. If we can scare those bastards up in the canyon and down in the capital, maybe we can get a boot in the door. Because of José—and because of your talk in the church—I think some people will sign this petition, and once they sign this petition it will be possible to form as a group, and once we're an organized legal group, then maybe we can tax ourselves enough to pay you to help us, if you will . . ."

Bloom lowered his eyes, a surge of hopelessness maybe destroying his life. She was talking about engaging him to do a twenty-four-hour-a-day job for peanuts—no, not even for peanuts, probably for a couple of abrazos, some sacks filled with illegal deer meat, and a bag of beans. She had no idea what it would take to stall or defeat a conservancy district in the courts, the cost in dollars and time of the paper work alone, the cost of transcripts for the inevitable appeals. She had no concept of how emphatically the conservancy laws were stacked against her people. To put up even a half-decent fight they would need a billion dollars. She was crazy, foolhardy—she and Joe and anybody else in this town who thought the small farmers had (or even deserved) an outside shot at survival against Ladd Devine's conglomerate, the state, and the Government of the U.S.A.

"I dunno," Bloom said, wondering where to begin, begging himself to muster the guts to refuse.

Ruby stubbed out her cigarette, saying "We will be like the Vietnamese."

Bloom glanced at her sharply. She was smiling; for the first time he noticed her almost mystical loveliness, her beautiful wind-toughened face, the crow's-feet ranging out from the corners of her sharp green eyes, the strength glowing from her; clean and pure, copper-colored, indomitable. She made him feel incredibly weak and flabby.

The lawyer shook his head. "I don't think here could be like Vietnam." His voice sounded ridiculous; but for God's sake, the *thought* was ridiculous. "Who have you really got?" he asked petulantly.

"Me. Claudio. My son Eliu. Marvin LaBlue. Amarante Córdova. Tranquilino Jeantete. There are others. A lot of people are thinking. And what about José? And Nancy? And Onofre Martínez? Sparky Pacheco?"

The lawyer said, "You can't make a revolution with a bunch of decrepit old men."

"Bullshit. If the spirit is willing I can make a revolution with a bunch of three-legged burros, or a sackful of bullfrogs."

Bloom smiled, sighed. "This petition you're going to circulate, what will it be basically, just against the conservancy district and the dam?"

"Sure. You know, that, and with a couple of reasons, like you mentioned in the church, written out. That we will be taxed too heavily to pay for Zopi Devine's lake; that we will lose our land—"

"And you plan on sending it where?"

"To the governor. To our representatives in the Congress."

"You know that's a useless, almost a foolish gesture, a complete waste of energy and time?"

"The point isn't to change their minds," Ruby said quietly. "The point is to have our people sign. The point is to make an action together. Signing a petition will draw us together. It's a kind of official beginning."

Bloom said, "Okay, but I'll bet you something. We'll draw up the petition right now, and if you want I'll take a draft to Chamisaville later this afternoon and Xerox a lot of copies, no problem. But I'll bet you this: I'll bet you five dollars that if you take the petition over to Joe Mondragón this afternoon, he won't sign."

"That's a bet," Ruby said, smiling at him almost pityingly. "Now, let's begin . . ."

An hour later, crestfallen, Ruby returned; Bloom was out back with his children, helping them feed hay bale flakes to their Shetland ponies. She walked up to the corral and, without a word, handed over a five-dollar bill. Bloom laughed, pushing it back at her:

"Oh, come on, Mrs. Archuleta. It was a joke, you know, I wasn't that serious, I mean, you know—"

Ruby nodded, shrugged, and slipped the five spot into her blue jeans pocket. Then she offered him a clipboard holding a copy of the petition, saying, "What about you, Mr. Bloom? If you're defending

José, if you're willing to work for us, you should
sign—"

Bloom stared at the petition, at the two names on
it, Ruby's and Claudio García's, and he thought: Oh
my God, how do I get out of this? Then, absolutely
not wanting to make the commitment, he took the
cheap ball-point pen she offered and signed his name
the way a prisoner, by confessing to some heinous
crime, might sign his own death warrant.

Ruby grinned. "From now on," she said, "I'm gonna
call you Charley. Carlito. And you just call me Ruby,
okay?"

The lawyer smiled sickly and nodded, thinking:
Don't do me any favors.

"I'll tell the people they can trust you," Ruby said.

Bloom wanted to say, No, don't tell them that, because they can't, but he couldn't say it; he laughed
hollowly and could not really think of a proper way
to react at all. Then of a sudden he truly hated her
guts and Joe's guts for holding him up, for jamming
him back into a corner from where there could apparently be no escape.

❧

Whenever Joe Mondragón felt really nervous, he
charged into his chicken shed and started madly catching the English sparrows that fed on the hen scratch
Joe kept in a long aluminum hopper in there. The
birds became so panicky at Joe's appearance they forgot where the door was and just kept battering from
window to window until Joe had caught ten or fifteen
of the obnoxious little fluffballs, which he stuffed into
his front shirt pockets. Of late, the scruffy yellow,
snake-eating reincarnation of Cleofes Apodaca had
taken to accompanying Joe into the shed. And, while
Joe raced around trapping sparrows against the window panes, the cat, like a great glove at third, repeatedly leaped up and snagged the frantic little birds
in midair as they flew away in line drives from Joe's
grabbing hands. Not one to stand on ceremony, the cat
killed each bird with one crunch, ate it with two bites,

digested it with three swallows, burped out four feathers, and leaped to catch another.

Now, even though he had been shot at by Harlan Betchel four hours before, and even though he had just refused to sign Ruby Archuleta's petition, when Joe staggered huffing and puffing from the shed with his pockets stuffed chock-full of English sparrows, he felt much better. So also did the cat, its stomach gorged with tiny crumpled wings. Joe tromped loudly into the house and transferred the twelve birdlets from his pockets into an old-fashioned, hexagonal glass-paneled ballot jar which he had bought for five bucks at a Monte Vista, Colorado, auction. This ballot jar Joe then set on the kitchen table, and, snapping open a beer, he ordered Nancy, who was in the living room reading a book, to fix him some lunch.

Nancy said, "Fix it yourself."

Joe ignored that by remarking, "Look at all the birds I caught."

"I think it's dumb to terrify those little birds like that. Now don't bother me, I'm reading."

Okay. Joe got up. He browsed through the refrigerator, fashioned himself a peanut butter, mayonnaise, and green chili sandwich, drummed up a Baggie full of cracklings that he wished had come from Seferino Pacheco's ravenous thundering pig, turned on the radio to "Heartbreak Theater," and settled himself regally at the table, munching on his sandwich and chugging swiftly through two beers while bemusedly regarding his fluttering centerpiece and listening to the lovesick deeds of one Big Bill Killeen and his small-town starstruck consort, Melody Applebaum, coming from the radio.

Nancy said, "How can I read with that crap on the radio?"

Joe felt perky, saucy, wicked, cool. Damned if he would pay her even an ounce of attention. So Nancy got up, stomped into the kitchen, and clicked off the radio. Smiling like Pancho Villa, Joe looked right through her; he didn't even arch his eyebrows; he said not a word.

"What's the matter with you?" Nancy cast a curious

glance over the ballot jar at her husband. "You're acting goofy. And by the way, since when don't you take your hat off at the table?"

"Since when don't you turn your mouth off when I'm eating?" Joe said haughtily, laughing on the inside, suddenly in love with his wife and proving it by this kind of jeering banter.

Making a sort of squinched, twisted face, Nancy flopped back onto the couch in the living room area. The house was very quiet because the kids were four houses down the road, driving their grandparents crazy.

Joe brushed some crumbs from his fingers and, polishing off his second beer, decided to go make some hunting knives in his workshop. On the way out he lifted the lid off his centerpiece, liberating all the sparrows inside the house.

He was outside, laughing, running for his shop, when Nancy bellowed: "You son of a bitch!"

"Hah!" Joe laughed. Suddenly, just like that—for only a moment, maybe, but for a good moment, at least—he was in love, on top of the world, and just about as tough as they come. The mood wouldn't last long; these moods never did with Joe. But still, he was grateful for them: they were one of those small miracles that somehow kept recurring to make his life worthwhile.

∽

That same night, at 10:42 P.M., a call came into the state police headquarters at Doña Luz to investigate vandalism at the state trout hatchery, which was located about midway between Doña Luz and Milagro, about a mile west of Ruby Archuleta's Strawberry Mesa Body Shop and Pipe Queen, on the Rio Lucero. Officer Bill Koontz and the Staurolite Baron's son, Bruno Martínez, were dispatched to the scene. On arrival they found the hatchery head, Glen Wesley Gore, standing beside the lunker pool with a hurt and extremely puzzled expression on his face. The lunker pool was the smallest of the fish "bins," a circular structure about fifteen feet across, in which from thirty to forty-five enormous trout usually swam. On a pole beside the pool was a vending machine that, for a dime, dispensed small packets of fish food for tourists to feed the lunkers. The pool was the hatchery's main attraction.

"What's the problem, Glen?" Bruno Martínez asked. "Seems pretty quiet around here. Nobody on the road leading in, and nobody on the highway either."

"Look at this frigging pool, will you?"

They looked. Bill Koontz whistled softly, "Where's all the fish?"

"That," Glen moaned, "is for me not to know, and for you boys to find out."

Removing his hat, Bruno scratched his head. "You mean somebody came in here tonight and stole all those fish?"

"You bet that's what I mean," the director said bitterly. "We had one fish in there, old Yellow Belly, a cutthroat, that must have weighed fifteen pounds."

"What in crissakes is somebody gonna do with all that fish?" Bill Koontz wondered aloud.

"They ain't gonna use them for fertilizer," Glen said.

"When did this happen, Glen?"

"Just now. I had to run over from the house. I heard voices, somebody laughing, but by the time I got dressed they were heading out. I heard the vehicle, but when I came round the corner of the path leads up from the house, they'd already squealed around that bend in the road over there, so I got no idea what they were driving. Sounded like a truck to me . . ."

A few minutes later, as Koontz and Martínez drove off the hatchery spur onto the highway, where they could see for a number of miles north, Bruno said, "Hey, Bill, you tell me. Isn't that a fire up there, say just around the Milagro turnoff?"

Koontz squinted his eyes, trying to make out the patch of red beside the road. "Yeah, I think you're right, man. I think that is a fire."

"What do you figure it could be?"

"Beats me—wait a minute. Isn't that just about where Ladd Devine's Miracle Valley sign is located?"

The radio dispatcher, Emilio Cisneros, cut into their conversation. "A–47–A . . . you guys at the fish hatchery?"

"Naw, we went there," Bruno radioed back. "We just pulled onto the highway."

"Can you see a fire up north?" the dispatcher asked. "We just got a call Devine's sign, you know, that big wooden one south of town, is on fire."

"No shit, Dick Tracy."

"Well, you fellas better proceed on up there and see what goes. After that gunplay this morning, who knows what's going to happen."

"Check," Bruno said. "We're on our way."

When they arrived, everything except the concrete base of the sign was demolished. Worried, haggard, fitfully puffing on a cigarette, Bernabé Montoya separated himself from the group of about a hundred onlookers and trudged over to the state cops.

"Who did it?" Koontz asked.

"Now Bill," Bernabé said slowly, "if I knew that would I be standing around here with the rest of this town, warming my nuts and toasting marshmallows?"

"We just came from the hatchery," Bruno said. "Somebody stole all the fish out of the lunker pool."

"Somebody what?"

"You heard him," Koontz said. "Somebody stole all the lunkers."

"So what we're all supposed to be on the lookout for, I suppose, is somebody driving a truck full of fat fish and gasoline cans, qué no?"

"This hasn't been a very funny day," Koontz said.

"He's telling me," Bernabé snapped at Bruno.

"Let's go in and arrest Joe Mondragón," Koontz said.

"That's what whoever set this would love for you to do."

"What's that supposed to mean?" Koontz snapped.

"That's supposed to mean," Bernabé said wearily, "that the situation is such in this town that all we got to do is pick up José Mondragón on a trumped-up

or even on a legitimate charge, and people will just
line up and start shooting at each other."

"Ladd Devine know about this?" Bruno asked.

"I sent Naranjo to the store to call him."

Koontz laughed. "Some operation you run up here,
Bernie. Police calls from a fucking pay phone on the
porch of a general store."

"Take it easy, Bill," Bruno cautioned. "Everybody's tired. Been a bad day."

"What was the evidence at the scene?" Koontz
asked. "Or did you bother to look?"

"Nothing much. Except the concrete and part of
the ground around it is soaked with gasoline."

In a notebook, Koontz wrote down some times and
mentioned the gas.

"If you fellas don't mind, I think I'll just ask
around a bit and see what comes home on the grapevine before I move on anybody," Bernabé said.

"Sure. Be our guests," Koontz said. "What the
hell . . ."

Later that night, while dark clouds obscured the
moon, a person or number of persons ushered about
twelve sheep belonging to Eusebio Lavadie from the
narrow hay field in which they were grazing into a
neighboring field, also belonging to Lavadie, of green
alfalfa. At dawn, the sheep began to eat; by 9:00
A.M., when Lavadie discovered what had happened,
three of the sheep were already lying on their sides,
dead and bloated. Lavadie, who in spite of his rural
background was squeamish about such things, rushed
back into his house and phoned Joe Mondragón,
gurgling frantically at him to come running with a
trocar. A trocar being a sheathed sort of ice pick
instrument you stab into the bellies of foundering
ruminants to let out the deadly gases. "I'll give you
three bucks for every animal you can save!" Lavadie
shouted hysterically.

"De acuerdo," Joe said. "Be right over."

Joe hung up and returned to the kitchen table,
slumped back into his chair, and lazily sipped from
a cup of lukewarm coffee.

"Who was that?" Nancy asked.

"That yellow-bellied pendejo, Lavadie," Joe murmured lazily.

"What did he want?"

"Somebody let some of his sheep into one of his green alfalfa fields and a bunch of them got bloated. So he asked me to come and punch holes in them with my trocar."

"Well—?" Nancy said.

"Well, I guess when I finish this cup of coffee I'll amble on over there and punch a few holes in his woolly balloons," Joe giggled.

"At the rate you're going his sheep will all be dead by then."

"Now wouldn't that be a crying shame." Joe frowned concernedly as he pushed out of his chair and moseyed into the bathroom to brush his teeth: "I guess I better get my ass in gear, qué no?"

The following morning, a package mailed from Chamisaville and addressed to Ladd Devine arrived at the Dancing Trout. Flossie opened the package—which contained about twenty huge trout heads—and burst out crying.

Fifteen minutes later her husband, Horsethief Shorty, and Jerry Grindstaff entered the Pilar Café, where Bernabé Montoya, over cherry pie and coffee, was talking fishing with Fred Quintana.

Devine set down the fishheads in the center of the table; Shorty and Jerry G. pulled over chairs from another table.

Bernabé sighed. "The lunkers from the fish hatchery, I presume?"

"None of *our* guests caught them," Shorty grinned.

"Any leads develop over that sign burning?" Devine asked.

"I went over to José's. We chatted a little, and he mentioned that Brazo Onofre, remember? And then he asked me to leave. I questioned a couple other people. Naturally nobody knows a thing."

"No witnesses?"

"If a hundred naked people wearing Indian headdresses and shooting off pistols and shouting 'Que

Viva Snuffy Ledoux!' had set that fire, Mr. Devine,
I wouldn't be able to dig up a witness."

Shorty said, "It appears the natives are getting ever
more restless. Cigar—?"

"The natives been restless a long time," the sheriff
said, accepting the cigar.

"It's this conservancy district and the dam, isn't
it?" Devine asked.

Bernabé shrugged. "That's the whatchamacallit—
you know, the . . . the thing, it's a chemistry term,
when you put something into a test tube that starts
everything else in to bubbling and smoking—"

"A catalyst." Shorty moved over as Harlan Betchel
joined them, took a peek in the cardboard box, and
whistled softly.

"Those the hatchery trout?"

"One and the same," Shorty piped.

"What are you going to do?" Devine asked.

Bernabé shrugged again. "I dunno. What do you
want me to do, look for fingerprints on these fishheads?"

"I don't mean about these fish, Bernie. I mean just
in general. Wouldn't you say things are getting a bit
out of hand?"

The sheriff shrugged yet again, gloomily regarding
the fishheads. At length he admitted, "Yeah, I guess
things are a little out of hand."

"When are you going to arrest somebody?"

"Who do you want me to arrest, Mr. Devine? Right
now the only person I got anything on is that VISTA
kid for discharging a firearm within the city limits."

"Arrest Joe Mondragón for irrigating that beanfield."

"You honestly think that would stop anything?"

"If that field doesn't get irrigated, that's the end of
the symbol, and people will calm down. Besides, these
men and women are conservative folk. Plus they scare
easy. Put Joe away and the rebellion is over."

"You want to bet?" Bernabé said softly.

"If you don't, things might go rough on you," Devine threatened quietly. "You haven't been the world's
best sheriff, you know."

"I've kept the lid on, Mr. Devine."

"You call what happened yesterday keeping the lid on?"

Bernabé flushed. "At least nobody died."

Devine said, "I think you better pick up Joe before somebody does die."

Bernabé shook his head. "It wouldn't do no good, sir."

"I think it would."

"Nope. Somebody else would irrigate that field for him."

"Like who?"

"Like maybe me," Bernabé said angrily.

Ladd Devine tried to face him down. After a long tense silence, the Dancing Trout owner dropped his eyes and said, "Why you, Bernie?"

"Because I don't like getting pushed around, Mr. Devine. I don't like being ordered to do things that go against my nature or against the nature of the situation. I'm handling this the best I know how and I'm praying nobody gets killed. I seen this coming ever since I was with my grandfather with his sheep when I was a kid. I've lived here all my life, Mr. Devine, I've bought most of my groceries and a lot of my ammunition from your store. Right now I'm eating cherry pie in your café. When I had an affair with Mabel Mascarenas from Doña Luz, we used to spend every Thursday afternoon in your Enchanted Land Motel across the highway over there. I've seen this coming, I've watched it building for a long time. And I'm scared because I'm afraid it's gonna cost me my job. And I don't know what to do. I don't know how to handle it. But I know how *not* to handle it. So I won't handle it the way I don't think it should be handled, even if I don't know how it should be handled. I'd just as soon put up with a thousand burned signs and a million dead trout, as make an arrest that would start the human bloodshed."

Devine stood up. "Do you want to take these fish-heads down to the state police, Bernie, or would you rather I did it?"

"I'll take them. What the hell."

"Okay. Let's go, Shorty, Jerry G. Maybe we'll talk to Joe Mondragón ourselves."

"Anything happens to Joe," Bernabé called after them, "and I'll be damn sure to arrest the three of you!"

"God forbid," Shorty grinned. "Jesus Christ himself couldn't command any more respect from me than does José Mondragón."

After they'd left, Harlan Betchel asked, "What's the matter with you, Bernie? You gone soft in the head?"

"How much do I owe you?" the sheriff growled.

"It's on the house. It's always on the house. You know that."

"How much?" Bernabé insisted morosely. "Once a decade I get this overpowering urge to pay. In fact, from now on I'm gonna insist on squaring my tab—"

"Screw you." Harlan pushed back, rising—he walked away. "I'm not giving you a bill because you don't owe me anything."

"They'll hit your fucking Buck-A-Fish trout pen next," Bernabé said nastily. "And if you don't gimme a bill I won't give a shit."

"So don't give a shit, then, Bernie. You couldn't catch a common thief anyway, not even if he took a crap in your back pocket in broad daylight." Harlan disappeared into the kitchen.

Bernabé tore the floppy wrapping paper off the fishhead package, crumpled it in a ball which he left in the ashtray, then lugged the box out to his truck. Turning south on the highway, he pulled over to pick up a hitchhiker, the VISTA volunteer, Herbie Goldfarb.

"Going someplace?" Bernabé asked.

"Just down to Chamisaville, sir," Herbie said timidly. "I need a break. Also a shower. Also I'm pretty scared."

"What are you scared of?"

"I don't know. I guess it's just everything that happened yesterday. I don't want to get shot, sir, I really don't. When I came out here I was a conscientious objector. I came here to avoid a war . . ."

"Nobody's gonna get shot," the sheriff said stubbornly.

"Well, I don't know . . ." Herbie lapsed into silence. They drove that way, listening to a religious program in Spanish from KKCV in Chamisaville, down to the Doña Luz state police headquarters where Bernabé let off the volunteer on the highway shoulder, then turned in.

He banged the carton of fishheads on the counter. Bruno Martínez was on duty, along with Granny Smith; a woman, Tina Valerio, was typing.

Bruno peeked into the box and made a wry face. "Where'd these come from, Bernie?"

"They were mailed to the Zopilote from Chamisaville yesterday morning."

"What time yesterday morning?"

"Doesn't it say on the postmark?"

"What postmark? The address, the postmark, the stamps, they've been tore off or something."

Ai, Chihuahua! Bernabé sat down and shakily lit a cigarette. I am a dumb cop, he thought, remembering the crumpled ball he'd left in the Pilar Café ashtray. I don't know my ass from a hole in the ground. Pancho Armijo, that S.O.B., he's gonna win by a landslide in November.

And then what'll I do for a living? the depressed sheriff wondered sarcastically: dig cesspools for Ladd Devine?

❧

When Amarante Córdova was young he used to throw stones at birds in flight. Of course he never hit a bird with one of those stones, and that was probably why it was fun to throw them—knowing absolutely that the birds would always dodge, or be going too fast for either his pitching arm or the missiles it released. In fact, as he remembered it, there had always been a kind of joy in attacking a thing that could not be hurt, a kind of satisfaction to be derived by all parties involved.

Amarante had stopped chucking rocks at little birds around the time he became sheriff, but in an old age that might be called a reversion to his childhood, he suddenly returned to a variation of his former pastime. The precise moment that he reverted into his former self occurred during one of the old man's daily jaunts into town, when he spied a redwing blackbird drinking from a small rain puddle in the Milagro–García spur and for some reason decided to throw a stone at it. With considerable effort he stooped over and selected a golf ball–sized weapon, straightened up, tiptoed a little closer, and then flung the rock at his target. But as his skinny, bent fingers could not release the projectile in time, he wound up drilling it against his own foot instead of at the bird. This smarted a little, and Amarante croaked a string of feeble curses as he limped around in the road, amazed by what a flabby uncoordinated old geezer he had become.

And then the butt of his mammoth, archaic six-gun collided with his wandering gaze; abruptly he quit stumbling around.

Obviously unafraid of such a decrepit old fart, the redwing blackbird was still dawdling around down by the puddle, nailing whatever insect tidbits had drifted close to shore.

Moving—now that he'd decided to hunt the bird—with a deliberate and cunning dexterity, Amarante removed his huge Peacemaker from its scabbard, and, holding it in both hands after laboriously cocking the hammer, he aimed for almost a minute at the blackbird, then pulled the trigger. By some sort of miracle the bullet, which was immediately projected forth at a high rate of speed amid a flash of fire, a boom of noise, and a spurt of smoke, drilled the bird squarely amidships, causing it to disintegrate in a great puff of black and yellow and red feathers, some of which —as the smoke cleared—floated tenderly back down like autumn leaves, alighting delicately on the puddle.

Well, at first Amarante was shocked, because he had not intended to kill the bird, just as he had never intended to kill the little feathered creatures when he'd been a kid hurling stones at them.

But then it occurred to him that this was a sign,

a message, an omen—maybe even from God himself: Amarante Córdova, useless old man, protector of Joe's beanfield, had been blessed with an aim that was accurate and true, the better to defend the bean- field, to save Milagro, to conquer the forces of evil and Ladd Devine—

Amarante gathered up some feathers and waddled into town as fast as his bowed arthritic legs could carry him. Plunking onto a stool at the Frontier, he jubilantly splashed the feathers across the bar, then banged down his six-gun on the hard mahogany top.

"A rat killed a blackbird out at your place?" Tran- quilino Jeantete asked, adjusting his hearing aid and popping them both a beer.

"*I* shot a blackbird from a hundred paces," Ama- rante bragged, lying through his teeth because the bird had only been about twenty feet away.

"Sure. And I strangled a wolf bare-handed last night," the crusty old bartender retorted, sucking on his thumb because he had cut it a little on the second poptop.

"You make fun of me," Amarante complained. "Everybody makes fun of me. But then . . . everybody made fun of Jesus Christ himself."

"If Jesus Christ himself walked into my bar and ordered a shot of blackberry brandy or tequila, I wouldn't make fun of him," Tranquilino said. "But when Amarante Córdova walks into my bar telling me that with his lousy eyesight he could even see, let alone kill with a pistol that weighs a ton, a blackbird at one hundred paces, then I got a right to mock, because somebody is lying through their teeth, what's left of them."

Amarante was hurt. "But I did," he protested. "You can walk back over to the Milagro–García spur and see for yourself the rest of the feathers and all the blood and gore."

"No thanks, cousin. Every morning I walk a hun- dred yards to the bar, I'm out of breath all morning. But I'm a fair man, my friend—" And so saying he tottered around the bar and lugged a wooden stool over to the far end of the room and set an almost-empty sherry bottle atop the stool. Then, plugging in the jukebox so that its internal gleam would shed some garish blue light on the target, he said, "Okay, you go ahead and prove to me you killed a blackbird at one hundred paces."

"In the bar?" Amarante was astonished.

"In the bar," Tranquilino insisted firmly. "It won't be the first time somebody discharged a firearm in here."

Amarante scrutinized Tranquilino to see if his old friend had gone off his rocker, but the bartender had his eyes sarcastically trained on the bottle and his hearing aid turned off, so how could a Gunfighter Supreme by recent Order of the Lord refuse to accept the challenge?

Amarante creaked gingerly off his stool, took forever to sight in his blunderbuss—and, along with a million painful fragments of gunshot echo, a thousand pieces of amber-colored glass ricocheted off the wall and sprinkled across the floor like stars during the creation of a small universe.

"Hijo, Madre, puto, cabrón!" Tranquilino Jeantete commented.

Then he located another almost-empty bottle and set it up on the stool and retreated behind the bar, saying "Whenever you're ready, maestro."

Ignoring the sarcasm in his lifelong friend's voice, Amarante thumbed back the hammer, took careful aim . . . and blew the second bottle into just as spectacular smithereens.

The glass had barely tinkled to rest around their feet when Harlan Betchel, Nick Rael, Ray Gusdorf, Bernabé Montoya, Betty Apodaca, Carl Abeyta and Floyd Cowlie, and Sparky Pacheco and Tobías Mondragón careened into the bar to see who was getting laid out. Naturally, when they saw the two old men, or more specifically, when they saw Amarante's huge six-iron, all of them ground to a halt; but before anybody could speak, Tranquilino said matter-of-factly, "Watch this, friends," and he carted another bottle over to the stool.

Bernabé Montoya knew he should have called a

halt to the target practice right then and there, but like everyone else he was curious, so instead of saying no he said nothing, and, of course, having condoned the first demonstration, which ended with bottle fragments no bigger than BBs falling on all their heads like rain, he was powerless to stop the subsequent carnage.

By the time Tranquilino had begun setting up half-full liquor bottles, at least four dozen people were gathered in the back and in the doorway of the Frontier; Nick Rael had already donated a box of .45 shells free, and Amarante Córdova was so drunk with his own power and accuracy that he could hardly stand up straight, let alone focus on what he was trying to hit . . . and yet, thus far he had not missed a single bottle. So incredible was this feat that everyone present had become hushed, reverent, awestruck, aware they were probably witnessing a miracle. In fact, the tension among the onlookers had grown almost unbearable. Also ,the slugs from Amarante's Peacemaker had almost dug a small round hole in the bar's adobe wall.

Suddenly, however, Amarante felt a nerve somewhere deep inside his body: he held his fire, blinked his eyes, and then lowered the gun.

Nobody said anything. Finally Amarante announced, "That's enough."

"Whatta you mean, that's enough?" a handful of people complained.

"That's just enough," Amarante said complacently, because he knew—quite simply—that if he fired again he would miss.

He holstered the gun, and, shooting his three brown teeth at everyone from a wide grin as he politely tipped his hat to the onlookers, he walked outside and headed home.

Amarante veered off the road at Joe's beanfield, however, having decided it wouldn't hurt to stand watch for an hour or two; and he was almost asleep, with his back to a bleached cottonwood log, when he realized a plane was coming up from the south.

Now normally there would be nothing unusual in a

plane coming up from the south. But today was a strange day. Amarante's eyes popped open, and fumbled in his suit pockets for his glasses, which he finally located and lodged in front of his eyes so as to identify the oncoming aircraft. Pretty soon he could begin to make out the markings on the plane. By the time the small Cessna reached Milagro he knew it belonged to Ladd Devine, and he had already unconsciously cocked the hammer on his Peacemaker while waiting eagerly for whoever was at the controls to guide that Cessna within pistol range.

Amarante did not know it, of course, but there were four men in the plane: Ladd Devine, Bud Gleason, the state engineer, Nelson Bookman, and the governor. They were all guests at a real estate conference slated to begin in Chamisaville that noon; the governor would give a keynote address, opening the two-day festivities. They were all taking an opportunity to become a little more familiar with the situation in Milagro, and for this reason they had decided to make a pass over the scene while Ladd Devine and Bud Gleason ran down the various Miracle Valley enterprise facts and figures, and also offered off-the-cuff comments on the local flora, fauna, and fulleros.

Down below, Amarante wasn't thinking much about the consequences of shooting Ladd Devine's plane from the sky, he was more or less allowing himself to be led by divine guidance, as it were. And so, as the little plane buzzed closer, he raised the pistol, and, overcome with a great calmness inside, he began to sight on the merrily droning target, waiting for it to approach a little closer so that God could pull the trigger.

"There's the beanfield," Bud Gleason said, and all eyes in the plane turned left and downward to take in, almost with respect if not awe, the tiny green plot among those barren west side fields that was causing such a hoopla.

And as Ladd Devine tilted the plane slightly to give them a better view, Amarante pulled the trigger, causing the hammer to snap forward driving the firing pin into the center of the .45 cartridge aimed at the slowly turning plane.

Nothing happened, however.

The cartridge was a dud.

~§

Before Herbie Goldfarb arrived in Milagro he had a passing familiarity with cockroaches and silverfish, but he had a very spotty record vis-à-vis ants. A vague impression, floating around in his head like a wayward wisp of cloud, told him there existed one insect of that species called an army ant, which hailed from either Togo or Peru, and this ant liked to mow down everything—from forests to people—that got in its way. Herbie also had it on various untrustworthy authorities that ants profited from radiation, thus they would survive an atomic war, and the irony of their survival, of course, was that ants were one of the very few other living organisms which enjoyed waging organized war against each other.

Aside from this, Herbie had been led to believe ants could lift loads ten or fifteen or twenty times their own body weight, and supposedly they were fairly intelligent. He understood also that some people in foreign countries nibbled on chocolate-covered ants instead of on M & Ms. Too, various ants could fly, others couldn't; some ants were red and some ants liked to sting, and some ants were black and didn't sting that much except when you rolled them under your thumb against your bicep on a picnic, trying to do them in. As for ant mythology, Herbie knew the story about the grasshopper and the ant, but he was familiar with only two expressions: "She (or he)'s got ants in her (or his) pants." And: "He (or she)'s a little antsy."

But the fact is, Herbie really hadn't given ants or ant lore (he'd never even owned an ant farm as a kid) much of a tumble prior to his westward journey as a Volunteer in Service to America.

It didn't take Herbie long to become very aware of ants in his new home. This new awareness began (one week after he sprained his thumb shooting skunks) when he bought a hummingbird feeder from Nick Rael, filled it with boiled sugarwater and red food coloring as instructed, and attached it to a branch of the tipped-over cottonwood vivisecting his outhouse. Nick had cautioned Herbie against bees, so the volunteer outfitted his feeder's glass nozzle with a big yellow bee guard, which worked fine: it separated (or strained out) the bees from the rapacious ants, who then had the sugarwater all to themselves. They marched up the tree trunk, out onto the limb, down the plastic wire attached to the inverted feeder jar, and then, like lemmings, they ate their way up the narrow glass spout, became stuck in the sugarwater stickiness, and drowned. Three days after Herbie first dangled the feeder from a limb, only a few tiny red drops remained inside the jar—the rest of the feeder was crammed full of well-fed dead ants.

"What you wanna do," Nick advised, "is have you got any oil? Olive oil, like for salads? No? Well, buy yourself a small jar, they're on the other side of that row over there, and smear a ring of oil around the branch the feeder's hanging on."

Herbie followed these directions, cleaned about a quarter pound of dead ants from the hummingbird feeder, and poured in a fresh sugarwater solution. During this operation Herbie was a little sloppy, allowing some of the sweet formula to splash on his wooden floor. Then he hung the feeder back up, forgetting to replace the bee guard, and sure enough, the oil kept the ants at bay, although the bees, like lemmings, poured into the feeder's unguarded snout, gorging themselves and drowning, so that within a few days Herbie's bottle, devoid of liquid but jam-packed with dead or ecstatically dying bees, resembled an apiarist's ossuary.

Gagging sporadically, the volunteer patiently scraped out the corpses, cooked up another sugar solution, and rehung the feeder, although already he was beginning to despair of ever attracting a hummingbird to his humble, accursed digs.

As it turned out, there were ample grounds for the volunteer's despair. Because before hummingbirds could discover his upside-down bottle, a bunch of fly-ing ants happened by, and in no time they drove themselves like lemmings up the glass tube into Herbie's jar-shaped slaughterhouse.

Considerably conscious of ants, now that he was locked into frustrating mortal combat with them, Herbie began to notice thin and curiously unbroken straight lines of the tiny beasts trickling down his walls and parading out onto his floor, heading for all those spots where sugarwater drops had spilled while he was loading the hummingbird feeder.

Paralyzed by the implication of those determined lines, Herbie could only sit and stare. In due course, however, as the black circular mass around each errant—and by now dried-up—sugarwater splash grew to the size of a half-dollar, the volunteer bestirred himself into action. That is, he arose and, with apologies to Mahatma Gandhi and to all those other Indians who wore fine-gauze masks throughout their lives so as not to breathe in and snuff out even the smallest microbic bug, Herbie proceeded jerkily over to each little ant rally and stepped on it, almost able to hear thousands of tiny screams as those wee bugs were suddenly extinguished beneath his merciless heel.

Such quick, arbitrary, effective, and wholesale an-nihilation fazed the surviving ant armies not one whit. They kept steadily coming at about the same pace. So that even as Herbie rested, feeling slightly queasy from the executions, the dead ants were replaced at the sugarwater splashes by vigorous live ants, and in no time the busy black circles threatened to become as large as small Frisbees.

What else could this sad pacifist do? Donning his God outfit once more, in a matter of seconds Herbie stamped out the newcomers. But not even a quiver of apprehension rippled from the circles of death up along the descending lines, which were being steadily fed through little holes in the adobe walls around the vigas.

Herbie's heart sank as he observed new ants method-ically plodding into the death arenas around the sugar spots; they paid no attention to the shapeless compatriots over which their tiny feet scrabbled.

Grabbing a T-shirt, the volunteer ran outside, soaked the shirt in the irrigation ditch, raced back inside, stamped out the new ant congregations, and then scrubbed each sugar spot with all his might for about five minutes.

Meanwhile, at the hummingbird feeder, regular, nonflying ants, who had only been momentarily routed by the oil ring around the main feeder limb, were crawling onto the branch above the feeder and dropping down—like lemmings—onto the sticky glass jar, drinking out the liquid and drowning as they did so, again packing the feeder with their corpses.

Herbie shuffled wearily back into Rael's store, where he put this question to Nick:

"What have you got, Mr. Rael, that murders ants?"

"Well, I got this here powder; it's pretty good, if you like powder. Or these ant buttons; you just put a drop of water in each day and stir, and they do okay if you like buttons. Then there's these ant traps, if you like ant traps. They all got the extra added attraction of the ants don't die out in the open where you can see them, they eat the poison and go back into their houses and drop dead, out of sight."

"That's the way I want it to be," the volunteer admitted grimly. "If they'll just die in private I think I can handle it. I better get a half-dozen ant traps and buttons, and also a can of powder."

"Gettin kind of bloodthirsty in your old age, ain't you?" Nick teased.

"I can't help it," Herbie whined politely. "There's so many ants in my house, when I walk they just about crunch under my feet like peanut shells."

"Ants are one holy pain in the ass," Nick said. He might have added, "Ants are indestructible," but he didn't. Every year Nick made a mint unloading various half-baked ant-poisoning devices into the people of Milagro, who persisted in believing in the myth of the little Dutch boy with his finger in the dike, or in the story of David and Goliath, and so forth.

Herbie punched open his traps, wet his buttons,

spread his powder, and snuggled down comfortably into his rancid sleeping bag, secure in the knowledge that tomorrow morning his ants would be extinct.

He dreamed the ants crawling all over his hummingbird feeder and clogging it with their bodies were a special kind of Milagro piranha ant. Whenever hummingbirds hovered at the spout to take a sip, hundreds of ants jumped on them, and for about six seconds there was a furious blurry thrashing in the air, then a spanking clean hummingbird skeleton dropped with a minuscule clunk onto the earth. All day long this went on, so that in the evening when Herbie scuttled out back to the splintered outhouse, a pile of tiny hummingbird skeletons, sparkling like rare jewels, littered the ground underneath his feeder.

But in the morning, in real life, perhaps half a million, not-yet-dead ants that had fed at the volunteer's various poisoned banquets were writhing on the smokehouse floor. They limped about in crippled, teetering circles; on their backs they frantically scriggled paraplegic legs; on their sides, twisted into grotesque agonized shapes, they arched and jerked and quivered. Their swollen abdomens seemed to glow with an evil, slow-murdering phosphorescence; their antennae drooped like wilted lettuce.

Herbie hunkered, petrified, *horrified,* on his sleeping bag, watching them die like gas victims from the First World War, like Napoleonic soldiers on a Russian winter battlefield. They twitched and floundered, weaved and bumped into each other, staggered about and toppled over and dragged their half-paralyzed selves painfully along the floorboards, little damp smears of ant crap marking the floor behind them, describing the patterns of their death throes.

"Why," Herbie wailed, "am I such a clumsy, gullible schmuck?"

Meanwhile, ant lines, unbroken, unswerving, undismayed, still poured steadily out of all those little holes up around the vigas.

If it weren't for bad luck, thought Herbie Goldfarb, recalling a song made famous by Johnny Cash, *I'd have no luck at all.* And he wondered all the more intently if it might not be a good idea to transfer out of Milagro, forget about his high-falutin principles, and head for Vietnam.

᪅

Benny Maestas had already been to Vietnam. Most of the able-bodied sons of Milagro between eighteen and twenty-five were, or had been, in the army, because aside from the Doña Luz mine, the army was the only other "area" employer that issued relatively regular paychecks, allowed people to do something—namely, hunt living things—that was in their blood from birth, and had a life insurance plan if they happened to get offed.

Thumbtacked on the wall in his room, Benny Maestas had a yellowed cartoon depicting some G.I.'s on a jungle patrol in which one G.I., a Chicano, was saying to another G.I., a black, "Yo soy el único en mi família que tiene empleo." Which translates into: "I'm the only one in my family who's got a job."

In point of fact, the little town of Milagro had one of the highest death ratios in the United States of America. Of the fifteen boys sent from there so far to Vietnam, eight had already died: Tranquilino Apodaca, Meliton P. Trujillo, Chato Arguello, Johnny Mondragón, Elisardo and Juan Córdova, Joe P. Mondragón, and Onofre L. Martínez.

It is perhaps interesting to note that the previous year's entire seven-man senior class, except for Rumaldo Ledoux (a cousin of the noted absentee santo carver and rabble-rouser, Snuffy Ledoux), who died in a car accident graduation night, joined the army and four were subsequently sent to Vietnam.

Now, as the Asian festivities were apparently drawing to a close, a national pictorial magazine decided to do a "sensitive" and "searching" feature on Milagro's "anguish." With this article in mind, a hip young reporter, Abigail Tedesky, flew out to the capital, rented a car, and drove up to Milagro, intending to complete some necessary background work before the paparazzi and tape-recording experts were trundled in.

Abby Tedesky had what would have to be described as a "very traumatic experience" in Milagro. In the first place, the minute her swish Cardinal crimson rent-a-car floated like a cruising shark into town eight days after the beheaded lunkers were mailed to Ladd Devine, the inhabitants pegged her for either a flimflam woman, traveling puta, or Kyril Montana's other half, a lady cop, and, beginning with a pebble pelting by Mercedes Rael, they acted more or less accordingly.

Abby first contacted the mayor, Sammy Cantú, who was excessively polite to her. As she explained who she was and why she had come to Milagro, he nodded his head, saying "Yes, yes, yes, uh-huh," and he didn't believe a word she said. Smiling ingratiatingly, though, he also eyed her intently, waiting to catch a high sign—a wink, a hand signal—that would indicate her real reasons for coming to Milagro and wanting to grill people. But to his chagrin, and subsequent terror, that sign was not forthcoming. After she left, toting a list of names that he had supplied, the mayor sat in a chair wringing his hands, certain Abby was in town on Kyril Montana's, or perhaps even the FBI's, behalf to keep a tight watch over people like himself.

Nick Rael nodded his head, saying "Yeah, yeah, yeah," while Abby explained herself and her mission, and when she tried to probe more deeply into Milagro's war dead, he asked, with a knowing, sardonic wink: "Uh, which war, exactly, would you be referring to?"

And Abby wondered: Why did this tight-lipped store owner chuckle like *that* when she answered, "The Vietnam war, of course."

After Nick Rael, things grew steadily worse.

Tranquilino Apodaca's mother kept her standing on the bienvenido mat, and when Abby finished her spiel, the bright-eyed woman replied, What do you want to write about Tranky for; he was a good kid, but also a bum. It wasn't bad enough he did time for burglary, assaulting a chota, and rape, he had to enlist in the government too; they gave him a free gun, free bullets, and free people to shoot at. When he came home defunct there was a smile on his face. There was a smile on my face too, because the government sent a check for ten thousand dollars. You want to write a story, why don't you write it about José Mondragón's beanfield? You want to write about a war, just keep paying your rent over in Pedo Hirsshorn's Enchanted Land whorehouse for the tourists, and don't walk around town without your eyes open."

The other mothers did not react in quite such a vituperative manner, but they all more or less chorused similar sentiments: "What do you want to write about my boy for? Dead is dead, rest in peace. I don't want to be reminded he was working for the government when he died, or that the meat he killed nobody was allowed to eat. You want to write about something, why don't you write about José Mondragón's beanfield over there on the west side? You want a war story, just keep paying your rent over in Pedro 'The Pedo' Hirsshorn's Enchanted Land whorehouse for the tourists, wear a bulletproof vest, and keep your eyes open."

Abby had never, not on any assignment, experienced such hostility, such suspicion. People muttered their standard replies, told her to write about Joe's beanfield, and closed the door.

Eventually Abby decided that since she was making little progress with the Dead Vet–Town's Anguish angle, she might as well humor the people a little by checking out Joe Mondragón's beanfield. By chance, Benny Maestas led her there.

They stood on the bank, overlooking the tiny beanfield surrounded by desolate land, busted fences, rotting houses. Wind raged, the bean leaves were covered with dust; they looked bedraggled, unhealthy, dying. Abby squinted her eyes, peering at this pathetic little patch of vegetables through one-way Lolita sunglasses as Benny Maestas unfolded his arm in a magnificent sweeping gesture, intoning with awe, reverence, almost religious serenity: "There it is."

"*This* is Joe Mondragón's beanfield?"

"You better believe it."

"But what's so special about it—?"

Meanwhile, perturbed rumors had been scooting

around in high places. As a result, Ladd Devine phoned the state engineer, named the national magazine Abigail Tedesky worked for, and said, "For God's sake, Nelson, they're going to write a story about Joe Mondragón's beanfield!"

Bookman shit a brick. "Jesus, Ladd, have you talked to the governor?"

"That was going to be my next call."

"Well, okay. Get back to me right away, will you? This is too much."

The governor said, "Are you serious about this, Ladd? Is this woman for a fact up there right now?"

"I'm not making this up," Devine said testily. "This isn't my idea of a thing to joke about. She's been in town three days now, talking with people down in the valley, asking them about the beanfield."

"Okay," the governor said quietly. "I'll see what I can do." Hanging up, he dialed state police headquarters: "Give me Xavier Trucho, please. . . ."

And the governor and Trucho talked.

After Ladd Devine hung up, he sat in his black Naugahide swivel chair with his hands clasped underneath his chin, his brow furrowed, thinking hard. For about five minutes he was deadly silent, then he called in Emerson Lapp, asking his secretary to send for Jerry Grindstaff. When Jerry G. arrived, Devine asked Lapp to leave and close the door behind him. They were alone in the closed office like that, Devine and Jerry G., for about eight minutes, after which Jerry G. emerged, his face expressionless as usual. He walked downstairs and out front, slipped behind the wheel of a Dancing Trout station wagon, and drove out of the canyon and through town, turning left onto the highway, aiming south. A little past the Body Shop and Pipe Queen he turned right onto Strawberry Mesa, bouncing over a maze of rutted roads to the Evening Star hippie commune.

What Jerry G. planned to arrange was made all the more possible by the fact that recently—within the last three months, in fact—a methadone · program for heroin addicts had been set up in Chamisaville. It was a program of good intentions, perhaps, and the people running it were trying to administer it fairly, but it was having at least one rather bad side effect: namely, the free methadone handouts were drawing a different kind of freak, notably smack addicts and pushers, into the area, most especially into the communes surrounding Chamisaville. This had caused a hitherto unknown tension to exist in the communes, a tension that had developed into a war between the peace-love-flower-child-grass-acid-mushroom-peyote hippies and the hard-stuff junkies moving in and ruthlessly taking over, trying to promote skag. To this new element, bean growing and gorgeous sunsets were so much crap in the spiritual can if the daily nickel bag or its equivalent did not arrive in time.

Jerry G. chugged up to the Evening Star commune, parked his car, said hello to a spacey-eyed woman traipsing along behind a herd of mangy goats, and headed briskly toward a nearby hoganlike structure in which a recent commune arrival known as Lord Elephant holed out. Jerry G. knocked on the door, the door opened, he disappeared inside.

While Jerry G. talked to Lord Elephant, some five miles away another important confab was taking place.

"She's got *gall*," Nancy Mondragón said. "Just sitting around in the Pedo's whorehouse for tourists and driving all over in full view of everybody and grilling people about everything from soup to hay, pretending it really isn't their opinions about José's beanfield that she's interested in. I'd like to kick her ass from here to Chamisa V.!"

Ruby Archuleta chuckled, lit a cigarette and dragged deeply, let the smoke out pensively. "She must think we're pretty stupid," the Body Shop and Pipe Queen operator said. "She really doesn't give us credit for much brains at all."

"We can't let her keep parading around like this, asking everybody questions, can we?" Onofre Martínez asked, rolling a cigarette as only he could, without even using his missing arm.

Juan F. Mondragón groaned, "What are you going to do, you're gonna break the law some more? Then there's gonna be even *worse* trouble. You'll get caught,

and *then* you'll be sorry. They'll pull out your fingernails with little pliers—"

Ray Gusdorf said, "Maybe there's some way we
could make her leave."

"Maybe," Ruby said. "Maybe there is—"

As Ruby Archuleta, Marvin LaBlue, Claudio
García, Onofre Martínez, Juan F. Mondragón, Amarante Córdova, and Jimmy Ortega left Joe Mondragón's house by his kitchen door, so also did the
governor of the state walk out of a meeting with Xavier
Trucho and Kyril Montana. And at the same time
Jerry Grindstaff stepped up out of Lord Elephant's
hogan at the Evening Star commune, slipping his wallet into his left back pocket as he shook hands with
the hulking baby-faced doper. And on the west side,
having run down the Joe's beanfield saga for Abby
Tedesky, Benny Maestas chucked a pebble into the
Roybal ditch and turned to leave.

The next day, when Abby Tedesky emerged—fresh
from a shower and dressed to beat the band—to start
her day, there was no air in the rented car's tires.
Irately, she informed Peter Hirrsshorn of this fact,
and he immediately rushed over to Rael's for some
canned air, with which he obsequiously inflated the
flat tires, begging Abby's forgiveness for the locals'
crude sense of humor as he did so.

Abby then steered out of the Enchanted Land
parking lot, only to be pulled over by a wailing, flashing state police car.

"You got a license?" Bruno Martínez asked
brusquely. "Lemme see your license, lady. One of your
taillights is out."

"This is a rented car," Abby said tightly, hunting in
her purse for the license. "It's a brand new car, how
could the taillight be out?"

"Rented or not, it's still out," Bruno said, carefully
studying the license. "Hey, where's the registration of
this car?"

"In the glove compartment—" Abby said, leaning
across to open it. But the papers she had absentmindedly thrust in there three days before had disappeared. In point of fact, they were right now peace-

fully simmering in Peter Hirsshorn's office safe at the
Enchanted Land Motel.

"Oh for crissakes!" Abby exclaimed, and started
trying to explain.

"Don't gimme that line," Bruno said curtly. "You
just follow me on down the road, Missus Teshkadilly,
we're gonna straighten this out at headquarters."

By the time she stalked out of Doña Luz headquarters two hours later, having been badgered unmercifully and then vindicated at least partially by
rent-a-car records in the capital, Abby was fuming.
She hit the gas pedal going back up to Milagro . . .
and immediately Granny Smith pulled her over for
speeding.

"My radar clocked you going seventy-five miles an
hour in a sixty-mile zone," he said laconically.

"Bullshit!" Abby exploded. She had hit the pedal,
but not that hard.

"I'd watch that type of language in front of a cop
if I was you, baby," Granny said, flinching internally
at the "baby," but carrying out orders anyway like a
good boy.

"Who the fuck are you calling 'baby'?" Abby exploded.

"Okay, that's enough, sister, I'm taking you in,"
Granny said.

"The hell you say!"

Granny dropped his hand onto his gun. "You just
get out of that car, miss, really quiet like, understand? And you walk back to my car, is that very
clear?"

Suddenly Abby's anger was replaced by a feeling
of being scared stiff. Things like this just didn't happen. At least they couldn't happen to her. "W-what
are you doing?" she stammered. "What are you talking about? I just spent half the day with you cops,
and now you're threatening to pull a gun on me because you claim I was doing seventy-five when I was
hardly going sixty—"

Granny lifted his hand off the gun. "Look, baby,
I don't know what your problem is, I don't even
know who you are. It's just when my radar says

you're going seventy-five, who am I supposed to believe, my radar? Or you?"

In her panic Abby realized she had better be conciliatory, she had better lick boots, even asses if necessary, turn a trick for this redneck son of a bitch if she had to, just to get out of this place alive.

"Oh, listen, officer," she murmured contritely. "I'm sorry, oh brother, am I ever sorry. I've just had a rough day, that's all, I really apologize. Listen, I can pay the ticket, how much is the ticket—?"

Granny wrote her out a ticket for a hundred dollars.

"A HUNDRED DOLLARS? FOR SPEEDING?"

"I don't make the rules, ma'am, I just enforce 'em."

"A hundred dollars for a lousy speeding ticket? Mister, who do you think you're trying to hold up, some kind of backwoods chippie? I'll get a lawyer; I'll sue you bastards until you're blue in the face! *What the hell is going on around here?*"

"I think we better head on down to the station," Granny said.

"You bet your sweet bippie," she hissed. "And you better not forget I've got one phone call coming to me!"

At the Doña Luz headquarters, though, a compromise was worked out between Bill Koontz, Bruno Martínez, Granny Smith, and Abby Tedesky. They decided in the end not to fine her at all, if she would just drive that rent-a-car back to the capital in the next twenty-four hours and have the taillight attended to, and stay within the speed limit during the rest of her time in the state. Trembling, Abby agreed to the terms and departed, expecting those redneck, greaseball, tanktown fuzz to shoot her in the back on her way out.

But she made it to the car, drove it very sedately away from Doña Luz headquarters, and headed north at forty miles an hour, intending to pick up her clothes and get away as fast as the speed limit allowed.

About halfway home, though, Abby noticed she was being followed. By a grubby-looking, mud-

splashed van of some sort. But she was afraid to
accelerate for fear of running into a speed trap. The
other vehicle, almost tailgating her spiffy new car,
followed that way for about two miles, then it pulled
out to pass, but started to steer back in too soon.
Abby braked, the van braked too; she wrenched her
wheel and braked hard, coming to a stop half off
the shoulder as a tall thin man with a moustache
jumped out of the van's passenger door, and a big
heavyset man with cherubic features, wearing a motor-
cycle outfit, circled hastily around the front, and a
third man exited through the van's side doors.

"Oh Jesus—" Abby reached to lock her door, but
too late. The lanky man pulled it open and in the
same motion grabbed her arm, jerking her from the
car—her forehead struck the upper doorjamb a hard
blow, and she cried out sharply, then the lanky man
slapped her once and threw her to the big cherubic-
looking guy, who in turn shoved her roughly into the
arms of the third man, who struck her hard alongside
the head, shouting as she fell down: "You better get
the fuck out of here lady, dig?" She landed on the
pavement in the shadow of, almost striking her head
against, the flaming rent-a-car. One of them kicked
her shoulder, then there followed a brief scramble as
they jumped into their vehicle and peeled out—like
that, it was over.

What could she do—go to the cops? Who was
kidding who? Abby pulled herself up and into the car
and drove north in a daze, not even crying. Minutes
later she coasted across the Enchanted Land parking
lot, stumbled into her room, jammed clothes into a
suitcase, ran outside and dove into her automobile
and departed without stopping by the office that did
not care whether she paid her bill or not, and as soon
as she reached the highway, she floored it. Passing the
Doña Luz state police headquarters at eighty-five
miles an hour, she did not think it odd that although
two police cars were parked in front, neither of them
made a move to chase her.

To Abby the whole thing was not even remotely
funny.

But all the various interest groups involved in the Miracle Valley beanfield war were satisfied because Abigail Tedesky—journalist, undercover cop, whatever—had finally taken a powder.

❧

Pretty much from the moment he woke up after a bad night, Charley Bloom knew it was going to be one of those Saturdays. His spirits began, if not to sink, at least to cringe, the moment Linda announced, before either of them was fully awake, that she was going down to Chamisaville with Nancy Mondragón to shop at Safeway and J. C. Penney's, and the plan was to leave Pauline and María and the three Mondragón kids with Bloom.

The lawyer frowned, but then, deciding to extort something in exchange for what was obviously already a *fait accompli,* he nudged his crotch up against her behind and slid his hands around to cup her breasts, muttering sleepily, "How about a little hanky-panky before you go—"

She didn't really pull away from him, but he could feel her resistance; she wasn't in the mood. No matter though, Bloom persevered; and though his penetration was dry and slightly painful to her he carried it out over her weak protests, and once inside her all the way they just lay like that together, hardly moving. For Bloom it was a comfortable erotic moment and he felt close to his wife, sleepy and slightly woozy and very sexy all over. Linda dropped her arm back, laying one cool hand against his thigh, glad that he could not see her face, and neither of them said anything for a few minutes.

Then they heard a thump in the other room as a child got out of bed, and a moment later María appeared in the doorway, rubbing sleep from her eyes.

"Hey Mommy, are you getting up?" she asked in her shrill little baby voice, and Bloom immediately shot back at her, "In a minute, sweetheart. Go take a pee."

"I don't hafta take a pee, Daddy."

"Yes you do, now go on, shoo, scat. I don't want you puddling on the floor."

Frowning, María turned around and thumped through the living room to the bathroom. They both listened to her shuffle around in there for about ten seconds, then she started coming back toward them, crying, "Mommy, Pauline did a caca in the bathroom last night and I can't pee."

Bloom stiffened now, growing tense for real, defensive and angry. Because after all, how many untold times had his children intruded on a good moment of sex like this? In fact, it seemed that they were always around, a constant threat, ruining whatever private moments he and Linda had tried to salvage. And the bitterness that immediately made his eyes narrow, his lips tighten, and all his muscles go hard was a bitterness born from a thousand nights when their lovemaking had been punctuated, made uneasy, and often sabotaged by one child's coughing, another child's nightmare, a sudden vomiting, an abrupt and chilling wail as Pauline awoke, having peed in her bed—it had been an endless succession of interruptions, so that after a while whenever they began to stroke each other in the dark Bloom had automatically tensed, waiting for one kiddie crisis or another to break the spell. Thus, his lovemaking had changed over the years; somehow a hostility he held against the children had also become directed at Linda, and now he got set to bang her suddenly, brusquely, and hard—unpleasantly, is the way it would turn out—so as at least to come before the child returned to destroy their brief flirtation with intimacy.

"You can flush the toilet," he sang, his voice taut-tense, though trying to be reasonable and sunny even if on the verge of hysteria.

María had already padded into the doorway again. "No I can't," she whined. "I'm scared."

"Well then go wake your sister and tell her to flush the toilet," Bloom said. "But just leave us alone for a minute. Mommy and Daddy are tired."

"I want to get in bed with you," María said.

"Not before you take a pee, you don't," Bloom threatened loudly, losing the sunshine in his voice.

"But if I waked up Pauline she'll hit me," María said, starting to cry.

"Oh for Pete's sake—" Bloom uttered angrily under his breath.

Linda, glad for the excuse, started to pull off him, saying "I'll go . . ." but he clamped his fingers around her shoulders, hissing "Wait a minute, dammit—" and then shouted:

"Pauline, are you awake? Hey Pauline, wake up!"

"You don't have to shout," the six year old retorted grumpily, "I'm awake."

"Well, will you please go into the bathroom and flush the toilet so your sister can use it," Bloom called, struggling to keep his voice from sounding too strained.

"What's the matter with her, is she a cripple?" Pauline wanted to know. "I'm reading *Uncle Wiggily*."

Linda tried to get up again, but this time Bloom's fingers abruptly dug into her so sharply that she collapsed back against him with a tight little gasp.

"If you don't get up and flush that toilet I'm going to whack your fanny!" Bloom threatened. "You do as I say, dammit."

"Oh, alright." Angrily Pauline threw her book on the floor, starting to cry as she stomped across the living room. "But *she* never does *any*thing, *I* always have to do *every*thing! You watch out, María, you little pimple, when they're not looking I'm gonna get you!"

"Just shut up and do what I told you to do!" Bloom wailed.

Pauline flushed the toilet and thundered defiantly back into her room. "Okay," Bloom said sweetly to the little waif sucking her thumb in the doorway, "it's okay now."

"Well, who is gonna wipe me?" María wanted to know, stalling for time.

"I will, I will, you just holler when you're through,"

Bloom said, pulling himself not quite all the way out of his wife.

María stood her ground in the doorway, insisting, "But I don't have to."

"Of course you have to," her father said tightly, smiling like a specter from the looney bin. "You always have to in the morning when you wake up, you know that."

Obstinately, the child shook her head.

"Go!" Bloom suddenly bellowed, causing even Linda to jump. "If you don't go I'll spank you hard, *very very hard*!"

María burst into tears and turned around, and as she turned around Bloom drove himself viciously back into his wife with no warning, and she exclaimed "Oh *Jesus*!" as he came.

María stopped, turning back: "What's the matter, Mommy?" she asked through her own tears.

"Noth-nothing, honey—" Linda whispered, tears forming in her own eyes, while Bloom had his head buried in the thick hair behind her neck, wanting to bawl himself.

Then they all got up, wordlessly dressing, and congregated in the kitchen. In a hurry to meet Nancy, Linda had only a cup of coffee, pecked her children good-bye, and, avoiding Bloom's eyes, she hurried out the door.

Bloom knew he should fix them something nutritious, like orange juice, bacon, French toast; instead he poured out bowls of Cheerios, sprinkled on some milk and brown sugar, and sat down at the table with them to drink his own coffee, certain in the knowledge that it was going to be a very long day.

Later that same morning, with all five kids camped in front of the living room TV watching cartoons, Bloom sat at the kitchen table alone, quietly drinking coffee while penciling some notes on a legal pad before him. He just happened to glance up as a pink blimp floated nonchalantly around his woodpile and across the front yard, but for a moment this curious apparition did not even register. And then, after it

had already sailed quietly out of sight, he realized
that his yard was being invaded by Pacheco's pig.

Bloom got up so fast he splashed coffee on his
legal pad, and he had started to scream "GET OUT
YOU FUCKING PIG!" even before making it halfway to the door. Then, as he bolted headlong into
the yard with his pants practically down around his
knees because he'd forgotten to buckle his belt before
leaping to the attack, he was greeted by the sight of
that arrogant sow trotting briskly across the yard
toward him with a small white pullet in its mouth.
The pig's head was down; its little pink eyes hardly
noticed the man in its path; it assumed that Bloom
would move.

The lawyer's head went *pop!* however—his infamous temper exploding. Instead of stepping aside,
he took a single step forward, and, as if punting a
football, he kicked the sow squarely in her fat jowly
chops so hard that she fumbled the chicken. In fact,
the little white hen catapulted halfway across the
yard, feathers flying like the sparks from a comet,
before gaining control of its wildly flapping wings
and coming to an upright halt: then, clucking terrifiedly, it ran away. Later Bloom would recall with
some satisfaction that that particular chicken had gotten what it deserved, since it was the only hen that
kept flying out of the pen in order to forage among
the green bushes, grass, garden, and weeds; and it
was always laying eggs where Bloom or Linda could
never find them—months later Pauline or María
would race inside breathlessly announcing that the
Easter Bunny had left a few dozen rotten eggs in the
tall grass near the crab apple tree, or in the middle
of the dry ditch in the back field.

But right now Bloom was furious because his territorial imperative had been violated by this stubborn
gluttonous beast, and if he'd had a gun he most certainly would have started shooting.

He did not have a gun, though; a fact which the
pig instinctively understood. Bloom didn't have a
thing. And so he just stood there for a moment facing
three hundred pounds of mammoth porker, which in

turn just stood where it was, blinking its albino eye-lashes while staring rather blindly at the irate lawyer.

The impasse was broken by the pig, which decided, simply, to leave; choosing for its line of departure a path which passed directly between Bloom's legs. The lawyer stepped aside, to be sure, but as the arrogant sow went by he hauled off and gave it a kick in the gut which damn near broke his leg, and even made the animal expel air with a "Whoof!"

Unfortunately, this kick also enraged Pacheco's carnivorous sow, and, stopping on a dime, it twirled on two toes like a ballet dancer and ran right through the big, but flabby, lawyer, knocking him to the ground. Bloom was about halfway to his feet when the pig knocked him down and steamrolled right over him again. He was up and cursing at full scream while lunging toward the woodpile for his ax, when the pig neatly clipped through again, knocking him for another loop, and this time when Bloom got up he knew he was going to butcher not only that sow, but also maybe Seferino Pacheco, and possibly anybody else who came around his house during the next fifteen hours.

At this point, however, the devil himself, carrying a rope around one arm and shoulder, lumbered mournfully into the yard and cried, "Stop!"

The lawyer stopped; the pig skidded to a halt. Bloom was purple and panting loudly; the pig puffed a little; chicken feathers were scattered across the lawn.

"I wish I had a gun," Bloom threatened savagely. "If I had a gun I'd shoot you both."

Pacheco had heard this tune before: he shrugged. "Why kill a man just because his pig wandered into your yard? Help me catch that fucking marrana instead."

"You don't understand," the lawyer said. "That thing was trying to kill me. And before I stopped it it was going to eat one of my chickens."

"My pig, she don't eat chickens," Pacheco said firmly.

"What did she want to do, then," Bloom asked bitterly, "take my pullet home for a pet?"

Pacheco grinned weirdly, shrugging again; suddenly the lawyer felt weak and dizzy. It was anger causing him to gasp for breath, so he sat down and gulped in air, feeling queasy.

Pacheco advanced toward the pig, which backed up one step, snorting in either a threatening or a loving manner (it was impossible to say which), and its snout seemed to wrinkle in a kinky smile. Then the big mournful drunk shrugged yet again and scuffed over to the woodpile; seating himself on a piñon stump, he wiped his brow. Twelve feet away Bloom was hunched over, coughing a little, hawking up phlegm, gasping, trying to calm down so that he wouldn't be sick.

The pig checked them both out for a second, then tiptoed almost daintily toward a fence draped with sweet peas, and amused itself for a while snapping at, and occasionally catching, the hawkmoths buzzing around the lush pink and white flowers.

Noting this, Pacheco began rambling at random. "Look at that," he mused almost dreamily, "I never saw her do that before. My Melvin, when he was a kid he used to do that, catch those moths when they came to the sweet peas. He had an insect collection, he was always wandering around town catching different butterflies, just with his hands. He mounted them, too: he got a book about it from the school library, and then when they were dry he stuck the butterflies and moths on pins on his wall. He had half a wall covered once, but then the ants came down and ate them. Those fucking ants ate them so fast—hell, I remember my wife and me, she was playing the piano, and I was just sitting in a chair near his bed, he must of been, oh about six or seven years old, asleep, late at night, and she was playing maybe a Mozart, you know? Or a Chopin. And all of a sudden I noticed a whole colony of ants was eating the butterflies on the wall over his bed, and little pieces of those pretty wings were falling down onto my Melvin's sleeping face and onto his covers, it was like a snow of shredded butterfly wings—"

Bloom half-heard Pacheco's babble through his own gasps, his labored breathing; and then abruptly, realizing what this drunk lunatic was saying, the lawyer realized that he himself was almost on the verge of tears.

"Pues, who knows?" Pacheco asked rhetorically. "What can you do about ants? I got up and brushed those little wing pieces off his cheeks, that's all. It was a funny night. I reckon those ants must of eaten half his collection that night. Later, of course, he got killed in Korea . . ."

Bloom stopped wanting to cry, because he had heard before what was now coming: who hadn't heard about how Melvin got his in Korea? Nobody had ever heard about how Pacheco's wife died, though. She just disappeared one day— "She's in the hospital down at the capital," Pacheco explained. And then she was dead, and he walked the little cardboard government canister with her ashes in it down to the gorge and dumped that human dust into a sharp windy gust that dissipated the fine gray gauze among the flickering cliff swallows long before the wind ever rippled across the green river far below.

"Oh, when he was a chaval, that Melvin, he sure collected things," Pacheco reminisced, abruptly heaving to his feet and slouching over to the sweet peas, where the pig grunted and grudgingly moved over slightly to make room for its master. And as Bloom glanced up, Pacheco swiped at a hawkmoth, missing it by a fraction.

"Yeah," he called back to Bloom. "That Melvin, he was like his mom, qué no? I guess if he'd grew up he would of been a faggot. Like me he liked poetry. Books. He collected bird feathers and butterflies and leaves—he knew all about leaves and different kinds of trees. And in one cardboard box he always had some of them little hoptoads, and in another cardboard box he always had some crickets—sometimes I wonder how that kid could sleep at night, with all that racket in his room. Shit, he was always pinching ants off the portal posts to feed to some frogs or salamander or other comosellama—"

The pig inched forward until its snout was almost touching the tip of a feeding moth's abdomen, and then suddenly, with a little *click!* it inhaled the insect, chewed once, and swallowed. Pacheco swung clumsily at another pretty moth sucking on a sweet pea nearby and stunned both himself and the lawyer by catching it. Turning, he stumbled back to the stump by the woodpile, plunked down, and for a moment, absorbed in the act of trying to pinch the moth dead without rubbing the colorful powdery scales off its wings, he was silent.

Then he displayed the moth—quivering, shimmering faintly—in his palm: Bloom nodded, not knowing what to say, how to react.

Pacheco smiled, giggled absurdly, and shook his head wonderingly. "Yessir," he coughed sleepily, deep in the past. "There'd be little frogs peeping, and the grillos chirping, and you could practically hear those pinche ants chewing up the butterflies on his wall, and the little wing particles were falling onto his face like snow, and he just slept through all that—"

Bloom wanted to get up, go inside, lie down, be rid of this—this what? Doomsayer? Maudlin old drunk? And his ridiculous sow. He was too tired, though. He was weary already, even though it was hardly midmorning: last night had been nearly sleepless; the children up and down; and Linda so quiet— as she had been so quiet again this morning during their aborted lovemaking—awake in the darkness beside him, wanting to talk about amorphous, unmentionable feelings that somehow included everything important; both of them able to say nothing while roots of sadness spread into the dark. Their agony or despair or anguish, whatever it was—why did it have to be so quiet?

Pacheco, sensing that he would be allowed to stay for at least a while, settled into a groove, sing-songing on. "Maybe it was this morning, maybe a week ago —who keeps track of time anymore? I was sitting in the kitchen having a beer for breakfast, listening to the radio, to KKCV down in Chamisaville. They were giving the ski report, and I listened to that with interest until all at once it occurred to me, you know —I mean, what the hell was there a ski report for in the middle of summer? Hijo, Madre! And so then when I listened hard it wasn't there anymore, it was actually the fishing report. But after a minute the ski report came back on again so I turned off the radio. I guess I was scared—"

Lightly lunging forward, moving its gargantuan bulk with astounding delicacy and a deadly accuracy, the pig caught another hawkmoth.

And Bloom sighed.

And Pacheco talked.

و

Every now and then Horsethief Shorty liked to get off by himself, so early one evening shortly after Abigail Tedesky's sudden departure, he saddled up an old horse named Gingersnap that he had broken almost eleven years ago, stuck a .30-30 in the saddle scabbard, and rode down out of the canyon, through the village, and onto the western mesa beyond the ghost town. The moon was up and new, with its horns turned down, meaning rain, and even though it had been a dry, absolutely blue and sunny day, Shorty could smell rain on the evening, on the faint southern breezes, and that made him feel all right.

About a mile from where a foot trail led down to some hot springs in the Rio Grande gorge, Shorty dismounted and pulled the reins over Gingersnap's head, letting them dangle down so the animal wouldn't move. Then he squatted a little distance away and rolled and lit a joint, taking a couple of long lazy tokes. Shorty had been smoking marijuana ever since his adolescence, and he had his own private pot plot by the river north of the Dancing Trout. He never would have dealt with local growers or with the Evening Star pot farmers for his weed, because of late it had become too easy to get in trouble buying dope. In the old days around here, though, people had smoked grass much as they drank tea or chokecherry

wine. Why, when Shorty first turned up in Milagro
there had even been some old señoras dressed in
black who would sit in rockers on their porches in
the evening, smoking the *mota* in little pipes—

After a fourth toke, Shorty pinched out the spark
in his joint and tucked it into his front shirt pocket.
Then he removed the .30-30 from the saddle scabbard and walked north, into a faint evening breeze.
Above him, nighthawks fluttered jaggedly, uttering
their deep resonant beeps; a touch of sensual peace
and magic lay like a mist across the sagebrush and
snakeweed mesa.

About a quarter-mile from the horse, Shorty
stopped. He pinched off some yellow rabbitbrush
flowers and tossed them into the air just to be sure
of the slight wind, then squatted again at the edge of
a small open area populated by two medium-sized
anthills and a cluster of prickly pear cactus. With
the gun held across his knees, Shorty began to call
for a coyote, popping his cheeks and making a kind
of soft-harsh snuffling and grunting noise that sounded
perhaps more like a pig than anything else, inter-
spersing it with a succession of low, quick barks and
then some mouse squeaks, but staying away from
any high-pitched eager shrieks. He called for a while,
then rested, and then made the noises again, in no
hurry, and not really caring, growing mellow from
the grass.

It didn't take long, though, to get an answer. At
first it came hesitantly, quick, not that far away;
Shorty barked and chattered, keeping it very low and
unurgent. And then suddenly the coyote trotted right
out of the sage and saw Shorty and started to turn
away as he swung up the gun and, without aiming,
killed the varmint with one shot, firing again as it
flopped over, just to be sure.

He stayed there a little longer, still squatting,
watching the animal as it cooled. Shorty was tough,
not given to a literary frame of mind nor to particularly intellectual sensitivities, but he was moved
in curious ways by the sudden and almost gentle
death of this small, bony, and very ragged critter.

He wasn't quite certain, either, why he had shot it, because Shorty was not the type who slaughtered wild animals for fun. Maybe it was simply that he wanted to reassure himself of a skill he'd always had in his bones; maybe he wanted to make doubly certain that skill, that *sharpness,* hadn't leaked out of his body when he wasn't looking. Because Shorty had a feeling he was going to have to draw on those particular resources sometime soon.

It was almost dark; stars were out; the sage rustled, eager for the rain it could feel and Shorty could smell, rain that probably lay hidden beyond the mountains due east, waiting for the wind to change. Shorty straightened up, removed a hunting knife from the leather belt-sheath tucked into his back pocket, quickly skinned the coyote, and walked back to the horse with the pelt tucked under his arm.

Shorty rode off the mesa and across the highway as the first soft waves of night spread into town. Dismounting at Rael's, he bought some cigarettes and a tin of snuff, then crossed to the Frontier Bar, which was almost deserted, very quiet, and dark. Joe and Nancy Mondragón were hunched over beers at the bar; the Staurolite Baron, Onofre Martínez, was hunched over the pay pool table quietly shooting up a rack; and Tranquilino Jeantete was hunched in his wooden chair behind the bar. It was impossible to see anyone's face.

"Como te has ido, prim?" Shorty said, addressing the ancient bartender. "Sacame una cervezita." Then, "How's tricks, José? Howdy, Nancy. 'Lo, 'Nofre."

Everybody nodded, smiled. Tranquilino set a beer on the bar and snapped open the poptop for Shorty, who immediately drank off half the can, wiped his lips, opened the snuff tin and rolled his pinkie in it, then drilled the tobacco powder up either nostril with his little finger, sniffed hard and sneezed three times, and, gasping, polished off his beer.

"It's gonna rain," Shorty announced. "Que me la pongas una otra, Tranky."

"Sure it's gonna rain," Nancy said. "You can smell it. I could smell it this morning."

"I ain't got that good a nose," Shorty grinned.

Joe smiled in a not altogether friendly manner: "What do you expect from a gringo nose?"

"I was just out on the mesa," Shorty said, "and I shot myself a Chicano coyote."

Joe and Nancy laughed; Tranquilino grimaced comically; Onofre Martínez dropped the eight ball into a side pocket.

Nancy said, "What did you have to use to kill it, a howitzer?"

"Nope," Shorty grinned. "I just pointed my finger and spit and it dropped dead from fear, like a borrega. That's all it takes to knock off one of those ratty little Mexican foxes."

As he said this, Shorty lounged off his stool and scuffed across the hard-packed dirt floor to the jukebox. Thumbing a quarter into the slot, he selected three country and western songs.

"Boy, is this stuff ever God's music," he called tauntingly across to Joe and Nancy. Making a grotesque, mocking face, Nancy clapped hands over her ears. Joe, pretending to look bored, muttered loudly, "God blew a fart and that hillbilly music was born."

Suddenly, however, Shorty wasn't into the banter. It didn't feel right, it lacked a correct rhythm—there was something almost malicious and hostile in all their voices. For nearly thirty years Shorty had felt at home in this funky local bar, but tonight he was almost like an intruder. He had interrupted something when he walked in, and now his selection of country music only made it worse.

Well, it was not anything Shorty couldn't handle, but why stick around? He paid and tipped his cowboy hat and walked out.

For a while, as the night breezes picked up, growing cooler, shifting, Shorty sat on Rael's porch near his quiet horse, looking across the road at the Pilar Café. The plate glass windows had gotten a little steamy, figures inside were indistinct. The jukebox in there was playing taco pop music down low; the strains of his country and western songs issued from the bar. Then Shorty noticed a pickup parked in the

shadows between the café and the locked-up Forest
Service headquarters; its radio was tuned onto a Juárez station, and an old man and his thirty-year-old
son seated in the cab were silently killing a six-pack
between them.

Dogs barked; a couple of bats hunted moths around
Harlan Betchel's mercury vapor security lamp; the
evening pulsed gently like a calm heart. There was
peace; there was also this tension. Because of the
breezes not too many mosquitoes were out. So let's
thank God for small favors anyway, Shorty thought
dispiritedly. Trouble was brewing, even though you
couldn't exactly pinpoint what it would be or where
it would come from, just as you couldn't pinpoint the
pending rain. They were all going to wind up in it
as sure as flies wound up in molasses syrup, though.
And Shorty had not killed that coyote for nothing—
no sir.

Shorty mounted up and headed home. At the
Dancing Trout he stopped by the bunkhouse to shave,
change underwear, and squirt some deodorant in his
armpits, then he walked past the main building, the
pool, and down a sloping lawn that surrounded the
tennis courts, and knocked on the door of cottage
number twelve—Rattlesnake Roost—wherein a forty-
three-year-old woman from Houston, Texas, named
Sabrina Oatman awaited him. Every year this tiny,
shapely woman with a deep tan, peroxide yellow hair,
and an oil baron hubby spent six weeks at the Dancing Trout, and for eight years, now, she and Shorty
had been trysting.

Sabrina adored making love. But Shorty had always found it something of a trick to manage her
amorous quirks. To begin with, Sabrina didn't mind
shedding clothes, but she kept her jewelry on. Meaning that grappling with her was like grappling with
an Aztec–Navajo artifact museum: in Shorty's embrace, Sabrina rattled like a hundred ghosts of Christmas Past. Her arms were lined with crystal-sounding
bracelets; her fingers bulged with bright knobby rings
that made black and blue welts all over Shorty's skin;
her svelte lovely neck was circled with dozens of gold

and turquoise and squash-blossom beads and baubles and jangles; silver hoops and pearls and jade tongs laughed out loud in her earlobes; she even wore a slim, solid-gold buddy chain around one ankle. Sometimes Shorty wound up practically butchered, not from her long powder-pink fingernails, but from all that hardware. In fact, just last year Shorty had somehow gotten his penis caught in a bracelet, Sabrina had rolled away, he'd screamed, his wong had practically been severed in two, and, in fact, a vein had been crushed, some permanent damage done. So that now, where the bracelet had struck, he had a scar-tissue callous growing that was causing his penis to bend painfully at right angles to where it should have been when hard. And although he had seen a doctor, who whistled, shook his head, and prescribed some green pills, so far as Shorty could make out those pills hadn't done much good.

Sabrina's other peculiarity, when it came to love-making, had to do with her athletic vision of how and where the act should take place. She adored coupling in the bathtub, seated on the toilet, backed against a wall, in an easy chair, on her back under a bed, in a closet, bent over an ironing board, on a lawn, in the swimming pool, on a tennis court at midnight, up in trees or down in the river, in the back seats, front seats, or trunks of automobiles, in airplanes or in the changing room at the Chamisaville J. C. Penney's, in gas station restrooms or in the momentarily empty main salon of a ritzy art gallery; she loved to get it and dish it out from fore and aft, did not mind crawling on her hands and knees all over the place with Shorty riding her seated far back (and inserted) the way he would seat a burro, and in particular she dug doing it with her legs wrapped around an upright Shorty's waist, him lugging her around in his arms—they could even fuck like that while Shorty was at the kitchenette stove making a cup of coffee; and, in short, Sabrina loved making love in every way, shape, place, and form except on her back, on, or in, a bed.

Shorty was in no mood to trifle, however. Thus,

when Sabrina, jangling like the bells of St. Mary's, gleefully opened the door, he plunged inside and, without so much as a howdy (and also like a champion chicken plucker), tore all of her clothes *and* her jewelry off in about six seconds flat, pushed her back onto the neatly made bed, and, before Sabrina had time even to squeak, he embedded himself in her, but good, and right then and there did their loving up brown—in the most conventional way imaginable —like it had never been done up before.

When he had finished, Sabrina sat up, patted back her hair, said "Whew," and asked: "What's eating you, Shorty?"

But Shorty just lay there with his hands clasped behind his head, staring at the ceiling.

Sabrina kissed his lopsided penis, then crawled around the rug, gathering in her clothes and jewelry, and disappeared into the bathroom. While he listened to her shower melody, "I'm as Corny as Kansas in August," Shorty just kept on lying there, puzzled about the strange sensations buffeting his body. Something unusual was going on inside, something he could not for the life of him define, except that if pressed for a metaphor he might have talked about spring thaws and snow melting, about ice breaking up in the Rio Grande—and he wondered if such a metaphor could possibly make much sense. Whatever was happening, it had Shorty on edge and defensive; things, in Milagro and in Horsethief Shorty Wilson himself, were coming to a head.

Jangling like a carnival midway, Sabrina emerged from her shower looking mighty spiffed up and sexy in a tight black turtleneck jersey, purple pedal pushers, and little golden slippers, and she smelled like strawberry champagne.

"Put on your duds, Shorty," she whispered sexily, bending over to kiss his nose, "and let's you and me go for a little promenade."

Shorty got dressed, except for his boots and socks: those he left just outside her door. When she asked, "What do you want to do that for?" all Shorty could say was, "Don't ask me no questions, woman, and I won't tell you no lies."

They meandered across a damp lawn past the swimming pool, wandered down a slope, and circled the tennis courts, heading toward a simple white gazebo backed by a grove of yellow willows and some aspen trees near Indian Creek.

Sabrina halted, pointing at the sky: "Hey, there's the Big Dipper!" And they were both gazing at the bright stars when four men wearing cloth bags over their heads jumped from the willows and attacked. One thug whacked Shorty across the shoulders with a baseball bat, and, as the foreman tried to spin around, another man kicked him in the balls and he sat down, half-blacking out, half-vomiting. He heard Sabrina start to shout, but her cry was cut in half by a thud, and there followed another thud, accompanied by a great jangle of bracelets, and then they ran away.

"Oh shit," Shorty gurgled, trying to lift his head, but he couldn't, the pain was as if cement had suddenly hardened in all his veins. He gagged and rocked, unable to catch his breath, until finally he tumbled backward, and, like that, lying on his back, he finally managed, with a tortured gasp, to force apart the knot in his gut and throat and suck in a mouthful of air.

Shorty needed more than a minute to start breathing semiregularly; then he tilted a little onto his side and heaved and flopped back again, his eyes fixed on the starry sky.

He didn't hate them; he wasn't angry; he wasn't afraid; he had no bitterness. The only feeling inside, other than the pain, was one of extreme sadness. Times they were a-changing. And while waiting for his head to clear, for the cement to melt in his veins and arteries so that he could move, Shorty remembered one line from a cowboy song, and it drifted through his saddened fuzzy brain while he blinked at the stars and struggled to recover:

Oh bang the drum slowly and play the fife lowly . . .

The line floated through his dizziness, floated through the blue sensation of sorrow fogging his pain, floated through the smell of grass and sage and the smell of the West and the smell of horses and of that coyote and of Milagro-grown mota: Shorty's life.

Oh bang the drum slowly and play the fife lowly . . .

Maybe five minutes passed before he managed to sit up.

Sabrina Oatman was just a few feet away, on all fours, wagging her head at him, breathing hard, with one eye already puffed shut and blood splashed hysterically across her face, and most of her front teeth missing.

"Oh shit," Shorty groaned unhappily. "I'm sorry about your teeth."

But Sabrina smiled bravely through her tears and the blood as she lisped: "It ain't as bad as it looks, Shorty—they were all of them false."

Then, even though the sky directly above was clear and sprinkled with the glittering souls of infant children who had died, a wind sprang up and rippled across the grass, carrying rain.

᪥

It rained, all right. For four days and four nights the water came down, and the people in town agreed they had never seen anything like it before, leastways not during summertime when the most anyone could hope for were hour-long showers in the midafternoons of otherwise brilliantly turquoise days. But rain it did, nonstop for all that time. Immediately rivers rose, spreading out into the bottomlands; irrigation ditches overflowed; fields that were already pretty soggy became dyed-in-the-wool Okefenokees; and all the roads, which had been skillfully constructed by master craftsmen so as to have absolutely no drainage, turned into quagmires.

In short, everything that had been dust in Milagro turned into mud.

Milagro mud, called zoquete by the people, was

not just run-of-the-mill mud, however. A mixture of sand and fine brown adobe clays and gray caliche, it had the texture, viscosity, and crippling powers of a tar pit. It sucked off boots and shoes and ruined the brake linings on cars and trucks; it built up crippling deposits under horse and cattle hooves. It became as everpresent as a plague bacteria; it was like a mold or fungus gone berserk. The very air people breathed was somehow permeated with mud—nostrils grew clogged; ranchers hawked out great brown globs from their throats. The mud in the roads actually seemed to flow with currents, as in the river and streams, but when it hardened it would be worse than cement. People awoke in the mornings to find their eyebrows caked with mud, and somehow brown crud deposits turned up on toothbrushes and in refrigerator ice cubes. Nobody and nothing escaped the mud. It stuck to people, animals, and inanimate objects like peanut butter. The leaves, coated with mud shells, fell off their branches, landing with audible thuds. Sheep became bumpily sheathed with the stuff so that they looked like big ambulating wasp nests; birds, having absorbed the zoquete in their feathers, labored erratically through the air, almost unable to fly. Chickens laid eggs that had two shells, the outer one of mud. Dogs, lambs, and little pigs suddenly disappeared under waves of heavy goo, and some storytellers said you could actually hear the landscape burp contentedly after such a meal.

Only Onofre Martínez's three-legged German shepherd avoided the mud by refusing to stray from the Chateau Martínez's Astroturf lawn.

Pacheco's sow, on the other hand, reveled in the glop; she floated blissfully around town with her eyes half-closed, looking like a queer sensual dirigible, happy as a pig in shit. And people, trying to scrape the goo off their boots and shoes, were often heard to complain angrily: "This crap is as hard to get rid of as Pacheco's pig!"

The floors of Rael's and the Pilar Café became coated with mud. To clean his place, Nick chipped away with an adobe hoe. Harlan Betchel, on the other hand, just sat in a corner staring at the buildup on his floor, wondering if he should drill holes and plant dynamite or what.

Finally, all movement and motion in town broke down; the roads became blocked by stuck vehicles. Worms squiggled frantically from a billion holes in the ground and drowned, their pale bleached bodies floating everywhere. Milagro metamorphosed into one great gloppy bog, overrun with muskrats and water snakes. The grass alongside irrigation ditches bolted toward the sky like some jungle weed shot full of hormones. Trout, which became lost in the muddy streams, suddenly found themselves being plucked from the water by curious horses in alfalfa fields. A million short-tailed field mice, forced to flee from their pastureland homes, got bogged down in mud; within minutes their crusted bodies lined the roadsides like the bodies of Christians put to death in Roman times. And prairie dogs, attempting to make the higher ground of the Milagro foothills, became so heavily coated with mud that they soon grew exhausted, and when the mud hardened they died, looking like plump little fritters, croquettes, or corn dogs.

"I think I'm starting to shit mud," Joe Mondragón complained to Nancy one morning.

And, although Herbie Goldfarb didn't know it, he might have been glad to hear that approximately thirteen billion ants suffocated to death in the Milagro mud.

Bernabé Montoya, seated on his bed beside Carolina and peering curiously into the barrel of his service revolver one night, discovered that the barrel was permanently clogged with a brown, hardened, cement-like substance. He groaned, "Now I'll probably have to buy another gun!"

But men like Onofre Martínez and Sparky Pacheco, Tranquilino Jeantete and Amarante Córdova smiled, remembering how in the old days they had deliberately flooded the north–south highway with irrigation water and then waited nearby with teams of horses to pull out—for a small fee—all the northbound or southbound travelers whose horse-drawn rigs or Model

Ts became mired in the tenacious ooze. That had been almost as lucrative a racket as setting fires up in the Midnight Mountains and then hiring on with the Forest Service to fight them.

All motion ceased, except, that is, for Ruby Archuleta, who gunned her plumbing truck around town until she could no longer navigate through the brown glop; then she switched to a horse, until that became impossible; and then she proceeded on foot going from farmhouse to farmhouse, always with some petitions under one arm, talking to the people, asking them to sign, explaining a thousand times over the situation in the valley, pushing her concept of the Milagro Land and Water Protection Association. Some people listened courteously, drank coffee with Ruby, asked questions. Others argued, bitched, and shouted —both with her and at her. Almost every man and woman agreed with Ruby's assessment of the situation in the Miracle Valley; "Yessir, that Zopilote has got to go," they cried emphatically. But they were also afraid of Ladd Devine; they did not sign; they didn't want trouble, or not any more, anyway, "because we already got Trouble with a capital T, qué no?" They wondered, too: Could Ruby Archuleta really be trusted? And although admiring Joe Mondragón, they also thought he was a jerk—you had to be loco to ask for a kick in the ass like that. And again: they were as leery of taxing themselves to fight the conservancy district as they were of the conservancy taxes themselves.

Persuading somebody to sign the petition was hell. Ruby tried to explain it all, and then she tried to explain it again. When, for the umpteenth time, the same people asked the same stupid questions, the dauntless woman gave the same patient replies. Everyone was very friendly and understanding and polite and suspicious and afraid, and almost nobody signed, although many began to wonder if Ruby wasn't perhaps a saint. But all the same, Ruby, drenched, covered with mud, exhausted from plodding through the molasses muck, persevered. Ranchers got used to her coming around with the petitions: some folks even looked forward eagerly to her visits. Children cried, "Here comes The Ant again!" Women said, "Can you beat it, the bruja is knocking on our door once more." Seferino Pacheco, who was in favor of the petition, refused to sign it because he liked Ruby's visits so much. And, spurred on by a relentless and unflagging determination, Ruby kept dropping by. Their talk ran the gamut from the conservancy district to the death of Betita Córdova, who fell in the gorge in the snow on the same day John F. Kennedy was assassinated in Dallas.

Suddenly it stopped raining and a wind began to blow. Day and night the wind roared across the valley, knocking over old cottonwood trees and driving people crazy. By the third day the air was brown with dust that got between people's teeth and stung their eyes and ruined their sweaty lovemaking. In no time the roads dried hard as cement; trout were left baking in dry pasturelands. Like sea things retreating with the ocean's tide, water snakes and muskrats went back to the green areas along ditches and in the dampest vegas. At first people said, "Thank God, this will dry things out"; and then they began to curse the wind; and finally they tried to get their cars, trucks, and horses unstuck. They went at the hardened zoquete with pickaxes, hatchets, even acetylene torches. Men and women had to flood the areas around their cars and pickups in order to get them unstuck; they pulled them free with Ray Gusdorf's tractor. But then Ray's tractor broke down and wound up back in Joe Mondragón's shop and from then on Jerry Grindstaff, perched frostily behind the wheel of Ladd Devine's backhoe, had a monopoly on the towing business—at ten dollars a throw. People cursed, but what could they do? The wind died down for a minute, allowing dust to settle over everything and everybody, then it started blowing again. On his daily junket to town, Amarante Córdova had to climb over a dozen dead cottonwood trees that lay in his way like king-sized hurdles. A cottonwood landed atop a Forest Service pickup being driven by Carl Abeyta, who received a broken nose and a mild concussion from the incident, but, unfortunately, nothing worse. Another accident occurred when Flossie Devine, in a Dancing Trout station wagon late at night on her way back from a Capital City dentist, swerved to avoid a mammoth tumbleweed loping across the highway and wound up in a ditch with her new bridgework in her lap. And men irrigated, but the wind sucked up the water almost before it could seep into the ground.

"What the hell is this?" Joe Mondragón asked Nancy one day. "After the flood are we gonna have a drought?"

For a week the wind dried everything out. It even began to dry the people out. Skin shriveled; lips became chapped; hair grew stiff, caked with dust. Hundreds of little birds were blown into windows and adobe walls and killed, and, trailed by the everpresent scrawking magpies pecking at its mangy tail, the ugly yellow, snake-eating cat, that both Seferino Pacheco and Joe Mondragón had begun calling Cleofes after the legendary Cleofes Apodaca, had a field day trotting from house to house, feasting on all the little dead birds with broken necks.

Then, abruptly, the wind ceased; dust settled over the town almost gently, like a fine lace handkerchief. People stumbled outside, into their fields, slightly stunned by the peaceful silence. Birds ruffled their feathers, shaking out the dust. Horses that had been standing perfectly still for days with their asses just sweetly touching against barbed wire strands casually moved on stiffened legs back into their pastures, grazing again. A light rain fell; the sun shone; a light rain fell once more.

Dew turned up on grass tips again, compliments of the night; dogs dared to bark; flocks of hummingbirds returned to Onofre Martínez's gingerbread kingdom; life returned to normal. Ruby Archuleta started making her petition rounds in the Pipe Queen truck once more, and an army of men, led by Horsethief Shorty, Joe Mondragón, Claudio García, and Harlan Betchel, moved around town with chain saws, cutting up the trees blocking roads or crushing houses. And although cottonwood logs didn't burn that hot and made too much ash, it was free wood nevertheless, so it was distributed to many houses, which led Carolina Montoya to observe to her husband, the sheriff:

"You see, it's an ill wind that blows no good."

And by then it was time for the rodeo.

&

Every year, and this year was no different from any other year, Milagro had a rodeo of sorts. The town owned a rodeo grounds, enclosed by a low link fence that had a few stock pens down at one end, and there was a megaphone system that went on top of Ray Gusdorf's pickup, Ray being the rodeo announcer. There were no grandstands; people drove their cars and trucks up to the edge of the fence and sat in their front seats or on the front fenders, drinking beer and looking on. Nick Rael's son Jerry sold pop, candy bars, Hostess Twinkies, and gum from an impromptu concession stand, and that was about how things stacked up.

The stock for the Milagro rodeo came from local ranchers. There were no Brahma bulls, only a couple of bucking Herefords. And there were no lean, mean, powerful broncos, only a half-dozen pint-sized Shetland ponies, two of which, Orangutan and Sunflower, belonged to Charley and Linda Bloom.

There were four events in the rodeo: bareback bucking Hereford riding, bareback bucking pony riding, team roping of the same sad-sack cow by six entrants, and pony racing for kids.

Rodeo day dawned hot, simmering, dusty. Joe Mondragón and Jimmy Ortega drove over to Bloom's house early, loaded Orangutan and Sunflower into a trailer, and dropped them off in a pen at the rodeo grounds. Then they went and retrieved the placid little brown pony Pete and Betty Apodaca kept in their backyard. After that they fetched a milk cow, belonging to Rafael Maestas, that had bucked like hell last year if you zapped her in the udder—just before the chute gate opened—with a cattle prod.

By the time Claudio García, Onofre Martínez (accompanied by his two great-grandchildren, Chemo and

Chepa), and the sheriff's deputy, Meliton Naranjo, had chased down and brought in the team-roping cow, which was the entire herd of a rancher named Cleofes Mondragón (Joe's second cousin), the rodeo grounds were surrounded by various vehicles and men and children, and they were ready to begin.

Carrying some American flags, the state flag, and a sheriff's posse flag, Joe, Claudio García, Eliu Archuleta, Sparky Pacheco, Nick Rael, Eusebio Lavadie, and a few others rode their horses into the arena and lined up for the National Anthem. Ray Gusdorf dropped the needle onto the record, but his megaphones weren't working so hot, and it was pretty difficult to hear the song over the noise of the gas generator powering the announcing system anyway. In fact, the generator sputtered and whined so loudly nobody could hear a word Ray said during the entire proceedings, but that didn't seem to matter.

The action took place in a sunny, lackadaisical way, with long lags between riders. As often as not, when a pony or a cow came out of a chute, it would just lope harmlessly around the arena while the spectators laughed and clapped, and the rider furiously kicked, thrashed, and beat his animal about the head, neck, and rump to make it do something. The rides were also hard to time because Ray Gusdorf's eight-second buzzer either didn't work (thanks to a loose connection), or else couldn't be heard (because of the noisy generator) when it did work. No matter, though. There was no money to win in this rodeo, and nothing to lose, either, since a contestant paid no entry fee.

When the Blooms' pony Sunflower made her first appearance, the crowd went ape. She leaped clear of the chute like a crazy grasshopper, rearing and twisting, wiggling and kicking high, revolving in dizzying circles and whinnying even louder than Ray's generator, and the rider catapulted off her back like a flopping rag doll. Benny Maestas hit the dirt in his first second, picked up a stone and furiously winged it at the pony, but missed and instead broke one of the headlights on the Body Shop and Pipe Queen truck.

Later, Jimmy Ortega landed on his head and was kicked in the ass to boot. And after him Johnny Pacheco was knocked off when Sunflower bucked into the chute gate Nick Rael couldn't swing open fast enough; Johnny almost broke a leg.

Which left the way to first-prize kudos wide open for Joe Mondragón.

But he only lasted two seconds. Sunflower did a flip out of the chute, landing on her (and Joe's) back, and the crowd let out a shrill gasp because it looked as if Joe had been killed.

But he was up even before Sunflower, throwing handfuls of dirt and screaming obscenities at the pony. Then, dusting himself off, he shouted at the corral boys: "Get that fucking horse back in that goddam chute, I'm going again!"

Claudio García and Rafael Maestas galloped across the arena, shooing Sunflower back into the pen; Nick Rael and Onofre Martínez herded her up into the chute. And when the people saw Joe was going to ride again, they clapped heartily, whistled, and honked their horns and chucked a few dozen empty beer cans into the arena.

This time Sunflower emerged from the chute like a horse with a Pegasus complex, taking off and bumping the chute gate so hard it knocked Nick Rael over backward, and then dropping suddenly out from underneath Joe like the trap door in a gallows, so that for a second there was a sight to make the crowd "Ooohhh," and "Aaaahhh"; Joe extended perfectly vertical with his feet high in the air, his head down, his right arm extended further downward and ending where his hand still grasped the loose rope which had come unraveled . . . and Sunflower was twenty yards away grazing on imaginary grass. Then the crowd shrieked as Joe plowed face first into the turf like an ass-backward rocket.

He knelt in the dirt a moment, tenderly feeling his mouth, while the hundred or so spectators cheered and honked some more and clapped and bammed their hands against their hoods and fenders. After a minute all their noise became rhythmic, the people chanting

"Otra *vez!* Otra *vez!*" meaning they wanted to see Joe's skydiving act again and knew he possessed an ego that could be goaded into it.

Once more, Claudio García and Rafael Maestas herded the pony into the stock pen, and, calling the horse every swearword he could think of, Joe lowered himself onto her back for another try. After all, he was about the best rider in the county, and everybody out there knew it—hell, he'd even broken horses with Horsethief Shorty for the Dancing Trout! And so simply the idea, let alone the fact, of not being able to stay aboard a two-bit, slanty-eyed, pea-brained Shetland pony just about had Joe shitting cupcakes.

Nick Rael yanked open the gate; Ray Gusdorf's excited shouts couldn't be heard; and vehicle horns went berserk—as did the mighty little pony. On her first twisting leap Joe found himself riding sideways; on her second jarring heave he was upside down, clinging to her belly; and a split second later, the hooves chopping terrifyingly but harmlessly past his ears, Joe was flat on his back, lost to everyone's view in a miniature atomic bomb of dust.

Grabbing a beer can and screaming obscenities at the top of his lungs, Joe charged after Sunflower. The horse ran to a corner, whinnied and reared, then galloped past Joe, who furiously threw the can, hitting her in the butt.

More jeering, whistling, catcalls, and scattered boos accompanied this unsportsmanlike conduct. Then the horns commenced again, along with some rhythmic handclapping, and taunts of, "Come on, José, can't you ride that little teeny-weeny horse?" and "Oye, primo, don't eat all the dirt up, we got to use this place again next year—!"

"Get that bitch ready again," Joe snarled. "I'm gonna kill that fucking horse!"

They got her ready again and he hopped on, adjusting the loose rope until it set just right in his gloved hand; then he yelled, "Open that fucking gate, Nick!" and Nick did, and all hell broke loose. For although the gate was open, Sunflower had decided to do her act in the chute. The crowd saw Joe's head bob up and down a few times, they heard a chilling splintering sound accompanied by some spine-tingling human bellows, and then suddenly Sunflower trotted calmly into the arena, minus Joe, who was lying on his back not seriously hurt but out cold, in a pile of horseshit in the chute.

That evening, just before dark when nighthawks were flying over the meadows and robins were making a final run down freshly irrigated fields, Joe, sporting a noticeable limp and a sullen forehead bump, and toting a loose rope in one hand, knocked on the Blooms' door.

"I come to ride that pony," he said tightly when Bloom answered.

"Are you crazy?"

"I come to ride that horse," Joe reiterated. "Where is it?"

"Out back, in the corral."

"Let's go," Joe said, starting around the house. Bloom followed.

Joe let Bloom fit a rope around her neck and lead her into the back field. And, while Joe mounted and adjusted his rope, the lawyer held Sunflower tightly; she didn't move.

But when Bloom let got it was as if somebody across the field had pushed in a detonator's plunger, exploding a hundred dynamite sticks affixed to Sunflower's belly. Long before he knew what hit him, Joe was up to his elbows in alfalfa with a tingling, bone-jarred spine, and Bloom was laughing so hard he had dropped to all fours and commenced beating the earth with his fists.

"Oh shit, that was beautiful!" Bloom gasped. "If you only could have seen what you looked like, oh Christ, what a beautiful *beautiful* thing!"

Joe didn't think it was so diddly-fucking funny, though. Enraged, but this time outwardly calm, he wrenched painfully onto his feet and stood for a moment, rubbing his can, staring at the pony feasting deliriously on alfalfa ten yards away.

"I'll be back," he threatened miserably, heading

toward the house, toward his truck in the driveway beyond. "You just wait and see!"

A rage like nothing he had ever experienced burned throughout Joe's bruised and battered body. Maybe he was going off his rocker or something. Or maybe it was just that all this beanfield business was starting to get him down.

Back home Joe made sure his rifles and his pistols and his shotgun were loaded and within reach. Then he tumbled into bed beside Nancy. But how to sleep? He just lay there, all tensed up, waiting for a fusillade of bullets to come buzzing through his windows. In fact, he wished the real shooting *would* start so they could get this whole charade over with.

Joe was so nervous he had to get up every fifteen minutes to take a leak. And it wasn't until the town roosters had already begun to crow that he finally drifted uneasily into dreams.

❧

When a copy of the so-called Milagro Land and Water Protection Association's petition, compliments of Bud Gleason (who had received it from Harlan Betchel, who had found it under a table in the Pilar where Claudio García had accidentally dropped it), arrived at Kyril Montana's desk, the agent pored over it for a spell.

Then he phoned the state engineer, Nelson Bookman, and a half-hour later the agent, Bookman, and Bookman's mouthpiece, Rudy Noyes, met in the state engineer's office. Bookman read over the one-paragraph complaint and then handed it to Noyes, who read it expressionlessly; then Bookman called in a secretary and gave her the petition with orders to have some Xeroxes made. He offered the agent a cigarette, but Kyril Montana only smoked the filtered kind, and so lit up one of his own.

Bookman said, "There're no signatures on this copy. How many signatures do you figure they've got over-all?"

"I'm convinced the Milagro Land and Water Protection Association doesn't even exist," the agent said.

"At least, to date nothing has been filed with the State Corporation Commission. As to how many up there have signed—I think, and my sources inform me, practically nobody."

"Whose idea was this petition?" Bookman wanted to know. "Our friend Joe Mondragón?"

"No. It's the brainstorm of a woman named Ruby Archuleta who runs a garage and a plumbing business south of town. Apparently the meeting they had in their church was her idea too."

"Who is Ruby Archuleta?"

"I don't know for sure. Nobody up there really knows her that well either. She's been married three times, never stirred up any political trouble before. She's in her late forties, does the job of ten men, so I'm told; she's a midwife among other things, and some people up there think she's a witch."

Nelson Bookman leaned back in his chair, straightened out the Xerox copies a different secretary dropped on his desk, and suddenly grinned.

"Let's burn her at the stake," he said huskily, abruptly lurching forward to stub out his cigarette.

The agent smiled; Rudy Noyes did not drum up even the faintest wisp or flicker of amusement.

"Ah, fuck 'em," Bookman growled. "They give me a royal pain in the ass, those people up there. For thirty-five years, in one capacity or another, I've been tiptoeing through their lives. I've got cramps in my calves. What do you think, Rudy, should we quit crapping around and just go in there and lower the boom on Joe Mondragón and screw the consequences?"

Now Rudy Noyes smiled. "Well, Nelson, we know the case is cut-and-dried, so that really isn't the problem, is it? My feeling is if we go to trial, though, they've got something concrete to hang their cause on, which we'd still like to avoid, if possible. If we hit Joe Mondragón with an order to show cause he's got a right to that water, they'll know exactly what to protest against, we may throw them all together, they'll fill up pages of these petitions, find themselves in a position to organize, and, of course, that won't queer the conservancy district and the Indian Creek Dam, but it'll sure make them that much more difficult and expensive to realize. So I would say at this juncture still, the less we give them the better."

"Precisely the way I had it figured," said Kyril Montana.

"Then what's to discuss?" Bookman asked. "It seems to me there's nothing to do except wait for the break that will nab Joe Mondragón outside the framework of irrigation rights and that damn-beanfield."

"Good." Kyril Montana stood up, shaking hands with them both. "I just wanted to be sure you knew."

"Anytime," Bookman said. "Anytime at all. Thanks for keeping us posted—"

All the same, as he reached the street outside, Kyril Montana felt something uncomfortable nagging at the back of his mind. It was not, compared to many cases he had worked on, that big a deal. Yet he suspected there was something nobody had yet touched upon in this thing. Perhaps it was simply that all over the country people were changing, they were acting differently than they ever had before, so much so that it had become impossible to foretell how they might react in any given situation.

Or maybe it was simply that he was too far removed from the people and from whatever was going on up there in Milagro—

A car honked. The agent had almost stepped off the curb without looking both ways.

≈

The day after the rodeo, Nancy Mondragón left her three kids with Linda Bloom because she had to drive her mother-in-law to the Doña Luz clinic, and Linda decided to ferry all the children to the Rio Lucero gorge for a swim. Herding them into the VW bus, she set off gaily enough, heading south on the highway and across Strawberry Mesa for a ways, and finally into the narrow, pretty gorge. At a point where the stream flowed about forty feet below the road she pulled over and guided the children down a fairly steep slope to the water. The stream was shallow here, perfect for youngsters, running slowly along a wide pebbly bed for a ways, then curling around moderate-sized volcanic boulders to form several foot-high waterfalls and a string of foamy, but still quite shallow and gentle, pools.

After Linda helped the kids undress or roll up their trousers, she settled herself on a large warm rock, cradling their clothes in her arms. She kept a sharp eye on her charges as they waded peacefully, gathering stones or stalking lizards along the shore. It was a peaceful, wonderfully sunny day. A hundred swallows darted between the gorge walls overhead, their shadows blipping across the shining water, across the children's bodies and happy glistening faces. Linda, watching over her brood, thought: This is how I'd like my life to be. This is why we live in Milagro.

An old van halted on the road above; two men tumbled out. At first, owing to the stream's noise, Linda didn't notice them. The men, who had perhaps been drinking, teetered on the brink of the cliff as they unzipped their flies and pissed down the embankment, an act neither Linda nor the children witnessed. In fact, nobody looked up until a splash occurred in midstream, a splash obviously too large to have been made by a child throwing a stone. Startled, Linda lifted her eye just as another fist-sized stone loudly smacked the water just below her observation post.

Although both men, one hefty and yet almost cherubic looking, and the other very tall and lanky, seemed vaguely familiar, Linda recognized neither. Afterward, she would remember that the skinny one had a moustache and that they both appeared to have reddish, bizarrely bloated faces, maybe from excessive boozing. But at first, thinking they were merely trying to attract attention in order to say hello, Linda smiled self-consciously and waved. Instead of waving back, however, both men stooped over to gather more rocks. And with that menacing gesture, Linda suddenly realized something was terribly wrong.

Her mind struggled to deny what was about to

happen; so she bestirred herself almost languidly, sitting up and staying immobile for a moment, gazing perplexedly at the men, the buttery lazifying sunshine still in control of her flesh. Then dreamily she rose to her feet. Each man had collected an armload of heavy rocks, any one of which, hitting a child or even Linda in the head, could have been fatal.

And now the scene, their slow and deliberate gathering actions, broke apart insanely as the two men began to pelt Linda and the five children in deadly earnest, aiming their rocks, trying to murder them.

Linda shouted, "Hey kids, they're throwing rocks!" But the children, even little María, had sensed what was up, they understood perfectly the danger represented by those two men above their heads, and they were already moving, starting to run, heading automatically downstream.

"Run!" Linda shouted. *"Run! Run! Run!"*

Splashing into the shallow water, she pushed Larry Mondragón, his brother Billy, and his sister Luisa and her own Pauline ahead of her.

"They're trying to kill us!" she blurted. *"Run fast!"*

The kids stumbled through the water, over and around boulders, through sand and muck and thick bank grass and willow thickets. María toppled forward, Linda yanked her upright and practically flung her ahead into the other kids, who were in a loose bunch, running well. Later, Linda would be amazed by how quickly they all had reacted correctly to the situation, these silly little kids. She would remember how Larry Mondragón slipped and Pauline tugged him to his feet; she would remember how little Billy Mondragón, who was only four (and one of the clumsiest preschoolers she had ever seen), went over a series of black rocks in their path like a lizard or an agile mountain goat. And Linda herself: she sprinted among them with her head turned, always looking up, trying to keep track of the rocks coming down. Once she dropped to her knees to avoid a stone that nearly grazed her head; another time she shoved María sideways into a pool to avoid a rock.

Above them the men staggered along the rim, firing rhythmically, if drunkenly, shouting words she never heard, stopping occasionally to stock up on ammunition, which they pitched rapidly at the woman and children, striking at their heels, missing the fleeing kids by inches.

Then, as suddenly as it began, the terrifying assault ended. The men quit, gestured obscenely, about-faced, swayed leisurely back to their van, started it up, and drove out of the gorge.

Linda kept the children moving for another twenty-five yards, then ordered them to stop. They gathered around her, gasping, wide-eyed, speechless; but nobody, not even the smallest child, was crying. Linda said, "I think it's alright now, I think those men left, I think they went away."

And they had.

Cautiously, trembling now that there was time to think about what had happened and wanting very badly to generate a release through tears, Linda pushed them all ahead of her up the steep embankment to the road. Quickly, they trotted back to the bus. Linda slid open the side door, and, tossing in the bundle of clothes she'd hugged in one arm all during their flight, she was amazed to realize that somehow not even a sock had been lost.

There was another, more roundabout way out of the gorge, and Linda took it, afraid that if she headed back onto the mesa the way they had come the men might be waiting at an impromptu roadblock. Lined along the rear seat, bunched on the floor, the kids sat quietly; in fact, since it had all begun, not one of them had peeped. Finally, Linda called back to everybody: "Hey, you guys, let's sing a song!" And with that she leaped into "Row, Row, Row Your Boat."

So they climbed out of the gorge and sped along the mesa in a dust cloud, singing fervently and almost joyously together, until suddenly the car hit a confused jackrabbit and Linda burst into tears.

"Who the hell did it?" Nancy demanded furiously of her friend. "What did those bastards look like? Were they Anglos? Or Chicanos? Didn't you get the license number? You tell me who did it and José and me, we'll kill them for you, for all of us! We'll tie them to trees and shoot off their toes and let them bleed to death! So help me God!"

"What good will that do?" Hopelessly, Linda swayed her head. "It's over," she whimpered. "They were just drunk. They didn't know what they were doing. I don't think they were even from around here."

"Tourists?"

"No. I don't know. I just don't want to talk about it anymore."

"How can you let somebody attack your kids and not want revenge?" Nancy asked. "An eye for an eye, a tooth for a tooth, goddammit! They were from the Dancing Trout, qué no? A pair of the Zopilote's pendejos. It's because of José's beanfield, and because Charley's gonna help, that this happened."

"No." Linda kept shaking her head. "I told you, I never saw them before. It's over. They were drunk. They didn't know what they were doing. One of them even had such a pleasant, little boy face . . ."

Nancy sat down across from her friend, regarding her critically for a short while.

"Next time they'll kill one of our kids, Linda."

But again the exhausted woman shook her head. "Violence just makes more violence just makes even more violence," she whispered through silent tears. "I don't want revenge."

And then she sat there, never having felt this brittle before, waiting to calm down, waiting for the nightmare to end, slowly and desperately and like a little child shaking her head.

Suddenly it hit Nancy: Linda's statement about the "little boy face." "*I* know who they were!" she exclaimed. "At least I know who one of them was. What's the name, José, of that guy out at the Evening Star, the huge one with the pretty, little kid face, the one who works for the chotas?"

"Lord Elephant—?"

"*That's* who it was! That son of a bitch must be on the Zopilote's payroll too! *I'll cut off his balls!*"

᭣

Lord Elephant's real name was Bobby Joe Tucker; his hometown was Baton Rouge, Louisiana. He lived in his hogan on Strawberry Mesa with a woman, Lady Elephant, whose real name was Christina Cupcoe, and whose hometown was Silvermine, Connecticut. Like Benny Maestas, Bobby Joe Tucker was a Vietnam vet; unlike Benny Maestas, he was also a junkie. In Vietnam, Bobby Joe spent many months on the line, during which time he became hooked on skag; later he was stationed at Saigon's Tan Son Nhut airport, working in warehouses that gift-wrapped bodies of American soldiers in patriotic red, white, and blue for shipment back home. While thus occupied, Bobby Joe became part of a ring that sent drugs—heroin, opium, grass, cocaine—back to the States sewn up in the bodies of dead soldiers or stashed in their coffins or included with their personal belongings. In this way Bobby Joe built up some interesting and valuable connections and with their help, just before leaving Vietnam, he worked out a daring plan to send himself a "body." The plan worked, he picked up his body immediately upon touching down on North American soil, and then he disappeared into the Yankee heartland with both an honorable discharge and ten pounds of uncut horse riding on his hip.

With luck, Bobby Joe could have become a rich man. But lacking an excess of smarts to begin with, he had pulled off this caper largely due to the efforts of some brainier military personnel who set the thing up for him in Saigon; to make matters worse, right off the bat he shot himself up too pure on three occasions, almost killing himself with each exaggerated fix, and by the time he had just barely survived his third OD, the gears in his brain had become pretty well stripped. Then, in Kansas City, he bumped into one of the former soldiers who had helped land him in the States with that fortune of uncut H, and this soldier wanted in on Bobby Joe's business, which at that point Bobby Joe still hadn't figured how to set up.

During the next three months, Bobby Joe traveled with his friend to New Orleans, Miami, Washington, D.C., and finally New York, trying to arrange a big score for all their junk, but playing it very tight to the vest for fear of running into a bunch of undercover narcs, or else getting ripped off or just offed by the people with whom they wished to bargain.

In the end, in New York, Bobby Joe's friend simply up and split with the smack, leaving Bobby Joe high, dry, and very strung out. After that, Bobby Joe wandered, doing odd jobs, stealing for his daily fixes, moving with one old lady and then another, always more or less in a fog or on the nod and desperate for smack and bread, until he landed in the Evening Star commune out on Milagro's Strawberry Mesa with Lady Elephant, née Christina Cupcoe, on his arm.

Lord and Lady Elephant set up housekeeping in that Evening Star hogan without an invitation from the other members of the tribe, who disliked them intensely, afraid that his hard-drug habit would bring the cops down on Strawberry Mesa like a ton of blue bricks. By the time Bobby Joe staggered into the commune, however, he didn't much care about the social amenities. In fact, despite his cherubic, blue-eyed baby face that always put people off their guard, he had developed, over the past few years, into one big, mean, son of a bitch. Anybody who did not see eye to eye with Bobby Joe was likely to regret it. Bobby Joe even carried a piece, a little .32-caliber, single-action revolver, which further petrified the peace-loving Strawberry Mesa crowd. So when the lord and his lady showed up one day looking for a place to crash, and Bobby Joe smiled innocently at everybody while nonchalantly inspecting the barrel of his gun with his blank blue eyes, the occupants of the lord's and lady's present hogan politely bowed their heads, gathered in their belongings and kids, and moved into another building nearby.

Bobby Joe had a persistent habit, though, and it eventually led him by the nose into the Chamisaville methadone program. Of course, as soon as he was enrolled in the methadone program the various police agencies in town were led by their noses to Bobby Joe Tucker, and—metaphorically speaking—the police tied Bobby Joe's hands behind his back, touched the barrel of a cocked revolver to his head, and advised him of his rights in the following manner:

"Bobby Joe Tucker, alias Lord Elephant, we're gonna let you stay in Chamisa County up there in the Evening Star commune on Strawberry Mesa with that cute little girl with the big titties you're screwing whose folks back in Connecticut have a runaway warrant out on her, and we're gonna let you continue getting your treatment from the methadone clinic, and we're even gonna look the other way during many of the dope-related activities you're involved in, just so long as you cooperate with us in certain ventures; just so long as you hearken to our beck and call every now and then when we need you to do a job or provide some information for us."

Well, Bobby Joe was all played out by this time and tired of being hassled by the pigs; he even sort of *liked* Strawberry Mesa, and he was actually thinking vaguely about reforming himself enough to become more a part of the commune, helping out with animals and the garden and so forth, and he'd gotten used to Lady Elephant, too, who was a sexy lay, not too bright, but a rather tender person, maybe one of the most gentle souls Bobby Joe had ever traveled with. And so he told the cops, "Whatever you say, fellas."

That is, he became what might be called a police informer, supplying a certain amount of drug information that enabled the various police agencies to meet the quota of busts they needed to make themselves look good: he delivered reports on transients, too, turning in, for example, a whole slew of runaways in return for being allowed to cohabit with his own particular runaway, Lady Elephant. And he occasionally carried out strong-arm tactics for the cops and their allies, who either paid him in hard cash for his trouble, or else sometimes in confiscated hard drugs.

Yet several days after rocks were thrown at Linda Bloom and those kids in the Lucero gorge, Bobby Joe Tucker's Chamisa County sojourn came to an abrupt end.

There wasn't much fanfare to the incident that put him back on the road again. Toward sunset five rattle-trap pickups jounced along the final rocky slope to the Evening Star commune, and eight men carrying rifles descended from the trucks, which had coasted to a stop in a slight semicircle about fifteen yards from the front door of Lord and Lady Elephant's hogan. In a tight group these eight men walked up to the hogan and one man knocked on the door, which Lady Elephant answered. "Your husband, is he here?" the man who had done the knocking asked, and when Lady Elephant, smiling serenely, nodded yes, the man said, "Will you bring him to the door, please?" Lady Elephant, still smiling, backed into the darkness, and, naked from the waist up, Lord Elephant appeared in the doorway, his beautiful little boy face contorted into a harsh sneer as he said, "What do you people want?"

The man who had done the knocking said, "We're giving you and your wife about two minutes to gather up whatever you can carry, and then we're gonna take you for a ride up to the Colorado border, and if we ever find out that you came back to this county we'll kill you."

Bobby Joe's pale eyes flickered, then swiftly assessed the faces of the men confronting him. They were old and weather-beaten local faces, lined and brown and composed harshly, tight-lipped, unforgiving, determined that he should do this thing. Bobby Joe could smell their skin and their old dusty clothes, and he could smell their guns. It was unequivocally evident that if Bobby Joe went for his little .32 they would kill him harder and faster and with less emotion than most men, marked for extinction, had the opportunity to get killed. Still, Bobby Joe dropped his jaw to begin a protest, to ask an outraged question,

but some little movement, maybe just a slight altera-
tion in the expression of one man's eyes, or the way
another man's shoulders changed their set when Bobby
Joe's jaw dropped, shut him up. There was nothing to
argue about, his life in Chamisa County had ended;
he was lucky they offered an opportunity to walk out
alive.

Bobby Joe said, "Chris, get together some things,
we're splitting."

The men waited in the doorway while Bobby Joe
and his old lady scraped together a few clothes, some
books, and stuffed these and some rocks and feathers
and a branch of sagebrush into a small gray suitcase.
Then Lord and Lady Elephant walked quietly through
the little group of men to a pickup and got in. Es-
corted by that caravan of trucks, they were driven,
without a word, up through a crimson sunset and the
occasional energetic wing bursts of horned larks, to
the Colorado border.

Part Four

"I wish to Christ that all of a sudden
winter would come."
—Bill Koontz

&8

What might be called the deadly game of "Waiting
for the War to Start" was beginning to get a few
people down, and one Milagro citizen suffering more
than most was the sheriff, Bernabé Montoya.

It was the kind of day when mundane tasks were
needed to reduce the building tension. Bernabé carried the ash drawer from his kitchen stove out to the
chicken pen and dumped the ashes over the fence so
the chickens could fluff it into their feathers and kill
mites. Then he spooned a few dozen cat turds from
the blue plastic boat serving as their kitty's catbox into
a trash can, loaded four metal trash cans into his
pickup, and headed down the north–south highway
for the official Milagro dump.

There were, of course, a good many unofficial
town dumps, starting with just about every citizen's
backyard crammed full of useful "useless" junk, and
moving on to all the oil drums people owned in which
they still burned their paper refuse in defiance of
state and county antipollution laws strictly forbidding
this practice. And then there were spots in various
arroyos—for example, the east side Arroyo del Marrano and the south side Arroyo de la Urraca—where
people dumped all their empty cans and jars and
dead dogs and chickens that had died from en-
cephalitis and old washing machines and cars, because the official dump was too far—three miles!—
away. And finally, there was the favorite—what might
be called the "official unofficial"—dump, which was
located in a gravel pit on west side mesaland belong-

ing to Eusebio Lavadie, who had posted signs (to no avail) at the gravel pit, threatening, in both English and Spanish, to keelhaul, garrote, draw and quarter, fine, jail, and, in general, "prosecute to the full extent of the law" all trespassers, garbage dumpers, deadbeats, lewd lovers, and so forth. About once a month Lavadie had to tack up a fresh sign because the old one, perforated by bullet holes, became illegible—Lavadie's gravel pit also happening to be *the* place to sight in one's rifle during the several months preceding deer season, during which time Lavadie didn't even bother to replace his sign lest somebody decide to adjust his crosshairs against the bridge of Lavadie's nose, or across the third brass button from the top of his vest, which was situated more or less directly over his heart.

Lavadie's gravel pit was also where those people engaged in construction activities who did not rip off their earthen or mineral materials from State Highway Department pits alongside the major north–south route stole the sand and gravel necessary to their various enterprises.

But Bernabé Montoya, being the staunch upholder of law and order that he was, had to travel three miles south to the official dump, and when he got there this particular morning, in spite of state and local ordinances to the contrary, the dump was burning, and about a hundred ravens were stalking around in the foul-smelling smog, eating breakfast.

Theoretically, ever since the strict environmental laws of the year before (which forebade open-air trash burning), Milagro had been required to bury its garbage. To satisfy this requirement, the county had purchased a bulldozer for fifteen hundred dollars from Joe Mondragón; the county had then turned the bulldozer over to the Milagro mayor, Sammy Cantú, who, in turn, turned it back over to Joe, who was given the biweekly job of interring the garbage, but Joe promptly turned over the bulldozer, period. And somehow nobody, in the past eight months, had gotten together the necessary apparatus to right the machine, so there it lay, like a mammoth turtle in the hot sun, helpless and useless on its back, and Sammy Cantú, for the past eight months, had been siphoning several bucks a week out of the town treasury to pay one-armed Onofre Martínez and his great-grandchildren, Chemo and Chepa Martínez, to wake up before dawn once a week and steal down to the dump and soak the garbage in kerosene and touch a match to it. Of course, nobody ever knew how the dump was set on fire. Among themselves, people winked and giggled and attributed the mischief to El Brazo Onofre. In fact one morning Nancy Mondragón actually threatened her eldest son Larry in the following manner: "Lorenzito," she said, "if you keep shooting BBs at the hummingbirds trying to feed at that poor Herbie Goldfarb's feeder, El Brazo Onofre is gonna sneak into your room tonight and set your hair on fire and burn you up just like it burns up the dump!"

When some huffy environmentalists, accompanied by a Chamisaville *News* reporter, expressed outrage over the burning, most of Milagro's officialdom shrugged its shoulders, scratched its head, and piously attributed the greasily smoking mountains of garbage to a direct hit by lightning, or else maybe to spontaneous combustion. The State Environmental Protection Agency had even sent an investigator named Jon Nickerson up once, and Sammy Cantú had sincerely promised to station a cop out at the dump on twenty-four-hour watch for a week in case "teen-age vandals" were to blame for the flames. And although no cop, vigilante, or even teen-ager with a slingshot ever spent five minutes on guard at the dump, at the end of a week Onofre Martínez dictated a letter to Jon Nickerson from Sammy Cantú, elaborately explaining that unfortunately an around-the-clock vigil had netted no culprits. After that, the EPA probably saw the writing on the wall; in any case, it quit bugging Milagro's dump.

As for the bulldozer, Joe Mondragón kept promising "to see a man" in Chamisaville who had the kind of rig that could right the machine, and Onofre Martínez kept accepting bribes to set all that crap on fire—and to Bernabé Montoya, who couldn't have cared less one way or the other, it looked as if this kind of suspended animation was going to be the state of affairs at the Milagro dump until either hell froze over or the environmentalists in the Friends of Chamisa County organization attacked in force, surrounding the dump with four-wheel-drive vehicles sporting .50-caliber machine guns while they proceeded self-righteously to bury the garbage with picks and shovels wielded by high school students trying to brown nose their way into As in their "democracy in action" or civics projects.

So, one by one, grunting heavily, wheezing bitterly, Bernabé pushed the trash cans to the rear of his pickup, dropped down to the mucky ground, and heaved the cans off the truck, tipping them over into the oozing smoky sludge. The fourth and final can he swung off the tailgate onto his toe. Releasing a hideous frozen gurgle, he closed his eyes and shivered until his face was almost purple and the veins bulged across his forehead, then he bellowed and kicked over the garbage can, and almost at the same instant drew his revolver and fired six times at the most concentrated pocket of ravens. The huge birds flapped frantically skyward, bumping into each other in their haste to flee, and perhaps one bird broke its wing against another bird, or perhaps—the law of averages notwithstanding—Bernabé actually hit one. Whatever, after a hundred ravens had boiled noisily off, one mammoth black beast remained, flapping around hysterically in the smoke.

Nervously, Bernabé punched out the spent shells, reloaded from bullets he held in his gun belt, aimed carefully at the cripple, and fired. A fan of garbage spewed up to the left. He fired again—a fan spewed up to the right. He fired once more, hitting a tin can that ricocheted into the desperately flopping bird. The fourth time he fired a pop bottle six feet from the raven exploded straight up like a Yellowstone geyser.

Cursing, Bernabé stumbled through heaps of mud and refuse in order to get a closer shot, but the raven scrambled frantically away. So the sheriff stopped and shot twice more, aerating the dump but not the bird.

"Ai, Chihuahua!" he wailed, discovering he had only four shells left. When these were lodged in his weapon, he fired once more from a steady standing position, and then, insanely plowing through the redolent glop, slipping and pitching forward, sideways, and back, he blasted away on the run three more times, hitting in rapid succession: the windshield of a discarded car, a leaky plastic jerry can, and the upside-down bulldozer.

At this point the raven toppled over a small cliff into a gully. Bernabé ran to the edge and began pelting the bird with rocks. But it kept flip-flopping around down there, impossible to hit. So with a suicidal primeval cry, Bernabé leaped into the gully, landing atop the tiring raven, and for a moment he hugged that bundle of outraged black fury to his chest, until finally, sobbing, he grabbed the bird by the neck, guided its beak into his mouth, and, among bloody and very surprised and gurgling protests from both parties, savagely bit off its head and contemptuously spat it out.

The broad wings went through a final incensed salvo and then quit whipping Bernabé's aching body, and somehow the hole in the neck, bubbling blood, released a last defiant scrawk.

Dumbfounded, panting, astonished by his own stupidity and rage, and spitting blood, Bernabé just sat there for a while. After a long time, he shakily pushed onto his feet, picked up the head and threw it away over his left shoulder, pulled out some wing and tail and breast feathers the Pilar Café's short-order cook Fred Quintana might want to use for his fly tying, and, wheezing almost asthmatically, he crawled up the bank and spent a half-hour searching (successfully in the end, thank *you,* Saint Anthony!) for his pistol, which he had dropped before he leaped.

"I don't know why I did that," he bleated aloud to a couple of low-lying, inquisitive, and also disapproving clouds, "unless José Mondragón's beanfield has finally driven me up the wall!"

Still and all: better to have mangled a raven than

another human being. At least, that's what Carolina would have said.

꿍

Charley Bloom went fishing a lot. When he and Linda first moved to Milagro he bought a fiber glass fly rod and some salmon eggs, and that had been one way to work the tension from his system.

Nowadays, Bloom only used artificial flies for bait. Not because he had developed into a fishing snob, but simply because he had found that once you learned a few basics about fly fishing, it was as easy (and more fun) to catch the small trout in the streams around Milagro on artificial lures as it was to catch them on bait.

A half-dozen small but fine trout streams were within an hour of his home. There was, of course, Indian Creek, which practically ran through the backyard. This river received heavy fishing pressure during the summer months, particularly back up in the canyon past the Dancing Trout where the National Forest campsites began, an area the Fish and Game Department kept regularly stocked with stupid rainbows that were also bad eating. Every Tuesday morning in June, July, and August a huge tank truck driven by Glen Wesley Gore of the Strawberry Mesa State Fish Hatchery threaded its way slowly up the Little Baldy Bear road past greedily grinning, wall-to-wall, out-of-state tourists clutching fishing rods that dangled salmon eggs and marshmallows, backed up to a siding just below the Guachupangue Junction bridge, and, after Glen had crossed himself and begged the Lord's forgiveness, dumped a wriggling mass of ten-inch rainbows into the stream. Whereupon a mile and a half of blundering fishermen went berserk, jumping into the stream and charging after the prey with everything except hatchets and hand grenades. The first time Bloom witnessed this melee was also the last time. Men in chest-high waders wandered up and down the two-foot-deep waters excitedly flailing the currents, using their fishing rods like cat-o'-nine-tails to create a froth, splashing, chattering loudly to each other, throwing stones, casting across each other's lines, and yet somehow, probably because the fish were so confused, they caught the hatchery trout.

In fact, if Glen made the dump about nine, the river was usually cleaned out by noon, the shore for that mile and a half littered with discarded salmon egg jars, hook packages, snarled leaders, piles of fly-covered fish guts and children shit, candy bar wrappers, soda pop cans and tab tops.

It took about a month after the battles of June, July, and August for Indian Creek to work itself back into shape. But then, starting in about mid-September and continuing through the end of the season on November 30, Bloom often worked the stream from the Guachupangue Junction bridge all the way down through Milagro and into the narrow gorge that eventually ended at the Rio Grande. At the upper end, by the bridge and then west to Milagro, there were a few hard-to-catch surviving rainbows; farther down in the Indian Creek gorge, where the water rushed between huge and almost erotically sculpted lavic boulders into deep foamy pools, there were a number of foot-long brown trout, and even some two- to three-pound whoppers.

The Rio Puerco, Dixonburgh Creek, and the Little Baldy River were very different streams. They flowed out of the high country, and all three entered Indian Creek either before, or right around, Milagro. They were shallow, not more than ten or fifteen feet across at their widest points, and, for most of their journey from the snowpack down, they were lined by impenetrable willows, overhanging junipers, a million young aspens, bushes, brambles—a veritable flycaster's nightmare. The streams were also crisscrossed by rotting trees and logs that had been felled by age or by extensive logging operations. Adding insult to almost incomparable injury, the diminutive cutthroat and brown trout (an eight-inch fish was a monster) that lived in these waters were so spooky and wild that stalking prong-horned antelopes and mountain sheep was child's play compared to approaching these pint-sized fish.

"Those three creeks," Bloom once complained, "are the God damn ninth circle of trout fishing in America."

Bloom couldn't get enough of those streams, though. Local myth had it that of the last out-of-state tourist to try a Milagro creek nothing had been heard for months until Horsethief Shorty Wilson (who could have caught hummingbirds blindfolded with tweezers if he'd wanted) stumbled across his bones high up on the Little Baldy River. And that was at once the nemesis and the attraction: the Little Baldy, the Rio Puerco, and Dixonburgh Creek were for the people who lived in Milagro. Period. And even then, very rarely did you meet a local crazy enough to go through what you had to go through to harvest a skinny little fish from one of those narrow streams.

Just about the only way for a fisherman to work such tight waters was to bull through willows and brush and trees into the stream and then walk slowly up it, hunched over so that his nose was practically touching the water, snapping the fly ahead about ten or fifteen feet into likely pools and riffles. Eight out of ten times, no matter how far he could snap out the line, the fly always got caught in an overhang, and he had to destroy the fishing for the next twenty yards by straightening up to free the hook. In fact, fishing those creeks was like fishing a tunnel. And even if a person was lucky enough to snap the fly out to where he wanted it in the fast-flowing water, it was hell, in such cramped quarters, to retrieve the line fast enough to keep it taut so that he could successfully strike a fish if one hit. Then, if he did hook something, there was no such thing as playing it. A fisherman had about a tenth of a second, before the trout shot into sunken branches, logs, weeds, and roots, to horse it out of the stream. And, in whipping the fish clear of the water and into the willows, like as not (the line becoming entangled in a thousand interlacing branches) the fish would end up flopping in the air three feet above the river, and of course, at least half the time, as the fisherman lunged to grab it, his prey would loose itself from the hook and splash back into water so icy that, boots or no, middle of summer or not, a man's feet were always numb.

In one way, fishing these creeks required finesse; in another way there was nothing even remotely connected to the fine art of trout fishing about this angling process. For example, despite the small-sized fish, Bloom always used a ten- or a twelve-pound leader, simply because he had to have something that could withstand endless yanking as he tried to get the fly out of grasping branches. Even so, the toll on flies was terrific, frustration the inevitable state of affairs from the moment he entered the creek until the end. Yet there was triumph, too, for after he'd learned to fish the tunnels, Bloom always returned home not only exhausted and with his snapping thumb bloody and swollen from accidentally releasing the hook into it a few dozen times, but also with at least five or six delicious pan-sized native fish jammed in his denim work shirt's two front pockets. Which gave him among the most glorious feelings of accomplishment he'd ever known.

Then there were the Little Baldy Bear Lakes, hovering almost like aqua clouds in an exquisite Shangri-la at the end of a four-mile drive up the canyon, then a four-mile hike almost straight up: nine small, nearly round, amethyst and turquoise lakes, some lying in open meadows, others hidden among tall pines, the highest ones almost above the tree line and surrounded by scrub oak stubble and majestic boulders, reflecting a dozen twelve- and thirteen-thousand-foot-high peaks.

In these lakes you could tie a ten-foot-long, carefully tapered leader with a one-pound tippet on the end attached to a size 18 mosquito, and, using a three-hundred-dollar bamboo pole, lay that mosquito out on the water without creating a single ripple, and you couldn't catch fish any better than anybody else. A multiple paraplegic, using a marshmallow fork with twine tied to it and a monstrous size 6 green and yellow woolly bear with artificial teeth that clacked like castanets and eight-inch-long Day-Glo, lemon-colored wings attached, could haul cutthroat trout out of the Little Baldy Bears hand over fist. In fact, the only requirement for fishing those lakes was a fast unhooking technique and a pitching arm in topnotch shape for throwing the trout back in the water.

The first time Bloom traveled up to the Little Baldys he couldn't believe the fishing. He and the young Capital City lawyer Sean Carter had left home at a predawn 4:00 A.M., arriving at the ninth and lowest lake just before eight, when it was thoroughly light out, but the sun had not yet risen over the mountains to shine down into the alpine bowl. The beauty was breathtaking, the lake absolutely still. Some deer wandered off the meadow, disappearing into the trees when he and Sean appeared. Fine blurs of mist were sifting gently across the still, lavender surface.

"The fish around here are probably incredibly spooky," Bloom warned his friend. "We'd better approach on our hands and knees, and cast from a kneeling position, pretty far back, I would think."

"Whatever you say . . ."

They crept, crawled, got their knees soaked and muddy, their hands frozen. Painfully, they arranged themselves at separate points along the shoreline, made sure their flies were tied on securely, and then both, with their breaths held, cast out onto the lake—

Afterward, Sean claimed that his first fish had hit while the fly was about two feet above the water and still descending. Bloom surmised his fish had at first struck the shadow of his descending fly, and the only reason he hadn't then hooked a trout when his fly alighted on the water was that three fish had collided head-on trying to grab the lure.

Subsequently they each tried two more casts from a kneeling position, and both hauled in trout. By 8:01, after seven casts apiece, they had caught six nine- to eleven-inch trout. By 8:13 both men had twelve fish, their daily bag. And so, slightly stunned, they stopped, built a campfire, and cooked trout for breakfast. While they ate, and the sun topped the mountains, bathing the water in gold, fish began jumping, and pretty soon so many were breaking the surface so often it looked as if rain were falling on the water.

After breakfast they stood on shore, in arrogant full view of the fish, yanking one out with every cast. They had contests to see who could catch the most fish in ten minutes, and the younger lawyer won with an average of 2.1 fish a minute. They tried whipping the fly full speed across the water, and hooked a trout every time. Sean took off his fly, tied on a plain hook, picked a buttercup and stuck it on the hook, cast, and caught a fish. Then he tried a blade of grass, a pine cone chip; there was no way to throw something—anything—into that water and *not* catch a trout.

So they went swimming. Or tried to anyway, tiptoeing out on shallow rocky ledges, ducking under the icy water for a second, then stampeding noisily toward shore. And while Bloom lay in the grass in the sunlight, the other lawyer stood naked on the shore, smoking his pipe and laconically pulling in a few dozen more fish just for the hell of it.

That was the Little Baldy Bear Lakes.

And, as the tension in Milagro grew, that was where Bloom wanted to go for a couple of days with Linda. So they turned the kids over to Joe and Nancy Mondragón and took off.

They parked their VW bus in a meadow where the road ended, helped each other into their packs, and started up the trail. It was a lax sunny day, warm and with the scent of pines heavy on the air. The path was here rocky, there carpeted with pine needles, occasionally damp and mucky where tiny springs trickled across. Birds flitted quietly into the trees; tiny white moths sprayed off from under their feet; the trail led sharply upward in shadow.

It always startled Bloom that his feminine, self-effacing wife not only liked to be in front of a hike, but also could maintain a strong, even pace. Behind her now, Bloom let his thoughts drift; mindlessly he stared at her legs, her butt. And, as the Milagro tension quietly oozed away, leaving him almost woozy with relief, Bloom began to anticipate sex, increasingly looking forward to it as they rose higher and the way became steeper, slowing them down. After a few miles, he was climbing with a hard-on.

They took five in a grassy spot among aspens alongside the Little Baldy River. While Linda peeled an orange and the smell of that prickled his nostrils, Bloom lay on his back, head resting on his pack, facing up into the airy green aspen foliage. Not for several years had they been off alone together like this, minus the kids. Bloom's body was infused with good feeling, compassion, love, and as Linda gently stroked his forehead, singing a song in Spanish, he fell asleep.

Back on the trail an hour later the Blooms felt renewed. Uptight, frightened adversaries only a few hours before, now there was almost a mystical closeness and sense of companionship between them. The lawyer's desire returned, and by the time they pulled into the meadow surrounding the ninth Little Baldy Bear Lake, he had metamorphosed into a sex maniac, grabbing for her breasts even before he had his pack off, begging her, "Let's make love, come on, sweetheart, let's do it—"

Linda cupped his crotch, feigning surprise, but shook her head playfully. "Climb that mountain with me," she said, pointing to Little Baldy Peak, "and we'll make love on the top of it."

"Oh shit, how corny and perverted at the same time can you get?"

"Well, if you don't want to that's okay by me."

"I want you right here, now, this minute," he whined happily, thrusting his hands up under her sweater, but she wrenched loose, trotting a few yards away like a cocky pony.

"On top of the mountain," Linda said. "It's that or nothing."

So they dumped their packs, pitched the tent, and resumed climbing. At first there was a grassy slope, then a thin sheep trail that zigzagged up a shale slide and through some mammoth gray boulders; after that they carefully crossed several snow fingers maybe thirty yards wide, reached the ridge, and walked up through flowing brown grass that seemed to be crushed flat against the mountainside by invisible snow.

At the top some mottled-red boulders provided shelter from wind, and between the rocks grew more thick brown grass. Below them, to the west, they could see the nine Little Baldy Bear Lakes, tiny and almost unbelievably beautiful, each lake pocked with hundreds of silver circles from the feeding fish. To the south and east the brown grass sloped gently into forested mountains, and they could see far down along the mountains, way beyond the snowcapped Hija Negrita peak that overlooked Chamisaville forty miles south. To the west lay the mesa and Doña Luz and Milagro; and about twenty miles beyond the mesa and the Rio Grande gorge was the small timbering town of Ojo Prieto, almost lost in a low-lying milky band of pollution that had probably drifted over from the power plants a hundred and twenty miles away.

They were each reminded of that morning after their honeymoon night, when the pheasants and the yellow-headed blackbirds had adorned the road back to Alamosa.

Bloom reached for Linda again, and this time she offered no resistance. Laughing, she attacked him, tugging off his shoes and his jeans and underwear while he worked on her boots and slacks and underpants, and then, up among the boulders in the flattened brown grass, still wearing their undershirts, shirts, sweatshirts, sweaters, and jackets to keep warm, their bare asses speckled with blue goosebumps, they began to make love.

Later, all tension gone, Bloom fished and Linda read in the sun beside the lake. They cooked the trout, toasted a few marshmallows, turned in early, and had another long delicious screw, after which they both floated into a relaxed, deep slumber while rain pattered softly against the tent.

Next day they hiked to all the lakes, fished a little more, lazed about in the warm misty weather, and, strangely, encountered not another soul. They had no

adventures, talked but little to each other, and everything was unabashedly beautiful and peaceful. They
felt momentarily young and untroubled, almost like
teen-age lovers, and they instinctively shied away
from talking much for fear of upsetting this fragile
miracle, a gift they had never expected to receive.

After another good night, during which they hardly
slept, choosing instead to have one of those endless
lovemaking sessions that had so characterized their
first six months together ages ago, it was time to go
home.

And in the morning when Linda mentioned casually
"I wonder how the kids are doing? I hope they're
okay——" Bloom could feel himself suddenly grow tight
again. Silently fighting off an onslaught of tension and
hostility, they broke camp. Later, as they treaded
rhythmically down the trail, Bloom began to feel
afraid; he knew something would go wrong to wreck
their mini-vacation. In fact, he could picture exactly
what it would be. As they came within sight of the
VW, and Linda gasped, letting out a small cry, his
worst fears would be confirmed. Somebody would
have thrown a large rock through the front windshield, and soaped across the rear window would be:
KEEP YOUR LEGAL NOSE OUT OF MILAGRO'S BUSINESS!

But the bus was all right when they got there;
nothing had happened. Still, Bloom had worked himself into such a state that the relief was overwhelming. And as Linda started the engine, he reached for
her, saying unhappily, "Hey, one more time . . ."

"Are you kidding?"

"No. Come on. When was the last time we made
love in the car?"

For a minute they dangled across the narrow aisle
between seats, kissing, toying awkwardly with each
other, then Linda pulled out the emergency brake
and together they grappled back to the rear seat
where they sat, making out for a while longer, until
Bloom skinned off her slacks while she unzipped his
fly and pulled his pants down onto his hips and sat
astride him. He penetrated past the elastic band of
her panties and groaned. Her head over him, her

arms around him as he chewed on her sweater-covered breasts, she whispered softly, desperately, "I love you, Charley, I really do . . ."

"I love you too."

The VW began to move. It had been parked on a vague slope, and now it proceeded quietly down that slope, neither of them noticing, until suddenly there was a drop, a rock, and the bus bounced high throwing them off the seat and off each other onto the floor. And then, crashing into a bank, tipping halfover, Bloom's worst fears were confirmed as the branch on a dead pine tree shattered the front windshield.

"You forgot to pull the brake all the way out!" Bloom shrieked, but then they were both giggling frantically and uncontrollably as they watched sperm bubble excitedly from the tip of his shining, stupefied, and unrequited penis.

∽

Harlan Betchel in Banlon pants and a sport shirt, Bud Gleason in a drip-dry summer suit and bow tie, and Eusebio Lavadie in Levi's and a work shirt stained with sweat were sitting together over cups of coffee at the same table in the otherwise empty Pilar Café when Marvin LaBlue parked the Strawberry Mesa Body Shop and Pipe Queen wrecker in front of Milagro's lone parking meter and walked in. Marvin had a toothpick riding on his teeth and a holstered .38 revolver decorating his right hip.

First off, soon as he entered, Marvin paused with his head tilted back so he could survey the Pilar from under the low tilted brim of his cowboy hat as he dug in his pocket for a coin. Locating a quarter, he ambled over to the jukebox, thumbed his coin into the slot, and punched out three songs by Charlie Pride, Tammy Wynette, and Loretta Lynn. After that, as Marvin clomped up toward the counter, Eusebio Lavadie called, "Hey, Marvin, come on over here and set a spell with us," so Marvin shrugged and reset his course. He turned the fourth chair at their table around and slumped down, straddling it with his arms folded over the top of the back, cowboy style.

"How about a cup of joe on the house, Marvin?" Harlan Betchel suggested chummily.

Marvin politely removed his hat, setting it down carefully on the floor, then he fished cigarette papers and a tobacco pouch from the right front pocket of his denim shirt, and, as he dribbled tobacco from the pouch into the cigarette paper cupped in his other hand, he grinned sort of slowly, shyly, and secretly to himself—Marvin never looked at who he was talking to—and said:

"How about a couple a rolled tacos, a bowl a chili, a Dr. Pepper, *and* a cup a coffee on the house, Mr. Betchel, huh?"

Harlan smiled. "Aw, come on, Marvin. A cup of coffee's one thing. If you want to use that gun to hold up the café, that's another thing—"

"You give an Anglo cowboy an inch, he'll sure as hell try to take you for a mile," Eusebio Lavadie joshed in a friendly manner, nervously eyeing Marvin's gun belt.

Bud Gleason made a great show of looking at his watch: "Oh hey, excuse me, fellows," he gasped in fake alarm. "I got a two o'clock appointment in Doña Luz." And, like a grizzled extra scurrying out of the bar just before the climactic final shootout in a grade B Hollywood Western, Bud dropped a dollar onto the table and hurriedly split.

Marvin giggled to himself as he licked his home-made cigarette, then he spit out his toothpick, replacing it with the weed in a casual but studied motion, and, shaking off the lighted match Harlan Betchel offered, he chose instead to strike his own kitchen match with his own thumbnail, the motion so pleasing him that again he smiled and giggled to himself, and he snapped out the match with one wrist flick; then, for dramatic emphasis, he touched the hot tip to his tongue—it actually sizzled, going out—before breaking the match in two and dropping it in an ashtray. Finally, Marvin took a big puff from his cigarette with his eyes still trained shyly down at the table,

and, as he exhaled from that first deep, satisfying
puff, Marvin shifted his weight a little in order to
reach down and pluck his shooting iron from the
holster. The gun he set quietly on the table in front
of him. With his left hand, then, he unsnapped his
left front shirt pocket, latching onto the box of bullets he had in there, and, with the cigarette between
his lips, and the smoke from it curling around his
pale, small-eyed, southern face causing him to squint,
Marvin untucked the flaps on his bullet carton, carefully selected six cartridges, closed the box and slipped
it back in his pocket, and, while Harlan Betchel and
Eusebio Lavadie watched in something akin to horror, he opened the cylinder on his gun and fed the
bullets into their proper chambers before closing the
cylinder with a click that might have been heard all
the way up the canyon in Ladd Devine's office if it
had not been for the country voice of Loretta Lynn
wailing on the Pilar Café's jukebox.

Betty Apodaca appeared at the table, pad in hand,
pencil, asking cheerfully, "What'll it be, Marvin?"

Harlan Betchel laughed a mite too loudly. "Hell,
Betty, bring this starving young lad a couple of rolled
tacos, a bowl of chili, a Dr. Pepper, and a cup of
coffee, and don't worry about the check, this one is
on the house, ain't that right, Marvin?"

And Marvin LaBlue, with the cigarette growing an
ash a mile long at his lips tilted his head back, nodding, and with his strange shifty eyes that never
looked at anybody trained at the ceiling, he chuckled,
"Yessir, Mr. Betchel, that's right."

And this statement he abruptly followed with, "By
gum, Mr. Lavadie, I sure have took me a lot of miles
in my life!"

Then, when the food arrived, Marvin chortled:
"Wow, I bet all this good grub is gonna bloat me up
'til I'm as fat as Pacheco's pig!"

❧

And so then there was Seferino Pacheco.

One dusty hot morning as that morose lonely man
was blundering awkwardly about town in search of

his pig, he almost stepped on a baby robin crouched in the road, its eyes closed and its cavernous yellow beak wide open, plaintively chirping for worms. Not much bigger than a golf ball, and with feathers only beginning to sprout from its tiny pink body, the baby bird certainly had no tomorrow in the middle of the road, let alone in life, and so the sensible thing for Pacheco to do was step on it, putting it out much as he extinguished his cigarette butts. But for many years this hulking heartbroken man had been about as sensible as the fourth-floor "hopeless" ward at the state mental hospital down in the capital, and so instead of squashing what should have been squashed, he leaned over, gently plucking up the scrawny little robin, and dropped it in the front pocket of his Big Mac work shirt. Then he continued to search fruitlessly for his pig.

Toward noon Pacheco decided screw the pig, angrily gulped a beer in the Frontier with Tranquilino Jeantete, and—to kill a bad case of runs he had—bought some blackberry brandy in Rael's, then limped home. There, having settled the baby robin in a clay bowl padded with grass, he lumbered outside to dig up some food, returning a short while later with twelve worms, all of which the tiny naked bird downed voraciously; then it fell asleep in the bowl. For an extended pensive time, his shaggy head held sadly in his hands, Pacheco stared at this minuscule thing on which he had so omnipotently decided to bestow a future. "I'm so lonely," he groused cynically, "that when it grows up I'll probably try to fuck it."

They were destined to become great pals, and why not? With nothing much better to do when not out tracking down his pig, Pacheco had all the attention in the world to lavish on the robin. Awaking at dawn, he immediately tugged on irrigation boots and a sweater and plunged outside to dig worms from the rich damp earth along his irrigation ditch. Then, while his morning coffee perked, he dangled worms into the robin's open beak. For a while, that was the extent of their relationship: three, four, then five times a day Pacheco excavated for worms, and three, four, five times a day his little friend—gulping them the way an elephant gulps hay bales—put away whatever Pacheco offered, then either clunked asleep or cheeped for more. How something so tiny could be so bottomless was a mystery to Pacheco: it was like clowns getting out of, or rather into, a Volkswagen beetle.

At night Pacheco set the bowl under a light bulb so the robin would stay warm. And after a while, since he was a man who enjoyed literary and spiritual allusions as well as symbolism, Pacheco decided to call the robin "Joe's Beanfield." Whereupon the air in his house, which for a long time had been so lonely it screamed, grew soft with the warmth of smiles that kept creeping out of nowhere to adorn Pacheco's craggy features as he cared for the infant bird.

Joe's Beanfield, who devoured worms as if they were about to be declared illegal, grew like a Walt Disney time-sequence movie of a desert flower unfolding after a rain. In no time at all, the stiff barbs of his minuscule feathers broke through their pale blue quillskins, and Pacheco found himself feeding a greedy, plump fluffball instead of a naked starveling.

In due course, Joe's Beanfield began learning how to feed himself. Pacheco filled up another bowl with earth, generously laced this earth with worms, and set the worm bowl beside the nest bowl, so that whenever Joe's Beanfield craved a snack between meals he could just hop onto the worm bowl's rim, cock his head—which still had some white baby tufts on it—and then jab down to spear a squirming goody.

Pretty soon, Joe's Beanfield quit spending all his time in the nest bowl and began to hop around the kitchen table, rummaging through a chaotic landscape formed by empty beer cans and old liquor bottles, by empty Spam and corned beef hash and chopped-green-chili tins. And eventually, of course, though he did so in fear and trembling, Pacheco had to take his pal outside. Tremulously, he set the robin down on a dandelioned patch of lawn, but Joe's Beanfield wasn't interested. He sat there for a few seconds alertly listening, quivering nervously, then he hopped into

Pacheco's hand, deposited a friendly little turd in the palm, fluffed up, and contentedly went to sleep. Thereafter, Joe's Beanfield passed whatever time he had to spend outside either on Pacheco's knee, or in his front shirt pocket, or else sometimes perched on his head or on his shoulder.

All too soon Joe's Beanfield was almost grown. Though still snoozing at night in the bowl under the light bulb, during the day he gamboled all over the topsy-turvy house, busily inspecting the wreckage of Pacheco's life, the piles of garbage and dirty clothes and rotting memorabilia strewn about; he spent a lot of time pecking at flies and moths that got caught in the corner spider webs. That mangy, snake-eating reincarnation of Cleofes Apodaca showed up from time to time to share a tin of sardines with Pacheco, but he never went for Joe's Beanfield. Once, though, Pacheco caught the cat gazing sleepily but interestedly at the bird, and, without even raising his voice, the sentimental, illiterate lunatic quietly intoned: "Gato, if you ever touch that bird, I'll bake you in the oven over there like a Red McClure potato." And, while Cleofes Apodaca the Second didn't nod, he did sleepily lower his lids a little more until his eyes were almost closed, and, as he started purring lazily, you could tell there existed between the three of them—the cat, the bird, and the man—a perfect understanding.

Outdoors, while Pacheco irrigated squash, Joe's Beanfield took baths in the icy water. Leaning on a hoe one day, observing his little pet while cottonwood seed fluff alighted without a ripple on the spreading silver pools that nourished his garden, Pacheco realized that, except for his pig, he had not felt this close to a living thing since his wife died. And with that he became unnaturally terrified of losing the bird.

Out in the garden next afternoon, Joe's Beanfield was startled by a black dung beetle fleeing the irrigation tidal wave with its butt aimed skyward in a threatening posture, and the bird flew onto his master's shoulder. This marked the first time Pacheco had seen him fly, and his heart twanged like a melodramatic soap opera chord. Immediately, the poor man felt more doomed than he had for ages; and the thought crossed his warped disintegrating mind, Maybe I should kill Joe's Beanfield and stuff him, and that way I'd never lose him.

Joe's Beanfield had no intention of taking a powder, however. The robin might fly up to the roof, or up into Pacheco's apple trees, but always he returned immediately to his master's head or shoulder, on which he usually shat just to prove to the huge dark man how much he loved him. And once, when by accident Pacheco entered his house without Joe's Beanfield, the bird battered so noisily against the screen door that the commotion could be heard all the way over at Joe Mondragón's house, two fields away.

But Pacheco knew the scoop on wild things. And because their imminent parting made him so sad, he went on a drinking binge to end all drinking binges. Lurching dazedly into town every day with the robin on his shoulder, he bought bottles of hundred-proof Old Grandad at Nick Rael's; and back home, seated at the kitchen table listening to mariachi music, soap operas, triple-A baseball games, and news on KKCV from Chamisaville, while Joe's Beanfield perched on his food bowl laconically sniping at worms, Pacheco tackled that Old Grandad like it too was about to be declared illegal.

The robin grew worm fat and night-crawler sleek. Pacheco's back ached from all that digging in the damp earth along the ditch. And after a while he had dug so many holes along the ditch bank that water began to leak into his field. Which was good for the field, but against ditch regulations. Thus, as soon as the mayordomo on that ditch, Sparky Pacheco, discovered Seferino Pacheco was flooding his front field around the clock, he came by positively reeking with dire threats.

"Hey, you can't steal the water like this, my friend," Sparky complained excitely. "You have to wait your turn!"

Wavering unsteadily on the ditch bank with Joe's Beanfield nailed to his shoulder, Pacheco growled,

"Go fuck yourself, Sparky. And besides, the musk-rats made all those holes, not me."

(In Milagro, whenever you got caught illegally trying to irrigate your fields, you always blamed it on the muskrats. And blessed was the man whose ditch bank actually *was* infested by the tunneling little animals.)

Sparky Pacheco returned next day with three shovels, one boy, Jimmy Ortega, and a man, Ricardo L. Córdova, and between them they patched Pacheco's ditch wall. Then they left, warning him to be more careful in the future about how he dug for worms.

Pacheco lunged inside, stuck the mouth of a half-full Old Grandad bottle in his lips, tipped his head back, and let the contents glug down his throat. Then, blundering about and bellowing like a wounded rhino, he staggered out front and shoveled a big sluiceway in the recently patched ditch bank, allowing almost the entire acequia flow to cascade into his already soggy front vega. After that he wove along the bank a ways, stabbing nastily with his shovel at little gray water snakes slithering hastily into the ditch, and he dug up a big shovelful of soggy dirt teeming with worms for Joe's Beanfield. The robin dropped off Pacheco's shoulder and began to inhale worms as fast as the man could gently prod apart the clods with his spade.

Having exhausted the first clump, Pacheco moved to stab up another shovelful, but as he did so his foot thrust into some soft earth, and, losing his balance, he sat down abruptly, directly on top of Joe's Beanfield.

Horrified, Pacheco flung himself drunkenly side-ways, but the bird had been flattened: Joe's Beanfield squeaked once, fluttered his wings, and expired.

Whimpering desperately, already starting to cry, Pacheco snatched up his friend, lunged to his feet, and flung the bird far out into the soaked field, letting out an anguished wail that was prolonged almost a full minute, after which he fumbled inside to seek solace in booze.

When Sparky Pacheco and Ricardo L. Córdova again arrived to cut off the water flooding the front field, they found Pacheco, tears clotting his nearly blind eyes, seated on his porch, a loaded .22 pistol lying ominously beside a bottle of Old Grandad on the cement at his feet, knocking off the last of Joe's Beanfield's food bowl worms.

"What do you think you are, cousin," Sparky teased gently, "a robin?"

But Pacheco just glared at them out of baleful, exhausted eyes. He was resigned, already, to what had happened. It served him right for messing around with a wild thing and for giving it such an ill-fated name to boot.

All the same, though, Pacheco felt mean enough to kill the first son of a bitch who dared to step on his shadow.

ട

About this time, a very popular movie came to the General Custer Drive-In in Chamisaville, and by curious coincidence about half the citizens of Milagro, who wanted a break from the tension building up in their town, attended the show on the same night.

Horsethief Shorty Wilson, Jerry Grindstaff, Emerson Lapp, and Flossie Devine drove down in a Dancing Trout station wagon, and, while Shorty sat contentedly behind the wheel guzzling a six-pack held in his lap, and teetotaler Jerry G., seated in the front passenger seat beside him, stared stonily ahead, Flossie and Lapp bounced around in back like a couple of starstruck adolescents, munching on popcorn and loudly sipping on a bottle of Southern Comfort as they giggled nonstop over private—usually risqué—jokes. Which provoked Jerry G., who was constantly having to turn half-around and bark "Shhh!" or order them, in his puritanical Okie voice, to "please pipe down back there, will you?"

Joe and Nancy Mondragón hit the road in their pickup with all the kids and Benny Maestas—still limping slightly from his self-inflicted knife wound—in back. On the way down Joe stopped once to fix a flat, twice to let various kids pee, a third time to buy two cold six-packs from Crown Liquors in

Chamisaville, and once again to stock up on buckets of Colonel Sanders' Kentucky Fried drumsticks. They arrived late, but in high spirits.

Joe parked in front of Bernabé Montoya, who was sharing a pint of bourbon and their mutual flesh with his girl friend, Vera Gonzáles.

Not too far away, in Onofre Martínez's mottled-green, 1953 Chevy pickup, the toothless Senile Brigade, featuring Onofre, Amarante Córdova, and Tranquilino Jeantete, were dividing their attention between two six-packs, a pint of blackberry brandy, and a paper bag full of A & W rolled tacos, while on the roof Onofre's three-legged German shepherd snarled happily at the big screen.

Nearby, the Strawberry Mesa Body Shop and Pipe Queen crowd was located, Ruby Archuleta behind the wheel of the wrecker, with Claudio García beside her. Marvin LaBlue and Ruby's kid, Eliu, stood behind the cab drinking beer along with everyone else.

Charley and Linda Bloom and their two kids were the only Milagro representatives at the movie not boozing. Bloom was in a foul mood; Linda was angry at him because of the mood. Bloom was pissed because he had to keep leaving the VW to go buy goodies at the snack bar for the girls—here a hot dog and an Almond Joy and a Coke; there a hamburger, barbecue chips, and a Dr. Pepper—and he deeply resented having to bribe the kids, who weren't interested in the movie, to keep quiet. As their demands increased, upping the ante, so to speak, Bloom's temper threatened to flare. He couldn't concentrate on the film, he kept missing dialogue; finally, he thought he would explode.

By contract, when Joe Mondragón's eldest kid, Larry, attempted to put the bite on his daddy for a candy bar, Joe merely leaned out the driver's side window and told his number one son, "Larry, you bug me again and I'm gonna take off my belt," and all the kids cooled it, silently watching the show like a trio of well-behaved angels.

Lightning flickered over the Midnight Mountains to the east; stars twinkled over the gorge in the west.

Suddenly it began to rain. Joe Mondragón turned on his windshield wipers; Bernabé Montoya didn't bother to turn on his wipers because he and Vera weren't watching the movie anyway; Onofre Martínez flicked on his windshield wipers; as did Horsethief Shorty, and Ruby Archuleta did likewise. But when Bloom twisted his wiper knob, nothing happened. Angrily growling, "I don't know why we came—" Bloom tumbled out with a screwdriver and a pair of pliers to fix the wipers.

"It was your idea to come," Linda accused.

"I'm never bringing those goddam kids to another movie," Bloom vowed.

"Don't talk like that in front of them," Linda barked.

In the Dancing Trout vehicle, Jerry Grindstaff turned around and, very frostily, said, "Em and Flossie, would you mind keeping it down to a dull roar? *Some* of us are trying to watch the show."

Horsethief Shorty belched and farted, exclaiming, *"Ai, Chihuahua,* excuse *me!"*

But that made Flossie and Lapp giggle. Lapp said, "Gerald G., accept our humble apologies, also our lack of couth; we will kibbutz, I mean kibitz, on the action no longer, we promise to keep it down to your dull roar."

Rain drummed against the roofs, it splashed violently against windshields, and Bloom who had further fucked up, instead of fixing, the wipers, sat there fuming with his hands tightly gripping the wheel, wishing he had never come. Beside him, arms folded tightly, Linda couldn't concentrate on the film either, and she wanted to cry. Behind them the kids crunched on Frito Lays and noisily sucked pop up through peppermint straws. Then there was a gasp in the back seat.

"María spilled her Dr. Pepper on my sleeping bag," Pauline wailed.

"I don't give a shit . . ." Bloom hissed between clenched teeth.

In Onofre Martínez's mottled-green, 1953 Chevy pickup, the three old men laughed and nudged each other and tugged on their beers, having a wonderful time, while on the roof Onofre's three-legged German shepherd stoically waited out the storm.

With the rain, Marvin LaBlue and Eliu Archuleta had ambled over to shelter under the snack bar awning. Benny Maestas joined them with little Larry Mondragón, who immediately hit up the soft-hearted hillbilly for a quarter. The other two Mondragón kids moved into the pickup cab with Joe and Nancy, who were halfway high on beer and finger lickin chicken.

The windows in Bernabé Montoya's truck steamed up, becoming so opaque that you couldn't see what was happening inside. You could make an educated guess, though.

Next door, Jerry G. finally became so disgusted by the back seat's muffled guffaws and raucous whisperings, not to mention Horsethief Shorty's noisy and highly redolent anal explosions, that he decided to seek a moment of relief by going to take a leak in the men's room behind the snack bar.

No sooner had Jerry G. left, though, than Shorty got the urge, too. Pleasantly aiming a "Hold down the fort, kids," at the back seat, he headed for the bathroom on Jerry G.'s heels.

At approximately this same moment, Bloom's youngest daughter, María, Joe Mondragón, Benny Maesta, Marvin LaBlue, and all three members of the Senile Brigade also felt the call, and they tumbled from their vehicles into the rain, scurrying toward the john.

Then Flossie Devine said, "Em, honey, you'll excuse me for a moment if I go to the little girls' room," and, imitating her accent, Em drawled, "You be mah guest, hear?" In unison with this exchange, down the row a bit, Nancy Mondragón was saying, "You kids sit tight, I gotta take a leak. You do anything wrong while I'm gone and I'll tell José to take off his belt."

And, as Nancy opened her door, Vera Gonzáles squirmed out from under Bernabé Montoya, gasping, "Wait a sec, amor, I better put on the diaphragm, I didn't know you wanted to here . . ." And, snatching her purse off the floor, she ran through the rain, almost colliding with Flossie Devine.

Jerry Grindstaff entered an empty men's room, and, positioning himself at the center one of three urinals, unzipped his fly. On this cue, Joe Mondragón bounced in loudly but happily cursing the downpour, and on his heels came Amarante Córdova, Onofre Martínez, and Tranquilino Jeantete, rain dribbling in gay rivulets off their cowboy hats. Laughing, these archaic human beings slapped each other's backs and engaged in some cackling all-Spanish bathroom humor having to do with the size and potency of their eighty- to ninety-year-old pissing instruments.

Joe Mondragón crowed, "Hello there, Jerry G.," to the taciturn Dancing Trout foreman, then he shouted, "Hola, primo!" to Amarante Córdova, who lumbered bowleggedly over to Jerry G.'s other side and with much grunting, giggling, and groaning, commenced unbuttoning his fly while at the same time attempting to peer across Jerry G.'s chest at the grinning Joe, who was peering past Jerry G.'s chest at Amarante. Somehow, in the midst of such confusion and noise, while fumbling to free his shriveled pecker, Amarante dislodged his Colt Peacemaker instead, which fell into the urinal with a clang, announcing the arrival of Horsethief Shorty, followed closely by Marvin LaBlue, and then Charley Bloom with his daughter, María, who immediately freaked at the sight of these old and middle-aged men laughing and chattering in Spanish and smoking cigarettes, completely and cacophonously cluttering up the tiny room.

Jerry G. had a bad thing about taking leaks, namely, when others were present, he couldn't. And now there was a terrific commotion as Horsethief Shorty shouted cheerful boozy greetings to the old men and to Joe, and as Amarante Córdova bent over to retrieve his blunderbuss, and as Marvin LaBlue's voice suddenly cut through the laughter (and through little María's bloody blue bawling), saying "That ain't a Peacemaker, Amarante, that's a *pissmaker*!" And Amarante stood there, weaving and grinning proudly at his gun and bumping into Jerry G.'s butt with each weave, while Bloom nodded hello to everybody as he grimly pushed through the crowd to the one toilet cubicle, in which a chair with a roughly scrawled cardboard sign saying "Out of Order" wired to its two front legs was set upside down on the toilet.

Meanwhile, only a plywood foot or so away in the women's restroom, Vera, Flossie, and Nancy almost collided trying to get in out of the storm through the same door at the same time. All three were breathless from running through the rain. A week earlier there had been a rumble in the women's head, during which one high school student had stabbed another, and somehow the door and the divider of the lone toilet cubicle had been uprooted and tipped over, and the management hadn't gotten around to replacing it, so now the john was completely exposed.

Flossie said to Vera, "You go ahead, honey." But Vera shrugged, saying politely, "No, you go first if you want, ma'am, I'm not in a hurry." Flossie was a little embarrassed, though, so she told Nancy, "I can wait." And Nancy replied, "So can I."

On the other side of the wall, Joe Mondragón was taking a satisfying, totally clear, absolutely endless beer leak, while Jerry G., very redfaced by now, strained to release his own stream as Amarante Córdova kept bumping into him while happily waving his mammoth gun. Bloom, with his wailing daughter cupped in the crook of one arm, started pushing back through the people, the smoke, and the Spanish babble.

Onofre Martínez said, "If you ain't gonna use that urinal, Amarante, I might as well," but the Staurolite Baron lost his footing on the way over, bumping hard against Amarante who bumped hard against Jerry G., who lost his footing and bumped hard against Joe Mondragón, who lost his balance and sprayed a few drops of pee on Jerry G.'s pant leg. With that, Jerry G. exploded. "Look what you did!" he yelled at Joe, stuffing himself back into his pants.

At that instant Bloom set María down in the dirt outside the men's room and drew off her panties, saying, "Just go here, sweetie, the toilet's broken in there."

"But it's raining," she complained. "I'm all wet."

"Oh for God's sake, dammit, go *here*," Bloom cried in agony, "or don't go at all."

"I can't," she blubbered. "It's raining."

"Well then *drown*!" Bloom sobbed between clenched teeth.

In the ladies' room, Nancy Mondragón said, "Aren't you Mrs. Devine?" And Flossie smiled, saying, "That's right, dear, and you must be Mrs. Mondragón."

"That's right," Nancy said. "Boy, I sure never thought I'd run into you in a dump like this."

Flossie didn't know how to react to that, so she shrugged, fluttered a hand, smiled, and finally cooed, "Well, honey, even rich people have to go to the bathroom, you know."

In the men's room, Joe Mondragón answered Jerry G. with: "Whatta you mean 'Look what *I* did'? Who bumped into who?"

"Well, it wasn't my fault," Jerry G. said. "This old fucking greaser bumped into me."

Whereupon a silence, like the silence of Hiroshima ten minutes after the bomb, struck the men's room with an audible thud. Of course, the instant Jerry G. let the word out of his mouth he realized that if he escaped from that men's room in the next minute more or less alive, he would have to light candles to some saint for the rest of his life in gratitude for the reprieve.

One man whispered, *"Ai, Chihuahua."* After that nobody said anything or made a move. Amarante stood there toothlessly half-grinning with his big gun held laxly, almost limply in his hands. Onofre Martínez was poised at the urinal with a cigarette between his lips, staring at a "SUCK MY BIG DICK, MOTHAFUCKAH" on the wall as the smoke from his cigarette gathered under his cowboy hat and then slowly curled around the brim, rising toward the ceiling. Tranquilino Jeantete, who'd been propped against the back wall, looked down at the floor, ashamed for Jerry G. Marvin LaBlue, also ashamed of, and afraid for, his fellow Anglo, did the same thing. The only sound was the noise Joe Mondragón made slowly and menacingly zipping up his fly.

The next sound was the one made by Horsethief Shorty taking out and opening his snuffbox, and drilling a powder-covered pinkie up either nostril. Following this rather bold action, Shorty sneezed. At that, everybody in the men's room heard Flossie Devine in the women's room say, "Well, if neither one of you sweet things is in that much of a hurry, you'll excuse me if I camp first, because I got a bladder that's ringing like a fire alarm."

On the heels of this statement, Bloom raged back into the men's room with red-eyed María in his arms, explaining to all those present, "I don't give a shit if it *is* out of order!"

Jerry G. took a tentative step toward the door, then another. Shorty closed his snuffbox, letting him pass. Jerry G. proceeded cautiously to the door, opened it, and slipped into the rain. Shorty raised his eyebrows to all of them, shrugged a *What can I tell you* to each and every one, said, "Caballeros . . . ," and backed out.

Little María Bloom piped, "But I don't *want* to anymore, Daddy," and Bloom wailed like a stricken baboon. With that, the old men suddenly giggled, while on the other side of the partition Flossie Devine crowed to the two Chicano women who had their backs turned to her, "Honestly, when it rains cats and dogs like this I swear I start thinking about going into the kennel business, you know?"

"I figure," Shorty said, drawing even with Jerry G. on the way back, "that you just came within a half-inch of getting your head blowed off."

"Oh screw you, Shorty."

And in the Dancing Trout station wagon, unaware of the high drama that had just taken place in a very low setting, Emerson Lapp suddenly fell asleep.

≈§

Still pretty much oblivious to the gathering storm, but very much aware of his own troubles, Herbie Goldfarb decided an escape into love might be just what the doctor ordered for his floundering soul. And there was a VISTA volunteer named Stephanie Milligan living in the Alamito section of Chamisaville who offered just such an escape; a tall, bony girl with tremendously vague blue eyes, who hailed from East Orange, New Jersey, she had only recently graduated from Skidmore College in upstate New York.

Herbie and Stephanie had often met during those times when Herbie traveled south on the Trailways bus to gather with his fellow volunteers, and also to take showers at the KOA Kampground north of town. At first Herbie shied away from Stephanie because she was a moody person who seldom spoke, and somehow her silence, her lack of complaints, placed her above the other VISTAs in an almost accusatory fashion. Too, Stephanie appeared to be involved with several community projects that had a halfway decent shot at success, and she was the only one in their group who could speak Spanish.

Stephanie wore peasant blouses, long colorful skirts, and sneakers; and the tall straight way she moved was almost regal. Unfortunately, she also sported a very flat chest, and never in his life had Herbie been attracted to such a titless wonder. Plump and rosy and Renoirish, Marilyn Monroe, Anita Ekberg, and Lainie Kazan—that's where Herbie's head had always been at, ever since his earliest pubescent fantasies. Even today, through all his dreams, there cavorted huge-breasted, olive-skinned, Ashkenazic, perpetual-motion, earth-mother, Sabra lovemaking machines. In fact, almost all Herbie's affairs to date had been with nubile, occasionally musclebound, Westchester County kibbutzim girls named Rachel or Ruth or Hanna, warm and fiery-eyed, black-haired people of his own race and faith, whose flesh in the hay had enveloped him in a plump fermented way like fresh bread dough. If he was destined to travel through life shelling out double, and in spades, for being a Jew, Herbie had always figured at least his love affairs with these women enabled him to skim some kind of interest off his personal checking account before paying the required dues. Hence for Herbie, nirvana was snuggling deeply into sunburned and throbbing female pectoral chub that cushioned him against the sensual beats of an eastern Mediterranean heart.

At first, then, he wasn't very turned on by this un-obtrusive, gaunt woman, whose abstraction bordered on the ethereal. But little things began to prickle his interest. For example, even though Stephanie was apparently the most competent volunteer, she never bragged about her accomplishments; she hardly deemed them worth mentioning. Which tantalized Herbie: What was her formula? Maybe she could teach him, if not to relate, at least how to defend himself when his neighbors started shooting bullets or chucking spears.

Also, in a way, Herbie had never met a less phony person. It got to him after a while, the fact that Stephanie waved no flags, had nothing to prove.

In the final analysis, though, it was probably her odor that nailed him to the cross. Stephanie smelled like freshly baked bread, sagebrush, and black to-bacco: she chain-smoked French cigarettes called Gauloises, always blowing the smoke out with dis-passionate and unselfconscious slowness, like a tired Depression farm woman (photographed by Dorothea Lange), or an exhausted, withdrawn whore. However she did it, her exhalations were sexy beyond belief.

So finally, more than anything else, that's what wrapped a metal loop around Herbie's heart and snapped the wire tight. My God, but he found himself almost crying out loud as she puffed her Gauloises during the volunteers' weekly discussion periods!

Herbie fell in love.

He imagined Stephanie's passion would be slow and lax and dreamy, unhurried and erotically vague, like warm moss in a southern swamp, not lush in the true sense of that word, but terribly profound.

Herbie was a romantic; he had loved *Elvira Madigan*; he had cried reading *The Sorrows of Young Werther*. In his daydreams, pebbles metamorphosed into sparkling rubies; chickens became peacocks; Stephanie Milligans dissolved into Greta Garbos. A day arrived, he popped the question: "May I come over to your place? Can I see what you're doing?"

Stephanie shrugged, not unpleasantly, her face shifting from one vaguely preoccupied expression to another so curiously removed and yet unselfconsciously tender that Herbie's heart did a back-flip, his guts began to ache, he was transformed into a carnal beast, a predator, a rapacious golem: tonight there would be a notching of pistols.

Together, with rolled-up towels under their arms, they hitchhiked into town from the KOA Kampground and caught another ride for several miles on the eastbound highway into Alamito. Stephanie lived in an old adobe farmhouse with eight empty rooms, a wood stove in the kitchen, and a refrigerator full of garden vegetables and chunks of goats, pigs, cows, and sheep donated to her by the neighbors. On raised screens beside the front door squash slices were drying. Graceful purple martins congregated around an elaborate miniature apartment house on a pole nearby. Chickens clucked lazily as they scratched in her yard; apples and pears were forming on fruit trees; fuzzily buzzing bees floated indolently through the lambent summery air; and, on the dirt roof of Stephanie's bucolic mansion, radiant yellow sunflowers bloomed.

Herbie gawked at this serene woman who traipsed so placidly about her Shangri-la. They didn't converse much as the peaceful afternoon waned toward suppertime. Shirt off, Herbie sat on a bench at a front-yard picnic table browsing through old *Time* magazines while Stephanie puttered around, doing her unobtrusive thing. Some local women involved in a day-care program came over and, speaking in hush-hush Spanish with Stephanie, they hung around for a while, occasionally laughing softly or smiling at Herbie who smiled back, amazed that these people could be so gentle and pleasant—what was the matter with Milagro? Or more to the point, what was wrong with Herbie Goldfarb?

The women departed. Some kids riding a horse bareback came by and shouted impertinently at Stephanie, who fed the sloe-eyed horse a carrot, ruffled the kids' hair, then whimsically teased them while stroking the horse's sleek neck—how could that Spanish language, which had always come on like a machine gun to Herbie's ear, so suddenly be transformed by this lanky, shy woman into almost velvet, French-textured syllables?

By suppertime Herbie loved her so much it hurt. Whereupon Stephanie appeared—miraculously!—with steaming enchiladas, a bottle of homemade beer, freshly baked bread, and locally grown grapes. They ate while a church bell languidly rang the Angelus. Herbie had never been so smitten. He could barely look at her, afraid that on close scrutiny she might dissolve into sainthood and be blown like holy pollen into the sky. The few times he dared to look up, she looked up, too; her eyes drifting coolly, calmly, collectedly across his face, probing with a vapory lack of concern. Stephanie, aglow with a sort of ivory luster, ate like someone at home with food, at home with this place, at home with the weather, at home with the time of day—in tune with everything: life, strained through the aura of her personality, was a rhapsody in champagne.

Herbie sighed.

Tenderly he cupped his erection.

Stephanie drifted inside, returning with coffee that tasted of chicory and cinnamon. Its steam, curling through the windless evening air, caused Herbie's nostrils to dilate sensually. Under the table their naked feet touched, they played a gentle game of footsie. It grew dark, the approaching night—languinous, honey-mellow, luminous—gleamed with a seraphic effulgence. It became time to go inside; they carried the dishes in to a sideboard and floated beyond, to her bedroom, coasting arm in downy arm onto her wide mattress on the floor, where they shed their clothes in a mystical trancelike manner, emerging into youthful nudity the way melodies are born.

They kissed: Stephanie's lips radiated a celestial glow. She was the most even-tempered resplendent woman he had ever met. The pungent darkness, pregnant with intimate prickles, sparkling, too, bubbling like honeydew wine, flowed over their skin. She draped her arms around him. They pressed together, thighs, groins, stomachs, like slow-motion, enchanted ballet dancers. It was going to be like fucking a Madonna.

About eight feet away, in a dark corner, there was a sudden and violent *snap!* followed by a salvo of hysterical, tiny bloodcurdling squeaks, then a skittering, scuffling, scraping, frantic bouncing little scramble, all of which caused Herbie to stiffen abruptly in an attitude of abject terror.

"Don't worry," Stephanie cooed. "It's only a mouse."

The scuffling weakened, the scraping stopped, a last pathetic squeak—like a miniature champagne cork—was ejected into the darkness. And a small whiff of death, like a wisp of cigarette smoke, drifted through the gentle gloom, slid swiftly between their bodies (causing her nipples to stiffen), rose to the windowsill, curled outside, and was dissipated on a wholesome apple blossom breeze.

Herbie was paralyzed for thirty seconds. Then gradually, untensing muscle by painful muscle, he slumped against her, his hard-on gone.

They waited. Stephanie had all the time, all the patience in the world. Lightly, her fingers stroked his shoulder blades; quietly they plucked the long hair scruffing his neck. Slowly, he became aroused again, their lips met like butterflies in a flowery glen, they entwined spiritually and bodily in a long, smooth embrace. Honey replaced the blood in Herbie's woozy veins.

Farther away this time, though still emphatically, there sounded another *snap!* that stabbed like a steel-tipped arrow driven from a hundred-pound bow into that part of Herbie's spine located between his shoulder blades. The frantic and all too graphic squeaks, scuffling, and scraping followed, and when she felt him go rigid Stephanie again explained: "Don't worry, it's only a mouse."

"What do you mean, 'It's only a mouse'?"

"This place is crawling with mice," Stephanie said.

"So . . . so what do you do?" Herbie stuttered. "You set traps all over the place?"

"Sure. I've been catching five or six mice a night."

Herbie rolled off her and lay on his back, staring at the ceiling. Sitting up, Stephanie lit a cigarette and blew her first exhale out across his stomach. Reaching down, she lightly stroked his penis, handling it the way she might handle a baby rabbit. But nothing happened: every muscle in Herbie's body *except* his penis was so rigid that if she had chosen to pluck him he would have reverberated like a giant guitar chord. Leaning far over, Stephanie sucked his limp nub into her smoky mouth . . . just as another *snap!* and death struggle took place in the nearby kitchen.

"I'm sorry," Herbie bleated hysterically, leaping to his feet, "but I better leave now if I wanna catch the nine o'clock bus!"

And their love, so immortal a moment ago, died in an instant like a little mouse.

❧

For years the Pilar Café basement had been decorated more or less like an Edwardian brothel, with one-dimensional naked trollops, rather than real whores, debauching around on feed calendars, and framed *Playboy* centerfolds lining the golden walls. Off in a corner a small bar carried essential bottles of bourbon, Scotch, and some wine; a little refrigerator was always well stocked with beer. In the center of the thickly carpeted room, directly beneath an adjustable ceiling lamp, was a large round table covered with green baize. On any given late afternoon or evening, up to a dozen serious men might be seated around this table intently playing cards—poker, blackjack, monte, hearts, even bridge occasionally, you name it. And it was the habit of these men to wager rather heavily upon the cards they held.

In short, the Pilar Café's basement was a gambling den.

By and large, only regulars inhabited this casino. Harlan Betchel, of course; and Bud Gleason; the Enchanted Land Motel manager, Peter Hirsshorn;

and occasionally Peter's brother Jim, Ladd Devine's mouthpiece, drove up for the game. Ladd Devine himself had never attended a session; and Horsethief Shorty Wilson was persona non grata because although everyone knew he cheated, nobody could catch him at it; hence, Shorty was impossible to beat. Sometimes Jerry Grindstaff muddled ponderously through a game, but most players considered him too morose to begin with, and they grew gloomier as he grew gloomier as his losings inevitably multiplied. Therefore, Jerry G.'s attendance was discouraged in any way possible.

Nick Rael spent every other night in this den of mild iniquity. As did Carl Abeyta and Floyd Cowlie, the Forest Service personnel, and also Eusebio Lavadie. Rounding out this nefarious *Who's Who* of Milagro gambling were the two state cops Bruno Martínez and Granny Smith, who whiled away plenty of time and dollars down there when they weren't above ground keeping a sharp eye out for the heinous shenanigans of pernicious and unruly characters like Joe Mondragón, Benny Maestas, and Amarante Córdova.

There was one night, however, when crime returned the compliment by taking the mountain to Mohammed, so to speak: that is, Evil Doings came to El Casino Pilar where they caught Granny Smith holding three kings, Bruno Martínez scratching his balls after having folded, Bud Gleason staring disbelievingly at a royal straight flush, Eusebio Lavadie drunk as a coot and pouring another, Harlan Betchel breathlessly dealing himself a final card, and both Jim and Peter Hirsshorn anxiously scrutinizing Harlan in an effort to interpret his reaction as he peeked at that card. Almost one hundred and fifteen clean greenbacks glowed vociferously in the center of the table, waiting for the lucky winner to claim them all.

This hand's lucky winner turned out to be none of the men seated around the table, however. For just as Harlan took a hefty glaum at the card giving him a full house in sixes and sevens, the stairway door clattered open and three desperadoes entered the room, changing the name of the game from Poker to Armed Robbery.

"Anybody moves, and especially either one of you state chotas so much as breathes a little too loudly, and all of you will be kissing worms tonight," the first person into the room announced calmly, poking a double-barreled, over-and-under, sawed-off shotgun at Granny Smith. This peppery person, who was barely over five-feet tall, and who had a strange rasping voice, wore a black cowboy hat pulled low, a woman's stocking and a red-checkered bandanna over the face, a puffy dark blue ski jacket, dungarees, and plain brown cowboy boots.

The man behind the sawed-off shotgun, who was six-feet tall and dressed and disguised similarly, brandished a pump shotgun, which he waved a little, explaining: "Gentlemen, this is a 12-gauge shotgun and I got number 4 Winchester express duckloads in it, and I took the hunting pin out, so that means I got five shells instead of three, understand? Okay. I want everybody's hands *in* sight, *on* the table, *palms* up, *now*."

These were clear enough instructions, easy to follow, and, needless to say, immediately complied with.

"Don't nobody even *twitch*," the third person now said. He was of medium height, dressed like the others, with a thick Spanish accent when he spoke, and his perhaps excessive authority derived from a .357-magnum pistol held tightly in his right fist.

All three stickup men were somehow very familiar to each person in the room. But because their hair was hidden under dark hats and their faces were obscured behind stockings and bandannas, and also because each robber was obviously putting on an act and an accent with his voice (not to mention the fact that the cardsharks, from Bruno Martínez through to Bud Gleason, were shitting ice cubes), it was difficult to say just which local personalities were responsible for this outrage.

"Take the money," Harlan stammered. "You can have all of it—"

"Thanks," said the sawed-off shotgun, "don't mind

if we do. How about raking all that moola into a neat little stack, okay?"

"Sure," Harlan agreed, but he wasn't so terrified that he would let them trick him into dying. "Can I move my hands to do it?"

"*Slow*-ly," said the .357 magnum. "*Ver*-y slowly."

"Is this too fast?"

"No, that's *per*-fect. Just like that. Nice and *eas*-y."

Harlan carefully scraped together all the cash, patting it and tunking it softly until it was in a single neat stack.

"Okay, now, draw that stack over near the edge of the table by your right arm," the pump gun hissed melodramatically. "And remember, one false—"

Bud Gleason blurted, "Excuse me, sir, but I . . . I think I'm gonna sneeze—"

"No tricks!" snarled the sawed-off shotgun. "You sneeze and I'll paint the table with your brains!"

"Aim so the money doesn't get gooey," the .357 magnum advised.

"Listen, you assholes—" Granny Smith began.

"I'll give *you* a second asshole right between your *eyes* if you finish that *sen*-tence!" the .357 magnum barked.

"Say, isn't that a line from a movie—?" Eusebio Lavadie began.

"Oh God," Jim Hirsshorn whispered between clenched teeth. "Take it easy, everybody. Shuttup, Granny, please. You too, Lavadie. Don't anybody be smart. Don't anybody move."

"But I got to sneeze," Bud Gleason moaned, sniffling up some snot. "Can I please pinch my nose?"

"Pinch your nose and you're gonna be kissing worms tonight instead of your wife," the sawed-off shotgun snorted.

"I'm sorry, but you'll have to kill me then," Bud groaned—and he sneezed. Gasping, he twitched his head painfully, and immediately uncorked another blast, a gigantic phlegm-spraying detonation that scattered money all over the table, all over Harlan Betchel's shirt front, and all over the floor.

The .357 magnum crossed behind Bud, touched

the barrel to the back of the real estate agent's head, and said, "You son of a bitch."

The sawed-off shotgun moved behind Peter Hirsshorn and poked his weapon against the back of the motel manager's head.

"Oh no," Peter moaned. "Oh please not me, oh no, oh please no . . ."

"You," said the pump gun, pointing his weapon at Harlan Betchel. "Clean up that money. Fassssst."

"Yessir."

"But slowly, too, understand? Move deliberately, I mean. I wanna see every move—"

"Yessir."

Harlan did exactly as he was told and had the money in a stack again in a jiffy.

Bud Gleason, eyes closed, about to faint or suffer his fourth major coronary, moaned, "I'm gonna sneeze again."

"Grab the *mon*-ey," the .357 magnum ordered, and the pump gun picked it neatly off the table, slipping the wad into his front blue jeans pocket.

Bud sneezed. And sneezed again. These attacks, which happened occasionally, were nearly impossible to stop. Each time he sneezed Bud's head bumped against the .357 magnum. Everyone else in the room, the three gunmen, all seven card players, stared at Bud, waiting for him to stop so the holdup could proceed. But once started, how could he stop? Bud sneezed and gasped, choked, and sneezed some more. Two, three times he begged the bandits to let him pinch his nose, but each time the .357 magnum warned, "You move your hands, wise guy, anybody moves their hands, in fact, and this room is gonna look like what happened on St. Valentine's Day in St. Louis."

And so the tableau of the sweating terrified card players with their palms turned up on the table and the three Jesse Jameses awaiting one false move persisted while Bud—popeyed, redfaced, and with sweat droplets spraying off his cheeks—continued to sneeze.

Finally the pump gun declared, "Oh shit, let's get on with it. He ain't gonna stop."

"Okay." At the same time that the sawed-off shotgun moved quickly behind Granny Smith and relieved him of his service revolver, the .357 magnum collected Bruno Martínez's pistol from its holster, and, after unloading the guns, they tossed the useless weapons onto the table.

"Anybody else got a piece?" the sawed-off shotgun asked.

Seven heads shook no in unison.

"Okay, now listen very carefully," the sawed-off shotgun continued. "I'm gonna give you some directions, and I want everybody to follow these directions just the way I tell them to you, comprendes? Because if you make even just a little itty-bitty mistake, tonight, instead of kissing your wives and sweethearts, you'll be kissing worms. Okay?"

Sucking in wind and making a sound like a train getting derailed, his eyes positively apoplectic, his chest rioting with pain, Bud Gleason crashed out another mucus-splattering sneeze.

"Okay. Now you're gonna do this with the right hand, not the left hand, the right hand, see? This one. Everybody raise their right hand just a little bit, say about six inches off the table, so I can see is there anybody can't tell his right hand from his left hand, okay? Okay. So do it."

Everybody except Bud raised his right hand as ordered. The .357 magnum jabbed Bud's head: "Do it!"

Confused, faint, and feeling nauseous from sneezing, tears streaming down his flushed cheeks, Bud raised his left hand. "Other hand," the .357 magnum snarled, jabbing again, and this time Bud raised the correct hand.

"Okay. Using this right hand you will all reach into your back pants pockets and remove your wallets and set them very, *ver*-y quietly on the table."

The men did as they were told, the sawed-off shotgun chuckled "Splendid," and the pump gun moved swiftly around the table plucking swag from the wallets. The highest contribution—eight hundred dollars —came from Bud Gleason; the lowest contribution— a hundred and fifty—from Granny Smith. In between, Bruno Martínez coughed up two hundred, Peter Hirsshorn two-eighty, his brother three-forty, Eusebio Lavadie lost an even four hundred, and Harlan Betchel shelled out five hundred and twenty-seven. They had been planning to gamble all night.

"Well," the .357 magnum sniggered, "I guess that just about wraps it up, Chet."

"Tell them about the newspapers, David," the pump gun smirked contemptuously.

"Oh yeah." The three gunmen backed toward the door while the sawed-off shotgun spoke. "We just want you gentlemen to know: you try to find out who's responsible for this heist, and we'll blow the whistle on this little gambling joint and who was here tonight to the Chamisaville *News,* to the Capital City *Reporter,* and to every other newspaper, publication, and civic crusader we can uncover in the northern half of this state."

"So just sit tight, amigos," the .357 magnum chortled. "Think it over. And keep your little handsies just like that for as long as you can stand it, we don't wanna end this little fiesta with no gunfight, qué no?"

With that, they flitted away. But they did so very quietly. In fact, strain as they might, not one card player heard a door open or close upstairs, nothing, no sounds at all. For all they could ascertain, the bandits had turned into ghosts and melted through the upstairs walls; they had simply evaporated.

Thoroughly mortified, the men eyed each other cautiously. The first one who dared move was Bud Gleason; raising a hand, he wearily pinched his nose.

"Do you think it's safe?" Harlan Betchel whispered.

"I guess so." Furiously, Granny Smith reached for his gun.

"Okay," Peter Hirsshorn said. "I'm going upstairs to notify the police."

"The police is here," Bruno Martínez growled bitterly.

"And nobody," Granny Smith added, "get that—*no*body reports nothing to nobody because the police *was* here, and gambling in this fucking state, especially unlicensed gambling, is very, *ver*-y—like the little man said—illegal."

Each man stared at his hands on the table; you could have heard a mosquito crawling across the green baize.

"Tell anybody about this," Bruno Martínez sighed ruefully, beginning even to smile a little, "and I swear to Christ you'll *all* wind up kissing worms."

"This just never happened," Granny Smith insisted. "Does everybody understand that?"

Bud Gleason sucked in a tortured gasp, shot up his eyebrows and lowered his eyelids, wrinkled his upper lip and twitched his nose, going "Ah . . . ah . . . aaah . . ."

But it didn't come.

Suddenly—at last—he couldn't sneeze.

"Wasn't that St. Valentine's Day massacre in Chicago?" Eusebio Lavadie asked.

Several days later an event probably unrelated to the Casino Pilar robbery occurred. A deposit of over two thousand dollars, in the name of the Milagro Land and Water Protection Association, was made in the Doña Luz branch of Jim Hirsshorn's and Ladd Devine's First State Bank.

᠀

Amarante Córdova, guarding Joe's beanfield again, may or may not have been dreaming when he encountered his second angelic apparition. Afterward he just could not recall if he'd fallen asleep. But anyway, there he was in his customary lookout beside a large dead cottonwood log, letting his eyes drift lazily from Joe's robust bean plants to the permanent rainbow that was still glimmering faintly but persistently in the dusty afternoon sunshine choking Milagro, when that same coyote angel reappeared, limping desultorily off the Milagro–García highway spur and along the Roybal ditch bank to Amarante's outpost. The one-eyed angel nodded a perfunctory "Hola" to Amarante, folded its beat-up wings—whose feathers rattled obscenely like those of a zopilote—and, like someone catering to hemorrhoids, eased painfully down nearby with an audible "Whew." After mopping its brow with a filthy handkerchief, the angel lit a cigarette by clicking together two nails on its left paw, inhaled deeply, and immediately had a long drawn-out coughing jag. When this had somewhat abated, and the coyote angel was only wheezing and gasping a little, Amarante dared to speak.

"I see that rainbow is still there," he murmured politely. "That's one tough rainbow if you ask me."

The angel glowered at the rainbow for a second, then shifted its sullen, yellowy eye onto Amarante.

"Listen, cousin," it said wearily, "the way things are supposed to work out, one day the struggles of all you little screwed-up underdogs will forge a permanent rainbow that'll encircle this entire earth, I should live so long."

"I still don't understand exactly how come the rainbow," Amarante said.

"It's like this, man," the disgruntled coyote figure said, its lone jaundiced eye staring blankly at the sky. "You know how down in the Chamisaville Headstart at the end of a day those teachers paste a little gold or silver star on the forehead of any kid who did good that day—?"

"I don't," Amarante said. "But I'll take your word for it."

"Well, this rainbow is kind of like that."

After which the exhausted angel suffered yet another smoker's hacking jag that lasted a full minute. When this fit had subsided, the ethereal being struggled wearily to its feet and snapped the butt into Joe's beanfield.

"Jesus Christ," the angel whimpered, staring forlornly at the healthy bean plants. "Three hundred years, and just about all you old farts got to show for it is seven-tenths of an acre of frijoles. And I hadda draw the assignment. You people don't deserve a gold star, let alone a rainbow. I'll see you around—"

Whereupon, with a grotesque rattle of its vulture wings and a little pained, snuffling grunt, the angel disappeared.

෴

At this point, the first manifestation of what developed into a singularly curious and imaginative terrorism campaign was noticed by Jerry Grindstaff on his way down to Rael's for some hot dogs and rolls, relish, mayonnaise, and mustard to be consumed by the Chamisaville Boy Scouts led by their scoutmaster, Jim Hirsshorn, who was taking them on a picnic using Dancing Trout horses and other paraphernalia that afternoon.

Having passed the dude ranch softball field, Jerry G. was just negotiating the curve around Ray Gusdorf's small spread when he noticed a freshly painted and inscribed wooden cross beside the road. In normal times Jerry G. probably wouldn't have given the cross a tumble; such roadside markers were a common occurrence. When people died in car accidents, for example, their relatives often erected similar humble monuments on the spots where they expired, and the victim's relatives usually kept the crosses brightly adorned with no-fade plastic flowers for years. Also, during some funerals, wherever—along the route to the camposanto—a cortege on foot halted to rest, the mourners erected a cross to sanctify that place, called a Descanso, and they often inscribed this cross with the following: *Passerby, pray for the soul of Onofre González* (or *Ricardo Tafoya,* or whoever inhabited the box they were lugging to the graveyard).

But something about this particular cross made the foreman do a double take about thirty yards below it, and he braked the Dancing Trout station wagon so hard the car fishtailed a little, causing Jerry G., who detested seatbelts, almost to catapult through the windshield. Hurriedly, in reverse, he sped back to the roadside marker, and, after the dust cloud had drifted away from his vehicle, gazed perplexedly for a full sixty seconds at the insolent inscription on the cross before angrily kicking open his door and circling around the car and ferociously tugging that hallowed symbol from the ground and chucking it irreligiously into the rear of the station wagon.

Then he backed over a cattleguard into a drive-way, turned around, and sped home to the dude ranch where, puffing laboriously, he barged into Ladd Devine's office and dramatically displayed the cross's message to Devine and Emerson Lapp, who had been double-checking some figures.

"I don't understand," Lapp said. "What does that mean?"

Devine let out a weighty sigh, asking quietly: "Where the hell did that thing come from?"

"Beside the road, sir. A short piece beyond Ray Gusdorf's place."

"Just erected by the side of the road?" Devine asked.

"That's right. The ground was fresh. It must of been stuck in there only last night or early this morning."

"What is it, somebody's idea of a joke?" Lapp asked bemusedly.

"Not a very funny joke, Em, if you'll pardon my saying so. Okay, Jerry G. Take that thing out to the incinerator and burn it for now."

"You don't want to hold it as evidence? I'll show it to the state police. They could dust for finger-prints—"

"All I want is for you to take that thing over to the incinerator and burn it," Devine ordered. "When I want mountains made out of molehills, when I want to legitimize their puerile actions by paying attention to them, I'll let you know."

"Yessir." Jerry G. carried the cross downstairs, heaved it back into the station wagon, and drove a half-mile south through sagebrush land to the dude ranch incinerator. There he bumped into Horsethief Shorty, who was lifting a similar cross from the bed of a Dancing Trout pickup.

"Good Christ! Where'd you find that one, Shorty?"

"Right across from the entrance to our beloved driveway. Where'd you get yours?"

"Just a little bit farther down the road."

"Somebody's feeling their oats," Shorty said. "But I figured, what the hell, if I showed it to the old man he'd probably drop a nut or lose a good night's sleep, so why bother?"

"I showed him this one," Jerry G. said.

"Oh yeah? How'd he take it?"

"He told me to burn it."

"You see?" Shorty chuckled. "The difference between you and me, Jerry G., is I got ESP."

"I don't see what's so funny," the foreman muttered.

"Nobody sees what's so funny, that's the trouble with this outfit. We're all a bunch of impotent, wrinkled-up prunes, if you ask me."

"Shorty," Jerry G. remarked in his most caustic drawl, "when are you going to grow up?"

"I dunno. I reckon maybe I'll grow up about the same time you manage to work that broom handle clear of your pinched asshole, cousin."

Jerry G. retreated silently to the station wagon, fetched a gas can, and soaked the crosses. Shorty struck a match on his zipper and casually flipped it at the two markers, which exploded into flame. Within seconds the fire had devoured both identical inscriptions, to whit:

Passerby, pray for the soul of Zopilote Devine!

This petulant auto-da-fé did not herald the end of the roadside crosses however: quite the contrary.

It signaled the commencement of their almost delirious proliferation.

ৡ

Come rain, come shine, come whatever, Bernabé Montoya had eyes that functioned just about like everybody else's eyes in Milagro: they popped open, wide awake, each morning at 5:00 A.M. In summertime this event occurred around sunrise; in the winter, of course, it happened well before dawn. During the summer Bernabé had no special early-hour chores to do: he owned cattle, but they grazed on National Forest permits up in the hills; he also harbored a few ratty chickens in the backyard. But he was not irrigating fields, milking cows, or otherwise performing feats of agricultural masochism which might warrant such early rising. Nevertheless, at 5:00 A.M. Bernabé's eyes snapped up like runaway window shades, and whether he wanted it to or not, his day began.

Usually the sheriff lay in bed, his skin flushed and silky from sleep, quietly regarding the ceiling while inwardly contemplating a number of subjects ranging from his soul to his navel, until finally he swung out from under the old-fashioned, home-sewn quilts, dressed slowly and luxuriously, and padded into the kitchen to fix breakfast for himself and for Carolina, a late riser who usually didn't make an appearance until after six.

Always, then, just before starting the coffee, Bernabé ambled into his backyard to check out the sun. Every morning he did this in unison with three-quarters of the other people in Milagro whose eyes had also snapped open (almost with the sharp, whip-crackling, wide-awake pops of little Chinese firecrackers) at 5:00 A.M.

In fact, you might say that any longtime Milagro resident who did not wake up shortly before, or at least right *at,* dawn and hurry outside to check on the sun (just as he had checked on the moon the last thing before bed eight hours before) had probably died in his sleep sometime during the night.

But in any case, on the particular morning now in question, Bernabé's eyes boinged open as usual, and he stared at the ceiling for ten minutes cogitating about useless things; then, because early mornings were also his sexiest times, the sheriff prodded Carolina a little, and, still mostly asleep, she nevertheless responded ardently while he assaulted her with that mute desperate urgency of his, asking, always asking with his body, inarticulately pleading for impossible answers.

After that, humming "Nothing could be finer than to be in Carolina in the morning," Bernabé dressed, then trotted outside to make sure the sun was rising directly above Pancho Armijo's rabbit hutch a quarter-mile away. And sure enough it was not only there, but also—Bernabé having checked his watch with the time-of-day recording on the free long-distance line to Sierra Bell's castle in the capital—right on time.

Satisfied that neither Mother Nature (nor Sierra Bell, God forbid) had gone berserk overnight, Bernabé turned around, along with two hundred other people in Milagro, and walked back inside to start, along with two hundred other people in Milagro, a piñon fire in his kitchen's combination wood and gas stove. No matter that it was a relatively warm summer morning: if you had lived in Milagro all your life, you started a fire in your combination stove first thing after checking out the sun.

Just as Bernabé commenced feeding piñon logs and kerosene-soaked wood chips into the left-hand side of his stove, however, the phone rang. When it did, the sheriff felt his heart dive-bomb down to his toes. And sure enough, who should be on the other end but a frantic Nick Rael.

"Bernie? Last night some punks broke into the store and cleaned me out of rifles, half my handguns, and all the rest of my ammo!"

With an *"Ai Chihuahua,"* Bernabé sat down.

Then he added, "Oh shit."

After that he asked hopefully, "Did you call the state chotas?"

"Sure I called them. But nobody answered down there. So get your tail over here, will you please? I haven't disturbed a thing. I'm even calling from the pay phone on the porch."

Hanging up, Bernabé poked a gun-shaped finger against his temple and made a wry face as he softly sputtered, "Bang."

Swaddled in an old-fashioned robe, Carolina appeared in the doorway: "I heard the phone."

"Yeah." Bernabé dropped a match onto the kerosene-soaked wood chips. "I'll bet you did."

"Trouble always comes in threes," she said vaguely.

The sheriff nodded. "Somebody stole guns from Rael last night."

"Oh dear."

"You're not kidding, 'Oh dear.' It's gonna be like World War III," Bernabé sighed. "I bet old man Devine up there is already pouring concrete for pillboxes. Welcome, ball fans, to the World Series of Death."

"It's an ill wind——" Carolina began.

"You're not kidding it's an ill wind."

Strapping on his gun belt, Bernabé stopped in front of her, slipping one hand inside her robe to cup a heavy breast. Tits, her tits, Vera's tits, everybody's tits mystified him. Maybe he loved tits more than any other thing, piece of anatomy, or even person on this earth. When Bernabé's rough hand curled around or crept over or grabbed onto or crushed a breast, no matter what the size, shape, age, or weight, it was always as if for a moment, at least, he had plugged into The Crucial Connection, the one that supplied All the Answers. Afterward, the rest of their female bodies, all of womankind, either disappointed him or disturbed him like painted cattleguards. And no breast, even though he often found himself pressing hardened nipples into his ears, had ever whispered words to Bernabé, unveiling answers that could placate his insatiable curiosity about the souls of people, the conditions of the universe.

Bernabé cupped Carolina's breast for a moment in a comradely and loving manner, slightly amazed—as always—by its sexy resonant pudding texture, then he kissed her, saying, "Wish me luck," and departed.

Perched glumly on the front porch, Nick Rael had invisible smoke curling quietly out of his ears when Bernabé arrived. The sheriff overshot where he wanted to park by a few feet, so he jammed the truck into reverse, but it was muddy here and his wheels spun a little; he rocked the truck, dug small holes with the tires, finally managed to go forward, braked, and leaped back; killed the engine; got out.

This performance Nick observed with a jaundiced eye that proclaimed: Asking Bernabé Montoya to investigate this case, or any case, is like asking a pet goldfish to eat a crate of bananas.

"Hey, Bernie," Nick called sarcastically as Bernabé

squucked through the muck. "Don't tell anybody, but your boots are on the wrong feet."

"I was in a hurry . . .", the sheriff mumbled, sitting down beside Nick in order to correct the goof. "When did you discover they robbed your place?"

"Thirty seconds before I called you. I just got here, saw they broke the glass in the door and jimmied it open, and I went in and took maybe a five-second look around, then I called you."

Boots on the right feet, Bernabé heaved up and slouched over to the door. For no particular reason he wiggled the handle, observing "Hell, it still works," and then he startled the piss out of Nick by kicking in the rest of the glass.

"Hey!" the storekeeper protested. "What'd you do that for?"

"It was already broken. Somebody could of got cut. Now, show me where they took those guns from."

After Nick, behind Bernabé's back, had derisively crossed himself, he walked around the store, describing the crime. "Well, see, these are their footprints in the sawdust because I swept up last night and put fresh sawdust down. You can tell they came over here and grabbed the handguns, and then went down this row to where the rifles were, see, on all these racks, and then moved over here—"

Bernabé tagged along behind Nick. Leaning against the glass counter in which the handguns had been kept, he sourly contemplated their empty display boxes, then trundled over to the rifle racks where he ran his finger in several empty U-hooks that had held the guns, and blew the dust from his fingers. Likewise, he smeared dust off the half-empty ammo shelf, unconsciously slapping his palm on his pants to clean it, then shook his head.

"You got any idea what time they might of hit this place, Nick?" As he spoke, Bernabé paced between rows, casting his eyes nervously—but actually blankly —about, as if searching for clues.

"I dunno. I leave around eight, you know that. So it hadda be after eight."

"Yeah." Bernabé uncorked a wry, despondent

smile. "I don't suppose I could get so lucky, like if they just wandered in and stole everything while you were standing behind the cash register smoking a cigar, and gave you their calling cards as they left."

"Very funny." Puffing out his cheeks, Nick went up and down on the balls of his feet a few times, cautioning himself to stay cool. He grumbled, "Uh, why do you figure they wanted all those guns?"

"Dunno." Bernabé quit pacing, he scratched his head. "Way things have been going, though, I got a feeling they ain't gonna use 'em for deer hunting." He fished unsuccessfully in his pocket for a coin. "Say, Nick, got a dime?"

"What for?"

"I wanna try the Doña Luz pendejo factory again."

"Use the house phone, for crissakes."

This time Bill Koontz answered. And about twenty minutes later, after both the Bunny bread and the Coors beer trucks had made their early-morning deliveries to the store, Koontz and Bruno Martínez arrived, bundling sleepily out of their patrol car with a fingerprint kit in tow. Immediately Nick's mom appeared in the Rael front yard and started winging pebbles at the state cops, who paid no attention.

"Shit," was Bruno's first remark. "Why did they have to shatter the entire front door?"

"Maybe to make it tough to find prints," Koontz theorized, already powdering the doorknob. "Boy, this thing is an unholy mess."

Nick Rael cast an Oh-Christ-Almighty-God-Please-Save-Us eye at Bernabé Montoya, who cast an Oh-Christ-Almighty-God-Please-Save-*Me* eye at the floor.

Bernabé's eye bounced on the sawdusted floor about the same time Bill Koontz's eye bounced on that same floor, causing Koontz to exclaim: "Hey— what was there in here doing this job anyway, a fucking army?"

Astonished, Bruno added, "Jesus. They did so much shuffling and scuffling we'd never get a decent footprint. Looks to me like somebody ran twenty head of buffalo through here just to destroy the evidence."

Bernabé cleared his throat once while ambling nonchalantly onto the front porch. There his eyes met his own pickup, and he was staring at this vehicle feeling uncomfortable, though unable to ascertain the reason for his disquiet, when Bruno Martínez sauntered out the front door and articulated the reason for Bernabé's discomfort:

"Oh for the luvva Mike," Bruno complained. "Who's truck is that? No, wait a minute, lemme guess. That's your truck, Bernie?"

"Yeah, that's my truck."

"Nick's back door is still locked," Bruno said quietly, "which means they must of parked in front."

Koontz joined them, incredulously surveying the damage that Bernabé, by parking in the mud, getting stuck, rocking his vehicle, sideslipping and whatnot, had done.

"Well, that's that," Koontz said quietly.

"Yessir. That sure is that," Bruno echoed. "You sure can't say that isn't that, not unless you're crazy."

Colored blue, Nick proceeded shakily to one end of the porch and sat down, placing his head in his hands, staring dismally at the muddy mess caused by Bernabé's pickup.

"Okay," Bernabé mumbled, seating himself at the porch's other extremity: "I fucked up."

"But good," Koontz observed.

"It was early in the morning," the sheriff explained, knowing that for Milagro there could not be a more feeble excuse.

"On top of everything else you let those deliverymen carrying bread and beer tromp all over the store?"

"He even *helped* them," Nick groaned.

Later, state police reports from the capital confirmed that the only legible fingerprints in Rael's store belonged to Bernabé Montoya. "And they literally coated every surface," Bill Koontz said with a relish, "the way flies coat hot horseshit."

And so the stolen guns and ammunition became just one more event in the Miracle Valley beanfield war that would never be explained. In due course conflicting rumors claimed the theft had been engineered by Horsethief Shorty (acting for Ladd Devine) or by the state police themselves, in order to deprive Milagro's more humble (and more militant) citizens of their God-given constitutional right to buy and bear and flaunt and discharge all manner of lethal instruments in the no-holds-barred shooting conflagration which was certain to break out soon.

≈§

The last job James ("Dust Devil") Vincent ever did for the state police was the dynamiting of the Milagro District Forest Service Headquarters.

He was recruited to do this job, not by Kyril Montana, but rather by some other higher-up undercover police functionaries who had decided Montana's approach to the whole affair was much too conservative.

Of course, the state police's undercover wing was not dynamiting the Milagro District Forest Service Headquarters just for kicks, or just because of an intragovernmental feud either, but because they planned to pin the job on Joe Mondragón, thus railroading him into disgrace, jail, or worse, and ending once and for all the dangerous game people were playing up there.

The plan was simple enough, and James Vincent and a friend, Leroy Middleton, carried out the first stage of it without a hitch. Arriving in Milagro at 3:00 A.M. on a very dark night, they immediately steered onto the narrow dirt lane leading past Joe Mondragón's house and the many ramshackle outbuildings surrounding it. Cruising slowly into Joe's territory, these two shady operators cased the outbuildings for about fifteen seconds, then, braking the car, Middleton pointed and James Vincent jumped from the car and heaved twenty bundled-together dynamite sticks into an open lean-to structure crammed with junk.

Back in the car, as they proceeded stealthily on, both men suffered brief grim giggle fits, an understandable reaction, as the provocateurs were very keyed up, about to be rich, and not a little surprised at how easy it had been, up until now, to earn their loot.

About five minutes later, however, they aborted the caper. Afterward, James Vincent could not figure out for the life of him what happened. But it had to do with the careless handling of a blasting cap which somehow exploded while he was setting two dynamite sticks alongside the cement foundation of the Forest Service headquarters. And this explosion—which immediately atomized three fingers on James Vincent's right hand—caused both Vincent and Leroy Middleton to panic.

In fact, almost simultaneously with the blasting cap's roar, Leroy Middleton jammed the car into low and, minus his partner, hauled ass, nearly clobbering James Vincent on the way out. After that, the deserted saboteur staggered around the plaza area bellowing the word "Shit!" at least two hundred times before Granny Smith and Bruno Martínez, who had received an anonymous phone tip fingering Joe Mondragón, squealed into the plaza area, almost flattening the dazed and bleeding Vincent. Granny braked; and Bruno jumped from the car, gun drawn, just as Harlan Betchel, toting a shotgun, came running from his house behind the Buck-A-Fish trout pond.

"Don't kill me!" James Vincent screamed. *"I'm on your side!"*

"Holy cow!" Bruno shouted. "Look at his hand!"

"Let's get this poor bastard to the clinic fast," Granny said.

"Who is he?" Bruno wondered, ushering Vincent into their vehicle.

"I don't know who he is, but I know who he ain't. He ain't Joe Mondragón."

"Radio Emilio to call Trucho and tell him what happened."

"First go check if there's dynamite over by the headquarters."

Harlan Betchel, who had been standing there, mouth agape, asked, "What happened?"

"If I knew, Harlan, would I—" And then suddenly something registered in Granny Smith's brain, a warning, an instinct telling him to order everybody to wait just a goddam minute here—

"I got it!" Bruno called, running back. "Two sticks, that's all!"

"Harlan," Granny Smith said, "you're a witness. You better come right down to the station."

"Sure, Granny, if you say so. But I got to put on my shoes. I—"

"Fine, Harlan. You do that. But move your tail, hear? And Harlan, don't tell anybody, huh? Do all of us a big favor: no phone calls, nothing; just don't tell anybody. Put on your shoes and jump in your buggy and open-throttle that car down to Doña Luz as fast as you can. Okay?"

"Yes . . . sure . . . fine."

"Come on," Bruno urged, working to get a tourniquet on James Vincent's arm. "Let's make tracks."

Signal light flashing, they were speeding down the highway at eighty miles an hour when Bruno said, "Wait a minute, you better slow down, look, up ahead—hey! What's with that guy? Jesus, Granny— STOP!"

Leroy Middleton, having just survived unscathed a ninety-mile-an-hour crash during which his car had sailed almost twenty yards through the air and then rolled over thirteen times, staggered like a blind drunk onto the highway directly into the path of the on-coming patrol car, which swerved and screeched to a halt, then reversed and backed up to where the would-be victim stood swaying. Bruno jumped out and grabbed his shoulders, shoving him into the car.

"Radio Emilio," Granny said. "Tell him to wake Doc Gómez and open that clinic!"

The dispatcher took the call, then informed them: "By the way, Trucho is having a fit. He says lay off Joe Mondragón, and if there were any witnesses get them out of that town and down to headquarters here ten times faster than on the double. That's a direct quote, that 'Ten times faster than on the double.'"

"We're gonna drive these guys to the clinic, Emilio, then we'll be in. Harlan Betchel should be down. Hold him there if you have to shoot him to do it.

Call Koontz and order him to get his ass in like it was on fire!"

James Vincent babbled, "Don't kill me, don't kill me, please, I'm really on your side—" Then he fainted.

Leroy Middleton groaned. "Oh boy, this is the living end, this is really the cat's pajamas, this is sweet, oh this is really *dynamite,* oh we did it, we're gonna get a *medal* for brains."

"What the hell is going on?" Bruno demanded.

"Oh you wouldn't believe me if I told you. You really wouldn't."

They arrived, with James Vincent alive but very pale, and both men considerably shaken, at Doña Luz headquarters about an hour later. Bill Koontz was there; so was Harlan Betchel.

Koontz, who'd had an incredibly scary confab with Xavier Trucho in the capital, said, "I think everybody better siddown. It's gonna take me a little time to explain this, see, but all of us here are gonna have to get things very straight, because if we don't, if any of this ever gets out . . . and that means you, Harlan, and me, and you, Granny, and you two boys there, Mr. Vincent and Mr. Middlesex—"

"Middle*ton* . . ." the getaway driver whined.

Four days later, while rummaging in an outbuilding for a hose that wasn't so moth-eaten it looked like a sprinkler system, Joe Mondragón discovered the dynamite bundle meant to pin the Forest Service explosion on him. Of course, Joe understood immediately that this dynamite had not just fallen from heaven in order to increase the personal wealth and power of Joe Mondragón, all-around handyman and bean farmer par extraordinaire. In fact, putting two and two together—even though (miraculously) no word as yet of the blasting cap incident had reached his ears—Joe had a pretty good idea that he at least ought to go tell Bloom about his discovery and ask for some legal advice.

But then Joe got to thinking what a person might do with this much boom if his lawyer never had a chance to make him turn it in. Like, suppose a fellow wanted to dig a big hole or move a big rock or knock down an old house in order to build a new house in its place, or blow up a dam——?

With these considerations firmly in mind, Joe carried the dynamite into his shop, wrapped it in thick plastic sheeting and tied it all together tightly, and then he stored it where no team of state chotas, no matter how stupid, would ever be able to find it.

ᴥᶽ

Ladd Devine reclined under the midsummer stars in a chaise longue on the roof over his office; Flossie was arranged quietly beside him, bathed in gentle light, at peace, and as usual killing a bottle. Devine was not at peace. That morning his nineteenth El Brazo Onofre note had arrived.

> Querido pendejo Devine:
> El Brazo Onofre is weaving a hangman's
> noose to fit around your money-green
> miser's neck. Sleep tight tonight.
> Don't let the vampires bite!

The letter came at ten. Around noon, Emerson Lapp phoned the dude ranch all in a twit because while he'd been parked at the Forest Service headquarters downtown somebody let the air out of all the station wagon's tires, and since Rael's hose was broken, Horsethief Shorty had to go down there with several cans of Instant Inflate to bail him out.

Lapp had been at Forest Service headquarters trying to convince Carl Abeyta and Floyd Cowlie to run more patrols along that section of Indian Creek running through Dancing Trout territory, because lately prowlers had been violating the National Forest land that Ladd Devine owned special-use permit rights to. Poachers were even harvesting trout at night, using large electric lamps. Worse, only three days ago two Dancing Trout swinglers from Kansas City had been startled by a bunch of arrogant midnight anglers who had spot-lighted them nakedly intertwined in a leafy grove near the creek. Obnoxiously giggling and firing off crude and lascivious remarks, the nocturnal fishermen had kept a light on the petrified lovers for at least thirty seconds before hee-hawing back into the blackness.

The embarrassed swinglers had not complained to Devine, but Horsethief Shorty had gotten word of the incident from Sabrina Oatman, who immediately wanted to make love with Shorty in that same grove where the swinglers were caught with their pants down in hopes a similar incident could happen to them. "I mean, wouldn't *that* be a ball to end all balls!" she trilled excitedly to Shorty, who was not very excited by her enthusiasm.

In the end, this noon Lapp had returned empty-handed from Forest Service headquarters, reporting to his boss: "They're not even going to venture out of the office, Carl said, until their request to the regional headquarters for bulletproof vests is filled."

Which left Devine wondering whether Carl Abeyta and Floyd Cowlie hadn't flipped, and also whether he should hire armed men to patrol his recreation fiefdom's borders after the sun went down. A practical idea, perhaps, the way things were going, but suppose an accidental shooting took place? And how would Dancing Trout guests react if it suddenly occurred to them they were vacationing in a state of siege?

Ladd Devine did not know about the Pilar Café stickup, nor had Shorty told him about getting rolled with Sabrina Oatman. All the same, a great many little things—like the Forest Service's refusal to patrol, and the men's room incident at the Chamisaville General Custer Drive-In (which Jerry G. had duly reported)—were pockmarking the normally smooth texture of Devine's summer days. Only just last Tuesday Flossie was thrown from a horse that had apparently been stung in the flank by a ball bearing or BB fired from an unseen slingshot.

"I heard it hit the horse," Flossie explained sadly, "and everything turned upside down."

But the worst outrage was those crosses. Like mushrooms in damp leaves, they sprouted every night by a dozen roadsides—downtown, up in the canyon, out on the north–south highway. Their inscrpitions always either advised the passerby to *Pray for the soul of Zopilote Devine,* or to *Pray for the dear departed soul of the Miracle Valley Recreation Area.* A few times, even, flowery bouquets had been laid at these contemptible monuments commemorating a death or deaths which had not yet occurred. It was impossible, of course, to ignore the crosses, and each morning Jerry G. and Horsethief Shorty, occasionally aided by Bernabé Montoya and the state cops, had to uproot a dozen epitaphs. Devine, obsessed by those repugnant crosses, could not stomach the thought that one of them, somewhere, somehow, might survive, mocking him into eternity. He had taken to counting the crosses, and he had also personally begun to saturate them with gasoline each day around 11:00 A.M. when the men returned from their patrols. If the crosses were meant to intimidate, they had succeeded: Devine simply could not stand the ridicule. He had even paid off-duty state policemen good money to patrol the highway and the town at night, but some-how the culprits were never caught; because the cross planting was just another prank by the mystical and ubiquitous El Brazo Onofre? Or could the lack of a pinch be more accurately attributed to the fact that the off-duty cops simply pocketed Devine's dough, parked in a deserted place, and logged eight hours of shut-eye every night?

Whatever, the crosses were still officially considered a "jest"; and they certainly had everybody chuckling no end, everybody, that is, except Devine, whose dignity was on the line. Wasn't mockery of an almost hundred-year-old reign involved?

What had begun as a mere nuisance had become a pain in the royal ass.

So now, under the stars beside his outrageous and gentle amazon of a wife, Devine felt slightly be-wildered. For years his intricate affairs had rolled along smoothly; he and his partners, his backers, his help, the people on his team—they had all proceeded cautiously, carefully, conservatively, successfully. Devine had only tackled and moved ahead with sure things; he had seldom received any flak; he could not recall ever having seriously misjudged the peasants downtown; like his roguish grandfather, he was used to winning.

But today a spiritual claustrophobia had set his internal organs to aching, sapping his strength. To be honest, the boss was a little pooped; a bit under the weather; unhappy, and baffled too; call it at loose ends. Somehow life had become fragmented, confusing; for a moment he had lost his unwavering drive. A dangerous lassitude hovered just out of range in his body; it was accompanied by a defeatist torpor. He was scared. And in this somber condition, his pale skin iridescently gilded by the bright stars while Flossie casually stroked his thighs, Devine remembered his grandfather; he remembered boyhood days in these mountains and canyons that his family had for so long controlled.

In particular, Devine remembered a single day in his youth, an experience, a brief moment of horror that had not returned to plague him for decades.

They had been up in the mountains on horseback, little Ladd (who was nine at the time) and his arrogant grandfather, collecting raspberries. All morning they picked, filling jars with lush red fruit and loading the jars into saddlebags. Then a rainstorm suddenly struck. "Follow me," the old man said. "If I remember correctly, we ain't too far from Bear Wallow cabin." Swiftly they drove their horses across a meadow, through shivering aspen groves until, sure enough, the small log edifice his grandfather called Bear Wallow cabin turned up. The crusty old man helped little Ladd dismount, telling him, "You go on inside out of the rain, Sonny, while I tend to these horses." And, obeying him, Ladd pushed open the door.

Three men, or rather the mossy, spider-webbed skeletons of three men, hung from a ceiling beam. In one skeleton's pelvic area mountain bluebirds had built a nest, and in it the female bird, surrounded by peeping young, stared beadily at the startled boy.

Rain clattered loudly in the surrounding forest; lightning and thunder boomed. After a moment Ladd Devine Senior appeared in the doorway behind his grandson, laid powerful hands gently on the boy's shoulders, and jovially mused: "Well, ain't *that* a queer place to raise a brood!"

On the roof over his office almost forty years after this incident, Devine shuddered. Drowsily, Flossie unbuckled his belt and undid the zipper, lifting out his penis—gently she caressed it. Devine closed his eyes, trying to remember why it was so important to keep growing, building, expanding and absorbing and accumulating things and power and making money, and making more money on top of that. What did it all add up to: something as incongruous and as crazy as raising a brood in a skeleton? Lowering her head, Flossie quietly slipped her lips over his penis, sucking him off tenderly. He glided a hand laxly into her loose hair, twisting those soft yellow strands around his thin fingers which felt fragile and likely to snap, as if made of hollow, unhinged porcelain. He didn't like himself very much; he never had. And he guessed he did not really love anybody at all.

Too bad.

Or as the French said: *Tant pis.*

Time passed. Devine opened his eyes startled, and his fingers gripped her head tightly, his body—coming—rigid . . . and the flagrant untouchable stars were so stilled they seemed to have been painted up there. Or they were chips from imaginary skeletons; lost virgin souls; pieces of pretty, insensitive ice; their loveliness an untouchable joke. Flossie swung her head to meet his, and Devine experienced a terribly powerful but undefined longing as they kissed, and he licked his own sperm from off her tongue.

That had not happened in a while, and he whimpered, almost like a little boy.

"It's alright," Flossie consoled sadly. And: "I'm sorry," she added. And then of course, with an utterly serene melancholy: "I reckon I love you even if nobody else does, you sweet thing, you sorrowful bastard, Ladd Devine."

❧

As much, perhaps, as Bernabé Montoya wished to communicate with his wife, Carolina, or with his girl friend Vera Gonzáles, his wife, Carolina, would have liked to communicate with him. But she could not talk to her husband, and had never understood the reason for this. Somehow, they shared a compatibility that allowed them to be loving, to make love, to discuss business and gossip and the weather, things of that nature; but they could never communicate in words the human passions, the thoughts and feelings, fears, frustrations, and joys underlying everyday mundane existence. Often it felt to Carolina as if they tacitly understood each other; but times came when they were as hopelessly estranged, she thought, as if a witch had cast a spell, making their lives and human emotions mute, irrevocably voiceless and sad.

Already, for too long the house had been silent. And often these days, with Bernabé gone and she alone among her saints, Carolina would find herself seated in a chair by a rear window, with her hands tucked under the band of her skirt, lightly massaging the still-prominent stretch scars across her plump belly, all that remained to her today of the six children she had carried and given birth to, even before reaching twenty, children already long gone, although she and her husband were hardly middle-aged. Five boys and a girl had forged those scars with the bulks of their unborn selves. Now two of the five boys were in the army overseas; a third had died from leukemia in childhood and was buried in the west side camposanto; the two other boys had married and moved away, one settling in Oregon, the other in Utah; and the girl—married, divorced, and recently remarried—lived in Tucson. All the children were still so young, and yet lost, as Carolina saw it; forever gone; communicating with their parents erratically, on postcards, in badly written and awkward letters, as they adapted to the outside modern world that Carolina had never liked, nor even remotely understood.

She was not unhappy; she had friends. Betty Apodaca, Stella Armijo, Nancy Mondragón and many others, for Carolina was a part of the girls, the women, the town. But when not with her friends or her husband, when she caught herself in a rare in-between time, the house carefully scoured, the groceries put away, dinner prepared, the week's baking done, her vegetable and flower gardens manicured, new squashes drying on racks in the sun, and the time she usually spent every day on exquisite colcha embroidery which she sold at two craft outlets (one in Chamisaville, the other in the capital) over—when those moments of sunny and almost languorous late-afternoon solitude arrived, she would sit by that open rear window gently stroking her scars, feeling slightly dizzy from, and a bit puzzled by, how fast it had all happened.

The curtains fluffed slightly in a summer breeze, ticking gently against an old gray cat drowsing on the sill; her saints were comfortable in the shadowy silence behind her, their sanctity practically murmuring softly; hummingbirds made buzzing sounds as they crisscrossed the backyard, feeding at tall hollyhocks. And her children were gone. So many postcards—from Disneyland, Tijuana, the Golden Gate Bridge—perched among the saints over the fireplaces, in wall crannies, but the boys and the girl were gone. And looking back it seemed to Carolina as if the children had been an explosion of no more than a moment's duration, instead of a twenty-five-year travail. Her memories were clouded, jumbled together, confused; it had all happened too quickly, and there were so many years yet to go, and her grandchildren would be born and raised in cities faraway.

Often this summer, and particularly as the beanfield tension mounted, she had found herself suddenly pausing during a labor to cock an ear as if she had heard something, either just behind her shoulder, a minute whisper, or else faraway and faintly transposed across miles of sagebrush, like a distant coyote or the tremor of a train.

Whatever it was, it startled Carolina, giving her a brief, undefined chill that stayed with her for a minute or sometimes throughout the day, nagging, inarticulate, untouchable, mysterious—perhaps like the aura from her saints.

On occasion it was not so much a sound that she seemed to have heard, but rather a smell that was in the air; and this smell, although never quite caught and confirmed, was an autumn aroma, an unsettling wisp of yellow aspen, smoking grass, apples, and frost. On the evening of a hot July day it would suddenly be there; or rather, she would think that it had just been there, over her shoulder, or on a puff of air carried through the open window as she sat lovingly touching her child-bearing scars. Autumn, crisp, and smelling of piñon and cold ditch water and tangerine clouds and hay; and the sound of the dry brown and twisty sweet pea shells suddenly splitting open, spitting out their seeds, while crickets crackled in dry grass —was *that* the sound she heard? It was suddenly there, that's all—the essence of those things . . . yet always gone before she could decide if it had been there or not. And how was she to explain why it gave her such a start, that far call or near whisper that was never quite there, that sudden whiff of autumn that always disappeared into the lazy hot July dust and sunshine and summer rain smell before she could decide if it had actually been on the air.

One day, with her hands pressed gently against her stomach, Carolina fell asleep in her chair by the window. And asleep, she dreamed. It was early autumn, years ago, during a rare year when a late frost in the springtime had not killed the orchards, and the trees were almost overburdened with glistening fruit. The air was jubilant with meadowlark songs. But then it started to snow, a gentle October snow, and the birds stopped singing. There was no wind, and this snow fell quietly; perched on a thousand fence posts, the meadowlarks waited for it to be over. It snowed all morning and part of the afternoon, and then it ceased. The air was not very cold; the mountains were lost in varying shades of gray mist; the sky was overcast, quiet—everything was immersed in lull. A few inches of snow lay on the ground; every apple on their trees bore an icy white cap. After a while the meadowlarks began to sing again, but their melodious calls were out of place, foreign in this gray, snowy landscape.

Then Carolina saw her child Benjamin, the boy who had died of leukemia, in a strange lonely pose under an apple tree. He had soft brown hair and small frightened eyes and a strained smile on his tight thin lips. He reached up and touched an apple, tipping it slightly, causing the snow to fall off in a little powdery swoop that brushed past his face, leaving a vague white fan across his dark jersey—

Carolina awoke, her skin prickling all over, tears in her eyes; and she didn't understand.

On another day, too, she fell asleep in that chair at the window after her work was done, with her fingertips pressed lightly like a blind person's against those stomach scars, and again she dreamed about her dead son, the only child who had stayed home.

This time she was out in a field with the boy, holding his hand, and it was raining, not hard, but steadily, although almost everywhere around them on the horizon sunshine gleamed.

Benjamin said, "Mama, is the rain alive?" And she answered him, "I think so, isn't everything alive and infused with the spirit of God?"

And he said, "Then does the rain have dreams too, like us?"

" 'Dreams?' Does the rain have dreams—?"

He pointed, smiling, toward the mountains, some of whose slopes were spangled with sunlight. "Rainbows are the rain's dreams," he said. "Look at that one over there."

She looked. "But where?" she asked; she could see nothing.

"Right over there, Mama. Right in front of us. Right there."

But it wasn't there: she couldn't see—

Carolina awoke afraid, goose-pimpled, and again crying. She took her hands off her belly and pressed them for several minutes against her face, saying Hail Marys until the fear imparted by the dream faded.

For too long this house, her home, had been silent.

❧

Early on a Wednesday morning, the Trailways bus made its regular stop outside Nick Rael's store, and the driver, Bill Thorpe, told his lone passenger he could have a five-minute rest stop in order to stretch, buy refreshments, or whatever. The passenger, a grizzled old fart reeking of booze (later, Bill Thorpe found eight empty beer cans in the bus restroom), staggered out, clumsily negotiated the warped wooden steps leading up to the store, and entered the freshly sawdusted interior just as Nick was bending under the counter to hunt up a package containing legal papers Charley Bloom was sending north to a Colorado client.

Exactly what happened next, or why it happened, nobody—least of all Nick Rael—ever managed to figure out. "All I know," a trembling, almost-hysterical Nick told Bill Koontz, Granny Smith, Bernabé Montoya, and Bruno Martínez fifteen minutes later, "is I'm just starting to raise my head when this ax blade comes down, blam! right into the counter there where you can see the chop mark, about six inches from my nose. And that crazy-eyed old son of a bitch —" Nick added, pointing to where Bill Thorpe's lone passenger lay on his back, still clutching the ax, with blood from the hole made by a soft-nosed .38-caliber bullet Nick had fired into the center of his concave chest running out into the damp sawdust, "is on the other end of it. Shit, I almost dropped a ripe tomato into my pants right then and there!"

"Okay, Nick, okay," Granny Smith said. "Easy on the graphics, huh? Just the story. Just give us the story like it happened."

"Well, I dropped the freight package but fast, and he pulled out the blade and swung again. Only this time he hit the cash register, the motherfucker. Look at the cash register! What am I gonna do about the cash register?"

"Don't you got insurance?" Bruno Martínez asked.

"Sure I got insurance. Who doesn't? But Christ Almighty, man. I'm gonna need a whole new cash register. You know how long it could take to order another one like this? And in the meantime what am I supposed to use, an abacus?"

"So he swung," Granny Smith said, "and hit the abacus."

"The cash register."

"Yeah, the cash register."

"Where'd he get the ax?" Bill Koontz asked.

"I dunno, I guess from over there in the rack. Does it look like one's missing? Sure, that's our brand he's got. Count 'em. I oughtta have eight axes in that rack."

"Nope, there's only seven there now," Bruno Martínez confirmed.

"Well then, so that's where he got it from," Nick said.

"Okay, okay." Granny Smith let his eyes flick nervously over the dead man. "Then with the next swing he hit the cash register."

"That's when I started for the gun," Nick said. "What, I'm supposed to let this stark raving lunatic chop off my head? I'm supposed to ask him politely why he's going berserk? Jesus! I keep the gun under the counter, on the second shelf, you know, within easy reach. But I hadda reach up for it this time, see, because I'm on the floor, and I just got it in my hand and pulled the hammer back when he comes running around the counter, grunting and babbling, with the ax raised over his head, so Christ, man, I wasn't gonna ask him about his problem, I just pulled the trigger."

"You fired once?"

"Once my *ass*. I fired six times!"

"Ai, Chihuahua."

"Well what did you expect? At the first shot he stops, but he didn't fall over or anything. He just stopped and stared at me, babbling and frothing at the mouth with his eyes rolling all around the place like sheep's eyes in a hot skillet, so fuck it, I emptied the gun at him, and he still didn't fall over right away. Christ, I was even reaching up for a box of shells when all of a sudden, slowly like, he just tipped over backward with a thump."

"It looks to me like you only hit him once," Bernabé Montoya said. The sheriff, the only person standing over by the dead man, was staring down at his froth-flecked, unshaven, bulbous, and starey-eyed frog face. Perhaps Bernabé was waiting to see if an apple-shaped, pearl-colored, white winged soul was going to blurt out of the corpse's gaping mouth.

"He had a ticket for Denver," Bill Thorpe said. "He was my only passenger."

"He must of been crazy," Bruno Martínez said. "This world is filling up with crazies."

"No wallet?" Bill Koontz asked Granny Smith.

"No wallet. No money. No nothing."

"What do you think, Bernie?" Nick asked.

"Oh, I dunno," the sheriff said slowly, still not taking his eyes off the dead man's face. "Who knows? Maybe he was lonely."

Everybody else in the store harrumphed sarcastically. At which point, Herbie Goldfarb, on whom all the cop cars outside somehow hadn't registered, tripped gaily through a pebble barrage and into the store to buy a candy bar.

"You see that son of a bitch?" Nick screamed at Herbie, pointing to the dead man. *"That's why you should carry a gun!"*

Four days later, about three in the afternoon, the storekeeper was standing at the counter reading the sports page of the Capital City *Reporter,* and although he didn't hear anybody enter the store, suddenly something made Nick look up, "and here was this big, wavy-haired, bearded, supersmiley, Jesus freak-looking creep standing in front of me," Nick told Bill Koontz." I never seen him before in my life. I figured, though, at first, he was probably from over at the Evening Star commune, qué no? One of them. So I asked him what did he want, and he points to all the staurolites I got in the pan to left of the register, you know, and he asked me what were those. So I told him. I don't remember exactly what I said, but I guess it was the usual spiel. I bullshitted about how they were called fairy crosses, and about how this is one of the few places in the world you can find little cross-shaped crystals like that, and then you know what he did? He took out his wallet which was bulging with cash—like maybe I never saw so much loot in a single wallet all at once—and he said 'I want to buy them all.' Well, shit, porqué no? I got a whole bunch more in a cardboard box in back that Onofre Martínez sold me, so I said sure, go ahead, and after counting them the freak hands me thirty-eight dollars and just scoops all those staurolites off the tray, stuffs them into his pockets, and makes the sign of the cross or something . . . and smiles at me and walks out."

"Well, the reason I asked, see," Bill Koontz said, carefully tucking the man's photograph back into his wallet, "is we found this same guy pulled off the highway in a little MG convertible last night down by Doña Luz, dead as a doornail."

"Hijo, Madre," Nick said, closing his eyes, "not another one."

"Yeah. And this one's just as weird. Like we thought at first it was dope, probably he OD'd. So we sent him down to Shroeder in the capital for an autopsy, and guess what Shroeder found in this guy's stomach—"

"Thirty-eight staurolites?"

"Thirty-five."

Nick let out a slow, lamenting sigh, at the end of which he asked: "I wonder what happened to the other three?"

"There's something in the air," Koontz said, starting to leave. "I don't know exactly what, but I wish to Christ that all of a sudden winter would come."

❧

Stella Armijo called up Harlan Betchel's wife, Greta, with some disquieting news.

"Hey Mrs. Betchel," Stella fairly shouted to Greta and the two other anonymous party-liners listening in, "I just saw Mercedes Rael drive past our place behind the wheel of your car!"

"Oh nonsense," Greta Betchel, a petite woman who

fancied herself both a nineteenth-century graveyard poet and the world's last jardinière suprême à la Louis XIV, replied. "First of all, Stella dear, you know Mercedes Rael is *much* too old to drive. And second of all—"

Then she stopped.

And she called to her son Albie, who was out back in the palace gardens shooting butterflies with a BB gun: "Albie, darling, be a dear sweet thing, would you, honey, and toddle around front to see if the car's still there?"

"Nope, it isn't," Albie said, squeezing the trigger on a bright orange monarch; "Dad just drove off a minute ago; I heard him leave."

"Excuse me, Stella, I've got to call Harlan." Greta hung up suddenly, lifted the receiver immediately, and dialed her husband, all in one smooth, only quasi-hysterical, motion.

"Why would I take the car?" Harlan wanted to know. "It's maybe fifty yards to the café, maybe less. When did I ever take the car?"

"Stella Armijo just called to say that she saw Mercedes Rael drive past her house in our car."

Harlan frowned: "Well, just a sec, honey, lemme check."

"Bad news?" Nick queried uneasily as Harlan lumbered through the door.

"Where's your mother, Nick? Stella Armijo just called Greta, said she saw Mercedes driving past her house in our car."

"You gotta be kidding," Nick laughed. "My mom hasn't had a license for fifteen years, not since she totaled that brand new '51 Ford pickup I had up in the canyon by rolling forty feet into Little Baldy Creek with one of Eusebio Lavadie's cows in the back. C'mon, Harlan, don't make bad jokes."

"Where is she, Nick?"

"In the front yard, in the backyard, in the bedroom taking a nap."

"You mind if I have a look-see?"

"Suit yourself."

As Harlan left, Nick's phone rang. "Hey, Nick?"

"Yeah. Who's this?"

"Bertha Gleason here. Now maybe you aren't going to believe this, and I don't think I would if I were you, but you better trot on over next door and check if your mother's at home, because if she isn't I think I just saw her drive by here in that pink and white Dodge belongs to Harlan and Greta Betchel."

Nick sat down. "Which way was she headed?"

"I'm not sure."

"That bad—?"

"That bad, I'm afraid," Bertha said sympathetically.

Nick poked a finger against his temple and pulled the trigger, mouthing a silent *pow*! As he did, Harlan's large shadow fell across the sawdusted floor.

"She isn't there," Nick said in a monotone, staring blankly ahead.

"How did you know?"

"Bertha Gleason. She just called. I guess Stella was right . . ."

"Which way was she headed, did Bertha say?"

Nick flung out finger-spread hands: "Right now, apparently, it's up for grabs."

"Oh Lord!" Harlan clapped a hand to his forehead. "It's all because I clocked her with that shoe, isn't it? Gaga or not, she's still got a memory."

"Like an elephant." And this was shaping up as such an all-encompassing disaster that Nick couldn't move.

"How did she stay on the road all the way to over there?" Harlan asked weakly.

"How can she climb trees, survive in the forest for a week, and eat all my daffodils without getting sick to her stomach?" Nick replied.

"You better call Bernie. We ought to let him know she's loose, right?"

"I guess so—"

"I know," the sheriff muttered disconsolately. "I know, I know, I know. I wish I didn't know, but I do. Already Nancy Mondragón called—your mama, she almost ran over Larry. Four seconds later that VISTA kid, the Jewish hermit from New York, he called from Onofre's place; he was on his bicycle when a little old lady in the Betchel's car deliberately ran him off the road. Six seconds later Lavadie called, wanting to know could he shoot her or not, because she went through a fence on his property and zig-zagged around a field, killed a couple of sheep, then left."

"Heading which way, Bernie?"

"He couldn't say for sure. Maybe east or west; maybe north or south. It was hard to tell. He said mostly she was sort of spinning around like a dust devil."

"Okay, Bernie, I guess we'll head out after her."

"I dunno now what's the point, Nick. Me, I figure I might just as well sit tight and man the phones until the motor stalls or she collides head-on with a tree. About all more cars on these roads can do is just get in her way, that's how I see it."

Nick banged down the phone. Immediately it rang.

"Nick? Nick? Is that you, Nick? Do you know what your mother is doing right now? Do you? *Do you?*"

"Who is this?" Nick asked.

"Who the hell do you think it is?" a hysterical voice on the other end screamed.

Nick hung up. Before he could release the apparatus, however, it rang again.

"Mr. Rael?" a woman's voice jabbered irately, "you ain't gonna believe this, but guess what?"

Whereupon Horsethief Shorty walked into the store laughing. "Relax everybody, relax," he chortled. "It's all over."

"She totaled my car," Harlan groaned.

"She's dead," Nick whispered.

"She just stopped," Shorty chuckled.

"She didn't crash?"

"Not exactly."

"She's alive?"

"More alive than a grasshopper on a hot skillet."

"Where is she?"

"Up at the Dancing Trout."

"Oh God help me—" Nick cringed in preparation

for the answer to his next question: "Where, up there, Shorty, did she stop?"

"In the swimming pool," Shorty sputtered. "But don't worry, man. For some reason that car of yours, Harlan—it floats."

Slowly, Nick sank back into his chair:

"Que milagro!" he squeaked hoarsely.

᪣

Supper was over, the children scrubbed and put to bed, Bloom in his study working. Linda sat down at the kitchen table with a cup of coffee and lit a cigarette. She was hot, tired from dealing with the children all day; the wind had been blowing, filling her hair with dust—but now everything was quiet. The house was straightened up and neat; the kitchen soft, bare, and shining. Everything was in order . . . except that her period was coming on. No big deal, but still she wanted to weep. It was too hard trying to keep life under control.

As the night thickened, dew forming, a grassy smell drifted in through the screen door. Already, small moths decorated the screen; they pinged deferentially against the windows and fell away.

Linda turned on the radio, locating a faraway California station that was playing quiet waltz music, and listened for a moment while sipping coffee, smoking; then she brought in some of the kids' clothes and set to work sewing on buttons. At first the music soothed; later it jarred, growing loud then fading to nothing; lightning from a storm located somewhere in that vast fifteen hundred miles separating the transmitter from the Blooms' radio kept intruding, causing bursts of jagged static. Finally Linda angrily turned off the radio and just sat at the table with her head resting in the fluff of clean kiddie togs, overcome by an almost pristine sadness, a feeling of hopelessness. She could not stand the idea that her husband was falling into the almost maudlin trap of defending something lost from the start; she knew it was lost because she had grown up among the losers; and Linda resented the fact that she still very much loved them, her people the losers, even while she was terrified of being nailed to the cross of her upbringing, her culture. All that could happen, with Bloom tilting at windmills, was the ruination of them both . . . of them all.

Little feet padded from the children's bedroom across the living room, into the kitchen; María cuddled up sleepily against her, whining softly, "Mommy, there is spiders all over the place. They are hopping on my bed."

Linda draped an arm around her daughter, softly shook her head: "But they won't hurt you, honey. They don't bite—" The house was literally crawling with daddy longlegs.

"I'm afraid," María whimpered, and so Linda put on a bright, sympathetic smile as she hoisted her daughter, and, heading for the bedroom, soothed, "Come on back to bed, love, and Mommy will sing you a song."

In the darkness, with Pauline in the other twin bed gently whistling as she dreamed, Linda sat beside her youngest daughter and sang "Oh Little Town of Bethlehem," the song—the lullaby—that for some reason she always sang to relax her children, calm their fears, make them drowsy—

> *Above thy deep and dreamless sleep*
> *The silent stars go by . . .*

And:

> *How silently, how silently*
> *The wondrous gift is given . . .*

But little María, tonight, was not immediately sleepy. She tucked a pudgy hand into her mother's warm crotch, saying "Tell me a story, Mommy, so I won't be afraid of the spiders."

And Linda, seated on the bed in the soft blue summer night, snug within the cheerful, mute universe of dolls and bright clean clothes and Little Golden Books, thought for a moment, but could invent no story, until abruptly she heard herself talking about home, Colorado, the old days, childhood—

"Well . . . a long time ago, sweet, Mommy used to be a cheerleader, did I ever tell you that?"

And, incredulous that this could actually be herself speaking, that the moments she was describing had actually taken place during her early life, she added: "We used to practice on summer afternoons and evenings, all of us girls, there were maybe eight or ten of us in junior high school then who were cheerleaders. We would ride our bikes to the football field and park the bikes on the dirt track, and then walk out into the middle of the field. Sometimes the grass was wet because they had had the sprinklers on, watering the grass. And sometimes the field was almost yellow because of the dandelion blossoms, and then they all went to seed and the field was white, it fluffed when we walked in it, just as if we were walking in dreamy tufts of sheep's wool—"

"Was this when you were a little girl like me, Mommy?" María asked.

"No, I was a little older than you, sweetie. I was thirteen or fourteen, I think. And so we would sit out in the middle of the field in the evening and talk about our routines, and then sometimes we lined up in formation and worked on the cheers—"

And she stopped, able to see them all, pert and young, high-strutting in the dusty golden evenings. Sometimes cars would stop on the other side of the track, and high school boys would look on, whistling softly, making lazy comments; or other times it would just be older people, men, women, grandparents, who parked their rattletraps along the road running parallel to the field, peacefully looking on. The moon might be up in the pastel aqua blue overhead while the sun flamed orange in the west, and other kids, younger boys and girls on bikes, might also stop by. Yet everyone kept a respectful distance, as if that small corps of lively, pretty girls was something inviolate, almost sacred, bouncy, virginal, clean—and the peace and the sense of youth and of well-being, for those moments, had been like a cloud.

She had never qualified to cheer for the rites of autumn, however; in the end they didn't pick her, she was too clumsy; she was not lively enough; she was too somber, too severe, too gloomy, perhaps—she lacked vitality. Maybe she had been too self-conscious; maybe she had been too mature.

But the thing is, Linda had forgotten about that time, those glorious evenings, the solitude, camaraderie, and the green football field, the gentility and serenity of those times, the peppy, shining brown girls dressed in sweatshirts and baggy letter sweaters and short-shorts, chanting lazily while moving happily through their cute, sexy routines, unassailable for a moment, secure.

She checked the telling, afraid of tears. María struggled to keep her sticky eyes open; they closed, fluttered groggily open, closed again, the little hand still embedded warmly between her thighs. Daddy longlegs noiselessly crisscrossed the floor; innocence whispered around the walls creating eddies in the air that set Linda's heart to aching, because more than anything she wanted to give her children a feeling of security, even though she knew this was ultimately impossible. Nothing would ever exactly fit together and solidify; she would never grow calm, never feel at ease; life was a hell on earth of loose ends, uncertainty, violence. The Chicano roots she had rejected had refused to shrivel and die; the culture she had hoped to adopt had refused to compensate. Her true language kept twirling into her head unannounced, replete with an arrogant dazzling laughter, boisterous, obscene, illiterate, tickling her mind on twinkletoes of murder.

Quietly, listening to the creak of her limbs, the crinkle of the cloth that clothed her, Linda roused herself, left the room, turned into the bathroom to draw a tub. At least a dozen daddy longlegs were arranged along the bottom of the cool porcelain tub, quiet, quivering when the light blared on and her shadow fell. She did not like to handle them, squashing the spiders the way Bloom squashed them—she usually opted for drowning. And so now she opened the spigots, shivering a little as the spiders scrambled, lost their footing, struggled momentarily in the hot water, and died, immediately bedraggled, soggy, long gone. Scooping them up in her hand, she shook them off into the wastebasket; when the water was high she shut it off and doused the lights.

In the dark, the bathroom door open, Bloom's typewriter faintly clicking in the distance, Linda undressed and, having gingerly sunk into the hot water, simply lay there, drowsy, the water murmuring around the islands of her breasts and her knees, relaxing.

Bloom's typewriter stopped, his door opened, she listened to him come.

"You in here?" he asked hesitantly from the doorway, trying to adjust his eyes, the smoke from his pipe smelling nice.

"Don't turn the light on——" she said hastily, fearing the harsh, knifing blast of fluorescence.

"Don't worry. I wasn't going to. I'm not that insensitive."

"I didn't say you were insensitive."

"Well, I guess it was what your voice implied then."

"Charley, *please*."

"Can I sit here a while?"

"If you want."

"But you don't want me to, do you?"

"Did I say that? Did you hear me say that?"

"Well, your voice sounded . . ."

Struggling for control, unhappy that he'd come, she said, "Honey, I would like it if you would sit here with me for a little while."

Bloom eased the lid down on the toilet, seated himself, released a pungent comfortable puff from his pipe.

"Let's not talk," Linda pleaded. "We ruin everything when we talk."

"I'll wash your back if you want."

"No, no, please." Because he would soap her back, and then he would not stop, he would start to soap her thighs, her breasts, he would force it to become a sexual encounter, no matter if he promised not to, and right now she only wanted peace. She wanted peace, an absolute quietude; she wanted an interlude of darkness, warm water, the pipe tobacco smell, security.

They sat, both silent, trying to relax with each other, to have a good moment. Linda cupped her breasts loosely, steam eddied thoughtfully in the dark air. Her exhaustion flowed into the hot water; she drowsed. She wished that the experience would never end. She wished that right now she could gently die. Bloom shifted, rustled, tapped his pipe out into his palm; the ashes made a sprinkling noise going into the wastebasket. A rainy whiff came through the open window, a few large drops spattered against the dusty leaves of a pear tree just outside. It was so warm, so cool, so relaxing—

Light, like a bomb burst, exploded in the tiny bathroom; and in the doorway, squinting groggily, stood little María again, the quietest child on two feet since Baby Jesus in the manger. "Mommy," she said, in that willful, winsome, half-whine of hers, triumphantly smiling at having caught her parents in an intimate pose, "the spiders are still crawling all around."

"Hey," Bloom blurted, immediately tense, angry, "turn off that light!" And then, looking down at his wife in the tub: "Oh Christ, what—"

"It's only my period," Linda said, shocked, not quite comprehending: the water was tinged with menstrual blood.

⊷⧵

Joe Mondragón, off on a wood run, drove like a maniac over the mesa's potholed dirt roads, a beer in one hand, the radio blasting. Nancy sat morosely beside him holding a six-pack minus one tallboy in her lap. Crows flapped off an occasional jackrabbit carcass; a black-and-white shrike sat on a fence post with a dead kangaroo rat dangling from under its talons; cows lumbered moodily off the dirt path into the sagebrush. Joe bapped his horn angrily at the cows, shaving their asses with his front bumper as the truck careened by, and, because they were Eusebio Lavadie's cows, he wouldn't have minded plowing into a couple of them either; the only reason they were grazing out here on this Bureau of Land Management land was because Lavadie had gotten money from Ladd Devine to buy up the permits of a Colorado rancher who'd decided to give up his cattle business. Joe had wanted some permits to graze cattle here, but he hadn't been able to come up with the cash and wouldn't have been able to swing the deal anyway, because these cows were Lavadie's payment for putting the Chamisa County Rural Conservation and Development Corps directly behind the Miracle Valley Recreation Area development project.

Joe suddenly braked the truck, grabbed his .30-06 from the window rack, and banged open his door.

"What are you doing?" Nancy asked.

"I'm gonna shoot one of that bastard's cows!"

"You do, you'll get caught, and that's what they want, José, you'll see."

Walking to within fifteen yards of a pregnant cow, Joe bolted a bullet into the chamber. The cow retreated a few steps and regarded him with watery, mooning eyes that indicated a massively substandard intelligence.

But Joe no more could have shot a cow he wasn't going to eat, much less one that was going to drop a calf, than he could have refused a free beer, or put more than a dollar's worth of gas at any given moment into his truck. At the same time, now that he was out here, having announced in no uncertain terms what it was he had planned to do, he couldn't just shrug and return to the truck.

So he compromised, opting to scare the shit out of the cow, which he promptly did, both figuratively and literally, pulling off three rapid shots that sprayed dirt and pebbles and bits of dead sage branches up into the cow's face and hide before it could turn and gallop lumberingly away, splatting a terrified patty onto its own heels as it fled.

Back in the truck, Joe felt better; Nancy stared noncommittally ahead. They had to slow up at the gorge, inching slowly down along the narrow, twisting road, pulling over twice before they hit bottom to allow other, wood-filled pickups on the way home to pass. They crossed the narrow wooden bridge over the Rio Grande, chugging through a swarm of olive green and russet-colored swallows that had mud nests under the bridge, and started the bumpy climb out. At the top, a wide, flat plain dotted with huge ant mounds stretched for a mile, and Joe left the dirt ruts to slalom between the mounds for a ways. Then they were in sagebrush again, barreling along with the windows rolled up against the adobe dust that enveloped their vehicle.

The sage became dotted with a few junipers in a landscape that seemed almost African. Then suddenly stumpy piñon pines surrounded them as they lurched onto an old railroad trestle road, banging along in well-worn ruts for another six miles, at which point they came to the territory of the Big Jack.

The Big Jack was a forest eater, a mammoth, three-story-high machine with three gargantuan steel-toothed wheels that not only knocked over piñon trees, but also crunched them up into bite-sized fireplace-perfect logs. For the past year, in this area of Chamisa County, the Big Jack had been pulverizing the scrubby pine forests in order to make more grazing land—"for the small farmers" insisted all the political brochures, although already most of the leveled acreage had been spoken for by two or three out-of-state cattle companies.

In the meantime, the local people were allowed to come in and lug away all the free wood they wanted, which saved the powers that be the considerable time and expense of carting their slash away themselves or else burning it, which was theoretically illegal.

All the same, Joe and Nancy couldn't help but feel a slight glow as they gunned through the dusty wasteland toward where pickings were best. Loading up on free wood was like gathering manna from heaven, and how could a person be completely cynical about that? For years in the north, part of the measure of a family's wealth had been its woodpile, and even though people like Joe and Nancy had propane heaters in their living rooms now, there would always be fireplaces in the other rooms and a combination gas-wood stove in the kitchen. And if, sometime in the future, not even the combination stoves and fire-places survived, it's an even bet there would still be a woodpile outside, hanging on as a kind of vestigial, nostalgic heartbreaker, like those horses in Charley Bloom's *Voice of the People* article.

Then too, maybe someday—if Zopilote Devine had his way—all the subdivision houses he was planning would pay their respects to Milagro's cultural heritage by having realistic-looking plastic piñon piles in their backyards, adding just the correct dash of authenticity to make their flimsy split-level ranch houses indige-nous to the area.

Totally unconcerned about getting stuck, Joe swerved off the beaten path at a good spot, bucking through loose dirt, sand, and muck to where busted trees lay all about. Without a word they both hopped out and set to work, Joe scavenging bigger logs that burned well in his shop's heater, Nancy gathering smaller branches that would fit easily into the kitchen stove. They each carried an ax, splitting with one or two easy blows what the Big Jack had not completely sectioned, and within an hour the pickup was stacked so high one more log probably would have snapped a spring or cracked the axle.

Joe fetched a cigarette from his shirt pocket, tossed one to Nancy, lit them both. Plunking tiredly down on an uprooted stump near the truck, he snapped open another tallboy; she leaned on the front hood, facing him, wearily letting the smoke drawl out be-tween her lips. A strange but harmonious feeling infused the surrounding desolation. In a far tree line crows scrawked; there was no other animal noise. But here and there small purple flowers shone irides-cently, and in the upturned earth and ragged dunes a few delicate asters grew; for some reason, hundreds of tiny fuzzy caterpillers were chewing on the asters. In its own way that barren area was beautiful, and, although the dust blowing and drifting and shifting in the erratic but constant breezes had dirtied their faces and colored the chinks between their teeth, they felt okay.

That is, Joe felt okay until Nancy, who had some things on her mind that wanted airing, asked, "How come you won't sign that petition Ruby Archuleta keeps bringing over?"

"Huh?"

"How come you won't sign that petition?"

"What, there's a law says I got to sign that petition?"

"I signed it."

"Good for you. I didn't. So what?"

"How come you won't sign it?"

"Because every time we signed something we signed away our noses, our ears, even our testicles."

"This is different."

"Well, I dunno," Joe grumbled defensively. "I just don't want to put my name on anything, that's all."

"Who are you gonna scream to when the chotas pour honey all over you and start eating you like a sopaipilla?" she asked grimly.

"Well, I just haven't figured it out yet. It's too complicated. I ain't that smart. Plus you know that as soon as that petition goes to the governor, five seconds later it's gonna be in the hands of the state cops . . ."

"If there's only a few names on it they sure will have a hearty chuckle, too."

"Well, fuck it."

"I think we should stop on the way back so you can sign, José. You started all this. It's time to quit monkeying around."

"Oh shuttup," Joe whined petulantly, and for some odd reason that ended the conversation.

On the way back Joe drove slowly, stopping a couple of times to piss. Distant clouds, rich and dark and rumbling threateningly, were rolling slowly off the mountains. In the far south, from a high line of transparent golden clouds, yellow and pink rain wisps dangled. Directly behind them in the west everything was a deep and placid early-afternoon blue.

On the north–south highway, instead of turning north toward Milagro, Joe steered south, pulling off a mile down the road into the Strawberry Mesa Body Shop and Pipe Queen complex. Ruby and her son, Eliu, Marvin LaBlue, and Claudio García were at work in the body shop on Benny Maestas' 1948 Pontiac which had killed a horse the night before. Over in the Pipe Queen, Onofre Martínez and his retarded son, O. J., and his two great-grandchildren, Chemo and Chepa, were using Ruby's tools to cut and thread some pipe.

Brushing metal bits from her hair, Ruby walked over to the truck. "What's up?" she asked, releasing a warm smile.

"I guess I'll sign that petition," Joe mumbled.

"It's up at the house. Follow me."

In her kitchen, surrounded by a half-dozen curious yellow cats and threatened by a placidly snarling mutt lying in a basket under the table, Joe affixed his signature to a handwritten petition claiming that "We, the undersigned residents of Milagro, representing the Milagro Land and Water Protection Association . . ." were opposed to the formation of the Indian Creek Conservancy District and the Indian Creek Dam, essentially because they were costly projects designed to aid the few rich landholders in town, projects that the poor people could not afford.

There were only about ten or twelve names before his, and the whole thing made Joe terribly uncomfortable, as if somehow he had just signed up for a hitch in the army or in a jail cell. He was being robbed of a certain freedom he had enjoyed, despite his poverty, all his life. He was being trapped into going farther than he had ever intended to go. Now somebody else besides himself had a real stranglehold on his future. And maybe (Joe thought for the ten-thousandth time) I shouldn't have cut that water into that fucking beanfield after all.

"You don't have too many names on this thing, do you?" he mumbled nervously.

"People just haven't decided yet. Everybody understands though, qué no? They just don't know what we should do about it. But you'll see——"

In the truck, going home, Joe suddenly exploded: *"Shit!"*

"What?" Nancy asked.

"Just shit," Joe whined uncomfortably, gripping a tallboy between his thighs in order to pop the top more easily.

ॐ

Early next morning Carl Abeyta arrived at the Forest Service headquarters to discover a weathered ten-year-old statuette of Smokey the Bear tied with red ribbon to the doorhandle of the office building. A long, thin adobe nail had been carefully hammered through its heart.

Carl was a local boy who knew a thing or two about hexes and about Milagro history, and so he reacted accordingly.

First he took the Smokey out back, splashed kerosene on it, and burned it up.

Next he turned around the desk in his office so that he was sitting at it with his back to the wall instead of to the window.

Then he sent an application off to regional headquarters, begging for a transfer.

That same afternoon, the real estate agent Bud Gleason awoke from a late-afternoon nap in dire need of taking a leak. Swinging his feet to the floor, he sat groggy and unmoving for a moment, lit a cigarette, then pushed his feet into some slippers and padded painfully into the bathroom. As usual his whole body ached. He unzipped his fly, prodding the old sad-sack penis into the clear, then stood there with one arm extended, his hand against the wall, his head propped desultorily against that arm's bicep, taking an occasional drag from the cigarette in his other hand while he waited for the pee to leave his throbbing bladder. Instead, just as a huge ash falling from his weed splashed against his penis, he sneezed. He hadn't closed the door, and so his wife, Bertha, who was downstairs stretched out on the living room divan reading last month's *Redbook* novel, heard the sneeze and called up to him:

"Somebody is thinking about you."

"Bullshit," Bud grumbled. "I'm catching a cold; maybe pneumonia; probably I'll die."

"Don't try and wriggle out of it that way," she said. "Somebody is thinking about you. I know you been horsing around on the sly, especially when I flew East in April to bury Grandpa."

"Oh yeah, me with my one ball that screams Rape! every time I have half an orgasm, and my heart that goes into shock every morning when I wake up because it's so surprised to be alive. After three and a quarter coronaries I should wear a black suit or something. Just to save everybody some time when I keel over . . ."

"Well, maybe somebody else is thinking about you for some other reason," she insisted.

"Like maybe God is thinking about my heart condition and wondering if it's time to pull the rug out from under, thanks a lot," Bud complained, tugging his penis impatiently, eager to get this leak over with, wondering why he couldn't pee.

"God—*hah*! Listen to him brag, would you? Whatever happened to the Devil in this scheme of things, he lost our address? We're too rich for God."

"I'm a condemned man," Bud wailed, grimacing, "and my wife thinks it's funny."

"What do you want me to do, cry?" she called. "You drop dead I'm a couple hundred thousand richer, plus I don't have to put up with you farting between my satin sheets anymore."

"Don't feed me all that Mexican crap and I won't fart in bed anymore!"

"You farted in bed when we lived in Brooklyn and all I fed you were potato pancakes and knishes!"

"*Ai*—" Bud doubled over, sneezing like a whale clearing its blowhole, and some urine finally popped out willy-nilly in the process.

"How about would you believe maybe it's somebody thinking about you for different than a loving reason? Like how about if Joe Mondragón is thinking about you?" she teased.

Their precocious eleven-year-old daughter, Katie, appeared in the doorway, staring inquisitively at his penis. "Why would Joe Mondragón be thinking about you, Daddy?" she asked, giggling when he sneezed again and some more urine squirted painfully out, most of it missing the bowl.

"Close the door, will you please?" Bud groaned. "What is this anyway, I'm not entitled to a little privacy? The whole family's gotta kibitz while I'm trying to void myself?"

"Well, if you wanted privacy why didn't you close the door and lock it?" his daughter asked.

"When I woke up the coast was clear. Now I look back on it my head must be getting soft not to lock and barricade the door when I'm in here."

"You peed all over the floor," Katie observed.

"Bertha!" Bud howled. "Will you tell this kid of yours to bug off and leave her father alone?"

"Your daughter she isn't? What happened to *your* voice?"

"Oh Lord—!" Bud couldn't believe it. He couldn't move, his bladder was going to burst, he couldn't stop sneezing . . . he sneezed again.

"Maybe Joe Mondragón made a little voodoo doll of you and is sticking pins into it," Bertha laughed. "Like during the Smokey the Bear santo riot."

"Funny—" He blasted another sneeze. "Get out of here, Katie, or when I'm finished, if I'm still alive, I'll spank you."

"You couldn't catch me," snotnosed Katie said, flouncing away and galumphing loudly down the carpeted stairs.

"You think it's so damn funny!" Bud screamed in frustration at Bertha, whom he could hear laughing.

"Funny? Getting the air let out of three tires on my Mustang yesterday afternoon is funny? No, I don't think it's funny. But what the hell did you expect after you let Ky Montana use our living room for his CIA headquarters—a dozen roses from the local poor people?"

Bud sneezed, and sneezed again, his whole body convulsing violently, and as it did so urine suddenly burst forth, describing the sort of dancing arcing patterns in the air kids make waving Fourth of July sparklers. Bud gasped and grabbed, getting his hands all wet and dousing his cigarette; his ass bumped against the sink and he yelped.

"Oh my gosh!" Bertha hooted from downstairs. "You alright? Take some digitalis!"

"No," Bud whined miserably, emptying the last portion of his bladder with some semblance of order, "I'm okay." Then, after washing his hands and blowing his nose, he groped behind the toilet for the scented pink sponge. Maybe after all she was right; maybe Joe Mondragón had been thinking about him, causing those sneezes. Who else in this town could have conjured up such a torture?

"Daddy peed all over the bathroom," he heard Katie tell her mom. And "That's alright," her mom replied loudly, "if he wants to write his name on the wall, more power to him. You only live once."

Bud plopped the sponge in the sink and sank tiredly onto the tub rim. He was terrified, of course. Terrified that somehow Joe Mondragón was going to halt all the Miracle Valley projects, and if he did that Bud's fortune, which could be frosted with caviar and Cadillacs if Ladd Devine pulled off everything that was planned, would take a precipitous nosedive. Already he'd borrowed heavily to redo their house, to buy into the west side subdivision and golf course, and to wheedle a position on the proposed ski valley's board of directors. And if those deals fell through he was dead, figuratively and probably literally, too. He had a heart inside—after three major attacks in the past ten years—that must look like the aftermath of a head-on collision.

Bud sneezed again, so hard his chest felt as if an innertube in it had suffered a blowout. "Oh Christ," he sniffled.

"I just saw it!" Bertha screamed from downstairs. "Bud? Can you hear me? I tell you, I just saw it!"

"Alright," he called sarcastically. "I'm a shlemiel

or I'm a shlamozzle or whatever it is you people call them, I'll bite—what did you just see?"

"The angel that flew over the house."

"I saw it too, Daddy!" Katie bellowed. "I saw it too!"

"Oh shit," Bud groaned to himself. "A bunch of comedians I live with. Laughs from sunup to suppertime. *Very* funny. A bunch of hooligans I live with is more like it. *Go away!*" he shrieked vehemently. "Go out back and stick your heads in the mud! You —Bertha—it might improve your looks!"

Suddenly his chest constricted, pain clobbered a shoulder, he almost toppled backward into the tub. For a moment, staying absolutely still in an almost iridescently humming moment that reeked of mortality, he waited, not even feeling sad or particularly cheated; he merely waited for Death to drive a stake through the center of his chest. But nothing happened. So after a moment he whispered, "God, I'm only forty-nine, please let me live until I'm fifty." Then, gingerly, he roused himself, took a pill, blew his nose again, and went back to the bedroom to put on fresh clean clothes. After all, it was late in the day and he had to drive down to Chamisaville to have dinner with a man interested in some land.

Ten minutes later, as he was about to slip behind the wheel of his late-model General Motors womb, Bud heard one, two, three, four, five, six tiny gunshot pops from over on the west side, and directly on the heels of the sixth pop he heard a high-powered rifle explosion that echoed across town and ran right up Milagro Canyon into the Midnight Mountains . . . and he didn't need anybody to draw him a picture in order to understand that all of a sudden—and finally —the chickens that had been fluttering around Milagro for the past few months (for the past one hundred and fifty years) had come home to roost.

Part Five

"Welcome, ball fans, to the World
Series of Darkness."
—Bernabé Montoya

Herbie Goldfarb had never owned a car. But after a while he became convinced that if he was ever going to do anything in Milagro besides vegetate and play the fool, he needed mobility. So he begged his father for bread, received two hundred dollars by return mail, and, early one morning, he clambered joyfully aboard a Trailways bus bound for the capital. Once in the big city Herbie headed directly for Joe Feeny's Conquistador Used Car Lot, and, following an hour of indecision, fear, cold sweat, and haggling, Herbie drove onto the capital's main thoroughfare behind the wheel of a 1956, two-door Chevy convertible with a cracked engine block and a leaky radiator. About fifteen seconds after his first left turn in this vehicle, Herbie was stopped by a cop who ticketed him for a nonfunctioning blinker signal system, an incident which took the edge off his glow. Still, once he had made it onto the north–south highway, that glow, that utter pride in ownership returned, and Herbie clicked on the radio—*it worked!*

It was a gorgeous sunny dry day. Locusts wailed in occasional cottonwoods; ravens, magpies, and buzzards drifted indolently through the clean air; and grasshoppers and butterflies smashed against the windshield in lovely patterns, while warm winds engulfed Herbie like an athletic whirpool bath, making his skin feel tender and good. The top was down and the volunteer's heart was buoyed up; he sang along with the rock 'n' roll on the radio.

Ten miles into the trip home a red light on the dash suddenly glared. Pulling over into a gas station, Herbie discovered that his engine was out—*out!*—of oil, and he fed in two and a half quarts. It was then he noticed the drip-drop exiting from the block, and when the garage attendant took a gander at that he muttered *"Ai, Chi-hua-hua!"* rolled his eyes, and sold Herbie three extra quarts of oil for the remainder of his trip north.

A little farther on, while climbing a steep hill, the radiator overheated, and Herbie had to coast back down on the shoulder several hundred yards to the only gas station within five miles, where the radiator exploded and boiled over. Eventually, the slightly frazzled volunteer calmed it down and filled it up with cool, fresh water, and he was able to hit the road again.

The steep, winding curves in the gorge he conquered like a combination Mario Andretti–Juan Fangio–Steve McQueen. On this, the most difficult stretch, his new car performed like a dream. Atop the gorge, however, with Chamisaville and Hija Negrita Mountain visible eleven miles ahead, the red oil warning light blinked again, and Herbie had to feed his voracious automobile another two quarts. Then, just as he started to pull back onto the highway, six small black clouds scudded off the nearby foothills and proceeded to attack him with rain.

Unfazed, still feeling gay about his—*his!*—car, Herbie veered onto the shoulder, unsnapped the straps holding down his folding canvas roof, and punched the button that raised the roof into place. A grinding whirr sounded under his hood, but nothing else happened. Already soaked by the rain, Herbie tried to tug the roof into place by hand, but the folding stays and struts were permanently rusted together—his roof wouldn't budge.

The volunteer stared at his car for a moment, then slipped behind the wheel into a puddle of water, pushed soaking wet hair from his eyes, and clicked on his windshield wipers, which did not function.

At that, Herbie's glow faded perceptibly, and he

putted about five miles in the rain, his teeth chattering, planning to revisit Joe Feeny's Conquistador Used Car Lot with his .38 pistol and do a Texas Tower massacre number on Joe Feeny and all his unctuous, hand-rubbing, oily-tongued, sycophantic henchmen.

Herbie's spirits improved, however, when the anti-Semitic clouds retreated just the other side of Chamisaville; in no time the hot sun and warm mesa-country air had dried out both himself and his car, and also his spirits. In fact, the volunteer had to admit it was funny: he'd been had, but what else was new? His car was still running, and when the oil alarm light became hysterical again it was almost joyfully that Herbie tended to the motor's gluttonous needs.

Two miles farther on he stopped again to pick up a hitchhiker, a hefty young woman with a broad and sensual face—such blue eyes—and dirty blond hair in pigtails. Flinging her pack and guitar in back, she announced, "Hi, I'm the Butterfly of Love—you wanna turn on? I've got a whole lid of Columbia two-toke, no shit. This guy I met down south laid it on me because I had a cute nose. Can you dig that? Me with a cute nose? Boy, he was sure a weird heavy dude. This state is crawling with heavy weird dudes —thanks for picking me up. You do wanna turn on, don't you?"

Herbie said, "Well, I guess I wouldn't mind—"

"Goody!" Leaning over the seat, she fiddled with her pack. The girl wore a peasant blouse and a nondescript ankle-length skirt; her calloused and dirty feet were bare. Herbie's spirits, and also his carnal lust, soared.

They chugged along at fifty miles an hour with the radio blasting and the late-afternoon wind whipping their hair, getting high on her Columbia two-toke. After his third drag Herbie looked at his passenger and grinned and she grinned back at him, and Herbie let his right hand float over and settle against one of her huge peasant breasts as he asked, "Where you headed?"

The Butterfly of Love giggled, flinging her head back gaily as she said, "Oh, you know, just wherever the roll of the dice takes me," and they laughed heartily together. Herbie suggested, "You can crash with me, if you want," and she answered, "Far out! That'd be groovy!" And she actually took his right hand back off the wheel, placing it on one breast, then she dropped her hand into his lap, and Herbie thought: Oh Jesus Christ, everything I always dreamed about is finally happening to *me!*

"Listen," he giggled, as they halted at Rael's store in Milagro, "do you wanna go for a picnic up in the Milagro Canyon?"

"Anything you say," his nubile, effervescent maiden sputtered happily. "This is so incredibly beautiful around here. This is really outtasight! This is *gorgeous!*"

Oblivious to Mercedes Rael's pebble onslaught, Herbie flapped into the store, and, while he selected bread and a Spam tin, some mustard and mayonnaise and beer, the Butterfly of Love played her guitar, singing so mellifluously that Amarante Córdova and Tranquilino Jeantete appeared in the Frontier Bar doorway with silly grins plastered across their faces and waved to her; she stopped the song just long enough to wave back.

The bottom fell out of Herbie's sack on the porch, but so what? Laughing out loud, he fumbled around for a moment gathering in the picnic goodies; then they were off, jolting through town and up past the Dancing Trout, singing together now, Beatles songs and Simon and Garfunkle, the Beach Boys, and even Chuck Berry; and the air, evening-cooled and foamy from their own dust, washed over them like fluffy, diaphanous whipped cream.

"Oy vey," Herbie murmured ecstatically, "for the first time this summer everything is *beautiful!*"

Following the road for about three miles, they pulled off into a lush grassy area beside a stream. Herbie killed the motor, and they both remained immobile for a moment, grinning stupidly through the windshield at the lovely stream and at the golden sunglow on pine tree tips rising along the slope beyond.

"Oh God, I feel good," Herbie murmured reverently.

"Oh Jesus, I feel good too," she whispered dreamily.

They faced each other. Herbie tugged the décolletage of that peasant blouse down over her breasts, which were enormous, unbelievable, like albino watermelons with huge organically grown strawberries in the center—for a second he could only ogle them in gluttonous awe. When had he ever been offered anything more luscious to devour? He would slake an entire summer's thirst at this golden slattern's overwhelming font!

A mosquito landed on one nipple; she brushed it off. Herbie slapped his cheek, squashed an insect that was punching a hole in his ear, then brushed three more off his arm. Languidly, he caressed her flesh zeppelins; a mosquito landed on his knuckle, he flicked it off with his other hand. His fingertips began to serenade a nipple; three mosquitoes alighted at once on her tantalizing tit; he gently shooed them off and pressed into that tumescent snow-white flesh; she murmured "Ouch," and clouted a fat mosquito sucking on her other breast, in the process smearing blood across the unbelievably succulent jug, and then Herbie had to remove his clutching paw from her bosom in order to crucify a mosquito that had punctured his lip, which is when she said, "What the fuck is the matter with this place? It's crawling with *bugs*!"

Herbie had a sensation that for the rest of his life he was going to hate the Southwest more than he had ever hated any place before, or would ever be able to hate any place again.

"I'll turn the radio up loud," she said, "maybe the noise will drive them away—"

And with the radio blaring Herbie suddenly forsook his debonair approach, lunging at her and grabbing what he could get before the roof caved in, inhaling one breast so lustily that the nipple must have kissed the scar where once his tonsils had been. Starting to respond, she ran her strong fingers eagerly through his hair, then clobbered his head—"I got one of the little motherfuckers!"—so hard he released her breast with a loud sucking *pop!*, exclaiming "Ouch, for crissakes!" as his ears started to ring from her blow.

With that, the Butterfly of Love exclaimed, "Oh Jesus, man, they're piranha bugs! They're cannibals!" Wrenching away from each other, they slapped cheeks, heads—she hitched her blouse up and croaked, "Hey, man, let's get out of here!"

Desperately, frantically, while the Rolling Stones cackled sadistically at full volume on the radio, Herbie shifted into reverse, and, without looking backward, furiously popped the clutch, causing his wonderful convertible to bolt back onto the dirt road and directly into a rattletrap pickup barreling along at a high rate of speed. The collision spun Herbie's car around so that the passenger side collided with the pickup's rear end, knocking the convertible off the road sideways and propelling the Butterfly of Love out her door into a somersault on the road.

Miraculously, nobody was hurt. Joe Mondragón, carrying a rifle in his left hand, leaped from the pickup and ran around it screaming obscenities in Spanish. When Herbie got a load of who he had backed into he clapped his hands over his eyes, waiting to be executed. When Joe realized who had clobbered his truck, he paused only long enough to unleash a string of gory expletives, then he turned tail, galloped up a slope into the woods, and disappeared.

"Shut off that radio!" the Butterfly of Love hollered. Fumbling blindly, Herbie located the knob and gave it a vicious twist to the off position.

The girl stood up, again fitted her chest back into her blouse, gestured obscenely at the car, and angrily retrieved her pack and guitar from the rear seat.

"I'm sorry," Herbie mumbled through his hands. "If you give me your pack, I'll carry it back to town . . ."

"Oh no you won't," she growled, sliding her arms through the straps and hunching the weight up into place. "You stay away from me, man. I think you got the worst karma of anybody I ever met."

And she took off down the road, leaving Herbie behind the wheel of his accordion, moaning into his hands.

❧

As the ten o'clock nightly news was ending, Kyril Montana's phone rang. Marilyn answered, spoke briefly with an undercover cohort of her husband's, and called the agent into the den from the living room. "It's Gil," she whispered, shrugging a little and smiling quizzically as she handed over the phone and left the den, closing the door behind her.

"Gil—?"

"Yeah. Listen. You know that guy up in Milagro? The little schmuck with the beanfield? He shot somebody a couple hours ago. Fellow by the name of Pacheco, owns a pig got into his field. Shot him once in the chest with a .30-06. He's not dead yet, but they say, depending of course on how the wind blows, that he could croak. They took him to the clinic at Doña Luz. Right now they should be transferring him to St. Claire's down here. But nobody thinks he'll make it."

Kyril Montana asked, "Where are they holding Mondragón?"

"They're not. He's gone."

"Gone? Gone where? Who's up there, anybody?"

"Sure. Trucho—believe it or not—he's even up there, with Granny Smith and the Doña Luz boys, Bill Koontz and Bruno Martínez. By the time anybody arrived, though, he'd flown the coop."

"Which way?"

"Up," Gil said.

"North—? Did they set up blocks?"

"East," Gil said, chuckling.

"East? There's not a thing to the east except mountains."

"Yessir," Gil laughed. "That's all she wrote."

"Up into the *mountains*?" Kyril Montana frowned. "Who knows for sure that's where he went?"

"They asked around. Everybody pointed to the mountains. So they drove in every available access road for miles and found his pickup at the end of one. He ran it into the back of a 1956 Chevy convertible belonging to—catch this, are you ready? Belonging to a VISTA volunteer named Harry Goldstein, who had a girl in the car with him called— guess what?"

"I can't guess, Gil. Come on, quit horsing around."

"The Butterfly of Love. No shit, I swear to God. The Butterfly of Love. Five thousand miles from nowhere Joe Mondragón runs his pickup into a 1956 Chevy convertible carrying a VISTA volunteer named Harry Goldstein and a hippie chick who calls herself the Butterfly of Love."

"And he's gone."

"But not forgotten. The volunteer, Goldstein, he said Mondragón had a gun, screamed something in Spanish, and ran up a hill into the trees."

"Listen, Gil, this isn't funny."

"Oh, come off it, man. How long is he gonna last in the mountains? He'll freeze his ass off tonight. When they arrest him tomorrow they'll have to thaw him out with a blowtorch in order to get a statement."

The agent took out his pad and started to write on it.

"What time did he shoot Pacheco?"

"Well, probably around six-thirty, while it was still light out, so far as they can tell."

"Where did he shoot him?"

"Out at the field. The new one. The illegal one, the *symbolic one*. He was half-down in the ditch, Pacheco was, soaking wet, almost drowned, when they found him."

"Out at the field? What the hell do you mean, Gil, 'out at the field'?"

"Apparently this guy Pacheco, him and his pig, they're a legend in that town. Pacheco's pig, everybody knows the story. The pig's always breaking loose, and this Pacheco, that's all he ever does up there, he drags his ass around from field to field, neighbor to neighbor, looking for his pig. He receives about two hundred death threats—or at least his pig does—per annum, according to the locals. Pacheco, he just couldn't build a fence strong enough to hold that pig. Neighbors, they've shot that pig four or five times, apparently, but mostly with .22s, never did it much damage."

"Anybody witness the shooting?"

"Sure. Two men. Guy named Mondragón, no relation, and another old coot named Mondragón, no relation either. What happened, is, Mondragón, our pal, *Joe* Mondragón—he showed up at the field, found the pig in it, went to his pickup and got the gun from the rack, walked back to his field feeding shells into the gun, and then shot the pig six times from about ten yards. That was around five-thirty."

"And then—?"

"Nobody knows how Pacheco found out about it. But they got some grapevine up there, I'm telling you. That Pacheco, he's lived alone six, seven years, ever since his wife died. I guess he really loved that pig. Maybe he was duking it for all I know."

"What happened when he heard about what Joe did to the pig, Gil?"

"He went hunting for Mondragón with a .22."

"Pistol or rifle?"

"Pistol. A fifteen-dollar cheapshit revolver."

"And—"

"And when he found Mondragón irrigating that beanfield with the dead sow off in a corner he stopped and ripped off a chamber load at our hero from a distance of about thirty yards."

"Shit," Kyril Montana murmured under his breath. "Did he hit him?"

"You kidding? That's another thing Pacheco does, apparently—he drinks. He's a bottle-a-day man, sometimes more. He really stokes it away. He's got some money, seems his wife was loaded; she wasn't a local filly, and she had education too. She bequeathed him a small bundle of eastern paper, and he hasn't worked a lick since."

"So he missed six times."

"You betcha. And I guess around the fourth miss Mondragón picked up his rifle, sighted carefully, and pulled the trigger."

"Gil, how come he ran?"

"I dunno. Least nobody can piece that one together. Except maybe he figured nobody saw it, and he knew no cop or judge was going to believe his story. Maybe he had a feeling it was some kind of setup . . ."

"Listen, Gil, this isn't a good situation. Who's on those witnesses? Is there anybody with those witnesses?"

"I imagine Trucho has explained a few things to them. So far I'm not even sure if the press is up there. But, if possible, of course, we'll try to get it handled like just another bar-type killing."

"Give me the names, the first names, addresses if you have them, of the two witnesses," the agent said.

Gil gave the names; he didn't have addresses.

"Where's Dave Edsell?" Kyril Montana asked. "He up there?"

"Last I heard, probably not. As I understand it, though, he's already spoken with Halversson over at the *Reporter*. So if Halversson wants to play it, that bastard should know how to play it, at least until we know more about how things stack up. Trucho wants your butt in Milagro, though. He doesn't know from shit about those mountains."

"Too many people up there could blow it, Gil. In fact it was probably stupid to send anyone up there at all. Maybe we should keep out and let the locals handle it . . ."

Gil laughed. "Unmarked cars all the way, man. Everybody's lying low down at headquarters in Doña Luz."

"If Halversson's interested and he sends Johnnie Dicus up there, that's the first goddam place Johnnie will stop. He's got a nose for this sort of thing, he's no greenhorn."

"Johnnie likes his job," Gil said. "What do you think he is, some kind of radical rinky-dink reporter? He's drawing a decent weekly salary from Halversson; he's got a wife, a brat, a mortgage, and a '71 Oldsmobile on time."

"So what's the plan?" Kyril Montana asked.

"They're gonna go in after him in the morning, I reckon."

"Who?"

"I dunno. Ask the boss. Maybe a couple local boys. And you."

"Damn. This isn't right at all."

"Maybe it will work for us, man. Every cloud has a sil—"

"Too much publicity," Kyril Montana interrupted. "If this thing gets away from us it's as full of explosives as an atom bomb. What are they planning to do, go over the mountains with choppers?"

"They got the little bubble copter up in Doña Luz already."

"God damn— Okay, Gil. Call Trucho. Tell him I'm getting ready right now to drive up there. I think maybe you better keep the line open to Halversson, but don't get too pushy. He knows where it's at, but sometimes he gets a little jerky and unpredictable. I don't see where he'd care to run much more than a couple of blotter-type inches, unless he gets wind something funny's in the air. I don't think he's capable of an act of courage, but his ego could do us a little harm if it got bruised."

"No problem," Gil laughed sarcastically. "I anticipate no problems from that quarter."

"Well, don't underanticipate," the agent warned. "This might be sticky, Gil, and it could use a little finesse."

"Call me Mr. Finesse," Gil chuckled.

"Fuck you," Kyril Montana swore petulantly. "And by the way, why wasn't I informed of this sooner?"

"At first Trucho didn't exactly think you'd be Mr. Right for this particular moment in that particular town, all things considered."

"But now he's scared."

"Let's just say he's quietly shitting in his pants," Gil corrected. "You and him better talk it over. He's got the background on the shooting; now he wants your background material, you know, on Mondragón and the others. And just exactly what you did up there, anything that never turned up in the official paper work. Maybe you better stop by for the file—"

"I know the file," the agent said tightly. "Or maybe you'd like me to drop it on Halversson's desk on my way out—?"

"Halversson, shmalversson. What about that other guy, the lawyer works for the *Voice*?"

"The *Voice* folded. Has anybody run into him up there?"

"Not so far as I know."

"Maybe somebody better talk with him. Or at least put a man on him," Kyril Montana said, more to himself than to Gil. But how could you talk to Bloom without arousing his suspicion and drawing a surefire story that might appear somewhere sometime?

"Okay, Gil. Yeah, you better tell Trucho to put a guy on Bloom, or at least keep half an eye on his place. Thanks for calling."

"Sure, pal. See you up there, maybe. . . ."

Immediately on hanging up, Kyril Montana began to move. He fetched a rifle from a polished walnut gun case that he had made when still in high school, and from a locked drawer at the bottom of this case he removed the bolt for the rifle, which he fitted into the gun. He also retrieved from the drawer a black plastic case containing the rifle's scope, a box of high-powered shells, and a .357-magnum pistol in a hip holster. He set this equipment on his desk and lifted his binoculars from off a peg beside the gun case. Then he went through the kitchen to a utility room, located a padded canvas gun-carrying case in a jumbled corner, and, back in the den again, he fitted the rifle, the scope box, the magnum, and the shells in the bag and zipped it up. After that he carried the equipment back through the kitchen and utility room, placed everything in the trunk of his car, locked the trunk, and started the car, letting it idle as he returned inside.

Marilyn was watching TV. Briefly, he outlined what had happened; she accepted the news quietly. While he was upstairs changing into flannel shirt, khakis, tennis socks, and tan leather hiking boots, she fixed black coffee in a thermos and some chicken salad sandwiches. With the sandwiches in a sack and the thermos under his arm, and having kissed her good-bye with a promise to call once he had gotten up there, the agent snagged a goosedown ski parka off a hook in the utility room, and he was seated behind the wheel ready to back clear of the garage when suddenly he remembered he had forgotten the pack.

It was a lightweight nylon-frame job, and all the necessities, from toilet paper to a flashlight and matches, extra socks, a plastic see-through poncho, and a lightweight sleeping bag were already in it. There was a pocket for fishline and flies; another pocket jammed tight with first aid equipment, a snakebite kit, a small whetstone, and other necessities of outdoor life. The agent added some dehydrated foodstuff packets, an aluminum mess kit, kissed Marilyn again, and left.

On the empty highway going north, he reviewed all the available information in the case and all the moves he had made, analyzing what had been done, where the weak links were, where the possible conduits of exposure were located, what the implications and possible consequences of Joe Mondragón's actions were, not only for Joe, but for himself, Kyril Montana, and for the state police. He went over in his mind the people who were familiar with all or even bits and pieces of his own and his office's actions up to this point, and composed a mental list of those few men who might possibly cause trouble. There was nobody in the capital, but in Milagro, although he felt certain of Lavadie, Bud Gleason, and Nick Rael, he wondered about the sheriff, Bernabé Montoya. And that stupid mayor, Sammy Cantú, could blunder into trouble. He probably ought to speak with Cantú, then, going over the facts so that the mayor would understand this incident was spontaneous, *not planned*—Pacheco had acted on his own. And, because the shooting was unpremeditated, they were all off the hook, so long as they kept their mouths shut.

Gliding down a hill into the small settlement of Arroyo Verde, Kyril Montana made a note to arrange a meeting with the governor and Bookman and Noyes, in order to explain what had happened. For as quickly as possible, now that they apparently had the goods on Joe Mondragón, whatever undercover provocateur groundwork had been laid and developed regarding him and his beanfield had to be erased; any and all confusion among those who had some knowledge about what had been afoot had to be dispelled.

At a Lota Burger stand the agent ordered coffee to go. On the road again, beyond the town's last street-light, he sipped the coffee and quit thinking about the various ramifications for a while. The radio crackled intermittently, he paid no attention; if his personal call number, or a ten-code related to the shooting, came up, he would automatically tune in. In the meantime he guided his powerful car along the highway, driving fast, over seventy, up toward Milagro.

For thirty miles there were no towns. The moon was partially hidden behind ragged summer thunderheads, but the agent could still see the surrounding landscape. On one side flat sagebrush plains trailed off into soft round foothills that led into mountains beyond. To the west, passing a lumber mill teepee burner whose tip glowed red, was an orchard valley along the Rio Grande. At one brief point where the road was slick from a local cloudburst he could smell a combination of fruit trees and heavy sage. Then the road suddenly started winding as it entered the river gorge.

Kyril Montana slowed down to fifty-five. For a half-hour, in the gorge darkness, no other cars came at him. When the moon emerged from behind thunder-head darkness the river gleamed. No guard railings lined the road, and in spots where rain had fallen the road was slippery and treacherous; small rocks that had oozed loose from the cliffside and scattered across the road forced him to brake down even further. Toward the end he climbed sharply for about ten min-utes, past a deserted motel and a few ghostly cotton-wood groves where dwellings lay, rising to the 7000-foot-high plateau he would follow all the way to Milagro.

It was a lovely sensation, one the agent had always

appreciated, catapulting from the twisty dark gorge onto that flatland, with a straight highway aiming exactly north. The treeless panorama ahead was among the most breathtaking sights in the state, even on a darkish night like this. To the left, across gently sloping sageland, the gorge opened for a startling instant. To the right stretched the Midnight Mountains, snowcapped for all but a few summer months and boasting the highest mountain in the state, 13,180-foot Hija Negrita, in the shadow of which lay—scattered like stars in the dark plain—Chamisaville's twinkling lights.

The car tires thrummed over a cattleguard and Kyril Montana stepped on the gas. From some roadside carrion an owl, huge and dark, its large yellow eyes glinting briefly in the headlight beams, took off, flying directly into the car's path. The agent neither lifted his foot off the gas, nor swerved, as—with a staggering wing-flapping whoosh—the bird swooped across the windshield and over the roof, missing death by inches. In another wet area a few miles closer to Chamisaville, tiny toads gallantly hopped across the road. Farther on the car whizzed past or over some kangaroo rats. to the west lightning flickered in sheets broken by jagged streaks. And, bound for El Paso, a Trailways bus boomed by.

Two miles outside Chamisaville the agent stopped at the state police bungalow. Although lights burned inside, the doors were locked. He had a passkey, entered, and called ahead to Doña Luz.

"Pacheco's still alive," an operator whom he did not know informed him. "In fact, they think already his condition is improving. Apparently he's a tough old fart."

"Where's Trucho?" the agent wanted to know.

"He's still up in Milagro chewing fingernails. Him and Bruno Martínez and Bill Koontz. Sal Bugbee, too. I guess they're still talking with the people. Things are pretty quiet up there. They got a posse organized to go out tomorrow around dawn."

The agent signed off and checked the gas pump outside, but it was locked and he didn't have a key, so five minutes later he pulled into a station on the northern outskirts of Chamisaville, filling up the tank on his credit card.

After that he kept his mind fairly blank over the eighteen miles to Doña Luz. It hailed for a minute, then the sky was empty and luminescent; clumps of sagebrush along the roadside glowed like torches. But soon lightning began flickering again off to the west while mist drifted from the close eastern mountain canyons toward the road. He passed a group of big, gaunt, slope-faced horses walking dumbly in a line along the shoulder—Indian horses, the agent guessed instinctively—and after that he crossed the Rio Colorado into Doña Luz.

One state police car and one county car were parked outside the small headquarters building. Inside three men sat around drinking coffee and chewing the fat—the radio operator with whom Kyril Montana had spoken, a handsome young kid by the name of Emilio Cisneros; the jovial gray-haired county sheriff, Ernie Maestas; and a crew-cut state highway patrolman the agent knew, though not well, Bill Koontz.

"That José Mondragón, that little son of a bitch," Ernie Maestas laughed. "I knew that bastard was gonna kill somebody someday. You know what he did to me once? I had him in the isolation tank, county jail, maybe three years, two—ahhh, I don't remember —a while ago, anyway. Johnny Roop brought him in, remember Johnny Roop?"

"Didn't he shoot himself dicking around with somebody else's gun in the jail a couple years ago?"

"Horseplay," Maestas chuckled. "He grabbed Pete Lujan's gun out of Pete's holster and somehow he shot himself in the stomach, and the assistant DA— that chingón Robertson—he called it an accidental death due to 'horseplay.' "

"Who's got a full report on the Pacheco thing?" Kyril Montana asked impatiently. "Did anybody make out a report yet?"

"Who's gonna call Tina and ask her to type out a report at 1:00 A.M.?" Koontz joked dryly.

"Type it," Maestas laughed. "Fuck it, who's gonna *write* it at 1:00 A.M.?"

"Well, let me see the preliminary folder at least," the agent said wearily as Ernie Maestas chortled on about Joe Mondragón.

"Like I said, we had him in the pit. I don't remember what for. I think he went after some drunken bastard with a timing chain, who the hell remembers? But anyway, he asked me for a blanket, said his nuts were cold, I told him to suck his dick to keep warm, So you know what that feisty little rat did—?"

Annoyed—though his features remained impassive —Kyril Montana leafed hastily through some scribbled sheets in the Pacheco–Mondragón folder, but came across no new information.

"He took his pants off, stuck them in the crapper, and started flushing like a madman. He had the whole cell plus half the county jail flooded before we could turn off the water—"

"How come all the downstate cheese is crawling around up here?" Koontz asked, offering Kyril Montana a cigarette the agent refused.

"We get out of touch down there," the agent joked humorlessly, heading for the door. "Every now and then Mr. Trucho likes us to participate in something like this just to keep our hands in."

"Yeah, God forbid you should ever get out of touch with us poor Chicanos up here," Ernie Maestas laughed, slapping the agent's shoulder as he went by. "You got to hunt down a cabrón from the norte every now and then just to test how good you are, verdad? The gabachos down south, they don't know assault and murder from a hole in the ground, qué no? Going after them is like shooting patitos in a pinball gallery, right? But up here things are different—"

Kyril Montana closed the door gently, backed his car around, pulled onto the highway again, and ran the last thirteen miles up to Milagro in less than ten minutes. A mile below town he stopped at a one-car block manned by the two Chamisaville state personnel, Loren McKay and Buddy Namath, who added nothing to the plethora of noninformation he already had.

Then, instead of stopping immediately in Milagro, the agent drove north to the other block, manned by a county undersheriff and another state cop, Sal Bugbee, who also had nothing to report.

With that he turned around and drove to Bud Gleason's house.

ᰤ

When Joe Mondragón shot Seferino Pacheco, Charley Bloom practically jumped for joy. *Saved!* he cried to himself when nobody was around. He would defend Joe on an assault or a manslaughter charge, and in the process the beanfield would be forgotten. It was what everybody wanted—qué no? He almost wished he had the guts to tell Bernabé Montoya, or the Doña Luz state cops, or the county sheriff, Ernie Maestas, to set an excessively high bail so that Joe would cool his heels out of action while the beanfield went to hell.

But after that first sensation of relief, the bottom fell out. He despised his gutless reaction to Joe's dilemma; he couldn't stand his cowardice. And he knew, too, there was no way that beanfield could go to hell; Joe or no Joe it would flourish, maybe now even more than before.

Whereupon, like a man doomed, he called up Bernabé Montoya. "Bernie? Charley here. Charley Bloom. Listen, I don't know the extent of what Joe's done, I don't even know if he did anything, and I don't know where he's hiding *if* he's hiding. But I want you to understand I'm his lawyer, and he has certain rights I'm sure you're familiar with. And if you and your deputies go after him like a pack of crazy wild dogs and shoot him down in cold blood or even manhandle him a *little,* I'm telling you right now I'll do everything I can to hang the lot of you from the rafters by your balls, if I have to go all the way to the Supreme Court to do it, understand? I don't know how you're going to handle it, but you better make damn sure you haven't got some trigger-happy boob in your posse, if that's what you're planning to form. If Joe shot Pacheco, he did it in self-defense, the

way I understand it, and if he doesn't come out of
the hills alive and in good shape, I'm going to hold
you personally responsible, and, like I said, I'll try
to have the book thrown at you, I'll make damn sure
you get hit with everything including the kitchen sink."

"Take it easy, take it easy," Bernabé replied nervously. "Don't get so excited, dammit. Nobody's going
off half-cocked, I assure you."

"I just want to make sure you understand this is
a ticklish situation that could have severe consequences," Bloom said.

"You think I don't know that—?" Bernabé croaked
desperately. "Jesus *Christ,* man!"

He hung up on the lawyer.

Bloom cradled the phone, and, bowing his head,
pressing his palms against his eyes, he shed a few
quiet tears.

Linda had just put the kids to bed. She sat down
in a chair staring helplessly at him from across the
room.

"I don't know how to handle it," Bloom moaned,
swaying a little. "I just don't know how to handle it.
I feel so ambiguous. What kind of wishy-washy person am I anyway?"

"Handle exactly what?" Linda asked.

"This: That. Anything. Everything. I don't *want*
to be involved in Joe's affairs. He *shot* a man, for
God's sake. I'm like you, I never wanted to spend my
life in the company of violent people. I don't want
to be associated with a man who killed another person.
I don't want to defend that kind of human being ..."

Bloom's face looked shocked and unholy and
drained. "I'm afraid," he whispered tiredly. "I'm
afraid of losing, afraid of winning, afraid of the
fight. I've always been afraid. I want to be safe. Like
you too, right? I spent my whole life looking around
for the big rock-candy mountain. I can't stand the
fact there isn't a Santa Claus. The people around
here—" He stood up abruptly, waving one hand.
"The people around here, if they ever saw Santa
Claus in the neighborhood, they'd fall all over themselves scrambling for their .30-30s so they could put

a little reindeer meat in their freezers! I hate their illiterate guts! I'm sick and tired of doing their dirty work. And of *not* doing their dirty work. Why don't you teach one of your own bloody people to be a lawyer? Why don't they learn to read and write? Every damn Friday when we come back from Chamisaville with the Sunday before's *New York Times* I feel guilty as sin. And I'm sick and tired of feeling guilty as sin!"

In pain he gripped his temples, ran fingers through his hair, turned away from her, toward her, paced across the room and back, stopped at a window, lowered his voice.

"We should get a gun," he said. "Learn how to shoot it. A rifle. A pistol to keep in the glove compartment. This autumn I'll get a hunting license, I'll go out and kill a deer."

Bloom sat down.

"I don't want a gun. I don't want to have to feel we need to protect ourselves like that. I came out West to escape that kind of shit. So what are we doing in a medieval little town where everybody and his brother practically sits around picking their teeth with bayonets all day? You know how kids around here get lead poisoning?—from eating .30-30 bullets, that's what from. And you know what I'm tired of? I'm tired of every time I pull up in back of a pickup truck there's a fucking gun on a fucking rack on the fucking rear window."

Silence. This was her speech in his mouth, and Linda just sat there, staring at her hands in her lap, a sense of imminent disaster riding like ice through her bones.

"I don't know," Bloom said, shaking his head. "I just don't know. Maybe I never should have left the East Coast. Maybe I shouldn't have been a lawyer. I don't have the temperament to be a lawyer. I'm not tough enough. I don't have the kind of compassion it would take to be good. I don't know what I have the temperament to be, you want to know the truth. Probably we shouldn't have gotten married. What's going to happen if everything falls apart again? Where will you go? Who gets the children? How will we support each other and the girls when everything is split apart—?"

Quietly, without moving, Linda started crying.

"Oh brother." Bloom stood up, turned stupidly in circles, slumped down, picked up a pencil off the desk and aimlessly broke it in two. Then he selected another pencil from a leather cup, broke it, and set the pieces in a row on the wide green blotter, and selected another one to break. And another.

He broke them all, lined the pieces up carefully, and sat there, elbows on the desk, hands covering his face, breathing heavily.

"I don't get any exercise," he murmured unhappily. "I'm fat, bloated, I jiggle when I walk. How much booze do I consume in a day? Two beers for lunch. Bourbon before dinner. Wine with the meal. I wake up in the morning, I start nibbling. I can't stop eating. I light a cigarette, smoke it, light another: I chain-drink coffee. My hands are always trembling; my nerves are shot. My veins bulge. My whole flabby body shakes from caffeine jitters, and I can't stop. What's the matter with me? Why don't you do something about it? Why don't you tell me to stop killing myself? What are you doing, counting the minutes until I die and you'll be free?"

Bitterly, the lawyer laughed. His veins bulged, his eyes were sore, his head ached: in the vernacular, he was strung—far fucking—out. Maybe he *was* killing himself; it was true he couldn't breathe right. Self-pity clogged all his pores.

"I used to think life was beautiful," Bloom moaned. "Everybody in my family thought life was beautiful. We grinned at each other morning, noon, and night. We had real-life Pepsodent smiles. Nobody ever got angry at anybody else. Life was a bed of roses!"

He was shaking his head again, back and forth.

"All my life I been waiting to grow up," he whispered. "Instead I only grow old. I hate growing old. I'm gonna go down to the capital tomorrow and buy a wig and some of that magic cream that hides liver spots and makes people look ten years younger. How come there isn't any Geritol in our medicine cabinet? When are we going to get a color TV?"

Linda sniffled and wiped her nose on the back of her hand.

"We don't have enough sex anymore," Bloom blurted suddenly. "I beat off at least twice a week, how about that? And, except for when we went up in the mountains, we always make love in the dark now, and we always make love the same way, the same tired old positions. I want to *fuck*. I wish I was married to somebody who knew better what to do in bed. We used to be so erotic. We used to laugh and joke in the hay. I don't think I can stand much more of this sugar-is-sweet bullshit, timid do-nothing hanky-panky anymore. Oh God."

Bloom rose and wandered dazedly around the room touching things, avoiding Linda's chair, stopping once to cough. He went to the kitchen, located a toothpick, and began busily to pick his teeth. From the kitchen he could see her sitting there, in her hair—already—streaks of gray. She was a dark, once-sensual girl—he had never been able to call her a woman—who'd had two lovely daughters by cesarean, and he guessed he loved her, but she was nothing like his first wife, whom he had hated while also lusting after her sensual way in the hay.

Bloom dug into a clay jar, latched onto a chocolate chip cookie, ate it.

"Forget what I said," he called softly in to her. "I'm not a good person. I'm sorry."

Linda didn't move, said nothing, he could not hear if she was crying—he hoped she was crying—but he couldn't reenter that room to find out.

"Let's forget about it," he whispered, eating another cookie, gulping it almost hysterically. "I should keep my mouth shut. When you get this old you should keep your mouth shut."

But he had to laugh ironically over that. "All my life I kept my Casper Milquetoast mouth shut. When they bury me they better gag me, because I'll probably start screaming from the grave, everything I never said."

"Oh shut up," she whispered unevenly. "Go away."

"I don't want to go away. Where would I go? There's probably some violence freak outside waiting to plug me. And anyway, suddenly I really feel like hurting you."

"Maybe there isn't somebody out there waiting to shoot you because you're not as important as you think," Linda said.

"Oh screw you," he spat sourly, and went outside.

In the moonlight, tears streaming down his face, he wandered around their place, their house but not a home. Since birth had he ever lived in a home? And what now for Charley Bloom? He sighed. The ponies whinnied quietly as they trotted over to see if he had sugar, a carrot, or anything else. He scratched Sunflower's forehead, gazing at the mountains, struck by their clear, ghostly peace. Once he had sworn never to leave the ocean, convinced that his soul craved sand and the green expanse stretching all the way to his ancestral home in Europe. But mountains did as much for a soul as the ocean, and they were more mystical and more alive, and more accessible, too.

Bloom journeyed into his back field. The grass was silvery, damp with dew. The valley all around him, what he could see of it, was dark and secretive, beautiful and serene.

Tomorrow he would leave. Good-bye, Linda: adios, my children: so long Joe—roast in hell, kids.

No, he wouldn't leave.

He was exhausted.

His daughters dreamed the rainbow-colored Raggedy Ann dreams of contented children. And he loved them. And he loved his wife. And fuck it. His life was over. The adventures he had always dreamed of, also the serenity and the security, were already a part of the past, impossible fantasies. If he had ever been free, he didn't know when. Joe Mondragón was important right now, he needed a defense if he survived, and Bloom could probably do a decent job, so he would do a decent job.

What the hell.

He returned to the house. In her puffy blue robe, eyes red rimmed, Linda leaned against a kitchen counter waiting for coffee water to boil. He nodded hello; she nodded back, dropping her eyes. Bloom fetched a sweater from the bedroom and came back to the kitchen, buttoning it up. She put a teaspoon of instant coffee into two mugs and poured the water. They stood in the kitchen, Linda leaning against the counter, Charley leaning against the fridge, sipping the coffee. Dogs started to bark and howl, kept it up for a few minutes—the racket died down. Then the faint odor of a faraway skunk drifted into the kitchen.

"I apologize for my outburst," Bloom said slowly.

She shrugged, making a small sound.

"I don't know," he said. "I just don't know."

"I don't either," she whispered, staring at the floor.

"Everything will be alright in the morning," Bloom said. "Or at least it will be better."

And after a long silence he added: "I love you."

Much later on that night, Bloom suddenly awoke out of a bad dream and discovered that she was up on one elbow staring at him.

"Oh shit," Bloom whispered despairingly. "I just feel too . . . God . . . damn . . . *mortal*."

❧

"So," Bernabé Montoya sighed wearily, "Pacheco's pig tried to eat José's beanfield, so José shot Pacheco's pig, so Pacheco tried to shoot José, so José shot Pacheco, and all because of that damn pig and that damn drunk *I* got to go up into the mountains and bring back José, only José ain't gonna want to come back, so somebody else will get shot, probably me."

Carolina, who was seated in her chair by the open rear window, said vaguely, "Cheer up, querido, things could be worse."

"Sure they could be worse," Bernabé muttered morosely, applying shoe polish to one of his boots. "The bullet José put in the middle of Pacheco's chest could of ricocheted off a rib, traveled a half-mile across the highway, passed in one of Mercedes Rael's ears and out the other just as she was throwing a stone at Harlan Betchel, and then bounced off one of those tin gutters on the Frontier Bar, come through that window you're sitting at, and struck you right between the eyes. Sure, it could of been worse—"

"I didn't mean . . ." Carolina began defensively, startled by her husband's bitter tone. "I didn't think . . ."

"Oh yeah . . . heck . . . I'm sorry . . ." Bernabé fumbled with words, came up mute. And then abruptly released what he'd not admitted before: "I guess I'm a little scared, that's all." He smiled weakly, shrugged self-effacingly.

It was a curious, lambent time then, in their house, in that room. A late-afternoon sprinkle had stirred up the dust, and now a slow breeze carried in an almost-radiant smell of dust and dry piñon pine and sage.

The room was growing dark; something had happened. They both felt raw, tender, exposed. A crack, a minute fissure had opened between them: Carolina, with her fingertips still touched against her child-carrying scars, held her breath; the evening's dusty pulse was almost too reminiscent, too saturated with a call to memory. Then Carolina, whispering, admitted, "I'm scared too."

And they waited. And they had much to say. Because they loved each other. Because they had failed each other. Because they were embarrassed to try and be articulate. Because life was half-over. Because, because, because. . . .

Bernabé, the human piñata; Carolina, with her shiny stretch marks, her dreams about Benjamin, her all-day-every-days in the house among sacred murmurations.

Last night in the bathroom, while seated on the can, Bernabé had noticed a spider spinning its web in a corner several feet away. He watched it passively for a moment, until of a sudden he realized it was a female black widow doing her thing not three feet from his toes. When he had finished, drawing up his pants and buckling his belt, Bernabé knelt on the floor near the spider, watching it work. A hundred times he had confronted black widows, and—BLAM! —always, unthinkingly, he had smashed them with his hand the way most men and women in Milagro eradicated the pests. But last night, on his knees, curious, fascinated as this most beautiful of all spiders wove her web, he held back for a second, impressed by the delicate geometric designs that deadly little creature was making in order to survive.

Then, on one of those impulses that are among the most impenetrable and yet somehow also most joyous of mysteries, he reached out and interrupted the spider's work, touching it with his finger, making it freeze, startled, in a defensive posture, and then he cupped the puzzled black widow in his palm, and the spider remained in that wrinkled bowl of brown skin poised high on its thin aristocratic legs, wonderfully dangerous, unmoving. Carefully, then, Bernabé raised the poisonous thing until the thread extending from the abdomen broke; after that he sat down on the edge of the bathtub, just staring at the small ebony spider, which, with a single bite, could probably cause him more discomfort than he had ever known; which, with a single bite, could kill a child, an old woman, an old man. And he remembered—

Being a teen-ager, working one summer at the Dancing Trout. In those days the old man, the senior Ladd Devine, had kept a small greenhouse; and for a while Seferino Pacheco had been his gardener— Bernabé, Pacheco's assistant. Whenever they transferred seedlings from table beds into small flowerpots, they always ran into a slew of black widows nesting in the little stacked flowerpots that were kept in a dark shed beside the greenhouse. The first time Bernabé unstacked and cleaned those pots for the transplantings, Pacheco ordered: "Collect all them spiders in a milk bottle, and I'll show you something." So Bernabé tapped the female spiders into a milk bottle, and when there were about thirty in the bottle, Pacheco told him: "Watch this."

Whereupon the alcoholic, who was not yet an

alcoholic back then, turned over the bottle, and, as if pouring nothing more dangerous than milk, sprinkled the spiders onto his bare forearm. They scrambled out; they fell; they plopped onto his muscled hairy arm and quivered there, uncertain, frightened, dangerous—and then they began to walk all over his arm while he smiled quietly at Bernabé, not even deigning to look at the creatures decorating his vulnerable flesh as they promenaded gingerly about, threading among each other, deadly and confused, but unwilling to bite.

"Jesus!" the teen-ager Bernabé exclaimed.

"Have you ever heard of Orozco?" Pacheco asked. Bernabé shook his head no.

"Have you ever heard of Diego Rivera?"

No again.

"How about García Lorca?"

No again. No again. No.

"Well—this is just a literary sort of exercise," Pacheco told him scornfully, at last awarding the spiders a disdainful glower. "They could kill me, but they probably won't. All the questions and games concerning souls, mortality, life and death, religion, great art, and banality are brought into play here. And as for me? I say fuck these stupid spiders!"

And as for Bernabé—? Last night, with the black widow in his palm, he had finally muttered, "Fuck this stupid spider," after which, practically overwhelmed by acute feelings of sadness, he had clapped his hands together, killing the thing.

Carolina at the window, feeling her scars, wanted to verbalize a memory, but couldn't. They were young, she and Bernabé, courting. He was working at the Dancing Trout that summer; for Pacheco the florist. One Sunday they took a picnic far up the Little Baldy River: Bernabé immediately set to fishing. Carolina, who did not especially like to fish, wielded a rod anyway, because she was in love with her husband-to-be. But while he fished upstream, she was downstream picking the lush red, wild raspberries that grew along the banks and whole handfuls of mint. Other bushes were laden with purpling currants; butterflies abounded; and at every step grasshoppers whirred off, some crackling like the snappers kids placed against their bicycle tire spokes.

Later in the afternoon clouds drifted over the mountains, over the Little Baldy: it was the rainy season; hail began to fall. They joined for a meal of tortillas and beans and chokecherry wine; they ate sheltered by spruces and pines. All around their place hailstones bounced, laying down a white cover that soon resembled snow. Since they were in love, urgent and alone, they made love. Bernabé smelled of fish, her body smelled like mint, and both their hands were stained red from the wild raspberries they had been eating. Afterward, while rain, instead of hail, fell steadily, they lay in the shallow brook, laughing and joking, washing off the raspberry stains their hands had left all over their bodies. . . .

Thirty years later, with Carolina quietly kneading her scars and Bernabé shining his boots before heading to the meeting at Bud Gleason's house, they both stopped their restless activities, captured and imprisoned, if only for a breath's length, by memories; and the air became almost heavy and damp with the urge, the need, the lust to speak, reveal, articulate, tell, talk at last—

But the opportunity passed: the moment—along with the air—cooled. The darkening room gave way to the damp, dusty odor, the beautiful aroma of rainy sage. Bernabé, Carolina, both wishing to touch and support each other, coo and fondle, maybe even weep in each other's arms at this crisis time, stared out the window instead, silent until one, or the other, commented upon how lovely was the land they lived in.

After another long silence, Carolina felt compelled to say: "Well, it's always darkest before the dawn."

At which Bernabé rolled his eyes, half in frustration, also half-lovingly, as he sarcastically crowed: "Welcome, ball fans, to the World Series of Darkness!"

And Carolina, although a little distressed by his tender mockery, quietly smiled.

ⲟⲟ

Many who were involved in it now and would be involved in it tomorrow were gathered in Bud Gleason's living room. They had been almost ready to pack it in for the night when Kyril Montana arrived. Xavier Trucho, a lean, hangdog, yet almost delicate-looking, cynical man, was slumped disconsolately in an armchair, smoking a cigarette. Bernabé Montoya and his deputy, Meliton Naranjo, stood tiredly with their backs to an adobe fireplace. Scattered about the room were Granny Smith and Bruno Martínez, the mayor, Nick Rael, Harlan Betchel, Eusebio Lavadie, and four other men: two Anglos, a Chicano who had been deputized to help lead the posse in the morning, and the helicopter pilot, Mel Willard. The room was stale from smoke; a few beer cans were scattered around.

"That crazy bastard Pacheco won't die," Trucho whined. He had a thin, almost high, almost effeminate voice.

"I heard."

"Everything is very quiet, though," Trucho added. "Thank Christ for small favors. This town is so quiet you could hear a throat being slit, isn't that right, Mr. Cantú?"

The mayor nodded hopelessly. All he had ever wanted in life was his petty share of what others skimmed off the top, and maybe a good time.

"There ain't anybody doing anything," Trucho said. "Nothing stirring, not even a ratoncito." He smiled at that. "All we can do now is we're waiting for the morning. There ain't any press here, nobody, so everything is very cool. It's very very quiet. It's so quiet you could hear blood drip . . ." And he smiled at that, too.

"What do people think?" Kyril Montana asked.

"Our people or his people?" Trucho asked.

"I'm not sure I'd put it exactly that way."

"How would you put it?" Trucho wanted to know.

"What about the posse? How many people do we have signed up for the posse?"

Trucho nodded toward Bernabé Montoya. "Mr. Montoya, how many men have you contacted for this posse tomorrow?"

"Thirty, maybe thirty-five men. All with guns," Bernabé said.

"Hello, Mel," Kyril Montana said to the helicopter pilot. "Sorry, I didn't notice you at first."

Mel Willard nodded back, smiled.

"The people here," Trucho said after an uncomfortable pause, "they don't think Joe Mondragón's been in these mountains for a long time. They feel he's gonna stick to the established routes, the tourist trails. There's a handful of little lakes about four miles up in the direction where he's headed—"

"The Little Baldy Bear Lakes," Kyril Montana said.

"Yeah. What do you call them around here, Mr. Montoya?"

"Osito Calvo."

"The Osito Calvo Lakes," Trucho said, leaning forward to stub out his cigarette. "Now he may or he may not be heading for those lakes, we don't know, we can't tell. In fact, we don't know a thing. He could of doubled around back into town for all we know. He could even be hitchhiking for Juárez. Or Denver. We got an all-points out . . ."

Bud Gleason sneezed. Eusebio Lavadie said, "I don't think he's gonna leave his home territory."

"What Mr. Lavadie here means," said Trucho, "is this is where Joe has people. His people. His gente, know what I mean? So we got to figure he's not gonna stray too far. We got Pete Gilliam keeping an eye on his wife's house, and on that lawyer's house, too. Mr. Martínez and Mr. Smith here are probably going to visit the wife, and maybe even that lawyer, Mr. Bloom, sort of surpriselike tomorrow sometime, just to make sure they don't have any guests we're looking for. But I doubt it. I figure Joe Mondragón is up in those mountains getting his butt frostbitten and I figure also that even if he hasn't been up there in quite a while, he knows those hills like the inside of his asshole, and we're not just going to beat him from the brush like a rabbit the first fifteen minutes out. As for me," said Trucho, abruptly heaving to his feet, "I got other things to look after, now. I'm going back to the capital; I'm going home. Kyril, check with Mr. Montoya here, and Granny and Bruno, they'll fill you in." He nodded perfunctorily, shrugged, put on his hat, and walked out.

"We're going to assemble where in the morning?" Kyril Montana asked.

"Right here," Bernabé said. "We told everybody right here, qué no?"

"Sure," Bud Gleason nervously confirmed. "I guess that's okay . . ."

"I assume," the agent said, "that this is going to be handled basically as a local thing—?"

Bruno Martínez nodded. "Yeah. That's the way we been asked to play it. Bernie here—it's his bailiwick, his jurisdiction, as the saying goes, right Bernie?"

The sheriff nodded glumly. "I'm afraid it looks that way . . ."

"Who's in charge of the weapons count?" the agent asked.

"Huh?"

"This morning, every man that shows up here who's a part of this posse, who's carrying an arm, you got to take down a description of that weapon, a serial number, and the amount, make, and type of ammunition that man is carrying. Somebody gets shot up there in the hills it won't hurt to know who did it. Although the best thing that could happen, I don't think I need emphasize, is that we return with Joe Mondragón hale and hearty and very much alive."

Bruno Martínez said, "Don't forget, the little bugger's got a gun."

The agent sat down. Quietly, and suddenly quite tiredly, but wanting to say this now before a lot of witnesses, he warned, "If our thirty-five guns kill Joe Mondragón tomorrow it's only going to be the beginning of a real bad time. A real bad public time and a real bad all-around time for this little town, know what I mean? Did anybody here talk with his wife?"

"She slammed the door in Trucho's face."

"Anybody talk with the lawyer?"

Nobody said anything until finally Granny Smith spoke. "Trucho figured at this point, what the hell. Maybe tomorrow."

"So who's slated for what until daybreak?"

Granny Smith said, "The boys on the highway will stay there until dawn, then Bruno here and me, we'll take the north end position, and I don't know who's coming up from Chamisa V., but they'll have two people up sometime for McKay and Buddy. Trucho said hang in until noon, and then fuck it."

"What about Mel, here? He's not going to fly alone—"

The Milagro deputy sheriff, Meliton Naranjo, raised his hand to waist level and mumbled unintelligibly. Mel explained, "He's going with me. Unless you want to change what Trucho decided."

"Whatever Trucho decided is more than good enough for me." The agent added, "So I guess we might as well get some shut-eye."

Bud Gleason said, "Whoever wants to can sleep on the couch here, or in a guest room, and we could even put an extra mattress in Katie's, in my daughter's, room."

The two uniformed state cops and Kyril Montana shook their heads. "We're going back to Doña Luz," Bruno said. "There's a couple bunks in back, so we'll probably stay right at the station case anything breaks."

"Thanks Bud, but I think I'll look around," the agent said. "I'll catch my winks in the car . . ."

"You're welcome, Ky—" Bud began, but his friend, smiling coldly, interrupted: "Like I said, I'll probably drive around a little. Maybe later I'll come back and park in your yard, if that's alright. But most probably I'll wind up on the highway with one of the block teams."

Uneasily, they broke up, going home or heading down the highway, whatever. Kyril Montana waited in his car until the others had left, then moved slowly out the muddy driveway, but instead of going west toward the highway he turned right, aiming toward the mountains, and once again he climbed the winding road up Capulin Hill to the water tank on which so many junior high schoolers had painted their class years.

There, with the radio off so its static would not disturb his concentration, he gazed out the open window at the town. Bright, silent sheet-lightning still flashed occasionally across the gorge in the west. Somber but not thundering clouds remained stationary near the eastern mountaintops behind him, and Kyril Montana wondered if it had either hailed or snowed in the high country, not an uncommon occurrence at twelve to thirteen thousand feet, even in July.

The moon directly over Milagro was clear and bright, almost full, the town dully luminous, trees and houses casting shadows. Few lights burned; but from a half-dozen chimneys slow, almost phosphorescent piñon smoke emerged, dissipating in a flat way over the town, seeping into bushy cottonwood foliage. Cows were lying down in some fields, horses still moved about in others. The police cars and officers manning the roadblocks were clearly visible. Every ten or fifteen minutes a lone car careened up or down the highway, at which point the patrol car emergency lights went on and snap-flickered as the car was waved to a stop and tiny flashlight needles jerked across the road for a moment—then the car started on and everything went out, returning to stillness again.

Strangely, no insects sang; all dogs and coyotes were quiet. The agent waited alertly for some movement down among the adobe houses, for some telltale stir in the shadows between buildings or in the cottonwood darkness along Indian Creek. At any moment he expected a car to start up and swing, with its lights extinguished, onto a muddy back lane, heading surreptitiously out. But nothing happened. Not in the heart of the minuscule town, nor in the surrounding fields, nor in the area around Joe Mondragón's house, nor around the lawyer's home either.

A few bats fluttered in the air near the car and he could hear their high screeching sonar—then they were gone. A cow groaned, something coughed, a sheep bell clinked once as the animal changed position. Never stopping, the agent's eyes roved slowly around town, along roads, through trees and the animal herds, probing, pausing to inspect anything that seemed even slightly out of place, quartering the community and circling around it and returning to quarter it again, waiting for something to happen, for Joe Mondragón to appear down there somewhere heading for home or for the highway—what would the man do? He didn't, couldn't, know.

At one point, without relaxing his vigil, the agent poured himself a thermos cup of coffee and ate Marilyn's chicken salad sandwiches. After which he got out and stretched his legs. The night had become chilly, almost cold enough to lay down a frost, he thought; it must be freezing at the higher elevations.

Around three-thirty he realized, abruptly, and with a real shock, that he had forgotten to call his wife. That kind of slip up bothered him a lot, and for maybe five minutes he could not concentrate as he should have on the ground below. It wasn't his style to make a goof like that. But if he let it get his goat now that would be even less his style, and so he forced it to the back of his mind and had some more coffee. Then all at once he realized he was exhausted, and with that he rolled up the driver's side window part way, slumped behind the wheel, and fell asleep.

But he was awake—suddenly—about an hour later, just before dawn. There was activity below him now, cattle and horses and sheep moving, the sheep bells clanging, and birds—magpies and bluebirds and killdeer—everywhere. The air was full of sound, and from out the valley's chimneys a white and pungent smoke arose.

Already several cars and some horses had gathered in Bud Gleason's front yard. The agent snapped on his radio and, as he watched more cars head for Bud Gleason's, contacted Doña Luz and the highway roadblocks to see if anything had happened. He was informed that a sixty-year-old woman, her twenty-two-year-old-daughter, and the daughter's five-month-old son had died at 2:45 A.M. when their pickup hit a horse on a Chamisaville bridge and flipped over into the Pueblo Creek; nothing else had occurred.

Kyril Montana spent a final peaceful moment on the hillside overlooking Milagro, listening to the magpies' chatter and to roosters crowing. Then, as the wide sky became translucently pink and azure with the moon still shining brightly from the center of it, he drove down the hill to Bud Gleason's house.

Five cars were parked in the yard when he arrived; eight men had gathered in a single group smoking and talking quietly—one man had a bottle. As soon as the agent drove in, Bernabé Montoya detached himself from this group and walked over to the un-marked car. Squatting down beside the front door so that his head was below the agent's, he said:

"That field over there—somebody irrigated it again last night."

"Joe's field?"

"You guessed it."

"Who did it?"

"How should I know? There's something else, too . . ."

"Namely—?"

"They took the pig. Pacheco's pig. We just left it there, you know? So they took the pig. Probably they slaughtered it, I dunno. But somebody took that pig."

Kyril Montana opened the door, got out. "Nobody saw anything?"

"You must be kidding."

"You think it was Joe irrigated it?"

Bernabé shook his head. "I know it was others."

"How do you know?"

"You can feel it," the sheriff said morosely. "That's all."

Then, after an almost desperate silence on his part, Bernabé added: "You really think it's worth going into them mountains today?"

"Yes."

Kyril Montana looked at the sky. Already the pink had faded; it was being replaced by delicate mauve interlaced with cottony cloud wisps. He heard the chopper coming up from the south, and within a few minutes Mel Willard had set the small bubble copter down in the alfalfa field directly behind Bud Gleason's opulent adobe home. By that time almost twenty-five men had gathered in the front yard; some were poring over U.S. Geological Survey maps spread out on the hoods of their automobiles.

It was dawn; it was time to start hunting Joe Mondragón.

❧

While the posse moved tensely on foot into the Midnight Mountains, Milagro began its day in the same old way. In a hundred valley houses fires started burning in combination wood and gas stoves, and men, dressed already in irrigation boots, quietly ate breakfast with their wives and children. The Valley Star milk truck halted at Rael's grocery before full daylight infused the small community, and the driver, Johnnie Gómez, swung milk crates down to Nick and his son Jerry who lugged the crates inside. Even before the Valley Star truck had sloshed out of the muck near Rael's front porch, Tim Goldhorn guided the Coors beer truck to a stop near the store, and while cartons of six-packs, tallboys, and quintos were going into the Rael coolers, along came the Trailways bus.

As he parked his cumbersome vehicle, which immediately came under attack by Mercedes Rael, the bus driver, Bill Thorpe, announced over the intercom that this was Milagro. In response a pale, taut little man wearing a floppy, sweat-stained cowboy hat and carrying a cheap cardboard suitcase held shut with greasy twine, pushed along the aisle through a blue smokers' haze and the gulping snores of strung-out voyagers and tottered unsteadily down the steps to his native earth. There he stood somewhat bewilderedly beside his suitcase as Bill Thorpe raised the side hatches and Nick flung a package into the luggage space. Then Bill swung a bundle of Capital City *Reporters* onto the ground; and as he did this a gaunt, crew-cut man wearing a T-shirt, dungarees, and high-top basketball sneakers propelled himself awkwardly off Rael's porch and hoisted the heavy bundle into his arms.

This middle-aged man was Onofre Jesus Martínez, the mentally retarded son of one-armed Onofre Martínez, and he was also the town's paperboy.

Lugging the papers over to the porch, O. J. produced pliers with which he cut the wires holding the bundle together, and, brow furrowed darkly, he counted off the ten copies that went in the store.

"So how they hanging?" Bill Thorpe asked, sticking his tongue out good-naturedly at Mercedes as he got the tickets on the package from Nick.

"Oh, can't complain, can't complain," Nick said.

"Christ, you oughtta thank your lucky stars you live in a nice peaceful place like this where all you got to contend with is ax murderers and a mother who's crazy as a loon," Bill joked. "You should of seen the smog down south this morning. And the *stink*."

Nick smiled, stowing the receipts Bill had signed in his shirt pocket. The driver nodded toward the passenger who had disembarked. "You know that guy? He from here? He don't speak a word of English. Maybe he's a wetback. He got on in the capital . . ."

"Sure, that's Snuffy Ledoux," Nick said. "He's from around here. Been gone a long time, though. Maybe ten years." And in Spanish, to Snuffy, Nick said, "Hey, cousin. Welcome back."

Snuffy smiled at him, but puzzledlike.

"You think he's alright?" Bill asked. "I'd hate to let another one like that ax nut get off here."

"Well, you know—" Nick smiled. "Snuffy is as alright as anybody else around town."

Bill laughed and swung up into his bus. "See you later, alligator," he called as the door hissed shut. Having begun his stint in the capital three and a half hours ago, he would drive the bus another hour north into the Colorado town of Fort Dempsey, eat a second breakfast at the Fort Dempsey Taco Wagon, hang

out for a few hours, then bring the southbound El
Paso bus through around one o'clock.

After the blue bus-exhaust clouds had dissipated,
Snuffy Ledoux came unglued. Leaving the suitcase
where it stood, he crossed to the porch, and, nodding
at O. J., who merely glared back, he walked inside.

"I been gone a long time," Snuffy said in Spanish
to Nick.

"Boy, you can say that again. I haven't seen you
for I don't know how many years."

"Nine years," Snuffy said. "I been working in the
capital. I been a groundskeeper out at the triple-A
baseball stadium."

"You lucky stiff. You got to see all those ball
games."

"I didn't earn much money, though," Snuffy said
sadly. "I got no money in my pocket, in fact. So
I need a couple things on credit."

Nick shrugged. "Sure. You get a severance check?"

Snuffy nodded. "It should be here Monday."

"Fine," Nick said. "That'll be just fine. Take your
pick of the store. Live a little."

"Okay. Gimme a pack of Camels and a Coors
tallboy. No, wait a sec, make that Hamms, there's a
boycott on Coors."

"You can get the Hamms yourself back in the
cooler." Nick dropped the cigarettes on the change
mat, raised the lid on his charge account box, dialed
L, and wrote out a sheet with Snuffy's name on top
and the items he had bought underneath and the
price. Placing the box on the counter, he handed the
man a ball-point pen, Snuffy made a shaky *X,* and
Nick wrote in his name.

"That okay?" Snuffy asked.

"One hundred percent correct."

"Well, thanks . . ." Outside, Snuffy seated himself
on the porch, smoking a cigarette and tugging luxuriously on his beer while O. J. Martínez counted and
recounted his newspapers. The Frontier Bar was still
closed: butterflies danced nervously in the air, zig-
zagging across the road, and on the other side of the
dirt area some big yellow swallowtails were sucking

nectar from flowering lilacs beside the Pilar Café. Harlan Betchel hadn't opened up yet; his guard dog, Brutus, sat in the window, staring alertly across the street at O. J. and Snuffy Ledoux. As always, the plaza area was littered with a thousand fragments of recently torn-up parking tickets that looked like muddy stars.

Pointing with his beer, Snuffy asked O. J.: "Tranquilino Jeantete, does that old man still run the bar?"

The forty-year-old paperboy, who didn't understand Spanish, just glared at him suspiciously.

"Sure is quiet around here," Snuffy said goodnaturedly. "What's happening, man?" He grinned. "Who's doing what to who?"

O. J. frowned more darkly and cocked his head.

"I been gone nine years," Snuffy said. He held up nine fingers so the retarded man would understand. "I been gone nine fucking years. That's a long time. What happened since I went away? Did anything happen at all?"

O. J. said, "Talk English."

Snuffy shrugged, crumpled the aluminum beer can and dropped it in the weeds alongside the porch, stood up and stretched. And kept smiling. "Nine years, son of a bitch. That's a helluva long time. Nine years I worked down there and I didn't save no money." He patted his pockets to prove it. "I don't got a single peso, how about that?" He removed a wallet from his back pocket, demonstrating to O. J. Martínez that it was empty. The paperboy shrugged, jerking his hostile eyes away.

"Well," Snuffy cooed happily, "I guess I'm home, ain't I? Yep, I guess I'm home, alright." He lit another cigarette, and, with a fat smile crinkling his whole face, he chuckled to nobody, to the town, to the gorgeous crystal morning: "I didn't earn a God damn fortune down there after all. I didn't come home in a silver Cadillac, no sir, I sure did not do *that*." He went back inside the store and signed another *X* for another tallboy.

With thirty-odd newspapers tucked under one strong arm, O. J. Martínez moved out on foot into the town's narrow dirt roadways to deliver the news to Milagro. Dogs barked at his heels wherever his long-legged stride carried him, and he snarled back at them, sometimes even spitting, which only made the flea-bitten mongrels yap more hysterically. Men and boys who were already in the fields irrigating looked up, laughing, and the women of Milagro watched O. J. come and go from their front doorsteps or parlor windows. Frowning, deadly serious lest he make a mistake, the half-wit loped through town, oblivious to hummingbirds whistling around the abundant hollyhocks, casting knifelike glances at shimmering magpies, recoiling almost in pain whenever turkeys, guinea hens, or geese added their shrill gobbles and honks and squeals to the furious canine cacophony that every morning except Saturday (when the *Reporter* didn't publish) trailed at his heels wherever he went.

O. J. returned to Rael's around eight, the papers safely distributed; the town quieted down. Exhausted, the half-wit bought a Nehi orange and a peanut butter Nabs from vending machines on the front porch, and sat down as far away as possible from Snuffy Ledoux, who was working on his fourth tallboy.

"Christ, man, you sure make a racket delivering those blats," Snuffy laughed. "You're like a cat with a bunch of tin cans tied to its tail."

A faded yellow pickup sputtered to a stop nearby. Esquipula Gurulé, his wife, Fructosa, and their children, Emma Jean, Filiberto, and Bobby, all carrying burlap feeding sacks, jumped from the truck and fanned out across the immediate area scavenging for aluminum beer cans. Already, this early in the day, they had a dozen filled-up sacks in the back of the truck; by midmorning, after they had canvassed the area down by the river where everyone went to drink or get laid, they would have a pretty full load. Then they would head for the Capital City recycling center, filling their quota on the way down, usually from the Doña Luz lover's lane. On every day of the week, beginning at 6:00 A.M. usually, and collecting until a little after noon, they worked various areas in the county, never failing to arrive in the capital with a full load. Working at this job full time, the family made a living.

Now, as the Gurulés scurried about casting their haunted, hunting eyes busily through weeds and in and out of likely looking nooks and crannies, Snuffy Ledoux suddenly shouted, "Hey, everybody, I'm back! Miren! Miren! Miren! Estoy p'aca!"

Fructosa Gurulé straightened up and, with her hands on her hips, matter-of-factly asked "How come you returned?"

"I got homesick."

"Well," Fructosa whined bitterly, "it's worse than when you left. Welcome back to nothing."

"What's happening?" Snuffy asked eagerly. "Who's alive, who died since I been gone? How much money did the Zopilote make off my brothers and sisters since I went away?"

Esquipula said, "Seferino Pacheco is dying because José Mondragón shot him yesterday after he shot at José because José shot to death Seferino's sow who was eating the bean plants in José's old man's bean-field José is irrigating illegally over there on the west-ern side of the highway."

"Don't tell me, lemme guess," Snuffy cackled. "They got José down there in the Chamisa V. cage hanging by fishhooks stuck in his ears and attached to the ceiling."

"It's not funny," Fructosa whined. "He ran away to the mountains, and there's a posse up there right now looking for him and when they find him they're going to kill him."

"No, they're not going to kill him," Esquipula con-tradicted. "They wouldn't do that. He's one of *us*."

"Oh, they'll kill him, alright," Fructosa declared. "Zopi Devine, they say he's gonna pay them to kill him. You'll see. You'll see what happens," she threat-ened darkly, suddenly commencing to canvass again.

"Don't listen to her, they're not going to kill him," Esquipula repeated apologetically. "But it's not a happy state of affairs no matter what happens. There's going to be a lot of trouble."

"All I hope and pray for," Fructosa groaned, "is that you stay out of it whatever happens."

"There's going to be a war—?" Snuffy asked incredulously.

"A war? What is a war?" Fructosa complained. "Everyday life here is a war. Survival is a war. Look at us. Look what we are doing now for a living. Now that you're back, what will you do for a living? God forbid it should be to carve more Smokey the Bears."

"I'm gonna carve santos and sell them to the tourists up in the canyon," Snuffy laughed. "That's my suitcase over there, and it's full of beautiful carvings."

"You have no shame," Fructosa moaned.

"The queen of the beer cans tells the santo carver he has no shame?" Snuffy hooted, pitching over to the suitcase. "Wait till you see *this*!" Deftly he snapped open the blade on his pocket knife, cut the cords holding the suitcase together, and the two halves fell open. There were half a dozen newspaper-wrapped bundles inside. Snuffy unwrapped one, holding in his hand an awkward wooden carving of a hollow-eyed and gaunt virgin squeezing a bellowing fat kid against her breasts.

"Ai, Chihuahua!" Fructosa sneered disdainfully. "That's too ugly. What's it supposed to mean? If it's a santo it's unreligious."

Esquipula squinted his eyes, cocked his head, wrinkled his upper lip: "That's crazy," he muttered at length. "Who'll buy something crazy like that? It's not nice at all. What happened to you down in the capital?"

"Okay," Snuffy said. "I guess I'll go back to Smokey the Bears."

"Oh God," Fructosa wailed, rolling her eyes. "Things aren't bad enough, yourself arrived to make them worse!"

Amarante Córdova lurched into view, staggering—it appeared—from the weight of his archaic six-gun. Ignoring everybody, he loped through the scene without so much as an hola, veered into the bar door, banged it open, and plunged inside.

Snuffy rewrapped his carving and closed the suitcase. "Amarante Córdova is still alive," he murmured incredulously. And then he shouted joyously: *"Amarante Córdova is still alive!"*

"God works in strange ways," Fructosa whined unhappily. "My brother Donald, he was a good worker, he never drank, he took care of his family, he never stayed out at night, he never had a car accident or an operation, not even for his tonsils, but he caught a chicken bone in his throat last New Year's Eve and choked to death. But *that* old brujo is still around, drunk morning, noon, and night, winter, summer, spring, and fall, scaring all the kids with his toothless mouth. I don't understand it, that's all."

The Gurulés regrouped at their truck, swinging sacks over the tailgate, the kids scrambled into the back, and Esquipula and sulky Fructosa, bidding Snuffy a forlorn adios, hoisted themselves wearily into the cab. As the truck chugged toward the highway, Amarante Córdova emerged from the Frontier Bar hugging a six-pack to his chest.

"Hey, cuate, where you headed with that beer?" Snuffy called. "You gonna drink all that beer yourself?"

Pretending not to hear, Amarante hurried as fast as his bowed and decrepit legs would carry him toward home, scattering a slew of yellow and red grasshoppers in his wake.

"Hey, Mr. Amarante, *sir!*" Snuffy cried, but the old geezer refused to be deterred.

Snuffy went through a few complicated contortions to regain his feet, wavered unsteadily for a moment, then wove back into the store to sign up for another six-pack of tallboys, some Slim Jim sausages, and a package of roasted piñon nuts. Outside again, he spent a bungling five minutes sloppily tying the cords holding his suitcase together, and, when that was more or less accomplished, he hoisted the suitcase with a grunt and began walking west.

A few minutes later Snuffy stood on the ditch bank overlooking Joe Mondragón's beanfield.

"What do you know," he laughed, fanning his

sweaty face with his grubby hat. "Would you look at that, my friends!"

Squatting, he lit a cigarette, and for about five minutes did not take his eyes off the field. It was quiet here, the sun had grown sultry, and although magpies were gathered in the cottonwoods by Indian Creek, they made no noise now. To the south, a red-tailed hawk circled—suddenly it dove toward a prairie dog settlement, but came up empty-handed. The mountains, those immediately to the east and the far humps and flat mesas in the south, were not etched as sharply as Snuffy remembered: a low-lying, parchment-colored haze almost obscured them in some places; elsewhere a milkiness made their outlines vague. The view extended for perhaps fifty miles, but people said you would never again be able to see for a hundred miles. Most of the crap in the air, experts said, came from new coal-fired power plants a hundred and fifty miles west of Milagro. Someday, these same environmental pontificators who knew about such things were saying, the deserted mesaland and the small green villages like Milagro would lie under polluting clouds as thick as those now found in Los Angeles and New York City.

Snuffy didn't know pollution from a duckbilled platypus. So he stood up, unbuttoned his pants, and, letting his eyes riffle almost sensually across the green mountain slopes above town, he pissed into Joe's field. Tomorrow, Snuffy thought, or the next day, or whenever the chotas and the trigger-happy posse got out of there, he would head into the hills for a spell with his sleeping bag, a lid of Mary Jane, some fishline, and a dozen artificial flies. Years ago he had been a mountain boy like most other kids from Milagro, passing time up there with sheep and goats, spending summers in a tent looking after cattle or taking care of his uncle's scare gun, lying under the stars with the gun booming and the animals making their comfortable and stupid summer noises—

All at once Snuffy experienced almost crippling waves of sadness and remorse. He patted his slight paunch; he flexed his trembling, nicotine-stained hands. But damned if he was the sort of person who wallowed for very long in past glories or failures; Snuffy just couldn't get steamed up about lost opportunities, or about his present and its infinite insecurity. In fact, he didn't give much of a shit about the future either. Who cared about the opportunities he would never have? Life was life, and one day followed another, and Snuffy took those days one at a time.

With a last affectionate glance at the beanfield, the santo carver pushed on, walking, sometimes stumbling, erratically along the dusty road, leaving rattled grass-hoppers and nervous little butterflies in his wake. He advanced past Amarante Córdova's decaying house to another crumbling building which had once belonged to the Ledouxs, most of whom were presently em-ployed in the steel mills of Pueblo, Colorado.

The roof had caved in since the day Tommy Bas-comb drove off with a hundred and ten Smokey statu-ettes; the windows were broken; the rooms were full of tumbleweeds; the outhouse had fallen apart; the well housing was menacingly aslant—so what else was new? A few outbuildings, a toolshed, a little barn had all sagged into piles of faded slabs and rusty nails. A cultivator, a striped tractor, a horsetrailer with no side panels and no tires, and other inoperative farm ma-chinery lay about. Old as the hills, Snuffy chuckled, and twice as worn out.

Depositing his suitcase in the kitchen beside a door-less icebox, he walked out back past the dead ma-chinery and into the fields where you could still see traces of old ditches that used to carry water, veins and arteries of the land's life. He crossed one field, then another, climbing through barbed wire fences, his beer and Slim Jims in a bag cradled carefully in one arm, and, traversing a mile of fallow, though once irrigated, earth, he reached the sage.

Contentedly, almost joyously, Snuffy entered the waist-high sage, proceeding for another mile due west toward the gorge. In a likely spot in the middle of nowhere, with nothing but pungent lavender all around, he sat down and popped open a beer. Another mile west some buzzards circled over the gorge. A raven

lumbered by. Then Snuffy was immersed in a downright religious, windless silence. He hadn't been so
happy or so sad for almost a decade. The quiet was
brilliant, stunning, miraculous. Snuffy drank a beer
and rolled a joint and smoked the joint and drank
another beer. He glowed, and the mesa hardly breathed
—the day was suspended, as still as a frightened rabbit. A blue-tailed lizard skittered near his feet. And
ants crawled around; they had built high sandy mountains everywhere in the sage.

After a peaceful sojourn Snuffy stood up and advanced farther, working his way slowly westward until
eventually he arrived at the gorge rim. Eight hundred
feet below ran the green river that extended all the
way from the Colorado mountains to the Gulf of
Mexico. Snuffy hurled a beer can into space, fascinated by its trajectory. Swallows darted on and
off the cliffsides far below, their burnished green
backs and white tailspots flashing. Pushing about a
hundred yards north, Snuffy discovered the trail into
the gorge he had known would be there, a narrow
descent to the river bank where two small hot springs
were located.

At times, descending it, it appeared Snuffy would slip
and fall, sailing out between silent echoing walls,
floating like a romantic, suicidal dreamer toward the
green ribbon far below. But he never completely lost
his balance, not even a decade had taken that away,
and in fifteen minutes he arrived at the Rio Grande.

A rattlesnake buzzed; Snuffy picked up a stick and
lazily beat it into a pulp.

One hot pool, surrounded by large boulders, was
about thirty yards from the river's edge, a shallow
puddle twenty feet wide. The other pool, not much
larger than a bathtub, had formed right at the bank of,
and on a level with, the river. You could bask there in
tingly bubbles, your nose on a level with the icy river
and only inches away from its swift currents that pulsed
just beyond a thin wall of lavic rocks.

Striping naked, Snuffy settled with a tallboy and a
joint in the bathtub-sized pool, his head resting against
a smoothly sculpted rock, the chilly Rio Grande rolling

by inches from his pigeon-toes. And, sipping on the beer, he remembered romantic days of yore when they'd had parties down here, the youth of Milagro, skinny dipping together and hustling nookie in the bushes, daring each other to leap into the nighttime river and swim through the ugly, murderous trolls and other aquatic banshees lurking within the strong black currents.

One day long ago Snuffy was fishing toward the hot springs from downriver when he heard voices at the bigger pool. Joe Mondragón was in there, grappling with a lovely girl named Nancy Quintana. Snuffy crept quietly into some bushes and saw that they were naked in the big shallow pool, Joe passionately munching on Nancy's plump flesh; chill autumn winds whistled down the river. And then, while Snuffy looked on, Joe and Nancy made love in that sandy bowl, their bodies steaming in the frosty dusk, their teeth chattering despite the heated water bubbling against their young bodies . . . and it started to snow. But the lovemaking continued until both were exhausted, then they lay on their backs in the pool, everything but their heads and Joe's persistent hard-on immersed in the warm water, watching the snow drift earthward out of the darkening October sky.

It was among the most beautiful sights Snuffy had ever seen. And right now remembering it made him cry, not because he felt sad, but because he was so delighted to be home again at last.

ఌ

Mist lay low in the trees, but he figured the sun would soon burn it off. In the meantime the helicopter was useless, and so Mel Willard was holding off until later. The helicopter pilot did not know the area well, but he'd flown over it a few times before in light planes out of the Chamisaville airport, and the deputy sheriff with him, Meliton Naranjo, knew the area as well as anyone, having been born and brought up in Milagro. So the helicopter might be some use, Kyril Montana was thinking, as he climbed slowly through the trees. But only if Joe Mondragón had gone up toward more open country, which was hard to believe. Rather, the agent speculated that his man had probably stayed around the lower, heavily wooded canyons where his truck had been found last night and where you'd practically have to trip over him to find him. Stayed there, or doubled back to or toward the town. Possibly he was already hanging out in somebody's home, although they knew for sure it wasn't the home of either his wife or his lawyer. It was a cinch he hadn't gone far, up, down, or sideways, because it would have been impossible to advance through the dark pines at night. Hence, if Joe Mondragón was heading for the high country, he hadn't had but a half-hour start on them, and they could make that up quickly.

At the edge of a small moss-lined streamlet he paused, listening. Other men on either side, mostly out of sight but within easy hearing, moved noisily through the trees, calling out to each other, mostly in Spanish. They were laughing, lighthearted, excited. Several had walkie-talkies, as did the agent. He also had a radio for communicating with the state team back in Milagro or down at Doña Luz, and with the helicopter once it was up and flying.

Kyril Montana did not like working with other men. He mistrusted most men and he believed (and had often had his beliefs confirmed) that very few were as dedicated as himself to whatever job was at hand. Most men, including (and maybe especially) policemen, were erratic, sometimes good at what they did, often bad, always unpredictable. When you were teamed up with them it meant you were in part responsible for, or at least affected by, their mistakes. And the agent could not stand to have something he was doing get derailed by someone with whom he'd been forced to work. There had been nobody, down through his years as a policeman, that the agent had ever trusted entirely. And today he felt especially uncomfortable in these woods with a bunch of northern Chicanos speaking a language he did not understand, hunting down a man who had a gun and just might use it, in a situation that could become extremely volatile if only one little thing went wrong.

And so as he climbed quietly up the steep, wooded hillsides expertly canvassing the forest in front of him and to all sides, Kyril Montana wished that he were somewhere alone in this vast and peaceful wilderness, searching for Joe Mondragón. For alone, he felt—one on one the *way all good hunting should be—his chances of coming upon the quarry would have been infinitely improved. These noisy, slaphappy, and, no doubt, trigger-happy people were probably either in cahoots with Joe Mondragón anyway, or else by their blundering, foolhardy attitude they'd telegraph all their movements to him well in advance, entirely blowing the search.

Dark indigo steller's jays flickered briefly out of black shadows, disappearing into the mist. There followed silence for a few yards, then shouts off to the left, laughter on his right. A man wearing a cowboy hat and a sheepskin jacket plunged into sight a short way ahead and waved, then veered out of sight again speaking rapid-fire Spanish into his walkie-talkie. The agent wondered if he was drunk.

It was slow, frustrating going. Proceeding cautiously, Kyril Montana advanced through underbrush and dead leaves, automatically avoiding twigs and small branches that cracked underfoot. But sometimes off to either side the dry limbs breaking sounded like gunshots, causing him to cringe and swear softly to himself. It occurred to him that the operation was hopeless, that Trucho had set it up all wrong, but there was nothing he could do about it. Barring a miracle, they'd be like this today, and maybe tomorrow, and then it would be called off. And *then* perhaps Kyril Montana could take over and do it his way, the quiet way, stalking Joe Mondragón one on one the way he should be stalked, or maybe just waiting for him like a man waits for a deer, on the crest of a hill overlooking a trail, or else back in town, waiting patiently for him to blow his cover. That's the way Kyril Montana would have done it, and if he had needed help it would only have been to station a man on Mondragón's house, on the lawyer's perhaps—though he was beginning to feel the lawyer didn't know diddlysquat—and on that beanfield.

Which somebody, not Joe Mondragón, had irrigated last night, and which someone (or two or three—how many?) would be irrigating indefinitely unless this thing were quickly resolved.

Kyril Montana was uneasy. He had long since admitted to himself that although he understood the generalities of this case, and although he was more than passing familiar with the north and the northern people, there was much to this particular situation he did not understand, or at least that he did not really know how to deal with. It had seemed to him back in the beginning, back during that first conference with the governor and Bookman and Noyes, that probably the most logical way to handle the situation was the legal way: take Joe Mondragón to court, find against him, make him stop irrigating, or—if he refused to quit—throw him in jail and be prepared to take the consequences. It had been obvious, however, that none of the men present in that room, men intimately concerned with land and water squabbles these past fifteen or twenty years (and familiar, also, with Ladd Devine's Miracle Valley project), had favored that solution. If Joe Mondragón were to be prosecuted, it had to be for something not directly connected to the symbolic use of irrigation water in that particular field, and the agent had seen the logic in that, because the last thing you wanted to do in this type of situation was hand the people a martyr on a silver platter. The only problem being, of course, that whenever you ran an operation that was not aboveboard there was a certain risk of it backfiring into a worse situation than it had been before. But right now, theoretically, they had Joe Mondragón more or less where they wanted him. Of course, according to the two witnesses, Joe had fired at Pacheco in self-defense; hence there was no way to bring a serious charge against him unless the witnesses were coerced into changing their testimony, which probably wouldn't be a difficult thing to accomplish, if necessary. Essentially, though, Joe was in the clear. Legally, right now, there was no way to hang him, although prior to a trial or a hearing he could probably be kept under wraps. Whether this would be a wise move or not, especially if others in Milagro were willing to irrigate that beanfield, was another question. The fact of the matter was, if you thoroughly reviewed all the alternatives, there really was no solution to the problem, no way to play it safe or to take chances yet be assured of success.

Then Kyril Montana started thinking another way. If Joe Mondragón failed to walk out of the Midnight Mountains alive, the whole thing might be over. Say if Joe took a potshot at one of his own trigger-happy compatriots and they blew him ass-backward down the canyon into eternity, scream as the liberals and the Charley Blooms might, they wouldn't have a leg to stand on. Too, death was a lesson these poor people would understand: when the killing started, and maybe *only* if the killing started, the irrigation of that field would abruptly end.

Still, this question remained: Could they—could his side, the police side—weather the storm that might result if Joe Mondragón were killed? In what ways would the Milagro people, downstate militant Chicano groups, or even out-of-state political groups pick up on his death? Suppose that lawyer Bloom latched onto and publicized Kyril Montana's previous trip to Milagro; suppose a leak developed in the capital—

The helicopter was up and about, approaching from the west. The mist was dissipating quickly, allowing the sun—in streaks and dazzling, abrupt splashes—to shine through. The agent made contact with Mel Willard, told him where they were, and went over the bubble copter's suggested search area. Basically, the copter was useless over these deep woods. So Willard had orders to fly up Deerhair Canyon toward the wide open meadows and rocky, treeless slopes around the Little Baldy Bear Lakes. Hence, in a very short time they'd have a pretty complete aerial report on what amounted to about a three-square-mile area.

Kyril Montana, a patient, methodical, unemotional man, searched through the luminous morning for Joe Mondragón. Although occasionally aware of, and slightly disturbed by, the action around him, the boisterous excitement and stupid techniques (or lack of techniques) of inexperienced men on a hunt, the agent was for the most part tuned in to only his own well-trained and modulated senses. He made doubly sure that nothing receded behind him without his inspection; he kept his eyes weaving through upper branches, determined not to miss a trick. When tiny ground squirrels popped up in front and zipped through the brush, he didn't flinch, nor did he ever raise his gun as if to shoot the tiny animals. When Bernabé Montoya's doleful voice crackled over the walkie-talkie, the agent replied succinctly, thoroughly, and then absorbed the information, or rather, lack of information, from the sheriff with equal automatic aplomb. And although he did not for a minute believe this herd of thundering clowns was going to flush Joe Mondragón, he never let that belief disturb his concentration on the job at hand.

By eight o'clock they had completed the first of the five circles that would eventually take them up Deerhair Canyon to the lowest Little Baldy Bear. The mist had lifted, disappeared. They had risen some four hundred feet and were now into tighter aspen stands, well above all piñon trees. From small clearings, now, they could see in the distance the rocky peaks rising above the Little Baldy Bear Lakes; some saddles between peaks still carried slim patches of snow. The sky was an ultrabright blue, but everyone in the posse knew that around noon clouds would begin to gather, and by three o'clock it would probably begin to rain, hail, or perhaps (who could ever tell?) it might even snow.

Together for a moment, they rested. Kyril Montana spread out a map; some of the men gathered around. He pointed to where they were, to where they would be going this next circle. While he talked they could hear the helicopter a mile or so above, flying low, sidedrifting suddenly into open places, Meliton Naranjo beside the pilot quickly sweeping the tree lines with binoculars, hoping to catch sight of a sudden evasive movement.

Bernabé Montoya sat with his back against a tree, smoking a cigarette and trying to look stern and dedicated, although his wishy-washy mind was boggled by this useless amateur bush-beating.

"I think if we catch him in an operation like this," the sheriff finally said guardedly, "it will only be because he wants to get caught."

Kyril Montana asked, "How would you do it?"

Bernabé shrugged self-effacingly. "Oh, I dunno really. I guess I wouldn't be in no hurry, though. Probably I'd wait."

"Where?"

"I'd go home and wait," the sheriff said. "Sooner or later he's got to come home for a meal or a piece of ass, qué no? He'll get tired of the mountains. It's boring in the mountains. José isn't exactly a Boy Scout."

"How long before he might come down out of here?" the agent asked.

"Oh two, maybe three days."

"That's all?"

A young man who'd been listening chortled, "Shit, man, it gets *cold* in these mountains at night."

"What's he gonna eat up here?" Bernabé asked. "Berries? Trout? He don't have no fishline."

"Yeah. And you shoot these truchas with a .30-06, you got no fish," the young man laughed.

"He isn't gonna kill a deer either," Bernabé added. "Or roast a bird. Hell, he's probably got a freezer full of beef from that feedlot in Colorado. He's got a wife that makes tortillas, enchiladas. José is probably so fucking hungry right now——"

"He's probably back there with Nancy right now, stuffing himself with beans," the young man griped good-naturedly, "while we're chasing his ass to hell and gone up in these hills."

Kyril Montana looked around at the men taking five. They were dressed in a ragtag assortment of dungaree jackets and old army coats; some wore straw cowboy hats; most wore Levi's and boots, all carried their own personal deer rifles, .30-06s and .270s and .30-30s, and a few carried pistols in hip holsters. Half to three-quarters of them were smoking hand-rolled cigarettes. Mostly, too, these were middle-aged to old people, with grizzled faces, many teeth missing, and sly—occasionally almost giggling—smiles.

"If everybody is so sure we're not going to flush Joe Mondragón, what are we all doing up here?" Kyril Montana asked.

Bernabé shrugged. "It's what you people want, ain't it?"

"You're the sheriff," Kyril Montana said. "What do you want?"

"I dunno. A man got shot, of course. A man should be brought to justice, I guess," Bernabé said. "At best, we got to keep up some appearances, qué no?"

Whereupon Kyril Montana experienced a rare sensation. These men were all Chicanos, and he was a white man, the person theoretically in charge of this search. That's all, it was nothing more than that, but it gave him a start all the same, made him uncomfortable for a minute. Only rarely, in fact maybe never, had he really *felt* that these kinds of people, that these Chicanos, belonged to a race not his own. Most of his partners, his immediate superiors and inferiors down in the capital, were Chicanos, and this had never bothered him. But up there, high in the wilderness behind Milagro with this lax, motley crew, he experienced a momentary and an almost terrifying race-consciousness, and felt like a foreigner, a real stranger and intruder in their territory.

The agent stood up to show that the break was over. Obediently, the men all stood with him, flicking cigarette butts into the damp brush and they spread out to start beating the bushes again.

∽

"I'm going over to see Nancy," Bloom said to his wife, "Maybe you better come along."

"I don't want to. But you go."

"She's your friend."

"They're *your* clients."

"Well, God damn . . ."

Bloom stopped himself from slamming the door,

closed it gently, crossed his front yard. He could smell fresh-cut hay and alfalfa; their immediate next door neighbor, Eusebio Lavadie, was on a tractor nearby starting his second cutting. Bloom waved at the man, whom he disliked intensely, and Lavadie waved back, grinning broadly. The pastoral valley calm, that bastard Lavadie serenely cutting hay while Joe Mondragón fled for his life, struck the lawyer like a brutally unfair blow.

He bent expertly between barbed wire strands and crossed a wide, soggy, overgrazed field, part of which was honeycombed with treacherous hummocks and leached-out grass clumps. Several massive, shaggy work horses stood up to their knees in muck among dense cattail stands in which hundreds of noisy redwing blackbirds cavorted. Killdeer, dragging false broken wings, ran screeching ahead of him on the shaved ground. In the next field grasshoppers burst up from under his feet like the shrapnel from land mines, and with a swipe of his hand Bloom caught one in midair.

And stopped.

Oh brother, he thought miserably. Turning slightly in wonderful, thick grass almost as high as his waist, he confronted the mountains, pale green on their lower slopes where the piñon and juniper were, dark, rich green higher up where the ponderosa began, interspersed with lovely summer-green aspen, and then higher up bald and rocky gray, patched with snow. Today, last night's tomorrow, was not better as he'd promised Linda it would be, but rather a little worse.

He felt very bad. He was thirty-seven years old and it was all going to fall apart again. He would never know security or flow peacefully and rapturously into his wife or any other woman when he made love. His eldest daughter, Miranda, no longer wrote him the happy illustrated letters she'd regularly sent his way throughout her earlier girlhood. They hadn't met in eight years; no longer could he bear the thought of their reunion, but he loved her desperately, and loved her mother too, even yet, yearning for a final session in her bed before he died, knowing he would probably

murder her if she ever granted him a last shot like
that.

Bloom felt sorry for himself. He was supposed to
be a professional, in control. Instead he was a child,
perpetually on the verge of a breakdown. It was insane, pathetic, almost criminal for a man pushing
forty to feel so inept, so ashamed of his body, his
heart, his work ethics, his Tinkertoy soul. He wanted
to drive the car a hundred miles to someplace where
he was not known, shack up with a sexy lady and a
lot of booze, and end it that way—with a bang (he
chuckled miserably) instead of all these sackfuls of
whimpers he carried around night and day.

He wanted to lie down in this redolent field, curl
up in the green womb in the dazzling aura of these
mountains, growing warm and drowsy under the sun,
abdicating all responsibilities—and sleep. Instead he
had to push on, face Nancy, console her, advise her,
be strong.

Dogs, all happy, bent-legged cripples, barked and
danced ferociously as he entered the yard: Nancy
opened the door before he knocked.

"Hi, Charley," she said cheerfully, backing up as
he scraped mud off his feet on an iron half-moon
sunk into the earth beside the door and entered the
warm kitchen. "How you doing this morning?"

"Oh, so so, I guess, thanks. I don't suppose Joe is
around, that I might talk to him?"

"He's up in the mountains."

"Yeah, I know, I heard all about that. I've got a
tendency not to believe all I hear around here,
though," Bloom said with what he hoped was a wry,
at-ease smile.

Halfway to the living room he suddenly stopped.
Ten old men, all wearing cowboy hats and faded
jeans and work boots or western-style boots, each
with a rifle held butt against the floor between his
knees, were sitting around watching a giveaway program on TV. Nearby, the three Mondragón kids were
stretched out on the threadbare carpet, intent on the
tube.

Bloom nodded, "Hello, Sparky; hi, Panky; how

are you, Onofre?" and the men nodded, mumbling hello back.

"What'll it be, Charley? Tea or coffee? Or would you like a beer?"

"Oh, nothing, nothing, Nancy, thanks. Can't stay too long, really. Just wanted to come over and see if there's any way I could get in touch with Joe."

"Not so far as I know. He ran into those mountains like a beep-beep last night."

"Like a what?"

"Like that roadrunner in the cartoons. Beep-beep." She smiled. "The one Wiley Coyote is always chasing, but never catching. Don't you watch TV, Charley?" The silent men in her living room didn't smile, but they looked amused.

"I guess not that much." Bloom laughed awkwardly. The guns, the quietude, the serenity of those old geezers, and the idiotic TV program, the enthralled children without a care in the world—it had upset him, he couldn't get his bearings straight. "But as Joe's lawyer," he said, "I wanted to get word to him."

"You could tell me. Then I could send him a telegram or something like that."

"Or 'something like that'?"

She nodded brightly. Several men chuckled audibly.

Bloom waved a hand carelessly, trying to seem nonchalant. "What have you got going here in this living room of yours, a reunion of the 101st Cavalry Unit of the Grenadine Fusiliers?"

"José just thought me and the kids should be protected in case anything funny developed." She smiled again, a pretty little butterfly burst of sunshine.

"This isn't funny, Nancy. There's thirty or forty heavily armed men up in the forest looking for Joe. Half those men, I'd bet, if they see him, they'll shoot him. Whether he's got a gun, whether he shoots at them first or not, they'll kill him on sight, claim it was self-defense, and get away with it because everybody knows about Joe's temper—"

Nancy sat on a couch beside a hunched, watery-eyed old man named Tranky Apodaca, the uncle of Betty who worked in the Pilar.

"The thing is," she said, flippantly lighting a ciga-rette, "they aren't going to find José. You can be assured of that."

"He can't hide out forever."

"You wanna bet?" This time Nancy's smile had no fun in it; it was hard, sailing frostily across the room. "If he doesn't want to be caught there's nobody gonna catch him. We've lived here all our lives."

"The longer he's gone, I think the worse it's going to be. Maybe you're right, maybe you're not. Just remember, there's others who've lived here all their lives looking for Joe. In another ten hours, somebody like Ladd Devine—is going to make an offer of one thousand dollars, or maybe more, for information leading to Joe's arrest. With that kind of price on his head you know there's going to be people digging up prairie dog holes and uncovering fresh graves in the camposanto looking for Joe. And those people, they know Joe won't be taken peacefully, so if they get a lead he's in this outbuilding or that shack, they're liable to shoot up the building backwards and for-wards before they even knock on the door or give him a chance to walk out peacefully."

"So what happens if he turns himself in?" Nancy asked angrily. "The chotas will kill him."

"They won't be able to if he's with me."

"Excuse me for laughing, but that's bullshit. The cops would spit in your face."

"I'm his lawyer. I'm trying to help you both. Le-gally, so far, he's got all the grounds in the world to stand on. There's no doubt it was self-defense. But the longer he stays out, the more everybody gets on edge, the more likely we are to have a tragedy in this town."

"The Zopilote already has a price on José's head."

"He's got no such thing. But he's as scared as both of you. He can't be expected to act rationally much longer either. This has been building for a long time. Everybody is just too damn uptight."

"Who said *we* were scared?" she shot back at him with a clipped little sneer.

"Nancy, what do you want me to do, get down on

my knees and beg? I've been your lawyer. I think I know how to handle this case. I'm afraid of the violence that might develop. I don't want Joe or anybody else to get killed. Everybody, at this point, is afraid. Even Ladd Devine is probably looking for an honorable out. But if he or Joe, or I don't know who —the state cops, Bernie Montoya—if among them one or two people get pushed to the brink, or their nerves crack, well shit, we'll pass a point of no return."

"Charley, this isn't putting you down, but for many years everybody around has been letting things get settled by the Mr. Devines and Jimmy Hirsshorns and Bill Koontzes and Bruno Martínezes, people like that. On their terms. Maybe now it's time to decide something for ourselves. On our terms. And in our own sweet time."

"This could be suicide," Bloom said.

"To fight for what you believe in isn't suicide," Nancy said.

"Oh cut out that stupid patriotic bull." Bloom felt like crying. It was hopeless. These people were bound and determined to slit their own throats.

Everybody stayed silent, all staring at the flickering screen.

"How do you know so much about everything anyway?" Nancy finally asked.

"Oh hell, I don't. You should know that. Mostly I'm just guessing. Look, so far a kind of miracle has happened. Namely, nobody is dead. Pacheco will probably survive; a couple dozen trout were beheaded; a sign was burned—"

Nancy stood up. "Come here, Charley." She opened the kitchen door. "I want to show you something." When Bloom was beside her, she pointed to the town's water tank on Capulin Hill. A Dancing Trout pickup and a Forest Service truck were parked under the tank, cigarette smoke drifting out the driver's window of the dude ranch vehicle.

"That's Horsethief Shorty up there, and both Carl Abeyta and the new guy, Floyd what's-his-name. They've got a radio, telescopes, binoculars, everything. They're just sitting up there waiting for José to show himself in case he doubles back into town, then they're going to radio the chotas and the chotas are going to come in and kill him. They've got two cars on the highway, and there's a bunch of them drinking champagne and telling jokes up at the Dancing Trucha, and another bunch of them at the Doña Luz pendejo factory. There's some in the Floresta too, looking for José. And you want me to tell José to just walk out into the open and say 'Here I am everybody, kill me?' You're asking me to do that?"

"If I'm with him nobody would dare try anything," Bloom said.

"You think so?" Nancy picked up a stone, throwing it at a magpie on a nearby fence post. "I've heard a lot of things lately, Charley, maybe I better tell you where it's at with you in their eyes. A man up from the capital not too long ago, an undercover police agent, he talked with some of our citizens here. And he talked about your first wife, you know? And about your divorce, and about what they said you did to your daughter back East. He said it was your fault that José was irrigating his father's beanfield. He said it was a plot. He told these citizens you were a radical because you defended César Pacheco—"

Bloom sagged back into the kitchen and leaned against a counter. "An undercover cop—?" Was it the FBI? How come he hadn't heard?

"I don't know what they know, or what's real and what isn't," Nancy said. "I don't care either. I wouldn't believe anything those creeps said in the first place. And I pretty much trust you. But that's what this undercover man said, and he's the one who went into the mountains with the posse today. So it's not just José, Charley. It's not just him at all."

Bloom actually felt faint. Turning, he poured a glass of water from the kitchen spigot, drank it slowly. Then, lowering onto a stool, he stared at the giveaway program without hearing or seeing it, without thinking, either. He was aware of his face being hot. And of a queasy sensation in his stomach. His ears, too, burned. His legs were weak. He sat there among the old men and the three kids and Nancy, more terrified than he'd ever been in his life, more terrified, even, than he'd been toward the end of his divorce when the whole thing had gotten so ugly that he had wanted to murder his wife.

Nancy settled nearby with coffee, sipping quietly from the cup, her alert eyes fixed on the tube.

"So we're waiting," Nancy said without taking her eyes off the program. "We're waiting for them to make their moves and for them to finish making their moves and for them to go away. If we have to wait a year for them to leave, we'll wait a year. Who's in a hurry? Not us."

She seemed astonishingly brave and strong. Bloom stood up. "I'm going home," he said. "If you change your mind about Joe going in with me, give me a call."

Outside in the pastoral quiet, Bloom felt threatened, exposed; he was a target. Up there they had glasses trained on him, on this house, probably on his house too. They had rifles with telescopic sights that could easily kill him from that distance—and he had nothing. He was a plump, not even middle-aged, man with a wide ass who'd never really wanted to become involved. He was a fainthearted, well-educated eastern white person you could push over with a semistiff turkey feather, a terrified human being who had always wanted to be decent, but had never been willing or able to pay the price. And now, in a town where he'd sought to get away from it all, he had somehow backed into a showdown. They'd have him disbarred; Bud Gleason would no doubt see that Hirsshorn foreclosed on his house. . . .

Bloom stood quietly in the warm summer sunshine, absorbed by the two trucks parked beneath the water tank. A man—not Horsethief Shorty—got out of one truck, circled behind it, took a leak.

In a trance, Bloom bent between barbed wire strands into the first field. He had always admired Horsethief Shorty from a distance. The man had character and spunk and Bloom had considered him an attractive original, had always known he was the real McCoy.

He had heard a hundred stories about Shorty's feats, always told with admiration, much laughter, occasionally envy. No one, so far as Bloom could ascertain, bore a grudge against Shorty. Men and women who disliked Ladd Devine, who had nothing but scorn and ridicule for Flossie and Jerry Grindstaff and Emerson Lapp, liked Shorty, maybe even loved him: his boisterous wild-card personality had carved for him a niche of welcome, or at least of respect, on both sides. Shorty had the stories, the personality, the deadeye with a rifle in deer season. Shorty spoke Spanish and understood the ways of white people and brown people and Indians. Shorty could mend anything, lay pipes, design houses, make adobes, read and write, talk crops and politics, and he'd parlayed his talents, some people felt, into a big piece of the Devine empire, but they didn't begrudge him what he had gotten, because he'd fought like a son of a bitch to get there; he hadn't been born into it; he had made it the hard way, and he'd never truly left the people.

But he was up there right now, with his glasses trained on the valley, on the town, a radio by his side, searching for Joe Mondragón.

Suddenly, Bloom was enraged. Raising one arm he carefully formed an exaggerated obscene gesture, aiming it emphatically at the pickups. For a long time nothing happened, they didn't notice, they had not been watching. Bluebirds flew low across the field, butterflies drifted, oily blue smoke coughed out of Eusebio Lavadie's tractor as he mowed his fields, and several cats, one of them pure white, trotted into the cut part to catch distraught field mice, to eat their babies in butchered nests.

Then Bloom saw it, caught the motion, a hand out the Dancing Trout pickup window, Horsethief Shorty's hand, up in a gesture, not obscene, but friendly—he waved.

"Fuck you," Bloom whispered, dropping his arm. And he headed for home where his wife's haunted eyes awaited, where his children's bright smiles would flutter through the sunny rooms like all these pretty summer butterflies.

 At about noon that day a backhoe driven by Jerry Grindstaff emerged from the Dancing Trout's white gravel drive, turned right, and descended the bumpy road past thick pastures in which Morgan horses grazed, and past tennis courts where Bostonians and Dallasites, clad in snowy white, exercised. Then it chugged slowly past orchards that eventually gave way to the valley's overgrazed fields, which were pocked with animal shit and smelled strongly of ammonia, and the backhoe continued on through the tightly clustered houses at the heart of town, past Rael's, the Frontier, the Forest Service headquarters, and the Pilar, and across the highway onto the Milagro–García spur. Jerry G. braked at Joe Mondragón's beanfield and, as he surveyed the scene, motor idling, he lit a cigarette.

 There was nobody around. Jerry G. had come on orders from the boss, who felt that policies so far had only led to more trouble than might have occurred had the beanfield been leveled long ago, Joe Mondragón arrested, and the matter fought out then and there, perhaps savagely—but at least it would have ended quickly, and by now would have been all but forgotten. As it was, things had gone much too far. A hands-off policy had backfired, the insurgents had gathered strength. And so, with Joe on the run and half the town chasing him, and with the rest of the town hiding behind barricades (and having consulted neither the state engineer nor the state police nor his own partner, Jim Hirsshorn, nor Horsethief Shorty), Ladd Devine had decided to kill the heart of the controversy, namely Joe's tiny beanfield.

 Letting his eyes laze around, Jerry G. took his time with the cigarette. Wind puffs rattled the cottonwoods, dust swirled in the road stirring grasshoppers up into their crackling, chili-red flights. A dust devil twirled eastward from the sage across the flat deserted fields, catching tumbleweeds, bouncing them along and letting them go, weaving among the crumbled houses and rusty car hulks—a truly desolate scene.

Increasingly, Joe's beanfield had made Jerry G. mad. He hadn't gone into exactly why, but the damn field threatened everything he had worked for all his life, it was holding a knife to the throat of the established order. Somehow just a few lousy green plants that wouldn't bring a plug nickel on anyone's market were a menace to Jerry G.'s future. So he sure hadn't balked (as he never balked) when Ladd Devine told him to have at it. In fact, for the first time in almost a week, he had smiled.

Flipping the cigarette, Jerry G. shifted into gear, climbed off the roadbank, chugged along the flatland beside the Roybal ditch, and hopped off the machine to open the barbed wire gate into Joe's beanfield.

But when he swung the gate open and turned around, a little old bespectacled man whom Jerry G. had seen often around town (usually drunk), but whose name escaped the foreman just now, was standing beside the backhoe's rear wheel, aiming the biggest goddam shooting iron Jerry G. had ever seen directly at his heart.

"Hey . . . what—?"

"You come a step closer," Amarante Córdova said in Spanish, "and I'll blow your head into pieces like it was a rotten pumpkin."

Now the foreman did not understand these words, but there was enough unmistakable authority in the ninety-three-year-old voice and also in the size of his Colt Peacemaker's snout to make Jerry G. freeze.

"Put the gate back up," Amarante ordered. "You put it back up right now." He gestured slightly with the gun, and Jerry G. savvied; he hopped to do as he was bid.

"Okay, go home," Amarante said. "Or I'll make a hole big enough for an owl to nest in in your chest."

The drift of this, too, Jerry G. managed to grasp perfectly. Hands awkwardly raised, he circled warily around the old man, backed up to the ditch bank, and walked sideways along the bank to the road. At the road he halted, briefly apprehensive about the backhoe, but he recommenced his hasty retreat with a jump as the old man bleated, "Get going! Beat it! Go home!" On the double, Jerry G. hightailed it for the highway.

Amarante grinned, giggled, holstered his oversized blunderbuss, and, grimacing awkwardly, trembling from the effort, clawing a bit like a man falling off a cliff, he somehow managed to haul his ancient bones up into the driver's seat of the powerful yellow machine.

In his younger days Amarante had often run a backhoe, but now he had trouble holding the clutch down long enough to push the shifting lever into gear. In the end, though, cursing his old bones and grunting like a hungry pig, he succeeded; the backhoe lurched forward, and as it did Amarante's floppy hat jolted off his head.

It was no picnic for a derelict that old to wrestle with the wheel, guiding the heavy machine, but the angels were on his side, saluting him, no doubt, with heavenly laughter as they gave strength to his feeble hands and as they gave the joyful determination of all legendary heroes from John Henry through Emiliano Zapata to his tenacious heart. Amarante cackled, hugging the wheel with all his might, aiming the backhoe westward. Fences snapped with melodious twangs as he plowed through, the strands sometimes whizzing past his ears. The machine jolted into gullies, lurched and coughed; Amarante bounced out of his seat, clinging for dear life; fence posts splintered. An adobe wall crumbled like stale cookies; the backhoe punched aside a wrecked car, then chewed mighty tracks through flat empty field after flat empty field, bursting at last through a final fence into the purple sage.

Bouncing, rocking, tipping, Amarante rode his mammoth mechanical bronco across the wide and lovely mesa—jackrabbits fled for their lives. The old man's chin hit against the wheel, the blow almost knocking him out. Yet he had determined to do this thing; his ninety-three-year-old pride would not allow him to fail. His fingers felt broken, his ribs and shoulders were certainly smashed, his head ached from the beating and from the noonday summer sun also, but he refused to die. His father's huge gun popped out of the holster, disappearing forever into the sage— Amarante did not notice. His final three teeth (though not—miraculously—his glasses) were jarred loose—he swallowed one and the other two fell to the ground . . . then he pissed in his britches. But he whooped also, croaking hoarsely, glutinous, joyful sounds, riding that bright yellow Ladd Devine backhoe westward, ever westward—

Toward the gorge.

And he could see it now, the break in the earth, faintly ahead, and then more clearly, and then he could make out a far sunny wall dropping sheerly; with the gorge in sight he stepped on the gas and all hell broke loose. What a way, he thought, his wrinkled lips flapping as he laughed and sputtered: *What a glorious way to go!*

The split in the earth widened, became immense. The ground sloped more, became smoother. Around here somewhere was a path down to the hot springs where Amarante had gone many years ago, courting, drinking, swimming, fishing sometimes, and he'd driven sheep up that path after taking them to graze on the rich bottomland beside the river. . . .

Betita's death—he suddenly remembered, then just as suddenly forgot as the backhoe glanced off a boulder, and he was thrown from the yellow machine, crashing atop a sagebush and bouncing from it into a small cholla cactus, and with that, abruptly—incredibly—the violence and the noise, the jerking and the bolting and the chugging were gone, and Amarante, on his feet for this sensational and emotional good-bye, saw the backhoe nose out into space and then keel over, diving from sight. Summoning his last reserve of strength, the old man limped to the edge in order to watch it fall.

Sideways it skidded through the air, hit an outcropping and flipped; turning several somersaults and bursting into flame, the backhoe sailed down trailing a brilliant fantail of sparks. Then, hitting a slope, it continued to roll, or rather to lope toward the river, and the fireball struck sandy earth a few yards south of the largest hot spring, where, overturning five or six times, it then leaped ten feet over Snuffy Ledoux, who was still lounging in the bathtub-sized hot spring putting the finishing touches on his last tallboy, and with a stupendous sizzle splashed into the Rio Grande, sinking instantly, leaving a fat greasy smoke ball hovering like a concerned mother over the bubbling spot where it had disappeared.

Snuffy Ledoux splashed to his feet. Screaming, *"You son of a bitch, I'll get you!"* he scrambled to his clothes, tugged them on in fifteen seconds, jammed his feet into the wrong boots, and hit the narrow path out bent on revenge.

Nobody in Milagro had ever made it up that gorge trail in even triple the time it took Snuffy Ledoux— who'd been at peace with the world for the first moment in ten years when that fireball thundered over his head—to make it. And nobody in Milagro had ever been even one-half as surprised as was Snuffy when he panted over the gorge rim to discover, not a. sly, conniving villain with handlebar moustaches and shifty eyes who'd attempted to end his life, but rather the old man, Amarante Córdova, looking like a thing that had just gone sixty-three rounds with seven bald eagles, staggering in zigzagging circles, gasping and bubbling out ding-y sounds, with nobody else around.

Snuffy hobbled over to Amarante, waved hi, and collapsed. The old man sat down. They gaped at each other, unable to talk, huffing and puffing.

It was Amarante who spoke first. "I can't walk back," he croaked. "I'll have a heart attack. I'll drop dead. I'm an old man."

Without thinking, Snuffy said, "I'll carry you on my back."

"Thanks," Amarante gasped. "You're a good boy. When did you return from the capital?"

"Just this morning. I saw you. What was that thing you tried to kill me with?"

"I wasn't trying to kill you. Nobody told me you were there."

Snuffy held his hands apart like a man describing a four-inch fish: "You missed me by that much."

"I apologize."

"What was that thing?" Snuffy insisted.

"A backhoe."

"Ai, Chihuahua!"

They sat there a while, not speaking, awaiting heart attacks. But nothing happened. The sun traveled farther westward; sage and cholla shadows shifted slightly; some ants crawled up their pant legs.

"I guess we might as well begin." Snuffy said, slowly unbending his aching limbs, arising. He pulled Amarante onto his feet, then turned around, squatting down, and hoisted the old man piggyback.

Lurching to the right, to the left, halting, leaning forward, taking a step, they began. Amarante held onto Snuffy Ledoux, smiling with a mouth that had no teeth now, and Snuffy's head began throbbing. He bit his lower lip until the blood flowed, carrying the old man a hundred yards, then halting to rest for five minutes, then starting off again.

In this way they progressed across the mesa, through the pale lavender sageland. Amarante began to sing in a high hoarse voice, a song with no notes, really, it was more of an Indian-style chant, high and sing-song wonderful, with no words anyone could understand, his radiant face tilted to the blue sky, shining like the face of a little boy or of an old old being as powerful as God, and his eyes were fixed on the permanent rainbow he could still see arching delicately over his hometown. And although blisters formed on Snuffy's feet, and although they began to bleed, he found himself marching farther between rests, the old man growing lighter with this triumphant outpouring of song; and by the time they reached the deserted west side beanfields the sun was hanging like a fiery orange in the west, and Snuffy Ledoux had also broken out into victorious song.

～§

When Herbie Goldfarb, responding to a soft knock, had opened his door late the night before and found himself staring into the broadly grinning mouth and clenched, *Viva Zapata!* teeth of Joe Mondragón, he figured his life was about to come to an abrupt and, no doubt, gory end. But Joe just kept grinning, chuckled, "Hello, Goldy, how they hanging?" and stepped over the threshold to wait out the storm.

Now, next day, after tipping up the last beer in Herbie's stack of six-packs, Joe said, "Herbert, we need some more cerveza."

"If I go for beer," Herbie protested, "they'll get suspicious."

And he could picture it already: his miserable hovel surrounded by state cops and by the National Guard, a bullhorn blaring—"We know you're in there, Joe!"—sirens wailing and red lights blipping, TV cameras whirring, and then Joe yelling back, "Come and get me, you pinche, pendejo-brained, yellow-bellied, motherfucking cabrones!" as he ripped off a shot through the high little window while Herbie cowered in a corner by the stove, and then all of them out there would open up at once, their high-powered rifle and machine gun bullets chewing the adobe walls to pieces, opening holes big enough to drive tanks through—

"Suspicious?" Joe asked incredulously. "Who, Tranky Jeantete? Shit, man, if he knew for sure I was with you he'd give us the beer free of charge!"

Herbie cringed. Then he thought: suppose I actually escape from this predicament alive (or at least only partially maimed, still breathing) and catch a plane for home. I'll still have no peace. They'll track me down, kicking open the door of my crummy railroad apartment just as me and some indescribably delectable woman are about to ball, and they'll throw me in the Tombs for a week, and if I survive it down there—if I'm not beat up or gang-raped—they'll extradite me back out here and nail me to the cross for harboring a felon, or for being an accessory to a murder, or for obstructing justice, or for conspiracy to commit a crime—

"And anyway," Joe added, "who's gonna look for me here? I mean, who even knows you exist?"

Thanks, Herbie thought grimly, I needed that.

Joe blinked away some beer fuzz that was making blue streaks across his eyeballs, and remarked, "You don't even know what all this is about, do you?"

Talking through the walnut-sized knot in his throat, Herbie croaked, "You shot a person. You killed a man . . ."

"Oh for crissakes," Joe muttered impatiently. "That old fart don't even have anything to do with it."

"With what?" Herbie asked timidly.

"Listen," Joe said. "Lemme tell you about the way things been around here. Lemme tell you about my father—"

Herbie was in no position not to listen, so he just sat there, letting Joe talk.

"Most of his life my old man was a sheepherder," Joe said. "He rented his borregas from the Zopilote, from old man Devine, he did his credit business at the Zopilote's store . . ."

Yet naturally—because of coyotes, bears, bad weather, you name it—Esequiel Mondragón had never been able to return the lambs per rented ewes the company required, and then when the capital began to enforce the termination of west side water rights, which eliminated the garden that at least fed them, he almost collapsed. He was sixty-three years old then, as Joe remembered, and dying. Joe's mother, Sylvia, had tuberculosis; suddenly she died, leaving the old man heartbroken on top of everything else. Pride made Esequiel hit the road for a while instead of taking welfare. He did seasonal work in the lettuce and potato fields up north for a few years, then he stayed home, with the family, trying to keep up the west side house. But the family soon broke up, moving to jobs in other towns and cities, to the army, and Esequiel was alone. Heavy rains washed the outside mud plaster off their house, and he was too feeble now to mix up fresh plaster. All his neighbors were leaving then, sadly

pulling up stakes, moving on. But Esequiel stayed put.
He refused to travel down to Chamisaville to fill out
the government forms for welfare, for food stamps.
The old man dry-farmed beans and some corn two
years hand running, but during those two years
the rains never came, or they came too late, and his
crops failed. Often he fished in those parts of Indian
Creek that ran near his home, but he was fined
several times for doing so without a license, and eventually gave that up.

His land was barren; the prairie dogs moved in. To
most Milagro citizens prairie dogs were anathema to
life, and they shot, killed, poisoned, drowned, blud-
geoned, hexed, cursed, and, in general, vilified the
pesky tunnel burrowers in about every way possible,
because those varmints would ruin a field before you
could say "Filiberto Mascarenas!" But Esequiel's head
had gone soft, and he let the critters into his front
field; he damn near welcomed them with open arms, in
fact. He liked to sit out front whittling on some
rough little santo, watching the prairie dogs establish
themselves.

Neighbors who had not yet gone took umbrage at
this. Soon the Milagro prairie dog war began. Cars
and trucks would stop in front of the field on the
Milagro–García spur, a rifle would poke out the window, and *blam!* there'd be one less prairie dog. The
third time this happened, the old man shot back with
his .22. After that, concerned Milagro citizens commenced picking off the varmints from a distance,
using high-powered guns and telescopic sights. Esequiel
went a little crazy. He began to sit out there all day
ànd part of the night, and finally he took a potshot at
an innocent truck that was just passing by. At which
point Bernabé Montoya drove over, arrested him,
and hauled him kicking and cursing down to the
Chamisa County Jail, where he stayed about a week
before using a stolen cell key to walk out the front
door; nobody stopped him because somehow nobody
was on duty.

"My old man died one month later in the hot sun

in the middle of a potato field outside Saguache, Colorado," Joe finished quietly.

There was silence, an almost gentle quiet in Herbie's gloomy hovel. Joe suddenly squashed his beer can and chucked it into the pile in the corner.

"So that's how come," he said morosely.

"That's how come what?" Herbie had the audacity, or the stupidity, to ask.

"That's how come all this," Joe said. "That's how come I'm sitting here drinking beer with a chickenshit, East Coast smarty-pants Jew bastard like you."

"Oh," Herbie said. Joe certainly had a way of making everything as clear as mud. As clear as *Milagro* mud, he added in afterthought, and, despite the tense situation, Herbie almost caught himself in a ridiculous smile.

∽ঽ

At 1:00 P.M. the posse reached the lowest Little Baldy Bear Lake. Gasping, thoroughly pooped, the men trudged into the half-mile-wide grassy alpine bowl with the small circular lake in the center and collapsed.

Mel Willard had set the bubble copter down midway between some trees and the lake. Meliton Naranjo was sitting in the doorway of the chopper, desultorily hunched over, smoking a cigarette; the pilot had stretched out on the grass nearby. Most of the posse's men collapsed closer to the tree line, on mossy ground, among large rocks. A few, having put down their guns and taken leaks, staggered over to the lake, where they knelt and drank. Kyril Montana propped his rifle against a tree, eased off his pack, and sat on a small boulder. He tried making a radio call to Doña Luz, but the static was so bad he couldn't understand the answer, except just barely to decipher that nobody down there had run into Joe Mondragón, so they might as well keep searching into the afternoon, weather permitting, or else go home.

There were several packs filled with sandwiches. Now an old man distributed these and some tiny boxes of raisins to everyone. Quite a few men had brought their own tortillas and cold beans, or bean dip; in the helicopter there were large thermos jugs of coffee. While they ate, the men were subdued, talking quietly, all played out.

Bernabé Montoya slipped off his gun belt and lowered himself onto a rotting log near the agent. He bit into a burrito, cold beans and green chili wrapped in a tortilla, and chewed thoughtfully for a while, gazing up at the first gray threatening afternoon clouds.

"So what do you think?" he finally asked the agent.

"I think you're right. This posse could have walked right over Joe Mondragón and never have known the difference."

"If he was there, one of these men would have spotted him," Bernabé said.

"You don't think we missed him?"

The sheriff shrugged, smiled vaguely, gestured at the nearest mountain peak with his burrito. "He could be anywhere. But he's not in shape; he didn't go even this far."

"What's on the other side of that ridge between Little Baldy Mountain and Latir Peak?" the agent asked.

"There's a trail goes down to Truchas Lake. If you follow it far enough it leads to Dixonburgh. When I was about twenty-five and he was fifteen or sixteen, me and José we used to come up here a lot on horseback. We hunted up here all year round before they made you buy a license and kill in a certain season. José's father, he had some sheep, and sometimes we were up here with those sheep, too. We moved all around these mountains with those sheep. And you know something? I haven't been up here for ten years. We even shot a wolf once . . ."

"Did you have a favorite place he might head for now?"

Bernabé smiled again. "These whole mountains, they were our favorite place. You don't know how we used to roam around here. There was a rancher, a gabacho, used to own a big place down in Dixonburgh, had a permit to run his cattle up here, and we used to shoot those cows, two or three a year, and take them home and smoke them. We did things like that which were not nice, I guess you could say, but we were pretty poor, you understand . . ."

"Do you think he might go over the ridge to Dixonburgh?"

"I dunno. I don't know his mind. We haven't been together for a long time. Him and me, we always used to hate cops. José still does."

Kyril Montana went over to the helicopter and got a paper cup of coffee for himself and one for the sheriff. When he returned, Bernabé was chuckling to himself. Accepting the coffee, he pointed to the lake:

"One time, José and me, we came up here in the springtime, you know? We had some dynamite and we set a charge off in that lake, and five minutes later there was five hundred cutthroat trout floating around on the surface. We waded out on the ledges and collected them into burlap feed sacks and packed them out on two burros we had brought along. Other times we used to come up with rods at night and build fires at the edge of these lakes, and you could catch eighty, a hundred fish in just a couple hours. We did that most often right after the Floresta stocked the lakes for the Dancing Trout tourists . . ."

Kyril Montana said, "It looks like rain."

Bernabé studied the gathering clouds for a moment. "Looks more like hail to me."

Mel Willard came over. "What's the plan?" he asked.

The agent said, "I'm going to climb Little Baldy Peak and then hike north along the ridge there, overlooking Deerhair Canyon. I'll probably go down the eastern slope of Grande Mountain up there, and circle around to where we began this morning. As far as I'm concerned the rest of you can go home; take the trail straight down the canyon. Whatever the weather, rain, hail, it's probably going to get ugly. I think Bernie here's right, I think we'll just wait for Joe Mondragón to come home. He can't last more than a couple days at most up here."

Bernabé stood, buckling on his gun belt. "Sooner or

later somebody will reach José and tell him it's not as bad as he thinks. That will bring him in. And this will all be resolved to everyone's satisfaction." He tipped his hat to Kyril Montana, then moved among the men, nodding, speaking a few words, slapping a back here, pointing to the northeast there, he rounded them up for the march home.

"What about me?" Mel Willard asked.

"Go home," Kyril Montana said, almost gently. "This is the wrong way, the absolutely wrong way to go about it."

"What about my partner, that gloomy S.O.B.?"

"Send him back with Montoya."

"Okay—great!" Mel grinned. "Think I'll lift off right now, if you don't mind, to get out of this wind tunnel before some of the shit up in those clouds hits the fan."

Kyril Montana watched the chopper start, lift jerkily off the meadowland, and rise at an awkward slant, then whizz down the canyon, almost clipping treetops.

After that he talked briefly with Bernabé and Meliton Naranjo, discussing how to brief headquarters in Doña Luz, and what kind of line to send Trucho in the capital.

"In the end," he told them, "the essential thing in this case is to keep a low profile. When you get back I want you to talk with his wife again. After that, make sure everyone in town understands that there were witnesses to the shooting who will testify it was in self-defense. I assume the grapevine will take it sooner or later to Joe Mondragón. Whatever the case, we don't want him to come home shooting. One way or the other he's got to understand he's really not in that much hot water."

"You'll excuse me, but the people in this neck of the woods are mighty suspicious about that kind of declaration," Bernabé said. "But we'll put the word out and then see what happens."

Kyril Montana and Bernabé shook hands, the sheriff rounded up his men, and suddenly they disappeared into trees; the agent was alone.

He had planned to start up immediately. But for a moment the intense loneliness and beauty of the open alpine setting held him. This was where he liked to be. It was in this country, in this kind of fluctuating weather, that the agent experienced his only real, deep feelings of awe and perhaps of humility. A marmot whistled, and he searched through the gray boulders beyond the lake for the animal, but you could never see them in rocks like that. And as the somber clouds gathering from the east extended farther out over the peaks, threatening to cut off the sun, a tentative wind swept down the Caballo Peak slope, riffled across the lake, and a few seconds later streaked on by the agent. A few gray jays, so tame they would eat from his hand, landed nearby and started hunting for sandwich scraps in the flattened grassy area where the posse had been.

Suddenly the agent noticed all the refuse that had been left behind, pieces of waxed paper and tinfoil, discarded Baggies, a few aluminum bean dip cans, empty cigarette packages, and some crushed coffee cups. And it angered him, the way people mistreated wilderness. So before shoving off, cursing softly under his breath, he canvassed the area, collecting the garbage, which he crushed and buried in his pack. Then he pushed in the antenna on his radio and also stored that in the pack. Now he was outside communication, truly alone. A lightness entered into his body as more small cyclones of increasingly icy wind rippled across the lake and through the luxuriant summer grasses. He had an afternoon to himself, alone in this magnificent high country, on top of the wilderness world.

Kyril Montana opened the breech on his gun to make sure there was no bullet in the chamber, then to make doubly sure once he'd driven the bolt back he fixed the gun on safety, and, with the binoculars slung round his neck and bumping softly against his chest, he pushed off, walking up to the lake shore where, for a few more minutes, he watched the scores of lovely, slim cutthroats swimming slowly in the clear, shallow water, occasionally—laconically—surface-feeding . . . such lovely, dumb fish.

Kyril Montana walked swiftly through the damp meadow past several curious Herefords. Five minutes later, as he climbed through the rocks and shale along a narrow sheep and pack mule trail, he noticed perhaps fifty sheep far to his left, high on the steep slopes of Little Baldy Mountain. Later, halfway up the ridge, he paused once more to take in the scene below. By now he could see two more azure, nearly circular lakes above the ninth Little Baldy Bear. There were some more cattle grazing near the shore of the fifth, and largest, lake. Two ravens skimmed deliberately along the distant treetops, floating into the open over the ninth lake and drifting down through the subsequent meadowland, heading into Deerhair Canyon, where the Milagro posse had retreated.

The agent climbed three-quarters of the way up the ridge and stopped again. The wind was blowing steadily; clouds obscured the sun. Perhaps two hundred yards across the small valley, Antelope Peak and Cabresto Mountain were still brightly lit and summery. Setting down his gun, the agent braced himself against a rock and began to scan the area with his binoculars. All nine Little Baldy Bear Lakes were visible now, and at the uppermost lake a pair of campers in a bright yellow rubber boat were fishing. The other lakes were quiet, unpeopled. Slowly, occasionally stopping at an area that his instincts told him was a likely exit from or entrance into the trees, he probed with the glasses along the pines bordering each lake. Once he paused for almost a minute at what appeared to be thin wisps of smoke rising from a recent campfire near the fifth lake's shore—but he surmised, after lengthy inspection, that it was some curious configuration of mist rising, perhaps from a warm spring in the muddy ground.

It was while panning his field glasses on the horizon along the tree line at the upper reaches of Deerhair Canyon that he came upon a man standing about two hundred yards directly opposite his position, and this man was aiming a rifle at Kyril Montana.

At almost the exact instant the glasses touched on the man and the agent registered his enormous bulk, he also registered a slight white puff of smoke from the gun, and at that he automatically collapsed himself sideways as a small piece of the rock he'd been leaning against exploded with a pop that was followed by a ricochet whine. Hitting the rocky earth hard, he kept rolling three or four times, down over jagged terrain, and while he rolled he heard the report of the shot that could have killed him, and then, after he'd stopped, tucked up tight behind a small boulder, he heard two more gunshots from bullets that must have been fired at him while he was rolling.

❧

Milagro's old men liked to hang out on Rael's porch. The men who most often, and for the longest times, frequented the porch were Amarante Córdova and the doomsayer Juan F. Mondragón, Onofre Martínez and the church custodian Panky Mondragón, Sparky Pacheco, and also Tranquilino Jeantete when he wasn't catering to the local drunks inside the Frontier. These members of the Senile Brigade, who endlessly discussed the latest rumor, political skullduggery, adulteries, and other carnal shenanigans on Rael's porch, were, of course, only the most constant nucleus that hung out there. For there was nobody in town, men and women alike, who did not spend some time on that porch during any given day, knocking off a soda and a peanut butter Nab or some piñon nuts or Slim Jims while the news got passed around and fondled affectionately, embellished when necessary, exaggerated where possible, and twisted if the occasion called for twisting.

People on the porch were also very adept at listening to each other with one ear, while the other ear stayed cocked on the radio Nick always had going inside the store, always tuned to KKCV in Chamisaville. And when, say, the "Barton Gas Birthday Club" came on the air, everybody shut up to see who was growing a little older today. Likewise, when the "Pet Parade" came on, some people hushed up so as to hear if there were any bargains on free puppies at the Chamisaville Animal Shelter, or whether or not any frustrated hippies were giving away their nubian milk goats. Just about nobody—unless Marvin LaBlue happened to be slouching around—listened to the country and western music on the "Platter Hoedown" show. Many people, however, perked up again for the shape of Edward Morgan's opinion, and for the "Swap Shop"; and then a real lull occurred on the porch as literally everybody clammed up for the "Hello, America" man, Paul Harvey. After that the afternoon faded away into syrupy mariachi and taco pop music, which the people tolerated with friendly bemusement. The Mexican songs were constantly punctuated by irrelevant spotshots nobody listened to, such as the "German Press Review" and a show featuring a well-known beauty queen talking to teen-agers about their diets and their pimples.

People also stationed themselves on Rael's porch because that was where the mail came in, and it was also where the various government checks that arrived by mail were cashed. The post office, an official-looking cage in back of the store, had about twenty-five combination boxes to one side of the grille. Nick was the postmaster. In the old days, Nick had had a nasty habit of shaking people down for their government checks, refusing to advance more credit until entire checks were signed over to him to settle up outstanding debts. But about three years before, Onofre Martínez, with some help from Charley Bloom, had put a stop to this by threatening to take Nick, not only into court, but also to the cleaners.

So for one reason or another, Rael's porch was Milagro's social center; and it almost always supported a large and animated crowd.

Yet by one o'clock on the day after Joe Mondragón planted a single .30-06 bullet in Seferino Pacheco's chest, not a single person was loafing on that porch. In fact, the heart of town was so deserted, and the air was so quiet, you could almost hear Mercedes Rael's heart pumping as she waited behind a lilac bush (with her hands full of pebbles) for somebody she didn't like to enter the plaza area.

Nick Rael was seated behind his counter trying to read an old issue of *Field & Stream,* and across the plaza area Harlan Betchel was seated at a back table in his empty Pilar Café trying to do the crossword puzzle in the day's Capital City *Reporter.* Catty-corner to the Pilar, in Forest Service headquarters, Carl Abeyta was trying to review the most recent multiple use plan for his chunk of forest.

Suddenly a grasshopper crackling across the deserted plaza area made all three men *and* Nick's mom jump as high as if they had just been bitten by a rattlesnake.

❦

A knock on the door.

When Charley Bloom answered, two men in state police uniforms, both men wearing sunglasses, were standing on the front stoop.

"You Charley Bloom?" Granny Smith asked.

"Yes," Bloom said, and, before he could catch himself, he had added a "sir."

"Where's José Mondragón?" Bruno Martínez asked.

"I'm supposed to know that?"

Granny Smith lifted a warning finger. *"Please.* Don't get smart with *us,* Mr. Bloom. We asked you a simple question."

"Could you repeat the question please?"

"Sure, gladly. Where the fuck is Joe Mondragón?"

"I don't know."

"Mind if we come in for a minute?" Granny asked.

"Yes, very much," Bloom said, as Linda appeared at his elbow.

"Huh. Are you absolutely *sure* we can't come in?" Granny insisted.

"I have nothing to say to you," Bloom told them. His heart was beating, almost fluttering, his legs were weak, his palms close to spurting sweat.

"You mean you're just gonna keep a couple of state policemen standing on your doorstep?" Bruno Martínez asked disbelievingly.

"Yes."

They looked at each other, shrugged; both faintly smiled. Bruno took out a pad and a pencil. "Okay, Mr. Bloom, when was the last time you saw José Mondragón?"

"I don't know. Maybe yesterday, maybe a couple days ago. I don't remember. You know, I might have seen him in Rael's, or waved when he drove by in his pickup, I don't know?"

"How about you, Linda?"

"Mrs. Bloom to you," the lawyer said angrily.

"How about you, *Mrs.* Bloom?"

"I have nothing to say."

"I see. Uh . . . Mr. Bloom, you've been writing about Milagro, I read one of your articles, I didn't like it too much, know what I mean? I mean, you know, it gets a little heavy sometimes when an outsider comes in and writes about my people, because I grew up here," Bruno said. "But you been writing about things up here, about José and his stupid field over there on the west side, so you must know a lot about this town."

Bloom shrugged. "I don't know. Maybe I know a little . . . maybe not so much after all."

"Oh come on, please, don't be humble now. I mean, I saw you over at that meeting the other day, remember? When you took all those maps into the church to incite those people to riot; let's not have no false modesty here, okay? I saw you then, and we've been thinking that maybe you're one of the ring-leaders of this thing, know what I mean?"

"No, I can't say that I do."

"Where's Joe Mondragón?" Granny Smith suddenly snapped.

"I told you, I don't know."

"He was here last night. One of our men saw him."

"Bullshit."

Granny Smith cocked his head. "What did you say? What did you say to a police officer?"

"You heard what I said. I'm not going to repeat it. It's not illegal, you know, according to the Supreme Court—"

Bruno Martínez interrupted: "Did anybody ever tell you, Mr. Bloom, that maybe you're not too smart?"

Bloom flared. "Did anybody ever tell you—"

"Hush!" Linda gripped his arm.

"Go ahead, Mr. Bloom. Did anybody ever tell me what?"

"Nothing," he mumbled. "Nothing."

Granny Smith said, "After Joe shot the poor old man, he ran by here, told you to hide the gun, borrowed a pack, a flashlight, and some food from you two, and headed for the hills."

"What in hell are you talking about?"

"Listen, Mr. Bloom, watch that language, okay? You're talking to police officers, understand?"

"Yes. I certainly do understand."

"He always pop this easy, Linda?" Granny Smith asked.

"Mrs. Bloom to you," the lawyer said tightly.

"Of course, ma'am, Mrs. Bloom. Excuse me. Now, *Mr.* Bloom. You better think real careful about when you saw Joe last and where, see, because like I said, we've been watching you, and, you know . . . you're in the legal profession, you understand these things, it wouldn't be too smart to lie. All we're asking for is a little cooperation. Because we're afraid somebody else's gonna get hurt bad, like with a bullet in the brain, and, well, you know, that just fucks up our jobs. That fucks up everybody, know what I mean?"

"Look," Bloom said, reaching back for the door, "we don't know anything, we have noth—"

"You shut that door in my face, Mr. Bloom," Bruno Martínez snapped, "and I don't *care* if you are a lawyer. I'll kick it down, understand? Now you listen to me, we don't have all day to mess around with a stuck-up eastern college person with a legal degree playing hide-and-seek games, right? Now you're in this thing and you're in it deep, and let's quit beating around the bush before there's some serious trouble here, okay? We want some facts."

As he said this a mottled-green, 1953 Chevy pickup with a three-legged German shepherd riding atop the cab rattled down the road, coasting to a stop behind the police car. Three members of the Senile Brigade wearing beat-up old cowboy hats sat in the front seat, and another younger man neither Bloom nor Linda recognized squatted in the back, smoking a cigarette. They did nothing, opened no doors, just stayed in the truck staring over at the Bloom front door.

"Who's that?" Granny asked.

"I don't know," Bloom said. "I guess just somebody."

"That ain't just somebody, that's my father's dog and that's his truck, too, and what the hell are they doing behind our car?" Bruno muttered darkly.

"I'll go see," Granny said.

"Hell you will—" Bruno grabbed at his arm. "I don't like the looks of that truck. Stay here."

Bloom said, "We have nothing more to say," pulled Linda back, shut the door and locked it, and leaned against it, shaking, unable to believe the way in which he had stood up to them.

Granny Smith and Bruno Martínez waited there for a moment, facing Onofre Martínez's battered green pickup. Granny said, "You think they got guns?"

Bruno scoffed. "Do rabbits have ears?"

"You figure each *one* has a gun?"

"That's probably a safe assumption."

"Would your own father shoot you?" Granny asked incredulously.

"You bet your sweet ass. He hates chotas."

"Ho-ly shit."

"Time to go home," Bruno said bitterly. "Time to get our fannies out of here."

"This town is going crazy," Granny moped, unbuttoning the strap that kept his revolver in the holster. "I'm gonna put in for a transfer. Better free your gun."

"This town has always been crazy," Bruno said. "Don't worry, it's free."

"Christ Almighty, man, would you shoot your own father?"

"I dunno. It never came up like this before. I guess so, though."

"You think that asshole or his wife knows anything about Joe Mondragón?"

"Probably not. I dunno. Who am I? Superman with X-ray vision?"

The two cops walked slowly along the muddy walk and through a gate to their car. Granny Smith called Onofre's license plate number into headquarters, re-affirmed their prior location call, and explained they were going to move out before trouble started. The men in the cab had their hats pulled down low, and between that and clouds of cigarette smoke and the cracked windshield, Bruno couldn't tell who the others were, except they all looked old enough to be Egyptian mummies. Their guns were probably rifles, he surmised, and they were probably held barrel up, between their knees. The three-legged German shep-herd, which had been staring at him through opaque but threatening eyes, suddenly growled.

"Jesus," Bruno muttered, shooting his father and the rest of those old geezers a finger. "Jesus H. Christ." And he swung into the passenger seat.

"We need reinforcements," Granny said. "Do you think we should call down south for reinforcements?"

"What, just because one guy tried to kill another guy for bumping off his pig and the other guy shot him and ran away? As far as they know down there, everything is almost hunky-dory. And anyway, Trucho don't care if we all get killed."

Granny Smith pulled onto the road and cruised slowly away from the green Chevy. "Watch behind," he said. "See if that lawyer comes out and talks to them."

"Not so far."

"We should of got a warrant, I guess, and gone in and tipped over a little furniture."

"Shit, man, they were scared. He was so scared he could hardly talk. But she didn't seem that scared to me."

"*I* was scared," Granny said. "When your old man's truck pulled up I thought those bastards were gonna open fire. I'm forty-six years old, Bruno, and I never pulled a gun on anybody in my life."

"I shot a junkie once," Bruno said. "Down in the capital. He was running away from an arrest."

"What happened?"

"I killed him. I didn't mean to kill him. It was gonna be a warning shot, only I was so pissed-off I hit him in the back of the head. That was—shit—ten, eleven years ago, I guess, before you came into the state."

"Texas is a tea party compared to around here," Granny complained. "The Mexicans in Texas are different. These goddam people of yours are weird. They're crazy."

"Yeah," Bruno said. "They're weird, alright. Should we drop in on José's wife?"

"I dunno, I don't really feel like it right now. I heard everybody and his brother, except the lawyer, bought guns the other day—Nick Rael told me. Not to mention the gun robbery at Nick's Bernabé did such a wonderful investigation on. Nobody ever shot at me before, you know? I wish to Christ we could get out of here before these people jump right out of their pants and start butchering each other. Screw Ladd Devine and all the rest of 'em. Why should I get killed so he can make another fifty million dollars?"

"What'll happen if they kill José up there, I wonder?" Bruno said.

"They'll have to call in the National Guard, I shit thee not."

"I'm getting an ulcer," Bruno whined. "If I could find another job at the same pay, I'd quit tomorrow."

*

Crouched behind, and hugging tightly to, his rock, Kyril Montana waited for a moment without budging. His rifle was ten yards above him, leaning against the rock up there, useless. The field glasses were on the ground three yards to the right of the gun. His hat was lying on the ground midway between the rifle and his present position. And he dared not move.

Although the agent felt some sharp pains, in his legs, in one hip, and under his ribs, he could not tell immediately if he'd been hit or not. Probably, he figured—as soon as his mind jammed back into gear after the shock of being fired upon had receded slightly —his pain came from the rocks he had bumped against diving out of the way and frantically heading for cover. But now he forced himself, without moving, to turn his mind inward, to trace physical patterns along his limbs and torso, to ascertain what, if any, damage had been done, and within a minute he realized that no bullets had touched him.

After that, Kyril Montana swiveled his head slightly, checking out the immediate terrain to see what cover it offered. There were larger rocks and some scraggly bushes eight or nine yards to one side of him; it was all open on the other side. And the first real cover up the slope was the rock against which he had originally been leaning.

Suddenly his wide-brimmed, khaki-colored hat popped about two feet into the air, and as it came down he heard another gunshot, and he thought: Very funny, you bastard! Several seconds later a piece of the rock against which his gun was leaning exploded inches from the rifle, and then, as he heard the report from that shot, the rifle went haywire, kicking up with a sharp jerk and bouncing sideways off the rock, a useless weapon when it hit the ground; the scope also splintered, and another gunshot echoed across the valley.

"You son of a bitch," he whispered tightly. "You miserable God damn son of a bitch." Now he was in more trouble than he had ever been in before.

Kyril Montana needed to get in a position from which he could see. But sure as hell whoever was doing the sharpshooting from over there had sized up his situation and knew which way he would be breaking. So the bastard must just be sitting over there with his telescopic sight trained between the agent's rock and the larger cluster to the north, waiting for him to make a dash for it.

But the gunman would tire, the agent knew. His eye would blur, he'd have to go off the hold for a minute. His arm would ache; he'd relax it for a few seconds at a time. Hence, the longer the agent sat tight, the better chance he had. He shifted his weight slowly, trying—without exposing any piece of himself beyond the outline of his small rock—to work into a position, into a crouch from which he could spring. Once in position he waited a full two minutes, then suddenly broke, lunging up and forward; legs driving hard, he dived behind the big cluster of rocks, in the process bashing the knuckles on one hand so hard he cried out, but no gunshot carried over to him; the man had not even fired.

He still had the radio. Kyril Montana worked his arms clear of the pack straps, but then, judging from the multiple rips and tears in the pack's fabric, he knew, even before opening the nylon cover to take it out, that the radio would be in bad shape. And he was right, of course: it was dented, smashed, useless.

Kyril Montana was panting; his heart beat rapidly, almost fibrillating, and he felt queasy, slightly nauseous. It took a strong effort of his will and a dozen steady deep breaths to quiet down his heart, and when it was quiet and his panting had stopped he ventured a look between two rocks and a tangle of dead gray branches toward the opposite valley rim. Squinting against the gray glare and against the cold and by now steady wind that made his eyes water, he searched the opposite timberline for the gunman, but could see nothing. He had good vision but that was a far distance, and it was difficult to pick out a figure among the gray rocks, scraggly pines, and greasy green bushes.

He needed his field glasses.

They were to his left, now, uphill, one lens glinting slightly. If he lunged for them he would be in the open all the way. He would have to snag them on the run and continue maybe ten more feet to the large rock against which he had been standing when the original shot had been fired.

As he was going over the terrain, planning exactly how to run it, memorizing the rocks and rotting logs that could trip him up, his mind abruptly veered away into the absolute and irrefutable realization that he had been caught in a trap. At the same instant this thought hit him, he realized the odds were much better than even that the gunman across the valley was not alone.

In fact—and this was only instinct, he had no way to prove it—there were probably at least four or five men in this vicinity or down in Deerhair Canyon hunting him now, determined to kill him. Kyril Montana shuddered.

Then he rubbed his eyes and refocused on the binoculars. Because of the wind, which would make the shooting much more difficult, he could probably afford to go slowly enough so as to assure snagging the glasses. Counting to five, then, he lunged into the open and ran exactly as he had planned to run, zig-zagging slightly, hunched over, avoiding all obstacles, grabbing the glasses as he passed by, and swinging around the large rock. There he crouched, panting, waiting to hear the report of a gunshot for a good minute before deciding he'd better make use of the glasses, locate the gunman if he could, and decide how to get out of there.

The boulder was large, plenty wide, but its silhouette was smooth. There was no place, really, that he could poke his head out and not be conspicuous. In the end, stretched on his belly and inching ahead a little with his elbows, he peered out from behind the bottom upward-starting curve of the rock. The tree line leaped at him from across the way, but there was nobody over there. Slowly, very slowly, he inched the binoculars along the trees, probing among the lower-down rocks, finding nothing. The man must have descended into the forest, heading his way.

Swinging the glasses west, the agent focused on the highest Little Baldy Bear Lake where the two fishermen, about a mile upward and thus probably deaf to the firing, were still drifting around on the silver surface, their parka hoods up now, casting lines into the water.

Kyril Montana brought his glasses swiftly down from that lake into the wide meadow directly below and onto a horseman progressing slowly around the eastern shore of the lake beside which the agent had eaten lunch. He thought he recognized the horse, a big dappled gray—had he noticed it in a Milagro field last night? Or on his other visit? The rider could have been any one of a hundred citizens from that town: small and wiry-looking, his face completely shadowed by a straw cowboy hat with the front brim bent down, he wore a faded denim jacket, Levi's, brown cowboy boots. And a gun belt. There was also a rifle in a saddle scabbard.

As the agent watched, this small man lifted a hand in greeting; swinging his glasses across the water and the meadow grass, he arrived at another figure—the man who'd been firing at him—just as that man emerged from the trees leading a small spotted pony. He waved back, then drew the reins over his animal's head and mounted up.

The two horsemen came together in the meadow at almost exactly the spot where the helicopter had been parked. They spoke briefly, then the bigger man fixed his binoculars on Kyril Montana's rock. He seemed to stare directly at the agent for almost a minute, then lowered the glasses, said something to his small partner, and, turning half-around, matter-of-factly removed his rifle from the saddle scabbard. Taking his time he raised the rifle, aiming directly at the agent, who was watching, for some reason mesmerized, who saw the white puff whipped away from the rifle by the wind but couldn't move. The rock shattered a foot above his head splashing pulverized dust and sharp slivers into his face and arm, and only then—howling with pain—did he jerk back sharply, incredulous at his own stupidity . . . and he never heard the report, it had been carried north into Deerhair Canyon on the wind.

A slight tear in his jacket's forearm indicated where the largest sliver had entered, and when he pushed the sleeve up about eight inches from the wrist he discovered a blue and only slightly bloody hole where the sliver had punctured his skin. As there was nothing he could do about it, he pulled the sleeve down again and wiped what he thought was sweat off his forehead. His hand came away bloody. For a second, as he stared at his hand, something in his stomach squeezed in tight making him nauseous again—had the bullet hit him in the head? Was he right now starting to die?

Quickly he took off his jacket, then his shirt. Immediately, his skin prickling, he put the jacket back on, then gingerly pressed the flannel shirt against his face, holding it there gently, eyes stinging slightly from the blood, and when he felt that enough blood had soaked into the fabric he tenderly wiped his face, after which he patted himself carefully all over his features, half expecting to come upon some huge gaping hole, but there were only scattered small pockmarks from the stone fragments.

Cautiously, lowering forward onto his stomach, he checked on the two horsemen again. One, the smaller man, was heading up the ridge on his horse, but way off to the side safely beyond pistol range. As his horse picked its way quietly up through the rocks and low brush, the bigger man remained down below, dismounted, kneeling behind a rock with his rifle aimed directly up at Kyril Montana.

It didn't take a genius to figure out their plan. And without a rifle the agent was helpless. Advancing up the ridge out of pistol range the little man would eventually get a line on the back of Kyril Montana's rock. The agent would inch around the side of his rock as the little man climbed, but he had no room for maneuvering. Sooner or later his ass would become a target for the man down below, who obviously had a fine telescopic sight and a gun that was sighted in true and had been very accurate at a far greater distance than the one from which he now had a bead drawn on the cop.

The valley had darkened, grown gray and momentarily still; almost icy cold.

Kyril Montana could do one of two things. Make a dash for his second shelter, empty his pistol at the mounted man, and then, in hopes that he might create at least momentary confusion, he could run for the timberline which began about eighty yards below those rocks. Only a miracle, he knew, would get him to those trees.

Or he could break for the top of the ridge about fifty yards above. It was a steep climb through tough little foot-high bushes and a million small jagged stones. It would be slow and hellish going, and that would give both gunmen plenty of time to empty their rifles at him.

Which meant his chances that way too, were nil.

His pistol was loaded, but he checked to make sure, nervously thumbing the hammer back and in a few times. He didn't know what to do; either way he was cooked. He whimpered, not believing that his mind was incapable of figuring a way out. To just sit there and wait for whatever might happen would be stupid. Those men meant to kill him, and if he didn't hit on something they would rub him out with consummate ease.

The agent flattened himself against the rock, thumbed back the hammer of his revolver, and waited for the horseman to show. When the rider did not appear within a minute he set the gun down and spent a moment removing the cartridges from his gun belt and putting them in his right-hand coat pocket where they could be more easily reached. He had eighteen extra cartridges, six in the gun. Then he put the bi-noculars' strap around his neck so that if he made a dash for it and somehow escaped he would be sure to have a pair of long-distance eyes; his survival might depend on it.

Almost by accident he glanced up the ridge, in time to see a third man not one hundred yards away, on foot and also carrying a rifle, rise into view. Even before he raised the glasses he knew it was a boy, a teen-ager, gangly, lanky, tall. Even with the binoculars, the agent could not see the boy's face, which was also nearly hidden by the downturned brim of a straw hat. But it was a kid, all right, maybe eighteen, dressed in a droopy old army jacket, dungarees, and boots. He was carrying a lever-action rifle without a scope, and he was close enough for the agent to hit him with the pistol, though it would take one hell of a lucky shot. The kid obviously had not seen Kyril Montana: he stopped, silhouetted against the sky, and waved downhill at the horseman riding up and at the other man farther below. Fascinated, watching him close up, the agent saw the boy's lower features and posture change as the men below obviously gestured, pointing, and then the kid's head turned and he was staring at the agent.

Kyril Montana lowered the glasses and blinked his eyes. He rubbed them quickly to get out the wind tears, raised his pistol, held his arm steady at the wrist with his other hand, aimed upwind a foot or so to the right of the silhouette and a little above his head, cocked the hammer with his thumb, and pulled the trigger. The explosion whacked him in the face like a fist, but up on the ridge nothing happened. The kid didn't move, didn't even lift his rifle, and there was no way to mark his shot, no splash of dirt, no splintering of rock, nothing. So he pulled back the hammer, took careful aim directly on the target, and fired again. This time the kid moved in a strange sideshuffle a couple of yards to his right, where he stopped and raised his rifle. There was nothing the agent could do except fire again, and so he pulled back the hammer, aimed quickly, and shot; cocked the gun right away and fired once more.

Then the kid was shooting, rapidly, excitedly, popping his shots off fast, and the first two went high, one just clipping the top of the rock, another one whining off with a violent spurt of granite fragments almost three feet away from his shoulder, a fourth punching up a fan of dirt and stone splinters five feet in front of the agent, and the fifth zipping harmlessly by on his open side. During this flurry the agent crouched flat against the rock with his arms crossed, his own gun held sideways across his face, eyes clenched shut and everything tensed waiting to get hit, and when the firing stopped and he had not been hit he extended his pistol arm again, cocked the hammer with the thumb of his trembling other hand, and squeezed off another useless shot at that amazingly immobile silhouette up there, in a squat, now, reloading; and then he swung his arm to the right because the small horseman had come into view and the agent wildly punched off his last shot.

Without even waiting to see if he'd hit the man, though certain he had not, the agent triggered open the chamber, bapped out the spent shells, and quietly, almost calmly, reloaded the gun. When he clicked the chamber back into place he looked up and saw the kid above him, reloaded, rising, and the rider off to the right dismounting off the wrong—the far and protected —side of his horse, and at that moment it started to hail.

It happened so suddenly that at first the agent cringed and doubled over thinking the hailstones were bullets from somebody behind or off at a slant below his exposed rear. But as soon as he saw hundreds of tiny white balls about the size of his little fingernail popping all over the ground he understood what was happening and scrambled to his feet, spun around, and began sprinting toward the trees. The hail was so furious and thick he could barely see a faint gray tree line down the hill. Within seconds the ground was white with the icy stones and the agent slipped once, pitching sideways, he struck hard, did a half-somersault and was on his feet again, galloping crazily down the slope, pelted by the hail, falling again and getting up, and falling once more and rolling several times and crawling insanely a few yards, scrambling and bashing his knees, and then bolting up again and plummeting the last few yards into the trees where the covering pine branches were so thick that suddenly it wasn't hailing anymore.

Swinging behind a tree he shouted *"Hah!"* triumphantly and giggled crazily, sobbing, laughing, panting with his chest tight and stricken with pain.

Kyril Montana looked at his hands: they were raw and bleeding. His pants were split at the knees, his kneecaps scraped raw and bloody. The side of one hiking boot was torn open. But he was alive, still mobile, and in the trees, and from here on in it was a whole new ball game—

But he had dropped the gun.

He had lost it in his scramble across that open area; and his binoculars were gone too.

Kyril Montana stared at the amazing storm, a sheet of violent white between him and three men with guns and, even as he watched, the storm slackened, the white thinned so that he could see back up the slope, at first faintly, and then more clearly to where he had been.

And with that he turned around and plunged deeper into the trees, grabbing trunks to swing around and down, skidding in thick meshes of slick, rotting leaves, barreling clumsily through brushy tangles, staggering pell-mell down through the forest and the canyons toward his car four miles below.

Eliu Archuleta was surprised, shocked, and almost knocked down by the sudden onslaught of hail. When he saw the agent whirl and make a break, he was firing and jamming down the lever and yanking it back up with his finger on the trigger so that the shot automatically got off, even as the agent suddenly disappeared into the violent white explosion. Swinging the rifle in the direction Kyril Montana was running, he fired three more times, clicking the pin into an empty chamber once, and then he started trotting down through the pelting hailstones toward the rock, shouting in Spanish, "How was that? How was that?" to his mother, who had been dismounting seconds before the blinding storm struck and Eliu had commenced his second barrage.

They met at the rock, both on foot, Ruby leading her horse. And while the woman stood a few feet uphill, shoulders hunched against the stinging pellets, her son anxiously inspected the rock, nervously touching the bullet scars, shaking his head and pretending to be ashamed over how many times he'd missed.

"I should of come closer," Eliu said with a shrug, staring through the storm toward where he knew the woods were. "I missed that son of a bitch by too much every time."

"You came close enough," Ruby said. "In fact, for a second I thought you might have hit him."

Eliu kneeled and, taking an old tobacco can wrapped in dirty adhesive tape from his back pocket, he dumped five more shells into his hand, shoved the can back into his pocket, then fed the bullets one by one into his gun.

"Even so, you shoot like hell," Ruby said, smiling a little.

"He was shooting at me. He didn't know I wasn't trying to kill him."

"So he shoots like hell too, thank God," Ruby said wearily. "You both shoot like hell so you're both alive and God is smiling. But I'm not. I'm unhappy because I think Claudio shot too close and maybe hit him." Then she added, "We'll lay off him now because it's going to be one cold chingadera up here tonight, and we don't want him to freeze to death."

"If he did, so what?"

"We don't need that kind of trouble," she said sadly, still hunched patiently against the storm like a horse, with her eyes squinched half-shut, immobile. "He's got the idea now and we don't want to push our luck."

Once he had reloaded, Eliu was up and moving nervously about again. He trotted down the slope for the pack and brought it uphill, along with the radio, depositing them at the base of the large rock. Then he collected the rifle and the agent's hat. There was a clean bullet hole in the hat, and he stuck his finger through the hole and wiggled it, grinning up at his mother, who said, "That was a nice thing for Claudio to do. He's got a real sense of humor."

Eliu pointed at Kyril Montana's rifle, with part of the stock and the bolt area blasted and bent and the scope shattered, asking, "What about that?"

"That was a nice shot, a very important shot for us. It's lucky the wind wasn't blowing this hard when he took that shot."

The hail abated, and they both looked down the slope to where Claudio García, kicking hard, was driving his horse up toward them. As he joined them and swung off his mount the storm ended. The sky remained gray, threatening, the valley dark, their ridge and part of the meadow around the ninth Little Baldy Bear Lake a sheer, dully gleaming white.

"Bravo," Claudio growled, standing there staring at the pack, the radio, the rifle, the hat. Eliu turned the pack upside down and kicked through the things that fell out, the dehydrated food packages, socks, extra shirt, matches, and the posse's picnic garbage.

"Put it all back in," Ruby said. "And when it's all together we'll tie it to the saddles and take it down to where the earth is soft and bury it. We don't want to get caught with any of this stuff."

She set a cigarette between her lips and thumbed a wooden match to light it, blew out the match and put it back in her jacket pocket. Moving quickly around the rock then, she scuffed in the hail to see if any other equipment belonging to the agent was scattered around, and in the process she collected all the expended shells that she could find. Satisfied nothing else was there, she moved quickly down the slope to the small rock behind which the agent had first crouched, scuffing all the way down and all around that rock, and after that she loped quickly over to the larger rocks where the pack had been and kicked around in the hail until certain that nothing else remained.

Claudio squashed up the hat and stuffed it into the pack and, with Eliu's help, lashed the pack and the useless rifle to the back of his saddle.

"Did you see where he entered the trees?" Ruby asked.

Her son shook his head. Claudio laughed: "I couldn't see the end of my own nose."

"We better get going," she said, leading them on foot slowly up the slope toward the ridge, away from the direction Kyril Montana had taken. "I don't want to freeze my ass off up here tonight."

"I guess we scared him enough," Claudio said uneasily, snapping his cigarette butt downhill. He was tired and a little shaken; frightened, actually, because maybe the agent could identify them, or maybe they had hit him; maybe they had botched this thing badly, maybe they should have killed him—Claudio, for one, had wanted very much to kill him, and he was still shaking from how difficult it had been to miss.

"I wonder," Eliu said quietly, "if we should have killed him."

Ruby cuffed him gently behind the head. "What are you, a total pendejo?" she asked unhappily. "If we had killed that cop they would have rounded up all the men in town and cut off their heads and hung them from their patrol car antennas."

"Well . . ." Eliu said uncertainly, "at least I guess he got the point." And he felt a little sick.

Claudio García shrugged tiredly: "Yeah, I think he got the point."

They were on top of the ridge. Smiling unhappily, Ruby mounted her horse. "Come on, you stupid men," she muttered quietly, affectionately. "Let's go home where it's warm."

❧

At 2:00 P.M. on the afternoon of the first day's hunt for Joe Mondragón, the subject of this hunt, accompanied by his wife, by a brother-in-law, Eloy Quintana, and by Jimmy Ortega, walked into state police headquarters at Doña Luz. The dispatcher, Emilio Cisneros, was the only man holding down the fort.

"I hear somebody's looking for me," Joe said cockily. "Where in hell is everybody?"

"You're supposed to be up in the mountains," the dispatcher said.

"Does it look like I'm up in the mountains?"

"No."

"Well, then, why don't you get on that radio and call in one of your trigger-happy goons so's I can find out what's supposed to happen to me."

"Sure . . . listen," said the flustered dispatcher. "Bill Koontz is parked up at Louie's Café. Why don't you just drive up there . . ."

"Wonderful."

Joe and his entourage left state police headquarters, piled into Eloy Quintana's dilapidated pickup, and in a cloud of violet-colored exhaust, drove back up the highway to Louie's Café.

Bill Koontz was sitting at the counter tapping up tostada crumbs with his middle finger and licking them off when Joe and his people walked in.

Joe sat down beside him. "Emilio down at the pendejo factory said you was up here, so that's why I came. What am I supposed to do now?"

"Well, shit now . . ." And after the state cop had picked up his jaw, he asked: "Ain't you supposed to be up in the mountains? There was thirty-five guys up there looking for you early this morning and they're not back yet."

Impatiently, Joe said, "Look, all I want to know is what am I supposed to do, that's all."

"The guy you shot, Pacheco, he's gonna be okay."

"That asshole came at me with a gun," Joe said. "He was crazy—"

"Yeah, I know. There's even a couple witnesses . . ." Koontz removed a dollar from his wallet and paid the girl behind the counter. "Let's go back down to headquarters," he said, adjusting his cap. "There's a bunch of stuff's gotta be filled out. Then I guess we'll turn you over to Bernie when he gets back, I don't know . . ."

"What am I gonna be charged with?" Joe asked nervously.

"I'm not sure. Where's that gun you shot him with?"

"Out in Eloy's truck. On the rack."

"Maybe you better give that to me," Koontz said.

Joe got the rifle from his brother-in-law's truck and gave it to the state cop who put it in the back seat of his patrol car, and then the Quintana truck followed Koontz's car back to the Doña Luz state police headquarters. Once there, Koontz called Xavier Trucho.

"We got Joe Mondragón," he said. "Now what exactly do you want done?"

"How'd you get him? Did the posse smoke him out of the mountains? Is he alive?"

"He walked into headquarters about two-fifteen. I wasn't here, I was up at Louie's Café having a bite to eat. So Emilio sent him up there. He just walked in and sat down beside me and we talked a little, and he gave me the rifle."

"Which rifle?"

"The one he shot Pacheco with."

"Where the hell is he now?"

"Right here. He's just sitting over there on a bench reading a magazine."

"You're kidding me, you son of a bitch!"

"He's over there. Honest to Christ. I swear to it."

"There's an assault warrant out on him, ain't there? That fucking Pacheco refused to die."

"Well, I'm not positive . . . I'd have to check with either Bernie or Maestas down in Chamisaville. Is that what we decided? If it is it don't make no sense . . ."

"I'll decide what makes sense," Trucho said. "Is Montana back yet?"

"Not that I know of. I assume he's still out with the posse."

"Why don't you try calling Bernabé Montoya on the phone," Trucho said sarcastically.

"Sure. I'll do that soon as I hang up—"

"Look, hold him there for a while. Kill him if he tries to walk out the door. I want to go over everything we got in this case and consult with a few people."

"Anything you say," Koontz said. "But what'll I tell Mondragón?"

"Tell him it'll be aggravated assault or something. Be vague. Like I said, Pacheco refuses to die. But don't let that little S.O.B. out of your sight. I'll get back to you real soon. Stick around the phone, because if I have to try and communicate through that asshole Cisneros I'm liable to have heart failure. I mean, don't go back up to Louie's with Joe for a piece of birthday cake or something, comprendes?"

"Yeah, okay. Whatever—" Koontz said.

He hung up and told Joe: "You'll have to stick around for a while until we get some things straightened out."

"Am I under arrest?"

"Let's just say that right now you're cooperating with us."

"I'm not under arrest—?"

"I told you—" Koontz began.

"If I'm not under arrest I'm getting out of here," Joe said.

"In that case you're under arrest."

"What for?"

"Aggravated assault, assault and battery, flight to avoid prosecution, resisting arrest, suspicion of attempted murder, conspiracy, attempted manslaughter, illegal use of irrigation water, discharging a weapon within city limits, and destruction of private property—namely, Pacheco's pig. Will that be enough for you or do you want me to start running down some of the peripheral charges that could go along with the major ones?"

Joe snarled, "You can't put any of that on me."

Koontz, who angered almost as quickly as Joe, said, "We can cut you up in eight seconds and spread you out on the highway for crowbait if we want, so you just shut up and siddown right where you are until we get a couple things straightened out around here!"

Eloy Quintana shrugged and put his hand on Joe's shoulder. "Siéntate, primo. What the hell."

But Nancy stalked to the counter behind which Bill Koontz was standing, and, eyes narrowing, she hissed, "Listen, chota, you don't talk to my husband like that—"

"Okay!" Koontz swung fast around the counter, and, pointing at her, Eloy Quintana, and Jimmy Ortega, he said, "You, you, and you—out! You want to sit in the truck, go sit in the truck. But get out of here. Pronto. Vamoose, understand? You don't, and you're under arrest for disobeying the order of a police officer."

"He gets a phone call," Nancy said.

"Yeah," Joe said. "I want my phone call."

"You'll get it when I'm ready to give it to you," the state cop said. "Now tell your wife and these two men to get the hell out of here, Joe, otherwise you ain't getting so much as a flea on a donkey's ass, savvy?"

"Hey, you son of a bitch, you can't talk that way in front of my wife—"

Eloy Quintana put his arm around his sister, motioned to the teen-ager to follow, and started outside. Jimmy Ortega got up slowly, arrogantly; eyes narrowed and lips in a sneer, he gave the cop a bitter glance, then sauntered slowly, tauntingly, out. Joe stared at the cop for a good ten seconds, then said "Huh!" and suddenly sat down, picking up a magazine again. Bill Koontz went to the front door to make sure Nancy, the brother-in-law, and the kid got in the truck.

They did. But as they closed the door another old pickup and then another turned off the highway and parked next to Eloy Quintana's vehicle. There were a couple of old men at the wheels of these trucks, some younger men, and a fat belligerent-looking woman on the seat beside one of them. They nodded and smiled at the passengers in the Quintana vehicle, then the woman and two men got out and walked over to the Quintana pickup and started to talk. Two more trucks, one a one-ton flatbed carrying two bundles of unedged pine slabs, pulled in almost immediately, and several more old men got out and came over to talk. One of the old men, wearing a torn and dirty sheepskin jacket, had on a gun belt; in all the truck cabs, gun racks held rifles.

Bill Koontz locked the front door and turned to Joe. "Those your friends out there?"

Joe looked up and gazed out the window with veiled, nonchalant eyes. He shrugged with an exaggerated lack of concern: "Yeah, those are my friends out there."

"What do they want?" Koontz asked.

"Who knows?" Joe said, suddenly very interested in his magazine. "Maybe they just think the state cop pendejo factory is the most exciting show in town."

"I hope to God, for your sake, that nothing funny starts to happen."

"Why don't you tell them to leave?" Joe said, laboring a little to queer his cocky grin.

"Sure. And if they don't—?"

Joe couldn't hold it back any longer. He lifted his head and allowed a cool-as-a-cucumber, on-top-of-the-world, infinitely arrogant shit-eating grin to illuminate his snotty features.

Marvin LaBlue in the Body Shop and Pipe Queen wrecker and two more muddy pickups swerved in and parked, then a 1957 Oldsmobile stripped of its fenders and muffler and riding high on its springs pulled up beside them, and six school-age youths including Benny Maestas got out and began sauntering loudly around, flicking combs through their hair and laughing raucously and adjusting the crotches of their tight trousers as they cast bold, threatening glances at the state police headquarters.

Bill Koontz told the dispatcher, "Get Chamisaville on that machine. Tell them to send up anybody they got available. Explain the situation." Then he called up Bernabé Montoya in Milagro; Carolina answered.

"Listen, Caroline, this is Bill Koontz down in Doña Luz. Is Bernie back yet?"

"He just got in. You want to talk?"

"I sure do."

She fetched him. "What's the problem?" Bernabé asked, his voice trudging down the fifteen miles of telephone wire like a funeral dirge.

"I got Joe Mondragón sitting in the office here reading a magazine, and there's about a dozen cars and trucks parked outside full of Milagro citizens who suddenly decided to come out of the woodwork, and I don't like the looks of this one bit. I'm alone here with Emilio, so I figure you and Naranjo better get down here on the double, if that's not too much to ask."

Bernabé sighed, "Sure, Bill. Be right over." And he hung up.

Most of the Senile Brigade, featuring Onofre Martínez and Tranquilino Jeantete in the cab of Onofre's 1953 Chevy pickup, with the three-legged German shepherd atop the cab and Joe Mondragón's gloomy uncle Juan F. Mondragón and the uncle's friend Panky Mondragón in back, now arrived. No sooner had this truck found a parking place, than Ray Gusdorf, accompanied by Sparky Pacheco, Fred Quintana, Gomersindo Leyba, and Tobías Arguello quietly pulled in. And Ray had no sooner turned off his ignition, than Betty Apodaca's pickup, carrying the Frontier barmaid, Teofila Chacón, and Amarante Córdova's dying son, Ricardo, coasted to a stop nearby.

Staring out at all these new arrivals, Bill Koontz thought: Holy Cow, there's more friggin' hardware out there than we got in Vietnam!

"I want my phone call," Joe said.

Koontz said, "When I'm ready, you'll get it." And he told the dispatcher, "See if you can get Bruno on the radio. Where's his car at anyhow?"

"He was over at Dixonburgh talking with Carl Murphy, remember? They were thinking, maybe, of sending some of the guys from the Double T Ranch over there up to the Little Baldy Bear Lakes from that side. He hasn't been in the car, though, for twenty minutes."

Koontz dialed Carl Murphy's number. "Hello, Carl?"

"Naw, this is Scotty Cotton. Carl, he's busy right now."

"This is Bill Koontz, State Police in Doña Luz, Scotty. Lemme talk with Bruno Martínez right away. It's urgent."

"Yes *sir*—"

The policeman waited nervously for about a minute. "Bill—?"

"Yeah. Look, we got Mondragón, he's sitting here in the office."

"Well, hot dog—"

"Don't celebrate too soon, Bruno. Maybe we also got a problem. There's about thirty or forty of his neighbors sitting outside in a bunch of pickup trucks, and it looks like it wouldn't take much for things to get ugly. So how about heading back here on the double."

"I'm leaving right now, Bill. Hold the fort."

Two more old and rusty cars pulled up in front of state police headquarters.

Koontz called Granny Smith at home. "Granny? We got Joe Mondragón. Yeah, yeah, I know, but we got trouble, too. A bunch of his friends are camped in maybe two dozen vehicles outside, and I'm here alone with Emilio, and I got the front door locked, but there's a lot of guns out there—"

"Jesus! Look, don't panic, Bill. I'll be over as fast as I can. You call Bernie? He back yet?"

"He's on his way. At least he said he was on his way. If he don't fall flat on his face in a mud puddle or something."

"See you in about five, then. For crissakes, stay cool, Bill. Whatever you do, don't pull a gun."

"I won't if I don't have to . . ."

The dispatcher said, "Sal Bugbee, Buddy Namath, and Ernie Maestas are all on the way."

"It'll take them half an hour to get here."

"What about my phone call?" Joe wanted to know.

"When *I'm* ready you'll get your phone call."

"I got to take a leak," Joe smirked.

"You know where the bathroom's at."

"Sure." Joe grinned like a prince and cast a significant glance outside as he circled around the counter past Bill Koontz, who followed him to the john.

"How about a little privacy?" Joe complained.

"The door stays open."

"What are you afraid of? You think I'm gonna crawl out that window or something?"

"Take a leak if you want to take a leak," Koontz said. "But hurry up about it."

Joe took his own sweet time about it, flicked droplets of urine all over the floor, zipped up his pants with a flourish, and turned away without flushing the toilet.

"Flush it," Koontz ordered.

"Flush it yourself. It's your toilet, qué no?"

They stared, unmoving, at each other.

"You flush it, you half-pint piece of horseshit," Bill Koontz said, unbuckling his holster's safety strap and letting his fingers touch the butt of his pistol, "or I'll crack your smart-ass fucking skull open."

"Hey," Emilio Cisneros called. "That lawyer just drove in."

"Oh Christ—" Koontz jerked his head sideways. "Up front, Joe. Let's go."

"You getting a little nervous?" Joe asked solicitously.

Koontz didn't answer. He followed Joe back out front and went over to open the door. Charley Bloom stepped through, and Koontz closed and relocked the door behind him.

"I'm Mr. Mondragón's lawyer," Bloom said. He extricated a cigarette, offered one to Joe, who declined, and to Koontz, who just batted the air irritatedly by way of refusal. "What are you holding Joe for?" the lawyer asked.

"We're not really holding him for anything. He more or less just got here."

"Well, if you haven't charged him, Officer Koontz, I don't think you can hold him."

A state police car with the red light flashing bounced frenziedly off the highway, swung around the cluster of rattletrap vehicles, and screeched to a stop with its nose practically touching the front door. Bruno Martínez tumbled out, leaving the emergency flasher on, grabbed the doorhandle, and thudded loudly into the locked door.

"Hey—!" he scrawked, staggering back grasping his forehead where it had crashed against the glass.

"Hold your water," Koontz snapped as he crossed the room and unlocked the door.

Bruno barged in, looking every which way, all out of breath.

"This is Mr. Bloom," Koontz said, "Mr. Mondragón's lawyer."

"Yeah." Bruno nodded perfunctorily at Bloom. "You get in touch with Trucho?"

"We talked—I dunno—maybe ten minutes ago."

Another pickup, stacked high with green hay bales, pulled in, and Bernabé Montoya stepped out. The sheriff nodded to this man, that woman, slapped a teen-ager on the back and grinned, accepted a cigarette and a light, and said something joking to several old-timers on his way to the headquarters, reached for the handle, and walked into the locked door.

"Hey," he muttered loudly. "Open the door."

Bruno Martínez flipped the lock and Bernabé sidled in bent over, rubbing his knee. "The first thing I'd do," he said bitterly, "is turn off that flashing light, unless you want to incite those people to riot."

"Oh yeah, I forgot—" Redfaced, Bruno went out and attended to the matter.

"And the second thing I'd do," the sheriff said, going over to flick an ash into the ashtray on the counter, "is I'd formally arrest José over there for assault or for discharging a weapon illegally or something, and then I'd release him on his own recognizance, or in the custody of his lawyer here."

Bill Koontz was going to say something, thought better of it, turned to Emilio Cisneros, and muttered, "You heard him, make out the forms." The dispatcher crossed to the typewriter, inserted some forms and carbon paper in the machine, and waited. Koontz motioned Joe over and had him empty his pockets onto the counter and take off his belt. Then while he made up a possessions ticket, he fed down the time of arrest and other information to the dispatcher, who typed it out rapidly, one-finger style. When he had finished, he gave Joe a copy, just to check over the personal data, and Joe said:

"Right here, in this little box, you got it I'm white. I ain't white, I'm brown."

"You're either white, or your're black, or you're oriental," Bill Koontz said.

"I'm brown, you son of a bitch."

"I think that about raps it up, qué no?" Bernabé Montoya said uneasily, edging between them and giving Joe a dark hairy eyeball. "I think Mr. Bloom and Mr. Mondragón ought to leave, now. So long, boys, you be careful on that road going back, And José—?"

Joe turned around at the door. "Yeah?"

"Stick around home, okay? This isn't quite over yet."

"Sure." Joe grinned obnoxiously. "I lived here all my life, didn't I?"

When they were outside, Koontz said, "I wonder if that wasn't a dumb thing to do. I should of just put him in the car and took him down to Chamisaville."

"He's not going anyplace," Bernabé said.

"I can't help feeling he shouldn't be out there with them—"

"This place was gonna explode," Bernabé said. "You dumbbells were sitting on a stick of dynamite."

"Suppose they don't leave—?"

"They'll leave. They're not crazy. And anyway, they won."

The policemen watched as Joe talked with a group of about ten people. Others just sat in their trucks, half-obscured behind dusty and cracked windshields, placidly looking on. One of Ruby Archuleta's Milagro Land and Water Protection Association petitions was making the rounds, and, laughing triumphantly, people were signing like mad. Bloom hung back while Joe bragged about what he would have done to Koontz and the rest of the chotas if they had tried to work him over, but the lawyer also kept glancing nervously at the headquarters, waiting for somebody to rescind his noisy little client's freedom; finally he got so nervous that he interrupted Joe's animated obscene oration, suggesting it was about time everybody split.

"That lawyer," Bruno Martínez growled. "I'd like to cut his balls off."

"Leave him alone," Bernabé said. "It's not gonna work out the way you wanted it to work out. But you can still salvage it, maybe. And that's about all. Try for anything more and we're all in a lot of hot water."

Koontz sat down, lighting a cigarette. "You really think those people out there mean business?"

Bernabé said, "I know it. Did anybody here call the DA?"

"I talked with him yesterday," Bruno said. "He and Trucho had talked. They were batting around an open charge of murder, but, you know how it is, that Pacheco won't die."

"The way I'd play it, if anybody asks me," the sheriff said, despite the fact that nobody had asked, or was going to ask, "is I'd fine him for destruction of property, making a disturbance, and discharging a weapon within the town limits. The assault you got him on now won't stick, not with those two witnesses."

"Period—?" Koontz said glumly.

Bernabé stubbed out his cigarette and sucked in a

deep breath, which he expelled very slowly, never having felt quite this heady before. "Listen," he said quietly. "I sat in a room while that man of yours, that Montana fellow, outlined the plan he had. Now, I know somebody didn't just make up those plans for fun and games, but I do know they didn't work. And although personally I've kicked José Mondragón's ass from here to breakfast and back again, I also realize times are changing and there isn't room for the same type of people up here that there used to be when I was growing up. But that agent don't understand the situation, and I don't think any of you do either, and you're in deep trouble if you let that boss of yours, that Trucho, shoot off his theories half-cocked. I know the Zopilote can win in Milagro, but after these couple of days I know he can't win without a war, and wherever those orders on José came from, I know they came with the express intention of avoiding a war. Or a little revolution. Or whatever the hell it's fashionable to call it these days—"

With that Bernabé suddenly walked outside and almost stunned everybody by signing Ruby Archuleta's petition. But just as he was about to put his name on the wrinkled page, his steady salary as sheriff clobbered him like a stroke, and instead of signing, he read over the petition, nodded a sort of noncommittal approval, and, with an audible sigh, passed it on.

Pretty soon men, women, and a few children—people with one-acre farms and barren ten-tree orchards and horses they never rode and ranchers with three-cow herds and no place to graze them—returned to their dilapidated vehicles, backed up, and pulled out, heading north toward home. In a moment only two state cars and Bernabé Montoya's pickup remained in the parking lot.

At which point the county sheriff, Ernie Maestas, accompanied by two deputies, arrived. And right behind them came Granny Smith, emergency signal flashing. And then Sal Bugbee and Buddy Namath showed up, each in separate cars.

"What happened?" Ernie Maestas chortled. "How come you're all still alive?"

"Oh fuck off," Bill Koontz said.

Ernie slapped him on the back. "When you gonna at least learn to swear in Spanish, you tight-assed gabacho marrano, huh?"

"When I'm dead, bury me in one of your lousy camposantos and I'll learn it from all the skeletons of your people."

The phone rang. It was Trucho. "Look," he shouted excitedly, "don't do anything with Mondragón. Arrest him for something petty, release him on his own recognizance. Things could be a lot more ready to blow than we suspect."

"We already did all that," Koontz said wearily.

"Fine. Lemme talk with Montana."

"He ain't back yet."

"He didn't come in with the rest of the posse?"

"Not so far as I know."

"Well, when that bastard comes in have him call me. And that don't mean five or ten minutes after he checks in, either. I want him to call me the second he walks through that door. Who's talking to him on the radio?"

"Nobody. There's a lot of weather disturbance up there. Nobody's been able to get in touch with him since around noon, I guess."

"Keep trying, dammit. We got to talk."

"Yes sir."

Bill Koontz hung up the phone and wiped his brow. In an hour he would be off duty, thank Christ. He went back to the bathroom and flushed the goddam toilet.

Part Six

"We wouldn't none of us have even been here
tonight . . . if it wasn't for the love of all them
stupid Coyote Angels."

—Onofre Martínez

Part Six

"They're scared," Bloom said quietly. "Devine is scared; the cops are scared. Down in the capital they're scared. They're scared even more than we are."

Linda sat across from him at the kitchen table, a coffee cup in front of her. She wore one of his old lumberjacket shirts, her hair was tied back in a pony tail. Her dark eyes were beautiful, her lips sad.

"Nobody was killed," Bloom continued. "That's amazing, isn't it? In that police station I thought it would all suddenly go haywire, but it didn't. That's the thing I don't understand. I guess in the end they were just too scared so they backed off."

"Did you collect the eggs today?" Linda asked.

"Are you kidding?"

"We should collect the eggs," she said.

They went out back to the chicken shed. A goose, which never slept inside, preferring instead to sit under the stars, honked gently as they entered the pen. Linda unlatched the coop door, and the door tilted awkwardly, jammed.

"I better put a new hinge on tomorrow," Bloom said.

They entered. The hay on the floor and in the egg boxes smelled dusty and sweet. The grubby yellow, big-balled, snake-eating reincarnation of Cleofes Apodaca was curled up in an egg box, purring. The chickens were roosting. Their two turkeys were sitting

on the ground under the roosting chickens, getting shat
upon as they snoozed.

Both five-cubicle egg boxes were on the ground.
Bloom sat down on one of them; Linda took a seat
on the other across the shed. Bloom lit a cigarette and
smoked slowly as they listened to the chickens
ruffling their feathers, clucking sporadically. Bright
moonlight reflected softly in the dusty window frames.

"I love it here," Bloom said gently. "You know,
suddenly I think I honestly love it here. In Milagro."

"What will happen now?" Linda asked.

"I don't know. But they can't do anything to Joe.
They don't dare. And I really believe that. I'm not
even sure they'll try to stop his irrigating. We may
never go to court."

"What about Devine? What about the conservancy district and the dam?"

"They're going to get cold feet," Bloom said simply.
"We may never have a hearing on that. Or at least,
not for a while. That'll give us time and we need time
to launch a fight, to forge out-of-town allies. Look at
all the people who signed that petition today—"

"Do you believe what you say, Charley?"

"Yeah. At least I think I do. Listen, for three hundred years, in one way or another, they've been
trying to drive the people out of this valley. But somehow some of them kept hanging on. And they can't
sell homesites up in the canyon or draw skiers or
expand the dude ranch if a whole bunch of angry people are walking around down here with loaded guns
looking hostile, now can they?"

Linda said, "All my life I had dreams of peace."

Bloom fetched a couple of eggs, one from under
the cat, and he held the warm eggs against his cheek.

"All my life, everybody around me, it was always
fighting," Linda said. "Everybody was always angry,
or always shouting or singing—I used to sit on my
bed with my hands over my ears. Everybody was so
noisy and tough and loudmouthed. And hysterical.
Automobiles never had any mufflers, half the Friday
night dances ended in brawls. I was always driving
into town to the jail to bail out a brother, a cousin,

my father. My mother never complained, not even when she was dying. She had cancer, she whispered Hail Marys nonstop to herself for a month, but she never complained. Guns, hunting, death, car crashes, frustration. The police were always hanging around. In town the air itself held a threat. There were always so many of us in such small rooms, and somebody was always banging a fist on the table, shouting out words of hate. All of us always hated so many people. We got so tired being so full of hate. I don't know where my brothers and sisters and my father got all their energy. Always talking, shouting, laughing, crying, bitching. Somebody who could only play three stupid chords was always banging away like an insane idiot on some tinny guitar. The radio was always on, the TV always going—when it worked. Everybody was always talking about money, shrieking about it, hating who had it, sobbing in the arms of who didn't have it. All the passion was so noisy. You'd go to the drive-in with somebody and all they did was joke and fart and drink beer and talk about the movie so much they never knew what was going on. And everything was a fight. And everybody always walked around armed. And when we came here I didn't think it would be that way ever again."

Bloom said, "I'm sorry."

Linda was crying. "I don't want to struggle like that anymore," she said. "I wish I could melt."

"What does that mean?"

"I don't know. Like snow . . ."

She looked up. "When it snows, when there's a fresh snow on the ground covering all the fields, flat and silent and white, with no marks on it—well, everybody I know wants to run across the white, make footprints, make marks, run, jump, thrash, create patterns, write their names, bust it up. But I never want to do that. I just want to stand at the edge of the field and look at the unbroken white. I don't want to mark it up in any way. I want to just watch it, and breathe in its serenity. I want to let it melt slowly without ever having been disturbed, except maybe by tiny mice—they never really break the crust; or by rabbits, or by a magpie landing and taking off, so you can see where its tail touched and where the wingtips pushed off, but that's all. There's no tension in that kind of field. Everything is so lovely and untouched and serene. I'm so tired of tension, Charley. I'm only twenty-nine years old, but I feel worn out. I feel so fragile. I feel like a crystal glass that's going to shatter if the noise and the tension, if the struggle and the fighting, if the *loudness* of it all rises even one decibel more. I'm not even afraid, I don't think— I'm just waiting."

Bloom said, "Amen. Funny. I've decided to go back to Rael's tomorrow and buy a gun."

Linda did not respond.

They sat across from each other in the feathery, hay-smelling chicken coop. One turkey released a contented trilling little cluck. An owl, off by the river hunting mice, uttered its muffled cry.

Bloom stood up, walked outside. The air was thick and moist, freshly mown grass smelling nice. The ponies stirred in their corral, moonlight glinting off their shiny backs. The mountains hovered over everything like benevolent, serene elephants.

The lawyer suddenly threw an egg, underhand, straight up into the air. It rose about twenty yards, fuzzily gleaming, then whizzed straight back to earth only a few feet away, hitting with a hard thud, but it didn't break.

Bloom couldn't believe it. He stared at the egg. Then he went over and picked it up—it wasn't even cracked. And for a long time he held the egg in his hand, both frightened and astonished and unable to move, his eyes fixed upon the moon.

⌘

Amarante Córdova sat on the stump beside his doorway; Snuffy Ledoux stood several feet away pensively smoking as darkness fell. For a moment the mountain peaks were crimson, then the sunlight blurred and ancient blue shadows drifted swiftly over the foothills, until only the mountaintops were bathed in rich warm rouge for seconds before suddenly it was night.

"Well, I'm home," Snuffy said tiredly, snapping his cigarette away. "And I ain't ever gonna leave again."

"You came at a good time," the old man said.

"Yeah, maybe I did." Snuffy sat down on the warm earth. "Or maybe I didn't. Now I got to make plans, though, I got to figure out how to live. I got to carve a lot of santos and peddle them down in Chamisaville, do something like that, I guess, who knows? I'm broke."

"Do you own your parents' house?" the old man asked.

"You kidding?" Snuffy picked up a stone, chucking it aimlessly at the nearby pile of piñon. "When I left I sold it to Devine. I needed the dough."

"You can live here," the old man said.

"What do you mean?"

"You can live here. In this house." He paused. "We could fix the house."

Snuffy swiveled his head, giving the dilapidated house a skeptical once-over. "There's a lot of work to be done," he said unenthusiastically.

"When I die you inherit the house and the land," Amarante said. "Others will move into the houses over here and begin to irrigate the land. You'll see. We're going to buy all this land back one way or another."

"When you die—shit!" Snuffy exclaimed sarcastically. "I better chop some wood for that stove of yours," he added, standing. Taking the ax in hand, he approached the piñon pile.

Before he reached for a log, the silver sparkle off shiny bean leaves several fields away caught Snuffy's attention. And although he was forty-five and kind of pooped out and lonely and wondering how in hell to turn a buck tomorrow, he suddenly smiled, allowing himself a vision he only half (maybe not even a quarter, to be honest) believed. It was not a vision of the future as totally unknown, but rather a vision of the future as composed, in part at least, of what had been okay about the past. He saw the west side houses whole again, their chimneys releasing pungent smoke, the houses inhabited by a new generation of men, women, and children whose fathers, aunts, and grandparents had been phased off the land and onto wandering migrant trails, whose roots had shriveled and died. If one beanfield, why not three? Or how about a dozen? And people would return from faraway places, and chilies and pumpkins would grow in the cornfields, and you would be able to smell bread baking—

"Ah, shit . . ." Snuffy reached for a log. Who was kidding who with a dream like that? And what had been so great about the old days anyway? You couldn't read or write and half the people died of TB. I'd like a car, Snuffy thought, I never wanted to spend my life on a horse. And what's so much fun about hoeing a row of beans, or about sitting in the crapper with wind howling up your asshole on a night that's thirty below?

A coyote, out on the mesa, howled. It had been a long time since Snuffy had heard that sound. He turned with the small log in one hand: Amarante nodded and grinned.

"Those damn coyotes," the old man croaked. "You're not even allowed to poison them anymore."

"There ain't enough coyotes left to waste your poison on," Snuffy said, abruptly dropping the log at his feet. And, with one savage, angry blow, which held in it a curse for every hour of every day of his life that he'd spent chopping wood, he busted the log neatly, downright exquisitely, in two.

&

His car was sitting there, exactly where he had left it, exactly as he had left it. Kyril Montana leaned on the hood panting heavily, big sweat droplets falling off his forehead onto the shiny metal. For possibly five minutes he was positioned that way trying to recover his breath, calming down, and then he began to feel chilled as the late-afternoon winds sweeping off the mountains hit him. Moving wearily, he swung behind the wheel and turned on the engine and the heater. Almost immediately, the police radio crackled inquisitively, asking his whereabouts. Taking a deep breath the agent lifted the mike, pressed the transmitting button, and, having dispassionately fed in his call number, he informed the dispatcher: "I'm okay; I just got back. I made no contact with Mondragón; the entire result of this search was negative."

"We got Mondragón," the dispatcher said. "Can you hear me? Joe Mondragón has been here and gone. Everything is cool, man. But you better come in quick and get in touch with Trucho, he's after your *ass*!"

Kyril Montana said "Thanks" and hung up the mike. By the overhead light he checked his face in the mirror: it was moderately scratched, but otherwise not so flushed now, not that bad. The agent ran fingers through his hair, combing it as best he could. After that he got out and opened the trunk where he always kept a fresh sport coat and slacks, a white shirt and a tie, in case of emergency. Stripping quickly, he donned the fresh clothes and then drove out of there.

Katie Gleason, who answered his knock grinning like a dervish, bounced off toward the kitchen shrieking, "Hey, it's Ossifer Wyoming, I mean Ossifer Dakota, I mean Ossifer Mon*tana*!"

From the den, where he was stretched out on a couch with a green eyeshade over his eyes listening to the evening symphony from a Capital City FM radio station, Bud called, "Ky, is that you? Is that *you*, Ky? Where the hell you been?"

Bertha emerged from the kitchen just as Bud, in his stocking feet, staggered groggily from the den.

"Where you been, at a cocktail party with a bunch of elk up there?" Bertha wanted to know. "Everybody else got back hours ago. Joe, he walked into the Doña Luz station just after noon and gave himself up, and they let him go an hour later when half the town showed up outside looking to burn the joint down. You missed all the fireworks, how about a cup of coffee? You look like you could use it."

Bud said, "They say Pacheco's alright. He's like his pig used to be, indestructible."

"That's fine," the agent said. "Can I use the phone?"

"Be our guest—"

The agent first dialed his wife. "I'm fine," he told Marilyn. "I just got in. No. I just wanted to stay up in the mountains a little longer, to be sure. Right, I've heard a little about what happened; I'll stop in Doña Luz for the details, and I'll probably be home round eleven unless I'm needed up here. No, don't wait up. And don't worry about that either, I'll grab a bite, probably here or on the way down. Right. Yes, everything is okay. I'll see you soon."

He hung up, waited a moment to make sure his poise was the way he wanted it to be, then dialed Trucho.

"He went home," the state police switchboard informed him. So he dialed Trucho at home.

"He's still at the office," Mrs. Trucho said.

"They told me there he went home."

"Well, if he did he didn't arrive yet."

"You tell him I called, tell him I'll check in at Doña Luz before I head south, he can leave a message for me there if he gets home. Otherwise we'll talk in the morning."

"I'll do that. But maybe you better call back in a little while, Mr. Montana, I heard he really wanted to talk to you—"

Hanging up, the agent went back to the kitchen, sat down at the table across from Bud, and was very grateful for the coffee Bertha set before him.

"Look," he said, exhausted but struggling hard to keep his eyes open, alert, and to keep from slurring his words, "I'm all out of cigarettes."

"Katie," Bud called, "go get me a pack of cigarettes from the silver box on the coffee table in the den."

"Get 'em yourself, I'm not your slave," Katie screeched. "Besides, I'm watching TV."

"Listen, you obnoxious little shrimp, you do what your daddy tells you to do!" Bertha hollered, bending over to peer into her oven at a rib roast and some baked potatoes.

"What is Daddy, a cripple? Is he a multiple paraplegic, huh? Is he, huh?"

"Oh Christ Almighty," Bud groaned, pushing himself up. "*I'll* get the cigarette myself."

"You always do that," Bertha said. "How do you expect the kid to learn if you always give in like that?"

"It's just easier. I'm sorry."

"Well then don't get mad at her if she never does what you ask her to do," Bertha harped, stirring some flour into a gravy base in a frying pan on the stove.

Kyril Montana sipped the hot coffee and his entire aching body tingled it tasted so incredibly good. Kitchen smells, of the roast, of baking cheese, of the gravy, a mixture of onion and garlic and strong seasoning, went to his head—he couldn't wait to eat.

Bud dropped an unopened pack of filter-tip cigarettes on the table. Kyril Montana took the pack and carefully tore off the wrapper.

"What happened to your hands?" Bud asked.

"Oh, you know. Just fending off brush, stuff like that. I lost my footing once and landed on some rocks, nothing serious." Reassuringly, the agent smiled, "There's nothing wrong that an invitation to share whatever it is Bertha's got going in that oven won't cure."

Bud looked down at his own clasped hands on the table. "You're not staying for dinner, Ky. Drink the coffee, take the cigarettes if you want, but then leave, please. Actually, I'm not asking you to leave, I'm telling you to leave, do you understand?"

Kyril Montana glared evenly at the top of Bud's head in the charged silence, trying to make him look up. "Bud, you're not really in a position to tell me to go to hell."

"If you won't accept it from him, then accept it from me—" Bertha began.

"Shuttup," Bud snapped, glancing up fleetingly at the agent, but immediately dropping his eyes again.

Kyril Montana said, "I don't want to stay where I'm not wanted, Bud, but you have to understand this is fairly sudden. I'm a little tired, you know, I've had a long afternoon in the hills. So this comes as a relative surprise—"

"I don't care, Ky. Do what you will, think what you will, plan some kind of revenge, but just finish your coffee and get out of here. Whatever happens from here on in, I'm not gonna be a part of it. And that includes letting you use my house for your red-baiting meetings or whatever. It isn't because I've got high and mighty scruples against what you're doing, understand; I haven't had any great change of heart. I'm just finally more scared of them, now, than I am of you."

"Well. You son of a bitch."

Bud nodded. "Right, you're right, I'm not up for any civic awards, Ky, I'm just looking after my own skin, you're absolutely right. But do me a favor and finish that coffee and get out of here, and steer clear of our lives from here on in."

Katie suddenly pranced into the kitchen, blurting, "Show's over!" And then, noticing her father's downcast face and the calm, infuriated agent, she said, "Hey everybody, guess what pennies are made out of—?"

For a second Kyril Montana felt murderous enough to turn around and slug that obnoxious kid; he wanted to knock her bratty little head right off her shoulders and send it splattering against the kitchen wall like a rotten tomato.

Instead, he shook loose a smoke from the pack Bud had given him, set the weed in his mouth, and lit it— flame flared up before his eyes.

"Hey," Bud said, amazed, and then abruptly, nervously giggling: *"You lit the fucking filter!"*

◖ʒ

It was a bright, beautiful night. Troubled, off-balance, and feeling strange, Horsethief Shorty wandered. He circled the dark swimming pool in which he had never splashed and crossed damp silver grass to the tennis courts, leaning against the wire with his hands hung in the steel webbing above his head. He had forgotten to loosen the nets at dusk and sweep the base lines, making sure they were securely tacked into the clay. Tomorrow evening he and a Chicano kid would sweep the courts and roll them flat.

But right now Shorty didn't want to loosen the nets. He leaned against, laxly hung onto, the fencing, gazing across the courts down toward the scattered town lights, toward the few mercury vapor lamps his boss had installed around the store, the café, and the Enchanted Land Motel. Across the highway in the ghost town Amarante Córdova's light glowed softly from the open door of his crumbling adobe.

Shorty rolled a cigarette, lit it, smoked quietly. After a while he snapped his cigarette butt through the wire onto the near court. "I sure spent my life kissing a lot of assholes," he mused wearily. "And I guess maybe I chose the wrong side."

Which was a thought that had been eating away at him for a while now, and it had really been driven home sharp as a lightning bolt when Bloom tossed that finger at him this afternoon: for some reason, the lawyer's bitter gesture had made Shorty almost want to cry.

Well, tonight it all made him sad. But shit, he thought, he'd been lonely all his life; loneliness was the absolute condition of his days, and it had been that way ever since he was a kid opening his eyes at first dawn and lying still for a minute, listening to the roosters crowing in a tiny pen out back and thinking in a minute he would have to get up and plod off to the war that was his school.

Hell, Shorty had shared Ladd Devine's dream about the golf course over there on the west side, and about the entire Miracle Valley project. He'd cast his hand in with that kind of progress, betting on the new people who were going to come in and make the town grow, and he was going to be a big part of that growth. You wouldn't have caught Shorty dead on a golf course, but he owned some of that land over there, some of the choicest parcels, and he would be a strong partner in the corporation that developed it, and there was an excitement to that kind of life.

But there they were down there, those Spanish niggers at the bottom of the proverbial heap, their little lights twinkling—and goddam if Shorty didn't have a yearning to traipse on down there and put away a few enchiladas and a quart of chokecherry wine with Joe Mondragón or Pancho Armijo, or even with that decrepit, ninety-three-year-old miracle, Amarante Córdova.

"Shorty? Is that you—?"

Flossie was up by the pool, wearing a swimsuit. Her long hair hung loose, shimmering like Christmastime fiber glass angel hair.

"Yep, this is me," Shorty said, and on his way to the pool he rolled another cigarette. At poolside, he stretched out in a chaise longue and lit the weed.

"I'm going for a swim in the nude," Flossie said.

"You go right ahead. Don't mind me."

Unselfconsciously, she undid the side zipper, let the top fall, and peeled the suit down her long legs. Her big breasts drooped a lot, and her belly had gotten pretty plump, but her legs were strong and lovely. She lifted her breasts a little wistfully with her palms, then let them fall, turned around, and slipped slowly backward into the cool water.

Flossie breaststroked quietly around for a minute before swimming to the poolside nearest Shorty, where she rested, arms folded on the tile border, chin resting on her arms.

"How's the water?" Shorty asked.

"I guess it's pretty cold, but I'm so drunk it's hard to tell. You can't swim, can you Shorty?"

"Nope. I'd sink like a stone."

"What do you think happens now?" she asked after a silence.

"I don't exactly know. They've won a small victory, but they won't know how to take advantage of it. It might delay the dam and the conservancy district, though, also the golf course on the west side, and the Miracle Valley crap, too."

"I wonder," she said. And then: "Shorty, is it wrong for me to be on their side?"

"I dunno. I feel kind of funny about things, too."

"There'll be a fight, won't there?"

"Sure, one hell of a fight. But then there's always fights."

"I'm pretty drunk, Shorty. I've been drinking ever since that posse went out early this morning. Ladd won't talk to me at all. He's very tense. He screamed at Jerry G. for losing a bulldozer or something, then he locked himself in the office for an hour. After that he took the Lincoln and drove down to the capital. I don't know what's going to happen. You know what?"

"What?"

"I wish I could fly," Flossie drawled.

"What then?"

"I'd get the kind of drunk I am right now and fly Ladd's plane over the mountains and crash it into a high meadow, or into one of those deep dark comfortable canyons nobody ever goes to."

"Hell, I can fly that plane," Shorty said quietly.

For a long moment, licking chlorinated bubbles off her lips, she said nothing. Then, closing her eyes, she asked, "Would you want to, Shorty?"

"I don't see why not. It's all over here for me, Flossie. I don't want to be on one side or the other in what's coming up."

"You really think it's over for you?"

"Sure. I was up by the water tank this afternoon looking for Joe Mondragón, when his lawyer walked into a field down below and gave me the finger. It was sort of like he shot me in the heart. Suddenly I felt like a big creep. I can't understand why something like that didn't happen to me when I was twenty."

"I just don't want to die in a hospital, in a straight-jacket, hollering and screaming from the DTs," Flossie said. "And besides, Shorty, I'm so sick of being so comfortable, I'm so sick of this gentle life."

"I suppose so," Shorty mused.

"We could go right now."

"Why not?"

Like somebody twenty years younger, all gleaming and graceful as a trout, she swam to the shallow end of the pool, water drops rolling off her big, growing-flabby body like sparks of liquid moon. And she paused there, profiled to Shorty, looking at the sky. A breeze whisked through orchard branches, rippled aspen leaves, stirred across the lawn, and slightly tickled the swimming pool water.

Flossie toweled dry and tugged the swimsuit back on. "Let's go," she said softly.

They walked up the hill, Shorty a little behind her, appreciating her ass, and around the corner of the lodge: a station wagon was parked in the driveway. Shorty drove; slowly they swung away from the house, heading down through the canyon into the valley. Flossie clicked on the radio, then clicked it off. They turned onto the highway, aiming south.

During that forty-five-minute drive to the Chamisaville airport neither spoke very much. Flossie sat with her hands in her lap, her long peroxide hair lovely and rich against her bare shoulders, and she smelled Horse-thief Shorty's smell, of animals and tobacco and sweat, and something she couldn't exactly define, a little bit like sagebrush, she guessed. And Shorty drove slowly down the highway smelling the sad, sagging woman beside him whom he had known so much of his life, her hair, the damp chlorine, faint traces of a lilac perfume, cherry lipstick on her lips. They drove south in the powerful car, while outside on the right the sagebrush plain stretched west, and the mountains rose on their left, dark and shining.

The airport was shut down for the night, Chet Premminger at home in the Chamisaville suburb of Arroyo Seco. Shorty unhooked the tiedown cables and helped Flossie into the plane.

When they were airborne she asked timidly, "How do you feel, Shorty?"

"I'm okay," he answered thoughtfully. Then smiled: "I've had an okay life."

"I had such a subdued life," Flossie said, not with rancor, no hurt feelings there. "I've always been so comfortable, you know."

He steered the plane over the mountains. The dark-ness in the canyons and valleys below was rich and soft. Neither spoke. Flossie looked down, looked up, gazed straight ahead, let her eyes unfocus and film over, fell asleep. Deer on a bald ridge halted, gazing skyward—Shorty waved. He was relaxing too, growing woozy; he cut the engine and settled back, eyes almost bemusedly on the silvered, shadow-casting landscape below. They were over a thickly forested, deep-canyoned region, inaccessible to most people.

The plane glided silently. And then the nose began to tip down toward the mysterious high country forest where they would not be discovered in years.

Laconically, almost too slowly. Shorty started the plane again, chuckled and shook his head, pulling them out of the glide, and he turned around, aiming away from the mountains over the mesa, heading south toward the airport. Everything gleamed, reflecting the moon so strongly he needed no lights to land. The plane bumped on the runway, straightened out, slowed down, and stopped: he cut the engine.

Flossie woke up.

"Hey," she murmured. "What happened?"

"Nothing," Shorty said, smiling broadly. "Nothing at all."

"You bastard," she whispered, tipping over and cuddling against him.

"I got to thinking about my life," Shorty said matter-of-factly, cupping her breast. "I got to thinking about where I been and what I done and what it was I always wanted, and I reached a conclusion."

"Which was—?" she murmured sleepily.

"I dunno, I guess mostly I just realized up there I was still curious. You know? I mean, I'm too old and too much of a bastard to change sides, but I'd like to stick around a while longer and see how things turn out."

&

There had never been such rejoicing in the Frontier Bar. The jukebox blared mariachi music, everybody was very drunk, and, because more women than usual were on hand, people tried to dance. Joe and Nancy Mondragón were both so bombed they could hardly stand up, let alone walk, God forbid knock off La Raspa, a foxtrot, or the Monkey, but they had decided to perform a flamenco number to a trio of unabashedly drippy accordions, chunk-a-chunk guitars, gagging fiddles, and hysterically sobbing south-of-the-border voices, so they cleared the floor by elbowing everybody else aside, and—Nancy gritting an imaginary rose in her teeth, Joe with a fist clenched against his belly holding together an imaginary skintight gypsy jacket—they began to "dance." And, as they insanely tattooed the floor with their uncontrolled feet, close to fifty intoxicated buffoons commenced clapping completely out of rhythm, and of course they hooted and shrieked, making vivid gestures and bearhugging each other deliriously while also commenting grossly on the Mondragón effort. Joe stomped, reeking of haughty sneers; Nancy stomped, twining a serpentine hand sensually in the air before losing her balance and zigzagging into the sodden crowd, which heaved her back into the center ring. The record ended, but so what? Nobody had heard the jukebox while it was going; nobody noticed when it was gone. They clapped and hollered while Joe rat-a-tat-tatted his feet and collided with Nancy, clip-clopped wobbly-kneed away, wavered off-balance, recovered, and kept on thumping his feet. And so it went until Joe keeled over backward, his head striking the floor with a sickening crunch. Stars did "La Bamba" in his brain. On awaking, he found himself propped up dazedly in a corner, his hair bloodsoaked; Tranquilino Jeantete was bumbling through a weird little jig with Nancy who suddenly burped loudly and plunged uncontrollably once more into the soused hordes. Instantly, another reeling and reeking woman took over where Nancy's rollicking had left off.

Joe clambered back into the spotlight and spread his arms, demanding silence. "Turn off the jukebox!" he shouted. "I'm gonna sing a song!"

Whereupon God cut his strings, and Joe sat down with a rude bump. The gathering hooted mercilessly. Somebody pulled the jukebox plug. Joe raised his arms, urgently wiggling his fingers until everybody piped down. All you could hear for a moment was labored breathing, carbonated bubbles going berserk in two dozen beer bellies, the beer coolers humming, and the ice machine tumbling chunks into its aluminum trough.

Joe's plan was to sing "Malagueña Salerosa" so soulfully, mournfully, sadly, and beautifully that after the first verse he would need a rowboat in order not to drown in the mob's tears.

But when he opened his mouth the first line sallied forth sounding like a mouse being squeezed to death by a king snake. Which made Joe and about twenty other men and women giggle. Ineptly smothering his own sputtering guffaws, Joe frantically thrust up his hands, again wiggling the fingertips for silence. This produced a chain reaction during which eighteen other blotto boozers uplifted their arms and wiggled their sweaty fingertips. And when Joe opened his mouth, instead of crooning like an Antonio Aguilar, he belched.

That broke up the fiesta. They hee-hawed and laughed, sputtered and chattered and babbled—a dozen cracked voices assassinated "Malagueña Salerosa," jubilantly they murdered it up to the spider-webbed rafters and well beyond; rasping words collided against rasping words, gurgling carousers collided against gurgling carousers, and the magic of that breathless soap opera moment Joe had intended to create departed.

Nancy tried to lift Joe, instead she collapsed over him.

"Let's get out of here," Joe mumbled woozily. "I'm gonna barf."

Painfully, laboring to help each other up, they became hopelessly entangled instead. Finally, they got to their feet and, arm in supporting arm, careened toward a wall, thinking that's where the door should have been; they wound up recharting their erratic course twice more before plummeting into the crisp night air.

Joe lurched about ten steps ahead, and, bending over with a hand braced against either knee, he erupted. Harlan Betchel's Doberman watchdog, Brutus, danced excitedly in the front plate glass window of the Pilar Café, barking and snarling while Joe heaved. Nancy wobbled over to the café and pressed her nose against the window, infuriating the dog. "Shuttup, Brutus," Nancy muttered, "or we'll make a sausage out of you, comprendes? A great big sizzling sausage."

Loping unsteadily over, Joe also pressed his nose against the window, merrily tapping on the glass with his knuckles. The dog retreated abruptly, neck hairs bristling, and knocked the salt and pepper shakers off one table.

Joe barked and snarled; Nancy growled and gritted her teeth. Brutus barked and snarled, yelped, retreated, charged forward, and crashed around in circles, going insane.

Onofre Martínez swerved gracefully out of the Frontier's ruckus, caught himself and regained his balance, and then, oozing one-armed dignity, he navigated over to the café and, draping his left arm around Nancy's shoulders and the invisible right arm around Joe's shoulders, he commenced barking and growling and snarling along with them. Brutus leaped forward, skidded to a stop, danced about, and kicked over a chair, howling back.

Soon eight more addled rabble-rousers joined the fray. Lined arm in arm along the plate glass front of the café, they barked and growled and snarled and meowed and cock-a-doodle-dooed, while the infuriated dog danced like a demented devil, leaping and jumping and snapping at them with foamy jaws. He knocked off more salt and pepper shakers, then tipped over a table, yelping in fright, and, fangs bared, he repeatedly charged at the crazies gathered outside.

Joe roared like a lion. Nancy baaed like a sheep. Snuffy Ledoux crowed and clucked and cheeped; Amarante Córdova brayed like a mule. Benny Maestas growled and whistled; Sparky Pacheco bammed his palms against the window; Jimmy Ortega neighed; Betty Apodaca tugged her cheeks out with her fingers, grimacing and loudly clacking her teeth. Both terrified and incensed, the savage watchdog thundered around, tipping over another table and three more chairs—napkin holders bounced across the floor; a sugar bowl shattered. Brutus cut his paw and began splattering blood over everything. The motley conglomeration of joyful, tanked-up ruffians outside laughed until tears came; they continued to imitate animals, they sang songs and gestured obscenely at the livid dog.

Bernabé Montoya, with his pants tugged up over his pajamas and his gun shoved backward into his holster, plodded wearily out of the shadows accompanied by Harlan Betchel, who wore a raincoat over his pajamas and carried a 16-gauge shotgun.

Bernabé dropped his cigarette in the dirt and ground it out. Then, after sucking in and sadly letting out a deep breath, he bawled:

"Okay, everybody: CUT IT OUT!"

They stopped and turned their heads and backed sheepishly away from the window, giggling at the sheriff and at Harlan Betchel and at Harlan's quivering shotgun.

"Now," Bernabé muttered grimly. "Would somebody mind telling me just what is going on?"

Nobody spoke; several burped. The revelers lurched a few feet sideways and back.

Bernabé started to walk over for a closer look through the Pilar window, but as he took a step his gun fell from the holster, plopping loudly to earth. While he bent to pick it up, the drunks unleashed a chorus of sniggers.

"Shuttup," Bernabé growled. Then he peered through the window. Brutus lay in the rubble gingerly licking his bloody paw.

Facing the culprits, Bernabé sighed, *"Ai Chihuahua,"* and removed a pad from his back pocket.

"Okay, okay, okay," he groaned. "Lemme get your names. You're gonna have to pay for this."

"Oh, hey Bernie, wait a sec," Harlan stammered. "It doesn't look like that much damage to me. They were just kidding around. I don't want to press any charges."

"Quit pointing that gun at us," an angry tipsy voice snarled, and Harlan quickly lowered the weapon, discharging a minute of profuse apologies in the direction it had been aimed.

"That's better," the same gruff voice allowed. Somebody else tee-heed derisively.

Bernabé asked, "Are you kidding me, Harlan—?"

"No sir. I'm absolutely serious. It's nothing, really. You can't hurt that furniture. And anyway, it was the dog that did it. There's no problem. None at all."

"Are you okay upstairs?" Bernabé gave Harlan a screwy look, refusing to believe he could get off the hook this easily.

"Absolutely," Harlan insisted. He smiled at the revelers. "It was all just in fun, right everybody?"

"Right, all in fun, that's right, Harlan, it was just all in fun, you bet." They sputtered and chuckled, loving their power, the way it reflected off the fear in Harlan Betchel's face. You could practically see the imprint of Joe Mondragón's bean plants across his ashen countenance.

"Okay, then. If you say so." Bernabé shrugged, replacing the pad in his pocket. "You people go back in the bar, though, okay?"

"Sure—" Everybody except Joe and Nancy tilted forward, and, in one manner or another, plunged, sashayed, tiptoed, or soft-shoe-shuffled into the Frontier Bar.

"Come on, José," Bernabé said warily. "Life is tough enough. Let's not have any more trouble."

"No trouble," Joe grinned. "We just decided to take a walk. What, there's a law in this town against taking a walk?"

"No law," the sheriff said. "Just laws against getting in trouble."

"Well, you know me," Joe laughed. "I'd walk a mile outta my way to steer clear of just one single tiny itty-bitty ounce of trouble."

Bernabé nodded, smiling in a joyless, on-guard manner.

Joe tucked his arm around Nancy's waist, swinging her roughly around, facing west—they began walking toward the highway.

"See?" Joe called back. "We're just a couple of turtledoves taking a little moonlight stroll."

Bernabé fished for a handkerchief in his pocket and

blew his nose. Then, while Harlan opened the café to check on his dog, the sheriff ticketed Onofre Martínez's mottled-green, 1953 Chevy pickup which was parked in its usual place, and after that he crossed the street and settled heavily onto the edge of Rael's porch. Laughter, and the raucous tinny jukebox music tripped out of the Frontier into the peaceful night. The sheriff muttered, "Welcome, ball fans, to the World Series of Borracheras." Then he drew his revolver, opened the cylinder, and, doing what he had forgotten to do when Harlan sounded the alarm, he slowly and quite sheepishly loaded the gun.

A night like this, after recent events, could lead a man to reflect on life in general, and so that is what Bernabé did while things were momentarily peaceful. And what he reflected on could be summed up thusly: It was all going to change now, the life in the valley, the way people looked at themselves and at each other, and the way they looked at the Ladd Devines and at the Jim Hirsshorns, at the Harlan Betchels, and even at the themselves. To be sure, life wouldn't return to what it was yesterday, but neither could it continue to be what it was today. The people had been apart for a long time, and now he sensed a small coming together—although who knew what those who had survived could do with a future nobody had defined? Bernabé knew the valley, he understood the people, and in the end he liked his life here, maybe he even had an embarrassing love for it all. But he was cynical and gruff, too, and sometimes he wished all the Joe Mondragóns would become cripples or at least eat poisonous mushrooms that would impair their vocal cords so he wouldn't have to listen to their stupid, abusive rantings all the time. But Bernabé understood roots and he understood the fractured culture, loving what was good in the past while refusing to romanticize it, at the same time that he admired all his stubborn neighbors who had survived on a wing and a prayer, on bootleg liquor, on a half-dozen illegal deer a year, and on a handful of overgrazed alfalfa fields. And any man or woman or half-grown kid who, come hell or high water or Ladd Devine, had hung onto a piece of land, a ragtag goat, a rifle, and the Spanish language, was okay in Bernabé's book. In fact, he sometimes envied his neighbors whatever it was some of them still possessed—call it cultural integrity—that he had mostly turned his back on by accepting the sheriff's job.

But what the hell. Bernabé was sad, sitting there on the porch tapping his heels lightly against the baseboards. He got up once and bought a Coke from the pop machine beside the door, sat down again, and stared at the cheery elongated shadows dancing in the yellow rectangle cast through the open Frontier door.

Bernabé saw no leaders; he had no idea how folks might get themselves together and forge viable new lives. If he had seen a way, or if he had believed a little more in his gente's ability to overcome their own confusion and internal disorders, he would have turned in his star tomorrow, grabbed a shovel, put on his irrigation boots, forsaken the security of his salary, and dived like a hungry muskrat into the heart of his own background in hopes of creating a better compromise for the unfathomable future.

But how could it be done? Friends tonight at the Frontier, these clowns would leap at each other's throats tomorrow. In the morning, hung over and nasty, bitching at the wives and kiddies and throwing stones at their sheep or at their useless horses, they would realize that a victory hardly lasted much longer than did a climax when they made love. They would realize that yesterday's triumph had ended when the moon rose, and that today new battle lines would be drawn, and that the fighting never stops.

Fuck it, the sheriff thought. He was tired. Getting up again, he crossed the street, took out his keys, and opened the lone parking meter which—*Que milagro!* contained a single dime. Bernabé lugged this rare coin back across the street and dropped it into the pay phone beside the soda dispenser, dialing home.

"Carolina? Everything's okay, no problem. They were just yelling at Betchel's dog that guards the Pilar. I'm gonna stick around a while, though, just sit on Rael's porch while they're drinking themselves into a stupor in there, make sure nothing else happens."

As an afterthought, he added, "It's a nice night out. You can really hear the frogs."

Whereupon Onofre Martínez—once the town's most noted bard—stumbled from the Frontier, and, teetering in the middle of·the plaza area, with his one arm upraised shaking a fist at the heavens, he launched immediately (and very loudly) into an epic corrido hailing the afternoon's triumph:

> *In the century of nineteen hundred*
> *In August of this year,*
> *A neighbor in our village,*
> *Made a chota's milk turn clear.*
>
> *Don José of Milagro,*
> *Last name of Mondragón,*
> *Led us into a battle—*
> *And the battle we have won.*
>
> *When Seferino Pacheco,*
> *That man with the awful pig,*
> *Invaded the blessed beanfield,*
> *Don José made him dance a jig.*
>
> *Pacheco was first to fire,*
> *Six shots at José's head—*
> *With one bullet Mondragón answered,*
> *Que milagro Pacheco ain't dead!*
>
> *The police came up from the capital,*
> *The woods were crawling with coppers,*
> *But Don José was invisible,*
> *Even to the noisy choppers.*
>
> *Swift as a deer he outraced them,*
> *Quiet as a fox he ran,*
> *He thumbed his nose as they blundered,*
> *He laughed to beat the band.*
>
> *When the time was ripe, he entered*
> *Their headquarters in Doña Luz,*

And laughed in the face of the chota
Whose name was William Koontz.

The cops were eager to beat him,
And shut him up behind bars,
But then the Angels of Milagro
Arrived in their jalopy cars.

William Koontz turned pale,
He crapped in his pants that day,
He groaned and dropped to his knees,
And loudly started to pray.

For his heart was heavily beating,
His heart was pounding hard,
And his ugly chota features,
Were colored the color of lard.

"Spare me," he cried, "I'm sorry—"
But José only sneered,
To see such a frightened copper,
So full of pathetic fear.

José marched out of the station,
He greeted us with a clenched fist,
And while everyone applauded,
His pretty wife he kissed.

So we'll sing this song of José,
Whose beanfield started a war,
That the people of Milagro,
Have won forever more!

Onofre stopped, blinking at the sheriff, his eyes lop-sided and terribly fierce. Then he staggered over to within two feet of the lawman and, swaying like an aspen in a stiff wind, he gurgled, "You know what, Bernabé, you know who's looking over us people in this town?"

Bernabé frowned, sensing more trouble, and tried to glower in both a no-nonsense and also semifriendly way: "No, what?"

"You mean 'No, who?' "

"Okay: No, who?"

"The Angel of Mud, that's who," Onofre blurted, tipping back and almost over. "And the Angel of Skinny Cows. And the Angel of Eighty-nine Cents a Six-pack Cerveza. And the Angel of Dysentery. And the cross-eyed, greasy Angel of Broken Trucks. And the Angel of Bad Luck—"

Onofre paused, blinking as he tried to focus on Bernabé.

"Oh brother, you never saw such a bunch of motley angels as we got hovering over this town," he crowed. "In fact, you know what? If Jesus Christ himself was up there he'd have thistle burrs stuck in his beard and scars from an old bullet wound in his belly and only three and a half fingers on his right hand and no more than four teeth in his mouth."

Bernabé felt like laughing, yet instead he set his face in a glower, hoping to drive this one-armed poet back into the heart of the revelry where he belonged.

But Onofre was only just getting started. Flinging his visible arm starward he babbled on: "We got the Angel of Leaky Outhouses up there, and we got the Angel of Overgrazed Pastures and the Angel of Always Being Broke up there—why, we got so many offbeat, grizzled angels floating around over this little town that sometimes I get claustrophobia from all their wing rustling—from them that *has* any feathers left in their wings, that is. And from their stink, too. Why, I bet there ain't another town on earth with so many *sweaty* angels hanging around on top of it. There's the Angel of Going Crazy up there, and the Angel of All the World's Cripples. You ask me, this town is like a pile of horseshit attracting every kind of ugly fly and winged insect in the neighborhood, only what we got is every kind of deformed, outcast, feathered ghoul from heaven looking after our people and their earthly affairs. Lame, half-blind, one-armed like me, retarded—you name it. This place just reeks of crippled glory!"

"Well, yeah. I guess so. Uh-huh," Bernabé replied, shifting uneasily.

"There's a whole chorus of cojo, manco, and tuerto angels up there!" Onofre shouted at him.

Bernabé nodded, silently praying as he did so: Mother of God, please return this blotto lunatic to the bar.

"And as of today," Onofre rattled on, "we got a new one just joined the crowd up there."

"Oh yeah?" Bernabé sighed warily. "And which one is that?"

"The Half-pint Beanfield Angel," Onofre hooted insanely, tattooing the earth with his boots.

"Maybe you better head on back into the celebration, cousin," Bernabé suggested unhappily.

The one-armed man ignored him. *"Hijo Madre!"* he shrieked. "They're all just a bunch of limping, chewed-up, noisy, useless, blind drunk, flea-bitten, tail-dragging, shifty-eyed Coyote Angels!"

Bernabé nodded again and muttered incoherently.

"But you know something?" Onofre added abruptly, now reeking with sentiment. "We wouldn't none of us have even been here tonight like we are, celebrating like this, if it wasn't for the love of all them stupid Coyote Angels."

And with that, Onofre aboutfaced, heaved over to his truck, daintily extricated the most recent parking ticket from under the driver's side windshield wiper, and RIPPED IT TO FUCKING SHREDS!

The shreds he let trickle gleefully off his hand onto the ground, then he smugly tipped his cowboy hat to Bernabé with his invisible arm and lurched jubilantly back into the bar.

To nobody in particular, Bernabé said, "Although we are a town of unbelievably shitty poets, we sure can rant and rave with feeling."

Some parking ticket confetti, caught in a frail wind puff, tumbled across the dirt and settled around the sheriff's boots, which were on the wrong feet. Then a Dancing Trout pickup chugged erratically past Forest Service headquarters and stopped in the middle of the plaza area. Jerry Grindstaff, drunk for the first time in maybe fifteen years, lurched out of the cab, clumsily worked the lever to chamber a shell in the .30-30 he carried, and started to swing around the truck, heading for the Frontier Bar.

"Hey!" Bernabé shouted. "Where you going with that gun?"

Startled, Jerry G. turned so sharply he lost his balance and sat down. But before Bernabé could even think about going for his own sidearm, Jerry G. had the rifle pointed up directly at the sheriff. He blinked his eyes confusedly, trying to focus them.

"Who's that?"

"It's me, the sheriff. Bernabé Montoya."

"The sheriff?" Jerry G.'s eyes rolled up and inward as he tried to grasp what "sheriff" meant."

"Quit pointing that rifle at me," Bernabé ordered.

With that the foreman's eyes clicked into a clearly focused and downright vicious glare. "I oughtta kill the whole bunch of you. Maybe I will. You people think you won something today, well let me tell you something: you didn't win *shit*."

"You're drunk," Bernabé said, and then abruptly his body went almost woozy with terror, because Jerry G. had more hate and deep-down murder in his eyes than Bernabé had ever seen in a person. Immediately all his stomach muscles involuntarily bunched in as if preparing to take a bullet.

He added: "You kill me, Jerry G., and I'll beat your ass down to the Chamisa V. jail and have Ernie Maestas lock you up and—"

"You fucking Mexicans . . ." the foreman growled thickly. "You fucking Mexicans don't have a snowball's chance in hell."

"We'll see."

"Sure you'll see. You'll see us hang you up by the balls. You'll see us cut the tits off all your sluts and nail them to the barn door. You want a war, we'll show you about a war . . ."

"We'll see—" Bernabé choked out again, his ears literally ringing from fright and his stomach cramping it was so tensed.

"For starters I'm gonna kill you and that toothless old man wrecked the backhoe and Joe Mondragón,"

Jerry G. snarled. "Then I'm gonna take a big crap in that beanfield, and afterward . . . and after that—"

With no warning his eyes unfocused and started rolling around again, and as they did he lowered the gun, looking befuddled for a moment, and then scared; and then his face took on the air of a queer, disconcerted drunk.

"You bet your ass you'll see . . ." he whined, starting to cry. And with movements as jerky as those of a windup toy, he struggled upright, wheeled around, plunged back into the truck, circled awkwardly around the plaza area, and drove back up to the ranch.

Bernabé sat there for a while unable to move, staring at the ground, stone-cold scared, and so tight and weak he thought he would vomit. There was inside his body a feeling of such inevitable danger and ultimate doom that it damn near took his breath away. Those people in the bar getting drunk, they didn't have enemies in the likes of Jerry G. and Ladd Devine and the politicos—they had executioners. Money, progress, numbers, and the American way of life were on the other side: Christ, those bastards even controlled the atom bomb—!

And Bernabé knew it was all hopeless.

And then as he calmed down a little he hoped that it wasn't.

Maybe I should sign their petition, he thought.

"Why don't you just shoot yourself in the head?" he whimpered out loud. "It would be simpler."

Gradually his hysteria drained, he cooled off, his fear changed, becoming more governable, he began to think again, his stomach relaxed, he noticed that his drenched armpits stank . . . then he realized that for the moment he, they—his drunken compatriots in the bar—were out of danger. Jerry G. had left and once again nobody was dead.

As the relief flowed into him like a fast-rising tide, Bernabé began to tell himself that he had handled the situation pretty competently.

In fact, he had actually faced down a momentarily crazy man who intended to kill him.

Why, he had "stared death right in the face" and sent that lily-livered son of a bitch packing!

A mysterious silence flowed over the heart of the town. In the Frontier, revelers' voices receded, seemed almost to dissipate like a morning mist. And after a minute Bernabé had to smile in spite of it all. Because, bumbling or not, he felt a little like either a God damn babysitter . . . or somebody's guardian angel.

❧

They arrived home shortly after dark, worn out and groggy from guiding the horses down through the forest at dusk. Marvin LaBlue, who was sitting outside in the evening quiet listening to the radio and smoking reflectively, waved as they guided their tired horses into the moon-whitened corral area, then he waited patiently while they dismounted and unsaddled the horses, turning them into the corral. Eliu Archuleta drummed up some pliers to cut the wire on a hay bale, half of which he dumped in to the horses, while Claudio García entered the house, emerging with his arms full of cold beer. He gave them each a can, knocked off his first one in a single deep draught, and then opened another. Eliu and Ruby drank theirs about like that also, and pried seconds from Claudio's arm. They smiled at each other. Marvin LaBlue said, "I took that petition with me when everybody went down to Doña Luz when Joe turned hisself in, and I figured damn near a hundred people signed, and about an hour later they turned him out again, free as a whistle."

"Who turned him out?"

"You know. Billy Koontz, and Granny, and Bruno Martínez. They were all scared stiff, those cops. You would of got a chuckle out of it."

Ruby said, "How did he get out so quickly?"

"They just suddenly come all together," Marvin drawled. "They heard Joe was down there, you know, and everybody went, I guess, just to make sure the cops didn't rough him up, and while they was there everybody signed your petition." Marvin handed her the petition.

Ruby stood there, a beer and a cigarette in one

hand, reading through the names on the petition. Eliu squatted with a fresh beer, gazing down the hillside at the Body Shop and Pipe Queen buildings; the wrecker parked in front gleamed like a magical apparatus. Claudio sat down heavily, hunched over, head hanging, staring at the ground, listening to the horses nosing apart the hay, listening also to the quiet country and western strains from Marvin LaBlue's radio.

Every name. Ruby read every name on the petition, though as she did so no elation spread through her body; she was too tired for that. And anyway, it was only the first step. There would have to be another meeting soon, and she would have to talk with Bloom and convince him to work for them, and she would have to talk with José, and they would have to harvest his beans in a symbolic manner, every person who had signed the petition picking a handful of beans. They would harvest them the same way churches had been built in the old days, with every family contributing some adobe bricks and pitching in with labor so that it was a symbolic labor of all with a part of everyone's earth in it. And they would have to decide about their demands and confront Ladd Devine, and they would have to notify the press sooner or later, which meant they would need reporters on their side, and they needed a leader, or, more importantly, they needed a group of leaders, and they needed to figure out how to raise more money for their association; needed to set up a defense fund, and no doubt they would have to find another lawyer because Bloom, would need help, *if* he stuck it out with them . . . Ruby worried about Bloom, he always seemed so on edge—

And then she wondered if everyone had signed her petition only in a moment of euphoria. Come tomorrow morning, would they all realize what they had done and come running, begging to erase their names? Or would they arrive in force in the morning, toting guns and shouting hallelujah, ordering her to carry that petition down to the capital and personally shove it up the governor's ass?

Ruby dropped the petition onto the ground beside

Marvin LaBlue's radio, gulped her second beer and
opened a third, then walked away from everybody,
maybe fifteen yards, and hunkered down, gazing at
the Body Shop and Pipe Queen, the wrecker, the
shining broken white line on the highway beyond.

They all rested like that, absolutely quiet, drinking
more slowly now that their thirsts had been quenched,
eyes vaguely fixed on shadow-casting objects downhill.
Eventually, Ruby crushed her third aluminum can and
went into the house for a towel, saying, "I'm gonna
take a bath." Moments later she emerged, skirted
around the house and entered the sagebrush, heading
for the few silvery cottonwoods and willows growing
along the Rio Lucero.

Bats fluttered through the moonlight sharply etched
against soft fluorescent clouds high in the night. Ruby
perched on a smoothly sculpted granite rock overlooking a foam-covered pool. Her muscles were tired, her
bones ached, her mind was going to sleep like a cat.
Once or twice she nodded, almost toppling into the
water. She had never been this weary before.

She shed her boots, jeans, her cotton underwear,
her shirt and bra, and slipped naked into the luxurious
foam. Tipping her head back into the gentle froth, she
gazed at the stars. Ruby sighed and held her breasts,
laxly rubbing the nipples until they grew stiff, letting
her body flow and twirl with the currents, her toes
stepping lightly off rocks, pressing gently along patches
of sand. She relaxed, allowing her body to be moved
however the water chose to move it, turning over once
or twice, loving the way her hair in lazy strands caressed her windburned face. The water was very cold,
but long ago she had ceased to notice its iciness. Her
skin tingled, and that was all. She drifted around the
pool on her back, on her stomach, bent always at the
waist with her feet lazily pushing off, puttering along
the bottom, her limbs loose and almost disconnected,
floating serenely in the dark.

Claudio appeared and undressed, slipping into the
pool. His hand, like the powerful and barely restrained
paw of a cougar, touched her belly, her breasts, her
throat. His shaggy head blocked out the stars while

they kissed. Then he sank underwater and drifted around in the purple flow, eyes wide open, trying to pierce the gloom, seeing only, finally, her white body with the tan hands and the tan neck and the head cut off. Breaking the surface, he left the pool, dried his hands on his shirt and then rolled a cigarette and squatted on a sandy patch between boulders, smoking, watching her drift aimlessly around the foamy pool, relaxing, slowing down, floating almost as if in sleep.

Five minutes later Ruby walked out of the water into his arms. "Make me a cigarette," she murmured, staying nestled in his arms while he fashioned the cigarette, lit it, and transferred it to her lips. Then he lifted her easily, she curled her legs around his hips, sliding calmly onto his penis. They grinned, exhaling smoke into each other's faces, making love. Claudio walked away from the stream, carrying her into the sagebrush until they could no longer hear the water, until the land—the mountains, the mesa leading off to the gorge—was very quiet.

"Listen," she said, and together they listened, smoking while Ruby moved almost imperceptibly on him. They could hear the celebration in Milagro, the Frontier's jukebox, people singing. They were alone, though, and after a while Claudio began to walk quietly around on the windless mesa, lifting her a little by the buttocks now, and their weary white bodies were wreathed in cigarette smoke as, gently, they continued making love.

The governor himself poured the last two of them to arrive—Ladd Devine the Third and Jim Hirsshorn—a double Scotch on the rocks and a little brandy, respectively, and carried the glasses across the softly lit living room of the governor's mansion to where the newest arrivals sat. Others gathered in the room for this late-night emergency meeting included Nelson Bookman and Rudy Noyes; the district head of the Bureau of Reclamation, Roland Kyburz; a young aide to the governor who specialized in Chicano relations, Keith Trujillo; a noted educator and sociologist at the state university, Professor E. Clarence Boonam (whose work included several lengthy articles on how southwestern conservancy districts had traditionally destroyed small subsistence farming cultures); the woman who headed the Health and Social Services Department, Ursula Bernal; and the governor's wife, Peggy. A gloom, a peculiar sadness, an almost nostalgic heaviness clung to thick gold draperies that muffled a half-dozen French doors leading out of the room; it was manifested in the delicate cigarette haze that flowed almost sensually through two large yellow chandeliers.

After he had served these last two drinks, the governor sat down on a piano stool before a shiny black Steinway and plinked a single thoughtful note.

"I take it," he began, getting right down to brass tacks, "things aren't all that hunky-dory up in Milagro."

"That's a fairly correct analysis of the situation," Ladd Devine said with what tried to be, but failed to pass as, a wry grin. Then: "I wonder how much of this is going to make the newspapers?"

"None of it," the governor said. "Excepting whatever that lawyer writes, which probably won't see the light of day unless they resurrect that little magazine."

"And Pacheco's going to be okay?" Jim Hirsshorn asked.

"So I've been told."

"What the hell happened with the bulldozer?" Nelson Bookman asked.

"It was a backhoe," Devine corrected. "There's an old man, Amarante Córdova, who lives nearby—"

"A ninety-two, ninety-three-year-old old man," Jim Hirsshorn said disgustedly.

"He had a gun, what could my man do?" Devine continued. "He doesn't speak Spanish, my man doesn't, but he got the drift. He told me he figured the slightest misstep and that old guy would have shot him. Then, after Jerry—my man, Jerry Grindstaff is his name, a Dancing Trout foreman—after he left, this old Córdova fellow drove the backhoe across the mesa and into the gorge. At least, that's how the tracks read. We didn't go down in the gorge because we couldn't see anything from the rim. It must have fallen into the river."

Keith Trujillo whistled softly: "A ninety-three-year-old bastard did *that*?"

"So far as we know. Jerry Grindstaff, he'd recognize Amarante Córdova. And there wasn't anybody else around."

Nelson Bookman, consulting a notebook, said, "So recent events summarize, not necessarily in order, a bit like this. They burned the sign. They turned Lavadie's sheep into green alfalfa. They cleaned out those trout from the hatchery. They threatened your foreman with a gun, and destroyed one of your vehicles, a backhoe. When Joe Mondragón turned himself in this afternoon, at least thirty-five to forty persons with guns parked in a threatening manner outside the police station. A bullet was fired through Joe Mondragón's window. And apparently there's talk of other people moving back into and repairing the houses on the west side, in the ghost town area—"

"You're forgetting a softball game a while ago that almost developed into a riot," Jim Hirsshorn said. "It finally had to be suspended in the first inning."

"Apparently the people have banded together and are not readily going to be intimidated," Nelson Bookman said thoughtfully.

"There's an understatement for you," Jim Hirsshorn rasped miserably.

"Anybody who couldn't see this coming had to be blind," Ursula Bernal said. "Aside from Algodon County, Chamisa County is the poorest in the state. Fifteen, twenty, sometimes as high as thirty-five percent unemployment, sixty percent of the people on food stamps, a per capita income of a thousand, maybe even less than a thousand dollars a year. This is the 1970s" she added emotionally, "and the state has a per capita income of twenty-nine hundred, and nationwide it's about thirty-seven hundred, and nationwide the median income for a family of four is ten thousand dollars a year—"

She stopped, embarrassed, flushing while her words

rang out strangely in the ornate room. An overworked, frustrated, very decent woman, Ursula Bernal directed a handcuffed agency that erratically dribbled out pennies to men, women, and children who could have used hundred-dollar bills plus bushel baskets of health care, an entirely different school program, a lot of understanding and kindness, and so on, ad infinitum.

"Who here doesn't know all those figures?" Keith Trujillo said somewhat testily.

"The thing is, they haven't changed since I was born," Ursula Bernal said tightly. "And that event happened to take place forty-eight years ago."

"A-hem." Roland Kyburz, the Bureau of Reclamation head, cleared his throat prior to changing the subject. "What I'm interested in discussing this evening is the future of the Indian Creek Conservancy District and that Indian Creek Dam."

"If we want to put it in, legally there's not that much problem, is there?" Jim Hirsshorn said.

"No problem," according to Rudy Noyes. "You can't lose."

"Only somebody could dynamite the dam, sabotage the construction vehicles, terrorize tourists, and so forth," Ladd Devine whimpered gloomily.

"That begins to look like a possibility." Nelson Bookman drained his drink, and, even before he had it back on the coaster, the governor's wife, smiling gaily, had vaulted with a professional swirl of skirts across the spongy beige rug and lifted the glass gently but firmly from his hand. He didn't have to remind her what he was drinking—she knew; she had memorized the drinking habits of almost a thousand important people.

"We can't stop now," Jim Hirsshorn said. "We've already begun to develop the recreation plots up there; contractors are under contract; we've invested a hell of a lot in plans for the ski basin and preliminary excavation; it's cost us I don't know how much for the initial golf course designs. And we've already invested God knows how much—about how much would you say, Ladd?—in eastern and midwestern advertising for the Miracle Valley recreation home-sites."

"A lot," Devine said. "In the hundreds of thousands."

"Not to mention what the bureau has sunk into a dozen planning reports, hydrographical surveys, maps, cost-benefit analysis, and—you know," Roland Kyburz added. The state is entitled to that water, and if we pulled out, believe me, it wouldn't be that easy to find another suitable area."

"But it's all a joke," Ursula Bernal said grimly. "You pretend the water is for the people in that valley, who don't want it, don't need it, can't use it, but will have to pay for it, while Mr. Hirsshorn and Mr. Devine here make a killing."

"It depends on how you look at it," Ronald Kyburz said frostily.

Nelson Bookman said, "Everybody concerned will profit."

"Bullshit."

Bookman shot a swift bitter glance at the HSS head; the others in the room remained uncomfortably silent for a moment.

"If this gets held up for another six months I could lose the notes that have already been promised," Ladd Devine said. "In the end, the way interest rates are fluctuating, a serious delay could cost a mint."

"Suppose the dam were dropped altogether?" The governor plinked another note.

Devine turned gray. "Oh shit—excuse me. But, I mean, we're not thinking in terms of something like *that,* are we?"

"I don't know," the governor said.

"See, if this thing caught fire in Milagro, it could spread across the other five northern counties and we'd be in serious trouble," Keith Trujillo said. "Those people up there are ornery. You got to handle them with gid gloves."

"But this whole thing is *good* for them," Devine almost whined. "Hell, if it hadn't been for me and my grandfather, those farmers would have had to migrate out of there long ago."

Nobody responded to that.

"The problem is, apparently we've handled it wrong," Nelson Bookman said. "That's my fault as much as anybody. I assessed the risks, called in Kyril Montana, and I'm willing to wager it wasn't the correct thing to do, although I'm not sure how we could have proceeded in order to avoid what's happened. We probably should have jumped on Joe and taken him to court right away, playing it up front and screw the publicity. I don't know. The risk there was that we'd have challenged them, and they'd have met the challenge, and we'd have wound up arresting the entire town. We had hoped to sneak through the conservancy district, your dam, Ladd, without much hoopla. We underestimated the people's ability to comprehend the complexities and to react against what none of them actually understands, other than instinctively, to this day. I think it would have gone smoothly if not for that beanfield, which was their stroke of luck, or apparently their rallying point, whatever. Call it our temporary Waterloo, if you will. Now we've got to make some hard decisions, change our tack, so to speak, without igniting the type of conflagration in which everybody would lose."

"Those damn old-fashioned people are a real thorn," Kyburz muttered.

"Thank God for that!" Ursula Bernal blurted, her dark eyes flashing.

"I just meant—" Kyburz stopped himself, shrugged.

"I think, no matter what, there's going to be tension," Devine said. "There always has been. You can't escape it. You just have to go ahead and deal with the incidents one at a time. This whole thing has only been just that, a small incident. They have no real strength, and they never will have it. The people up there aren't united."

"They have strong roots," Ursula Bernal said.

The governor's small eyes appeared to see nothing, to be gazing stupidly at the rug. But the governor understood some things. He was a Democrat and he had strength in the north. Milagro itself did not have enough votes to tickle a heifer's balls, but if some publicity worked its way into this and the thing developed into a scandal or a truly delicate political issue, he and those with him might find themselves in hot water come the next election. Pork barrel projects, as this one might be called, were getting exposed across the nation; dams for the sake of dams were being questioned; the Bureau of Reclamation or the Corps of Engineers could not move in anywhere anymore expecting to be met with open arms. On the other hand, development swung votes; "progress" was the most important political card a man could play, and Ladd Devine's Miracle Valley project was the kind of thing people considered progress; it would bring outside money into the state. And if little or none of that money filtered down to the destitute farmers of the Miracle Valley, well—when had it ever? The enterprising ones would skim off their share, and if they were smart and wished to enjoy their lives, they'd learn how to ski and play golf. The others did not deserve what they wouldn't work for.

But he kept returning to this: suppose somebody, or a couple of people, or maybe even a cop, was shot up there? Suppose those illiterate, backward assholes actually tried to launch a kind of disorganized rebellion? It had happened before, and it had cost a territorial governor his head a hundred years ago, and it had cost another governor his political career only twenty years ago.

And if something like that took place, and if the militants got wind of it—as of course they would—and headed up to Milagro from the south, or down to it from Denver, things might get very rough. The governor had already been forced to alert the National Guard once during his tenure in office, to deal with barrio disturbances in the capital. And he sure didn't want to do that again if there was any possible way to avoid it.

"When was the conservancy district supposed to come up for a hearing?" the governor asked.

"Well, the district judge, Nate Jaramillo, hasn't decided on that," Bookman answered. "When he got in, the docket was so crowded—because of Mort Alexander's death and your delay in making the interim appointment—that he just hasn't, up until now, set any particular date. You could probably figure within the next three months, though."

"My feeling is we'd best back off on this, for the moment anyway," the governor said, "I'll speak to Nate about letting it ride indefinitely. I'll explain the situation."

"Any more delays and I'm going to be up to my ass in lawsuits." Ladd Devine had gone pale.

"Ladd, you jumped to some conclusions," the governor said. "So did I. But from now on we're just going to have to progress a little more slowly in the north."

"I didn't jump to any conclusions that your office and Nelson's office didn't lead me into."

"*Mister* Devine," the governor said, abruptly rising from the stool and commencing to pace deliberately up and down the center of the room. "You developed this project to where it is today because of certain arrangements that myself and my colleagues in state government were able to effectuate on your behalf. Now I can knock those arrangements apart like I can knock apart a castle made of toothpicks with my little pinkie if you start giving me a bad time. Right now I don't see this as a project that has to be killed indefinitely, but I'm God damn ready to see it delayed until either we can better assess the situation or the situation changes. In the meantime, if you crash-land it's not as if nobody is going to crash-land with you, or as if there'll be nobody to lend a helping hand. The complexities of the financial arrangements, the government and the private monies involved, I hope you understand, and I know I do. You may forget, but I have an investment in this thing, and I'm not the kind of man who throws an investment out the window. But at the same time I'm not the kind of man who cuts off his nose to spite his own face either. I fold when I'm not holding a winning hand and wait for better cards, do I make myself clear?"

Stopping, he looked down; his angry voice sagged. "We've done alright for a long time in this state, Ladd. Don't you try to cross me now."

His speech over, the governor retreated to his piano stool, sat down, plinked another note.

And as a late afterthought, he appended: "This is not a particularly happy moment in *any* of our lives."

It was then that the noted sociologist, E. Clarence Boonam, finally spoke. "Ursula," he said cheerfully to the HSS head, "let's you and me go downtown and have a little drink to celebrate."

◦§

Joe Mondragón squatted on the ditch bank overlooking his beanfield. Nancy sat against the trunk of a nearby cottonwood. Joe's eyes and his brain were so blurry he could barely see, let alone think, but he was *feeling* a lot of things. In fact, his feelings were all in a ball and twisting crazily in his stomach like those bunches of bait worms in cardboard canisters that Nick sold in his store. And among all the feelings, all the confusion inside, Joe—in spite of his muddled brain—could single out a couple for particular consideration: namely, the feeling of being triumphant and important; and another related feeling which translated into an emotion known as "being scared shitless."

It was his field, his bunch of crummy beans; he loved them, he loved enchiladas and burritos, and he would fart a lot because of these purebred Milagro beans. But when he'd planted them he had not really known what he was doing, and he had certainly not anticipated the particular consequences that had occurred. And he had an inkling of what some more of the consequences were going to be now that this officially was not just *his* beanfield anymore, and he didn't like them one bit.

One thought Joe had never entertained, even in his most uncomfortable dreams, was that somehow he would be singled out to be a leader. Which in this case, Joe figured, was tantamount to being singled out to be a human target on the state pistol range down in the capital. Or it was like getting chosen to be dressed in a deerskin outfit and then lowered from a helicopter into the Little Baldy Bear Lake region during the first weekend of the fall hunting season.

And Joe knew something about himself: he was not a leader. A fighter maybe, but no leader. He couldn't articulate things well enough for that, he couldn't think things out. His brain worked like his tractor; if you tinkered with it, drowned it in oil, kicked it and cursed it, and maybe threatened to shoot it, it would just barely function, plow half a field, perhaps, before breaking down again.

As for tomorrow—he could just see it: five, ten, maybe fifteen of them would come to his house, and after they were all together in the living room and had drunk a beer apiece or guzzled some coffee, they would ask, with big, lopsided, toothless, cheerful smiles plastered against their faces: "Well, José, what are we gonna do now?"

And he would stare at them, his head bowed under the weight of an excruciating hangover, and say, "What do you fellows think we *ought* to do?" And they wouldn't even have to think about that one. They'd all shrug and smile and nod their heads, and say "We don't know. It's for you to say." That—or, one would say this, the other would say that, a third would call both their plans ridiculous, a fourth would agree with the first, a fifth would have another idea, a sixth would stalk out in a huff never to return, a seventh would talk with the first, explaining the faults in his plan and causing the first to abandon his plan, which would leave only the fourth agreeing with the first's plan the first no longer believed in himself anymore, and finally somebody would say, "José, you and that lawyer Bloom, you go talk to Devine," or "You go talk to those motherfuckers in the capital," or—

Nancy came over, squatting beside him, resting an arm over his shoulder. "Heigh ho, José my love," she whispered drunkenly, tenderly kissing his shoulder.

The mesa coyotes were singing, calling to each other or challenging the moon. And, of course, there were a lot of silent ones out there hunting rabbits in their dogged, loping style. No matter how much you poisoned them, shot them, scared them, trapped them, hated them, caged them, or generally raked over their habitat, you could not entirely kill all the coyotes, Joe thought. And the cottonwood leaves were so still they could hear Indian Creek bubbling over smooth stones across the road a ways. They could even hear the jukebox music at the Frontier Bar in town, the music remote like a fiesta memory from the old days.

"When Seferino Pacheco gets back, you know what?" Joe murmured.

"I'm afraid to ask." She leaned over just slightly, touching her tongue to his earlobe.

"I'm gonna give him one of those piglets we got. For a present."

"*Ai, Chihuahua,*" Nancy laughed. "What do you wanna go and start that trouble all over again for?"

"So when the pig grows up I can shoot him again," Joe cackled, and suddenly, sputtering happily, he toppled out of her arms and rolled right down the short slope into his bean plants, laughing to beat the band—

At first the noise sounded like machine guns; then it enlarged into thunder, and Herbie Goldfarb stirred uneasily, dreaming of snakes and rain. But soon he was dreaming of the Butterfly of Love, of the way her jumbo tits had smiled at him before the piranha mosquitoes attacked . . . yet the thunder kept on thundering, even though now sunlight and whopping breasts flooded his dreams. Finally he realized all that urgent loud noise was coming from outside his dreams in the real world, heralding another calamity, no doubt, and with a fatalistic whimper the volunteer awoke.

"Coming. Just a sec. Wait a sec—I'm coming. *Christ*!"

Joe Mondragón was standing there, grinning like a hyena, a Tasmanian devil, a Cheshire cat; behind him, seated on the hood of Herbie's accordioned 1956 Chevy convertible (which hadn't budged since the wrecker dropped it off), was Joe's wife, Nancy, also grinning like a hyena, a Tasmanian devil, a Cheshire cat. Lord have mercy, they've come to kill me, Herbie thought.

But Joe flung an arm around Herbie's shoulders. "Hey kid," he shouted, "how come you're sleeping? This is a night for celebration. We *won*!"

"Oh," Herbie said, scratching behind one ear.

"Put your shoes and pants on," Joe ordered. "We're gonna have some *fun*!"

Oh Lord no, Herbie thought, anything but *fun*. But if he did not do what Joe wanted, no telling what the little punchdrunk maniac was likely to do to Herbie's flabby city-boy body, so he pulled on some pants, a shirt, and his sneakers, accepted a tug from the pint bottle of alcoholic gunk Joe offered, and shuddered as Nancy threw her arm around his shoulders, shouting, "Let's go!" Between them, silently saying good-bye to all that, Herbie teetered out of his yard.

It was a little before midnight when a very sleepy Charley Bloom opened his door, and there stood Joe and Nancy Mondragón flashing him a pair of the world's most lopsided pie-eyed grins, and caged between them, looking a bit like a duck that had just crawled out of an oil slick, was Herbie Goldfarb, drunk by now, greeting Bloom with a sort of apologetic —in fact, call it a sick—leer.

"We came to ride that horse," Joe said, and both he and Nancy, bumping into Herbie and swaying unsteadily, giggled. Herbie produced a faint "What-me-worry?" expression, and shrugged.

"Go ahead," Bloom said. "Just leave me out of it."

"You got to come, Charley. I can't get on her if you don't catch the bitch and hold her steady."

"Oh hell. Alright. Jees . . ."

Bloom put a raincoat on over his pajamas, shoved his feet into some mud-encrusted irrigation boots, and followed their reeking little entourage around the house. The moon shone brightly, the night was quiet and crisp, already an autumnal tinge rode the air. Bloom caught Sunflower, wrapped a rope around the pony's neck, and led her into the back field. With no further ceremony Joe hopped on, Bloom let go, and immediately Joe was revolving like a pinwheel about six feet above the ground while Sunflower just trotted out from underneath him.

Joe sat in alfalfa, momentarily stunned, while Bloom and Nancy writhed in paroxysms of wonderful idiotic laughter. Herbie Goldfarb just stared dumbfoundedly at the scene.

"You'll never ride that horse!" Bloom shrieked. "Never, never, *never!*"

"Maybe not," Joe said with a hurt, puzzled grin. "But I sure aim to keep trying."

With that, Herbie tipped up the booze bottle, killing it, wiped his lips with gusto, and was more than a little taken aback to hear himself boasting, "I can ride that horse."

Nancy snorted; Joe howled, "You can ride that horse my *ass!*" And Bloom, abruptly alarmed, quit laughing in order to scrutinize Herbie closely, wondering was the volunteer okay, or had he suffered a nervous breakdown, or what?

Herbie's hands flapped expressively in the night air: "I can ride that horse," he again declared.

"You can't even drive a car, how can you ride that horse?" Joe wanted to know.

"If he wants to commit suicide let him commit suicide," Nancy giggled.

Joe said, "Charley, go get that horse."

"Oh, hey, wait a minute," Bloom protested. "I mean, a joke is a joke—"

"I can ride that horse," Herbie insisted matter-of-factly, and suddenly he had never felt so cool and collected in his life.

"So get the horse," Joe repeated. "The man said he can ride that horse."

"Awe, why don't you all go home," Bloom suggested, distressed by the ugliness in Joe's voice. "What's the point—"

"Get him the horse, Charley."

"Yeah," Herbie chimed in. "Go get me that horse." And he giggled at Joe, who did not giggle back.

Cursing himself for answering the door, Bloom retrieved Sunflower and held her while the volunteer

mounted up and Joe helped adjust the loose rope.
Then Bloom kept holding onto the pony until Joe said
impatiently, "Let go," whereupon the lawyer released the horse and all hell broke loose.

Sunflower's hind end jerked up almost perpendicular
and, as her heels still touched stars, she twisted her
belly in a number rodeo people call a "sunfish," causing Herbie to swivel around sideways, but not only
did he hold onto the rope, he also kept his legs
wrapped tightly around her chubby guts. So Sunflower bounced up, down, sideways, and backward,
rearing and kicking and chopping, snorting furiously,
only Herbie still wouldn't come unglued. He held onto
that rope like it was a check for one million dollars,
and although it felt as if maybe his spine was already
busted and his balls had been split like fat grapes and
his teeth had been jarred right out of his mouth, he
kept holding on tightly, with the stars boiling around
in his eyes like sparks shot from a cannon, and he
saw Bloom and Joe and Nancy, too, rightside up
here, upside down there, but he didn't fall off Sunflower, because the minute he had upturned that liquor
bottle Herbie had known he was going to ride this
pony if it killed him, or else die trying.

Sunflower unleashed every dirty trick in the book,
she even twisted her head around and tried to bite his
forearm, but Herbie rode her across Bloom's tiny field
and back again, and within a minute the ferocious little
horse was exhausted; she came down off a spinebender
and stopped on a dime, twitched for a moment and let
out a whole series of strange indignant whinnies, and
then stood still, with Herbie still astride her, pleased
as punch.

Somehow—God forbid the volunteer should question how—a miracle had occurred.

Who could speak? Who was a great enough human
being to come up with words for this occasion? Nancy
stared, Bloom stared, Joe stared. When the ringing
departed from Herbie's brain, he realized that not
only had he ridden a very cantankerous horse, he'd
accomplished something nobody else had ever accomplished. And with that he understood that this

moment was probably one of the most precious moments, if not *the* most precious moment, in his life, a triumph he would treasure forever, a foolhardy act that had turned into a stupendous victory of mythic proportions, a single, violent, heroic experience that had made his summer worthwhile. He could brag about this for eternity, to his future lovers, to his wives, to his children, to his grandchildren. His tombstone would be a simple plaque, inscribed: "Herbert Goldfarb, 1948–?" And then: "He rode Sunflower."

In what could not be characterized as other than a patronizing manner, Herbie patted the horse. Then, letting go the rope, he quietly dismounted. Sunflower's ears lay back flat, but she was defeated; she couldn't move. And Herbie, standing there cupping his aching testicles as he faced Joe and Nancy and Bloom, grinned at them like a movie star.

A hush such as rarely fell over the Miracle Valley fell now. Crickets and frogs halted their nocturnal prattling for a moment as if in homage to this great event, owls ruffled their feathers and were still, the dogs in town and the coyotes on the mesa quit issuing bloodthirsty challenges to each other—the world grew remarkably still as a Jewish star was born.

Then, moving unsteadily more from amazement than from all the booze he had consumed, Joe Mondragón marched up to Herbie Goldfarb and punched that smart-ass East Coast son of a bitch right in his prissy little nonviolent mouth.

<s

And Pacheco, asleep, laboring for his life, breathing stertorously, dreamed.

It was five o'clock on a summer evening. Bees simmered; a lush apricot swoon weighted the air. His wife was playing the piano; Chopin, a prelude. Men, irrigating in the silver fields, paused, leaning contemplatively on their shovel handles, to listen. A deep bell clanked . . . animals lazing home. Dust, stirred up by the day's traffic on the roads, hung softly, a beige mist across the fields. Melvin, who died later on in Korea, caressed the slow August landscape, chasing butterflies. The laughter of children a half-mile away carried clearly across the fields, somehow releasing memories of making love early on a frosty autumn morning, when people could hear the ax blows of their neighbors chopping wood all across the small valley.

Then Death, decked out in a sombrero, a serape, and shiny silver spurs, a spicy carnival apparition, dancing over the little village, chuckled like a dove, winked in a joking, comradely fashion at Pacheco, and jitterbugged quietly on into the resplendent and remarkably spangled horizon.

Epilogue

"It's an ill wind that blows *no* good."
—Carolina Montoya

It was traditional in Milagro, at midnight every December thirty-first, for the people to congregate in their backyards or in their fields and spend a few minutes discharging various firearms at the stars in honor of the New Year.

Of course this particular summer night heralded no New Year, but all the same, around one o'clock on the morning after Joe Mondragón strutted out of the Doña Luz state police headquarters a free man, some shooting began, and it caught on, passing from house to house, from backyards to small fields, the people outside jaybird naked or in their pajamas or fully dressed and drunkenly weaving with open beer cans lodged in their back pockets, as, one after another, they happily fired bullets at the general cosmos, or aimed more carefully, trying to perforate the moon. And then as suddenly as it had started the barrage ended. Folks trundled inside and laid down their guns, and some began gently to make love, while others kept on drinking, and still others rehashed yesterday and wondered about tomorrow.

At the Chateau Martínez, the Staurolite Baron slumped onto his piano stool and played a walking boogie-woogie bass with his left hand and some jazzy treble runs with his nonexistent right hand, while the ghost of Pacheco's pig, whose inessential form had finally managed to pass through the white picket fence surrounding the Martínez digs, started eating Onofre's Astroturf lawn and his plastic garden flowers.

627

At the Joe Mondragón house not far away, Joe drowsily stroked Herbie Goldfarb's guitar and hoarsely croaked out a Tiny Morrie song, while Nancy set free the sparrows that had been imprisoned in the ballot jar ever since Joe caught them to celebrate his release from the pendejo factory. And, hands on her hips, tipping drunkenly to starboard, Nancy watched the tiny, confused birds flutter off helter-skelter into the night.

On the other side of the highway, Snuffy Ledoux was carving a little Smokey the Bear just for old time's sake, and nearby Amarante Córdova sat on his bed drenched in tears, bemoaning the loss of his old-fashioned Colt Peacemaker.

Down the highway apiece Claudio García and Ruby Archuleta were asleep, but Marvin LaBlue had wandered into the body shop and was on his back now, tinkering with a transmission as he listened to country and western music on WBAP.

Bud Gleason sneezed. And Bertha, throwing a fat leg across his stomach and chucking him under the chin, teased: "Somebody is thinking about you."

"Who?" Bud asked sleepily.

"Kyril Montana."

"Thanks," the real estate agent moaned, "I needed that."

"I almost signed their petition," Bernabé Montoya told his wife. "To tell the truth, I might still do it. Which would mean I'd lose the next election to Pancho Armijo by a landslide. In fact, I bet old Pancho already is in love with me for even thinking about signing that petition—"

"Of course he is," Carolina replied, uncorking a gigantic yawn. "After all, it's an ill wind that blows *no* good."

"Ai, Chihuahua . . ."

And, now that it had devoured most of the town's water snakes, that grubby yellow feline reincarnation of Cleofes Apodaca was pitter-pattering quietly along the irrigation ditches, hunting frogs. Thus does history turn in cycles.

At last, late late that night, or rather early in the

morning, Onofre Martínez passed out over his piano; Joe Mondragón slumped insensate beside Herbie Goldfarb's guitar; and Marvin LaBlue lost consciousness with two wrenches lying across his chest and a greasy smile on his hillbilly face.

A small brown bear waddled through the heart of town stirring up parking ticket flakes, but nothing else: the Doberman Brutus in the Pilar Café was much too tired to bark. A few minutes later the bear crossed through Herbie Goldfarb's yard, but this time the high-minded pacifist, conscientious objector, and VISTA volunteer manqué didn't notice because he was too busy dreaming about how to guillotine, garrote, gag, strangle, electrocute, bludgeon, and in general crucify Joe Mondragón for punching him in the mouth.

While over by Joe's beanfield, almost hidden in dark shadows, smoking a cigarette and hacking uncomfortably from time to time, sat Amarante Córdova's miserable Coyote Angel, trying to cop a weed and five minutes of tranquility before the bell rang for the next round.

Roosters began to crow. "I'm so tired I could sleep for ten years," Bernabé Montoya said, rolling onto his stomach. And with that he realized he was not going to wake up at 5:00 A.M.—not this morning. Nobody in Milagro was going to wake up at 5:00 A.M. In fact, they were all so drunk and exhausted and suffering from a release of tension that every last citizen would probably sleep until noon.

In light of this revelation, just before conking out, with one arm draped lovingly across Carolina's chest, Bernabé murmured happily:

"Welcome, ball fans, to the World Series of Peace."

The phone rang.

"Bernie?" Nick Rael gasped frantically. "My mom just escaped again, and I think she headed into the mountains. *We got to form another posse right now!*"